ROY'S WORLD

ROY'S WORLD
STORIES 1973–2020

BARRY GIFFORD

SEVEN STORIES PRESS
NEW YORK • OAKLAND • LIVERPOOL

Seven Stories Press
140 Watts Street
New York, NY 10013
sevenstories.com

Library of Congress Cataloging-in-Publication Data has been applied for.

LCCN: 2020032405
ISBN: 978-1-64421-022-2 (pbk)
ISBN: 978-1-64421-023-9 (ebook)

College professors and middle and high school teachers may order free examination copies of Seven Stories Press titles. To order, visit sevenstories.com/textbook or send a fax on school letterhead to (212) 226-1411.

Drawings by Barry Gifford.

Printed in the USA.

9 8 7 6 5 4 3 2 1

ACKNOWLEDGMENTS

A number of these stories have appeared in the following magazines, newspapers, books or anthologies:

A Boy's Novel (Santa Barbara), *A Good Man to Know* (Livingston, Montana), *Amerarcana* (San Francisco), *Another Magazine* (London), *Arizona Republic* (Phoenix), *Brick* (Toronto), *Bridge* (Chicago), *The Chicagoist* (Chicago), *City Lights Review* (San Francisco), *Confabulario* (Mexico City), *Dazed and Confused* (London), *El Angel de la Reforma* (Mexico City), *El País*, (Madrid), *Film Comment* (New York), *The Fireside Book of Baseball* (New York), *Flash Fiction Forward* (New York), *The Independent* (London), *L'Immature* (Paris), *La Nouvelle Revue Française* (Paris), *La Repubblica delle Donne* (Milan), *The Lifelovers ABC* No. 3 (Madrid), *Max* (Milan), *Memories from a Sinking Ship* (New York), *Narrative* (San Francisco), *New Sudden Fiction: Short Stories from America and Beyond* (New York) *Nude* (London), *The PEN Short Story Collection* (New York), *The Phantom Father* (New York), *Plan V* (Buenos Aires), *Ploughshares* (Boston), *Positif* (Paris), *Post Road* (New York), *Sad Stories of the Death of Kings* (New York), *San Francisco Chronicle*, *San Francisco Examiner*, *Santa Monica Review* (Los Angeles), *Southwest Review* (Dallas), *Speak* (San Francisco), *Vice* (New York) and *Wyoming* (New York).

"Roy and the River Pirates" and "Lost Monkey" originally appeared in *Vice* magazine (New York). "The King of Vajra Dornei" appeared, in different form, in *The Up-Down* (New York, 2015). "A Long Day's Night in the Naked City (Take Two)" originally appeared, in different form, in *The 2nd Black Lizard Anthology of Crime Fiction* (Berkeley). "Mules in the Wilderness" appeared in *The Collagist* (Ann Arbor). "Dingoes" appeared in *Contrapasso* (Sydney). "The Colony of the Sun" appeared in the *Santa Monica Review* (Los Angeles). "The Religious Experience" and "The Cuban Club" appeared in *Narrative* (San Francisco). Several of these stories also appeared in *Confabulario*, the cultural supplement of *El Universal* (Mexico City). "The Best Part of the Story" originally appeared in the *Los Angeles Times*. "Tell Him I'm Dangerous" appeared in *Zoetrope All-Story* (San Francisco).

The following stories were published in *The Chicagoist* (Chicago): "Mona," "Mud," "King and Country," "Dark and Black and Strange," "Sick," "The Italian Hat," "I Also Deal in Fury," "Creeps," "Dingoes," "Chicago, Illinois, 1953," and "Role Model."

"Bar Room Butterfly" appeared, in different form, in the anthologies *Berkeley Noir* (New York) and *Noir Journal* (Philadelphia).

To the memory of Jack Colby

"I listened and looked at them—there they were: the ones who would yet raise hell and kill a lot of bad people . . . I remember them all, I assure you. They pass and pass again through my memory, and I call them by their names as they go by."

—João Guimarães Rosa, *Grande Sertão: Veredas*

"Genius is the recovery of childhood at will."

—Arthur Rimbaud

CONTENTS

Preface 19

MEMORIES FROM A SINKING SHIP

Memories from a Sinking Ship 23
A Good Man to Know 26
The Forgotten 29
Mrs. Kashfi... 32
The Old Country 35
The Monster 37
The Ciné... 38
Dark Mink 42
Nanny 45
Island in the Sun 47
An Eye on the Alligators 50
The Piano Lesson 52
The Lost Tribe.. 53
The Lost Christmas...57
My Catechism 59
Sunday Paper 62
The Origin of Truth 64
The Trophy.. 68
The Aerodynamics of an Irishman.......................................72
A Rainy Day at the Nortown Theater 74
Renoir's Chemin montant dans les hautes herbes 76
Forever After 77
The Mason-Dixon Line...80
The Wedding 83
The Pitcher 84
A Place in the Sun... 86

The Winner 88

The God of Birds 92

Sundays and Tibor 95

Poor Children of Israel 98

The Man Who Wanted to Get the Bad Taste
    of the World Out of His Mouth 100

Johnny Across 103

The Secret of Little White Dove 109

The Delivery 112

The Deep Blue See 114

Radio Goldberg 116

Why Skull Dorfman Went to Arkansas 119

Wanted Man 123

The Bucharest Prize 127

Blows with Sticks Raining Hard 130

The Chinaman 134

The End of Racism 136

Way Down in Egypt Land 139

Bad Things Wrong 143

Detente at the Flying Horse 146

Shattered 150

A Day's Worth of Beauty 152

The Peterson Fire 156

Door to the River 158

Sailing in the Sea of Red He Sees a
    Black Ship on the Horizon 162

WYOMING

Cobratown 167

Chinese Down the Amazon 170

Bandages 171

Soul Talk 175

Skylark 177

Flamingos 180

Wyoming 182

Saving the Planet 184

A Nice Day on the Ocean 185

Perfect Spanish 187

Seconds 189

Roy's World 191

Nomads 194

Ducks on the Pond 197

Sound of the River 199

Red Highway 201

Lucky 203

K.C. So Far (Seconds/Alternate Take) 205

Concertina Locomotion 207

Imagine 208

The Geography of Heaven 210

Man and Fate 212

Where Osceola Lives 214

The Crime of Pass Christian 216

Cool Breeze 219

Night Owl 221

Islamorada 222

On the Arm 225

Look Out Below 227

The Up and Up 229

Black Space 232

Fear and Desire 234

God's Tornado 236

SAD STORIES OF THE DEATH OF KINGS

The Age of Fable 241

The Great Failure 243

Irredeemable 245

Sad Stories of the Death of Kings 248

The Sultan 252

The Liberian Condition 256

Six Million and One 259

War and Peace 263

Chop Suey Joint 266

Significance 270

Einstein's Son 272

The Albanian Florist 276

The Weeper 280

The Swedish Bakery 283

The Man Who Swallowed the World 287

Ghost Ship 292

Caca Negra 295

Roy's First Car 299

El Carterista 302

Crime and Punishment 306

The American Language 309

Lonely Are the Brave 312

Force of Evil 316

The Choice 319

Bad Girls 323

The Sudden Demise of Sharkface Bensky 328

Portrait of the Artist with Four Other Guys 332

The Starving Dogs of Little Croatia 335

In the Land of the Dead 339

The Secret of the Universe 341

Far from Anywhere 343

Rain in the Distance 347

Bad Night at the Del Prado 350

The Theory of the Leisure Class 355

Innamorata 358

The Exception 361

Close Encounters of the Right Kind 365

Blue People 370

Call of the Wild 372

Arabian Nights 376

Last Plane out of Chungking 378

The Vanished Gardens of Córdoba 380

Benediction 381

THE RED STUDEBAKER

Alligator Story 387
The Vast Difference 393
The Birdbath 397
Storybook Time 401
The Red Studebaker 404
The Trumpet 408
Unspoken 412
Haircut 416
The Invention of Rock 'n' Roll 419
Infantry 422
Drifting Down the Old Whangpoo 425
The Wicked of the Earth 428
Christmas Is Not For Everyone 431

THE CUBAN CLUB

Roy and the River Pirates 437
Dingoes 441
The King of Vajra Dornei 444
Real Bandits 447
Haitian Fight Song (Take Two) 450
The Cuban Club 454
Appreciation 458
The Awful Country 460
Deep in the Heart 462
Unopened Letters 464
Chicago, Illinois, 1953 467
The Colony of the Sun 470
Creeps 473
Achilles and the Beautiful Land 475
Men in the Kitchen 478
Anna Louise 481
Mules in the Wilderness 483

The Boy Whose Mother May
  Have Married a Leopard 487
Stung 489
El almuerzo por poco 492
Vultures... 494
I Also Deal in Fury 497
Hour of the Wolf.. 500
Lost Monkey...503
When Benny Lost his Meaning 507
Sick.. 509
The Best Part of the Story...514
Tell Him I'm Dangerous...518
The Shadow Going Forward...524
Feeling the Heat...527
The Sharks...530
Smart Guys 533
Apacheria..537
Dark and Black and Strange...541
The Vagaries of Incompleteness 544
King and Country...547
House of Bamboo.. 550
The Unexpected 553
The Way of All Flesh.. 557
Some Products of the Imagination 560
The Comedian...565
Lament for A Daughter of Egypt.......................................569
The Old West... 572
Incurable... 574
Shrimpers.. 577
Learning the Game... 580
The Fifth Angel..583
A Long Day's Night in the Naked City (Take Two).....586
The Religious Experience 589
The Familiar Face of Darkness...591
Las Vegas, 1949 595
In Dreams..598

Lucky 601

Danger in the Air 604

Child's Play 606

The Message 610

River Woods 612

The History and Proof of the Spots on the Sun 617

War is Merely Another Kind of
  Writing and Language 620

The End of the Story 622

Innocent of the Blood 626

The Italian Hat 630

The Senegalese Twist 633

Kidnapped 636

The Dolphins 639

Dragonland 642

Role Model 645

Mona 648

Mud 651

The Phantom Father 654

Roy's Letter 656

THE WORLD IN THE AFTERNOON

The World in the Afternoon 661

Wing Shooting 665

Acapulco 669

His Truth 675

Disappointment 678

The Navajo Kid 681

In My Own Country 685

Rinky Dink 688

Where the Dead Hide 691

Bar Room Butterfly 694

Absolution 697

The Goose 701

Spooky Spiegelman and The Night Time Killer 704

Constantinople..708
The Same Place in Space..709
The Good Listener...711
Garden Apartment..715
Kitty's World...719

PREFACE

In the company of eighteen new ones, which comprise the section "The World in the Afternoon," *Roy's World* is a compilation of my previously published Roy stories, an effort to evoke a portrait of a time and place that no longer exist, one I've been crafting for the better part of a half century. This is history on my own terms, a series of intertwined episodes based on events real and imagined, dosed with sense impressions designed to enable the reader to both visualize and, most important, feel them as does Roy and other inhabitants of this fictional universe. That said, the Roy stories come closer to comprising an autobiography than any other form I might have chosen. People have often remarked that I have a very good memory; perhaps, but memory is subjective beyond doubt or control and therefore unreliable, insufficient to present a viable or even acceptable, let alone accurate, compendium. My hope is that they prove entertaining and suggestive, perhaps even meaningful. Just as the real world keeps spinning, so does Roy's.

—B.G.

Memories from a Sinking Ship

ROY'S FATHER

Memories from a Sinking Ship

When Roy was five years old his mother took him to Chicago to stay with his grandmother while she went to Acapulco with her new boyfriend, Rafaelito Faz. Roy had been told that hell was boiling but when he and his mother flew up from Miami and arrived in Chicago during the dead of winter he decided this was a lie. Hell was cold, not hot, and he was horrified that his mother had delivered him to such a place. My mother must hate me, Roy thought, to have brought me here. I must have done something terribly wrong. The fact that his grandmother was there already was proof to Roy that she, too, had committed an unforgivable sin.

Roy's mother stayed in hell only long enough to hand him over. Rafaelito Faz would meet her in Mexico. "He's very rich," Roy's grandmother informed him. "The Faz family owns a chain of department stores in Venezuela." Rich people, Roy concluded, did not have to go to hell. His mother had shown him a picture of Rafaelito Faz clipped from the *Miami Herald*. His hair was parted down the middle and he had a wispy mustache that looked as if it might blow off in the Chicago wind. Underneath the photograph was the caption, "Faz heir visits city."

When Roy's mother returned from her holiday, she was wearing a white coat and her skin was as brown as Chico Carrasquel's, the shortstop for the Chicago White Sox. Roy did not tell his mother that he was angry at her for dropping him off in hell while she went to a fabulous beach in another country because he was afraid that if he did she would do it again. Roy asked her if Rafaelito Faz had come to Chicago with her. "Forget *that* one, Roy," she said. "I don't ever want to see the rat again."

The next time Roy went to Chicago to visit his grandmother, he was almost seven and it was during the summer. His mother disappeared after two or three days. Roy's grandmother said that she had gone to see a friend who had a house on a lake in Minnesota. "Which one?" Roy asked. "There are 10,000 lakes in Minnesota, Roy," his grandmother told him, "if you can believe what it says on their license plate, but the only one I can name is Superior."

While Roy's mother was in the land of 10,000 lakes, there was a sanitation workers strike in Chicago. Garbage piled up in the streets and alleys. Now the weather was very warm and humid and the city started to stink. Big Cicero, the hunchback with a twisted nose who once wrestled Killer Kowalski at Marigold Arena and now worked at the newsstand on the corner near the house, said to Roy's grandmother, "May they rot in hell, them garbagemen. They get a king's ransom as it is just for throwin' bags. Cops oughta kneecap 'em, put 'em on the rails. The mayor'll call in the troops soon it don't end, you'll see." Roy's grandmother said, "Don't have a heart attack, Cicero." "Already had one," he said.

One afternoon Roy looked out a window at the rear of the house and saw rats running through the backyard. A few of them were sitting in and climbing over the red fire truck his grandmother had bought for him to pedal around the yard and on the sidewalk in front of her house. "Nanny, look!" Roy shouted. "Rats are in our yard!"

His grandmother came into the room and looked out the window. The rats were climbing up the wall. She grabbed a broom, leaned out the window with it and began knocking the rats off the yellow bricks. They fell down onto the cement but quickly recovered and headed back up the side of the house. Roy's grandmother dropped the broom into the yard and slammed the window shut. Rats ran up the windows. Roy thought that they must have tiny suction cups attached to their feet to be able to hold on to the glass. He could hear the rats scampering across the gravel on the roof. A flamethrower would stop them, Roy thought. If the mayor really did call in the army, like Big Cicero said he might, they could use flamethrowers to fry the rats. Roy closed his eyes and saw hundreds of blackened rodents sizzling on the sidewalks.

By the time Roy's mother returned, the garbage strike was over. Roy told her about the rats sitting in his fire truck and climbing up the wall and his grandmother swatting them with a broom. "Not all the rats are in Chicago, Roy," she said. "They got 'em in Minnesota, too."

"And in Venezuela," Roy started to say, but he didn't.

A Good Man to Know

I was seven years old in June of 1954 when my dad and I drove from Miami to New Orleans to visit his friend Albert Thibodeaux. It was a cloudy, humid morning when we rolled into town in my dad's powder-blue Cadillac. The river smell mixed with malt from the Jax brewery and the smoke from my dad's chain of Lucky Strikes to give the air an odor of toasted heat. We parked the car by Jackson Square and walked over a block to Tujague's bar to meet Albert. "It feels like it's going to rain," I said to Dad. "It always feels like this in New Orleans," he said.

Albert Thibodeaux was a gambler. In the evenings he presided over cockfight and pit-bull matches across the river in Gretna or Algiers but during the day he hung out at Tujague's on Decatur Street with the railroad men and phony artists from the Quarter. He and my dad knew each other from the old days in Cuba, which I knew nothing about except that they'd both lived at the Nacional in Havana.

According to Nanny, my mother's mother, my dad didn't even speak to me until I was five years old. He apparently didn't consider a child capable of understanding him or a friendship worth cultivating until that age and he may have been correct in his judgment. I certainly never felt deprived as a result of this policy. If my grandmother hadn't told me about it I would have never known the difference.

My dad never really told me about what he did or had done before I was old enough to go around with him. I picked up information as I went, listening to guys like Albert and some of my dad's other friends like Willie Nero in Chicago and Dummy Fish in New York. We supposedly lived in Chicago but my dad had places in Miami, New York, and Acapulco. We traveled, mostly without my mother, who stayed at the house in Chicago and went to church a lot. Once I asked my dad if we were any particular religion and he said, "Your mother's a Catholic."

Albert was a short, fat man with a handlebar mustache. He looked like a Maxwell Street organ-grinder without the organ or the monkey. He and my dad drank Irish whiskey from ten in the morning until lunchtime, which was around one thirty, when they sent me down to the Central Grocery on Decatur or to Johnny's on St. Louis Street for muffaletas. I brought back three of them but Albert and Dad didn't eat theirs. They just talked and once in a while Albert went into the back to make a phone call. They got along just fine and about once an hour Albert would ask if I wanted something, like a Barq's or a Delaware Punch, and Dad would rub my shoulder and say to Albert, "He's a real piece of meat, this boy." Then Albert would grin so that his mustache covered the front of his nose and say, "He is, Rudy. You won't want to worry about him."

When Dad and I were in New York one night I heard him talking in a loud voice to Dummy Fish in the lobby of the Waldorf. I was sitting in a big leather chair between a sand-filled ashtray and a potted palm and Dad came over and told me that Dummy would take me upstairs to our room. I should go to sleep, he said, he'd be back late. In the elevator I looked at Dummy and saw that he was sweating. It was December but water ran down from his temples to his chin. "Does my dad have a job?" I asked Dummy. "Sure he does," he said. "Of course. Your dad has to work, just like everybody else." "What is it?" I asked. Dummy wiped the sweat from his face with a white-and-blue checkered handkerchief. "He talks to people," Dummy told me. "Your dad is a great talker."

Dad and Albert talked right past lunchtime and I must have fallen asleep on the bar because when I woke up it was dark out and I was in the backseat of the car. We were driving across the Huey P. Long Bridge and a freight train was running along the tracks over our heads. "How about some Italian oysters, son?" my dad asked. "We'll stop up here in Houma and get some cold beer and dinner." We were cruising in the passing lane in the powder blue Caddy over the big brown river. Through the bridge railings I watched the barge lights twinkle as they inched ahead through the water.

"Albert's a businessman, the best kind." Dad lit a fresh Lucky from an old one and threw the butt out the window. "He's a good man to know, remember that."

The Forgotten

It was snowing again and Roy couldn't wait to get out in it. Standing in line with the other second graders, all of them with their coats, mufflers, hats and gloves on, he was impatient to be released for morning recess. Roy had just told Eddie Gray that if the snow was deep enough they should choose up sides for a game of Plunge, when the teacher, Mrs. Bluth, called out to him.

"Roy! You know that you are not supposed to talk while I am giving instructions. You remain here while I take the rest of the class down to the playground."

Roy stood still while everyone else filed out of the classroom. As soon as he was sure that they were on their way down the west staircase, Roy walked out of the room and headed in the opposite direction. Nobody was in the hallway. Roy walked down the east staircase to the ground floor and through the exit to the street. Snow was coming down hard and Roy put up the hood of his dark blue parka as he headed north on Fairfield Avenue. He could hear the kids yelling in the playground on the other side of the school.

At the corner of Rosemont and Washtenaw, near St. Tim's, Roy passed an old man wearing a brown trenchcoat and a black hat who was holding a handdrawn sign that said, "I am a brother to dragons, and a companion to owls. JOB, 30:28."

"How old are you?" the man asked Roy.

"Seven," Roy answered, and kept walking.

"Read the Bible!" the man shouted. "Don't forget, like I did!"

When Roy entered the house, his mother was seated in front of the television set in the living room, drinking coffee.

"Is that you, Roy?" she asked. "I thought you were at school. It's only a little after ten."

"They let us out early today," he said. Roy went over to where she was sitting. "What's on?"

"*The Lady from Shanghai.* It's a good one. Rita Hayworth with her hair bleached blonde. Do you think I'd look as good as a blonde, Roy?"

"I don't know, Ma. I like you the way you are."

She kissed him on his forehead. Roy never drank coffee but he liked the odor of it.

"I'm going to play in my room," he said.

"Okay, honey."

About half an hour later, Roy heard the telephone ring and his mother answer it.

"Yes, this is she," she said into the receiver. "Uh huh, he is. He's in his room right now. Oh, really. I see. Yes, well, that will be between you and Roy, won't it? I'm sure he had a good reason. I understand. He'll be there tomorrow, yes. Thank you for calling."

Roy heard his mother hang up, then go into the kitchen and run water in the sink. A few minutes later, she appeared in the doorway to his room.

"Sweetheart," she said, "I have to go out for a little while. Is there anything you'd like me to pick up at the grocery store?"

"No, thanks, Ma."

"You'll be all right?"

"Sure, I'll be fine. I'm just playing with my soldiers."

"Which ones are those?" she asked.

"French Zouaves."

"Their uniforms are very beautiful. I've never seen soldiers with purple blouses before."

"These Zouaves are from Algeria," said Roy, "that's why their faces and hands are brown. They fought for France."

"And white turbans, too," his mother said. "Lana Turner wore one in *The Postman Always Rings Twice.* Do you remember that movie, Roy? Where she and John Garfield, who's a short order cook, kill her husband, who's much older than she is?"

"No, Ma, I don't."

"Thanks to a tricky lawyer, at first they get away with the murder, but then they slip up."

His mother stood there for a minute and watched Roy move the pretty Zouaves around the floor before saying, "I'm going now, honey. I'll be back in an hour."

"Okay, Ma."

"I'll make us grilled cheese sandwiches when I get back," she said, "and maybe some tomato soup."

It wasn't until after he heard the front door close that he took off his coat.

The next day at school, when he entered the classroom, Mrs. Bluth said, "Good morning, Roy. How are you feeling today?"

"Fine, Mrs. Bluth," he said, and took his seat.

The other kids looked at Roy but didn't say anything. Later, on the playground during morning recess, Eddie Gray asked Roy if he'd gotten into trouble for having left school without permission the day before.

"No," Roy said.

"Your mother didn't yell at you?"

"No."

"Why'd you leave?" Eddie asked.

"I didn't like the way Mrs. Bluth talked to me."

A few flurries began falling. Roy put up his hood.

"What about your dad?" asked Eddie. "What did he do?"

"My father's dead," said Roy.

"You're lucky," said Eddie Gray, "my old man would have used his belt on me."

Mrs. Kashfi

My mother has always been a great believer in fortune-tellers, a predilection my dad considered as bizarre as her devotion to the Catholic Church. He refused even to discuss anything having to do with either entity, a policy that seemed only to reinforce my mother's arcane quest. Even now she informs me whenever she's stumbled upon a seer whose prognostications strike her as being particularly apt. I once heard my dad describe her as belonging to "the sisterhood of the Perpetual Pursuit of the Good Word."

My own experience with fortune-tellers is limited to what I observed as a small boy, when I had no choice but to accompany my mother on her frequent pilgrimages to Mrs. Kashfi. Mrs. Kashfi was a tea-leaf reader who lived with her bird in a two-room apartment in a large gray brick building on Hollywood Avenue in Chicago. As soon as we entered the downstairs lobby the stuffiness of the place began to overwhelm me. It was as if Mrs. Kashfi lived in a vault to which no fresh air was admitted. The lobby, elevator, and hallways were suffocating, too hot both in summer, when there was too little ventilation, and in winter, when the building was unbearably overheated. And the whole place stank terribly, as if no food other than boiled cabbage were allowed to be prepared. My mother, who was usually all too aware of these sorts of unappealing aspects, seemed blissfully unaware of them at Mrs. Kashfi's. The oracle was in residence, and that was all that mattered.

The worst olfactory assault, however, came from Mrs. Kashfi's apartment, in the front room where her bird, a blind, practically featherless dinge-yellow parakeet, was kept and whose cage Mrs. Kashfi failed to clean with any regularity. It was in that room, on a lumpy couch with dirt-gray lace doily arm covers, that I was made to wait for my mother while she and Mrs. Kashfi, locked in the inner sanctum of the bedroom, voyaged into the sea of clairvoyance.

The apartment was filled with overstuffed chairs and couches, dressers crowded with bric-a-brac and framed photographs of strangely dressed, stiff and staring figures, relics of the old country, which to me appeared as evidence of extraterrestrial existence. Nothing seemed quite real, as if with a snap of Mrs. Kashfi's sorceress's fingers the entire scene would disappear. Mrs. Kashfi herself was a small, very old woman who was permanently bent slightly forward so that she appeared about to topple over, causing me to avoid allowing her to hover over me for longer than a moment. She had a large nose and she wore glasses, as well as two or more dark green or brown sweaters at all times, despite the already hellish climate.

I dutifully sat on the couch, listening to the murmurings from beyond the bedroom door, and to the blind bird drop pelletlike feces onto the stained newspaper in its filthy cage. No sound issued from the parakeet's enclosure other than the constant "tup, tup" of its evacuation. Behind the birdcage was a weather-smeared window, covered with eyelet curtains, that looked out on the brick wall of another building.

I stayed put on the couch and waited for my mother's session to end. Each visit lasted about a half hour, at the finish of which Mrs. Kashfi would walk my mother to the doorway, where they'd stand and talk for another ten minutes while I fidgeted in the smelly hall trying to see how long I could hold my breath.

Only once did I have a glimpse of the mundane evidence from which Mrs. Kashfi made her miraculous analysis. At the conclusion of a session my mother came out of the bedroom carrying a teacup, which she told me to look into.

"What does it mean?" I asked.

"Your grandmother is safe and happy," my mother said.

My grandmother, my mother's mother, had recently died, so this news puzzled me. I looked again at the brown bits in the bottom of the china cup. Mrs. Kashfi came over and leaned above me, nodding her big nose with long hairs in the nostrils. I moved away and waited by the door, wondering what my dad would have thought of all this, while my mother stood smiling, staring into the cup.

The Old Country

My grandfather never wore an overcoat. That was Ezra, my father's father, who had a candy stand under the Addison Street elevated tracks near Wrigley Field. Even in winter, when it was ten below and the wind cut through the station, Ezra never wore more than a heavy sport coat, and sometimes, when Aunt Belle, his second wife, insisted, a woolen scarf wrapped up around his chin. He was six foot two and two hundred pounds, had his upper lip covered by a bushy mustache, and a full head of dark hair until he died at ninety, not missing a day at his stand till six months before.

He never told anyone his business. He ran numbers from the stand and owned an apartment building on the South Side. He outlived three wives and one of his sons, my father. His older son, my uncle Bruno, looked just like him, but Bruno was mean and defensive whereas Ezra was brusque but kind. He always gave me and my friends gum or candy on our way to and from the ballpark, and he liked me to hang around there or at another stand he had for a while at Belmont Avenue, especially on Saturdays so he could show me off to his regular cronies. He'd put me on a box behind the stand and keep one big hand on my shoulder. "This is my *grandson*," he'd say, and wait until he was sure they had looked at me. I was the first and then his only grandson; Uncle Bruno had two girls. "Good *boy!*"

He left it to his sons to make the big money, and they did all right, my dad with the rackets and the liquor store, Uncle Bruno as an auctioneer, but they never had to take care of the old man, he took care of himself.

Ezra spoke broken English; he came to America with his sons (my dad was eight, Bruno fourteen) and a daughter from Vienna in 1918. I always remember him standing under the tracks outside the station in February, cigar stub poked out between mustache and muffler, waiting for me and my dad to pick him up. When we'd pull up along the curb my dad would honk but the old man wouldn't notice. I would always have to run out and get him. I figured Ezra always saw us but waited for me to come for him. It made him feel better if I got out and grabbed his hand and led him to the car.

"Pa, for Chrissakes, why don't you wear an overcoat?" my dad would ask. "It's cold."

The old man wouldn't look over or answer right away. He'd sit with me on his lap as my father pointed the car into the dark.

"What cold?" he'd say after we'd gone a block or two. "In the *old* country was cold."

The Monster

I used to sit on a stool at the counter of the soda fountain in my dad's drugstore and talk to Louise, the counter waitress, while she made milk shakes and grilled cheese sandwiches. I especially liked to be there on Saturday mornings when the organ-grinder came in with his monkey. The monkey and I would dunk dough-nuts together in the organ-grinder's coffee. The regular customers would always stop and say something to me, and tell my dad how much I looked like him, only handsomer.

One Saturday morning when I was about six, while I was waiting for the organ-grinder and his monkey to come in, I started talking to Louise about scary movies. I had seen *Frankenstein* the night before and I told Louise it was the scariest movie I'd ever seen, even scarier than *The Beast from 20,000 Fathoms* that my dad had taken me to see at the Oriental Theater when I was five. I had had dreams about the beast ripping up Coney Island and dropping big blobs of blood all over the streets ever since, but the part where the Frankenstein monster kills the little girl while she's picking flowers was worse than that.

"The scariest for me," Louise told me, "is *Dracula*. There'll never be another one like that."

I hadn't seen *Dracula* and I asked her what it was about. Louise put on a new pot of coffee, then she turned and rested her arms on the counter in front of me.

"Sex, honey," she said. "Dracula was a vampire who went around attacking women. Oh, he might have attacked a man now and then, but he mainly went after the girls. Scared me to death when I saw it. I can't watch it now. I remember his eyes."

Then Louise went to take care of a customer. I stared at myself in the mirror behind the counter and thought about the little girl picking flowers with the monster.

The Ciné

On a cloudy October Saturday in 1953, when Roy was seven years old, his father took him to see a movie at the Ciné theater on Bukovina Avenue in Chicago, where they lived. Roy's father drove them in his powder-blue Cadillac, bumping over cobblestones and streetcar tracks, until he parked the car half a block away from the theater.

Roy was wearing a brown and white checked wool sweater, khaki trousers and saddle shoes. His father wore a double-breasted blue suit with a white silk tie. They held hands as they walked toward the Ciné. The air was becoming colder every day now, Roy noticed, and he was eager to get inside the theater, to be away from the wind. The Ciné sign had a red background over which the letters curved vertically in yellow neon. They snaked into one another like reticulate pythons threaded through branches of a thick-trunked Cambodian bo tree. The marquee advertised the movie they were going to see, *King of the Khyber Rifles*, starring Tyrone Power as King, a half-caste British officer commanding Indian cavalry riding against Afghan and other insurgents. "Tyrone Cupcake," Roy's father called him, but Roy did not know why.

Roy and his father entered the Ciné lobby and headed for the concession stand, where Roy's father bought Roy buttered pop-corn, a Holloway All-Day sucker and a Dad's root beer. Inside the cinema, they chose seats fairly close to the screen on the right-hand side. The audience was composed mostly of kids, many of whom ran up and down the aisles even during the show, shouting and laughing, falling and spilling popcorn and drinks.

The movie began soon after Roy and his father were in their seats, and as Tyrone Power was reviewing his mounted troops,

Roy's father whispered to his son, "The Afghans were making money off the opium trade even back then."

"What's opium, Dad?" asked Roy.

"Hop made from poppies. The Afghans grow and sell them to dope dealers in other countries. Opium makes people very sick."

"Do people eat it?"

"They can, but mostly they smoke it and dream."

"Do they have bad dreams?"

"Probably bad and good. Users get ga-ga on the pipe. Once somebody's hooked on O, he's finished as a man."

"What about women? Do they smoke it, too?"

"Sure, son. Only Orientals, though, that I know of. Sailors in Shanghai, Hong Kong, Zamboanga, get on the stem and never make it back to civilization."

"Where's Zamboanga?"

"On Mindanao, in the Philippine Islands."

"Is that a long way from India and Afghanistan?"

"Every place out there is a long way from everywhere else."

"Can't the Khyber Rifles stop the Afghans?"

"Tyrone Cupcake'll kick 'em in the pants if they don't."

Roy and his father watched Tyrone Power wrangle his minions for about twenty minutes before Roy's father whispered in Roy's ear again.

"Son, I've got to take care of something. I'll be back in a little while. Before the movie's over. Here's a dollar," he said, sticking a bill into Roy's hand, "just in case you want more popcorn."

"Dad," said Roy, "don't you want to see what happens?"

"You'll tell me later. Enjoy the movie, son. Wait for me here."

Before Roy could say anything else, his father was gone.

The movie ended and Roy's father had not returned. Roy remained in his seat while the lights were on. He had eaten the popcorn and drunk his root beer but he had not yet unwrapped the Holloway All-Day sucker. People left the theater and other people came in and took their seats. The movie began again.

Roy had to pee badly but he did not want to leave his seat in case his father came back while he was in the men's room. Roy held it until he could not any longer and then allowed a ribbon of urine to trickle down his left pantsleg into his sock and onto the floor. The chair on his left, where his father had been sitting, was empty, and an old lady seated on his right did not seem to notice that Roy had urinated. The odor was covered up by the smells of popcorn, candy, and cigarettes.

Roy sat in his wet trousers and soaked left sock and shoe, watching again as Captain King exhorted his Khyber Rifles to perform heroically. This time after the film was finished Roy got up and walked out with the rest of the audience. He stood under the theater marquee and waited for his father. It felt good to be out of the close, smoky cinema now. The sky was dark, just past dusk, and the people filing in the Ciné were mostly couples on Saturday night dates.

Roy was getting hungry. He took out the Holloway All-Day, unwrapped it and took a lick. A uniformed policeman came and stood near him. Roy was not tempted to say anything about his situation to the beat cop because he remembered his father saying to him more than once, "The police are not your friends." The police officer looked once at Roy, smiled at him, then moved away.

Roy's mother was in Cincinnati, visiting her sister, Roy's aunt Theresa. Roy decided to walk to where his father had parked, to see if his powder-blue Cadillac was still there. Maybe his father had gone wherever he had gone on foot, or taken a taxi. A black and gold-trimmed Studebaker Hawk was parked where Roy's father's car had been.

Roy returned to the Ciné. The policeman who had smiled at him was standing again in front of the theater. Roy passed by without looking at the cop, licking his Holloway All-Day. His left pantsleg felt crusty but almost dry and his sock still felt soggy. The cold wind made Roy shiver and he rubbed his arms. A car horn honked. Roy turned and saw the powder-blue Caddy stopped in the street. His father was waving at him out the driver's side window.

Roy walked to and around the front of the car, opened the passenger side door and climbed in, pulling the heavy metal door closed. Roy's father started driving. Roy looked out the window at the cop standing in front of the Ciné: one of his hands rested on the butt of his holstered pistol and the other fingered grooves on the handle of his billy club as his eyes swept the street.

"Sorry I'm late, son," Roy's father said, "Took me a little longer than I thought it would. Happens sometimes. How was the movie? Did Ty Cupcake take care of business?"

Dark Mink

Pops, my other grandfather, my mother's father, and his brothers spent much of their time playing bridge and talking baseball in the back room of their fur coat business. From the time I was four or five Pops would set me up on a high stool at a counter under a window looking down on State Street and give me a furrier's knife with a few small pelts to cut up. I spent whole afternoons that way, wearing a much-too-large-for-me apron with the tie strings wrapped several times around my waist, cutting up mink, beaver, fox, squirrel, even occasional leopard or seal squares, careful not to slice my finger with the razor-sharp mole-shaped tool, while the wet snow slid down the high, filthy State and Lake Building windows and Pops and my great-uncles Ike, Nate, and Louie played cards.

They were all great baseball fans, they were gentlemen, and didn't care much for other sports, so even in winter the card table tended to be hot-stove league speculation about off-season trades or whether or not Sauer's legs would hold up for another season. Of course there were times customers came in, well-to-do women with their financier husbands, looking as if they'd stepped out of a Peter Arno *New Yorker* cartoon; or gangsters with their girl-friends, heavy-overcoated guys with thick cigars wedged between leather-gloved fingers. I watched the women model the coats and straighten their stocking seams in the four-sided full-length mirrors. I liked dark mink the best, those ankle-length, full-collar, silk-lined ones that smelled so good with leftover traces of perfume. There was no more luxurious feeling than to nap under my mother's own sixty-pelt coat.

By the time the fur business bottomed out, Pops was several years dead—he'd lived to eighty-two—and so was Uncle Ike, at eighty-eight. Pops had seen all of the old-time great ballplayers, Tris Speaker, the Babe, even Joe Jackson, who he said was the greatest player of them all. When the White Sox clinched the American League pennant in 1959, the first flag for them in forty years (since the Black Sox scandal of 1919), he and I watched the game on television. The Sox were playing Cleveland, and to end it the Sox turned over one of their 141 double plays of that season, Aparicio to Fox to Big Ted Kluszewski.

Uncle Nate and Uncle Louie kept on for some time, going in to work each day not as furriers but to Uncle Louie's Chicago Furriers Association office. He'd founded the association in the '20s, acting as representative to the Chamber of Commerce, Better Business Bureau, and other civic organizations. Louie was also a poet. He'd written verse, he told me, in every form imaginable. Most of them he showed me were occasional poems, written to celebrate corona-tions—the brothers had all been born and raised in London—and inaugurations of American presidents. In the middle right-hand drawer of his desk he kept boxes of Dutch-shoe chocolates, which he would give me whenever I came to visit him.

Uncle Nate, who lived to be 102, came in to Uncle Louie's office clean-shaven and with an impeccable high-starched collar every day until he was a hundred. He once told me he knew he would live that long because of a prophecy by an old man in a wheelchair he'd helped cross a London street when he was seven. The man had put his hand on Nate's head, blessed him, and told him he'd live a century.

Uncle Louie was the last to go, at ninety-four. Having long since moved away, I didn't find out about his death until a year or so later. The fur business, as my grandfather and his brothers had known it, was long gone; even the State and Lake Building was about to be torn down, a fate that had already befallen Fritzl's, where the brothers had gone each day for lunch. Fritzl's had been the premier restaurant of the Loop in those days, with large leather booths, big white linen napkins, and thick, high-stemmed glasses. Like the old Lindy's in New York, Fritzl's was frequented by show people, entertainers, including ballplayers, and newspaper columnists. Many of the women who had bought coats, or had had coats bought for them, at my grandfather's place, ate there. I was always pleased to recognize one of them, drinking a martini or picking at a shrimp salad, the fabulous dark mink draped gracefully nearby.

Nanny

From the time I was four until I was eight my grandmother lived with us. She slept in the big bedroom with my mother (my father had remarried by then) and was bedridden most of the time, her heart condition critical, killing her just past her sixtieth birthday. I called her Nanny, for no reason I can remember, and I loved her, as small boys suppose they do. My mother was often away in those days, and while I don't remember Nanny ever feeding me, (too sick to get out of bed for that) or dressing me, or making me laugh (there was Flo for that, my black mammy who later "ran off with some man," as my mother was wont to disclose; and then a succession of other maids and nurses most of whom, again according to my mother, either ransacked liquor cabinets or ran away à la Flo—anyone who left my mother always "ran off"), I do remember her scolding me, and once my mother was in Puerto Rico, for some reason I'm sure Nanny considered adequate (sufficient to pry her from bed), she backed me into a corner of my room against the full-length mirror on my closet door (thus I watched her though my back was turned) and beat me with a board, me screaming, "My mother'll get you for this!"; and when my mother returned my not believing it was really her (she being so brown from the sun), and my momentary fear of her being an impostor, some woman hired by my grandmother to beat me because it was too hard on her heart for her to do it herself.

This repeated paranoia, persistent tension, allowed no relief for me then but through my toy soldiers, sworded dragoons, Zouaves, and Vikings that I manipulated, controlled. Hours alone on my lined linoleum floor I played, determinedly oblivious to the voices, agonies perpetuated dining room to kitchen to bedroom.

And there was the race we never ran. Nanny and I planned a

race for when she was well, though she never would be. Days sick I'd sit in my mother's bed next to Nanny and devise the route, from backyard down the block to the corner, from the fence to the lamppost and back—and Nanny would nod, "Yes, certainly, soon as I'm well"—and I'd cut out comics or draw, listening to Sergeant Preston on the radio, running the race in my mind, running it over and over, never once seeing Nanny run with me.

Island in the Sun

"Oh, Roy, this poor thing!"

"Who, Mom? What poor thing?"

Roy was eating breakfast in their room at the Casa Marina in Key West, Corn Flakes with milk and red banana slices on it. His mother had a cup of Cuban coffee and a small glass of freshly squeezed orange juice on the table in front of her. She was reading the *Miami Herald*.

"This sick man in a big city up north who was beaten to death by teenagers. How terrible."

Roy looked out through the open French doors to the terrace and beyond to the Atlantic Ocean. The water was very blue and he knew it would be cold despite the bright December sun. If they decided to swim today, Roy thought, he and his mother would go to the other side of the island and swim in the Gulf of Mexico, where the water was always warmer.

"Why would they beat up a sick man?"

"He was mentally retarded and weighed three hundred pounds and wore a homemade Batman costume. The neighborhood kids liked to pick on him and call him names."

"What was his real name?"

"Jimmy Rodriguez."

"How old was he?"

"Forty-two. Listen, Roy: 'Mr. Rodriguez lived alone in the city's most crime-ridden district. Neighbors told police that he would often shout at drug dealers and prostitutes from the sidewalk outside the apartment building in which he lived.'"

"Does it tell about how it happened?"

"Two fourteen year old boys and one thirteen year old girl hit him with soda pop bottles until he fell. Then they kicked him and poured soda on him while they shouted, 'Fatman not Batman! Fatman not Batman!'"

"Even the girl?"

"Mm-hm. The kids kept beating and kicking him even after he was dead, a neighbor, Feliciana Domingo, told police. Oh, Roy, this is really sad."

"What, Mom?"

"Batman had bought the bottles of soda pop for the kids who killed him."

Roy had never lived in a real neighborhood. He was eight years old and had grown up in hotels. His mother put down the newspaper, picked up her cup and took a sip of coffee.

"What happened to the kids who did it?"

"I don't know, it doesn't say. They'll probably be sent to a reformatory."

Roy's mother put down her cup, lit a Pall Mall, inhaled deeply, then blew the smoke toward the terrace. White curlicues floated in the air for a few seconds in front of the dark blue water, then vanished.

"What does retarded mean?"

"Slow, Roy. Batman's brain didn't work fast."

"Mom, I'm full."

"Okay, baby, don't eat any more. As soon as I finish my cigarette, we'll go to the beach."

"Probably Batman never went to a beach."

Roy's mother puffed and turned halfway around in her chair to stare at the ocean.

"Why did he live alone? Somebody should have taken care of him."

"Yes, Roy, somebody should have. The poor thing."

Roy watched a horsefly land on one of the sugar cubes that were crowded in a small green bowl next to his mother's cup and saucer. He remembered his father once saying that he knew a guy named Art Huck who would bet on anything, even which cube of sugar a fly would land on.

"Mom, do you know a man named Art Huck?"

"No, I don't think so. Who is he?"

"A friend of Dad's."

His mother sat still, looking toward the water.

"What are you thinking about?"

"I'm not sure which is worse, Roy, an act of cruelty or an act of cowardice."

"Maybe they're the same."

"No, actually I think cruelty is worse, because it's premeditated."

"What's that mean?"

"You have to think about it before you do it."

"You're always telling me to think before I do something."

"You're not a cruel person, Roy. You never will be."

"Do you know any cruel people?"

Roy's mother stood up and walked out onto the terrace. She threw her cigarette away.

"Yes, Roy," she said, without turning to look at him, "unfortunately, I do."

An Eye on the Alligators

I knew as the boat pulled in to the dock there were no alligators out there. I got up and stuck my foot against the piling so that it wouldn't scrape the boat, then got out and secured the bowline to the nearest cleat. Mr. Reed was standing on the dock now, helping my mother up out of the boat. Her brown legs came up off the edge weakly, so that Mr. Reed had to lift her to keep her from falling back. The water by the pier was blue black and stank of oil and gas, not like out on the ocean, or in the channel, where we had been that day.

Mr. Reed had told me to watch for the alligators. The best spot to do it from, he said, was up on the bow. So I crawled up through the trapdoor on the bow and watched for the alligators. The river water was clear and green.

"Look around the rocks," Mr. Reed shouted over the engine noise, "the gators like the rocks." So I kept my eye on the rocks, but there were no alligators.

"I don't see any," I shouted. "Maybe we're going too fast and the noise scares them away."

After that Mr. Reed went slower but still there were no alligators. We were out for nearly three hours and I didn't see one.

"It was just a bad day for seeing alligators, son," said Mr. Reed. "Probably because of the rain. They don't like to come up when it's raining."

For some reason I didn't like it when Mr. Reed called me "son." I wasn't his son. Mr. Reed, my mother told me, was a friend of my father's. My dad was not in Florida with us, he was in Chicago doing business while my mother and I rode around in boats and visited alligator farms.

Mr. Reed had one arm around me and one arm around my mother.

"Can we go back tomorrow?" I asked.

My mother laughed. "That's up to Mr. Reed," she said. "We don't want to impose on him too much."

"Sure kid," said Mr. Reed. Then he laughed, too.

I looked up at Mr. Reed, then out at the water. I could see the drops disappearing into their holes on the surface.

The Piano Lesson

I bounced the ball against the yellow wall in the front of my house, waiting for the piano teacher. I'd been taking lessons for six weeks and I liked the piano, my mother played well, standards and show tunes, and sang. Often I sang along with her or by myself as she played. "Young at Heart" and "Bewitched, Bothered and Bewildered" were two of my favorites. I loved the dark blue cover of the sheet music of "Bewitched," with the drawing of the woman in a flowing white gown in the lower left-hand corner. It made me think of New York, though I'd never been there. White on midnight dark.

I liked to stand next to the piano bench while my mother played and listen to "Satan Takes a Holiday," a fox-trot it said on the sheet music. I was eight years old and could easily imagine foxes trotting in evening gowns.

I was up to "The Scissors-Grinder" and "Swan on the Lake" in the second red Thompson book. That was pretty good for six weeks, but I had begun to stutter. I knew I had begun to stutter because I'd heard my mother say it to my father on the phone. They ought just to ignore it, she'd said, and it would stop.

"Ready for your lesson today?" asked the teacher as she came up the walk.

"I'll be in in a minute," I said, continuing to bounce the ball off the yellow bricks. The teacher smiled and went into the building.

I kept hitting the ball against the wall. I knew she would be talking to my mother, then arranging the lesson books on the rack above the piano. I hit the ball once high above the first-floor windows, caught it, and ran.

The Lost Tribe

Roy looked for the tall black man whenever he walked past the yellow brick synagogue on his way to his friend Elmo's house. The man always waved to Roy and Roy waved back but they had never spoken. The man was usually sweeping the synagogue steps with a broom or emptying small trash cans into bigger ones. Seeing a black man working as a janitor was not an unusual sight, but what was unusual, to Roy, was that the man always wore a yarmulke. Roy had never before seen a black person wearing a Jewish prayer cap. Elmo was Jewish, so Roy asked him if anybody could be a Jew, even a black man.

"I don't know," said Elmo. "Maybe. Let's ask my old man."

Elmo's father, Big Sol, was a short but powerfully built man who owned a salvage business on the south side of Chicago. When Big Sol was home, he usually wore a Polish T-shirt, white boxer shorts, black socks and fuzzy house slippers. He was very hairy; large tufts of hair puffed out all over his body except for from the top of his head, which was bald. Big Sol was a kind, generous man who enjoyed joking around with the neighborhood kids, to whom he frequently offered a buck or two for soda pop or ice cream.

Big Sol was sitting in his recliner watching television when Elmo and Roy approached him.

"Hey, boys, how you doin'? Come on in, I'm watchin' a movie."

Roy looked at the black and white picture. James Mason was being chased by several men on a dark, wet street.

"This James Mason," said Big Sol, "he talks like he's got too many meatballs in his mouth."

Roy remembered Elmo having told him his father had been wounded at Guadalcanal. He'd recovered and was sent back into combat but later contracted malaria, which got him medically discharged from the Marines. Elmo was named after a war buddy of Big Sol's who had not been as fortunate.

"Hey, Pop," Elmo said, "can anybody be a Jew?"

"This is America," said Big Sol. "A person can be anything he wants to be. "

"How about Negroes?" said Elmo. "Can a Negro be Jewish?"

"Sammy Davis, Junior, is a Jew," Big Sol said.

"Was he born a Jew?" Elmo asked.

"What difference does it make? Sammy Davis, Junior, is the greatest entertainer in the world."

A few days later, Roy was walking past the synagogue thinking about how he had never been inside one, when he saw the black janitor wringing out a mop by the back door. The man waved and smiled. Roy went over to him.

"What's your name?" asked Roy.

"Ezra. What's yours?"

"Roy."

Ezra offered his right hand and Roy offered his. As they shook, Roy was surprised at how rough Ezra's skin was; almost abrasive, like a shark's.

"How old are you, Roy?"

"Eight. How old are you?"

"Sixty-one next Tuesday."

"How come you're wearing a Jewish prayer hat?" Roy asked.

"You got to wear one in the temple," said Ezra. "It's a holy place."

"Are you a Jew?"

"I am now."

"You weren't always?"

"Son, that's a good question. I was but I didn't know it until late in my life."

"How come?"

"Never really understood the Bible before, Roy. The original Jews were black, in Africa. I'm a descendant of the Lost Tribe of Israel."

"I've never heard of the Lost Tribe."

"You heard of Hailie Selassie?"

"No, who is he?"

"Hailie Selassie is the Lion of Judah. He lives in Ethiopia. Used to be called Abyssinia."

"Have you ever been there?"

Ezra shook his head. "Hope to go before I expire, though."

"How did your tribe get lost?"

"Old Pharaoh forced us to wander in the desert for thousands of years. Didn't want no Jews in Egypt. Drew down on us with six hundred chariots, but we got away when the angel of God put a pillar of cloud in front of 'em just long enough so Moses could herd us across the Red Sea, which the Lord divided then closed back up."

"Why didn't Pharaoh want the Jews in Egypt?"

Ezra bent down, looked Roy right in his eyes and said, "The Jews are the smartest people on the face of the earth. Always have been, always will be. Old Pharaoh got frightened. Hitler, too."

Roy noticed that the whites of Ezra's eyes were not white; they were mostly yellow.

"They were scared of the Jews?"

Ezra straightened back up to his full height.

"You bet they were scared," he said. "People get scared, they commence to killin'. After awhile, they get used to it, same as eatin'."

Ezra picked up his mop and bucket.

"Nice talkin' to you, Roy. You stop by again."

Ezra turned and entered the synagogue.

Walking to Elmo's house, Roy thought about Ezra's tribe wandering lost in the desert. They must have been smart, Roy decided, to have survived for so long.

Big Sol was sitting in his easy chair in the living room, drinking a Falstaff and watching the White Sox play the Tigers on TV.

"Hey, Big Roy!" he said. "How you doin'?"

"Did the Lost Tribe of Israel really wander in the desert for thousands of years?" Roy asked.

Big Sol nodded his head. "Yeah, but that was a long time ago. The Jews were tough in them days."

"Ezra, the janitor at the synagogue up the street, told me that Jews are the smartest people on the planet."

Big Sol stared seriously at the TV for several seconds. Pierce struck Kaline out on a change-up.

"Yeah, well," Big Sol said, turning to look at Roy, "he won't get no argument from me."

The Lost Christmas

In 1954, when I was eight years old, I lost Christmas. At about noon of Christmas Eve that year, I went with some kids to the Nortown Theater on Western Avenue in Chicago to see a movie, *Demetrius and the Gladiators*, starring Victor Mature and Susan Hayward. My mother and I had until earlier that month been living in Florida and Cuba, and were in Chicago, where I was born and where we sometimes stayed, to spend the Christmas holidays with Nanny, my grandmother, my mother's mother, who was bed-ridden because of a chronic heart condition. In fact, Nanny would die due to heart failure the following May, at the age of fifty-nine.

The ground was piled with fresh snow that Christmas Eve Day. The few cars that were moving snailed along the streets barely faster than we could walk. The first time I had come to Chicago as a human being old enough to be conscious of my surroundings was when I was five or six. Now that I was older, however, and was somewhat inured to the snow and ice—at least I knew what to expect—I could if not enjoy at least endure the weather, especially since I knew my situation was temporary.

I thought *Demetrius and the Gladiators* was a great movie, full of fighting with swords and shields and a sexy redhead, like my mother. I didn't notice if Victor Mature's breasts were larger than Susan Hayward's—an earlier (1949) film, *Samson and Delilah*, had prompted the comment by a producer that Mature's tits were bigger than co-star Hedy Lamarr's—I was impressed only by the pageantry of goofy Hollywood ancient Rome. Walking home Christmas Eve afternoon, the leaden gray Chicago sky heading rapidly toward darkness, I suddenly was overcome by dizziness and very nearly collapsed to the now ice-hard sidewalk carapace.

My companions had already turned off onto another street, so I was alone. I managed to steady myself against a brown brick wall and then slowly and carefully made my way the final block or two to my grandmother's house.

The next thing I knew I was waking up in bed dressed in my yellow flannel pajamas decorated with drawings of football players. The first image I saw was a large-jawed fullback cradling a ball in the crook of his left arm while stiff-arming a would-be tackler with his right. I was very thirsty and looked up to see my mother and Nanny, who, miraculously, was out of her sickbed, leaning over me. According to my mother, I asked two questions: "Can I have a glass of water?" and "Is it Christmas yet?"

In fact, it was December 26th—I had lost consciousness almost as soon as I arrived home following the movie, and had been delirious with fever for most of the time since then. The fever broke and I woke up. My mother brought me a glass of water, which she cautioned me to sip slowly, as the doctor had ordered.

"Was the doctor here?" I asked. Nanny and my mother told me how worried they had been. A doctor friend of Nanny's had come twice to see me, even on Christmas Day; he would come again later. Nanny and my mother laughed—in fact, both of them were crying tears of relief.

"This is the best gift of all," said my mother, "getting my boy back."

I've often wondered what I missed during my delirium, as if those twenty-four or so hours had been stolen from me. Once someone asked me if I had access to a time machine and could go forward or back anywhere in time, where would I go? I told him without hesitation that I would set the machine for Christmas Day of 1954. To paraphrase William Faulkner, that Christmas past is not dead, it's not even past.

My Catechism

It was during the winter I later referred to, in deference to the poet, as Out of the Clouds Endlessly Snowing, that I was dismissed once and forever from Sunday school. Mine was not a consistent presence at St. Tim's, due to my mother's predilection for travel and preference for tropical places, but the winter after I turned eight years old, she left me for several weeks with her mother, whom I called Nanny, in Chicago. Where exactly my mother chose to spend that period of time I've never been entirely certain, although I believe she was then keeping company—my mother and father were divorced—with a gunrunner of Syrian or Lebanese descent named Johnny Cacao, whose main residence seemed to be in the Dominican Republic.

I recall receiving a soggy postcard postmarked Santo Domingo, on which my mother had written, "Big turtle bit off part of one of Johnny's toes. Other than that, doing fine. Sea green and crystal clear. Love, Mom." The picture side of the card showed a yellowish dirt street with a half-naked brown boy about my age sitting on the ground leaning against a darker brown wall. A pair of red chickens were pecking in the dust next to his bare feet. I wondered if the chickens down there went for toes the way the turtles did.

On this blizzardy Sunday morning, I walked to St. Tim's with two of the three McLaughlin brothers, Petie and Paulie, and their mother. My mother and grandmother were Catholics but they rarely attended church; Nanny because she was most often too ill—she died before my ninth birthday—and my mother because she was so frequently away, swimming in turtle-infested seas. Petie and I were the same age, Paulie a year younger. The eldest McLaughlin brother, Frank, was in the Army, stationed in Korea.

After the church service, which was the first great theater I ever attended, and which I still rank as the best because the audience was always invited to participate by taking the wafer and the wine, symbolizing the body and the blood of Jesus Christ, Petie, Paulie and I went to catechism class. Ruled over by Sister Margaret Mary, a tall, sturdily built woman of indeterminate age—I could never figure out if she was twenty-five or fifty-five—the children sat ramrod straight in their chairs and did not speak unless invited to by her. Sister Margaret Mary wore a classic black habit, wire-rimmed spectacles, and her facial skin was as pale as one of Dracula's wives. I had recently seen the Tod Browning film, *Dracula*, featuring Bela Lugosi, and I remember thinking that it was interesting that both God and Dracula had similar taste in women.

During instruction, the class was given the standard mumbo jumbo, as my father—who was not a Catholic—called it, about how God created heaven and earth, then Adam and Eve, and so on. Kids asked how He had done this or that, and what He did next. I raised my hand and asked, "Sister, *why* did He do it?"

"Why did He do what?" she said.

"Any of this stuff."

"You wouldn't exist, or Peter or Paul, or His only son, had He not made us," answered Sister Margaret Mary.

"I know, Sister," I said, "but what for? I mean, what was in it for Him?"

Sister Margaret Mary glared at me for a long moment, and for the first and only time I could discern a trace of color in her face. She then turned her attention away from me and proceeded as if my question deserved no further response.

Before we left the church that day, I saw Sister Margaret Mary talking to Mrs. McLaughlin and looking toward me as she spoke. Mrs. McLaughlin nodded, and looked over at me, too.

The following Sunday morning, I was about to leave the house when Nanny asked me where I was going.

"To the McLaughlins'," I told her. "To Sunday School."

"Sister Margaret Mary told Mrs. McLaughlin she doesn't want you coming to her class anymore," said Nanny. "You can play in your room or watch television until Petie and Paulie come home. Besides, it's snowing again."

Sunday Paper

As he often did when I was about eight or nine and he still lived with us, Pops, my mother's father, asked me to go for the Sunday paper. For some reason on this particular day I decided to go to the stand on Washtenaw instead of the one on Rockwell, taking the shortcut through the alley where the deep snow from the night before was still undisturbed, no cars having gone over it yet that morning. I was shuffling through the powder, kicking it up in the air so that the flakes floated about in the sunlight like rice snow in crystal balls, when I spotted the police cars.

There were three of them, parked one behind the other on Washtenaw in front of Talon's Butcher Shop. A few people stood bundled in coats outside Talon's, trying to see inside the shop, which I knew was closed on Sunday. I stood on the opposite side of the street and watched. An ambulance came, without using its siren, and slid slowly to a stop alongside the police cars. Two attendants got out and went into Talon's carrying a stretcher.

A man came up beside me and asked what was going on. I looked at him and saw that he had on an overcoat over his pajamas and probably slippers on under his galoshes.

"I was just going for a paper," he said.

When I told him I didn't know, he crossed over and spoke to one of the women standing by the door of the butcher shop. The man looked in the doorway and then walked away. I waited, standing in a warm shaft of sunlight, and in a couple of minutes the man came up to me again. He had a rolled-up *Tribune* under his arm.

"He hanged himself," the man said. "Talon, the butcher. They found him hanging in his shop this morning."

The man looked across the street for a moment, then walked down Washtenaw.

Nobody came out of the butcher shop. I went to the corner and bought a *Sun-Times*. I stopped for a few seconds on my way back to see if anything was happening but nothing was so I turned into the alley, carefully stepping in the tracks I'd made before.

The Origin of Truth

When Roy was in the fourth grade, his class was taken on a field trip to the Museum of Science and Industry. Aboard the school bus on the way to the museum, Bobby Kazmeier and Jimmy Portis both said they couldn't wait to go down into the coal mine.

"They got a real working coal mine there," Portis told Roy and Big Art Tuth, Roy's seatmate, "like in West Virginia, where my daddy's family's from."

"It ain't real," said Big Art, "it's a reenactment."

"Not a reenactment," Roy said, "a reproduction, or a replica. It's to show what a coal mine is like."

"What's the difference?" asked Kazmeier. I heard you go down a mine shaft in an elevator."

"An open air one, Kaz," said Portis, "not like an elevator in the Wrigley Building."

"They've got open ones in the State and Lake Building," Roy said, "to deliver furs. My grandfather works there. Also in the Merchandise Mart. They're in the back; customers take the regular elevators."

"I hope we don't have to squeeze through any narrow places in the caves," said Big Art. "I don't want to get stuck."

Delbert Swaim, the dumbest kid in the class, who was sitting behind Roy, said, "I bet it's like in Flash Gordon, where the clay people blend into the walls and attack when nobody's looking."

In the museum, the class looked at outer space exhibits and architectural displays, which were pretty interesting, but the boys were anxious to go down into the coal mine. This was left for last. The class teacher, Mrs. Rudinsky, instructed the students to keep together.

"We'll descend in groups of ten," she announced. "That means three groups. When you reach the bottom, stay right there with your group until the others arrive. I will be with the third group."

Mrs. Rudinsky was not quite five feet tall, she was very skinny and wore thick glasses and a big black wig. She was forty-five years old. The story was that she had lost all of her hair as a teenager due to an attack of scarlet fever. Roy didn't know what scarlet fever was, so he asked Mary Margaret Grubart, the smartest girl in the class, about it.

"Fevers come in all colors," she told Roy. "Scarlet's one of the worst, it can kill a person. A man wrote a famous novel about it where a girl had to wear a scarlet letter on her dress to warn people not to get near her so they wouldn't get sick. In historical times, sick people were burned alive."

In the coal mine, the kids were shown around by a museum guide wearing a hard hat with a flashlight attached to the front of it, the kind that miners wear. There were blue flames that indicated gas deposits and a miniature railway on which carts carrying coal traveled. The guide explained how the operation worked and presented samples of different types of coal, which the students passed around. The hardest, blackest coal was called bituminous.

"This is the kind Superman can squeeze and turn into diamonds," said Roy.

The other kids laughed but the guide said, "You're right, son. Bituminous is processed over a period of hundreds if not thousands of years and can become diamonds."

"Superman can make a diamond in a few seconds," Roy said. "But he doesn't do it too often in order not to destroy the world economy. My grandfather told me that."

"Your grandfather knows what he's talking about, young man," said the guide.

After the tour had concluded and they were back above ground, Mrs. Rudinsky lined the students up preparatory to marching them out of the museum to the bus. Two boys were missing: Bobby Kazmeier and Jimmy Portis.

"Has anyone seen Portis and Kazmeier?" asked Mrs. Rudinsky.

"They're still down in the mine," said Delbert Swaim. "They said they wanted to explore more."

"You all wait right here!" Mrs. Rudinsky commanded, before going to find a museum employee.

While two security guards and the coal mine guide went down in the elevator to find the missing boys, Mrs. Rudinsky loaded the other students onto the school bus, where they were told to wait with the driver, Old Ed Moot. Mrs. Rudinsky went back into the museum.

"They could suffocate," said Old Ed Moot, "if they stay down there too long without masks."

It was more than an hour before Mrs. Rudinsky returned to the bus. Bobby Kazmeier and Jimmy Portis were not with her.

"Go!" she said to Old Ed Moot, and sat down in a seat at the front. Old Ed pulled the door closed.

"Mrs. Rudinsky, some of us have to go to the bathroom," said Mary Margaret Grubart.

"You'll just have to hold it until we get to the school," Mrs. Rudinsky told her.

"Where's Kaz and Jimmy?" asked Roy.

"They'll find them," the teacher said.

"You mean they're still down in the mine?" asked Big Art.

"No talking!" ordered Mrs. Rudinsky.

Roy noticed that her wig was turned slightly sideways and listing to port. Above her right ear, Mrs. Rudinsky's scalp was hairless.

She was the first person off the bus and headed straight for the principal's office, leaving the students to fend for themselves. The school day was over, everyone was free to go home, but Roy and Big Art stood by the bus with Old Ed Moot, who lit up an unfiltered Chesterfield.

"Those boys are in big trouble," said Old Ed, "unless they're dead. Either way, your teacher's in deep shit."

"Hey, Ed," said Big Art, "can we have a cigarette?"

Old Ed shook his head as he inhaled his Chesterfield. "Dirty habit," he said. "Don't start."

"We already started," said Art.

Just then a police car pulled up in front of the school. Two cops got out with Jimmy Portis between them and entered the building.

"Wow," Roy said, "where's Kaz?"

"Maybe suffocated," said the bus driver. "This one's the lucky one."

Two minutes later, another police car arrived and parked behind the first one. Two cops got out with Bobby Kazmeier wedged between them and walked into the school.

Old Ed Moot looked at the Timex on his left wrist and said, "Well, fellas, my day's done."

He dropped his cigarette butt on the ground and stepped on it, turning his steel-toed Sears workshoe so that there wouldn't be anything worth picking up, and walked away.

"What do you think will happen to them?" asked Big Art.

"I don't know," Roy said, "but if it hadn't been for Jimmy and Kaz staying in the coal mine, we probably would have got homework."

The Trophy

My dad was not much of an athlete. I don't recall his ever playing catch with me or doing anything requiring particular athletic dexterity. I knew he was a kind of tough guy because my mother told me about his knocking other guys down now and again, but he wasn't interested in sports. He did, however, take me to professional baseball and football games and boxing matches but those were, for him, more like social occasions, opportunities to meet and be greeted by business associates and potential customers. At Marigold Arena or the Amphitheater Dad spent most of his time talking to people rather than watching the event. He may have gone bowling on occasion but never in my company.

When I was nine I joined a winter bowling league. I was among the youngest bowlers in the league and certainly the youngest on my team. The league met on Saturday mornings at Nortown Bowl on Devon Avenue between Maplewood and Campbell Streets. The lanes were on the second floor up a long, decrepit flight of stairs above Crawford's Department Store. I told my dad about it and invited him to come watch me bowl. I wasn't very good, of course, but I took it seriously, as I did all competitive sports, and I steadily improved. I practiced after school a couple of times during the week with older guys, who gave me tips on how to improve my bowling skills.

There were kids who practically lived at the bowling alley. Most of them were sixteen or older and had pretty much given up on formal education. The state law in Illinois held that public education was mandatory until the age of sixteen; after that, a kid could do whatever he wanted until he was eighteen, at which time he was required to register for military service. It was the high school dropouts who got drafted right away; but for two years these guys got to sleep late and spend their afternoons and evenings hanging out at the bowling alley, betting on games, and gorging themselves on Italian beef sandwiches. At night they would go to Uptown Bowl, where the big, often televised professional matches took place.

The announcer for these events was usually Whispering Ray Rayburn, a small, weaselish man who wore a terrible brown toupee and pencil-line mustache. His ability to speak into a microphone at a consistently low but adequately audible decibel level was his claim to fame. Kids, including myself, often imitated Whispering Ray as they toed the mark preparatory to and as they took their three- or four-step approach before releasing the bowling ball:

"Zabrofsky casually talcs his right hand," a kid would whisper to himself as he stood at the ball rack, "slips three digits into the custom-fit Brunswick Black Beauty, hefts the sixteen-pound spheroid"—(one of Whispering Ray's favorite words for the ball was "spheroid")—"balances it delicately in the palm of his left hand. Amazing how Zabrofsky handles the ebony orb"—("orb" was another pet name)—"almost daintily, as if it were an egg. Now Zabrofsky steps to his spot, feet tight together. He needs this spare to keep pace with the leader, Lars Grotwitz. Zabrofsky studies the five-ten split that confronts him with the kind of concentration Einstein must have mustered to unmuzzle an atom." ("Muster" was also big in Whispering Ray's lexicon.) "Zabrofsky's breathing is all we can hear now. Remember, fans, Big Earl is an asthmatic who depends heavily on the use of an inhaler in order to compete. You can see the impression it makes in the left rear pocket of his Dacron slacks. Despite this serious handicap his intensity is impressive. He begins his approach: one, two, three, the ball swings back and as Big Earl slides forward on the fourth step the powerful form smoothly sets his spheroid on its way. Zabrofsky's velvet touch has set the ebony orb hurtling toward the kingpin. At the last instant it veers left as if by remote control, brushes the five as it whizzes past and hips it toward the ten. Ticked almost too softly, the ten wobbles like an habitué dismounting a stool at Johnny Fazio's

Tavern"—(Johnny Fazio was a sponsor of the local TV broadcasts)—"then tumbles into the gutter! Zabrofsky makes the tough spare."

On the last Saturday in February, the league awarded trophies to be presented personally to each team member by Carmen Salvino, a national champion bowler. My team had won its division despite my low pin total. Each team had on its roster at least one novice bowler, leaving it up to the more experienced members to "carry" him, which my team had managed to do. I was grateful to my older teammates for their guidance, patience, and encouragement, and thanks to them I was to be awarded a trophy. The only guy on the team who had not been particularly generous toward me was Oscar Fomento, who worked part-time as a pinsetter. Fomento, not to my displeasure, had left the team two weeks into the league season, after having beaten up his parents with a bowling pin when they gave him a hard time about ditching school. One of the other guys told me Oscar had been sent to a reformatory in Colorado where they shaved his head and made him milk cows in below-freezing temperatures. "That's tough," my teammate said, "but just think how strong Fomento's fingers'll be when he gets back."

My dad had not made it to any of the Saturday morning matches, so I called him on Friday night before the last day of the league and told him this would be his final chance to see me bowl, and that Carmen Salvino would be there giving out trophies. I didn't tell Dad that I'd be receiving a trophy because I wanted him to be surprised. "Salvino," my Dad said. "Yeah, I know the guy. Okay, son."

It snowed heavily late Friday night and into Saturday morning. I had to be at Nortown Bowl by nine and flurries were still coming down at five-to when I kicked my way on a shortcut through fresh white drifts in the alley between Rockwell and Maplewood. Dashing up the steep wet steps I worried about Carmen Salvino and my father being able to drive there. I lived a block away, so it was easy for me and most of the other kids to walk over. I hoped the snowplows were out early clearing the roads.

During the games I kept watching for my dad. Toward the end of the last line there was a lot of shouting: Carmen Salvino had arrived. Our team finished up and went over with the other kids to the counter area, behind which hundreds of pairs of used bowling shoes, sizes two to twenty, were kept in cubbyholes similar to mail slots at hotel desks. Carmen Salvino, a tall, hairy-armed man with thick eyebrows and a head of hair the color and consistency of a major oil slick, stood behind the counter in front of the smelly, worn, multicolored bowling shoes between the Durkee brothers, Dominic and Don, owners of Nortown Bowl.

Dominic and Don Durkee were both about five foot six and had hair only on the sides of their heads, sparse blue threads around the ears. They were grinning like madmen because the great Carmen Salvino was standing next to them in their establishment. The Durkees' skulls shone bright pink under the rude fluorescent lights. The reflection from the top of Carmen Salvino's head blinded anyone foolish enough to stare at it for more than a couple of seconds.

I was the last kid to be presented a trophy. When Carmen Salvino gave it to me he shook my small, naked hand with his huge, hairy one. I noticed, however, that he had extremely long, slender fingers, like a concert pianist's. "Congrajalayshuns, son," he said to me. Then Carmen Salvino turned to Dominic Durkee and asked, "So, we done now?"

When I walked back home through the alley from Maplewood to Rockwell, the snow was still perfectly white and piled high in front of the garages. At home I put my trophy on the top of my dresser. It was the first one I had ever received. The trophy wasn't very big but I really liked the golden figure of a man holding a golden bowling ball, his right arm cocked back. He didn't look at all like Carmen Salvino, or like me, either. He resembled my next-door neighbor Jimmy McLaughlin, an older kid who worked as a dishwasher at Kow Kow's Chinese restaurant on the corner of Devon and Rockwell. Jimmy worked all day Saturday, I knew. I decided I'd take the trophy over later and show it to him.

The Aerodynamics of an Irishman

There was a man who lived on my block when I was a kid whose name was Rooney Sullavan. He would often come walking down the street while the kids were playing ball in front of my house or Johnny McLaughlin's house. Rooney would always stop and ask if he'd ever shown us how he used to throw the knuckleball back when he pitched for Kankakee in 1930.

"Plenty of times, Rooney," Billy Cunningham would say. "No knuckles about it, right?" Tommy Ryan would say. "No knuckles about it, right!" Rooney Sullavan would say. "Give it here and I'll show you." One of us would reluctantly toss Rooney the ball and we'd step up so he could demonstrate for the fortieth time how he held the ball by his fingertips only, no knuckles about it.

"Don't know how it ever got the name knuckler," Rooney'd say. "I call mine the Rooneyball." Then he'd tell one of us, usually Billy because he had the catcher's glove—the old fat-heeled kind that didn't bend unless somebody stepped on it, a big black mitt that Billy's dad had handed down to him from his days at Kankakee or Rock Island or someplace—to get sixty feet away so Rooney could see if he could still "make it wrinkle."

Billy would pace off twelve squares of sidewalk, each square being approximately five feet long, the length of one nine year old boy's body stretched head to toe lying flat, squat down, and stick his big black glove out in front of his face. With his right hand he'd cover his crotch in case the pitch got away and short-hopped off the cement where he couldn't block it with the mitt. The knuckleball was unpredictable, not even Rooney could tell what would happen once he let it go.

"It's the air makes it hop," Rooney claimed. His leather jacket creaked as he bent, wound up, rotated his right arm like nobody'd done since Chief Bender, crossed his runny gray eyes, and released the ball from the tips of his fingers. We watched as it sailed straight up at first, then sort of floated on an invisible wave before plunging the last ten feet like a balloon that had been pierced by a dart.

Billy always went down on his knees, the back of his right hand stiffened over his crotch, and stuck out his gloved hand at the slowly whirling Rooneyball. Just before it got to Billy's mitt the ball would give out entirely and sink rapidly, inducing Billy to lean forward in order to catch it, only he couldn't because at the last instant it would take a final, sneaky hop before bouncing surprisingly hard off of Billy's unprotected chest.

"*Just* like I told you," Rooney Sullavan would exclaim. "All it takes is plain old air."

Billy would come up with the ball in his upturned glove, his right hand rubbing the place on his chest where the pitch had hit. "You all right, son?" Rooney would ask, and Billy would nod. "Tough kid," Rooney'd say. "I'd like to stay out with you fellas all day, but I got responsibilities." Rooney would muss up Billy's hair with the hand that held the secret to the Rooneyball and walk away whistling "When Irish Eyes Are Smiling" or "My Wild Irish Rose." Rooney was about forty-five or fifty years old and lived with his mother in a bungalow at the corner. He worked nights for Wanzer Dairy, washing out returned milk bottles.

Tommy Ryan would grab the ball out of Billy's mitt and hold it by the tips of his fingers like Rooney Sullavan did, and Billy would go sit on the stoop in front of the closest house and rub his chest. "No way," Tommy would say, considering the prospect of his ever duplicating Rooney's feat. "There must be something he's not telling us."

A Rainy Day at the Nortown Theater

When I was about nine or ten years old my dad picked me up from school one day and took me to the movies. I didn't see him very often since my parents were divorced and I lived with my mother. This day my dad asked me what I wanted to do and since it was raining hard we decided to go see *Dragnet* starring Jack Webb and an Alan Ladd picture, *Shane*.

I had already seen *Dragnet* twice and since it wasn't such a great movie I was really interested in seeing *Shane*, which I'd already seen as well, but only once, and had liked it, especially the end where the kid, Brandon de Wilde, goes running through the bulrushes calling for Shane to come back, "Come back, Shane! Shane, come back!" I had really remembered that scene and was anxious to see it again, so all during *Dragnet* I kept still because I thought my dad wanted to see it, not having already seen it, and when *Shane* came on I was happy.

But it was Wednesday and my dad had promised my mother he'd have me home for dinner at six, so at about a quarter to, like I had dreaded in the back of my head, my dad said we had to go.

"But Dad," I said "*Shane*'s not over till six-thirty and I want to see the end where the kid goes running after him yelling, 'Come back, Shane!' That's the best part!"

But my dad said no, we had to go, so I got up and went with him but walked slowly backward up the aisle to see as much of the picture as I could even though I knew now I wasn't going to get to see the end, and we were in the lobby, which was dark and red with gold curtains, and saw it was still pouring outside. My dad made me put on my coat and duck my head down into it when we made a run for the car, which was parked not very far away.

My dad drove me home and talked to me but I didn't hear what he said. I was thinking about the kid who would be running after Shane in about ten more minutes. I kissed my dad good-bye and went in to eat dinner but I stood in the hall and watched him drive off before I did.

Renoir's *Chemin montant dans les hautes herbes*

The path on the hillside is a stripe of light, a three-dimensional effect. There is nothing theoretical about this: everything is where it is supposed to be. Not merely light and shadow and balance and color but the unprepared for, the element that informs as well as verifies the work. As the light in the Salle Caillebotte in the Jeu de Paume changes the painting changes, too—like the sun slowly emerging from behind a cloud, it opens and displays more of itself.

The people and the setting are from a previous century: women and children descending the path. There is absolutely nothing savage about the picture. Flowers, fruit trees, foot-worn path, wooden fence—nothing to disturb. The element of feeling is calm; difficulty disappears.

An early summer afternoon in the house in Chicago. I'm ten years old. The sky is very dark. A thunderstorm. I'm sitting on the floor in my room, the cool tiles. The rain comes, at first very hard, then soft. I'm playing a game by myself. Nobody else is around, except, perhaps, my mother, in another part of the house. There is and will be for a while nothing to disturb me. This is my most beloved childhood memory, an absolutely inviolable moment, totally devoid of difficulty. It's the same feeling I have when I look at Renoir's *Chemin montant dans les hautes herbes*. I doubt very seriously if my father would have understood this feeling.

Forever After

Riding in a car on a highway late at night was one of Roy's greatest pleasures. In between towns, on dark, sparsely populated roads, Roy enjoyed imagining the lives of these isolated inhabitants, their looks, clothes, and habits. He also liked listening to the radio when his mother or father did not feel like talking. Roy and one or the other of his parents spent a considerable amount of time traveling, mostly on the road between Chicago, New Orleans and Miami, the three cities in which they alternately resided.

Roy did not mind this peripatetic existence because it was the only life he knew. When he grew up, Roy thought, he might prefer to remain in one place for more than a couple of months at a time; but for now, being always "on the go," as his mother phrased it, did not displease him. Roy liked meeting new people at the hotels at which they stayed, hearing stories about these strangers' lives in Cincinnati or Houston or Indianapolis. Roy often memorized the names of their dogs and horses, the names of the streets on which they lived, even the numbers on their houses. The only numbers of this nature Roy owned were room numbers at the hotels. When someone asked him where he lived, Roy would respond: "The Roosevelt, room 504," or "The Ambassador, room 309," or "The Delmonico, room 406."

One night when Roy and his father were in southern Georgia, headed for Ocala, Florida, a report came over the car radio about a manhunt being conducted for a thirty-two year old Negro male named Lavern Rope. Lavern Rope, an unemployed catfish farm worker who until recently had been living in Belzoni, Mississippi, had apparently murdered his mother, then kidnapped a nun, whose car he had stolen. Most of the nun's body was found in the bathtub of a hotel room in Valdosta, not far from where Roy and his father were driving. The nun's left arm was missing, police said, and was assumed to still be in the possession of Lavern Rope, who was last reported seen leaving Vic and Flo's Forever After Drive-in, a popular Valdosta hamburger stand, just past midnight in Sister Mary Alice Gogarty's 1957 red and beige Chrysler Newport convertible.

Roy immediately went on the lookout for the stolen car, though the stretch of highway they were on was pretty lonely at three o'clock in the morning. Only one car had passed them, going the other way, in the last half hour or so, and Roy had not noticed what model it was.

"Dad," said Roy, "why would Lavern Rope keep the nun's left arm?"

"Probably thought it would make the body harder to identify," Roy's father answered. "Maybe she had a tattoo on it."

"I didn't think nuns had tattoos."

"She could have got it before she became a nun."

"He'll probably dump the arm somewhere, Dad, don't you think?"

"I guess. Don't ever get a tattoo, son. There might come a day you won't want to be recognized. It's better if you don't have any identifying marks on your body."

By the time they reached Ocala, the sun was coming up. Roy's father checked them into a hotel and when they got to their room he asked Roy if he wanted to use the bathroom.

"No, Dad, you can go first."

Roy's father laughed. "What's the matter, son? Afraid there'll be a body in the bathtub?"

"No," said Roy, "just a left arm."

While his father was in the bathroom, Roy thought about Lavern Rope cutting off Sister Mary Alice Gogarty's arm in a Valdosta hotel room. If he had used a pocket knife, it would have taken a very long time. He had probably brought along a kitchen knife from his mother's house to do the job, Roy decided.

When his father came out, Roy asked him, "Do you think the cops will find Lavern Rope?"

"Sure, they'll catch him."

"Dad?"

"Yes, son?"

"I bet they never find the nun's arm."

"Won't make much difference, will it? Come on, boy, take your clothes off. We need to sleep."

Roy undressed and got into one of the two beds. Before Roy could ask another question, his father was snoring in the other bed. Roy lay there with his eyes open for several minutes; then he realized that he needed to go to the bathroom.

Suddenly, his father stopped snoring.

"Son, you still awake?"

"Yes, Dad."

Roy's father sat up in his bed.

"It just occurred to me that a brand new red and beige Chrysler Newport convertible is a damn unusual automobile for a nun to be driving."

The Mason-Dixon Line

One Sunday I accompanied my dad on an automobile trip up from Chicago to Dixon, Illinois. It was a sunny January morning, and it must have been when I was ten years old because I remember that I wore the black leather motorcycle jacket I'd received that Christmas. I was very fond of that jacket with its multitude of bright silver zippers and two silver stars on each epaulet. I also wore a blue cashmere scarf of my dad's and an old pair of brown leather gloves he'd given me after my mother gave him a new pair of calfskins for Christmas.

I liked watching the snowy fields as we sped past them on the narrow, two-lane northern Illinois roads. We passed through a number of little towns, each of them with seemingly identical centers: a Rexall, hardware store, First State Bank of Illinois, Presbyterian, Methodist, and Catholic churches with snowcapped steeples, and a statue of Black Hawk, the heroic Sauk and Fox chief.

When my dad had asked me if I wanted to take a ride with him that morning I'd said sure, without asking where to or why. My dad never asked twice and he never made any promises about when we'd be back. I liked the uncertainty of those situations, the open-endedness about them. Anything could happen, I figured; it was more fun not knowing what to expect.

"We're going to Dixon," Dad said after we'd been driving for about forty-five minutes. "To see a man named Mason." I'd recently read a Young Readers biography of Robert E. Lee, so I knew all about the Civil War. "We're on the Mason-Dixon line," I said, and laughed, pleased with my little kid's idea of a joke. "That's it, boy," said my dad. "We're going to get a line on Mason in Dixon."

The town of Dixon appeared to be one street long, like in a Western movie: the hardware store, bank, church, and drugstore. I didn't see a statue. We went into a tiny café next to the bank that was empty except for a counterman. Dad told me to sit in one of the booths and told the counterman to give me a hot chocolate and whatever else I wanted.

"I'll be back in an hour, son," said Dad. He gave the counterman a twenty-dollar bill and walked out. When the counterman brought over the hot chocolate he asked if there was anything else he could get for me. "A hamburger," I said, "and an order of fries." "You got it," he said.

I sipped slowly at the hot chocolate until he brought me the hamburger and fries. The counterman sat on a stool near the booth and looked at me. "That your old man?" he asked. "He's my dad," I said, between bites of the hamburger. "Any special reason he's here?" he asked. I didn't say anything and the counterman said, "You are from Chi, aren't ya?" I nodded yes and kept chewing. "You must be here for a reason," he said. "My dad needs to see someone," I said. "Thought so," said the counterman. "Know his name?" I took a big bite of the hamburger before I answered. "No," I said. The counterman looked at me, then out the window again. After a minute he walked over behind the counter. "Let me know if ya need anything else," he said.

While my dad was gone I tried to imagine who this fellow Mason was. I figured he must be some guy hiding out from the Chicago cops, and that his real name probably wasn't Mason. My dad came back in less than an hour, picked up his change from the counterman, tipped him, and said to me, "Had enough to eat?" I said yes and followed him out to the car.

"This is an awfully small town," I said to my dad as we drove away. "Does Mason live here?" "Who?" he asked. Then he said, "Oh yeah, Mason." Dad didn't say anything else for a while. He took a cigar out of his overcoat pocket, bit off the tip, rolled down his window, and spit it out before saying, "No, he doesn't live here. Just visiting."

We drove along for a few miles before Dad lit his cigar, leaving the window open. I put the scarf up around my face to keep warm and settled back in the seat. My dad drove and didn't talk for about a half hour. Around Marengo he said, "Did that counterman back there ask you any questions?" "He asked me if you were my dad and if we were from Chicago," I said. "What did you tell him?" "I said yes." "Anything else?" "He asked if you were there for any special reason and I said you were there to see someone." "Did you tell him who?" Dad asked. "I said I didn't know his name."

Dad nodded and threw his dead cigar out the window, then rolled it up. "You tired?" he asked. "No," I said. "What do you think," he said, "would you rather live out here or in the city?" "The city," I said. "I think it's more interesting there." "So do I," said Dad. "Relax, son, and we'll be home before you know it."

The Wedding

When my mother married her third husband, I, at the age of eleven, was given the duty, or privilege, of proposing a toast at the banquet following the wedding. My uncle Buck coached me— "Unaccustomed as I am to public speaking," I was to begin.

I kept going over it in my head. "Unaccustomed as I am to public speaking . . ." until the moment arrived and I found myself standing with a glass in my hand saying, "Unaccustomed as I am to public speaking—" I stopped. I couldn't remember what else my uncle had told me to say, so I said, "I want to propose a toast to my new father"—I paused—"and my old mother."

Everybody laughed and applauded. I could hear my uncle's high-pitched twitter. It wasn't what I was supposed to have said, that last part. My mother wasn't old, she was about thirty, and that wasn't what I'd meant by "old." I'd meant she was my same mother, that hadn't changed. No matter how often the father changed the mother did not.

I was afraid I'd insulted her. Everybody laughing was no insurance against that. I didn't want this new father, and a few months later, neither did my mother.

The Pitcher

One night when I was eleven I was playing baseball in the alley behind my house. I was batting left-handed when I hit a tremendous home run that rolled all the way to the end of the alley and would have gone into the street but an old man turning the corner picked it up. The old man came walking up the alley toward me and my friends, flipping the baseball up in the air and catching it. When he got to where we stood, the old man asked us who'd hit that ball.

"I did," I said.

"It was sure a wallop," said the old man, and he stood there, grinning. "I used to play ball," he said, and my friends and I looked at each other. "With the Cardinals, and the Cubs."

My friends and I looked at the ground or down the alley where the cars went by on Rosemont Avenue.

"You don't believe me," said the old man. "Well, look here." And he held out a gold ring in the palm of his hand. "Go on, look at it," he said. I took it. "Read it," said the old man.

"World Series, 1931," I said.

"I was with the Cardinals then," the old guy said, smiling now. "Was a pitcher. These days I'm just an old bird dog, a scout."

I looked up at the old man. "What's your name?" I asked.

"Tony Kaufmann," he said. I gave him his ring back. "You just keep hitting 'em like that, young fella, and you'll be a big leaguer." The old man tossed my friend Billy the ball. "So long," he said, and walked on up to the end of the alley, where he went in the back door of Beebs and Glen's Tavern.

"Think he was tellin' the truth or is he a nut?" one of the kids asked me.

"I don't know," I said, "let's go ask my grandfather. He'd remember him if he really played."

Billy and I ran into my house and found Pops watching TV in his room.

"Do you remember a guy named Tony Kaufmann?" I asked him. "An old guy in the alley just told us he pitched in the World Series."

"He showed us his ring," said Billy.

My grandfather raised his eyebrows. "Tony Kaufmann? In the alley? I remember him. Sure, he used to pitch for the Cubs."

Billy and I looked at each other.

"Where's he now?" asked my grandfather.

"We saw him go into Beebs and Glen's," said Billy.

"Well," said Pops, getting out of his chair, "let's go see what the old-timer has to say."

"You mean you'll take us in the tavern with you?" I asked.

"Come on," said Pops, not even bothering to put on his hat, "never knew a pitcher who could hold his liquor."

A Place in the Sun

The final memory I have of my dad is the time we attended a Chicago Bears football game at Wrigley Field about a month before he died. It was in November of 1958, a cold day, cold even for November on the shore of Lake Michigan. I don't remember what team the Bears were playing that afternoon; mostly I recall the overcast sky, the freezing temperature and visible breath of the players curling out from beneath their helmets like smoke from dragons' nostrils.

My dad was in good spirits despite the fact that the colostomy he'd undergone that previous summer had measurably curtailed his physical activities. He ate heartily at the game, the way he always had: two or three hot dogs, coffee, beer, a few shots of Bushmill's from a flask he kept in an overcoat pocket. He shook hands with a number of men on our way to our seats and again on our way out of the stadium, talking briefly with each of them, laughing and patting them on the back or arm.

Later, however, on our way home, he had to stop the car and get out to vomit on the side of the road. After he'd finished it took him several minutes to compose himself, leaning back against the door until he felt well enough to climb back in behind the wheel. "Don't worry, son," he said to me. "Just a bad stomach, that's all."

During the summer, after my dad got out of the hospital, we'd gone to Florida, where we stayed for a few weeks in a house on Key Biscayne. I had a good time there, swimming in the pool in the yard and watching the boats navigate the narrow canal that ran behind the fence at the rear of the property. I liked waving to and being waved at by the skippers as they guided their sleek white powerboats carefully through the inlet. One afternoon, though, I went into my dad's bedroom to ask him something and I saw him in the bathroom holding the rubber pouch by the hole in his side through which he was forced to evacuate his bowels. He grimaced as he performed the necessary machinations and told me to wait for him outside. He closed the bathroom door and I went back to the pool.

I sat in a beach chair looking out across the inland waterway in the direction of the Atlantic Ocean. I didn't like seeing my dad look so uncomfortable, but I knew there was nothing I could do for him. I tried to remember his stomach the way it was before, before there was a red hole in the side of it, but I couldn't. I could only picture him as he stood in the bathroom moments before with the pain showing in his face.

When he came out he was dressed and smiling. "What do you think, son?" he said. "Should I buy this house? Do you like it here?"

I wanted to ask him how he was feeling now, but I didn't. "Sure, Dad," I said. "It's a great place."

The Winner

My mother and I spent Christmas and New Year's of 1957 in Chicago. By this time, being ten years old and having experienced portions of the northern winter on several occasions, I was prepared for the worst. On our way to Chicago on the long drive from Florida, I excitedly anticipated playing in deep snow and skating on icy ponds. It turned out to be a mild winter, however, very unusual for Chicago in that by Christmas Day there had been no snow.

"The first snowfall is always around Thanksgiving," said Pops, my grandfather. "This year, you didn't need a coat. It's been the longest Indian summer ever."

I didn't mind being able to play outside with the kids who lived on Pops's street, but I couldn't hide my disappointment in not seeing snow, something we certainly did not get in Key West. The neighborhood boys and girls were friendly enough, though I felt like an outsider, even though I'd known some of them from previous visits for as many as three years.

By New Year's Eve it still had not snowed and my mother and I were due to leave on the second of January. I complained to her about this and she said, "Baby, sometimes you just can't win."

I was invited on New Year's Day to the birthday party of a boy I didn't know very well, Jimmy Kelly, a policeman's son who lived in an apartment in a three-flat at the end of the block. Johnny and Billy Duffy, who lived next door to Pops, persuaded me to come with them. Johnny was my age, Billy one year younger; they were good pals of Kelly's and assured me Kelly and his parents wouldn't mind if I came along. Just to make sure, the Duffy brothers' mother called Jimmy Kelly's mother and she said they'd be happy to have me.

Since the invitation had come at practically the last minute and all of the toy stores were closed because of the holiday, I didn't have a proper present to bring for Jimmy Kelly. My mother put some candy in a bag, wrapped Christmas paper around it, tied on a red ribbon and handed it to me.

"This will be okay," she said. "Just be polite to his parents and thank them for inviting you."

"They didn't invite me," I told her, "Johnny and Billy did. Mrs. Duffy called Kelly's mother."

"Thank them anyway. Have a good time."

At Kelly's house, kids of all ages were running around, screaming and yelling, playing tag, knocking over lamps and tables, driving the family's two black cocker spaniels, Mick and Mack, crazy. The dogs were running with and being trampled by the marauding children. Officer Kelly, in uniform with his gunbelt on, sat in a chair by the front door drinking beer out of a brown bottle. He was a large man, overweight, almost bald. He didn't seem to be at all disturbed by the chaos.

Mrs. Kelly took my gift and the Duffy brothers' gift for Jimmy, said, "Thanks, boys, go on in," and disappeared into the kitchen.

Johnny and Billy and I got going with the others and after a while Mrs. Kelly appeared with a birthday cake and ice cream. The cake had twelve candles on it, eleven for Jimmy's age and one for good luck. Jimmy was a big fat kid and blew all of the candles out in one try with ease. We each ate a piece of chocolate cake with a scoop of vanilla ice cream, then Jimmy opened his gifts. He immediately swallowed most of the candy my mother had put into the bag.

Mrs. Kelly presided over the playing of several games, following each of which she presented the winner with a prize. I won most of these games, and with each successive victory I became increasingly embarrassed. Since I was essentially a stranger, not really a friend of the birthday boy's, the other kids, including Johnny and

Billy Duffy, grew somewhat hostile toward me. I felt badly about this, and after winning a third or fourth game decided that was enough—even if I could win another game, I would lose on purpose so as not to further antagonize anyone else.

The next contest, however, was to be the last, and the winner was to receive the grand prize, a brand new professional model football autographed by Bobby Layne, quarterback of the champion Detroit Lions. Officer Kelly, Mrs. Kelly told us, had been given this ball personally by Bobby Layne, whom he had met while providing security for him when the Lions came to Chicago to play the Bears.

The final event was not a game but a raffle. Each child picked a small, folded piece of paper out of Officer Kelly's police hat. A number had been written on every piece of paper by Mrs. Kelly. Officer Kelly had already decided what the winning number would be and himself would announce it following the children's choices.

I took a number and waited, seated on the floor with the other kids, not even bothering to see what number I had chosen. Officer Kelly stood up, holding the football in one huge hand, and looked at the kids, each of whom, except for me, waited eagerly to hear the magic number which they were desperately hoping would be the one they had plucked out of the policeman's hat. Even Jimmy had taken a number.

"Sixteen," said Officer Kelly.

Several of the kids groaned loudly, and they all looked at one another to see who had won the football. None of them had it. Then their heads turned in my direction. There were fifteen other children at the party and all thirty of their eyes burned into mine. Officer and Mrs. Kelly joined them. I imagined Mick and Mack, the cocker spaniels, staring at me, too, their tongues hanging out, waiting to bite me should I admit to holding the precious number sixteen.

I unfolded my piece of paper and there it was: 16. I looked up directly into the empty pale green and yellow eyes of Officer Kelly. I handed him the little piece of paper and he scrutinized it, as if inspecting it for forgery. The kids looked at him, hoping against hope that there had been a mistake, that somehow nobody, especially me, had chosen the winning number.

Officer Kelly raised his eyes from the piece of paper and stared again at me.

"Your father is a Jew, isn't he?" Officer Kelly said.

I didn't answer. Officer Kelly turned to his wife and asked, "Didn't you tell me his old man is a Jew?"

"His mother's a Catholic," said Mrs. Kelly. "Her people are from County Kerry."

"I don't want the football," I said, and stood up. "Jimmy should have it, it's his birthday."

Jimmy got up and grabbed the ball out of his father's hand.

"Let's go play!" he shouted, and ran out the door.

The kids all ran out after him.

I looked at Mrs. Kelly. "Thanks," I said, and started to walk out of the apartment.

"You're forgetting your prizes," said Mrs. Kelly, "the toys you won."

"It's okay," I said.

"Happy New Year!" Mrs. Kelly shouted after me.

When I got home my mother asked if it had been a good party.

"I guess," I said.

She could tell there was something wrong but she didn't push me. That was one good thing about my mother, she knew when to leave me alone. It was getting dark and she went to draw the drapes.

"Oh, baby," she said, "come look out the window. It's snowing."

The God of Birds

While he was waiting to get a haircut at Duke's Barber Shop, Roy was reading an article in a hunting and fishing magazine about a man in Northern Asia who hunted wolves with only a golden eagle as a weapon. This man rode a horse holding on one arm a four-foot long golden eagle around the shore of a mountain lake in a country next to China from November to March looking for prey. Beginning each day before dawn, the eagle master, called a berkutchi, cloaked in a black velvet robe from neck to ankle to protect him from fierce mountain winds, rode out alone with his huge bird. The berkutchi scoffed at those who practiced falconry, said the article in the magazine, deriding it as a sport for children and cowards.

"Eagles are the most magnificent of hunting beasts," said the master. "My eagle has killed many large-horned ibex by shoving them off cliffs. He would fight a man if I commanded him to do so."

The berkutchi's eagle, who was never given a name, had been with him for more than thirty years. He had students, the article said, whom the berkutchi instructed in the ways to capture and train eagles.

"I can only show them how it is done," said the master, "but I would never give away the real secrets. These secrets a man must learn by himself, or he will not become a successful hunter. A man is only a man, but the eagle is the god of birds."

"Roy!" Duke the barber shouted. "Didn't ya hear me? You're next!"

Roy closed the magazine and put it back on the card table in the waiting area.

When he was in the chair, Duke asked him, "Find somethin' interestin' inna magazine, kid?"

"Yes, an article about a guy in the mountains of Asia who hunts wolves on horseback with an eagle."

"How old are you now, Roy?"

"Almost twelve."

"Think you could do that?" Duke asked, as he clipped. "Learn how to hunt with a bird?"

Duke was in his mid-forties, mostly bald, with a three day beard. Roy had never seen Duke clean shaven, even though he was a barber. His shop had three chairs but only one other man worked with him, a Puerto Rican named Alfredito. Alfredito was missing the last three fingers of his right hand, the one in which he held the scissors. When Roy asked him how he'd lost them, Alfredito said a donkey had bitten them off when he was a boy back in Bayamon. Roy never allowed Alfredito to cut his hair anymore because Alfredito always nicked him. He got his hair cut on Thursdays now, which was Alfredito's day off. Duke told Roy that Alfredito worked Thursdays for his brother, Ramon, who had a tailor shop over by Logan Square. Roy wondered if Alfredito could sew better than he could cut hair with only one finger on his right hand.

"I don't know," Roy answered. "Maybe if I grew up there and had a good berkutchi."

"Berkutchi? What's that?"

"An eagle master. The one in the magazine said the eagle is the god of birds."

The door to the shop opened and an old man wearing a gray fedora came in.

"Mr. Majewski, hello," said Duke. "Have a seat, I'll be right with you."

Mr. Majewski stared at Alfredito's empty chair and said, "So where is the Puerto Rican boy?"

"It's Thursday, Mr. Majewski. Alfredito don't work for me on Thursdays."

"He works tomorrow?" asked Mr. Majewski.

"Yeah, he'll be here."

"I'll come tomorrow," Majewski said, and walked out.

"You want it short today, Roy?"

"Leave it long in the back, Duke. I don't like my neck to feel scratchy."

"I used to shoot birds when I was a boy," said Duke, "up in Waukegan."

As he was walking home from the barber shop, a sudden brisk wind caused Roy to put up the collar of his leather jacket. Then it began to rain. Roy walked faster, imagining how terrible the weather could get during the winter months in the mountains of rural Asia. Even a four-foot long golden eagle must sometimes have a difficult time flying against a cold, hard wind hurtling out of the Caucasus, Roy thought, when he saw a gray hat being blown past him down the middle of Blackhawk Avenue. He did not stop to see if it was Mr. Majewski's fedora.

Sundays and Tibor

Roy hated Sundays. Sunday was the day his mother usually chose to pick a fight with her husband or boyfriend of the moment, to express in no unquiet way her dissatisfaction and disappointment with her current situation, making certain that the man in question was left in no doubt as to his responsibility for her distress.

Sunday was also the day his mother insisted on the family, such as it was, going out to dinner. Nothing ever pleased her on these occasions: the route her husband or boyfriend chose to drive to their destination; the service and food at the restaurant; everyone else's bad manners, etc. Roy dreaded these outings. Many times he purposely stayed away from his house, even when he had nobody to play with, there were no games going on at the park, or the weather was particularly foul. He'd walk the streets until he was certain his mother, her husband and his sister had left the house before returning, guaranteeing him two or three hours of solitude. Of course when his mother got home, Roy knew, she would yell at him for missing the family affair, but he had time to prepare an excuse: the game he was playing in went into overtime, or somebody got hurt and Roy had to help him get home.

Holidays were also potential trouble, time bombs set to Roy's mother's internal clock. The bigger the occasion, the louder the ticking. Once, Christmas fell on a Sunday. Christmas also happened to be the anniversary of his mother's marriage to her third husband, the father of Roy's little sister. This triple-barreled day of disaster resulted in his sister's father's belongings being thrown by Roy's mother down the front steps and scattered over the lawn in front of their house. As Roy's soon-no-longer-to-be stepfather picked up his soggy undershorts and other personal items from the snow, Roy, who bore the man no particular affection, felt something close to compassion for him. That day, Roy swore to himself that he would never get married.

For a period of time when his mother was between marriages, when Roy was nine years old, she kept company with a Hungarian named Tibor. Tibor worked as a concierge or receptionist at an elegant little hotel on the near north side of Chicago. He was a short, skinny, hawk-nosed man in his mid-thirties with a mane of unruly brown hair. Where and under what circumstances his mother had made Tibor's acquaintance, Roy never knew. Tibor had fled Budapest at the beginning of the Hungarian revolution. In his home country, apparently, he had been a musician of some kind, although Roy had never heard him play an instrument. Tibor never approached Roy's mother's piano.

One rainy Sunday afternoon in late autumn, Roy returned to his house from playing in a particularly bruising tackle football game. He was looking forward to collapsing on his bed, which was really a fold-out couch, but when he arrived, Tibor was stretched out on it with his shoes and socks off, asleep. Roy's little Admiral portable television set was on. His mother was making something in the kitchen.

"Hey, Ma, Tibor's on my bed."

"He had a long night at the hotel," she said, "it was very busy. He's tired."

"So am I. I wanted to lie down. Why can't Tibor sleep in your room, or on the couch in the living room?"

"He was watching television, Roy. And your room is closer to the kitchen. I'm making him a goulash."

"What's a goulash?"

"A ragout of beef with vegetables cooked with lots of paprika. It's the national dish of Hungary."

"Why don't you wake him up now so he can come in here and eat it?"

"The goulash isn't ready yet. I'll call him when it's done. Tibor had a hard time in Hungary, Roy. He had to escape."

Roy's mother turned and looked at him for the first time since he'd entered the kitchen.

"Your face is filthy," she said. "So are your clothes."

"I was playing football. The field was muddy."

"Roy's mother returned her attention to the goulash. Roy walked out the back door and sat down on the porch stairs.

"Close the door when you go out!" said his mother. "It's cold!" She closed it.

On another Sunday, Roy was walking behind his mother and Tibor next to Lake Michigan. Tibor was wearing a long, gray overcoat that was too big for him. Roy recognized it as one having belonged to his mother's second husband, Lucious O'Toole, a handsome drunkard she had divorced after six months. Lucious had a metal plate in his head from being wounded in the war and he couldn't hold a job. Years later, when Roy was in high school, he saw Lucious staggering along a downtown street, unshaven, wearing a torn and dirty trenchcoat. It was snowing but Lucious was hatless and, Roy noticed, now mostly bald.

Following his mother and Tibor, Roy thought about pushing Tibor into the lake. Roy didn't hate him, but he wanted Tibor to just disappear and for his mother never to mention Hungary or goulash again.

After Roy saw Lucious O'Toole downtown that day, he told his mother, who showed no emotion.

"He looked like a bum," said Roy.

"You never know what's going to happen to a person," she said. "Sometimes it's better that way."

Poor Children of Israel

"They got Harry the Butcher last night," the Viper told Roy. "Only after he piped a cop, though. I heard it on the radio."

The city had been terrorized for days by a gang of six escapees from the Poor Children of Israel Hospital for the Criminally Insane. Roy had read about them in the headlines of the *Tribune* all week. MADMEN STILL AT LARGE was one. Others were LUNATICS ON CRIME SPREE and TERROR GRIPS CITY AS CRAZY KILLERS ELUDE CAPTURE!

Roy and the Viper trudged through slush on their way to school. After two days of snow, the temperature had risen suddenly, turning the streets into a sloppy mess.

"Where'd they find him?" Roy asked.

"The Butcher and the other five broke into a room at the Edgewater Beach Hotel. A husband and wife were in there. Swede Wolf strangled the guy. The woman ran out to the balcony and tried to climb down from the fourth floor. She was screamin' and yellin' for help. That's how the cops found 'em."

"Did she get away?"

"No, they grabbed her and kept her prisoner for a few hours. The radio didn't say, but I bet those maniacs put it to her. Most of 'em had been locked up for years."

"How'd a bunch like that get upstairs in a big fancy hotel?"

A bus sped through a puddle and splashed muddy water on the boys' coats and pants.

"God damn it!" the Viper shouted. "I'll get that driver with an iceball, you'll see."

"They must have snuck in during the night," said Roy.

"Who was gonna stop 'em? Swede Wolf had murdered all kinds of people. Harry the Butcher, too."

"Did they have guns?"

"No, just crowbars and tire irons. The cops shot the Mahoney twins, the ones who raped and decapitated their mother."

"They cut her head off before they had sex with the body," said Roy. "I remember when it happened."

"Yeah, that's right. Anyway, those two are dead. The rest of 'em were captured. The cop the Butcher laid out is in the hospital. He might not make it."

The other big news Roy heard about that day was that the governor of the state of Georgia had forbidden the Georgia Tech football team to play in the Sugar Bowl on New Year's Day because their opponent, the University of Pittsburgh, had a Negro fullback. Students rioted on the Georgia Tech campus and were hosed down and beaten by Atlanta police.

When Roy got home after school, his mother was sitting at the kitchen table, reading a magazine.

"Hey, Ma, you hear they caught those escaped mental patients at the Edgewater Beach Hotel? They murdered a guy and the cops shot and killed two of them."

"How terrible, Roy," she said, without looking up. "There's some chicken left from last night in the refrigerator, if you're hungry."

Roy looked at the calendar on the wall next to the sink. The date was December 11, 1955. The calendar was from Nelson's Meat Market on Ojibway Boulevard. The top part was a photograph of the Nelson brothers: Ernie, Dave and Phil. The three of them had white aprons on and they were smiling. Ernie and Phil had mustaches. Dave was the youngest, still in his twenties. His right eye was glass. He'd popped it out and shown it to Roy once and told him Phil had poked his real eye with a toy sword when they were kids.

"What a shame," said Roy's mother. "The Edgewater Beach used to be such a nice hotel."

The Man Who Wanted to
Get the Bad Taste of the World
Out of His Mouth

Roy got thrown out of school on the same day the bodies of the Grimes sisters were found in the Forest Preserve. The Grimes girls were twelve and thirteen, one and two years older than Roy. It was a rainy April afternoon when Roy heard about the murders over the radio while waiting for an order of French fries with gravy at the take-out window of The Cottage. Marvin Fish, who had dropped out of school the year before at the age of sixteen, having not gotten past the eighth grade, was working the window.

"Jesus on a pony," said Marvin, when he heard the news. "I ain't lettin' my little sister outta the house alone no more."

"The Grimes sisters weren't alone," Roy said. "They were with each other."

"Wait a second."

Marvin Fish turned up the volume on an oil-spattered Philco portable that was on a shelf above the deep fryer.

"The sisters were reported missing on March fifteenth, three weeks ago," said the man on the radio, "one day after they did not return home after school."

"Nobody woulda never reported me missin'," said Marvin. "I didn't used to go home after school, which I hardly ever went to anyway."

"Authorities believe that the girls were kidnapped," the radio voice reported, "then driven to the woods, where they were assaulted and killed. Their decomposing bodies were discovered by a transient who apparently stumbled over the shallow graves. The transient, whose name was not released, is being held as a suspect. Police say he may have committed the murders and for some reason returned to the scene of the crime."

"What's a transit?" asked Marvin Fish.

"Transient, a bum," said Spud Ganos, who with his wife, Ida, owned The Cottage. He had come out from the back and was standing next to the fryer. "Just another friggin' guy tryin' the wrong way to get the bad taste of the world out of his mouth."

"Here's your fries," Marvin said to Roy, "with extra gravy. No charge for the extra gravy."

Roy put seven nickels on the counter.

"Thanks, Marvin," he said, and picked up the soggy bag.

"Where'd you get all the buffaloes?"

"Won 'em laggin' baseball cards."

"School ain't dismissed for two hours yet," Marvin said. "What're you doin' out?"

"Mrs. Murphy said the next time I was late she wouldn't let me into class. Told her I had to take a whiz was why I was late today, but she said I shoulda planned better and to take a hike."

"Murphy, yeah, I had her a couple times. Whenever there was a loud noise she'd say, 'Set 'em up in the other alley.'"

"Still does."

It was too early for Roy to go home, so he walked slowly toward the park, eating his fries with gravy. The rain had diminished to a cold drizzle. Roy had on a White Sox cap and a dark blue tanker jacket that according to the label was water repellent. He did not understand the difference between water proof and water repellent. Roy thought that they should mean the same thing but apparently they did not. Elephant or rhinoceros hides were water proof, he figured, like alligators and crocodiles, as opposed to swan, goose and duck feathers, which were merely water repellent. Ducks and geese flew sometimes, so perhaps that's how they dried off. Roy didn't remember if swans could fly or not.

When he got to the park, Roy perched on the top slat of a bench and looked at the muddy baseball field. What had happened to the Grimes sisters could happen to any kid, he decided, even if a kid didn't accept a ride in a car from a stranger. Someone who was bigger and stronger could grab a kid, or even two kids, especially if they were girls, and force them into a car.

The bottom of the bag was so wet from all the gravy that there was a hole in it. Roy had to keep one hand underneath the bag to keep the few remaining fries from falling out. The Grimes girls had been assaulted, the man on the radio said. Roy wondered if being assaulted and being molested were the same thing, or if there was some kind of difference, like between water proof and water repellent. It began raining harder again. Nobody would be playing ball today, that was for sure.

Johnny Across

Marcel Proust wrote, "One slowly grows indifferent to death." To one's own, perhaps, but not, Roy was discovering, to the deaths of others. Almost daily now, it seemed, certainly weekly, he heard or read of the death of someone he knew or used to know, however briefly, at some time during the course of his fifty-plus years. This, combined with the noticeable passing of various public persons who had made a particular impression upon him, had begun to affect him in a way he could not have predicted. What disturbed Roy most, of course, were the deaths of people he cared for or upon whom he looked favorably. The others—former adversaries, political despots, or murderers languishing behind bars—had been as good as dead to him already. Early on in Roy's life he had developed a facility for excising certain people from his con-sciousness. He simply ceased to care about those individuals he felt were unworthy of his friendship and trust. He really did not care if they lived or died; what they did or did not do concerned him not at all.

During the winters when Roy attended grammar school in Chicago, the boys played a game called Johnny Across Tackle. Often upwards of thirty kids aged nine to thirteen would gather in the gravel schoolyard, which was covered with snow, during recess or lunch break or after classes were over, and decide who would be the first designated tackler. The rest of the boys would line up against the brick wall of the school building, a dirty brown edifice undoubtedly modeled after the factories of Victorian England, which was perhaps fifty feet long. This would be the width of the field. Sixty yards or so across the schoolyard was a chain link fence. The object was to run from the wall to the fence and back again as many times as possible without being tackled. The wall and the fence were "safe." Nobody could be tackled if they were touching with some part of their body—usually a hand, sometimes as little as a toe—the wall or the fence.

Somebody would volunteer to be "it," the first designated tackler. The object, of course, was to be the last man standing. They mostly played when there was a thick layer of snow over the gravel, to protect them from being cut by the stones. Even so, boys would be bruised and battered during this game; broken arms, wrists, ankles and fingers and the occasional broken leg were not uncommon. Girls would play a tag version of the same game, a more sensible exercise. Roy thought he should have taken this as an early sign that women were, if not superior, the more sensible sex.

The boy who was "it" would survey the lineup, pick out his quarry—usually one of the weaker kids, an easy target—and shout, "Johnny Across!" All of the Johnnys would then take off for the opposite safety of the fence. Each participant wanted to be the last survivor, the "winner," except that whoever won knew he would be piled on by however many of the tacklers as possible.

If the last boy was well-liked, the others would take him down tenderly, with respect for his toughness and athleticism. If, however, "Lonely Johnny," as Crazy Jimmy K., an older friend of Roy's who claimed to have achieved that distinction more than twenty times, called him, was unpopular with the majority of the rest of the players, the result could be decidedly ugly. Often, in order to avoid an animalistic conclusion, a kid who knew he was going to get it if he managed to make it through to the end would go down on purpose early in the game and get in his licks on the tackles.

When Roy was eleven years old, he was troubled by frequent nosebleeds. As his doctor explained, this was a not uncommon occurrence during rapid growth spurts. Blood vessels in Roy's nose would burst at any time, even when he wasn't exerting himself. One weekday morning in the middle of February, Roy went to the doctor's office to have his nose cauterized. The doctor inserted what looked to Roy like a soldering iron up each of his nostrils and burned the ends of the broken blood vessels. He then lubricated Roy's nasal passages, packed them with gauze, and instructed him to avoid contact sports for ten days. He handed Roy a tube of Vaseline and said he should not let his nostrils dry out, not blow his nose, and not pick at the scabs that would form, even if they itched. Then Roy took a bus to school.

Just as he arrived, the guys were gathering in the schoolyard to begin a game of Johnny Across. Roy ran over and joined them. The first designated tackler had already been chosen, Large Jensen, a Swedish kid who volunteered to start at tackle almost every time he played. Large, whose real name was Lars, was, at six feet tall and two hundred pounds, the biggest twelve-year-old on the Northwest side of the city. At least none of the kids at Roy's school had heard of or encountered anyone able to dispute this claim. Large said he had recently run into a kid at Eugene Field Park who was an inch taller and almost as heavy, but that kid was already thirteen, which Large would not be until June. Large's mother, whom the boys called Mrs. Large, had the widest hands Roy had ever seen on a woman. He was sure she could hold two basketballs in each one if she tried. Mrs. Large was wide all over but not very tall. Large's father—Mr. Large—was six feet six and probably weighed around 350. He worked over in Whiting or Gary, Indiana, for U.S. Steel. Large told the boys that as soon as he was sixteen he was going to quit school and go to work for U.S. Steel, too. His father already had a silver lunchbox with LARS stenciled on it in black block letters, just like his own, which was labeled OLAF.

Roy kept to the edges of the field, holding his head steady as he could and running at moderate speed. For some reason Roy thought that if he ran fast the intensity might disrupt the healing process. For a while, he was able to avoid any serious contact, and in particular kept away from Large Jensen and his mob. When Roy found himself one of only twelve remaining boys, he knew he had to either allow himself to be brought down without a struggle or risk serious damage.

On the next across, two of the tacklers, Thomas Palmer and Don Repulski, targeted Roy. Palmer was cross-eyed and couldn't tackle worth a damn. A straight arm would fend him off. Repulski worried Roy, however. He was bigger than Roy, six months older, a little fat but strong. Roy was faster, so he knew he had to make a good fake and hope Repulski would go for it, then Roy could beat both of them to the wall.

The rule was that the tacklers yelled "Johnny Across" three times. If a kid didn't move off the safe—the fence or the wall—after three calls, he was automatically caught. Roy waited through two calls, then, just as Palmer and Repulski started to shout "Johnny Across!" for the last time, he broke to his left, toward the eastern boundary of the schoolyard. This gave him more room to maneuver and would, perhaps, even enable him to outrun them to the boundary before he cut downfield toward the wall.

Roy slugged Thomas Palmer right between his crossed eyes with the flat of his right hand just as he reached the edge of the field. Palmer's glasses flew off and he went down on his knees. Roy didn't wait to see if he had made Palmer cry or if the busted frame had gashed his forehead. Roy had Repulski to beat, and as Roy made a hard cut his left foot gave way on the wet snow. Roy's left knee touched the ground and Don Repulski, unable to brake, barreled past him out of bounds. Roy recovered his balance and hightailed it to the wall. He was safe.

Palmer was yelling his head off. He claimed that Roy had gone down as a result of their contact. Roy's knee had hit the ground, Palmer said, so he was caught. Palmer had an inch-long cut on the bridge of his nose and was holding the two pieces that were his glasses. "No way!" Roy shouted. "I hit Palmer before I made my cut. He went down and then I turned—that's when my knee touched the snow." Repulski backed Roy up, he'd seen what happened. He started to say something else but then he—and everybody else—stopped talking. They were all just staring at Roy.

Roy had forgotten about his nose. He looked down and saw that the snow directly below him was turning bright red. Blood was streaming from both of his nostrils. He pulled the packet of tissues out of his coat pocket, tore it open, took a wad and jammed it up against his face. Blood soaked through the tissues in a few seconds, so he threw that wad away and made another. Slowly, the bleeding subsided. Holding a third bunch of tissues to his nose, Roy leaned back against the wall. He took out the tube of Vaseline, unscrewed the cap, squeezed ribbons of it up his nostrils and set himself for the next Johnny Across.

There were only four kids left on safe. Four against thirty. Repulski and about seven other guys stood directly in Roy's path. Palmer was not among them but Large Jensen was. At the second call, Roy took off, faked left, went right and banged against Large Jensen's stomach. Roy hit the ground hard and sat still. He glanced down without moving his head much; a few crimson drops dotted the snow. Large and the rest of the gang ran off to tackle someone else.

The school bell rang, signaling the end of the lunch break. "Who's Lonely Johnny?" Roy asked Small Eddie Small. "Nobody," he said, as he walked by. Roy got up and followed him. All four of the remaining Johnnys had been tackled before making it to the fence, the last two or three at about the same moment, so there was no winner. Repulski came trotting by and punched Roy's right shoulder.

"Good game," he said. Vaseline had congealed in Roy's throat. He hawked it up and expectorated a mixture of clotted blood and petroleum jelly, then walked into the building.

What Roy didn't realize until much later was that Johnny Across had been a valuable learning experience for life—and death. This business of living and dying, Roy concluded, was just one big game of Johnny Across, with everyone scampering to avoid being tackled. Back then, though, his biggest concern was how to stop his nose from bleeding. Ten days after Roy's nostrils were cauterized, he returned to the doctor to have him remove the scabs so that Roy could resume breathing properly. By this time Roy had swallowed enough Vaseline to have lubricated his mother's Oldsmobile for the next six months.

Roy had played Johnny Across several times during this "healing" period, and had luckily avoided direct contact involving his nose except for one sharp blow by Small Eddie Small's left elbow that engendered only a brief trickle. The guys, Roy thought, did not want to witness another vermilion snow painting, so they mostly took it easy on him. He took it easy on himself, too, but Roy knew, even then, that if he kept playing it safe, in the long run he would never become Lonely Johnny.

The Secret of Little White Dove

The morning after Thanksgiving, Roy went to meet the Viper and Jimmy Boyle on the corner of Blackhawk and Dupré. The weather was miserable; icy rain sputtered out of a dark gray sky but there was no school and the boys didn't want to spend any more time than they had to cooped up inside with their families.

Roy had the hood of his blue parka up and he wore the pair of oversized Air Force gloves his cousin Bink had given him the last time Bink had been home on leave. Roy loved these gloves. They were supposed to keep a pilot's hands warm even if the temperature dropped to fifty below. The gloves were silver-blue and shiny; they almost glowed in the dark. Roy didn't mind the lousy weather so much now that he could wear his Air Force gloves.

He saw Jimmy Boyle talking to Red Fellows, a washed up prize-fighter in his late thirties who hung out at Beebs and Glen's Tavern. Roy had never seen Fellows box but the Viper said he'd heard Skull Dorfman tell Larry the Leg that Red had a left hook like his sister's and a right hand like his other sister's. Pops, Roy's grandfather, told him that Rocky Marciano had the best right hand in the business. "After his match with Marciano," Pops told Roy, "Joe Louis said, 'That boy don't fight by the book, but tonight I got hit by a library.'"

Roy arrived at the corner the same moment the Viper appeared from the opposite direction, just in time to see Red Fellows extract his left arm from his pea coat and roll up his shirtsleeve.

"See this?" he asked the boys.

On his biceps was a tattoo of a naked woman. Written under the legs were the words, "Little White Dove."

"I got it done in Germany," Red said, "when I was in the army. It's of a girl I met over there in a club in Berlin."

"Why does it say 'Little White Dove'?" asked Jimmy Boyle.

"I give her the nickname. Her actual name was Ingrid Meister."

"Why'd you call her that?"

Red Fellows grinned. The two teeth to the left of his only remaining front tooth were missing.

"It's what I called her most private part," he said. "Named it after the girl in the song, the Injun broad who fell in love with her brother."

Red rolled down his sleeve and put his arm back into his coat.

"You guys don't know what I'm talkin' about, do you?"

Nobody answered.

"Didn't think so. It's the secret to pleasin' a woman. She'll show you what to do with it but you gotta ask. Don't be afraid to ask."

Red Fellows walked away. Roy, Jimmy Boyle and the Viper, none of whom had yet turned twelve years old, stood under the black and orange-striped awning in front of Bompiani's Bakery and watched the rain turn to ice on the sidewalk.

"The name of the Indian girl's brother was Running Bear," said Roy. "That's the name of the song. Johnny Horton made the record."

"Red's a man of the world," Jimmy Boyle said.

"Where's he been other than Germany?" asked the Viper. "He never fought no further from Chicago than Fort Wayne."

"Red knows his way around," said Jimmy.

"He knows how to get to Beebs and Glen's," said Roy.

A hard wind swept water under the awning, soaking the boys' pants and shoes.

The Viper said, "Shit, at least Red knows enough to get in out of the rain."

That night on his way home, Roy cut through the alley behind Wabansia and Prairie. As he passed a passageway between two of the garages, Roy heard an eerie sound, some terrible combination of sobbing and snorting the way a horse does just after it stops running. Roy stopped and listened. The rain had quit a few hours before and the temperature had fallen. The surface of the alley was almost entirely iced over and glistened in the moonlight. Roy edged closer to the garage nearest him. The snorting noise became punctuated by a guttural sound, then ceased altogether. The sobbing lessened but continued.

A man walked out of the passageway. Roy flattened himself against the garage door. The man turned up the alley and walked in the direction from which Roy had come. He was average-sized and wore a short, dark jacket and a dockworker's cap. Roy heard another noise coming from the passageway, the sound of a person trying to stand up but slipping and falling in the attempt, scraping the wall with his body.

A second man came from the passageway. He stopped at the entrance to the alley and rubbed his face with both hands. When he dropped them, Roy could see that it was Red Fellows. Red blinked his eyes hard a few times, then worked them over again with his fists. He seemed unsure of where he was or in which direction he should go. Roy knew that he did not want Red to see him, though he was not entirely certain why. Roy had witnessed nothing and he did not even know what it was he had heard. Still, he was afraid. If Red looked his way, Roy decided, he would run and hope Red did not recognize him.

Red put his right hand against the brick wall to his right and leaned on it. He coughed and brought up some phlegm, then spat it on the ground. Red leaned there for a few moments, then stood up straight, steadied himself, and began walking up the alley in the same direction the other man had gone.

Roy watched Red negotiate the slippery, cracked concrete with mincing steps, stopping several times as he made his way, until Red was out of sight. Roy then peeled himself off the garage door and headed toward his house. The sky was now so clear that he could plainly see the seven stars that formed either the Big Dipper or the Little Dipper. Roy was not sure if the constellation was Ursa Major or Ursa Minor, but he did remember that the scientific name of the North Star was Polaris.

The Delivery

I went up the stairs carrying the two shopping bags full of Chinese food figuring on a fifty-cent tip. It was a good Sunday due to the rain, people stayed in. I had two more deliveries in the bicycle basket. I rang the third-floor doorbell and waited, feeling the sub gum sauce leak on the bottom of one of the bags.

A woman opened the door and told me to please put the bags on the kitchen table, pointing the way. I put down the bags and looked at the woman. She was wearing a half-open pink nightgown, her nipples standing out against the thin material. Her hair was black halfway down her head, the bottom half was bleached and stringy.

"How much is it?" she asked.

"Five dollars," I said, looking at her purpled cheeks and chin.

"Just wait here and I'll get it for you," she told me. "Be right back."

I looked around the kitchen. I was twelve years old and was not used to being alone in strange kitchens. There were dishes in the sink, and one of the elements of the overhead fluorescent light was burned out, giving the kitchen a dull, rosy glow, like the woman's face, and her nightgown.

The woman came back and gave me a fifty-dollar bill. She had put on a green nightgown similar to the one she'd had on before, and flicked her pink tongue back and forth through her purple lips.

"I don't have any change for this," I said. "Don't you have anything smaller?"

She smiled. "Well, I'll just go see!" she said, and went off again.

I sat down on the kitchen table. I was beginning to enjoy myself, and was disappointed when she returned in the same green nightgown. She handed me a twenty.

"Will this do?" she asked.

I dug in my pocket for the change but she stopped me.

"Don't bother, darling," she said, smiling, and put her hand on my wrist. Her nails were painted dark red, but looked lighter in the hazy glow. "Keep it all," she said, and took me by the hand to the front door.

She put my hand on her breast. I could feel a lump through the nightgown.

"Thank you very, very much," she said, heavily, like Lauren Bacall or Tallulah Bankhead. I thought she looked like Tallulah Bankhead except for her hair, which was more like Lauren Bacall's.

"You're welcome," I said, and she opened the door for me, letting me out.

It was still raining, but I stood for a minute under the Dutch elm tree where I'd left my bike and the bags of food covered by a small piece of canvas. I removed the cover from the bicycle and folded it over the bags in the basket. I felt the twenty-dollar bill in my pocket, and I smiled. If I could have two deliveries like this a day, I thought, just two.

The Deep Blue See

When I was in the eighth grade I was given the job of being one of the two outdoor messengers of Clinton School. Since I was far from being among the best behaved students, I could only surmise that some farsighted teacher (of whom there were very few) realized that I was well suited for that certain responsibility, that perhaps some of my excess energy might be put to use and I'd be honored and even eventually behave better because of this show of faith in my ability to run errands during school hours. Either that or they were just glad to get rid of me for a half hour or so.

I thought it was great just because it occasionally allowed me to get out of not only the classroom but the school. Escorting sick kids home was the most common duty but my favorite was walking the blind piano tuner across California Avenue to and from the bus stop.

For two weeks out of the year the old blind piano tuner used to come each day and tune all of the pianos in the school. My job during that time was to be at the bus stop at eight forty-five every morning to pick him up, and then, at whatever time in the after-noon he was ready to leave, to walk him back across, wait with him until the bus arrived, and help him board.

We became quite friendly over the two-week period that I assisted him. The piano tuner looked to me like any ordinary old guy with white hair in a frayed black overcoat, except he was blind and carried a cane. My dad and I had seen Van Johnson as a blind man in the movie *Twenty-three Paces to Baker Street*. Van Johnson had reduced an intruder to blindness by blanketing the windows and putting out the lights, trapping him—or her, as it turned out—until the cops came, but I'd never known anybody who was blind before.

I couldn't really imagine not being able to see and on the last day I asked the piano tuner if he could see anything at all. We were crossing the street and he looked up and said, "Oh yes, I see the blue. I can see the deep blue in the sky and the shadows of gray around the blue."

It was a bright sunny winter day and the sky was clear and very blue. I told him how blue it was, I didn't see any gray, and there were hardly any clouds. We were across the street and I could see the bus stopping a block away.

"Were you ever able to see?" I asked.

"Oh yes, shapes," he said. "I can see them move."

Then the bus came and I helped him up the steps and told the bus driver the old man was blind and to please wait until I'd helped him to a seat. After the piano tuner was seated I said good-bye, gave the token to the driver, and got off.

While I was waiting at the corner for the traffic to slow so that I could cross, I closed my eyes and tried to imagine what it was like to be blind. I looked up with my eyes closed. I couldn't see anything. I opened them up and ran across the street.

Radio Goldberg

Rigoberto Goldberg was a tall, lanky kid, an Ichabod Crane with thick glasses bordered by heavy black rims who didn't talk much. He also had a mustache, which no other twelve-year-old in Roy's neighborhood had. Dickie Cunningham thought it might have been because of Goldberg's being half Spanish.

"Puerto Rican kids grow up faster than we do," he said.

"Goldberg isn't from Puerto Rico," Roy told him. "He was born in the Dominican Republic."

"Where's that?"

"An island around Cuba, I think," said Roy. "And how do you know Spanish kids grow up faster? Mostly they're smaller than us."

"They're shorter," said Cunningham, "but they got hair on their chins when they're our age. Lookit that kid Luis went to Margaret Mary."

"One got thrown out for pullin' a switchblade on a teacher?"

Cunningham nodded. "Luis Soto somethin'."

"Sotomayor."

"Kid had a goatee in seventh grade."

"He was thirteen already. Got put back twice."

Rigoberto Goldberg was not an outstanding student. Once in a while he'd crack wise in class, but mostly he seemed content to sit in the back row and hope to be ignored by the teacher. None of the other kids even knew if he could speak Spanish. Cunningham asked him if he could but Goldberg just shrugged and walked away. He was a real loner.

It was a surprise, therefore, when one afternoon after school Goldberg approached Roy and Cunningham and asked them if they wanted to see his radio station.

"What do you mean, your radio station?" asked Cunningham.

"I got a radio station," said Goldberg, "in my garage. I built it."

"Sure," Roy said. "Let's go."

As they walked to Rigoberto's house, Cunningham said, "Do you have call letters for your station, like WLS or WBBM?"

"I got a name," he told them. "Radio Goldberg."

"Wait a minute," said Roy, "don't you have to have letters? I thought east of the Mississippi River radio stations are all K-something, and west of the Mississippi they begin with W."

"It's my station," said Rigoberto. "I can call it whatever I want to."

Inside his family's garage, Goldberg had constructed what appeared to be a gigantic crystal set. He sat down in front of the table it was on, placed earphones over his head, switched on the machine and began turning dials. With his thick black glasses, droopy nose, uncombed dark brown hair and mustache, Goldberg looked every bit the mad scientist. All sorts of squealy, squeaky, dissonant noises emanated from the equipment, rattling off the brick walls. Several voices filled the room simultaneously. Roy felt as if he were inside a fun house at an amusement park. Rigoberto remained calm, fiddling the controls with his spiderleg fingers. For the first time, Roy noticed that Goldberg had an inordinate amount of dirt under his fingernails.

Suddenly, the cacophony ceased and Rigoberto spoke into a large, wood-framed microphone.

"Hey there, you with the stars in your eyes," he said, "this is Radio Goldberg, broadcasting from the forty story Goldberg Building located in the heart of the heartland, Chicago, Illinois, U.S. of A. Seven hot watts for all you guys, gals and tots."

Goldberg at the mike was an astounding sight to Roy and Cunningham. He transformed himself from a geeky, shirt-buttoned-up-to-the-collar, four-eyed bed-head into a smooth-talking ball of fire. Amazingly, Goldberg's body language became that of a slinky jungle cat's, and his voice had the timbre of Vaughan Monroe's recording of "Ghost Riders in the Sky." Rigoberto talked about whatever was on his mind at the moment. He trashed teachers of his by name, castigated girls he deemed stuck up because they wouldn't give him the time of day, and he played records. Goldberg owned only a few 45s; these included such diverse platters as Patti Page's "How Much is that Doggie in the Window?," Little Richard's "Good Golly, Miss Molly," and Jim Backus's spoken word rendering of the story of "Gerald McBoing Boing."

Radio Goldberg's broadcasting area, Rigoberto told Roy and Cunningham, encompassed approximately the six blocks surrounding his house. He came on the air after school on weekdays for a couple of hours, occasionally at night if his parents were out, and early Sunday mornings while his parents were still asleep. On Sunday, he said, he liked to tell his listeners that sometimes he thought he was a son of God, like Jesus, and then he would play Elvis Presley's record, "I Believe." His parents, Rigoberto said, knew nothing about Radio Goldberg.

It wasn't long after he had revealed his secret station to Roy and Cunningham that Goldberg's neighbors began lodging complaints with the legitimate local radio stations whose signals were irregularly being interfered with. Three weeks into his broadcasting career, the police, armed with a search warrant, knocked on the Goldbergs' door. They discovered Rigoberto's garage set-up and confiscated his equipment. A small article describing the dismantling of Rigoberto Goldberg's operation appeared in the evening paper, the *Daily News*, under the heading, 'RADIO GOLDBERG' GOES OFF THE AIR. BOY, 12, CITED FOR BROADCASTING ILLEGALLY. The article quoted Arturo Goldberg, Rigoberto's father, who said, "My son is a genius. One day, you'll see."

"They fined me fifty bucks," Rigoberto told Roy and Cunningham. "My parents paid it but they're making me pay 'em back out of the money I earn from my paper route."

"Did the police return your equipment?" Roy asked him.

"Not yet. They still got my records, too."

"The cops are a bunch of crooks," said Cunningham. "One of 'em'll probably swipe 'Gerald McBoing Boing' and give it to his kid."

Why Skull Dorfman Went to Arkansas

Roy usually avoided Skull Dorfman's booth, but when Skull himself beckoned, Roy went over.

"Here, kid," Skull said, after reaching into one of his pants pockets and coming up with a five dollar bill, "get me a *Form* and an *American*." As Roy took the fin from him, Skull added, "Make that a *Sun-Times*, too. And don't forget to give the girl somethin'."

Roy walked to the front of Meschina's, where Flo, who'd been a blonde the last time Roy had seen her, was working the cash register.

"Hi, Flo," Roy said. "I like your hair."

Flo smiled, patted the back and sides of her head, and said, "Thanks, hon. I was a redhead once before, you know. I changed it to black after Tony Testonena and me went on the permanent outs. Feel like myself again. Ain't it late for you to be out, Roy? It's almost midnight."

"No, my mother doesn't care. She's probably not home yet, anyway. Can I have a *Racing Form*, an *American* and a *Sun-Times*, please? They're for Skull."

Roy handed Flo the five. He looked at her closely as she bent down to pick up the papers, put them on the counter, and then made change. Roy's mother was thirty-four years old and a real redhead. Flo had some serious creases in her face; cracks and crevices marred the thick, sand colored make-up around her eyes and mouth. His mother didn't have creases yet, at least none as evident as Flo's, and she didn't wear much make-up. Roy figured Flo had to be at least forty, if not older. She was skinny and her narrow breasts jutted out and up like steer horns. Cool Phil said they were falsies. Roy had only a vague idea of what falsies looked like. He wasn't crazy about Cool Phil because Phil was always in a bad mood and never had anything good to say about anybody. Roy thought maybe it was because Cool Phil, who was eighteen, six years older than Roy, had bad acne and was already losing his hair.

Flo gave Roy two dollars and fifty cents. "Here you go, hon," she said, and shot him a big smile. Her lips were thin, too, and she applied ruby red lipstick unevenly beyond the edges.

"Keep the quarters, Flo," said Roy, and handed them back to her. He folded the three papers under his right arm and kept the two singles in his left hand.

"Thanks, hon," Flo said, "you're a real gentleman."

Roy delivered the papers to Skull Dorfman, placing them carefully on the formica next to two empty and one half-eaten whitefish platters and a table barrel of old dills with three pickles left in it. He held out the singles toward Skull.

"I gave Flo four bits," Roy told him.

Seated across from Skull Dorfman in the booth was Arnie the Arm Mancanza. Arnie only had one arm, having lost his right in an industrial accident at Pocilga's sausage factory. The Arm carried a good three hundred pounds, and Dorfman had to go two-sixty or seventy, so Roy assumed the whitefish platters were merely a warm-up.

Skull plucked one of the bills from Roy's fingers and said, "The other one's yours, kid. I'm fat but I ain't cheap."

"You ain't fat, Skull," said the Arm. "I'm fat."

"Okay, Arm," Skull said. "Okay."

Roy joined his friends, who were occupying a booth in the back.

"How much he tip you?" asked the Viper.

"A buck."

"He pinch you on the cheek?" asked Jimmy Boyle. "I hate when he does that."

Roy shook his head no.

"He's a fat fuck," said the Viper.

"Arnie the Arm says Skull isn't fat," Roy said. "He says *he's* fat."

"Takes the Arm twice as long to eat since the accident at Pocilga's," said Jimmy Boyle. "His appetite ain't changed, just his velocity."

"What are you," the Viper said, "a fuckin' scientist?"

"My old man says Mancanza and Bruno Benzinger were feeding a stiff through the grinder is how it happened. Arnie got careless and caught his sleeve. By the time Benzinger turned off the machine, Mancanza's right arm was in slices."

"What happened to the stiff?" asked the Viper.

"Benzinger was a medic in Korea, so he tied a tourniquet onto what was left of Arnie's right arm to stop the bleedin', then finished off the stiff before takin' Mancanza to the hospital. My old man says if fuckin' Benzinger had taken the cut off parts of the arm, the doctors might have been able to reattach it, but he ground them up, too."

The next time Roy was in Meschina's, Skull Dorfman's booth was empty.

"Hey, Viper," Roy said, as he slid into a booth. "It's past midnight. Where's Skull?"

"You ain't heard what happened?"

"No."

"The Arm told Cool Phil Skull messed up. He got two jobs, you know, one tendin' a bridge on the river, the other as a parimutuel clerk at Sportsman's."

"Yeah, so?"

"You work for the city, you ain't supposed to work at the racetrack. It's a law."

"What happened?"

"Skull was at the track when he was supposed to be tending the bridge, and the fuckin' *Queen Mary* come through."

"The *Queen Mary* on the Chicago River?"

"One of them big god damn passenger liners. People want to

see a river that flows backwards, I guess. Anyway, Skull's got his key on him, the one unlocks the switch raises the bridge. They're goin' nuts, nobody'll squeal on Skull, so the river pilot and the police don't know where he is. The *Queen Mary*'s bobbin' up and down, can't go nowhere. Everybody and their mother's pissed as hell. Takes 'em forever to find another key or break the lock. Finally, they get the bridge up. Skull gets back there, they put his ass in a sling."

"What did they do to him?"

"The Arm says Skull's suspended indefinitely from the bridge job without pay, and for sure he can't work the track no more unless he quits the city, which'd mean he'd forfeit his pension, which he got more'n twenty years in."

Jimmy Boyle came in and sat down next to Roy.

"I just told Roy about what happened to Skull," said the Viper.

"Yeah, the Arm's out front on the sidewalk," Jimmy Boyle said. "Heard him tellin' Oscar Meschina that Skull's in Hot Springs, workin' at a dog track."

"Where's Hot Springs?" the Viper asked.

"Arkansas," said Roy. "I was there once with my mother. Gambling's legal."

A couple came in and sat down in Skull Dorfman's booth.

"I guess it's true," said the Viper. "Don't look like Skull's comin' in."

Jimmy Boyle nodded. "Nope," he said, "not tonight, anyway."

Wanted Man

The summer I was thirteen years old I worked in Cocoa Beach, Florida, building roads and houses for my uncle's construction company. One afternoon when we were paving a street in one hundred and five degree heat, a police car pulled up to the site, stopped, and two cops got out, guns drawn. They moved swiftly toward the steam roller, which was being operated by Boo Ruffert, a former Georgia sheriff. The cops proceeded without a word and grabbed Boo, dragging him down from his perch atop the steam roller. I was shoveling limerock off of a curb directly across from the action, and I watched the cops handcuff Ruffert and begin double-timing him toward their beige and white. Jake Farkas, who had been sweeping behind Boo, jumped up onto the steam roller and shut it down before the machine went out of control and careened off the road. My uncle came running out of the trailer he used as an office and intercepted the policemen before they locked Boo Ruffert into the patrol car.

"Wait!" my uncle shouted at the cops. "What are you doing with him?"

"This man is wanted on a charge of child molestation in Georgia," said one of them. "We have a warrant for his arrest."

"Want to see it?" asked the other cop. He was holding the nose of his revolver against Ruffert's right temple.

"Listen," said my uncle, "Boo here is my best heavy equipment operator. He's almost finished with this street."

My uncle pulled out a roll of bills from one of his trouser pockets.

"Let me buy you fellows some lunch. Ruffert won't go anywhere, I'll keep an eye on him. You boys have something to eat while he finishes up here."

He held two fifties out toward them. "How about it?"

The cops looked at the money in my uncle's hand, then stuffed Ruffert into the back seat.

"Sorry," said one, "you'll have to get yourself another man. This one's headed to the hoosegow."

I had walked over and stood watching and listening to this exchange. I looked at Ruffert through the left side rear window. Boo grinned at me, exposing several brown teeth, and winked his right eye, the one with the heart-shaped blood spot on the lower outside corner of the white. I guessed Boo's age to be about forty. Jake Farkas came up and stood next to me. Jake always had the stub of a dead Indian, as he called cigars, in his mouth, usually a Crook, and three or four days' worth of whiskers on his face. He was in his early thirties but had already fathered, he told me, approximately thirteen children.

"You think you can ride her down the rest of the way?" my uncle asked Jake.

"Sure thing," Jake said.

My uncle turned and walked back to the trailer.

"Did you know about Boo?" I asked. "That he was a wanted man?"

Jake chuckled and said, "My dear old Mama used to say it's always good to be wanted, but I'm older now and I know that my dear old Mama weren't always right."

Jake strode to the steam roller, hopped up into the seat and cranked it over. I went back to shoveling limerock.

That evening, after my uncle dropped me off at a local movie theater while he went off to play cards, a bizarre incident occurred. I figured he was going to see a woman and that he knew I knew but seeing as how he had a wife in Miami, I assumed he thought it prudent not to tell me any more than he had to. I was not particularly fond of my aunt; my uncle knew this and most probably also knew I would never have betrayed his confidence had he chosen to tell me the truth, but this way neither of us had to compromise ourselves.

The movie was *Zulu*, which depicted red-jacketed, heavily-armed British soldiers in South Africa battling against Shaka's spear-throwing warriors. The theater was segregated; white patrons were seated downstairs and black patrons were seated in the balcony. This was in 1964, so some small progress had been made regarding racial equality in Florida in that both whites and blacks were at least allowed to be in the movie theater together.

The redcoats were vastly outnumbered by the Zulus, but their highly-disciplined British square defense—one line kneeling and firing as the line behind them stood and cleaned and reloaded their rifles—kept the natives at bay. The outcome, however, was inevitable; at some point the Zulus would overwhelm them. As the battle raged, there came from the balcony increasing shouts of exhortation directed at the Zulus, which incited equally fervent vocalizing by the white members of the audience below. The din inside the theater grew louder and more and more heated, practically drowning out the soundtrack of the picture.

Suddenly, the lights in the theater came on and the film stopped. The cinema manager jumped up onstage and stood in front of the screen. He was a large, mostly bald, clean-shaven white man wearing a baggy green suit. He held a lit cigarette between the second and third fingers of his right hand, the one he used to gesticulate and point toward the balcony. The crowd was silent.

"Listen up!" he shouted. "Any further ruckus and I'm throwin' all you niggers out of here!"

The manager kept his two cigarette fingers pointed at the balcony section for at least twenty seconds longer; then he put them to his mouth, took a long drag on the cigarette, exhaled smoke so that it curlicued slowly away from him and vanished in the lights, and dropped the butt to the floor where he ground it out with his right shoe. He did not lower his eyes from the cheap seats until he jumped down from the stage and unhurriedly proceeded up the center aisle and out into the lobby. The sound of the doors swinging shut was the only noise in the theater until the house lights blinked out and the projector resumed rolling.

The film ended with Shaka's Zulus acknowledging the bravery and ingenuity of the British regulars by saluting them and deciding against slaughtering them wholesale, thereby emerging victorious by having made the grandest and noblest heroic gesture possible before disappearing over a distant rise. I waited until almost every other patron had left the theater before I did. There was no trouble outside. The manager stood in front of the ticket booth, smoking. Up close, I could see several dark stains on the jacket and pants of his suit.

My uncle was parked in front of the theater. I climbed into his white Cadillac convertible and he drove away.

"How was the show?" he asked.

"Good," I said, "there was lots of fighting. Did you win?"

"Win?"

"Yeah, at the poker game."

"A little," said my uncle. "I always win a little."

We drove for a while without saying anything, then I asked, "What do you think will happen to Boo?"

"He'll do some hard time, I'm sure," my uncle said. "It's a bad business, messing with children."

"Was it a boy or a girl that he messed with?"

"A girl."

"How old was she?"

"Jake told me she was ten."

"How does he know?"

"What difference does it make? Ruffert was a wanted man, you won't ever see him again. Tell me more about the movie."

The Bucharest Prize

Roy was closing up the Red Hot Ranch, a hot dog shack where he worked three days a week after school and on Saturdays, when through the front window he saw a white Cadillac pull up to the curb. His mother got out of the passenger side. She was dressed to the nines, wearing a black cocktail dress beneath an ermine stole. Roy went outside to meet her. It was just after seven p.m., the sky was beginning to seriously darken and the air was cool.

"Roy, darling," said his mother, "I'm glad I caught you."

She bent a little to kiss him but barely brushed her maroon mouth against his left cheek so as not to smear her lipstick. Before Roy could say anything, she handed him a five dollar bill.

"This is for dinner, baby, and something extra," she said. "I won't be home until later tonight."

Roy looked at the car. A man he didn't know was seated behind the steering wheel. The man was wearing a midnight blue suit-jacket over a tan shirt with a tie that matched his coat.

"Honey, you work so hard. Get some Chinese, the vegetables are good for you."

His mother's hair was flaming red, like Rita Hayworth's. She showed Roy every one of her spectacular teeth and waved goodbye to him as she got back into the Cadillac. The man had kept the motor running.

"Thanks, Ma!" Roy shouted as the car moved away.

Roy went back into the Ranch. He was thirteen years old and in a little more than an hour he would be playing in the city-wide All-Star baseball game. When he'd seen his mother arrive, he thought that she had come to take him to the ballpark, which was about half a mile away. He thought she had remembered his telling her the day before that he had been one of the youngest players chosen for the game; most of the All-Stars were fifteen or sixteen years old. She had never come to one of his games.

Roy did not start in the game that night but he got to pinch-hit in the sixth inning and he banged one off the lower right corner of the scoreboard for a triple, driving in two runs. Because he'd hit the scoreboard, Roy was awarded a case of Coca-Colas from the Bucharest Grocery.

After the game, knowing the case of Cokes would be too heavy to carry home, Roy passed the bottles out to the other players. They sat next to the field drinking Coca-Cola and talking about the game. The air had turned chilly but the boys were still perspiring and excited, so they joked and clowned around until they'd polished off most of the case.

Walking home, Roy felt sticky and cold from where sweat had dried underneath his wool uniform. He was proud to be seen wearing the shirt with the words All-Stars across the chest in big black letters. He hoped his mother would be home by now.

When Roy got there, the white Cadillac was parked in front of his house. He had one bottle of Coca-Cola left, stuffed in the left rear pocket of his baseball pants. Roy took it out and sat down on the steps of the Anderson house across the street. He'd given back the church key the boys had borrowed to open the other bottles to Marge Pavlik, the woman who ran the concession stand at the field. Roy had seen men take caps off bottles with their teeth but he didn't want to try it. Skip Ryan had lost part of his right front tooth that way; he could spit eight feet through the space.

Roy put down the bottle, closed his eyes, and thought about the ball he'd hit caroming off the scoreboard. It had rolled behind the rightfielder, who'd overrun it a little. After he'd slid into third base safely, Roy had stood up and looked back at the totals on the board, hoping the official scorer did not charge the outfielder with an error, which would have reduced the hit to a double. The Bucharest prize was given only for triples. No error was posted.

The third base coach, Eustache "Stash" Pavlik, Marge's husband, had come over, said, "Good goin', kid," and swatted Roy on the behind.

Roy heard a car door open and close, followed by the sound of an engine starting. He opened his eyes and saw the white Cadillac disappearing around the corner. Roy stood up and headed across the street, then he remembered the Coke, went back and picked it up. Mrs. Anderson opened the front door.

"Roy," she said, "can I help you?"

"No, thanks, Mrs. Anderson. I was just sitting on your steps for a few minutes. I'm going home now."

"You look very nice in your uniform, Roy."

"Thanks."

"Did your team win?"

"Yes, ma'am, we did."

"Mr. Anderson and I like baseball. Tell us the next time you're going to play."

"I will, Mrs. Anderson."

Roy started to go, then he turned back.

"Mrs. Anderson, I won a case of Cokes tonight. Would you like one?"

He held the bottle out toward her. She took it.

"Thank you, Roy, how kind of you to offer. Good night."

"Good night," said Roy, "say hi to Mr. Anderson."

"I will."

Roy stood there.

"Roy," said Mrs. Anderson, "are you all right?"

Blows with Sticks Raining Hard

Roy wanted to get home before dark, so he decided to hitchhike rather than wait for a bus. At ten past five, when he left Little Louie's, the sky was gray with black stripes painted on the clouds. Snow began to fall as Roy stood in the slush next to the curb with his right thumb out.

He'd been sitting in the back booth at Louie's reading Joseph Conrad's *Congo Diary*, which he'd checked out of the Nortown branch library after having read *Heart of Darkness*. Roy had decided to write his next book report on *Heart of Darkness*, and his English teacher, Mr. Brown, had mentioned Conrad's *Congo Diary* as being interesting background material for the story. Roy enjoyed reading passages from Conrad's diary to his friends, especially to the girls, who hung out in Louie's after school.

"To Congo da Lemba after passing black rocks long ascent," Roy read to them. "Harou giving up. Bother. Camp bad. Water far. Dirty. At night Harou better."

After hearing this, Bitsy DiPena said, "Africa sounds icky. Why would anyone want to go there?"

"For jewels and ivory and minerals," Roy told her, "and slaves, of course."

"There's no slavery anymore, I don't think," said Susie Worth, as she combed her long, blonde hair, which she did constantly. "Not in 1961."

"Arabs still have slaves," Jimmy Boyle said, "and some African tribes, too. I learned it in history."

"In the evening three women of whom one albino passed our camp," Roy read aloud. "Horrid chalky white with pink blotches. Red eyes. Red hair. Ugly. Mosquitos. At night when the moon rose heard shouts and drumming in distant villages. Passed a bad night."

"Spooky," said Susie Worth, biting on her comb.

"Spooky *and* icky," Bitsy DiPena said.

"Row between the carriers and a man about a mat. Blows with sticks raining hard."

"Stop it, Roy!" said Bitsy. "I don't want to hear any more."

It was getting colder as the light disappeared and snow came down harder. Roy kept his thumb out but nobody stopped. People were just off work, hurrying home or to the grocery stores. Roy began walking, turning every few steps to show drivers his thumb. Finally, a car pulled over, a dark green Plymouth sedan. It slowed, then idled a few yards ahead of Roy. He ran up to the Plymouth and opened the front passenger side door. The driver was a middle-aged man wearing an overcoat and a homburg hat. He had wire framed glasses and white hair.

"I'm going to Peterson," Roy said.

"Hop in," said the man. "That's in my direction."

Roy got into the car and pulled the door closed. The car heater was on full blast.

"Good to be out of this weather," the man said.

"Yeah, thanks," said Roy. "Didn't think anybody was going to stop."

"People are afraid to these days. You never know who you're picking up."

"I'm just a kid, though," said Roy.

"Even so," the man said, "you'd be surprised the things that happen."

Roy glanced again at the driver. He looked like he could be a minister. His face was bland, almost colorless.

"What's your name, son?"

"Roy."

"You go to high school?"

"Yes, sir. I'm a freshman."

"You're about fourteen, then."

"Almost."

"What are you interested in, Roy? What subjects?"

"Sports, mostly. I like to read, too."

"Good, good," the man said. "Are you reading a book now?"

"Yes. Joseph Conrad's *Congo Diary*."

"Really? That's impressive, Roy. Do you like it?"

"I like his descriptions of the people and places along the river where the boat stops. The crew walk inland sometimes and make camp. There's lots of insects and sickness. A boy gets shot. The boat has to avoid rocks that appear suddenly in the river. It's pretty exciting."

"You want to travel, Roy? Go to foreign places?"

"Uh huh. My uncle's been all over the world, he's always going somewhere. Right now he's in Mongolia. I'm going to be like him."

"What about the Bible, Roy? Do you read the good book? Are you a Christian?"

"My mother's a Catholic, but it doesn't interest me much. This is Peterson," said Roy. "You can let me out here."

"It's awfully bad outside," said the man. "What street do you live on? I can take you there."

"Rockwell, but you don't have to. I can walk over."

"It's only a couple of blocks out of my way. I'll take you."

The driver turned left on Peterson. The sky was completely black now.

"Where on Rockwell, Roy?"

"Near the corner," Roy said. "Here's okay."

The driver pulled the car over and stopped.

"You should go to church, Roy," he said. "You're a very bright boy. Christianity will help you to understand the mysteries of life."

The man placed his right hand firmly on Roy's left leg, up high, near his crotch. Roy yanked down hard on the handle of the passenger side door and got out of the car. He slammed it shut. The dark green Plymouth pulled away slowly, sliding through the snow, Roy thought, like a crocodile oozing off a Congo riverbank. He dropped his books and made a snowball, packing it hard with ice, then threw it at the car. The snowball hit the rear window, but the driver did not stop. Roy made another iceball. The Plymouth was almost out of sight. He didn't know where to throw it. Roy was not wearing gloves and his fingers were freezing. His eyes were tearing up from the wind. He hurled the snowball as far as he could across the street into the darkness.

"Night cold," Roy said out loud. "Natives hostile. Back to boat. Harou suffering again."

The Chinaman

I always spotted the Chinaman right off. He would be at the number two table playing nine ball with the Pole. Through the blue haze of Bebop's Pool Hall I could watch him massé the six into the far corner.

My buddy Magic Frank and I were regulars at Bebop's. Almost every day after school we hitched down Howard to Paulina and walked half a block past the Villa Girgenti and up the two flights of rickety stairs next to Talbot's Bar-B-Q. Bebop had once driven a school bus but had been fired for shooting craps with the kids. After that he bought the pool hall and had somebody hand out flyers at the school announcing the opening.

Bebop always wore a crumpled Cubs cap over his long, greasy hair. With his big beaky nose, heavy-lidded eyes, and slow, half-goofy, half-menacing way of speaking, especially to strangers, he resembled the maniacs portrayed in the movies by Timothy Carey. Bebop wasn't supposed to allow kids in the place, but I was the only one in there who followed the Cubs, and since Bebop was a fanatic Cub fan, he liked to have me around to complain about the team with.

The Chinaman always wore a gray fedora and sharkskin suit. Frank and I waited by the Coke machine for him to beat the Pole. The Pole always lost at nine ball. He liked to play one-pocket but none of the regulars would play anything but straight pool or nine ball or rotation. Sometimes the Pole would hit on a tourist for a game of eight ball but even then he'd usually lose, so Frank and I knew it wouldn't be long before we could approach the Chinaman.

When the Chinaman finished off the Pole he racked his cue, stuck the Pole's fin in his pocket, lit a cigarette, and walked to the head. Frank followed him in and put a dollar bill on the shelf under where there had once been a mirror and walked out again and stood by the door. When the Chinaman came out, Frank went back in.

I followed Frank past Bebop's counter down the stairs and into the parking lot next to the Villa Girgenti. We kicked some grimy snow out of the way and squatted down and lit up, then leaned back against the garage door as we smoked.

When we went back into the pool hall Bebop was on the phone, scratching furiously under the back of his Cub cap while threatening to kick somebody's head in, an easy thing to do over the phone. The Chinaman was sitting against the wall watching the Pole lose at eight ball. As we passed him on our way to the number nine table he nodded without moving his eyes.

"He's pretty cool," I said.

"He has to be," said Frank. "He's a Chinaman."

The End of Racism

One of my favorite places to go when I was a kid in Chicago was Riverview, the giant amusement park on the North Side. Riverview, which during the fifties was nicknamed Polio Park, after the reigning communicable disease of the decade, had dozens of rides, including some of the fastest, most terrifying roller coasters ever designed. Among them were the Silver Streak, the Comet, the Wild Mouse, the Flying Turns, and the Bobs. Of these, the Flying Turns, a seatless ride that lasted all of thirty seconds or so and required the passengers in each car to recline consecutively on one another, was my favorite. The Turns did not operate on tracks but rather on a steeply banked, bobsledlike series of tortuous sliding curves that never failed to engender in me the sensation of being about to catapult out of the car over the stand of trees to the west of the parking lot. To a fairly manic kid, which I was, this was a big thrill, and I must have ridden the Flying Turns hundreds of times between the ages of seven and sixteen.

The Bobs, however, was the most frightening roller coaster in the park. Each year several people were injured or killed on that ride; usually when a kid attempted to prove his bravery by standing up in the car at the apex of the first long, slow climb, and was then flipped out of the car as it jerked suddenly downward at about a hundred miles per hour. The kids liked to speculate about how many lives the Bobs had taken over the years. I knew only one kid, Earl Weyerholz, who claimed to have stood up in his car at the top of the first hill more than once and lived to tell about it. I never doubted Earl Weyerholz because I once saw him put his arm up to the biceps into an aquarium containing two piranhas just to recover a quarter Bobby DiMarco had thrown into it and dared Earl to go after. Earl was eleven then. He died in 1958, at the age of fourteen, from the more than two hundred bee stings he sustained that year at summer camp in Wisconsin. How or why he got stung so often was never explained to me. I just assumed somebody had dared him to stick his arms into a few hives for a dollar or something.

Shoot the Chutes was also a popular Riverview ride. Passengers rode on boats that slid at terrific speeds into a pool and everybody got soaking wet. The Chutes never really appealed very much to me, though; I never saw the point of getting wet for no good reason. The Parachute was another one that did not thrill me. Being dropped to the ground from a great height while seated on a thin wooden plank with only a narrow metal bar to hold on to was not my idea of a good time. In fact, just the thought of it scared the hell out of me; I didn't even like to watch people do it. I don't think my not wanting to go on the Parachute meant that I was acrophobic, however, because I was extremely adept at scaling garage roofs by the drainpipes in the alleys and jumping from one roof to the next. The Parachute just seemed like a crazy thing to submit oneself to as did the Rotor, a circular contraption that spun around so fast that when the floor was removed riders were plastered to the walls by centrifugal force. Both the Parachute and the Rotor always had long lines of people waiting to be exquisitely tortured.

What my friends and I were most fond of at Riverview was Dunk the Nigger. At least that's what we called the concession where by throwing a baseball at a target on a handle and hitting it square you could cause the seat lever in the attached cage to release and plunge the man sitting on the perch into a tank of about five feet of water. All of the guys who worked in the cages were black, and they hated to see us coming. Between the ages of thirteen and sixteen my friends and I terrorized these guys. They were supposed to taunt the thrower, make fun of him or her, and try to keep them spending quarters for three balls. Most people who played this game were lucky to hit the target hard enough to dunk the clown one in every six tries; but my buddies and I became experts. We'd buy about ten dollars worth of baseballs and keep those guys going down, time after time.

Of course they hated us with a passion. "Don't you little motherfuckers have somewhere else to go?" they'd yell. "Goddamn motherfuckin' whiteboy, I'm gon' get yo' ass when I gets my break!" We'd just laugh and keep pegging hardballs at the trip-lever targets. My pal Big Steve was great at Dunk the Nigger; he was our true ace because he threw the hardest and his arm never got tired. "You fat ofay sumbitch!" one of the black guys would shout at Big Steve as he dunked him for the fifth pitch in a row. "Stop complaining," Steve would yell back at him. "You're getting a free bath, aren't ya?"

None of us thought too much about the fact that the job of taunt-and-dunk was about half a cut above being a carnival geek and a full cut below working at a car wash. It never occurred to us, more than a quarter of a century ago, why it was all of the guys on the perches were black, or that we were racists. Unwitting racists, perhaps; after all, we were kids, ignorant and foolish products of White Chicago during the fifties.

One summer afternoon in 1963, the year I turned sixteen, my friends and I arrived at Riverview and headed straight for Dunk the Nigger. We were shocked to see a white guy sitting on a perch in one of the cages. Nobody said anything but we all stared at him. Big Steve bought some balls and began hurling them at one of the black guys' targets. "What's the matter, gray?" the guy shouted at Steve. "Don't want to pick on one of your own?"

I don't remember whether or not I bought any balls that day, but I do know it was the last time I went to the concession. In fact, that was one of the last times I patronized Riverview, since I left Chicago early the following year and Riverview was torn down not long after. I don't know what Big Steve or any of my other old friends who played Dunk the Nigger with me think about it now, or even if they've ever thought about it at all. That's just the way things were.

Way Down in Egypt Land

There was a one-legged pool hustler named The Pharaoh who used to eat his dinner every day at four o'clock in a diner under the el tracks on Blackhawk Avenue called The Pantry. The neighborhood kids didn't know his real name, he just went by The Pharaoh because he said he came from Cairo, the tail of Little Egypt between the Mississippi and Ohio rivers.

"It's the asshole of Illinois," The Pharaoh told Roy and his friends, none of whom had ever been there.

"My mother had a cousin named Phil Webster was murdered in a bar in Paducah," said Ralph McGirr. "That's near there, ain't it?"

"Paducah's in Kentucky," The Viper said, "across the Ohio. It's pretty close."

The Pharaoh said nothing, just finished his meatloaf and mashed potatoes and dug into a slice of blueberry pie. The boys sat on stools in The Pantry or stood around, waiting for The Pharaoh to be done with his meal so that they could follow him down the street to Lucky's El Paso and watch him shoot pool. The El Paso was an old poolhall that had been closed down for years until Lucky Schmidt took it over. He renamed it Lucky's but everybody around there still called it the El Paso, so he changed it to Lucky's El Paso to pacify the old-timers. The Pharaoh didn't care what the place was called as long as it had a five by ten foot table to play one-pocket on. The Pharaoh always dressed the same: he wore a red and black checkered flannel shirt buttoned up to the neck and dark gray trousers held up by black suspenders. Once Roy had seen what looked like part of a thick blue scar below The Pharaoh's Adam's apple; Roy guessed that was why he kept his shirt buttoned to the top.

After The Pharaoh had polished off the pie, he propped himself up on his crutches and swung out of The Pantry. Jimmy Boyle held open the door and The Pharaoh turned right, followed by six boys aged twelve to fifteen. He didn't wear a coat. Nobody knew exactly how old The Pharaoh was or how he lost his left leg. Roy figured The Pharaoh was around forty or fifty years old because his curly brown hair was thinning and his forehead and cheeks were pretty wrinkled. The Viper said he'd heard Lucky ask The Pharaoh about how his leg went missing. This was while The Pharaoh was sitting down waiting for Ike the Kike to miss and without looking at Lucky The Pharaoh told him maybe someday he'd tell him but first Lucky should go fuck himself and his sister. After that, said The Pharaoh, they could talk about it.

The Pharaoh did not use his crutches when he shot; he supported himself by balancing his weight between his right leg and the table. The boys closely studied every move The Pharaoh made. His practice routine never varied: he lined up four balls at one end of the felt, hit them one after the other just hard enough off the rail so that they came back to exactly the same spot at which he'd placed them. The Pharaoh did this three times with each ball unfailingly, then he was ready to play. Roy and his friends tried to emulate The Pharaoh's warm-up but none of them could do it right more than once or twice. The only advice The Pharaoh would offer anyone was to tell them to tap the ball as if they were kissing their dead mother in her coffin.

The Pharaoh preferred one-pocket but occasionally indulged someone at nine ball. He never played straight pool, which he said was for stiffs. "If I'd bought into boredom," he told Roy, "I'd have stayed in school."

The only time Roy ever saw The Pharaoh lose was the last time he saw him, on a February night when he and The Viper went together to Lucky's El Paso. The boys came in out of the beginning of a blizzard around nine o'clock and saw a very tall, skinny guy bent low over the match table, the one Lucky kept covered even when the place was full of customers. The other tables he sometimes let bums sleep on after closing but not this one. There were about fifteen men sitting or standing in close proximity to the match table, watching this tower of bones beating the bejesus out of The Pharaoh at his own game. The Pharaoh sat perfectly still in the ratty red armchair he always used, his lone leg stretched out in front of him, an inch and a half of white cotton sock exposed between his trouser cuff and a beat up brown brogan. He was smoking an unfiltered Old Gold, staring at his imperturbable opponent.

The tall, skinny guy was about the same age as The Pharaoh but he was better dressed. He wore a dark blue blazer over an open-necked pale yellow shirt and chino pants. His few strands of black hair were greased back on his skull. Everything about him was long: his fingers, nose, even his eyelashes. Nobody spoke. Roy and The Viper stood and watched what were the final moments of the match, and when it was over the other witnesses to the slaying of The Pharaoh dropped their cash on the table and marched out of the poolhall into the storm.

The victor picked up his winnings, folded the bills into a thick roll, wrapped a blue rubber band around it and stuffed it into a pants pocket. Then he went over to The Pharaoh and said softly, but not so softly that Roy and The Viper could not hear the words, "You're washed up in Chi, Freddie, and don't never go back to Cairo, neither."

The Pharaoh sat and let his Old Gold smolder while the thin man unscrewed his cue, packed it into his case, pulled on a shabby beige trenchcoat, shook loose a Chesterfield from its pack to his lips, lit it, and without looking back at The Pharaoh left the El Paso. Lucky was sweeping up butts and putting the folding chairs away. He did not speak to The Pharaoh, nor did the boys, though they stood and waited for him. Roy thought maybe he'd need help walking in the snow.

After a half hour, The Viper elbowed Roy and they headed for the door. Before facing the blizzard Roy stopped and glanced over at The Pharaoh.

"Come on," said The Viper, "I'm hungry. Let's get some Chinks."

"Think he can make it to his crib?" Roy asked. "Where do you think he'll go?"

"I don't know," said The Viper, "but it probably won't be Little Egypt."

Bad Things Wrong

Louie Pinna was a bad kid, everybody said so: his neighbors, relatives, teachers. He was a bad student, that was certain. Pinna never really learned to read or write, so he was stuck in the third grade until he quit school legally at the age of sixteen. Roy had been in that third grade class with Pinna, a situation that was embarrassing not only for Louie but for his classmates, as well. At fifteen Pinna was already six feet tall. His legs did not fit under the small desk he was assigned to, so he sat in the last seat of the last row and splayed his legs to either side. Everyone was relieved when Pinna was finally allowed to leave.

After that Pinna hung out on the corner of Diversey and Blackhawk in the afternoons and worked as a night janitor at a downtown office building. Roy and his friends would often stop and talk to him after they got out of school. Pinna had always been nice to them; Roy never understood why so many adults considered Louie Pinna to be a rotten apple. In the 1950s, the concept of learning disabilities was not widely discussed, so a kid like Pinna was considered dumb and labelled a loser, earmarked for a bleak future as a bum or a criminal.

By the time Roy was in high school, Pinna had disappeared from the neighborhood. Roy asked around about him but nobody he talked to seemed to know where Pinna had gone. Then one day when Roy was fifteen Pinna's face appeared on the front page of the *Chicago Tribune*. Under a photograph of the now twenty-three-year-old Louie Pinna, who had grown a fruit peddler mustache, were the words: NO BAIL FOR SUSPECT IN KILLINGS. The article accompanying the photo said that Pinna worked at a meat processing plant on the West Side of the city and was accused of feeding bodies of murder victims through a grinder, after which the remains were mixed with food products and packaged as pork sausage. Pinna had not actually been charged with committing any murders, only with disposing of corpses provided, investigators theorized, by The Outfit, Chicago's organized crime syndicate.

Alberto Pinna, Louie's father, a retired plumber, was quoted in the newspaper as saying that his son had "a slow brain," and that, "if Louie done such a thing, he was used by those type people who do bad things wrong." Louie's mother, Maria Cecilia, was quoted as following her husband's statement with the remark, "And there ain't no shortage of them in Chicago."

"You believe this?" Roy asked the Viper.

"Pinna goes to prison," the Viper said, "at least he won't have to worry about taking care of himself no more."

"Do you think he did it? Ground bodies up for the Mob?"

"What makes you think he wouldn't?"

Roy and the Viper were on a bus passing the lake, which was frozen over. Roy remembered seeing Louie Pinna with Jump Garcia and Terry the Whip, both of whom had done time in the reformatory at St. Charles, going into Rizzo and Phil's, a bar on Ravenswood Avenue, a couple of years before. The cuffs of Pinna's trousers came down only to the tops of his ankles and he was wearing white socks with badly scuffed brown shoes. Rizzo and Phil's, Roy had heard, was supposedly a hangout for Mob guys.

"Pinna never picked on younger kids," Roy said. "He wasn't a bully."

"He did the thing," said the Viper, "ain't no character witnesses from grammar school gonna do him no good."

"Can't see what good it'd do to put Pinna away. He didn't harm a living person."

That night, Roy's mother's husband, her third, a jazz drummer who used the name Sid "Spanky" Wade—his real name was Czeslaw Wanchovsky—almost drowned in the bathtub. He had been smoking marijuana, fallen asleep and gone under. Spanky woke up just in time to regurgitate the water he'd inhaled through his nostrils. Roy's mother heard him splashing and coughing, went into the bathroom and tried to pull Spanky out of the tub, but he was too heavy for her to lift by herself.

"Roy!" she yelled. "Come help me!"

Roy and his mother managed to drag Spanky over the side and onto the floor, where he lay puking and gagging. Roy saw the remains of the reefer floating in the tub. Spanky was short and stout. Lying there on the bathroom floor, to Roy he resembled a big red hog, the kind of animal Louie Pinna had shoved into an industrial sausage maker. Roy began to laugh. He tried to stop but he could not. His mother shouted at him. Roy looked at her. She kept shouting. Suddenly, he could no longer hear or see anything.

Detente at the Flying Horse

Roy had a job changing tires and pumping gas two days a week after school at the Flying Horse service station on the corner of Peterson and Western. This was during the winter when he was sixteen. The three other weekday afternoons and also on Saturdays he worked at the Red Hot Ranch, a hot dog and hamburger joint. Roy had taken the gas station job in addition to his long-standing employment at the Ranch because his mother had had her hours reduced as a receptionist at Winnemac Hospital. His sister had just begun grammar school and they needed the money. Roy knew that his mother was considering getting married again—for what would be the fourth time—as a way to support them, a move he wanted desperately to avert or, at the least, delay. None of his mother's marriages had been successful, as even she would admit, other than two of them having produced Roy and his little sister. They were her treasures, she assured them; their existence had made her otherwise unfortunate forays into matrimony worthwhile.

Domingo and Damaso Parlanchín, two Puerto Rican brothers, owned the Flying Horse. They were good mechanics, originally from San Juan, who had worked for other people for fifteen years and saved their money so that they could buy their own station. They were short, chubby, good-humored men in their forties, constantly chattering to each other in rapid Spanish. The Parlanchín brothers paid Roy a dollar an hour and fifty cents for each tire he changed, half of what it cost the customer. Damaso could patch a flat faster than Roy could get it off the car and back on again, and do it without missing a beat in the running conversation with his brother. Domingo was the better mechanic of the two, the more analytically adept. Damaso was superior at handling the customers, able to convince them they needed an oil change or an upgrade of their tires.

It was no fun changing tires in January in Chicago. The temperature often fell well below zero degrees Fahrenheit and icy winds off the lake scorched Roy's perpetually scraped knuckles and cut fingers. Prying loose frozen lug nuts was Roy's greatest difficulty until Domingo showed him how to use an acetylene torch to heat the bolts before attempting to turn them with a tire iron. "Cuidado con la lanzallamas," Domingo told Roy.

One snowy afternoon about a quarter to four, just before dark, a black and white Buick Century ka-bumped into the station on its rims and stopped. All four tires were flat. Roy could see that they were studded with nails. Two burly men in dark blue overcoats and Homburg hats sat in the front seat. They did not get out, so Roy went over to the driver's side window and nodded at him. The man rolled down the window. He was about forty-five years old, had a three-day beard and a four inch-long scar across the left side of his lips. The man in the passenger seat looked just like the driver, except for the scar.

"How fast fix?" asked the driver.

"It looks like you need four new tires, sir," said Roy.

"Not possible fix?"

"I'll ask my boss, but I doubt it. You're riding on your rims. We'll have to check if they're bent."

"Go ask boss."

Roy trudged through the thick, wet snow to the garage, where Domingo and Damaso were working over a transmission on a 1956 Ford Apache pick-up.

"There's a guy here who needs four tires replaced. Looks like he drove over a bed of nails."

"Tell him he can to leave it," said Damaso.

"And coming back at siete horas," Domingo added.

The wind ripped into Roy's face when he removed his muffler

from around his mouth to convey this information to the driver of the Buick. Roy's eyes stung; they watered as he waited for the man to respond.

"Cannot they fix now?"

"No," said Roy, "we're pretty backed up."

The driver spoke to his companion in a language Roy could not readily identify. The wind whined and shrieked, making it difficult for Roy to hear anything else.

"We wait," the driver told him. "Can fix sooner."

Roy shook his head. "Maybe you'd better try another station. But you'll damage your wheels."

The man produced a fifty dollar bill and shoved it at Roy. He held it between two black leather-gloved fingers. "This extra. Okey dokey?" he said. "You give boss."

Roy accepted the bill, marched back to the garage and handed it to Domingo.

"The guy says this is on top of the cost of replacing the tires, if we can do it now."

"Tell him drive in muy despacio," said Domingo.

After the man had done this, following Damaso's signals to pull up into the other bay and onto the lift, Damaso told the men to get out of the car.

"We stay in," said the driver.

"No es posible raise car with you inside. Insurance no good if you fall."

The driver held out another fifty. Damaso took it. He nodded to Domingo, who activated the lift.

"Lock doors!" Damaso shouted up at the men. "And no move!"

Roy pumped gas for several customers while the Parlanchín brothers worked on the Buick. The sky had gone dark and snow kept falling. Before the Buick pulled out of the station on four new Bridgestones, it stopped next to Roy. The driver rolled down his window.

"Yes, sir?" said Roy. "Is everything okay?"

"All okey dokey," replied the driver. "You young boy, work hard bad weather. How much Spanish men pay you?"

"Buck an hour and two bits a flat."

"Slave wage," said the man. "Now 1962. Take."

The driver extended toward Roy his black gloved left hand between two fingers of which protruded another fifty-dollar bill. Roy took the money and stuffed it into one of the snap pockets of his brown leather jacket.

"Thank you," he said. "Where are you guys from?"

"You know Iron Curtain?"

"I've heard of it."

"We are from behind."

After the Buick had gone, Roy went into the garage.

"Strange hombres, si?" said Domingo.

"The driver gave me a tip," Roy told him. "I don't know why, though."

"He give us a hundred extra," said Damaso.

"The Buick had diplomatic license plates," Roy said. "They're Russians, I think."

"Must be they are trying to be more friendly," Domingo suggested, "since they been forced to take missiles out of Cuba."

When Roy was eleven, he remembered, his mother had had a boyfriend from Havana, a conga drummer named Raul Repilado. She had met him in Coral Gables, Florida, when she and her third husband, Sid Wade, the father of Roy's sister, were vacationing at the Biltmore. Raul Repilado's band, the Orquesta Furioso, was appearing at the hotel. Raul had come to Chicago a couple of times to see Roy's mother, the last time during the winter. Before leaving, the conguero declared that he would never come back to such a terribly cold place, even for a beautiful woman. Roy couldn't wait to tell his mother that he'd made an extra fifty bucks that day.

Shattered

Roy was walking to his after school job at the Red Hot Ranch when a girl about his age, whom he did not know, came up to him and said, "Isn't it terrible? I just want to scream."

Roy looked at her face. The girl was crying but she was still pretty. She had blonde hair and gray eyes. At closer inspection, Roy realized that the girl was older than he'd first thought; she was about eighteen or nineteen.

"Isn't what terrible?" he asked.

"You didn't hear?"

"I don't know," said Roy. "Hear what?"

"The president's been shot. He's dead."

Fresh tears shot out of the girl's eyes and poured down her cheeks.

"Can you hold me?" she asked him. "I need to be held, just for a few seconds."

Even though he was two or three years younger than the girl, Roy was at least two inches taller. He put his arms around her. She sank her head into his chest and continued sobbing.

"I'm shattered," she said. "I never imagined anything so terrible could happen."

"Do they know who shot him?"

The girl moved her head side to side without taking it off of Roy's chest.

"A woman shouted it from the window of a bus."

"Maybe the woman was crazy," Roy said. "Maybe it didn't happen at all."

"No, it happened. I've been walking for blocks and blocks and other people said it, too."

The girl remained in Roy's embrace for about a minute before she pulled away and wiped her face with the end of her scarf. It was a windy, cold day; the sky was overcast. Roy could feel snow in the air.

"Thank you," the girl said. Her gray eyes were bloodshot. "This is the worst thing that ever happened to me."

Later that night, after Roy had gotten home from work and watched the news on television, he thought about what the girl had said, that the assassination of the president was the worst thing that had ever happened to her, even though she was not the person who had been murdered.

When things go wrong, Roy decided, people are shocked by the discovery of their own lack of control over events. Perhaps now the girl would understand just how fragile the appearance of order in the world really was. All Roy wanted to think about was how pretty she was and how good it felt to hold her.

A Day's Worth of Beauty

The most beautiful girl I ever saw was Princessa Paris, when she was seventeen and a half years old. I was almost seventeen when I met her. An older guy I knew from the neighborhood, Gus Argo, introduced me to Princessa—actually, she introduced herself, but Gus got me there—because he had a crush on her older sister, Turquoise, who was twenty-two. This was February of 1963, in Chicago. The street and sidewalks were coated with ice, a crust of hard, two day-old snow covered the lawns. Princessa attended a different high school than I did, but I had heard of the Paris sisters; their beauty was legendary on the Northwest side of the city.

Argo picked me up while I was walking home from the Red Hot Ranch, a diner I worked at four days a week, three afternoons after school and Saturdays. It was about eight o'clock when Gus spotted me hiking on Western Avenue. He was twenty-one and had worked at Allied Radio on Western for three years, ever since he'd graduated from high school. Argo had been a pretty good left-handed pitcher, I'd played ball with and against him a few times; he was a tough kid, and he had once backed me up in a fight. A gray and black Dodge Lancer pulled over to the curb and honked. I saw that the driver was Gus Argo, and I got in.

"Hey, Roy, where you headed?"

"Thanks, Gus, it's freezing. To my house, I guess. I just got off work."

"Yeah, me, too, but I got to make a delivery first, drop off a hi-fi. Want to ride over with me? Won't take long."

"Sure."

"Your old lady got dinner waitin'?"

"No, she's out."

"Okay, maybe we'll get a burger and coffee at Buffalo's. I just got paid, so it's on me."

"Sounds good."

"Ever hear of the Paris sisters?"

"Yeah, everybody has. You know them?"

"I'm makin' the delivery to their house. I been tryin' to get up the nerve to ask Turquoise Paris to go out with me for two years."

"Are they really so good looking?"

"I'd give anything to spend one day with Turquoise, to have one day's worth of her beauty."

"What about the other one?"

"Princessa? She's almost eighteen, four years younger than Turquoise. I only saw her once, at the Granada on a Saturday. She's a knockout, too."

Gus cranked up the blower in the Dodge. The sky was clear black but the temperature was almost zero. The radiator in my room didn't work very well; I knew I would have to sleep with a couple of sweaters on to stay warm. Argo parked in front of the Paris house and got out.

"Come in with me," he said. "You can carry one of the boxes."

Princessa opened the front door. She was almost my height, slender and small-breasted. Her lustrous chestnut hair hung practically to her waist. Once I was inside, in the light, I took a good look at her face. She reminded me of Hedy Lamarr in *Algiers*, wearing an expression that warned a man: If you don't take care of me, someone else certainly will. Princessa's complexion was porcelain smooth; I'd never before seen skin that looked so clean.

"You can just leave the boxes on the floor in the living room," she told us. "My father will set it up when he gets home."

"Who's there, Cessa?"

Gus Argo and I looked up in the direction from which the voice asking this question had come. Gene Tierney stood at the top of the staircase. Or maybe it was Helen of Troy.

"The delivery boys," Princessa answered. "They brought the

new hi-fi."

"Tell them to just leave the boxes in the living room. Daddy will set it up later."

"I just did."

The apparition on the staircase disappeared; she wasn't coming down.

"Thanks, guys," said Princessa. "I'd give you a tip but I don't have any money. I can ask Turquoise if she does."

"No," Gus said, "it's okay."

He glanced at the top of the stairs once more, then walked out of the house.

"My name is Roy," I said to Princessa.

"Hi, Roy." she said, and held her right hand out to me. "I'm Cessa."

I took her hand. It felt like a very small, freshly killed and skinned animal.

"Your hand is warm," I said, holding it.

"My body temperature is always slightly above normal. The doctor says people's temperatures vary."

"It feels good. Mine is cold. I wasn't wearing any gloves."

She withdrew her hand.

"Could I come back to see you sometime?" I asked.

Princessa smiled. Hedy Lamarr vanished. Princessa had one slightly crooked upper front tooth the sight of which made me want to kiss her. I smiled back, memorizing her face.

"It was nice to meet you," I said, and turned to go.

"Roy?"

I turned around. Hedy was back.

"You can call me, if you like. My last name is Paris. I have my own phone, the number's in the book."

I went out with Princessa a couple of times. She talked about her boyfriend, who was already in college; and about Turquoise, who, Cessa told me, was a party girl.

"What's a party girl?" I asked.

"She gets fifty dollars when she goes to the powder room, sometimes more. My parents don't know."

I didn't ask any more questions about Turquoise, but I did repeat what Princessa told me to Gus Argo.

"Fifty bucks for the powder room? You're shittin' me," he said.

"Does that mean she's a prostitute?" I asked him.

"I don't think so," said Argo. "More like she goes out with visiting firemen who want a good lookin' date."

"Visiting firemen?"

"Yeah, guys from out of town. Salesmen, conventioneers."

Many years later, I read Apuleius's version of the myth of Psyche and Amor. Venus, Amor's mother, was so jealous of her son's love for Psyche that she attempted to seduce Amor in an effort to convince him to destroy his lover, which he would not do. Venus even imprisoned Amor and ordered Psyche to go to the underworld and bring up a casket filled with a day's worth of beauty. Eventually, Jupiter, Amor's father, came to his son's rescue and persuaded Venus to lay off the poor girl.

I remembered Gus Argo telling me he would have done anything to have had one day's worth of Turquoise Paris's beauty. My guess is that he never got it, and I doubt that he knew the story of Psyche and Amor. Gus just didn't seem to me like the kind of guy who'd spring for the powder room.

The Peterson Fire

It was snowing the night the Peterson house burned down. Bud Peterson was seventeen then, two years older than me. Bud got out alive because his room was on the ground floor in the rear of the house. His two sisters and their parents slept upstairs, above the living room, which was where the fire started. An ember jumped from the fireplace and ignited the carpet. Bud's parents and his ten- and twelve-year-old sisters could not get down the staircase. When they tried to go back up, they were trapped and burned alive. There was nothing Bud Peterson could have done to save any of them. He was lucky, a fireman said, to have survived by crawling out his bedroom window.

I didn't see the house until the next afternoon. Snow flurries mixed with the ashes. Most of the structure was gone, only part of the first floor remained, and the chimney. I was surprised to see Bud Peterson standing in the street with his pals, staring at the ruins. Bud was a tall, thin boy, with almost colorless hair. He wore a Navy pea coat but no hat. Black ash was swirling around and some of it had fallen on his head. Nobody was saying much. There were about twenty of us, kids from the neighborhood, standing on the sidewalk or in the street, looking at what was left of the Peterson house.

I had walked over by myself after school to see it. Big Frank had told me about the fire in Cap's that morning when we were buying Bismarcks. Frank's brother, Otto, was a fireman. Frank said Otto had awakened him at five thirty and asked if Frank knew Bud Peterson. Frank told him he did and Otto said, "His house burned down last night. Everybody but him is dead."

I heard somebody laugh. A couple of Bud's friends were whispering to each other and trying not to laugh but one of them couldn't help himself. I looked at Peterson but he didn't seem to mind. I remembered that he was a little goofy, maybe not too bright, but a good guy. He always seemed like one of those kids who just went along with the gang, who never really stood out. A bigger kid I didn't know came up to Bud and patted him on the left shoulder, then said something I couldn't hear. Peterson smiled a little and nodded his head. Snow started to come down harder. I put up the hood of my coat. We all just kept looking at the burned down house.

A black and white drove up and we moved aside. It stopped and a cop got out and said a few words to Bud Peterson. Bud got into the back seat of the squad car with the cop and the car drove away. The sky was getting dark pretty fast and the crowd broke up.

One of Bud's sisters, Irma, the one who was twelve, had a dog, a brown and black mutt. I couldn't remember its name. Nobody had said anything about Irma's dog, if it got out alive or not. I used to see her walking that dog when I was coming home from baseball or football practice.

Bud Peterson went to live with a relative. Once in a while, in the first few weeks after the fire, I would see him back in the neighborhood, hanging out with the guys, then I didn't see him anymore. Somebody said he'd moved away from Chicago.

One morning, more than thirty years later, I was sitting at a bar in Paris drinking a coffee when, for no particular reason, I thought about standing in front of the Peterson house that afternoon and wondering: If it had been snowing hard enough the night before, could the snow have put out the fire? Then I remembered the name of Irma Peterson's dog.

Door to the River

Roy read in a science book about a parasite that lives in water and enters the skin of human beings, goes to the head and causes loss of sight. This condition, Roy learned, was sometimes called river blindness. Soon after he'd read this, Roy was taken on a Friday night by his cousin Ray to Rita's Can't Take It With You, a blues club on the West Side. Ray was twenty-two, six years older than Roy. Ray had recently enlisted in the Navy and wanted to celebrate before leaving for boot camp the following Monday. The cousins were accompanied to Rita's by Ray's friend Marvin Kitna, an accordionist in a polka band who had been to the club several times before.

"The Wolf's playing tonight," Kitna told Roy and Ray. "He's gettin' up there, but he's still the best."

Roy, Ray and Marvin Kitna were the only white patrons that night in Rita's Can't Take It With You. Kitna seemed to know almost everybody there, from the two bartenders, Earl and Lee, to many of the customers, as well as the two off-duty Chicago cops, Malcolm and Durrell, who were paid to provide security. Roy let his cousin and Kitna order beers and shots of Jim Beam for the three of them. The waitress, whom Marvin addressed as Dolangela, and who favored them with a dazzling dental display of gold and silver, did not ask any of them, even Roy, for verification of their ages.

Roy slowly sipped his beer and kept his mouth shut. He did not touch the shot of bourbon. The Wolf put on a great performance, crawling around on the stage, lying on his back while playing guitar and emitting his trademark howl. Ray and Marvin Kitna got up and danced a couple of times with girls Kitna knew. Roy was content to sit still and take in the show.

After the boys had been there for about an hour, a girl came over to their table, pulled up a chair and sat down between Roy and Ray.

"Hi," she said to Roy. "My name's Esmeraldina. What's yours?"

"Roy."

"You got beautiful hair, Roy. You mind do I touch it?"

"No."

Esmeraldina ran the fingers of her right hand through Roy's wavy black hair.

"You Eyetalian?" she asked him. "You an Eyetalian boy, huh?"

Roy shook his head. "I'm mostly Irish," he said.

"Pretty Eyetalian boy with turquoise eyes."

Esmeraldina draped her left arm around Roy's shoulders while she played with his hair.

"Just go along with her, Roy," said Marvin Kitna. "She won't bite."

"Oh yes, I do," Esmeraldina said. "I surely do can bite when a particular feelin' comin' on."

She poured Roy's shot of Beam into his glass of beer and picked up the glass.

"You mind do I take a taste?" she asked Roy.

Roy shook his head no and Esmeraldina drank half of the contents.

"What's that particular feelin' you're talkin' about, Esmeraldina?" asked Roy's cousin.

She grinned, revealing a perfect row of teeth unadorned by metal, and replied, "When a man get under my skin, crawl all up inside so's I can't itch it or see straight. Happens, I ain't responsible for myself, what I do until the feelin' wear off."

"How long's that take?" asked Marvin Kitna.

"Depends on the man," Esmeraldina said.

"Like river blindness," said Roy.

"What's that, honey?"

"A water bug swims in through a person's pores up to their head and makes them go blind."

Esmeraldina stared for a long moment into Roy's eyes, then she kissed him softly on the mouth.

"I bet you know all kinds of interestin' things, Roy," she said. "You want to dance with me?"

"Sure."

Esmeraldina picked up Roy's glass and finished off the shot and beer before they headed to the dance floor. Jimmie "Fast Fingers" Dawkins' "All for Business" was playing on the jukebox. She pressed her skinny body hard against Roy's and wrapped her arms around his back. Esmeraldina nudged him gently around in response to the slow blues. Roy guessed that Esmeraldina was in her early twenties but he didn't want to ask for fear she would in turn ask him how old he was and he did not want to have to lie.

"How old are you, Roy?"

"Old enough to be here," he said.

"You pretty sharp. Sharp and pretty."

"You're very pretty yourself, Esmeraldina."

After the record ended, Esmeraldina took Roy by the hand and led him out of the club. It was cold outside, too cold to be in the street without a coat. Roy had left his on the back of his chair at the table. Esmeraldina did not have one, either; she shivered in her short-sleeve blouse as she walked him to the right, around the corner onto Lake Street. A few yards ahead of them, two men, both wearing short-brimmed hats, were arguing with one another. One of them pulled a gun from a pocket and shot the other man in the forehead. The man who had been shot flew off his feet backwards as if he'd been caught off balance by Sugar Ray Robinson's quick left hook. The shooter ran and disappeared under the el tracks. Roy looked at the man on the ground: his eyes were open and his short-brim was still on his head.

"Bad timin'," Esmeraldina said. "We'd best go back indoors."

She and Roy hurried into Rita's Can't Take It With You, where Esmeraldina let go of him and lost herself in the crowd. Roy went over to the table where he'd been sitting with Ray and Marvin Kitna. They weren't there. Roy looked for them on the dance floor but he didn't see them. He took his jacket off the back of his chair and put it on. The music coming from the jukebox was very loud but Roy could hear a police siren. He saw Malcolm and Durrell, the security guards, go out the front door followed by Earl, one of the bartenders, and several customers. Roy ducked out, too, turned left and walked as fast as he could away from Lake Street. He could still see the dead man with a nickel-sized hole above the bridge of his nose.

"How could his hat have stayed on?" Roy said.

Sailing in the Sea of Red
He Sees a Black Ship on the Horizon

As a boy, Roy dreamed of going to sea, working as a deckhand on an oceangoing freighter, an ambition he was one day to realize. This vision took hold when he began reading the stories of Jack London and, later, those of Melville, Traven and Conrad. For awhile, he had a recurring dream in which he was a lookout positioned on the bow of a large boat at dawn. As the sun rose, the water turned red, and in the farthest distance Roy spotted an unmarked black cargo ship teetering on the lip of the horizon, as if it were precariously navigating a razor's edge of the planet. Roy felt that at any moment the mysterious freighter could tip over into the unseen and be lost forever.

When he was twelve years old, Roy's friend Elmo got his father to pay for him to take trumpet lessons. The old man operated a salvage business and didn't know much about music but he was proud of Elmo's desire to play the trumpet. The only tune Elmo ever learned to play all the way through, however, was "Twinkle, Twinkle, Little Star." Every so often, the old man would come home tired and dirty from the junkyard, plop down with a can of Falstaff in his favorite chair and ask Elmo to play something. Elmo would get his horn and stumble through "Twinkle, Twinkle, Little Star," which never failed to delight his father.

"How's the trumpet lessons goin', son?" the old man would ask him. "Makin' progress, Dad," Elmo would say. "Makin' progress."

When Elmo quit taking trumpet lessons, the old man was visibly disappointed. "Don't know why he stopped," he said, shaking his almost entirely bald head. "He was makin' progress."

Many years later, when Elmo's father learned that he was dying from stomach cancer, the old man refused to have chemotherapy.

All he wanted was morphine, to dull the pain. The old man had been a Marine during World War II and had seen combat in the Pacific, where he'd contracted malaria, of which he still suffered occasional bouts. He told Elmo and Roy that war was stupid.

"War's a business, boys," said the old man, "big business, a way for the fat cats to make more coin when things ain't goin' so swift. This way they figure the ordinary citizen'll appreciate what they got and spend more after the shootin' stops. The fat cats live to make suckers out of us regular Joes."

Every day for the last six months of his life, the old man sat in a lawn chair in front of his garage and never complained, even when his burly body shrunk down to the size of a boy's. He was never mean; all the kids in the neighborhood liked him.

"I want to go out being who I am," he said, explaining why he refused to undergo chemotherapy.

After he passed away, Elmo called up Roy and said, "The old man died today. He's on that black ship you used to dream about."

"He was a great man," Roy told him.

"That's what I always thought," said Elmo.

Wyoming

ROY'S MOTHER

Cobratown

"We're really fine when we're together, aren't we? I mean, when it's just the two of us."

"Uh-huh. How long till we get to the reptile farm?"

"Oh, less than an hour, I think."

"Will they have a giant king cobra, like on the sign?"

"I'm sure they will, sweetheart."

"I hope it's not asleep when we get there. Mom, do cobras sleep?"

"Of course, snakes have to sleep just like people. At least I think they do."

"Do they think?"

"Who, baby?"

"Snakes. Do they have a brain?"

"Yes. They think about food, mostly. What they're going to eat next in order to survive."

"They only think about eating?"

"That's the main thing. And finding a warm, safe place to sleep."

"Some snakes live in trees, on the branches. That can't be so safe. Birds can get them."

"They wait on the limbs for prey, some smaller creature to come along and the snake can snatch it up, or drop on it and wrap itself around and squeeze it to death or until it passes out from not having enough air to breathe. Then the snake crushes it and devours it."

"You're a good driver, aren't you, Mom? You like to drive."

"I'm a very good driver, Roy. I like to drive when we go on long trips together."

"How far is it from Key West to Mississippi?"

"Well, to Jackson, where we're going, it's a pretty long way.

Several hundred miles. We go north through Florida, then across Alabama to Mississippi and up to Jackson, which is about in the middle of the state."

"Will Dad be there?"

"No, honey. Your dad is in Chicago. At least I think he is. He could be away somewhere on business."

"Who are we going to see in Mississippi?"

"A good friend of Mommy's. A man named Bert."

"Why is Bert in Mississippi?"

"That's where he lives, baby. He owns a hotel in Jackson."

"What's the name of the hotel?"

"The Prince Rupert."

"Is it like the Casa Azul?"

"I think Bert's hotel is bigger."

"You've never seen it?"

"No, only a photo of it on a postcard that Bert sent."

"How old is Bert?"

"I'm not sure. I guess about forty."

"How old is Dad?"

"Forty-three. He'll be forty-four next month, on the tenth of April."

"Will he invite me to his birthday party?"

"I don't know if your dad will have a birthday party, Roy, but I'm sure he would invite you if he did."

"Some dinosaurs had two brains, Mom, do you know that?"

"Two brains?"

"Yeah, there's a picture in my dinosaur book that Dad sent me that shows how the really big ones had a regular-size brain in their head and a small one in their tail. The really big ones. It's because it was so far from their head to their tail there was too much for only one brain to think about, so God gave them two."

"Who told you God gave dinosaurs two brains?"

"Nanny."

"Your grandmother doesn't know anything about dinosaurs."

"What about Bert?"

"What about him?"

"Do you think he knows about dinosaurs?"

"You'll have to ask him, baby. I don't really know what Bert knows about."

"You said he was your friend."

"Yes, he is."

"Why don't I know him?"

"He's kind of a new friend. That's why I'm taking you to Jackson, to meet Bert, so he can be your friend, too."

"Is Bert a friend of Dad's?"

"No, baby. Dad doesn't know Bert."

"How far now to the reptile farm?"

"We're pretty close. The last sign said twenty-six miles. I can't go too fast on this road."

"I like this car, Mom. I like that it's blue and white, like the sky, except now there's dark clouds."

"It's called a Holiday."

"We're on a holiday now, right?"

"Yes, Roy, it's a kind of holiday. Just taking a little trip, the two of us."

"We're pals, huh?"

"We sure are, baby. You're my best pal."

"Better than Bert?"

"Yes, darling, better than anyone else. You'll always be my favorite boy."

"Look, Mom! We must be really close now."

"The sign said, 'Ten minutes to Cobratown.'"

"If it rains hard, will the snakes stay inside?"

"It's only raining a little, Roy. They'll be out. They'll all be out, baby, don't worry. There'll be cobras crawling all over Cobratown, just for us. You'll see."

Chinese Down the Amazon

"What do you think, baby? Does this place look all right to you?"

"Is it safe?"

"Safe as any motel room in Alabama can be, I guess. At least it looks clean."

"And it doesn't stink of old cigarettes, like the last one."

"We can stay here."

"I'm tired, Mom."

"Take off your shoes and lie down, baby. I'll go out and bring back something for dinner. I'll bet there's a Chinese restaurant in this town. There's Chinese everywhere, Roy, you know that? Even down the Amazon it said in the *National Geographic*. I can get some egg rolls and pork chow mein and egg foo yung. What do you think, baby? Would you like some chow mein and egg foo yung? I'll just make a quick stop in the bathroom first. Out in a jiffy."

"Could I get a Coca-Cola?"

"Oh! Oh, Christ! This is disgusting! Come on, baby, we're moving."

"What happened, Mom?"

"Just filth! The bathroom is crazy with cockroaches! Even the toilet's filled with bugs!"

"I don't see any bugs on the bed."

"Those kind come out later, when the light's off. Get off of there! The beds are probably infested, too. Let's go!"

"I've got to put on my shoes."

"You can do it in the car. Come on!"

"Mom?"

"Yes, Roy?"

"Could I get a hamburger instead of Chinese?"

Bandages

"I was very shy when I was a girl, so shy it was painful. When I had to leave my room at school, to go to class, I often became physically ill. I got sick at the thought of having to see people, or their having to see me, to talk to them. I think this is why I had my skin problems, my eczema. It came from nerves. Being sick allowed me to stay by myself, wrapped up in bandages. People left me alone."

"But weren't you lonely?"

"Not really. I liked to read and listen to the radio and dream. I didn't have to be asleep to really dream, to go into another world where I wasn't afraid of meeting people, of having them look at me and judge me. I really felt better, safe, inside those bandages. They were my shield, I suppose, my protection."

"Prince Valiant has a shield."

"I like this song, Roy. Listen, I'll turn it up: Dean Martin singing 'Ain't Love a Kick in the Head.' He works hard to sound so casual, so relaxed. I always had the feeling Dean Martin was really very shy, like me. That he affected this style of not seeming to care, to be so cool, in order to cover up his real feelings. That's his shield."

"Are we still in Indiana?"

"Yes, baby. We'll be in Indianapolis soon. We'll stay there tonight."

"Indiana goes on a long time."

"It seems that way sometimes. Look out the window. Maybe you'll see a farmer."

"Mom, are there still Indians in Indiana?"

"I don't think so, baby. They all moved away."

"Then why is it still called Indiana, if there aren't any Indians left?"

"Just because they were here before. There were Indians, many different tribes, all over the country."

"The Indians rode horses. They didn't have cars."

"Some of them had cars after."

"After what?"

"After people came from Europe."

"They brought cars from Europe?"

"Yes, but they made them here, too. That's where the Indians got them, the same as everybody else."

"There aren't so many horses here as in Florida."

"Probably not."

"Mom?"

"Yes, Roy?"

"You still wrap yourself up with bandages sometimes."

"When I have an attack of eczema, to cover the ointment I put on the sores, so I don't get everything greasy."

"You don't want anyone to see the sores?"

"One time, not long after I married your father, I had such a bad attack that my skin turned red and black, and I had to stay in the hospital for a month. The sores got so bad they bled. The skin on my arms and hands and face stank under the bandages. I couldn't wash and I smelled terrible. When the nurses unwrapped the bandages to sponge me off, the odor made me want to vomit.

"One day your dad's brother, Uncle Bruno, was there when the nurses took off the bandages. He didn't believe I was really sick, I don't know why, but he wanted to see for himself. It was costing your dad a lot of money for doctors to take care of me and to keep me in a private hospital. When they removed my bandages, Bruno was horrified by the sight of my skin. He couldn't stand the smell or to look at me, and he ran out of the room. I guess he was worried about all the money your father was spending on me. He probably thought I was pretending to be so sick. After that, he said to your dad, 'Kitty used to be so beautiful. What happened to her?'"

"But you are beautiful, Mom."

"I wasn't then, baby, not when I was so sick. I looked pretty bad. But Bruno knew I wasn't faking. I screamed when the nurse peeled off the bandages, my skin stuck to them. Bruno heard me. He wanted your dad to get rid of me, I was too much trouble."

"Did Dad want to get rid of you?"

"No, baby, he didn't. We separated for other reasons."

"Was I a reason?"

"No, sweetheart, of course you weren't. Your father loves you more than anything, just like I do. You mustn't ever think that. The trouble was just between your dad and me, it had nothing to do with you. Really, you're the most precious thing to both of us."

"When will we get to Chicago?"

"Tomorrow afternoon."

"Where are we going to stay? At Nanny's house?"

"No, baby, we'll stay at the hotel, the same place as before. Remember how you like the chocolate sundaes they make in the restaurant there?"

"Uh-huh. Can we sit in the big booth by the window when we have breakfast?"

"Sure, baby."

"Can I have a chocolate sundae for breakfast?"

"One time you can, okay?"

"Okay."

"Mom?"

"Huh?"

"Do I have nerves?"

"What do you mean, baby? Everyone has nerves."

"I mean, will I ever have to be wrapped up in bandages because of my nerves?"

"No, Roy, you won't. You're not nervous like I was, like I sometimes get now only not so bad as when I was younger. It'll never happen to you, never. Don't worry."

"I love you, Mom. I hope you never have sores and have to get wrapped up again."

"I hope so, too, baby. And remember, I love you more than anything."

Soul Talk

"Mom, when birds die, what happens to their souls?"

"What made you think of that, Roy?"

"I was watching a couple of crows fly by."

"You think birds have souls?"

"That's what Nanny says."

"What do you think the soul is, baby?"

"Something inside a person."

"Where inside?"

"Around the middle."

"You mean by the heart?"

"I don't know. Someplace deep. Can a doctor see it on an X-ray?"

"No, baby, nobody can see it. Sometimes you can feel your soul yourself. It's just a feeling. Not everybody has one."

"Some people don't have a soul?"

"I don't know, Roy, but there are more than a few I'll bet have never been in touch with theirs. Or who'd recognize it if it glowed in the dark."

"Can you see your soul in the dark if you take off all your clothes and look in the mirror?"

"Only if your eyes are closed."

"Mom, that doesn't make sense."

"I hate to tell you this, baby, but the older you get and the more you figure things should make sense, they more than sometimes don't."

"Your soul flies away like a crow when you die and hides in a cloud. When it rains that means the clouds are full of souls and some of 'em are squeezed out. Rain is the dead souls there's no more room for in heaven."

"Did Nanny tell you this, Roy?"

"No, it's just something I thought."

"Baby, there's no way I'll ever think about rain the same way again."

Skylark

"You know, sometimes you look just like your father, only much more beautiful, of course."

"You don't think Dad is beautiful?"

"No, your father isn't so beautiful, but he's a real man."

"And I'm a real boy, like Pinocchio wanted to be."

"Yes, baby, you're a real boy."

"Why isn't Dad with us so much anymore?"

"He's very busy, Roy, you know that. His business takes up most of his time."

"When will I see him again?"

"We'll go to Havana in two weeks and meet him there. You like the hotel where his apartment is, remember? The Nacional?"

"Will the little man with the curly white dog be there?"

"Little man? Oh, Mr. Lipsky. I don't know, baby. Remember the last time we saw him? In Miami, the day after the big hurricane."

"We were walking down the middle of the street that looked like it was covered with diamonds, and Mr. Lipsky was carrying his dog."

"The hurricane had blown out most of the windows of the big hotels, and Collins Avenue was paved with chunks of glass."

"Mr. Lipsky kissed you. I remember he had to stand on his toes. Then he gave me a piece of candy."

"He was carrying his tiny dog because he didn't want him to cut his paws on the broken glass. Mr. Lipsky said the dog was used to taking a walk every morning at that time and he didn't want to disappoint him."

"Mr. Lipsky talks funny."

"What do you mean, he talks funny?"

"He sings."

"Sings?"

"Like he's singing a little song when he says something to you."

"Sure, baby, I know what you mean. Mr. Lipsky's a little odd, but he's been a good friend to your dad and us."

"Does Mr. Lipsky have a wife?"

"I think so, but I've never met her."

"I hope when I grow up I won't be as little as him."

"As *he*, honey. As little as *he*. Of course you won't. You'll be as tall as your dad, or taller."

"Is Mr. Lipsky rich?"

"Why do you ask that, baby?"

"Because he always wears those big sparkly rings."

"Well, Roy, Mr. Lipsky is probably one of the wealthiest men in America."

"How did he get so rich?"

"Oh, he has lots of different kinds of businesses, here and in Cuba. All over the world, maybe."

"What kinds of businesses?"

"Lots of times he gives people money to start a business, and then they have to pay him back more than the amount he gave them or pay him part of what they earn for as long as the business lasts."

"I guess he's pretty smart."

"Your dad thinks Mr. Lipsky is the smartest man he's ever met."

"I hope I'm smart."

"You are, Roy. Don't worry about being smart."

"You know what, Mom?"

"What, baby?"

"I think if I had to choose one thing, to be tall or to be smart, I'd take smart."

"You'll be both, sweetheart, you won't have to choose."

"Do you know what Mr. Lipsky's dog's name is?"

"Sky something, isn't it? Skylark, that's it, like the Hoagy Carmichael song."

"I bet he's smart, too. A dog named Skylark would have to be very smart."

Flamingos

"Mom, after I die I want to come back as a flamingo."

"You won't die for a very long time, Roy. It's too soon to be thinking about it. But I'm not so sure that after people die they come back at all. How do you know about reincarnation? And why a flamingo?"

"How do I know about what?"

"Reincarnation. Like you said, some people believe that after they die they'll return in a different form, as another person or even as an insect or animal."

"Mammy Yerma told me it could happen."

"Mammy Yerma usually knows what she's talking about, but I'm not so sure about being reincarnated, even as a flamingo."

"Flamingos are the most beautiful birds, like the ones around the pond at the racetrack in Hialeah. I'd like to be a dark pink flamingo with a really long, curvy neck."

"They're elegant birds, baby, that's for sure."

"If you could come back as an animal, Mom, what would you be?"

"A leopard, probably. Certainly a big cat of some kind, if I had a choice. Leopards are strong and fast and beautiful. They climb trees, Roy, did you know that? Leopards are terrifically agile."

"What's agile?"

"They're great leapers, with perfect balance. They can jump up in a tree and walk along a narrow limb better than the best acrobat. Another thing about leopards, I believe, is that they mate for life."

"What's that mean?"

"It means once a male and female leopard start a family, they stay together until they die."

"People do, too."

"Yes, baby, some people do. But I think it's harder for human beings to remain true to one another than it is for leopards."

"Why?"

"Well, all animals have to worry about is getting food, protecting their young, and to avoid being eaten by bigger animals. Humans have much more to deal with, plus our brain is different. A leopard acts more on instinct, what he feels. A person uses his brain to reason, to decide what to do."

"I'd like to be a leopard with a human brain. Then I could leap up in a tree and read a book and nobody would bother me because they'd be afraid."

"Baby, are you getting hungry? We humans have to decide if we want to stop soon and eat."

"A leopard would probably eat a flamingo, if he was hungry enough."

"Maybe, but a skinny bird doesn't make much of a meal, and I don't think a leopard would want to mess with all of those feathers."

"Mom, I need to go to the bathroom."

"Now that's something neither a leopard nor a flamingo would think twice about. I'll stop at the next exit. I need to go, too."

Wyoming

"What's your favorite place, Mom?"

"Oh, I have a lot of favorite places, Roy. Cuba, Jamaica, Mexico."

"Is there a place that's really perfect? Somewhere you'd go if you had to spend the rest of your life there and didn't want anyone to find you?"

"How do you know that, baby?"

"Know what?"

"That sometimes I think about going someplace where nobody can find me."

"Even me?"

"No, honey, not you. We'd be together, wherever it might be."

"How about Wyoming?"

"Wyoming?"

"Have you ever been there?"

"Your dad and I were in Sun Valley once, but that's in Idaho. No, Roy, I don't think so. Why?"

"It's really big there, with lots of room to run. I looked on a map. Wyoming's probably a good place to have a dog."

"I'm sure it is, baby. You'd like to have a dog, huh?"

"It wouldn't have to be a big dog, Mom. Even a medium-size or small dog would be okay."

"When I was a little girl we had a chow named Toy, a big black Chinese dog with a long purple tongue. Toy loved everyone in the family, especially me, and he would have defended us to the death. He was dangerous to anyone outside the house, and not only to people.

"One day Nanny found two dead cats hanging over the back fence in our yard. She didn't know where they came from, and she buried them. The next day or the day after that, she found two or three more dead cats hanging over the fence. It turned out that Toy was killing the neighborhood cats and draping them over the fence to show us. After that, he had to wear a muzzle."

"What's a muzzle?"

"A mask over his mouth, so he couldn't bite. He was a great dog, though, to me. Toy loved the snow when we lived in Illinois. He loved to roll in it and sleep outside on the front porch in the winter. His long fur coat kept him warm."

"What happened to Toy?"

"He ran after a milk truck one day and was hit by a car and killed. This happened just after I went away to school. The deliveryman said that Toy was trying to bite him through the muzzle."

"Does it snow in Wyoming?"

"Oh, yes, baby, it snows a lot in Wyoming. It gets very cold there."

"Toy would have liked it."

"I'm sure he would."

"Mom, can we drive to Wyoming?"

"You mean now?"

"Uh-huh. Is it far?"

"Very far. We're almost to Georgia."

"Can we go someday?"

"Sure, Roy, we'll go."

"We won't tell anyone, right, Mom?"

"No, baby, nobody will know where we are."

"And we'll have a dog."

"I don't see why not."

"From now on when anything bad happens, I'm going to think about Wyoming. Running with my dog."

"It's a good thing, baby. Everybody needs Wyoming."

Saving the Planet

"Mom, what would happen if there was no sun?"

"People couldn't live, plants wouldn't grow. The planet would freeze and become a gigantic ball of ice."

"In school they said the earth is shaped like a pear, not round like a ball."

"So it would be a huge frozen pear spinning out of control. The planets in our solar system revolve around the sun, Roy. If the sun burned out, Earth and Mars and Venus and Saturn and all the others would just be hurtling through space until they crashed into meteors or one another."

"Will it ever happen?"

"What, baby?"

"That there won't be any sun?"

"I don't think so. Not in our lifetime, anyway. Oh, Roy, look at the horses! Nothing is more beautiful than horses running in open country like that."

"Dad's never going to live with us again, is he?"

"I'm not sure, baby. We'll have to wait and see. You'll see your father, though, no matter what."

"I know, Mom. I just hope you're right about the sun not burning out."

A Nice Day on the Ocean

"You know that friend of Dad's with one eye that's always mostly closed?"

"Buzzy Shy. His real name is Enzo Buozzi. What about him?"

"A waiter at the Saxony said Buzzy wanted to give him five dollars to let him kiss his fly."

"Who told you that?"

"I heard him tell Eddie C."

"Heard who?"

"Freddy, the waiter. Why would Buzzy want to kiss Freddy's fly?"

"Did Buzzy ever touch you, Roy?"

"He pinched me once on the cheek when I brought him a cigar Dad gave me to hand him. He gave me a quarter, then tried to pinch my face again, but I got away. It hurt."

"Buzzy Shy is sick, baby. Stay away from him. Promise?"

"Promise. He doesn't look sick."

"The sickness is in his brain, so you can't see it."

"Eddie C. said for *ten* dollars Buzzy could kiss his ass and anything else."

"Who's Eddie C.?"

"A lifeguard. I think at the Spearfish."

"These aren't nice boys, Roy. I don't want you talking to them."

"I wasn't talking to them, Mom, I was listening."

"Don't listen to them, either. I'll talk to your dad about it. I don't want Buzzy Shy bothering you."

"Dad and Buzzy are friends."

"Not really. Buzzy helps out sometimes, that's all."

"How did his eye get like that?"

"He was a prizefighter. Somebody shut it for him."

"Maybe his brain got hurt, too."

"I don't know, baby. He was probably born with the problem in his head. Don't go near him again."

"Mom?"

"Yes, baby?"

"I like the sky like this, when it's really red with only a tiny yellow line under it."

"Red sky at night, sailor's delight. Red sky at morning, sailor take warning."

"What's that mean?"

"Tomorrow will be a nice day on the ocean."

"Sailor's Delight would be a good name for a red Popsicle, don't you think, Mom?"

"Yes, Roy, I do. Remember to tell your dad. I'm sure he knows someone in the Popsicle business."

Perfect Spanish

"Before you were born, I got very sick and your dad made me go to Cuba to recover. I stayed in a lovely house on a beach next to a lavish estate. It was a perfect cure for me, lying in the sun, without responsibilities."

"Was Dad with you?"

"No, I was alone. There was a Chinese couple who took care of the house and me. Chang and Li were their names."

"How long were you there?"

"Six weeks. I was so happy, just by myself, reading, resting, swimming in the Caribbean Sea. It really was the best time of my life. I never felt better, until, of course, I had to leave."

"Why did you have to leave?"

"To make sure you were a healthy baby. I needed to be near my doctor, who was in Chicago."

"The ground is so beautiful here, Mom. It looks like snow, but the air is very hot."

"That's cotton, baby. Cotton is the main crop in Alabama. The temperature doesn't stay high long enough up north to grow it there. Also, the cost of labor is much cheaper in the South, and picking cotton is extremely labor-intensive."

"What does that mean?"

"It takes a lot of people to handpick the buds. That's why slaves were brought here from Africa, to work in the fields."

"They didn't want to come."

"No, baby, they didn't."

"There aren't slaves now, though, right?"

"Not officially, no. But too many people still live almost the same way as they did a hundred or more years ago. There's no work here, really, except in the cottonfields, and it doesn't pay much. The difference between then and now is that people are free to come and go, they're not owned by another person."

"I wouldn't like to be owned by someone."

"Nobody does. Slavery is against the law in the United States, but it still exists in some parts of the world."

"Let's not go there."

"We won't, Roy, I promise."

"Were there slaves in Cuba?"

"At one time, yes."

"Were there slaves when you were there before I was born?"

"No, baby, that was only a few years ago."

"Chang and Li weren't slaves, right?"

"Certainly not. They were caretakers of the property. Chang and Li were very happy to be working there. They were wonderful people and very kind to me."

"How did they get from China to Cuba?"

"I don't know. By boat, probably. Or maybe their parents came from China and Chang and Li were born in Cuba. They spoke perfect Spanish.

"Roy?"

"Yeah, Mom?"

"Are you all right?"

"I'm okay."

"Something's bothering you, I can tell. What is it?"

"I think I'd like to learn to speak perfect Spanish."

"You can, baby. You can start taking Spanish lessons whenever you want."

"Mom?"

"Yes, sweetheart?"

"I bet the slaves didn't think the cotton fields were so beautiful."

Seconds

"Are we going to see Pops and Nanny soon?"

"Yes, baby, we'll be in New Orleans for three or four days, then we'll go to Miami. I don't know if Pops will be there, but Nanny will."

"Why isn't Pops there so much?"

"I never told you this before, but I think you're old enough now to understand. Pops and Nanny haven't always been together. There was a time when I was a girl—more than ten years, in fact— when they were each married to another person."

"Who were they married to?"

"Nanny's husband was a man named Tim O'Malley. His family was in the trucking business in Chicago. Pops married a woman named Sally Price, and they lived in Kansas City. I used to go down on the train and visit them there. This was from when I was the age you are now until I went away to college."

"Why did they marry other people?"

"In those days Pops was a traveling salesman for a shoe company, and Kansas City was part of his territory. Sally was a girlfriend of his for a couple of years before Pops and Nanny got divorced. When he decided to spend more time with Sally than with Nanny, my mother divorced him and she married O'Malley, who'd always liked her."

"So O'Malley was like your other father."

"In a way, but we were never close. I lived most of the time at boarding school, Our Lady of Angelic Desire, so I didn't really see him so much. He died suddenly of a heart attack ten years to the day after he and your grandmother were married."

"How did she and Pops get back together?"

"Pops had divorced Sally two years before O'Malley's death and moved back to Illinois. He always loved my mother and would stand across the street sometimes to watch her come out of our house and get in her car and drive away. Pops wanted Nanny back, and after O'Malley was gone, she agreed to remarry him."

"I bet you were happy."

"No, I wasn't particularly happy, because I didn't completely understand why Pops had left in the first place. O'Malley was nothing special to me, and he wasn't as smart or funny or handsome as my father, but my mother blamed Pops for their separation and I guess I took her side, right or wrong. I don't feel the same way now. It's difficult to know what really goes on between people in a marriage, and I don't think anyone other than those two people can understand, including their children."

"What about you and Dad?"

"What about us, Roy?"

"You're divorced but you're still friends, aren't you?"

"Oh, yes, baby, your dad and I are very good friends. We're better friends now than when we were married."

"And you both love me."

"Of course, baby. Both your dad and I would do anything for you."

"It's okay with me that you and Dad don't live together, but sometimes I get afraid that I won't see him anymore."

"You can see your dad whenever you like. When we get to the hotel in New Orleans, we'll call him, okay? I think he's in Las Vegas now. Maybe he can come to see us before he goes back to Chicago."

"Yeah, Mom, let's call him. Remember the last time we were with him in New Orleans and he ate too many oysters and got so sick?"

"We'll make sure he doesn't eat oysters this time, don't worry. Try to sleep a little now, baby. I'll wake you up when we get there."

Roy's World

"Remember the time you caught a barracuda and brought it back to the hotel and asked Pete the chef to cook it for you?"

"It was the first fish I ever caught. I was out with Uncle Jack on Captain Jimmy's boat, fishing for grouper, but a 'cuda took my mullet."

"Pete thought you were so cute, bringing the barracuda wrapped in newspaper into the kitchen. You were only five then."

"He told me that barracudas aren't good eating, so he made me a kingfish instead."

"Grilled in butter and garlic."

"And he said he wouldn't charge us for it since I'd brought him a fish to trade."

"You really love your Uncle Jack, don't you, baby?"

"He's a great fisherman, and he knows everything about boats."

"You know he was a commander in the navy?"

"Sure, he told me about how he built bridges and navy bases in the Pacific during the war."

"Uncle Jack is a civil and mechanical engineer, Roy. He can draw plans, too, like an architect. He was a Seabee, and the navy offered to make him an admiral if he stayed in."

"Why didn't he?"

"He said to make money it was better to be in private industry. That's why he moved to Florida, to build houses. My brother can do anything, though."

"He can't fly."

"What do you mean, baby? You mean like Superman?"

"No, Uncle Jack told me he tried to become a pilot in the navy. They sent him to Texas to learn how to fly, but he washed out. He said there was something wrong with his ears that made him lose his balance."

"Yes, that's right. I remember when he came home from Texas. He was so disappointed. But Jack can do so many things. You know, baby, if you get really interested in something, you should follow it through all the way. I mean, find out everything you can, learn all there is to learn about it, try to do it or figure it out. That's what your Uncle Jack does, that's how come he knows so much about different things. He can't do everything so well, like flying a plane, but he tries. And you know he's been practically all over the world. Jack's a great traveler."

"I'm going to be a great traveler, too. We travel a lot, don't we, Mom?"

"Yes, we do, but except for Cuba and Mexico, only in the United States."

"I like to draw maps."

"You mean to copy them from the atlas?"

"Sometimes, just to learn where places are. But also I like to make countries up. Oceans and seas, too. It's fun to invent a world nobody else knows."

"What's your favorite country that you made up?"

"Turbania. It's full of tribes of warriors who're always fighting to take over all of Turbania. The largest tribe is the Forestani. They live in the mountains and come down to attack the Vashtis and Saladites, who are desert people."

"Where exactly is Turbania?"

"Between Nafili and Durocq, on the Sea of Kazmir. A really fierce small tribe, the Bazini, live in the port city of Purset. They're very rich because they own the port and have a big wall all around with fortifications not even the Forestanis can penetrate. The Bazinis also have rifles, which the other tribes don't. The Vashtis and Saladites ride horses, black and white Arabians. The Forestanis travel on foot because the woods in the hills are so thick that horses can't get through. And each tribe has its own language, though the Bazinis speak Spanish and maybe English, too, because of the shipping trade. The Forestanis can also speak like birds, which is the way they communicate when they don't want anyone outside the tribe to know what they're saying. It's a secret language that they're forbidden by tribal law to teach outsiders. If a Forestani is caught telling the secret bird language to a person from another tribe, his tongue is cut out and his eardrums are punctured."

"Well, Roy, we'll be in Chattanooga soon. Let's have a snack and you can tell me about some of your other countries. I hope they're not all as terrible as Turbania."

"Turbania's not so terrible, Mom. Wait until you hear about Cortesia, where all the people are blind and they have to walk around with long sticks to protect themselves from bumping into things and each other, so everyone pokes everyone else with their sticks all the time."

Nomads

"Where are we now, Mom?"

"Just outside Centralia, Illinois."

"This is sure a long train."

"I'll turn off the motor. Tell me if you get too cold, Roy, and I'll turn the heater back on."

"It's cold out, but not real cold yet, even though it's almost December. Why is that?"

"Weather is pretty unpredictable sometimes, baby, especially in the spring or fall. But you can bet before too long this part of the country'll be blanketed white."

"How come we never take a train?"

"You took a train a couple of times, don't you remember? When you went up and back to Eagle River, Wisconsin."

"It was fun sleeping overnight on the train, though I didn't really sleep very much. I stayed up looking out the window into the shadows, imagining what might be out there. I like the dark, Mom, especially if I'm protected from it, like through a train window."

"What did you think you could see, Roy?"

"Monsters, of course. Lots of large creatures crunching through the forest. Then I could see campfires, real quick little flashes of smoky light burning up through the trees. I thought maybe it was Indians, the last ones left living in the woods, moving every day and setting up a new camp at night."

"Nomads."

"What's that?"

"Nomads are people who travel all the time—they don't live in one place."

"Is Nomads the name of a tribe?"

"It used to be. They're in the Bible, I think. Now it's just a word used to describe anyone who's constantly changing their place of residence."

"We move around a lot."

"Yes, we do, but we mostly stay in the same places."

"That's what the Plains Indians did. I read that they would come back to the same campgrounds depending on the seasons."

"I think the Indians understood the weather better than most people do now."

"What do you mean, Mom?"

"People live mostly in cities, so they defy the weather. They stay in their buildings and complain when it rains or snows, or that it's too hot or cold. The Indians adjusted better to changes of climate. When it was too warm on the plains, they moved to the mountains, where it was cooler. When it snowed in the mountains, they moved down."

"This train is about the longest I've ever seen."

"Cotton Belt Route. Southern Serves the South. Don't you love to read what's written on the boxcars?"

"Yeah, but what do the letters mean? Like B&O?"

"Baltimore and Ohio. L&N is Louisville and Norfolk, I think. Or maybe it's Louisiana and Norfolk."

"It's almost ending, Mom. I can see the caboose. Start the car."

"It's nice to have heat, huh, Roy? If we were Indians in the old days we would've had to wait on our horses until the train passed."

"We'd be wrapped in blankets, so we wouldn't be too cold."

"I once saw a painting of an Indian riding in a blizzard, his long-braided black hair and blanket covered with ice. Even the pony's mane was frozen."

"I like cars, Mom, but horses are more beautiful. I'd feel more like a real Nomad if I were on a horse instead of in a car. Wouldn't you?"

"I guess so, baby. But it would take us a lot longer to get anywhere."

"Sometimes I don't care how long it takes. And when we get there I'm always a little disappointed."

"Why disappointed?"

"I don't know. Maybe because sometimes it's better to imagine how something or someplace is rather than to have it or be there. That way you won't ever be disappointed when you find out it's not so great as you hoped."

"You're growing up, Roy, you really are. Some people never figure that out."

"Probably the real Nomads knew, and that's why they were always moving."

"It's impossible to avoid being disappointed sometimes, baby, unless you learn to not expect too much."

"I like traveling, Mom. I like it more than being in one place, so maybe I'm learning."

Ducks on the Pond

"Roy! Roll up your window. It's freezing outside."

"I want to leave it open just a little, okay, Mom? I like the feeling when the heater's on high and we can still feel the cold air."

"Amazing how cold it can get in Mississippi, huh, Roy? And it's not even Christmas yet."

"Where are we now?"

"We just passed the Batesville turnoff. We'll stay tonight in Memphis, maybe at the Peabody if we can get a room. Remember that hotel, baby? The one with the ducks on the pond in the lobby."

"There was a kid there the last time who told me he drowned a duck once. Not one of the Peabody ducks."

"Drowned a duck? I didn't know ducks could drown."

"I guess they can. They have to come up for air, like people, only probably not as often."

"I wish I could pass this darn truck. Sorry, Roy, I don't mean to swear, but the driver won't let me get around him. Tell me more about the ducks. Who was it who drowned one?"

"A boy I met at the Peabody Hotel the last time we stayed there. He was older than me, twelve or thirteen, I think."

"It was in March. Bert came up."

"Is Bert still alive?"

"Of course, baby. Why would you ask that?"

"Just wondering. You said he was having trouble with his brain, so I thought maybe it exploded or something."

"He had something growing in his head, that's right. You remembered. I think the doctors took it out."

"Before his brain could explode."

"His brain wouldn't have exploded, baby. At least I don't think so. If the thing that was growing in there got big enough, though, it might have squeezed the inside of Bert's head so much that he wouldn't have been able to think properly. I'll call him when we get to Memphis."

"What if the doctors couldn't get it out?"

"I'm sure they did, Roy, otherwise I would have heard something. I think I can pass now, hold on."

"Mom, where did the seed in Bert's brain come from?"

"Just a sec, baby, let me get back over into the other lane. Okay, what did you say? How did a seed get where?"

"In Bert's brain. The thing that was growing began as a seed, right? How did it get planted there?"

"That's a good question, Roy. I don't think anybody knows exactly, not even the doctors."

"Remember the Johnny Appleseed song? 'Oh, the Lord is good to me, and so I thank the Lord, for giving me the things I need, the sun and the rain and the apple seed. The Lord is good to me.'"

"I like to hear you sing, baby. You have a sweet voice."

"It couldn't have been an apple seed in Bert's head."

"No, it wasn't. Don't think about it anymore, honey. Pretty soon you'll see the ducks on the pond at the Peabody."

"Maybe that kid will be there again."

"I guess it's possible."

"I wouldn't ever try to drown a duck, even if I could."

"No, Roy, I don't believe you ever would."

Sound of the River

"Is it okay if I turn up the radio?"

"Sure, Roy, but not *too* loud. What's playing?"

"I don't know, but I like it."

"Is that a man or a woman who's screaming?"

"He's not screaming, Mom, he's singing. Sometimes he shouts, but it's part of the song. But that's not the part I care about so much. What I really like is the kind of thumping sound behind him, the way it jumps up around his voice sometimes and almost swallows or drowns it or something."

"You mean the rhythm section. It's the part of the band that keeps the beat. They keep the song moving."

"I don't think I've ever heard music like this before. It reminds me of the noise water makes hitting against the rocks on the side of the river, like down behind the Jax brewery. The same sound over and over, only it's not exactly the same."

"That's the Mississippi, baby. Can you remember how the waves sound on the beach in Cuba? The way they slap down on the sand, then make kind of a hushing noise as the water rushes up before rolling back. It's different than the sound of the river in New Orleans."

"I remember being out on a little boat with Uncle Jack and on one side of the boat the water was green and on the other side it was blue. Uncle Jack told me to put my right hand into the water on the starboard side, into the blue, which was really cold. Then he told me to put my left hand into the water on the port side, and it was very warm. He said the cold blue side was the ocean, and the warm green side was the Gulf Stream. Wasn't that near Varadero?"

"No, honey, that was off Key West."

"Where are we now, Mom?"

"Macon, Georgia."

"What's here?"

"Oh, most likely the same as everyplace else. Men and women who don't understand each other and aren't really willing or able to try. Just what this man is shouting about on the radio."

"I think he's saying, 'Lucille, won't you do your sister's will? Oh, Lucille, won't you do your sister's will? Well, you ran away and left, I love you still.'"

"Sounds about right to me."

Red Highway

"You hit one that time, Mom. I felt the bump."

"I can't avoid them all, baby. They crawl out on the road and lie there because the asphalt absorbs heat and they like the warmth. I have to admit I'm not very fond of snakes, but I'm not trying to run them over."

"I know you wouldn't do it on purpose. There are a lot of good ones, like king snakes, who help farmers by eating rodents that destroy crops."

"You've always loved reptiles, Roy. Maybe when you grow up you'll be a herpetologist."

"Is that the big word for reptile handler?"

"Herpetology is the study of snakes, and a herpetologist is a person who studies them."

"There's another one! It must be six feet long. You just missed him."

"They're easier to see when they're crawling, otherwise they blend into the highway here."

"Why is this road dark red? I've never seen a red highway before."

"It must be the earth here, baby, the color of the dirt or clay."

"If it rained now, I wonder if the snakes would all crawl away."

"Probably they'd want to get down into their holes,"

"Why were you so mean to that man in the restaurant back in Montgomery?"

"He said something I didn't care for."

"Did he say it to you?"

"No, Roy, he said it to everyone who could hear him. He *wanted* people to hear him."

"What was it that he said?"

"He was showing off his ignorance."

"Nobody likes a show-off."

"Especially not his kind."

"What was he showing off about?"

"He used some words I don't like."

"He called you beautiful. 'What's the matter, beautiful?' he said."

"That wasn't what upset me. It was what he said before. Forget about him, honey. God punishes those people."

"Could God change him into a snake and make him crawl out on the red highway so he'd get run over?"

"Roy, don't believe you're better than anybody else because of the way you look or who your parents are, or for any other reason you had nothing to do with directly. Okay?"

"Okay."

"It sounds simple, but it's not so easy to do. Treat people the way you'd like them to treat you, and if you don't have anything good to say, don't say anything."

"Uh-huh."

"Sorry, baby, I don't mean to preach, but that man made me angry."

"Watch out, Mom, there's another snake!"

Lucky

"It's always raining in Indiana."

"Seems that way, doesn't it, baby?"

"I remember one night we were driving through Indiana like this and I saw a sign that said New Monster. Lucky was with us, and I asked him what it meant, and he told me there was a new monster loose around there and the sign was put up to warn people. I imagined a crazyman had escaped from an asylum, or a dangerous freak had run away from the sideshow of a carnival. I was really frightened and stayed awake for a long time staring out the window watching for the monster, even though it was dark."

"Poor Lucky. He was the one who wound up in an asylum."

"You told me he had to go to a hospital."

"He did, Roy, a special kind of hospital for people who can't control themselves."

"Lucky couldn't control himself?"

"In some ways, baby. He told terrible lies to people in business and got into trouble all the time. You know how handsome Lucky was, and he could play the piano so well and sing. When he was a young man he'd been a great athlete, too. He was a wonderful golfer and tennis player and swimmer. Lucky charmed everyone, men and women loved him, but he was insane."

"Later, Lucky told me the name on the sign was really New *Munster*, which is a town in Indiana. He was just joking around with me, Mom. That wasn't such a bad thing, even though I got so scared."

"No, of course not, baby. Lucky stole a lot of money from a big company he was working for, but he didn't go to jail for that, they let him off easy. Then a few weeks later he was arrested for taking off all of his clothes in front of some young girls in a park. I guess he'd done things like that before, or he tried to do something with one of the girls, I can't remember, so this time he was committed to an institution."

"Do you know where Lucky is now?"

"I think he's still locked up in Dunning."

"Where's Dunning?"

"A place outside Chicago."

"How long does he have to stay there?"

"Oh, Roy, who knows? I suppose until he's well. It's really terrible about Lucky, it wasn't his fault. He just couldn't control himself."

"Lucky liked to eat spaghetti with a spoon. He'd chop up his noodles with a knife and then eat them with a tablespoon. Do you remember that, Mom? I think that's a crazy way to eat spaghetti."

K.C. So Far
(Seconds/Alternate Take)

"How come we've never been to Kansas City before?"

"I used to come here often when I was a girl. From when I was your age until I was seventeen. I rode the train back and forth from Chicago to see my father."

"Pops was in Kansas City then?"

"Yes, for a few years, when he was married to another woman. Remember, I told you about her. Actually, I don't think they were really married. They lived together and she told people they were married. I never liked her."

"What was her name?"

"I called her Aunt Sally. She was a terrible housekeeper, very sloppy. She left her clothes lying around everywhere, always had dirty dishes piled in the sink. My father liked her because she was pretty and well-read. Sally liked to talk about politics, literature, art. She wasn't stupid, I'll say that for her. She was a chain-smoker. The ashtrays in that house were always overflowing with butts and dead matches."

"It's hot here."

"It can get very hot in Kansas City, Roy, especially in the summer. We used to sit out on the porch at three and four o'clock in the morning, drinking lemonade with shaved ice, when we couldn't sleep because of the heat."

"What did Pops do in Kansas City?"

"He was a hat salesman. He traveled all over the Midwest. Traveling salesmen were still called 'drummers' back then. It's where the phrase 'drumming up business' comes from. Or maybe the word 'drummer' came from the saying, I'm not sure. I think Pops had a girlfriend in every town in his territory, or most of them. That's what caused the breakup with Aunt Sally."

"Pops still wears a hat when he's outside."

"Yes, baby, a homburg, that's his favorite. Pops always was a sharp dresser."

"What happened to her?"

"Who? Sally?"

"Yeah."

"You know, I have no idea where she is now, and I doubt that Pops does, either. She stayed in Kansas City for a while after my father moved back to Chicago, then he stopped talking about her. Sally was a blonde with plenty of pep. I bet she found herself a guy and cut Pops off cold. It's strange how sometimes people can be such a large part of your life and then suddenly they're gone. I didn't miss her or those long, hot train trips."

"She wasn't nice to you, huh?"

"Sally wasn't bad to me. I guess I didn't want to like her because I was so close to Nanny, and I felt if I allowed myself to really like Sally then I would be disloyal to my mother. I'm sure most kids have the same conflict."

"If Dad got a new wife, would you want me to hate her?"

"Not at all, baby, of course not. You'd make up your own mind about her. It would depend on how she treated you."

"Even if she was nice and I loved her, I wouldn't love her the same as I love you, Mom. I'm sure I wouldn't."

"Roy, look at that airplane landing! It's coming in so low. The Kansas City airport is in the middle of the city. Planes fly in right over the houses."

"I'd be scared one would crash on us if we lived in a house here. You know, Mom, I don't think I like Kansas City so far."

Concertina Locomotion

"Sometimes it seems like things go very fast, and sometimes they go slower than an inchworm."

"Yes, honey, strange the way time moves, isn't it? I can't believe I'm not twenty or twenty-one or -two anymore. Years get lost, they fly by and you can't remember them. This is when you get older, of course. I'm sure that now you can remember almost exactly when everything happened."

"I like watching snakes crawl, the way their bodies fold and bend and curl up like a lasso, then straighten out."

"Time works sort of like that, in concertina locomotion."

"Is that a train?"

"No, Roy, it's the way some creatures move, especially tree snakes. They kind of coil and partially uncoil and this motion propels them. I read about it in a nature magazine. You know how a concertina or accordion takes in and lets out air when it's being played? Well, this type of snake looks like that."

"Snakes can see where they're going, can't they?"

"Sure, and they use their tongues as sensors."

"The car's headlights are kind of our sensors."

"I also read that blind people use hand gestures when they talk, the same as people who can see. Isn't that interesting? It has something to do with the way human beings think."

"I think Texas goes on forever."

"We just take it a little bit at a time."

"Like concertina locomotion."

"Yes, baby. As soon as we're east of Houston we'll get a whiff of the bayou. You'll know when we're there with your eyes closed."

Imagine

"Roy, do you remember the name of that man in Havana who used to give you a silver dollar whenever he saw you?"

"Sure, Winky. He had two tattoos of a naked girl on his arm."

"Winky Nervo, that's right. It was driving me nuts not being able to remember his name. Winky was in a dream I had last night. What do you mean, he had two tattoos of a naked girl? The same girl?"

"I think so. On one side of the muscle part of his right arm he had the front of the girl and on the underneath was the back of her. She had her hands on her hips the same way in both of the tattoos. I liked Winky a lot. He used to give silver dollars to all the kids."

"For some reason, Winky was in my dream. He was talking to a black woman outside of a restaurant or a bar or a nightclub somewhere, maybe in Havana, though it could have been Mexico City. There was a red and yellow sign flashing on and off behind them. The woman's dress was bright blue, and Winky stood very close to her. Under her, almost. You know how little Winky was, and the woman was very black and much taller. She leaned over him like a coconut palm.

"I liked Winky, too. Your dad said he was a terrible gambler, threw everything he had away on craps and the horses."

"Why don't we ever see Winky anymore, Mom?"

"Oh, baby, Winky's someplace nobody can find him. He owed a pile of dough to some wrong guys and couldn't pay it back."

"Maybe he's in the old country. Winky always said how when he got set he would go back to the old country and not do anything but eat and drink and forget."

"Honey, Winky's in a country even older than the one he was talking about."

"Maybe he was showing the woman his tattoos. Winky could make the girl's titties jump when he made a muscle."

"Remind me to call your dad tonight when we get to Tampa. You haven't spoken to him for a while."

"Not since my birthday. Mom?"

"Yes, Roy?"

"Winky always had lots of silver dollars in his pockets."

"That doesn't mean he had money, baby. Not real money, anyway."

"Does Dad have real money?"

"He might not have it, but he knows how to find it and where to get it, and that's almost as good. There's a big difference between your father and a man like Winky Nervo. Don't worry about your dad."

"I won't."

"Winky wasn't sharp, Roy. He didn't think ahead."

"It's important, huh? To think ahead."

"Baby, you can't imagine."

The Geography of Heaven

"Do you realize, Roy, that Cairo, Illinois, where we are now, is actually closer to the state of Mississippi than it is to Chicago?"

"I know we're next to the Mississippi River."

"That's right. We were on the Mississippi in St. Louis, Missouri, and now Cairo. From here it flows down to Memphis. What state is Memphis in, baby?"

"Tennessee."

"Good. Then it goes to Greenville—"

"Mississippi."

"Then to New Orleans—"

"Louisiana."

"Before flowing into—"

"The Gulf of Mexico."

"Great, Roy! You really know your geography."

"I think this is the best way to learn it, Mom, by traveling all over. The places are real, then, instead of just dots and names on a map."

"You should show me your maps, Roy, the ones you made up. I'd like to see them."

"I draw maps of real places too, Mom, not just imaginary ones. When we stop, I'll make a map of all the places we've been. Where are we going to stay tonight?"

"I thought we'd see if we could get to A Little Bit O' Heaven, in Kentucky. Remember, they have all those little cottages named after different flowers?"

"Oh, yeah. We stayed in the Rose Cottage because that's Nanny's name."

"There certainly isn't much color in the sky today, is there? It's just grey with tiny specks of black in it."

"It might snow, huh?"

"I think it's more likely to rain, honey. It's not cold enough to snow."

"Mom, if you had a choice between freezing to death or burning up, which one would you choose?"

"I'd take freezing, definitely, because once your body is numb all over, you can't feel anything. You die, sure, but it's better than feeling your flesh melt off the bones. How about you?"

"I like being in hot weather a lot more than cold weather, but I guess you're right. I saw in a movie where a guy who was lost in the wilderness made a blanket of snow for himself and survived until the rescuers came because his body stayed warm under the snow."

"I didn't know about that, Roy. Let's remember it, just in case we get stranded sometime in the mountains in a blizzard."

"You were right, Mom, here comes the rain. All the tiny black spots in the sky were raindrops ready to fall. I never saw rain that looked so black before. It's like being bombed by billions of ants."

"Yes, baby, it is strange, isn't it? Roll up your window all the way. I hope we can make it to A Little Bit O' Heaven before it gets too bad."

"Mom, is there a religion of geography?"

"Not really, unless you consider the ones where people worship places they believe an extraordinary event occurred."

"Probably something important to someone happened just about everywhere, and some people made more of a big deal about it than others."

"Yes, baby, you've got it right."

Man and Fate

"Vicksburg is really a sad place, Mom, I've never seen so many graves."

"It's spooky here, baby, I agree. It breaks my heart to think about all the young boys, many not too much older than you, who're buried here. You know, Roy, some people would think we're crazy, driving around like this in a cemetery in Mississippi in the rain. I can't help but imagine the lives these boys might have had if there hadn't been a War Between the States. A civil war is the worst kind of war. It's been almost one hundred years since this one ended, and the South still hasn't recovered."

"Soldiers from the North are buried here, too, Mom. Hundreds of 'em."

"How can a place be so dreary and beautiful at the same time?"

"I'll bet there are ghosts here who come out and fight the war all over again every night."

"It wouldn't surprise me, baby. Somebody could make a terrific movie of ghosts or even corpses rising from their graves and not fighting but talking with one another peacefully about how horribly wrong it was to have a war in the first place."

"That wouldn't be so exciting, Mom, not if they were just talking. It would be cool to see the corpses, though."

"The only real reasons people go to war anymore are religion and money, and often it's a combination of the two. In the Civil War, cheap labor in the form of slaves was the main issue. In World War II, Hitler used the Jews as scapegoats for Germany's economic problems, which were a result of World War I. He had to go to war to get Germany out of debt. Do you understand any of this, Roy?"

"Not everything. I know that sometimes people want the land that other people are on."

"That has to do with money. One piece of land might be better than another to grow crops on, or there's oil or gas or diamonds and gold or other valuable minerals in it. And as far as religion is concerned, everybody should be left alone and leave others alone to worship as they please."

"Why don't they?"

"Most do, Roy, but some people get carried away. They believe their way should be the only way. It's when people think they've got an exclusive on being right that the world goes ape."

"I once heard Dad say to a guy, 'If I had to get a job done right and I had to choose between you and an ape to do it, I'd take the ape.'"

"I've had enough of Vicksburg, baby. How about you?"

Where Osceola Lives

"Mom, did you know that the Seminoles are the only Indian tribe that never gave up? They hid out here in the Everglades and the soldiers couldn't defeat them."

"I know that the Glades was much larger then, so the Indians had more room to move around and evade the army."

"The Seminoles weren't really a regular tribe, either. They were made up of renegades and survivors of several different tribes who banded together for a last stand in what they called the Terrible Place. Their leader was Osceola, whose real name was Billy Powell, and he was mostly a white man."

"If I'm not mistaken, Roy, the road to Miami that we're on now was originally a Micosukee Indian trail. Imagine how difficult it must have been to build the highway here."

"Really dangerous, too. There's alligators and panthers and water moccasins all around. The Seminoles somehow survived everything, even swamp fevers that killed dozens of soldiers."

"In the movie *Key Largo*, there are two Seminole brothers who've escaped from jail and the cops are looking for them. Even though he's seen them passing in a canoe, the hotel owner doesn't tell the cops because he likes the brothers and believes they were treated unfairly. Later, just before a hurricane is about to hit, the Seminole brothers and other Indians come to the hotel for shelter, as they'd always done during a big storm, but a gangster who's taken over the hotel refuses to let them in."

"What happens to them?"

"They huddle together on the porch of the hotel and ride it out. The Seminole brothers survive."

"Remember Johnny Sugarland, my favorite alligator wrestler at the reptile farm up in St. Augustine?"

"Sure, baby. The boy with three fingers on one hand and the thumb missing on the other."

"He's a Seminole. Johnny told me about Osceola, so I got a book about him from the school library. Nobody except the Seminoles knows where Osceola's body is buried. Some of them say that Osceola is still alive and hunting with an eagle, an owl, and a one-eyed dog as old as he is way back in a part of the Terrible Place that no white man has ever seen."

"Crazy Horse, the Sioux warrior, is another Indian whose burial place is kept secret. Supposedly, no white man knows where his grave is, either."

"I'd go into the swamp with Johnny, if he'd take me. It would be great to see where Osceola lives."

"I'm sure he's dead now, Roy. For the Seminoles, it's Osceola's spirit that's still alive."

"I think I like the Everglades more than any other place I've been."

"Why is that, baby?"

"It's got the most hiding places of anywhere. If you don't get eaten by a gator or a snake, or get swallowed up in quicksand or die of a fever, you could disappear from everyone for as long as you wanted."

"Roy, there's a reason the Indians called this the Terrible Place."

"I know, Mom, but I think I'd be okay, as long as I remembered the way out."

The Crime of Pass Christian

"You know, Mom, the best time for me is when we're moving in the car. I like it when we're between the places we're coming from and going to."

"Don't you miss your friends, or sleeping in your own bed?"

"Sometimes. But right now we're not in New Orleans yet and it's kind of great that nobody else knows exactly where we are. Where are we, anyway?"

"Comin' up on Pass Christian, honey. Remember once we stayed in a house here for a week when your dad had business in Biloxi? An old two-story house with a big screened-in porch that wrapped all around the second floor."

"It's where I trapped a big brown scorpion under a glass and left it there overnight. In the morning the glass was still upside down but the scorpion was gone. You let it go when I was asleep, didn't you, Mom?"

"No, baby, I told you I didn't. I don't know how it got out. And your dad was away that night in New Orleans. It was a real mystery."

"I like that we don't know what happened. Maybe there's a ghost living in the house who picked up the glass, or somehow the scorpion did it with his poison tail."

"This part of the Gulf Coast always seems haunted to me. If the scorpion had gotten out by itself, the glass would have fallen over, or at least moved. As I recall, it was in exactly the same place the next morning when we looked."

"What kind of ghost do you think lives in that house?"

"Oh, probably the old lady who lived there all of her life. Someone told me she was almost a hundred years old when she died. She never married, and lived alone after her parents passed away."

"What was her name?"

"Baby, I don't remember. Mabel something, I think. There was a story about a kidnapping involving the woman. I can't recall exactly what happened, but she had been kidnapped when she was a child and held for ransom. The family was quite wealthy. It was a famous case."

"Did the police catch the kidnappers?"

"I guess so. Oh, wait, Roy, here's the sharp curve in the highway I hate. I always forget when it's coming up."

"You're a great driver, Mom. I always feel safe in the car with you."

"You shouldn't ever worry when we're driving, baby. Now, look, the road stays pretty straight from here on. Yes, the men who kidnapped Mabel Wildrose—that was the family's name, Wildrose—were caught and sent to prison."

"Did they hurt her?"

"Something bad happened, but it was strange. Mabel Wildrose was nine years old when she was kidnapped."

"The same age as me."

"Yes, your age. They cut off some of little Mabel's hair and sent it to her parents."

"She must have been really scared."

"I'm sure she was. But other than that, I don't think she was harmed. Her parents paid the money and the cops found Mabel wherever it was the kidnappers said she would be."

"You said the men were caught."

"Uh-huh, in New Orleans, when they tried to get on a freighter bound for South America. There was one crazy part of the deal I remember now: The men had left her wrapped in a blanket, and when they were caught trying to board the boat at the dock in New Orleans, one of them was discovered to be carrying Mabel's clothes, including her shoes, in his suitcase. The man had polished the shoes and asked the police if he could keep them with him in his jail cell. He was a nut."

"I wouldn't want to be kidnapped."

"Baby, nobody's going to steal you. Everyone knows who your dad is. They wouldn't want to get into trouble with him."

"What if they didn't want money? What if someone wanted to keep me?"

"It won't happen, Roy, really. Don't worry."

"One day I thought I saw a ghost in the house in Pass Christian, but I don't think it was Mabel Wildrose. It was too big to be her. I was lying on the floor in the front room, playing with my soldiers. It was rainy and kind of dark and cold, and a shadow ran through the room and went out the door. I didn't really see it, it was more like I felt it. The screen door flew open and banged shut behind the shadow."

"Probably only the wind, baby, blowing through the house."

"It might have been the ghost of one of the kidnappers, maybe the guy with Mabel's shoes. Do you think they're dead now?"

"Who, honey?"

"The men who stole Mabel Wildrose when she was nine."

"Oh, they've been dead a long time. They probably died in prison."

"I'd stab someone with my knife if he tried to take me. I'd try to get him in the eye. Probably Mabel didn't have a knife on her, huh, Mom?"

"I doubt that she did, Roy, but sometimes there's not much you can do to stop a person, especially if they're bigger than you."

"I'd wait until they weren't looking and then stab my knife in their eye and run away. They wouldn't catch me if I got outside."

"Forget about it, baby. Nobody is going to kidnap you."

"Sure, Mom, I know. But I'm gonna keep my knife on me anyway."

Cool Breeze

"What would you do if one of the men on the chain gang broke away and jumped in our car?"

"That won't happen, Roy. We won't be stopped much longer. Their leg irons are too tough to bust, and these prisoners are swinging bush hooks, not sledgehammers."

"The air is so smoky here. It must be really hard for the men to breathe when it's so hot."

"We're in the Bessemer Cutoff, baby. This part of Alabama is full of steel mills. If these men weren't prisoners, most of them would be working in the mills or mines or blast furnaces somewhere in Jefferson County."

"There are more black guys than white guys on this chain gang. On the last one we passed, in Georgia, there were more white prisoners."

"We're going to move now, honey. Get your head back in."

"Uncle Jack had two brothers working construction for him who'd been on a chain gang. Their names were Royal and Rayal."

"They told you they were in jail?"

"Uh-huh. They didn't murder anybody, only robbed a bank. Tried to, anyway. Rayal, I think it was, told me the reason they got caught was because they didn't have a car. They got the money, then tried to take a bus to get away."

"Where was this?"

"Jacksonville, I think. The bus didn't arrive when it was supposed to, so the cops arrested them."

"I'll never forget that movie with Paul Muni, *I Was a Fugitive from a Chain Gang*. At the end he escapes, and when he meets his old girlfriend, she asks him how he survives. As he disappears into the shadows, he whispers, 'I steal.' It's pretty spooky."

"I feel kind of bad waving back at the chain-gang guys, you know? We get to leave and they don't."

"Here we go. Oh, baby, doesn't it feel good to have a breeze?"

Night Owl

"It's dangerous to drive in the fog like this, isn't it, Mom?"

"We're going slowly, baby, in case we have to stop on a dime."

"Do you know how many bridges there are that connect the islands between Key West and Miami?"

"About forty, I think, maybe more."

"Does everyone have secrets?"

"Oh, yes, certainly they do."

"Do you?"

"One or two."

"Would you die if anybody found them out?"

"I wouldn't die, no. There are just a few things I'd rather other people didn't know."

"Even me?"

"Even you what?"

"You have secrets you wouldn't tell me?"

"Roy, there are things I don't want to think about or remember, things I try to keep secret even from myself."

"It must be hard to keep a secret from yourself."

"Gee, baby, I can't see a thing."

Islamorada

"Listen, baby, tonight when we get to the hotel I want you to call your dad."

"Is he coming to Miami?"

"No, he has to stay in Chicago. Your dad is sick, Roy, he's in the hospital. It'll cheer him up if you call him there."

"What's wrong with him?"

"He's got a problem with his stomach. I think he needs to have an operation."

"I remember when I was in the hospital to have my tonsils out. You stayed in the room with me on a little bed."

"You were such a good patient. After the surgery you opened your mouth to talk but you couldn't. All you could do was whisper."

"The nurse gave me ice cream."

"Poor baby, when the doctor came in you asked him if he would do another operation and put your voice back in."

"Is Dad scared?"

"Your dad doesn't scare easily, honey. He's a pretty tough guy."

"The doctor said I was brave. I didn't cry or anything."

"You were great, Roy. I was the one who was frightened."

"Can we stop at Mozo's in Islamorada and get squid rings?"

"Sure. Oh, there's a big sailboat, Roy. Look! She's a real beauty."

"It's a ketch."

"I never can tell the difference between a ketch and a yawl."

"The mizzenmast is farther forward on a ketch, and the mizzen sail is larger than on a yawl. Uncle Jack taught me."

"You know, I don't think your dad has ever been on a boat in his life, except when he was a little boy and sailed across the Atlantic Ocean with his family from Europe to America."

"How old was he?"

"About eight, I think."

"Did they come on a sailboat?"

"No, baby, on a big ship with lots of people."

"Why did they come?"

"To have a better life. After the big war, the first one, things were very bad where your dad's family lived."

"Were they poor?"

"I guess it was difficult to make a decent living. There were more opportunities over here. The United States was a young country and people from all over, not just Europe but Asia and Africa, too, felt they could build a new life for themselves. Everyone came to America this way, for work and religious reasons. They still do."

"Were you already here when Dad came?"

"I wasn't born yet. Your dad had been here for almost thirty years before we met."

"Dad didn't tell me he was sick."

"He'll pull through, Roy, don't worry. We'll call him as soon as we get to Miami. You'll see, he'll tell you he's going to be all right."

"I wish you and Dad were still married."

"It's better the way things are for your dad and me, baby. Some people just weren't made to live with each other."

"I won't ever get married."

"Don't be ridiculous, Roy. Of course you'll get married. You'll have children and grandchildren and everything. You just have to find the right girl."

"Weren't you the right girl for Dad?"

"He thought I was. It's not so easy to explain, honey. There were all kinds of reasons our marriage didn't work. The best part of it was that we had you."

"If Dad dies, I don't want another one."

"What do you mean, baby?"

"If you get married again, he won't be my dad."

"Look, Roy. Is that one a ketch or a yawl?"

"A yawl. It's got two jibs."

"We'll be in Islamorada in five minutes. I'm ready for some squid rings myself."

On the Arm

"Maybe we can go to a baseball game in Atlanta. I went once with Dad and his friend Buddy from Detroit. We saw the Crackers play the Pelicans."

"We'll look in the newspaper when we get there, baby, and see if the Crackers are in town. Don't hang out of the window, Roy. Get your arms back in."

"Mom, it's so hot. I won't get hit."

"Remember when we read about that boy whose arm got taken off by a truck?"

"Is Buddy from Detroit still in Atlanta?"

"Buddy Delmar, you mean? No, honey, I think he's in Vegas now. He works for Moe Lipsky."

"Buddy was a ballplayer. He knows a lot about baseball."

"Your dad told me Buddy could have had a career in the game, but he had a problem, so he didn't go on."

"What kind of problem?"

"He's a fixer, Roy. I guess he always was, even back when he played. Buddy bet on games. He paid pitchers to let batters get hits, hitters to strike out, and fielders to make errors."

"Did he get caught?"

"Somewhere along the line. I don't know exactly what happened, but according to your dad, Buddy had an umpire on the arm who had a big mouth. The ump spilled the beans and did Buddy in. I don't think he went to jail over it, but he was finished as far as baseball was concerned."

"He could tell me things that would happen before they happened. A player would do something and Buddy'd say, 'Didn't I tell ya?'"

"The first time I met Buddy Delmar, your dad and I were at the

Ambassador, in the Pump Room. Buddy paid for our drinks. He flashed a roll that could have choked a horse."

"You mean if he tried to swallow the money."

"Who, honey?"

"The horse."

"It's just an expression, Roy. Buddy likes to act like a big shot. Some women go for that routine, not me."

"I remember Buddy asked me, 'How's that good-looking mother of yours?'"

"Did your dad hear him say that?"

"I think Dad was getting a hot dog."

"Buddy Delmar thinks he's catnip to the ladies."

"I'd never take money to strike out."

"Of course you wouldn't. You won't be like Buddy Delmar. You'll be your own man."

"Is Dad his own man?"

"Sure, Roy, he is. Being his own man causes him problems sometimes."

"Buddy from Detroit had a problem, you said."

"Baby, you don't have to be like any of these people. Your dad is a decent person, don't get me wrong, but he does things you'll never do. Your life will be different, Roy."

"What about Buddy?"

"What about him?"

"Is he a decent person?"

"If Buddy Delmar had never been born, the world wouldn't be any worse off."

"Mom, if we ever have a house, could I get a dog?"

"Oh, Roy, you really are my own special angel. We won't always be living in hotels, I promise. Listen, if the Crackers aren't playing, we'll go to a movie, okay?"

"Okay. It wouldn't have to be a big dog. If he was too big, he wouldn't be happy riding in our car so much."

"Baby, remember what I said about keeping your arms in."

Look Out Below

"Mom, when you were a girl, what did you want to be when you grew up?"

"I thought I might be a singer, like Nanny. Other than that, I had no idea."

"Uncle Jack says I should be an architect, like him."

"If that's what you want to do, baby."

"I want to be a baseball player, but after that I'm not sure."

"Apalachicola. Doesn't the name of this town sound like a train? Let's say it, Roy. Slowly at first, then faster and faster."

"Apalachicola—Apalachicola—Apalachicola—Apalachicola—Apalachicola—Apalachi-agh!-cola! It gets harder the more times you say it."

"Isn't it just like a choo-choo? *Ap*-alachi-*co*la—*Ap*-alachi-*co*la—*Ap*-alachi-*co*la—"

"It's pretty here, huh, Mom?"

"Especially now, at sundown. Your dad and I were here once in a big storm. Almost a hurricane but not quite. Black sand was flying everywhere. We couldn't see to drive."

"I think it was close to here where Uncle Jack's boat got stuck on a sandbar when he and Skip and I were fishing. Remember, Mom? I told you about it."

"Tell me again, honey. I've forgotten."

"Uncle Jack couldn't drive the boat off the sandbar so he told me and Skip to jump in the water and push from the stern."

"Did it work, or did you have to call the coast guard?"

"It worked, but when we first got in and started pushing, Skip saw a big fin coming at us. He shouted, 'Shark!' and we climbed back into the boat as fast as we could. Uncle Jack asked, 'Where's a shark?' Skip pointed at the place where he'd seen the fin and

Uncle Jack said, 'Get back in the water and push! I'll tell you when there's a shark coming.'"

"That sounds like my brother. Did you both get back in?"

"Uh-huh, Skip's a lot stronger than I am—"

"He's four years older."

"Yeah, well, he pushed as hard as he could and so did I, and Uncle Jack cut the wheel sharp so the boat came unstuck. Then Skip and I swam fast to it and climbed aboard before the shark came back."

"I'll have to talk to Jack about this."

"No, Mom, it was okay. We had to do it. We were really stuck and only Uncle Jack could drive the boat."

"You wouldn't be much good as a baseball player if you lost a leg to a shark."

"There was a pitcher with the White Sox who only had one leg. I saw a movie about him. I think he lost it in a war."

"Roy, is this true?"

"Honest, Mom. He pitched on a wooden leg. I don't know how many times, but he did it."

"That's incredible. A person really can do just about anything if he works hard at it."

"When I find out what I want to do, I'll work really hard at it."

"After baseball, you mean."

"Yeah, after baseball. Mom?"

"Yes, baby?"

"Do you think Skip and I were really dumb to get back in the water? What if the shark had come up from underneath to bite us?"

"Please, Roy, even if there was a one-legged baseball player, I don't want to think about it."

The Up and Up

"Why didn't you tell me Dad was going to die?"

"Oh, baby, I didn't know he would die. I mean, everyone dies sooner or later, but we couldn't know he would die this soon."

"Dad wasn't old."

"No, Roy, he was forty-eight. Too young."

"I didn't know he was in the hospital again."

"We talked to him just after he went back in, don't you remember?"

"I forgot."

"Your dad really loved you, Roy, more than anything."

"He didn't sound sick, that's why I didn't remember he was in the hospital."

"It's a shame he died, baby, really a shame."

"After he came home from the hospital the first time, after his operation, Phil Sharky told me Dad was too tough to die."

"Phil Sharky's not a person worth listening to about anything. I'm sure he meant well telling you that, but he's the kind of man who if you ask him to turn off a light only knows how to break the lamp."

"What does that mean, Mom?"

"I mean Phil Sharky can't be trusted. You can't believe a word he says. If he says it's Tuesday, you can get fat betting it's Friday. Phil Sharky's a crooked cop who doesn't play straight with anyone."

"I thought he was Dad's friend."

"Look how dark the sky's getting, Roy, and it's only two o'clock. If we're lucky, we'll make it to Asheville before the rain hits. I thought we'd stay at the Dixieland Hotel. It has the prettiest views of the Smokies."

"Phil Sharky gave me his gun to hold once. It was really heavy. He said to be careful because it was loaded."

"Was your dad there?"

"No, he went out with Dummy Fish and left me at the store. He told me he'd be right back. I asked Phil if the gun wouldn't weigh so much if there weren't any bullets in it and he said if they went where they were supposed to it wouldn't."

"Baby, you won't ever see Phil Sharky again if I have anything to do with it. Did you tell your dad about this? That Phil let you handle his gun?"

"Dad didn't get back for a long time and I fell asleep on the newspaper bundles. When I woke up, Phil was gone and Dad and Dummy and I went to Charmette's for pancakes. I remember because Solly Banks was there and he came over to our table and said I was a lucky kid to have the kind of father who'd take me out for pancakes at four in the morning."

"Suitcase Solly, another character who couldn't tell the up and up if it bit him. So your dad didn't know Sharky showed you the gun?"

"Phil told me not to say anything to Dad, in case he wouldn't like the idea, so I didn't."

"We're not gonna beat the rain, baby, but we'll get there while there's still light. Tomorrow we'll fly to Chicago. The funeral's on Sunday."

"Will everyone be there?"

"I don't know about everyone, but your dad knew a lot of people. Most of the ones who come will want to talk to you."

"Even people I don't know?"

"Probably. All you have to do is thank them for paying their respects to your father."

"What if I cry?"

"It's normal to cry at a funeral, Roy. Don't worry about it."

"Mom, what was the last thing Dad said before he died?"

"Gee, baby, I really don't know. I think when the nurse came to give him a shot for the pain, he'd already died in his sleep. There was nobody in the room."

"Do you remember the last thing he said to you?"

"Oh, I think it was just to not worry, that he'd be okay."

"I bet Dad knew he was dying and he didn't want to tell us."

"Maybe so."

"What if he got scared just before he died? Nobody was there for him to talk to."

"Don't think about it, Roy. Your dad didn't live very long, but he enjoyed himself."

"Dad was on the up and up, wasn't he, Mom?"

"Your dad did things his own way, but the important thing to remember, baby, is that he knew the difference."

Black Space

"Isn't that terrible? Roy, did you hear that just now on the radio?"

"I wasn't really listening Mom. I'm reading the story of Ferdinand Magellan. Did you know there's a cloud named after him that's a black space in the Milky Way? What happened?"

"They found two cut-up bodies in suitcases in the left-luggage department in the railway station in New Orleans."

"Do they know who put them there?"

"The attendant told police it was a heavyset, middle-aged white woman who wore glasses and a black raincoat with what looked like orange paint stains on it."

"It's raining now. When it rains in Louisiana, everything gets fuzzy."

"What do you mean, things get fuzzy?"

"The drops are wobbly on the windows and that makes shapes outside weird."

"People are capable of anything, baby, you know that? The problem is you can never really know who you're dealing with, like this woman who chopped up those bodies."

"Were they children?"

"Who? The corpses in the suitcases?"

"Uh-huh."

"No, honey, I'm sure they were adults."

"But the crazy lady who did it is loose."

"They'll get her, Roy, don't worry. Maybe not right away, but they will."

"Do you think it's easy to kill someone, Mom?"

"What a strange question to ask. I don't know. I suppose for some people it is."

"Could you do it?"

"Maybe with a gun if I were being threatened. I've never really thought about it."

"Could you cut up a body like she did?"

"Roy, stop it. Of course not. Let's talk about something else. Are you hungry? We can stop in Manchac and get fried catfish at Middendorf's."

"I wonder if she wrapped the body parts up so blood didn't go everywhere."

"Please, baby. I'm sorry I mentioned it."

"Remember the shrunken head Uncle Jack brought back from New Guinea?"

"How could I forget?"

"Somebody had to chop it off before it got shrunk. Or do you think the whole body was shrunk first?"

"Roy, that's enough."

"I bet that attendant was really surprised when he saw what was inside those suitcases."

"They must have begun to smell badly so the attendant got suspicious. I think he called the police, though, and they opened the suitcases."

"Do you think the woman is still in New Orleans?"

"Baby, how would I know? Maybe she just took a train and beat it out of town. I'm sure she did. She's probably in Phoenix, Arizona, by now."

"Nobody really has control over anybody else, do they?"

"A lot of people don't have control over themselves, that's how a horrible thing like this can happen. Now stop thinking about it. Think about horses, Roy, how beautiful they are when they run."

"Mom, you won't leave me alone tonight, okay?"

"No, baby, I won't go out tonight. I promise."

Fear and Desire

"I don't like when the sky gets dark so early."

"That's what happens in the winter, Roy. The days are a lot shorter and colder because our side of the planet is farther away from the sun."

"The trees look beautiful without leaves, don't they, Mom?"

"I like when it's sunny and cold. It makes my skin feel so good. We'll stop soon, baby, in Door County. I'm a little tired."

"I think I dream better in winter."

"Maybe because you sleep more."

"Mom, what do you think of dreams?"

"What do I think of them?"

"Yeah. I mean, what are they? Are they real?"

"Sure, they're real. Sometimes you find out things in dreams that you can't any other way."

"Like what?"

"Some experts think dreams are wishes. You dream about what you really want to happen."

"Once I dreamed that I was running in a forest and wolves were chasing me. There was a real big red wolf that caught me in deep snow and started eating one of my legs. Then I woke up. I didn't want that to happen."

"Maybe it meant something else. Also, dreams depend on what's happening around you at the time. Dreams are full of symbols."

"What's a symbol?"

"Something that represents something else, like the red wolf in your dream. The red wolf was a symbol of a fear or desire."

"I was afraid of the wolf because I didn't want him to bite me."

"Do you remember anything else about the dream?"

"The red wolf didn't have any eyes, only dark holes where his eyes were supposed to be."

"This sounds like a case for Sigmund Freud."

"Is he a detective?"

"No, baby, he was a doctor who studied dreams and wrote about them."

"If I'd had a gun I would have shot that wolf."

"It's not always so easy to get rid of something that's chasing you, because it's inside your own mind."

"You mean the red wolf is hiding in my brain?"

"Don't worry, Roy, the wolf won't bother you again. You woke up before he could hurt you."

"The sky's all dark now. Mom, is desire bad or good?"

"It can be either, depending on what it is and why a person desires something."

"A person can't decide not to dream."

"No, baby, dreams either come or they don't. We'll stay at the Ojibway Inn. Remember that motel with the Indian chief on the sign?"

"I bet everybody has scary dreams sometimes."

"Of course they do."

"I hope the red wolf is chasing somebody else now."

God's Tornado

"Oh, Roy, I just love this song. I'll turn it up."

"What is it?"

"'Java Jive' by the Ink Spots. Listen: 'I love java sweet and hot, whoops Mr. Moto, I'm a coffee pot.'"

"That's crazy, Mom. What's it mean?"

"'I love the java and the java loves me.' It's just a silly little song that was popular when I was a girl. Coffee's called java because coffee beans come from there."

"Where?"

"The island of Java, near Borneo."

"Borneo's where the wild men are."

"It's part of Indonesia. Coffee wakes you up, makes you feel jivey, you know, jumpy."

"Who's Mr. Moto?"

"Peter Lorre played him in the movies. He was a Japanese detective."

"Why is he in the song?"

"I don't have the faintest, baby. I guess just because he was a popular character at the time, before the war."

"Look, Mom, there's tree branches all over the road."

"Sit back, honey, I don't want you to bump your head."

"There must have been a big windstorm."

"This part of the country is called Tornado Alley. I don't know why people would live here, especially in trailers. It's always the trailers that get destroyed by tornadoes."

"Where were we when a tornado made all those rocks fall on our car?"

"Kansas. Wasn't that terrible? There were hundreds of dents on the roof and the hood, and we had to get a new windshield."

"Where does weather come from?"

"From everywhere, baby. The wind starts blowing in the middle of the Arabian Sea or the South China Sea or somewhere, and stirs up the waves. Pretty soon there's a storm and clouds form and the planet rotates and spins so the rain or snow works its way around and melts or hardens depending on the temperature."

"Does the temperature depend on how close you are to heaven or hell?"

"No, Roy, heaven and hell have nothing to do with the weather. What matters most is where a place is in relation to the equator."

"I know where that is. It's a line around the globe."

"The nearer to the equator, the hotter it is."

"I think hell must be on the equator, Mom. The ground opens up like a big grave and when the planet turns all the bad people fall in."

"How do good people get to heaven?"

"A whirly wind called God's Tornado comes and picks them up and takes them there. People disappear all the time after a tornado."

"And what about purgatory, the place where people are that God hasn't decided about yet?"

"I think they wait on the planet until God or the Devil chooses them."

"Are they kept in any particular place?"

"I'm not sure. Maybe they just stay where they are, and they don't even know they're waiting."

"I don't know if you know it, baby, but what you say makes perfect sense. I wish I could write down some of these things, or we had a tape recorder to keep them."

"Don't worry, Mom, I've got a good memory. I won't forget anything."

Sad Stories of the Death of Kings

Nate

Jack
(Pops)

Ike

Lovie

ROY'S GRANDFATHER AND THREE OF HIS BROTHERS

The Age of Fable

Roy read a story about a tribe of female warriors who interrupted the conflict between the Greeks and the Trojans in their quest for males to assist in the propagation of their race. These women called themselves Amazons and were led by Penthesilea, who, as had the rest of the tribe, severed her right breast in order to more swiftly and easily draw back her bow. The most exciting part of the story, Roy thought, was the Amazon queen's confrontation with the champion of the Greeks, Achilles, whose ferocity in battle attracted Penthesilea as no man ever had before. For the first time she encountered a man whom she could consider her equal.

The idea of a tribe of brave, vicious, single-breasted women was almost beyond the comprehension of Roy's eleven-year-old mind. He drew pictures of the Amazons as he imagined them: naked, tall and lean, their long hair tied back with leather thongs.

Roy asked his grandfather if he'd ever read this story.

"Sure," said Pops, "it's in *The Iliad*, by Homer."

"That's right," Roy said. "I kind of found it by accident on a table at the library. Do you think there really ever was a tribe of savage women like that?"

"I don't think savage is the correct word for them, Roy. They knew what they were doing. The Amazons wanted to be independent of men, the problem being that they needed men to impregnate them in order to keep their race from dying out."

"But they only wanted girls, right?"

Pops nodded.

"Then what did they do with boy babies?"

"Killed at birth," Pops said. "Drowned them or slit their throats."

"It's just a story, though, isn't it?" Roy asked. "Homer made it all up."

"Yes," said Pops, "but there's a lot of truth to it. Even today many Chinese drown their female babies because they think they're worth less than men."

"But they need girls to keep China going."

"They don't drown all of 'em."

After talking to Pops, Roy walked over to the park to see if anybody was playing ball. Halfway there it started to rain, so Roy ducked under a canopy in front of the entrance to an apartment building. A very tall, sturdily built blonde lady wearing a thin black coat came out of the building. She stopped under a canopy and looked at the rain, which was falling hard.

"Damn!" she said. "Now it'll be a bitch to get a cab."

She turned around and walked back into the building without glancing at Roy. He waited under the canopy for a few more minutes until the rain let up a little, then ran back to his house.

Pops was sitting in the kitchen eating a chopped chicken liver sandwich and drinking a beer.

"I thought you were going to the park to play ball," he said.

"There won't be a game. Maybe I'll go when it stops raining."

Roy opened the refrigerator and took out a bottle of milk.

"What's the leader of the Amazons called?" he asked.

"A virago," said Pops.

"Is that the same as queen?"

"You need a king to have a queen, Roy. No, a virago is a termagant."

"Termagant? That sounds like an insect."

Pops bit into his sandwich.

"It means a big, tough woman," he said, as he chewed.

"I guess the Chinese don't want any of them," said Roy.

"Probably not," Pops said. "Close the refrigerator door."

The Great Failure

Roy was puzzled by the last words spoken by the dying father to his daughter at the end of the movie *The Great Failure*: "It is far more difficult to forget than to remember. How much happier I might have been had I sooner understood this simple fact."

Roy was nine years old when he saw *The Great Failure* at the Uptown theater with Jimmy Boyle. It was part of a double bill with *Taza, Son of Cochise*, the movie he and Boyle had gone to see, where Rock Hudson plays the Apache chief's kid who joins up with the renegade Geronimo.

"Rock must've spent a lot of time lyin' around his swimming pool in Beverly Hills to get that good a roastin'," said Jimmy Boyle.

"They rub grease on his skin to turn it dark," Roy said. "That way he doesn't get burned."

"He still don't look like an Indian," said Jimmy. "He looks like an actor with a Hollywood tan. Rocky Graziano looks more like an Indian than Rock Hudson."

Both Boyle and Roy were shivering in the late December wind as they walked home.

"And he don't talk like one, neither," Jimmy added.

"Mrs. Sweeney, the librarian at Clinton, doesn't sound like an Indian either," said Roy, "and she is an Indian."

"Oh yeah? What tribe?"

"Navajo. She told us she grew up on a reservation in New Mexico."

"No shit. How'd she get to Chicago?"

"Went to a college for Indians in Kansas, then got a job here."

"Her skin stay dark even in the winter?" asked Jimmy.

"Yeah."

"She ever talk Navajo?"

Roy shook his head. "Not at school. Maybe at home she does."

That night Roy thought more about what the dying father said at the end of *The Great Failure*. His daughter in the movie was about the same age as Roy and Roy wondered if she was supposed to have understood what her father meant about it being tougher to forget things than remember them. Roy remembered everything; he could read or see or hear something and it stayed in his brain and when he needed to recall it, or even sometimes when he didn't try to recall it, he could. Roy assumed it would always be this way, which was why he was curious about what the father said about being happy. Things happened and either they were good or bad and depending on what they were a person was happy or sad.

Before he fell asleep, Roy decided that the father thought he was a failure even though he had been a rich lawyer who had become governor of his state and run for president of the United States. He hadn't failed because he lost the presidential election but because he hadn't spent enough time with his wife and daughter and made them unhappy. His wife had committed suicide by jumping off a bridge into a raging river during a thunderstorm and was swept away and drowned; and his daughter liked to tear the arms and legs off of her dolls.

The family in *The Great Failure* lived in a mansion in New York and had servants and a big car. Taza, the son of Cochise, lived in a teepee in a desert, rode a buckskin horse bareback and spent most of his time fighting against the U.S. cavalry. Taza was not puzzled but he was not happy, either. Roy was almost always happiest when he was alone. Neither the father nor Taza were ever really alone, so maybe that had something to do with it.

Irredeemable

The Saturday afternoon that Roy and his friends heard about the fire at Our Lady of Abandoned and Irredeemable Boys, they were on their way to see a double feature at the Riviera. The movies were *Rumble on the Docks* and *Don't Knock the Rock*. Roy was eager to see *Don't Knock the Rock* because his favorite singer, Little Richard, was in it performing "Long Tall Sally." The boys were on foot passing through Greektown when a kid Jimmy Boyle knew named Martin Kenna, whose great-great-Uncle Hinky Dink Kenna had been a strongarm boss before Capone, came up to them and said, "You guys heard Irredeemable Boys burned down?"

It was an overcast, bone-rattlingly windy day in early March. A blizzard was supposedly on the way but the streets were clear of evidence from the last storm almost two weeks before. Neither Roy nor the Viper nor Boyle was wearing a hat; they kept their gloveless hands shoved deep into their coat pockets.

"When?" asked Jimmy.

Martin Kenna's nose was blue. He wore a black watch cap under the hood of his gray parka. His hands were buried in the pockets and Roy bet he had gloves on.

"Real early this morning," Kenna said, "before it got light out."

"They know how it started?" Roy asked.

Martin Kenna shook his head. "I ain't heard. Worst part is the main staircase collapsed as the orphans was comin' down it. Bunch of 'em died. Fried up. Don't know how many. You guys goin' to the Riv?"

Jimmy Boyle nodded.

"I thought so. Nick Kilennis said *Don't Knock the Rock*'s good but *Rumble on the Docks* is bunk."

"You goin'?"

"No, I gotta work today at the bakery. See ya."

"See ya," said Jimmy.

Kenna walked away and turned the corner onto Clark. The three boys continued toward the theater. Roy wished he'd worn a hat or had a coat with a hood.

"You think somebody torched Irredeemable Boys?" he asked.

"Why'd anybody burn down an orphanage?" said Jimmy.

"For the insurance," the Viper said. "Or maybe even an orphan was disturbed about bein' mistreated."

Roy got a kick out of seeing Little Richard do "Long Tall Sally" while he banged on the piano with his right foot, but *Rumble on the Docks* was phony like Martin Kenna said Nick Kilennis had said, with a pretty boy gang leader whose hair never got mussed during a fight. Roy couldn't get the thought of the orphanage fire out of his head, though, and after the show he told Jimmy Boyle and the Viper that he wanted to go by.

"It's a long way," Jimmy said. "It'll be dark by the time we get there."

"I got stuff to do," said the Viper.

Roy walked by himself up Ojibway Boulevard until he came to Terhune, where he turned east toward the lake. Roy kept his head down against the wind as best he could but it didn't do much good. He was freezing and considered giving up but Roy kept walking and when he turned onto Tecumseh Street the wind calmed down.

There were two hook and ladders and a red car parked inside the big iron gates of Our Lady of Abandoned and Irredeemable Boys. The sky was getting dark fast but from the sidewalk Roy could see the black, smoking skeleton of the orphanage. The gates were closed and no people were visible on the grounds. An old man and a woman passed by on the other side of the street but they did not stop or look over.

Roy was about to leave when he saw a white-haired man wearing a long brown overcoat appear from around the other side of the orphanage. The man got into the red car and started it up but did not drive away, just sat in it with the motor running. Then tiny dots of light flashed on and off from the ruins like fireflies. Roy figured it was the men from the hook and ladders looking for sparks and smoldering debris.

The part of the sky right over what was left of Irredeemable Boys was a very dark green while all around it was almost entirely black. For some reason Roy had stopped shivering. Instead of getting colder, the air seemed warmer. Maybe it was about to snow.

Sad Stories of the Death of Kings

Roy's friend Magic Frank had a job cleaning up the Tip Top Burlesque House on Saturday and Sunday nights, which, because he began work at three thirty on the following days, was actually Sunday and Monday mornings. According to the law, during business hours patrons and workers at the Tip Top had to be at least eighteen years old and Magic Frank was only sixteen, but since the girlie shows stopped at three the city ordinance did not apply to him. He'd gotten the job through his older brother, Moose, who played poker on Thursday nights with the Tip Top's owner, Herman "Lights Out" Trugen. Moose told Frank that Trugen's nickname derived from his habit of turning out lights to save money on electricity. Trugen, who was in his sixties, supposedly had been pals with the comedic actor W. C. Fields, another famous miser who kept padlocks on his telephones to which only he had the keys. In Berlin, Moose said, Herman Trugen had operated a whorehouse favored by the Nazis, several of whom helped him escape Germany during the Holocaust. Trugen's two sisters and a brother had died in Auschwitz.

Magic Frank did not like to go alone to State and Congress, so on Christmas Eve he asked Roy to accompany him, promising to buy Roy breakfast after he'd finished mopping the theater and taking out the trash. It was already officially Christmas on Sunday night when the boys got to the Tip Top early, at two thirty, in order to catch the last show.

"I thought you couldn't get in until the place was closed," Roy said.

"I got a key to the back door," said Magic Frank, "and Trugen don't come in Sundays. The other guys don't care, they just nod or wave and let me sit and watch if I want."

"What about the strippers?"

"What about 'em?"

"You know any?"

"Not really. By the time I come in, they're dog tired. They mostly just get dressed and leave."

A cold, sporadic rain pelted the boys as they walked down Dearborn past Van Buren, then turned left on Congress Parkway, where a gust of wind hit them flush in the face.

"Jesus H. Christ!" Frank cried. "As soon as I can, I'm movin' to Miami."

Magic Frank led Roy down an alley just west of State Street to the rear of the Tip Top and unlocked the back door. Roy followed him through the offices into the theater. The show was on so the boys snuck up a side aisle to the very last row and took seats. Two middle-aged, red-nosed men were on stage.

"Where was you last night, Al?" one asked the other.

"Inna cemetery."

"A cemetery?"

"That's right, Joe."

"What were you doin' inna cemetery at night?"

"Buryin' a stiff."

The dozen or so members of the audience barely acknowledged this stale joke despite an urgent roll on the snare drum and the cymbal crash that punctuated it. To Roy, the comedians looked as beat as the pit band sounded once they began an overture to the last stripper of the night.

"And now, for the delectation not to mention play-zeer of you germs out there," announced Joe, the fellow who had performed the apocryphal interment, "direct from Paris—that's a burg in southern Illinois—guaranteed to raise your spirits if nothin' else, the proud proprietor of the best breasts in the Middle West, Miss May Flowers!"

May Flowers entered stage left as the duo departed stage right.

Draped in a bodice-hugging, floor length, bright yellow gown, she sashayed around out of synch to the pit band's dull rendering of "Night Train." Her high-piled hair was fiery red.

"Sonny Liston uses this tune to jump rope by," Roy whispered to Magic Frank.

Before she stripped, Miss Flowers looked to be about forty years old. After her act was finished, Roy thought, she looked even older. Her breasts were long and narrow and set wide apart, the nipples sporting silver pasties; once released from imprisonment, they depended almost to her hips. During May's flounce and inevitable divestiture, the few witnesses who had paid to get in out of the cold expressed no particular emotions that Roy could easily discern. Most of them remained passive, if not in fact comatose, undisturbed by this jactitative offering. Those individuals deep in slumber went undetected by the performer, their snores rendered inaudible by the unenthusiastic strains of Jimmy Forrest's signature composition. May Flowers completed her act without much of a flourish. Once having shed all but a strategically positioned gold lamé triangle, she strode quickly out of sight and for all anyone knew directly out of the building.

Miss Flowers was not in evidence once Roy and Magic Frank went backstage. The musicians beat a hasty retreat as well, and two cadaverous-complexioned ushers hustled the patrons into the inhospitable night. It was part of Frank's job to turn off the lights and make sure the doors were locked, so the ushers took off as soon as they were certain all of the customers had gone.

Roy asked Magic Frank if there was anything he could do to help him, and Frank said he could empty the waste baskets from the office and dump them into a garbage can in the alley. Roy consolidated the contents of the several baskets into one and carried it outside, careful to prop open the door with a chair so as not to lock himself out. As he was emptying the trash, May Flowers walked out of the theater into the alley, carrying a bag and a box with a handle. She was wearing a big beaver coat with a small matching hat. Roy shivered in the icy rain.

"Nasty night, ain't it?" she said.

Roy looked at her and asked, "How do you get all of your hair under that little hat?"

"You mean the wig I wear durin' my act? It's in here," said May Flowers, lifting the box. "There's a pack of cigs and a lighter in the left side pocket of my coat. Could you be a good egg and take 'em out and light one up for me?"

Roy put down the waste basket, fished a hand into the pocket of May's coat and dug out a pack of Viceroys and a gold lighter.

"Pull one and torch it, honey," she said.

Roy put a cigarette between his lips and flicked the lighter. Up close, she looked a lot like his grandmother.

"Just stick it in," said May Flowers, parting her lips.

Roy transferred the Viceroy from his mouth to hers, then replaced the pack in the beaver coat pocket.

"You're a livin' doll," she said. "Don't you end up like these bums come in this dive don't do nothin' but tell each other sad stories of the death of kings. Merry Christmas."

May Flowers walked away. Roy picked up the waste basket and went back into the building. Magic Frank was putting a mop and bucket into a closet.

"I just saw May Flowers in the alley," Roy told him. "She asked me to light a cigarette for her."

"No kiddin'. What else did she say?"

"That I shouldn't end up like the men who come here."

Later, when the boys were in a diner, Frank said, "Wow, first night at the Tip Top and you got to meet May Flowers."

A scabrous Christmas tree, bedraped sparingly with tinsel, stood by the door.

"Yeah," said Roy, "but I wish I hadn't seen her breasts first."

The Sultan

James "The Sultan" Word died last week. I read his obituary in the local newspaper, one of the paid obits, not a byline in the sports section, which he deserved. The Sultan was a terrific prize fighter for fifteen years, a guy nobody liked to fight, a counterpuncher who made opponents come to him. If he got in with a hard charger who tried to wrap him up, Word would wade in quickly and catch him by surprise. According to the paper, James was one month shy of his fiftieth birthday when he died; no reason for his demise was given.

I remembered that he worked for the sanitation department as a garbage collector back in his boxing days because his income from matches was erratic. The Sultan was a sweet character, a soft-spoken, tan-complexioned, good-looking welterweight with a Ray Robinson mustache and permanent smile. He was given his nickname by Aroundel X, a Black Muslim friend of Word's, who told James that he resembled a Mohammedan Sultan and was put on earth to dominate any Turks who dared to defy him. I don't know that James bought into Aroundel X's concept, but the nickname stuck.

The Sultan and I played chess together on Saturday mornings at Yardbird's Gym when it was on Magazine Street while my sons worked out on the bags and sparred in the ring. One-eyed Eddie, James's trainer, let him rest Saturdays and tutored my boys while we played on a card table off to one side. The Sultan played chess the way he fought, shyly, staying away until I made an improvident move, depending on an opponent's impatience to provide him an opening so that he could sneak in a shot. Win or lose, The Sultan never stopped smiling.

I went to his funeral. It was on a Friday and the weather was awful, raining hard with thunder and lightning and even a little hail. I was one of three or four white men among about thirty or forty black people. After it was over I walked away alone and as I did I noticed a stocky young man with big ears who reminded me of a kid I once knew named Ernie Nederland. I first met Nederland when we were both in sixth grade. We went to different schools, so we ran into each other occasionally, at parties or hanging out at parks around town. Ernie was a good-looking guy, girls liked him even though his ears stuck out, and at twelve or thirteen years old he already had the reputation of being a tough kid. He and I got along well whenever we encountered one another; he never seemed particularly aggressive but it was clear that he thought highly of himself. Nederland's rep stemmed from his family being connected to The Outfit; his uncle was a federal judge who supposedly was in their pocket, and Ernie's old man was a big deal in the city sanitation department, which was famously controlled by organized crime.

A few years after I moved away, an old friend of mine from high school told me that Ernie Nederland had become a button man. Ernie owned a gas station on the West Side but he made his real bread by shooting people at the behest of The Outfit. According to my friend, as long as Ernie's victims were known or suspected criminals, his uncle the judge protected him; even if Nederland was arrested, he was never prosecuted.

I don't know what became of Ernie. When I was in my car driving away from The Sultan's funeral, I recalled watching Ernie Nederland in a fistfight on a school playground when we were about fifteen. Nederland kept a grin on his face while he fought, and like James Word he let his opponent come to him, taking punches on his arms and elbows without letting the other guy get a clean shot at his face. I'm sure Ernie lost a fight now and again but the time I'm talking about he slipped every roundhouse right and rabbit-punched the kid hard with his left hand, which he used like a hammer. That fight ended after Nederland dropped the other boy, then picked up a two-foot length of lead pipe he'd brought along and cracked the kid's skull with it. Ernie never stopped smiling the whole time.

The Sultan didn't, either. I watched him spar numerous times and fight a half dozen and he was always smiling, even when he got hit. I figured he did this to unnerve his opponent, to not let him know he was hurt, a common enough ploy. I thought it a little bit interesting that both The Sultan and Ernie Nederland's dad were in the sanitation business. As far as I know, Ernie never hoisted a garbage can so long as he could handle a lead pipe or a gun.

Nederland did tell me a story once, a year or so before I saw him pipe that kid. We were at a party and he noticed that I was watching one girl dance with more than casual interest. She had a ponytail and was wearing a yellow sweater. She was dancing with another girl.

"You know her?" Ernie asked me.

"No," I said. "Do you?"

"I know about her."

"What do you know?"

"She's dyin'."

I looked at him. "How do you know?" I looked back at her. "She doesn't look sick."

"She had a heart operation, got a thick scar on her chest from where the doctors opened her up."

"She showed you?"

Ernie shook his head. "An older guy I know, Al Phillips, done it with her a few times. He's seen it."

It was uncommon for kids in those days, especially girls, to have sex before the age of sixteen or seventeen, but I believed Nederland.

"How do you know for sure that she's dying?"

Ernie pulled a pack of Camels from a pocket, shook one out, lit it and inhaled.

"Want one?" he asked.

"No, thanks," I said.

Nederland blew a couple of smoke rings.

"Al Phillips told me," he said. "Doctors told her folks after she got out of the hospital a year ago, when she was twelve and a half, that she should enjoy herself for the time she had left. They didn't say how long that might be. It's probably why she started doin' it so young. Her name's Daisy Green."

I watched Daisy Green dance. She moved better than most of the other girls.

"Real slinky, ain't she?" said Nederland. "Al says she'll do anything."

He rapidly exhaled a trio of smoke rings and went to talk to somebody on the other side of the room.

The record that had been playing ended and "Good Golly, Miss Molly" came on. Daisy Green and the other girl continued dancing together. I thought about cutting in but I didn't. It felt strange knowing that she would be dead soon and that she was more sexually experienced than I.

A week after The Sultan's funeral there was a small article in the newspaper stating that police had arrested a man suspected of having murdered James Word during an attempted street robbery. The suspect, Tyrus Chatmon, had shot James twice in the chest. There were photographs of Chatmon and Word; only The Sultan was smiling.

The Liberian Condition

The day Omar Buell appeared in the schoolyard wearing only a pair of worn brown combat boots and holding a deer rifle is a day nobody who was there will ever forget. It was a windy, cloudy afternoon in late February or early March, just before the bell rang signaling the end of lunch hour. Dirty snow was piled up around the edges of the schoolyard and kids were running around playing tag or, like my friends and I, playing touch football. I was eleven years old and had known Omar Buell since we had both been in first grade. He always wore a wash-faded, longsleeved, checkered flannel shirt buttoned up to his neck, baggy green or gray trousers and raggedy, black and white high-top gym shoes. He didn't talk much to other kids and never hung around the playground after school. Buell was not an outstanding student, either; he always got passing grades but consistently placed near or at the bottom of the class. There was nothing to really distinguish him except, perhaps, for his hair, which he wore longer than most and was the color of August wheat. Once I heard Heidi Dilg, a girl in our fourth grade class, say she wished she had hair that color.

Omar Buell, naked except for combat boots and holding a Winchester .30-30, shocked everyone. All of the kids stopped playing and stared at him. Omar stood still without shivering even though the temperature was a smidge above freezing. Mrs. Polansky, who taught health and home economics and was a schoolyard monitor, ran into the building right after Raymond Drain, a sixth grader who was infamous for once having taken a shit on the floor in the back of a classroom in front of everybody, pointed him out to her. None of the kids approached Buell, but nobody ran away. He just stood there looking at us, but not at anyone in particular.

"You're gonna freeze your pecker off!" Jimmy Groat shouted.

A few of the kids laughed, but Omar Buell did not budge, not even his face muscles moved. I put on my gloves, which I'd stuffed into my coat pockets before we'd begun playing football. Several teachers, including Mrs. Polansky, and the school janitor, Bronko Schulz, came out of the school building and stood off to one side, sizing up the situation. Bronko Schulz was a big, easygoing guy who liked to tell the boys what he considered to be dirty jokes. He once asked me why a penis was the lightest thing in the world. I told him I didn't know and Bronko said, "Just a thought can lift it." The bell rang but we all stayed where we were.

"What's wrong, Omar?" said Mr. Brady, an eighth grade English teacher.

Everybody thought Brady was a pretty nice guy. He didn't shout at kids or tell them to take off their hats or pull up their pants and never told anyone to shut up. If he wanted a kid to stop talking, Mr. Brady would just pat him or her on the shoulder and go on with what he was saying.

When Omar did not respond to Mr. Brady, or even look over at him, Mr. Brady said, "Son, what do you need?"

Miss Riordan, the school nurse, whose father was the head priest at St. Tim's, handed a red blanket to Mr. Brady.

"You must be cold, Omar," he said.

The late bell rang. I could see that Bronko Schulz was holding something behind his back that looked like a tire iron.

Mr. Brady walked up to Omar and draped the blanket around his shoulders. Brady did not attempt to take the rifle away from Omar but he put one arm around him and together they walked into the school, followed closely by Bronko Schulz and the other teachers. Nobody said anything to the kids, so we just went back to playing tag and touch football.

I can still see Omar Buell and Mr. Brady walking in the school-yard with Omar wrapped in a red blanket carrying the deer rifle.

I never saw Omar Buell again, but a couple of weeks after the incident Jimmy Groat said that his mother told him Omar had an incurable condition so he had to be locked up in an institution with other incurable nut cases.

The other day I read an article in the newspaper about a Liberian rebel leader who made his men march into battle completely naked carrying only their guns in order to frighten the enemy. He claimed to have been responsible for the deaths of more than 20,000 people, and said that before a fight he made a human sacrifice to the devil, usually killing a child and plucking out the heart, which was divided into pieces for his men to eat.

"Did your mother say what they call Omar's condition?" I asked Jimmy.

"She don't know," he said. "Maybe she just made up the part about him being put away in an institution to make me behave better."

Six Million and One

Israel Rostov was a high school dropout who worked as a fur cart pusher in the State and Lake building. Roy was eight years old when he first saw him. Roy often accompanied his grandfather, Jack Colby, whom he called Pops, on Saturdays to the furriers' office that Pops shared with his brothers, Ike and Nate. Their brother Louie, who was the president of the Chicago Furriers Association, which he had founded, kept his office on the sixth floor of the building. The other Colby brothers' office was on the eighth floor.

Roy would sit on a high stool and cut up pelts with a stiletto-like knife Pops had taught him to use, while his grandfather and great-uncles sat around a marble-topped table and played cards. When Louie joined them, the game was bridge; otherwise, they played three-handed gin rummy.

Izzy Rostov delivered furs on carts from floor to floor. He was a short kid with thick, curly black hair and bushy eyebrows, small dark brown eyes and a huge hook nose that seemed to be trying to escape from his face. Rostov's thick red lips curved upwards at the corners so that it looked as if he were always smiling, except that his smile more resembled a sneer. He perpetually had a burning unfiltered Lucky Strike dripping from his mouth. Roy was fascinated by Izzy's ability to talk while never removing the cigarette from his lips, as if the butt end was glued between them.

Rostov called Roy "my little pal," and stopped his cart to talk to him whenever he encountered Roy in the hallways or in the freight elevator. This usually occurred when Roy was going to or from the eighth floor and the sixth floor to visit with his Uncle Louie. The delivery boy always had a future plan for himself that he told Roy about. Most of the time it had to do with his moving to Miami Beach to hang out in the luxury hotels so that he could "hook up with rich, lazy broads."

One afternoon, Rostov told Roy he had something special to show him but he couldn't do it in the hallway. Roy followed Izzy into the eighth floor men's room. After making sure that nobody else was in the bathroom, Rostov removed from one of his coat pockets a small, black handgun and held it out for Roy to look at.

"This is a .38 caliber snub-nose revolver," Rostov said. "A very accurate piece of hardware. I bought it from a spook on Maxwell Street."

"What are you going to do with it?" asked Roy.

"Stick up a few gas stations, what else? I gotta get a stake together before I travel, buy some slick clothes to impress the broads, you know. I can't make it on the peanuts these penny-pinchin' Hebes pay me around here."

Izzy Rostov tapped the tip of his prodigious nose with the barrel of his revolver, and said, "I might even have enough dough to get my beak fixed."

Then he laughed and put the gun back into his coat pocket. The ash from Rostov's cigarette dangled dangerously and Roy was certain it would fall off, but it didn't. Roy moved further away from him.

"Don't be frightened, little pal," said Izzy. "I ain't gonna shoot anyone. The piece is just to throw a scare into 'em, let the suckers know Israel Rostov means business. I could change my name, too, once I get down South. How does Guy DeMarco sound? Smooth, huh? The broads'll go for a name like that. Guy DeMarco."

"You think gas stations keep a lot of cash around?" Roy asked.

"Depends," said Rostov. "But I got bigger ideas."

Rostov came close to Roy, mussed up his hair and then walked out of the men's room. Roy waited for a minute before returning to his grandfather's office. Jack, Ike and Nate were playing gin.

"Hey, babe," said Pops, "I thought you were going to see your Uncle Louie."

"I decided not to. I just went to the washroom." Roy went over to his stool, climbed on and resumed cutting up pelts.

The next time Roy ran into Izzy Rostov, the delivery boy winked at him but did not stop to talk. His cart was loaded with mink and fox stoles.

"Gotta get these on a truck goin' to the Merchandise Mart," Izzy said, and pushed on toward the freight elevator.

A couple of Saturdays after that, all four of the brothers were playing bridge when Louie said, "You hear the Rostov boy got killed?"

"The delivery cart kid?" asked Ike.

"Yes. Apparently he tried to rob a liquor store on Huron the other night and the clerk shot him in the back before he could get away."

"You know about his parents?" asked Nate.

"What about them?" Jack asked.

"They were survivors of Auschwitz."

"Horrible," said Ike. "Imagine how they must feel."

"What's Auschwitz?" asked Roy.

The men were silent for a few moments before Nate spoke.

"It was a concentration camp, a prison death camp during the war where the Germans murdered Jews."

"They also murdered Gypsies and Communists," said Ike, "but mostly Jews."

"But Rostov's parents are still alive," Roy said.

"Some prisoners were rescued by the Allies before the Nazis could kill them," said Louie.

"How many people did they kill?" asked Roy.

"Too many to count," said his grandfather. "The accepted figure is six million."

"More," said Louie. "They murdered more."

"To think that the parents escaped the Holocaust," Nate said, "they come to America and their child is shot down in the street like a wild animal."

"He had a gun," Roy said. "He showed it to me."

The men all looked at Roy.

"It was a snub-nose .38," he said. "Izzy told me he was going to stick up a gas station and move to Miami Beach."

"What kind of home life could the boy have had?" said Nate.

Roy looked out a window onto State Street. The Chicago Theater was showing Alan Ladd in *The Badlanders*. Clumps of brown dirt the size of pigeons were blowing through the gray air.

"Let's play cards," said Ike.

War and Peace

Lots of guys went into the service from Roy's neighborhood. Most of them got drafted into the army and were sent to Germany or Korea. This was during the 1950s, between World War II and the Vietnam War, after the cease-fire of the police action in Korea, so the only guys who got killed bought it by accident. Stuffy Foster drowned during basic training in South Carolina. Little Goose Wentworth's older brother, Big Goose, went AWOL from Fort Polk, in Louisiana, and disappeared into a swamp; his body was found two weeks later covered with snake bites, his corpse half-devoured by varmints. Woody Crow drove a tank over a cliff while on maneuvers in Düsseldorf and broke his neck. The biggest success story came after Moe Israel stole a general's jeep in Belgium and drove it to Monte Carlo where he was arrested in a casino and then sent to prison. Moe's cousin Artie told Roy that Moe set up a book-making operation in the penitentiary at Leavenworth, Kansas, that was so successful he was able to send money to his mother every month.

When Phil Flynn told Roy that as soon as he could drop out of high school he was going to enlist in the navy, Roy asked him why. Both boys were eleven years old; they were sitting on upturned milk bottle crates in the alley behind Phil's house swapping drags on a Lucky Strike. Phil lived with his parents and two older sisters in a one-bedroom apartment above a meat market. His sisters slept in the bedroom and their parents slept in a Murphy bed that came down from the living room wall. Phil slept on a cot in the apartment's only hallway; every time someone had to use the bathroom during the night he or she invariably bumped into Phil's cot and woke him up.

"I figure it's the only way I'm gonna get to Tahiti," Phil said. "If

I let the army draft me, they'll stick me up on the DMZ in Korea where I'll fuckin' freeze to death, or in Germany where I'll also fuckin' freeze to death."

It was cold sitting outside in the alley. Brownish snow was piled up against garage doors and a thin layer of ice covered the cracked and potholed pavement. This was early March in Chicago and more bad weather was on the way.

"What's the DMZ?" asked Roy.

"Demilitarized zone," said Phil. "It's supposed to be the scariest place on earth, where the commies and our guys stand day and night with their rifles pointed at each other."

"Does the U.S. Navy go to Tahiti?"

"I went into the recruitin' office upstairs of the currency exchange," Phil said, "and the Chief Petty Officer in charge told me the navy would send me to the south seas if that's where I wanted to go."

"Why do you want to go there?"

Phil finished off the cigarette and flicked the butt away.

"Hot and breezy," he said, "and fabulous brown babes with big tits and almost no clothes. I saw 'em in my sister Mary's art book. Standin' around with flowers in their long black hair and lyin' down by a lagoon without tops on and nothin' to do. You gotta be on a ship to get there."

"You told your parents?"

"Nah. My old man wants me to go to college. He talks about it all the time, about how me and Mary and Wanda are all gonna graduate from college. It's a big thing with him since he never went past the third or fourth grade and works in a bottle factory."

"Was he in the service?"

"Uh-uh. He gets fits, so they wouldn't take him. Wanda gets fits, too. Next time you're around ask her to show you her tongue where she bit off part of it."

Roy stood up. "I'm goin'," he said.

Phil took a cigarette out of a pocket of his blue tanker jacket. "I got another Lucky. You wanna share?"

Roy shook his head and put up his coat collar.

"You oughta join the navy with me," said Phil.

He took out a book of matches and lit his cigarette.

"Warm breezes, naked women and no wars. Nobody would fight if they could lay by a lagoon all day with a girl with titties like coconuts and flowers behind her ears."

Roy grinned and nodded his head then turned and started walking toward his house. His nose was running and he wiped it with the back of his left hand. Roy had seen Phil's sister Wanda twice, once walking with another girl on Ojibway Boulevard, and once waiting for a bus on Blackhawk. Her skin, he recalled, was much darker than Phil's, and her hair was black, not ginger colored like her brother's or Mary's, and her eyes were big and brown, theirs were small and blue. She was probably the prettiest girl Roy had ever seen.

Chop Suey Joint

When Roy was eleven years old, he got a job delivering Chinese food on a bicycle. He was paid twenty-five cents an hour and a dime for each delivery, plus tips. He worked three nights a week from five o'clock until eight, and from four to eight on Sundays. Kow Kow Restaurant provided the bicycle, which was equipped with baskets attached to the handlebars and mounted on the rear fender. Roy was also fed dinner, for which he usually requested a hamburger on toast, vegetable chow mein and egg foo yung. He enjoyed this job except when the weather was really foul, which was when he often had the most deliveries. Riding in traffic over icy streets or in driving rain was difficult, but he was skillful enough to avoid any serious mishaps during the year or so that he worked as a delivery boy.

Every Sunday night a man came into Kow Kow at eight twenty, ten minutes before closing. This was also the time when Roy ate his dinner. The man always sat in one of the two red leather booths on either side of the front window and ordered the same items: won ton soup with extra dumplings, served extra hot; shrimp fried rice; and two pots of tea, also extra hot. He was in his late forties or early fifties, had a three or four day beard, was of medium height and size, wore the same brown sportcoat, a black shirt buttoned up to his neck and a weather-punished brown Fedora, which he did not remove while he ate.

Don Soon, the owner's son, always waited on him. Don was twenty-three, he smiled a lot and Roy liked him the best of anyone at Kow Kow, although all of the guys who worked there—waiters, cooks and kitchen help—were nice to him. No women worked at Kow Kow. Mr. Soon, the owner, tended the cash register while seated on a high stool behind a counter near the entrance.

He said the same thing to every customer after ringing up the bill: "You come back. We waiting for you." Mr. Soon spoke Cantonese to his employees but when speaking to his son and to Roy he used perfect English. When Roy asked Don why his father spoke pidgin to non-Asian customers, Don said, "He thinks they expect it, so he does his Charlie Chan act. This is a chop suey joint—you get egg roll and atmosphere."

One Sunday night, when Don was in the kitchen and Mr. Soon had left early, the man in the hat, as the employees called him, looked over at Roy, who was eating his dinner at a nearby table, and said, "Hey, kid, you work here, don't you?"

Roy nodded. "I do deliveries."

"You suppose you could go in the kitchen and tell 'em I'm ready for my second pot of tea?"

"Sure," Roy said, and stood up.

"Make sure you tell 'em 'extra hot.'"

"Okay."

"Sorry to disturb your meal."

"No problem," Roy said, and walked back to the kitchen.

He came back and sat down.

"Don's bringing it," he said to the man in the hat.

"Thanks, kid."

Thirty seconds later, Don Soon brought the man a pot of tea, smiled at him and walked away.

"These are nice people here," the man said to Roy.

"They are," said Roy.

"They pay you good?"

"Enough, I guess."

"This waiter, he's always smiling."

"His name is Don. He's the owner's son."

"He reminds me of an Arab I knew when I worked in the oil fields in Saudi. His name was Rashid bin Rashid. Bin means 'son of.' He smiled all the time, too. This Rashid, he captured falcons and sold 'em. He showed me how to do it. Took a pet pigeon and tied a long piece of string to one of its legs and the other one to a stone. We sat and waited until a falcon flew over, then Rashid threw the pigeon up into the air and we took off. The falcon swooped down and killed the pigeon and when he brought it to the ground we ran back and chased the falcon away. Then we dug a shallow pit in the sand downwind of the dead pigeon. Rashid got into the pit holding the end of the string tied to the stone. I covered him with a blanket and he told me to get far away. When the falcon came back to finish picking at its kill, Rashid slowly reeled in the pigeon. As soon as the falcon got close to him, Rashid reached out and grabbed it."

The front window behind the man was streaked with rain. Roy was glad he had finished his deliveries before it started. The man poured himself a fresh cup of tea and took a long sip.

"The Arabs mostly drank coffee," he said, "sometimes tea. They like it boiling hot. I got used to drinking it that way."

"How long were you in Saudi Arabia?" Roy asked.

"Three and a half years. Made a pile. Gone now."

Roy stood and picked up his dishes to take to the kitchen.

"Nice talking to you," he said. "I enjoyed the story about catching a falcon in the desert."

The man in the hat poured more tea.

"If you're here next Sunday, I'll tell you about the time I helped save a camel from drowning in quicksand."

"I'll be here," said Roy.

He never saw the man again. A few weeks after their conversation, Roy asked Don Soon if the man had come in at a time when he wasn't working. Don said no, that as far as he knew the man in the hat had not been back since that night.

"You must have told him about a better Chinese restaurant," said Don.

Roy asked Mr. Soon if he'd seen him, and Mr. Soon shook

his head and said, "White ghost all look same." Then Mr. Soon smiled and messed up Roy's hair with his right hand. "Just kidding, Roy," he said. "No, I don't know what happened to him. He always left a fair tip. I hate to lose a good customer."

In his second year of high school, four years after he'd stopped working at Kow Kow, Roy came across a book on a shelf in the school library about falcons and falconry. He immediately remembered the man in the hat's story. Roy looked through the book to see if there was any information on capturing falcons but there was not. Most of the text was about training the birds to hunt, which seemed silly to Roy because it was obvious that a falcon knows how to hunt without a man having to teach it. He put the book back on the shelf. There were millions of pigeons in the city, Roy thought. They shit on everything. Chicago would be a better place, he decided, if more falcons lived there.

Significance

Roy often wondered what the significance was of having a favorite color or number. His favorite color was blue, a common enough preference, he came to learn. His mother's favorite number was eight: whenever she asked him to guess what number she was thinking of, he always said eight and he was always right. One time she asked him and he guessed eight and his mother said, No, I was thinking of the number four, and Roy said, You're fibbing, you were thinking of eight, and she laughed and said, You're right, I was thinking of eight. I can't help it. You can't fool me, Roy said, and his mother said, No, Roy, you know me too well.

Roy and his mother played this game often when they were in the car and she was driving. When his mother tried to guess what number Roy was thinking of she usually guessed three or nine and she was correct about half the time, though neither three nor nine were Roy's favorite number. As Roy grew older, he and his mother played this game less frequently, and by the time he was ten or eleven they stopped playing it for good.

Many years later Roy was walking alone at night on a street in a city his mother had never been to when he thought about their numbers guessing game. He was thinking of the number five and he wished his mother were there because if he asked her to guess she would have said three or nine. Just then Roy passed a house with an open window from which he heard a record playing: Eartha Kitt singing "April in Portugal" in French. He stopped in the street to listen. "April in Portugal" had been one of his mother's favorite songs when he was a boy; she often used to play it on the piano and sing the lyrics in English, though she could speak French passably well.

Eartha Kitt finished singing and Roy walked on. Any number

divisible by three, he remembered, was in certain ancient cultures considered to have mystical or occult significance, but he could not recall why; the number eight placed horizontally was the mathematical symbol for infinity, as well as an overhand knot as illustrated in the Merchant Marine handbook.

The significance of April in Portugal, Roy knew, was that it was the month in which the people in the song had fallen in love. The importance of numbers or colors in one's cosmology was far more arcane, except, perhaps, to adherents of numerology and whatever students of color symbology might be called. (Colorologists?) Roy had an urge to stop the next person he encountered on the street and ask him or her if he or she could guess what number he was thinking of at that very moment, but he overcame it. Even if the person played along and guessed correctly, Roy knew no meaning could be discerned from it, that nothing profound would be revealed. More significant, Roy thought, was his having been reminded of his mother playing and singing "April in Portugal." There was no doubt as to its value in Roy's cosmology.

He could still remember the photograph of Eartha Kitt on the cover of her album *That Bad Eartha,* bare-shouldered in a black cocktail dress, slinky, cat-like, a vixen amused by the charade. The significance of her come-on-and-try expression had not been lost on him. Roy wondered what Eartha Kitt's favorite number was.

Einstein's Son

There was a man in Roy's neighborhood who claimed he was the son of Albert Einstein. Roy was ten years old when he saw a picture of Einstein on the cover of *Look* magazine. Einstein's long white hair starfished from his head, he had a droopy ringmaster's mustache and a slightly befuddled expression on his face that made Roy think of him as a dotty but benevolent scientist who would not seem uncomfortable throwing elbows in the headslapping, eyethumbing company of the Three Stooges.

The man who told people that he was Einstein's son was in his midfifties, tall, already bald and immaculately shorn of facial hair. He wore gold wire-rim glasses and always dressed in a blue suit with a white shirt and red tie under a shabby beige trenchcoat frayed at the cuffs, and battered brown wing tip shoes. His name, he said, was Baron Otto von Loswerden, so everyone in the neighborhood referred to him as the Baron. According to Steve the Newsie, who owned the newspaper and magazine stand on the northwest corner of Dupré and Minnetonka, and from whom von Loswerden bought a *Chicago Tribune* at eight o'clock every morning while stopping to chat for a few minutes, the Baron was an illegitimate child of Albert Einstein and his then girlfriend, Mileva, whom the young physicist later married and who bore him another child. The Baron, however, who was not yet Otto, nor, obviously, a baron, was given away to avoid scandal and financial responsibility. It was not until he was thirty years old, the Baron confided to Steve, and at the deathbed of his adoptive father, that he learned of his true parentage.

"Do you believe him?" Roy asked Steve the Newsie.

Roy's friend, Billy Murphy, who worked on Sunday mornings for Steve piecing together newspaper sections, was the only person Roy knew who had ever been in the newsie's apartment. Billy told Roy that the floor of the apartment was carpeted half a foot thick with old newspapers, and the walls were decorated with photographs of very young girls cut out of the papers.

"What difference does it make?" said Steve. "If a man wants to believe he's a baron or even a king, who am I to say he ain't?"

Steve was five foot two and weighed more than two hundred pounds. He had almost no nose, very few teeth and a cauliflower left ear. Billy Murphy told Roy that Steve's mother, whom Steve called The Army of Mary, lived in the apartment with him, but that nobody had seen her for a very long time.

"I think she died and Steve wrapped her in old newspapers like a mummy," Billy said. "He's got a padlock on a freezer up there. I bet The Army of Mary's in it."

Roy did not know where the Baron worked, or if he worked at all.

"Do you know where the Baron lives?" Roy asked Billy.

"No. I only see him walkin' back and forth on Minnetonka."

"Me, too," said Roy. "He must rent a room in a house around here."

One gray afternoon when Billy was holding down the stand while Steve the Newsie went to drain the snake, Roy was crossing the street and Billy shouted for him to come over.

"What's up?" Roy said.

"Look at this."

Billy showed Roy a nine-by-twelve-inch box with fancy writing on the cover.

"What is it?"

"The Baron gave it to Steve to read. He says it's a manuscript."

Roy read what was written on the box.

"What Albert Einstein Got Wrong about the Electrodynamics of Moving Bodies by Baron Otto von Loswerden, Son of Einstein."

"Did you ever hear the Baron speak?" asked Roy.

"Yeah," said Billy, "a couple of times."

"Does he have a German accent?"

Billy thought for a moment, then said, "I don't think so. Why?"

"If he was from Switzerland or Germany or Austria, he'd have an accent, wouldn't he?"

"Yeah, I guess. But maybe he's been livin' in Chicago for so long that he lost it."

"Cunningham's mother and father came over from Ireland forty years ago and they still have theirs," said Roy.

The back door of the newsstand opened and Steve came in.

"What you bums doin'?" he said.

"I just showed Roy what the Baron gave you," said Billy.

"Be careful with that," said Steve, taking the box from him. "It's his masterwork."

"Can you understand scientific stuff?" asked Roy.

"I haven't read it yet."

"Billy and I were wonderin' where the Baron lives."

"And how come he don't have a German accent?" asked Billy.

"My grandfather says Einstein's from Switzerland," said Roy.

"You boys ask too many questions."

Steve put the box on the floor under the front counter.

"Go on, both of ya, beat it before you scare off the customers."

That night, Roy asked his grandfather if he knew that Albert Einstein had an illegitimate son who lived in the neighborhood.

"No, I didn't," said Pops. "What's his name?"

"Baron Otto von Loswerden. He says Einstein and his girlfriend gave him up for adoption when he was a baby."

Pops said, "Loswerden. It means 'to get rid of.' The man may be an impostor but at least he's got a sense of humor."

"What's an impostor?"

"A phony, a pretender."

"He gave Steve the Newsie the manuscript of a book he wrote about something Einstein did wrong."

Roy's grandfather looked at him and smiled.

"America is a great country, Roy. A man can be whoever he wants to be."

"Is it a crime?"

"Is what a crime?"

"To say you're somebody you're not."

"That depends on your purpose, why you're doing it and what you do."

"What if someone died and nobody knew about it but you and you didn't want to give up the body and you kept it in your freezer? Is that a crime?"

"Roy," said his grandfather, "what is it you're not telling me?"

The Albanian Florist

There was a man named Cubar Shog who haunted the bus stops along Ojibway Boulevard late on weekday afternoons to pick up women, most of whom worked as maids in the neighborhood, on their way home. Cubar Shog was a middle-aged, completely bald Albanian who stood five foot six and weighed well over two hundred pounds. He looked like a wrestler, which he told Roy and the other kids he had been in Europe. Cubar emigrated to America from Tirana in his late twenties and worked for fifteen years smelting steel in a mill in Whiting, Indiana, before moving to Chicago and opening a flower shop on the corner of Ojibway and Dupré.

He always carried a bouquet of flowers with him whenever he approached a woman at a bus stop. Cubar spoke softly in the hope of diminishing the harshness of his Balkan accent, and smiled as he offered the bouquet to the object of his desire. If the woman seemed agreeable, Cubar would then propose they spend an hour or so together and mention a price. Of course many of the women were offended by his overture and threw the flowers to the ground, then turned away or even attempted to slap Cubar's face. His wrestler's reflexes were usually sharp enough to deflect an attacking hand and, once rejected, Cubar quickly retreated, picking up the fallen bouquet and walking swiftly down the street to the next bus stop.

Almost as often, however, the woman Cubar Shog propositioned was intrigued by the thought of earning some extra money and agreed to accompany the egg-shaped Albanian man to his nearby flower shop. Cubar kept a tiny room in the rear of the store just for this purpose. Neither Roy nor any of the other neighborhood boys knew where Cubar actually lived. His taste in women was fairly eclectic: they were white, black or brown, and short, tall or medium height; the one exceptional requirement was that the woman not be too skinny. Cubar preferred his ladies to have a bit of heft to them.

"Boys, is nothing satisfaction like woman of healthful size with good heavy leg," Cubar told them.

Jimmy Boyle worked after school for Cubar Shog delivering flowers. He was the only one of the boys who had seen the back room at Illyrian Brothers Florists. Cubar had given the store this name because of his belief that Albanians had descended from ancient Illyria, and he thought it sounded poetic, more suitable for a flower shop than Cubar's or Shog's. The "brothers" part was a tribute to his younger brother, Thracian, who had been bitten to death by rabid wild dogs on Crocodile Street in Tirana when he was five years old. A neighbor had discovered Thracian's dismembered body, chased away the pack of murderous mongrels and carried the pieces to the Shog house, where they were laid out on the kitchen table. Cubar, who was nine at the time, could never forget those several mauled and chewed chunks of flesh and bone that had been his little brother. Even as an adult it was a rare night that this ghastly tableau did not appear in the florist's dreams.

Around six thirty one Thursday evening, Jimmy Boyle knocked on the back door of Roy's house. The boys usually came and went through the rear entrances of each other's houses, preferring to use the Chicago alleys as their thoroughfares. It was well after dark when Roy let Jimmy in out of a freezing drizzle.

"You won't believe what I just seen," said Jimmy.

"What?" asked Roy.

"Let's go in your room and I'll tell you."

Roy and Jimmy went into Roy's room. Roy closed the door. He and Jimmy Boyle had known each other for five and a half years, since they were seven. Both of them were the only sons in their families and both of their fathers were dead. Jimmy had two sisters,

Roy had one. The fact that each of them were fatherless created an unspoken bond, and usually when one or the other had something important to tell, Jimmy went first to Roy and Roy to Jimmy.

Jimmy Boyle had orange hair, green eyes and a face full of freckles. "As Irish-looking a kid as there ever was," said Roy's mother. Jimmy was most often half-grinning but he was not grinning now: he looked scared, his eyes were wide open and his shoulders and arms were shaking.

"What happened?" Roy asked.

"Cubar's dead," said Jimmy. "At least I think he is. I come back from deliverin' roses to Mrs. Anderson on Maplewood, it's her and Mr. Anderson's anniversary today, and I seen the back room door at the shop was open about half way. I didn't say nothin' 'cause I thought maybe Cubar had a broad in there, so I hung out up front until after six, which is when I'm supposed to leave."

"You hear anything?"

Jimmy shook his head. "Nothin'. Finally I called for him. 'Hey, Cubar,' I said, 'you back there? I gotta go now.' He didn't answer so I went back and stood by the door and said, 'Cubar, it's Jimmy,' but he still didn't say nothin'. Then I figured maybe he went out before I come back, though that ain't never happened without him leavin' a note on the front counter or taped to the front door.

"I pushed the door to the back room open all the way and at first I didn't see him. His body, I mean. I almost left but then I went into the room. You know there ain't much in there, just a cot with a blanket and a pillow on it and a mirror and a crucifix on the wall facin' the bed. Cubar was lyin' face down on the floor at the foot of it with a big scissors stickin' in his neck."

"Was there a lot of blood?" Roy asked.

"Not really," said Jimmy. "Some, but not much. He didn't have his pants on, or underwear, neither. Cubar's got lots of fuzz on his ass."

"He must be dead," said Roy, "if he wasn't movin'."

"Yeah, I guess," said Jimmy. "I said, 'Cubar, are you alive?' But he didn't talk or move."

"You better go back and call the cops. Don't tell 'em you left the body alone."

Jimmy nodded. "My old man told me when I was eight not to ever call the cops."

"But Cubar's dead," said Roy.

"My old man said not to call the cops especially if someone was dead."

The boys sat on Roy's bed for a few minutes without talking.

When Jimmy stood up he said, "You know about Cubar's brother, the one wild dogs ate back in Albania?"

"Yeah, he told me and the Viper the story," Roy said.

"I figured," said Jimmy.

"Why?" Roy asked.

"Just thinkin' how Cubar and his brother both met violent ends."

"On different continents," said Roy.

"Right," said Jimmy, "on different continents."

Roy let Jimmy out the back door. It was still drizzling outside and there was no moon. Cubar must not have seen the woman coming up behind him, Roy thought, otherwise he probably could have wrestled the scissors away from her.

The Weeper

"You seen the Weeper around lately?" Roy asked Jimmy Boyle.

"I ain't," said Jimmy, "not for a couple months, maybe. You think somethin's happened to him?"

The two boys, both of whom were ten years old, kicked their way through the slush on Ojibway Boulevard. They were headed for the Pharaoh Theater to see a double feature of *Phantom from Chinatown* and *Nothing Left for the Dead*. It was a freezing cold Saturday morning in late January, and the boys walked quickly, looking forward to being inside the warm theater just as it opened.

The Weeper was a red-bearded bum who supposedly slept in a garage behind an abandoned building in the short alley between Bulgaria and Pasztory streets. Goat Murphy lived near there and said he'd seen him coming out of the garage a few times when Goat was on his way to school.

"We should ask Goat Murphy," said Jimmy.

"I did," said Roy, "and he hasn't seen him since before Christmas."

"Maybe he's at a hobo convention in Florida."

"Let's go by after the show," Roy said, "and see if we can find his garage."

Roy thought *Phantom from Chinatown* was dumb, with a fake-looking ghost going around strangling guys who resembled the man who'd murdered his wife; but *Nothing Left for the Dead* was pretty good, especially the part where the beautiful brunette in a tight white sweater who's the leader of a graverobbing gang begs her boyfriend to make love to her on top of an unearthed coffin in a cemetery. "Kiss me fast, Steve," she says to him, "remind me that I'm still alive."

It was still light out when Roy and Jimmy found the alley. The wind was blowing hard and an intermittent sleet bit at the backs of their necks.

"God, I hate this weather," said Jimmy Boyle. "When I get older I'm ditchin' Chicago and movin' to San Francisco."

"Why there?" asked Roy. "I think it gets cold and foggy in San Francisco."

"Yeah, a little," Jimmy said, "but not too bad. My Uncle Johnny lives there and he says it don't ever snow."

"What does he do there?"

"He's a bartender. Uncle Johnny's from County Cork, he says there's lots of Irish in San Francisco, like here. He used to be in the Merchant Marines."

The boys looked for doors that had broken or boarded-up windows in them. Roy found one that was more dilapidated than most and had cardboard wedged in several cracked or missing panes.

"Hey, Jimmy," he said, "let's try this one."

Jimmy came over and together they pulled on the door. The top hinge was gone so they had to pull hard to pry the door open against the snow packed in front of it. The garage was empty except for a pile of torn, dirty blankets and scattered trash.

"Look here," said Roy.

Hanging from a long nail in a board under a side window was a piece of paper on which were hand-printed the words: Gone for the Kilyazum if you make it away from the Dogs Sorcerers Hormongers Murderers Idolytors and Liars we shall meet again and Know the Reasons Why.

"Think the Weeper wrote this?" Jimmy said.

"He must have," said Roy. "He was always talkin' about how he wept every day for all the people who suffer in this life. That's why he's called the Weeper. But what's Kilyazum?"

"Father Jerry talked about it in Sunday school," said Jimmy. "I think it's when Christ returns and reigns in heaven with all the good people, even ones who already died, for a thousand years."

"What happens to the bad people?"

"The devil forces 'em to keep doin' bad things on earth."

"But if everyone who's good goes to heaven," said Roy, "that means they must be dead."

"I guess so," said Jimmy Boyle. "You think it's better to be dead than alive?"

Roy thought about the woman in the movie pulling her boyfriend down on her in the cemetery.

"No," he said, "I don't."

The Swedish Bakery

Martin Kenna was in a bad spot. The Lingenbergs had been good to him but he knew if he didn't do what his older brother, Brendan, wanted him to do, which was to leave the back door to the bakery unlocked when he left on Thursday night, Brendan and his friend Double Trouble would beat the daylights out of him. Bren would probably only cuff him around a little, but DT, Martin knew, would make him hurt. Once DT had it in his criminal mind to do something there was nothing Bren could do to stop him, even when it came to kicking the crap out of his would-be accomplice's little brother.

Martin had to talk to someone about his predicament, so he decided for the first time in his barely thirteen-year-old life to ask Father Ralph for advice. On his way to St. Rose of Lima, Martin Kenna ran into the Viper.

"Hey, Kenna, where you goin'?"

A cold drizzle began so Martin put up the hood of his blue parka. The Viper was hatless. His stringy black hair and glasses were getting wet, but the Viper didn't seem to mind.

"Nowhere special. Gotta see someone."

"A bunch of us is gonna play football at the empty lot on Ojibway. You want to come?"

"Maybe after. It's gonna be muddy."

The Viper grinned, revealing big green front teeth, and punched Martin Kenna lightly on his right shoulder.

"You can cut better in the mud," said the Viper, "make tacklers miss."

At St. Rose of Lima, Kenna entered the church and saw Father Ralph checking the rows, making sure the benches were clean. Martin walked down the aisle to the end of the row Father Ralph was inspecting and stood there.

"Hello, Martin," said the priest, "what are you doing here at this hour?"

"I wanted to talk to you about somethin', Father."

Father Ralph stood in front of the boy and studied his face.

"You can put your hood down, Martin, the roof doesn't leak."

Kenna shook off the hood. Father Ralph was five foot four, about a half-inch taller than Martin. His dark brown hair was thinning rapidly. Mrs. Kenna swore that Father Ralph used Sultan of Africa shoe polish to cover his bald spot; she said she could smell it when she stood next to him.

"What can I help you with, Martin?"

"It's Bren, Father, my brother. He wants me to do somethin' I don't feel right about doin'."

"Sit down," said Father Ralph.

Both the priest and the boy sat down on the nearest bench. Father Ralph had one blue eye and one green eye. Martin looked mostly into the green one.

"Now, tell me, what is it Brendan wants you to do?"

"You know, Father, I work four days a week after school at the Swedish bakery on Belmont and Broadway."

"Lingenberg's, I know. Your mother told me. Go on."

"Well, it's this way, Father. Bren hangs around with this older guy, DT—Double Trouble—his last name is Korzienowski, I don't know his Christian name."

"A Polish boy."

"Yeah, I guess. Anyway, he talked my brother into helpin' him rob the bakery. They want me to leave the back door unlocked next Thursday night so they can boost the receipts which Babe Lingenberg don't deposit in the bank until Friday mornin'."

"How do they know this, Martin? That the receipts will be there overnight."

Kenna unzipped his coat, then zipped it up again. "I told 'em,

I guess."

"And do they know where the receipts are kept?"

Kenna nodded. "In a desk drawer that's locked, but it'd be real easy to bust open."

"And you also told them where this desk is, did you?"

"Yes, Father."

"Why did you provide them with this information, Martin?"

Martin Kenna looked away from Father Ralph's green eye and down at the floor.

"I don't know," he said.

"Was the robbery Brendan's idea or the Polish boy's?"

Martin looked up again.

"DT put Bren up to it, Father, I'm positive. DT says he's from a real poor family and the Lingenbergs are rich, so they won't miss the money."

"As Jesus said, the poor will always be with us, but I am here now," said Father Ralph.

"Father, if I don't leave the door unlocked, Bren and DT'll beat me up. What should I do?"

"They won't lay a hand on you, Martin, don't worry."

"How can you be sure, Father?"

"Like Jesus, I am here now. I'll have a talk with your brother, and perhaps I'll have an opportunity to discuss the situation with this Polish boy. What did you say his name is? His real name."

"Korzienowski."

"Korzienowski, okay." Father Ralph stood up. "You go on now."

Martin Kenna stood up, said, "Thank you, Father," and turned to leave.

"Oh, Martin."

Kenna stopped and looked back at Father Ralph.

"You won't forget to lock the back door of the bakery, will you?"

"No, Father, I won't."

Later that afternoon, Martin Kenna saw his brother and DT

standing on the corner of Cristiana and Nottingham, smoking cigarettes. The drizzle had turned icy but neither Brendan nor DT had coats on. Both of them were wearing red and black checked flannel shirts, blue jeans with the cuffs rolled up twice and scuffed black Chippewa motorcycle boots. Martin was across the street, they didn't see him, so he kept going.

Years later, when Martin heard the news that Brendan had been killed in a knife fight in prison, he remembered seeing his brother and Double Trouble Korzienowski standing coatless in the icy rain. Martin didn't know what happened to DT or what Father Ralph had said to him and Brendan about their plan to rob the Swedish bakery so that neither of them mentioned it to Martin again. It had always bothered Martin Kenna, however, that he had told Father Ralph about it, that by doing so he had betrayed Brendan. Martin knew it was foolish, even absurd to feel guilty about this, but still he often wished he had not asked the priest to intervene. It might have served him better to have just taken the beating. Now his brother was dead and so, perhaps, was Father Ralph. It's not only the poor who will always be with us, thought Martin.

The Man Who Swallowed the World

Sid Roman, Roy's mother's first cousin, was a kind, handsome, intelligent man who dropped his marbles at the age of forty-six. Cousin Sid, as Roy and his mother and her brother, Buck, always referred to him, worked for many years as a clothing salesman, specializing in men's suits, at one of Chicago's most exclusive and expensive haberdasheries. This mode of employment lasted, as Roy's mother phrased it, "until Cousin Sid lost his looks."

Actually, Cousin Sid's loss of his looks coincided with the loss of his mind. One day Sid could not find the silver cigarette lighter with his initials inscribed on it, a gift from his wife, Norma, for his fortieth birthday, and he decided that he had swallowed it. Cousin Norma was an equally kind, intelligent woman, who was "high strung" (again, Roy's mother's words), with a history of nervous breakdowns. Cousin Norma, an unhealthily thin woman with stringy red hair, who chain-smoked unfiltered Chesterfields, told her husband that he must simply have misplaced the lighter.

"Look in the pockets of your charcoal suit jacket," she told Sid. "It's in the pile to go to the dry cleaners."

"I already did," he answered, and pointed to his neck. "Look at my throat. There's where my lighter is, I can feel it."

"That's your Adam's apple," said his wife.

"I'm going to the emergency room," said Cousin Sid, "to have it removed."

He walked out of the house and did not return until six months later, when he was released from the psychiatric ward at Pafko Hospital.

After this, Cousin Sid behaved normally for a while; although, as Roy's mother observed, his looks were gone. Before his breakdown, he had resembled the actor William Powell, except for his hair, which Sid wore slicked back in the style of the day, and was silver and thicker than Powell's. During his residence at Pafko Hospital, however, Cousin Sid's teeth went bad, resulting in his having quite a large number of them removed. This gave him the appearance of his cheeks having caved in. Also, his color had changed: no longer glowing and golden, his face was now bloodlessly pale, bordering on unearthly. His mustache was gone, too, exposing a wrinkled and shrunken or shriveled upper lip that no longer covered completely his front teeth, of which one was missing. For some reason, he could not grow his mustache back, freezing his mouth in an expression somewhere between a sneer and a contemptuous grin.

Cousin Sid lost his job at the clothing store. Norma supported them and their fifteen-year-old son, Larry, who was disabled by polio and confined to a wheelchair, by working as a secretary for a law firm. It was months before Sid found work at a discount shoe store on the south side of the city. The job required that he travel almost two hours on the elevated and two buses each way.

Four weeks after her husband began selling shoes, Norma received a call at the law office from the police informing her that Sid was in their custody at the Cottage Grove precinct. Sid had told a bus driver that he'd swallowed his transfer. When the driver ordered Sid to pay an additional fare, Sid refused, insisting that he was in possession of the transfer, it was in his stomach, and that he had also swallowed all of the money he'd had in his pockets so that it could not be stolen. The driver told him to get off the bus, but Sid took a seat and would not get up. The driver then radioed for the police, who came and removed him forcefully. Following this incident, Cousin Sid became convinced that he had swallowed everything from kitchen utensils to clocks, and Norma had him committed to an asylum in Indiana run by a nondenominational organization called Angels of Victims of Unfathomable Behavior.

Roy was nine when he accompanied his mother, Uncle Buck

and Cousin Norma to visit Cousin Sid in Indiana. It was a sunny, early October day, and Roy enjoyed riding in the backseat of his uncle's 1955 Cadillac Coupe Deville as they cruised through the Indiana dunes. Roy wondered how different they could be from the deserts of Egypt or Arabia, and imagined himself mounted on a camel among Bedouin tribesmen, his face shielded from blowing sand and intense sun by robes and gauzy scarves.

At the asylum, which was a huge black-and-gray stone building in the middle of nowhere that looked to him as if it should have been surrounded by a moat infested with crocodiles, Roy was made to sit alone in a waiting room while the others were taken by a woman wearing a gray nun's habit to see Cousin Sid. There was only one high window in the waiting room which admitted a narrow shaft of sunlight. It would be difficult to escape from this room, Roy thought, if the door were locked, especially because the six metal chairs were bolted to the floor and would have to be pried loose before they could be stacked high enough to reach the window. Roy remained there for an hour and was beginning to feel like the *Count of Monte Cristo* imprisoned in the Chateau d'If before the door opened and his Uncle Buck said, "Let's go, champ."

Seeing that his uncle was by himself, Roy asked, "Where are my mother and Cousin Norma?"

"Norma's pretty upset," said Buck. "Your mother is with her, taking a walk around the grounds."

Roy followed his uncle outside and they stood next to the Cadillac. Buck removed a cigar from an inside pocket of his navy blue sportcoat, bit off one end and felt in his other pockets for a book of matches.

"How's Cousin Sid?"

Buck located his matches and lit the cigar.

"He thinks he's swallowed everything he can't see."

"What do you mean everything? You mean including the Pacific Ocean and the Empire State Building?"

Buck took a few puffs. The smoke quickly disappeared into the crisp air.

"I suppose so," he said. "Whatever can't fit into his little room. I'm afraid it's the end of the world for Cousin Sid."

"He swallowed it," said Roy.

"What?"

"The world. He's got it all inside him."

Roy's mother and Cousin Norma came around the corner of the big, ugly building and walked slowly over to them. Cousin Norma was crying, a cigarette dangling from the left corner of her mouth. Her lips looked like two long, crimson scratches. Roy's mother was holding Cousin Norma's right elbow. They all got into the car and nobody spoke until after Buck had been driving for fifteen minutes.

"I envy Sid," said Cousin Norma. "He doesn't have to think anymore."

"The sisters will take care of him," said Roy's mother; then she added, "I mean, the Angels."

"What's unfathomable behavior mean?" asked Roy.

"It's when somebody behaves in a way nobody else can understand," said his uncle.

Cousin Norma, who was sitting in the backseat with Roy, lit a fresh Chesterfield off a half-inch butt, which she then tossed out the window on her side. Her fingers were stained and wrinkled like a weathered, well-oiled baseball glove.

"Kitty," she said to Roy's mother, "I remember when I was about Roy's age, maybe a year younger, and my aunt gave me a beautiful girl doll for my birthday. I looked at it and then handed it back to her. My mother said, 'You can't do that, Norma. Take the doll and say thank you to Aunt Rose.' I ran away and locked myself in my room. I couldn't keep that doll, she was too beautiful and I was too ugly. I didn't want to have her around to haunt me, to constantly remind me of how I looked compared to her. I remember how I felt that day. It's the same way I feel now."

Roy stared out the window on his side at the sand dunes. He wanted to tell Cousin Norma the same thing he'd said to his uncle, that he thought Cousin Sid's world was inside him now, but he kept looking out the window and thought about the Arabs.

Ghost Ship

Roy sometimes cut through Rosedale Cemetery on his way to play ball at Winnebago Park. Jews were not allowed to be buried at Rosedale, so Roy thought it interesting that next to the cemetery, on its western boundary, was the Zion National Home, a residential institution for elderly Jews.

One summer's morning, Roy was cutting across Rosedale when he saw an old woman walking with a cane along the same path ahead of him. As he approached her, the woman suddenly stumbled and fell. Roy ran up to her and took hold of one of her arms.

"Are you all right?" he asked.

The woman was wearing a pink housecoat buttoned up to her neck and fuzzy purple slippers. She wore thick glasses that magnified her hazel eyes.

"I'll survive," she said, "at least for a little longer. I'm used to this, unfortunately. When you get to be my age—I'm eighty-eight—you never know if your next step will be your last."

Roy helped the woman to her feet, then picked up the cane and handed it to her. She looked at Roy and smiled. A few of her teeth were missing.

"How old are you, son?" she asked.

"Eleven," said Roy.

"That's the age my granddaughter, Esther, was when we left Hamburg on the *Caribia*, bound for Cuba. This was in 1938. What year were you born?"

"Nineteen forty-six."

"Esther would have been thirty now, had she survived."

"What happened to her?"

"The Cuban government wouldn't allow the *Caribia* to dock because most of its passengers were Jewish. We were fleeing

Hitler's Germany. Esther caught the typhoid fever and she died on board. We were forced to bury her at sea. The *Caribia* truly became a ghost ship after that. Esther's ghost was with us as we sailed back and forth across the Atlantic Ocean in search of a safe harbor."

"Why didn't the Cubans want the Jews?"

"They were afraid if they took us, more Jews would come expecting to be taken in, too. This happened in many places, in many countries, on five continents."

"How long were you on that ship?"

"Four or five months, I think. Finally, we were granted permission to disembark at Baltimore, Maryland. All of the passengers were housed in the same buildings slaves were kept in after they were brought there from Africa. My daughter, Rebecca, Esther's mother, and I waited in those slave quarters for weeks—I can't recall now how many—until we were taken by train to New York City and deposited at the Jewish Orphans and Immigrants Home."

"Do you live at Zion National?" Roy asked.

"Yes, barely, as you can see."

"No Jews are allowed to be buried here at Rosedale. Did you know that?"

The old lady smiled again and said, "Even after death there are places Jews are forbidden to go."

She coughed a few times, very deeply, making a sound so loud it frightened Roy a little.

"Zion stretches out her hands," the woman said, "but there is none to comfort her; the Lord has commanded against Jacob that his neighbors should be his foes; Jerusalem has become a filthy thing among them."

"What's that?" said Roy.

"One of the lamentations of Jeremiah."

"Is it from the Bible?"

"Yes. The only words worth repeating are from the Old Testament or Oscar Wilde."

The woman coughed again and shuddered.

"I have to be getting back now," she said.

Roy accompanied her to the entrance of the Zion National Home and held her left elbow as she walked up the two front steps and went inside. He decided to walk all the way around Rosedale to get to Winnebago Park, even though he knew that would make him late for the game. On the way there he imagined the little girl's ghost roaming the decks of the *Caribia* as it sailed without a destination. The girl's name was Esther, Roy remembered. She was the only person he knew of who had been buried at sea.

Caca Negra

"You know Rubio, worked at Al's Auto Parts?"

"Wears thick glasses and sort of snorts after finishing a sentence?"

Bobby Kabir nodded. "Right," he said.

"What about him?" asked Roy.

"Was sent up on a fake counterfeit scam. Got seven years."

"Who told you?"

"My Aunt Nardis. She plays canasta with Rubio's old lady."

Roy and Bobby Kabir were standing and leaning against the north wall of the school building to stay out of the wind, waiting for the afternoon bell to ring. It was a drizzly, dark November day. Nobody was playing ball. Bobby Kabir was smoking a Kool, concealing it in his cupped right hand between puffs so the playground monitor wouldn't see it and report him. Kabir was almost fourteen, a year and a half older than Roy, but they were both in the eighth grade. Bobby was tall and thin, with a light brown pockmarked face. He had moved to Chicago from Detroit over the summer with his mother. They lived with her sister in an apartment above Victory Cleaners on Chippewa Street. Bobby had been set back a year in school, he said, because of his having been expelled from the one he went to in Detroit, for hitting a teacher.

"I didn't really hit him," Kabir told Roy and his friends, "just kind of threw him down when he put his hands on me. I don't like people puttin' their hands on me."

Jimmy Boyle asked Kabir why the teacher grabbed him, and Bobby said, "He thought I was botherin' a girl in the hallway and I told him to mind his own business. He got a little cut on his head when he bumped into a locker, then made a big deal out of it. After I got thrown out I didn't transfer to another school like I was supposed to. I got a job as a helper, deliverin' ice. Then we moved here."

"What kind of scam was Rubio in on?" Roy asked.

"Caca negra. Black money."

"What's that?"

"Sheets of uncut bills supposedly stolen from the government. They're covered with black ink because of bein' taken out of circulation. The ink's removable by a chemical. Problem was, Rubio's paper was phony. He got caught tryin' to sell it to an undercover cop."

"He looked dumb," said Roy. "I only know who he is 'cause the Viper used to work Saturdays in the stock room at Al's. I saw him when I went by there to meet Vipe after he got off."

About a week after Roy and Bobby Kabir had this conversation about Rubio being busted, Bobby was arrested during a break-in at Al's Auto Parts and charged with attempted burglary. Arrested with him was a thirty-five-year-old black Puerto Rican guy named Diezmo Blanks. Diezmo Blanks worked at the store for a year but had been fired for molesting a customer, a woman who had come in to buy a leather steering wheel cover. Blanks had apparently offered to put it on for the woman, who declined politely, saying her husband would do it. Diezmo Blanks followed her out to her car and tried to kiss her. She complained to Al and he fired Blanks on the spot, gave her money back and told her to keep the steering wheel cover. How Bobby Kabir had gotten mixed up with Diezmo Blanks, Roy didn't know, nor did any of his friends.

"You liked Kabir," Jimmy Boyle said to Roy. "You surprised he'd do somethin' like that?"

"I didn't know him so good," said Roy. "Just talked to him around school. He's only lived here a few months."

"I seen him once with his mother," the Viper said. "They were goin' in the door next to Victory Cleaners."

"He told me they lived over it with his aunt," said Roy. "I never met her or his mother."

"Kabir's mother's real tall," said the Viper. "She was dressed all in black and had a scarf around her head. I couldn't hardly see her face."

It was a Friday after school and Jimmy Boyle, the Viper and Roy were walking to Lucky's El Paso to shoot pool. Roy did not know exactly why, but he felt sorry for Bobby Kabir. An icy rain started to fall. Roy stopped on the sidewalk.

"I'm goin' home," he said. "I don't feel good. See you guys tomorrow."

Roy turned around and headed the other way. He knew he couldn't do anything to help Bobby Kabir, nor was there any reason he should. Kabir wasn't really even a friend of his. Roy walked faster. His head was already wet.

Since Bobby Kabir was a minor, he was sentenced to the Boys Reformatory at St. Charles for a year. Roy never saw him again. He figured Kabir's mother must have moved away because nobody he knew ever saw her again, either.

Diezmo Blanks, however, turned up in the news about three years later. He and a fellow inmate named Marvellis Nubarrón escaped from prison and murdered a gas station attendant in Johnson City, Illinois. They stole his car, a parakeet yellow 1961 Pontiac Bonneville, and drove to Wyoming, where they were apparently forced off the road during a blizzard. Highway patrolmen found Diezmo Blanks and his partner dead from exposure in a snowdrift next to Route 80, sixteen miles outside of Laramie. They had abandoned the Pontiac and attempted to walk into town during the storm. Photographs of Blanks and Nubarron were in the newspaper. The article said that Diezmo Blanks was a three-time loser who had been convicted once for indecent behavior with a child and twice for armed robbery. Bobby Kabir's name was not mentioned.

Victory Cleaners was sold and renamed for its new owner, Jet Wing. Roy's mother began bringing her dry cleaning there, and whenever Roy walked over to Chippewa Street to pick it up for her he couldn't help but think about Bobby Kabir. One time he asked Jet Wing if an older woman named Nardis still lived upstairs.

"Wing family live up," he said. "No Nardis."

Roy's First Car

"She's gone, she's solid gone, that's what the guy said just before he knocked back a shot of Wild Turkey and walked out of The Four Horsemen into the damn blizzard and got hit by a bus."

"That's how it goes sometimes," said Heavenly Wurtzel, a waitress at The Broken Arrow. "My dad says once your name's up there on that wall, that's it, game over."

Roy and Marvin Varnish were in a booth at the diner drinking Green Rivers. Marvin, a diesel mechanic for the Chicago Fire Department, was six years older than Roy, who was almost sixteen. Roy had met Marvin, who was a friend of Roy's cousin, Kip, to talk about getting a car from him. Varnish's side job was buying old cars that didn't or couldn't run, fixing them up and selling them. He had a 1955 Buick Century with Dyna-flo about ready to go, he told Roy, that he could let Roy have for three hundred dollars.

"Who's your dad say puts the names up on that wall?" Marvin Varnish asked the waitress.

Heavenly Wurtzel was twenty-six, a peroxide blonde, decidedly on the portly side. She still lived with her parents. Her father, Barney Wurtzel, owned a plumbing company that he advertised on the radio during White Sox games. Between innings a woman's voice promised, "Nobody lays pipe like Wurtzel." Heavenly told Marvin Varnish that her mother told her father that this sounded dirty and Barney Wurtzel said, "Plumbing's a dirty business, Ruth."

"God, I guess," Heavenly said.

"And where's this wall?" asked Roy. "I'd like to see it to know if my name or the name of anyone I know is on it."

"Bethlehem, probably," said Heavenly. "Jerusalem, maybe. Around where the Garden of Eden was."

Marvin studied Heavenly as she walked away.

"She wouldn't be too bad lookin'," he said, "she cut down on the sweets. Some men like 'em big, though. Eugene Kornheiser was that way. He worked hook and ladder out of Station Fifteen 'til he fell off a building and broke his back."

"Why do you think Heavenly's not married yet?" Roy asked.

"She had a kid when she was seventeen, gave it away. Pinky French told me."

"So? What's that got to do with somebody marryin' her now?"

Marvin shrugged and drained the remainder of his Green River through the straw.

"Guys find out about her havin' a kid already, it bugs 'em," he said. "They want a clean slate. Heavenly'd be better off movin' away, snaggin' a guy in another city won't find out so easy."

Roy walked with Marvin Varnish over to the firehouse to take a look at the Buick, which was parked in the alley behind the station. Snow was piled up a foot deep around it. The car was burgundy with dark green upholstery. Roy looked in the front passenger side window.

"The seats are pretty ripped up," he said.

"I'll throw in a roll of tape," said Marvin. "It's got Dyna-flo, like I said. You know what that is?"

"No."

"You turn the key in the ignition, then step on the starter button before you step on the accelerator pedal, then you goose it. Everything works. You smoke?"

"Uh-uh."

"Good, 'cause the lighter don't work."

Roy agreed to buy the car as soon as he turned sixteen and could get a driver's license.

"When's your birthday?" asked Marvin.

"Next month. I've got the money," Roy said. "I've been savin' up. Do you want me to give you somethin' now?"

Marvin shook his head. "It's okay, I trust you. I won't sell it to nobody else."

It was snowing like crazy as Roy trudged down Minnetonka Street. A red panel truck was parked in front of The Broken Arrow, its motor running. Roy saw Heavenly Wurtzel come running out of the diner, a black scarf covering her head, and climb into the truck on the passenger side. A big man smoking a cigar was in the driver's seat. Painted on the side of the truck in yellow block letters were the words NOBODY LAYS PIPE LIKE WURTZEL. Under the words was a telephone number, SOUTH SHORE 6-6000. The driver rolled down his window and stuck out his head to see if it was safe to pull out. He was wearing a short-brimmed brown hunter's cap with earflaps. A hard wind blew snow in his face, causing him to squint. He kept the cigar clenched in his teeth. Roy guessed that the driver was Barney Wurtzel.

Heavenly was only twenty-six, but unless she got out of town soon, like Marvin Varnish said, her life was pretty much over. Roy hated thinking this, so he did his best to imagine himself behind the steering wheel of the '55 Buick Century. Then he remembered Marvin's story about a guy stumbling out of The Four Horsemen tavern into the path of a bus. It was probably better, Roy thought, to not know if your name is on the wall.

El Carterista

When Roy was fifteen, he worked for the summer at WTVT, a television station in Tampa, Florida, assisting in-studio hosts of the morning and evening movies, and occasionally reporters or film crews in the field.

One morning, Roy was assigned to a freelance photographer named Ernie Walls, a man in his late forties or early fifties, whose claim to fame, the station manager told Roy, was that while working for *Life* magazine he had spent several weeks with Fidel Castro and his rebel army in the Sierra Maestra in Cuba before the ouster of Fulgencio Batista.

Ernie Walls was hired to direct filming of the groundbreaking ceremony for the University of South Florida. Roy rode with the photographer in Walls's 1959 Lincoln Continental convertible from the television station to the ceremonial site in North Tampa. They were followed by a WTVT van carrying remote equipment and the camera crew.

On the way, Ernie Walls regaled Roy with tales of his adventures taking pictures around the world, the highlight being his sojourn with the 26th of July Movement in Cuba.

"You don't mind riding with the top down, do you, son?" Ernie Walls asked. "I like to feel the breeze blowing through my hair, what little I've got left."

"No, sir, Mr. Walls," said Roy. "I like it, too."

"Call me Ernie."

The photographer was five foot eight, portly, pink-faced, with thinning red hair and bloodshot eyes. As he drove he removed from the left hip pocket of his dirty tan sportcoat a silver flask. He unscrewed the cap and took a long swig.

"Hope you don't mind my having breakfast while I tool along," said Ernie. "A screwdriver's the healthiest way to start the day. I'll pick up some orange juice later, I get the chance. Until then, the vodka will have to do."

It was shortly after 10:00 a.m. when Roy and Ernie Walls left the station. The photographer pulled steadily on his flask during the twenty-five minute trip. When he wasn't sipping, he talked.

"Castro wasn't a commie when I was with him. I think he figured he could cut a deal with the Mob. Made a mistake there. Batista was their boy, they could control him. Fidel was a wild card and the Mob only plays with a marked deck. Both the Mob and the United States government knew Castro couldn't be trusted, but he wasn't a hater. Che, though, now he's a hater. He could, he'd execute Kennedy and everyone in Washington. You watch, there'll come a time Fidel will have to get rid of him."

"Did you meet Che?" asked Roy. Ernie Walls sucked again on his flask before he answered.

"Slept in the same tent with him once. Man stinks. Doesn't bathe. Smokes cigars or a pipe to cover his fox. Always reading: Goethe, Nietzsche, Marx."

"Who are they?"

"German writers. You ever see that movie *The Stranger*, where Orson Welles plays a Nazi on the run after the war?"

"No."

"He's hiding in Connecticut, about to marry a professor's daughter, played by Loretta Young, and at dinner one evening someone mentions Karl Marx's name in company with other German thinkers and Welles says, 'But Marx wasn't a German, he was a Jew.' That's what tips off Edward G. Robinson, who plays a Nazi hunter, that Welles is the man he's after."

The shoot at the groundbreaking took about an hour, after which Ernie Walls invited Roy, who had done nothing more for the photographer than hold his camera case while he shot stills, to have lunch with him. Walls drove to Ybor City and parked his Continental in front of Las Novedades.

"They mix an honest drink here," he said, "and the food's good."

"I've been here a couple of times," said Roy, "with my uncle."

Ernie Walls and Roy got out of the car. Ernie took a cigar from an inside pocket of his coat, bit off one end, spit out the leaves and rested his small right hand on Roy's left shoulder.

"We'll order you up some pollo asado, son," he said. "Or do you prefer lechon? With black beans and yellow rice."

"I like them both," said Roy.

In the restaurant, Ernie Walls ordered two vodka martinis for himself. Roy ordered a Cuban sandwich and a Coke.

"That all you want?"

"I'm not real hungry," Roy said.

Ernie lit his cigar and puffed life into it.

"There was an Americano with the Escambray Brigade. William Morgan. Che never liked him. He poisoned Fidel against Morgan, said he was a CIA infiltrator, and they put him in front of a firing squad."

"Was Morgan working for the CIA?" Roy asked.

"No. He just didn't agree with Che, and Che hates Americans. There was some chatter about how Morgan cuddled up with Trujillo after Batista skipped to the DR, but nothing they could prove."

"Did Che hate you?"

"I'm sure he did, but at that point Castro needed all the good publicity he could get, so he kept Che in check. A reporter from the *New York Times* was there, too."

The martinis arrived. Ernie Walls immediately lifted one, said, "Death to all tyrants!" and drank it. He put down the empty glass and lifted the other.

"Death to all tyrants!" he said, and polished off the second martini.

"Know what Che called me?" he asked.

"What?"

"El Carterista, the pickpocket."

"Why?"

"He said I was stealing images from them with the camera, taking something that didn't belong to me. Curtis said some plains Indians said the same thing."

"Why didn't he call you El Ladrón?"

Ernie looked at Roy and smiled.

"You speak Spanish?"

"Un poquito," said Roy.

The waiter brought Roy's Cuban sandwich and a Coca-Cola.

"Two more of these, por favor," the photographer said, motioning to the two empty martini glasses.

The waiter took them away. Ernie Walls puffed on his cigar. Roy bit into his sandwich.

"They were special days," said Walls, "up there in the mountains with those brave, desperate men. I can honestly say I've been a witness to history."

The waiter returned with two more martinis and set them down on the table. Ernie stared at the twin glasses for a few moments before picking up the one closest to him.

"Lift your glass," he said to Roy.

Roy raised his Coke and said, "Death to all tyrants!"

Ernie Walls nodded. His nose resembled a red ping-pong ball.

"Where would we little people be without them?" he said.

Crime and Punishment

Roy and Jimmy Boyle had just reached the landing of the staircase leading to the second floor of the school when the Viper, who was coming down the stairs, stopped them and said, "You hear about the guy went to the gas chamber at midnight last night in San Quentin? They killed him even though he didn't murder anybody."

"I thought they couldn't do that," said Jimmy. "I thought only killers got executed."

"Maybe he had a bad lawyer," said Roy.

He and Jimmy Boyle were twelve years old, the Viper was thirteen. The Viper's uncle, Charlie Ah Ah, his mother's brother, was doing seven years at Joliet for armed robbery, so the Viper kept up on prison news. His uncle stuttered badly, so he was called Charlie Ah Ah because he always said "Ah, ah" before he could get a whole word out.

"The Red Light Bandit," said the Viper. "He raped and robbed people parked on lovers' lanes. The newspapers named him the Red Light Bandit because he pretended to be a cop by using a revolving red light on his car."

"When you're in the gas chamber you're supposed to take a deep breath right away so you pass out and don't suffer so much," Jimmy said to Roy as they continued up the stairs.

"Probably the gas chamber is a better way to go than the electric chair," said Roy. "I heard on the news once about how a guy's hair caught on fire when he got a jolt."

That evening, Roy's grandfather was reading the newspaper and Roy asked him if there was anything in it about the execution at San Quentin.

"Yes," said Pops, "the man they killed was actually quite bright.

He wrote two books while he was in prison appealing his sentence."

"Jimmy Boyle said he thought only murderers could be executed. Charlie Ah Ah's nephew told us this guy just raped and robbed."

"It depends on the law in the state in which a crime is committed," said Pops. "This case was in California. The law is different there than it is here in Illinois."

"Do you think a person should be executed even if he hasn't killed anybody?"

"Many people believe there should be no capital punishment no matter what crime has been committed, even murder. I believe there are some crimes so unforgivable that the world is undoubtedly better off if the person or persons who committed them will never again be able to repeat them, and there is, of course, only one way to be certain of that. It isn't just that they should be eliminated for what they've already done but what they may do in the future.

"In India, people believe that once a tiger has killed and eaten a human being, he develops a craving for human flesh and will then go after people almost exclusively. Usually it's older tigers who do this because they're too slow to chase down other animals."

"Like in the movie *Man-Eater of Kumaon,* with Sabu," said Roy.

"Just like those man-eating tigers," Pops said, "people can get used to doing things they've never done before, previously unimaginable things, even if those things are terrible and cause great suffering. They can get to like doing them."

It was drizzling the next morning in the schoolyard when Roy told Jimmy Boyle and the Viper what his grandfather had said.

"The Golden Rule is to do to others as they did to you," said Jimmy.

"Charlie Ah Ah says get the other guy before he gets you," said the Viper. "And James Cagney said, 'Get 'em in the eyes, get 'em right in the eyes.'"

"No," said Roy, "that was John Garfield in *Pride of the Marines*, after he gets blinded by the Japanese."

"Maybe Cagney'll play the Red Light Bandit," said Jimmy Boyle. "I'd go see that one."

"I don't think he will," said Roy. "Cagney went to the electric chair as Rocky Sullivan in *Angels with Dirty Faces*. I don't think he'd want to be executed twice."

"If I had to go," said the Viper, "and I could choose how, I'd ask for a firing squad. It'd be over quick and I could wear a blindfold."

"You get to choose in Utah," Roy said, "between a firing squad or a hanging."

The school bell rang. Rain started coming down a little harder but the boys were in no hurry to go inside. They stood and watched the other kids head for the doors. The Viper dug a butt out of one of his coat pockets and lit it.

"Hanging would take forever," said Jimmy Boyle.

"Probably not," said Roy.

The American Language

Djibouti "Jib" Bufera was one guy in the neighborhood of whom everyone was afraid. Roy was twelve when he first saw him, getting out of the driver's side of a black Cadillac in front of Phil and Leonard's restaurant on Bavaria Avenue. Jib was forty-four years old then, five foot eight-and-a-half, stocky, clean-shaven. He was wearing a black overcoat and a dark gray, medium brim Borsalino hat. Accompanying him was a shorter man about the same age who was very wide around the middle, had a mustache, also wearing a black overcoat but hatless, smoking a long, dark brown cigar. Bufera allowed this man to precede him into Phil and Leonard's. The Cadillac was parked in a space next to a sign marked Fire and Police Only.

"You see who that was?" said Chick Ceccarelli.

"Who?" said Roy. "Guys got out of the black Caddy?"

"Yeah. Jib Bufera and some goomba. Bufera's the guy tried to kill Castro."

The two boys were standing across the street from Phil and Leonard's. It was four o'clock on a Saturday in December and they were on their way home following a football game at Queen of All Saints, which boys from other schools called Queers of All Sorts.

"How do you know he tried to kill Castro?" Roy asked.

"My Uncle Paul, he's a federal judge. He told my dad the government gave the contract to The Outfit."

"Probably be impossible to get near Fidel in Havana."

"Uncle Paul says nothing's impossible, but Jib tried to hit him in New York, after he took control of Cuba and came to speak at the UN. Castro stayed at a hotel up in Harlem. There was always a big crowd outside and when he leaned out an open window to wave to people, Bufera took a crack at him with a rifle from a window in a building across the street. He missed and didn't get another shot."

Chick and Roy stood on the sidewalk with their hands in their coat pockets. The temperature was dropping as the sky faded from light gray to dark gray. Everyone in the neighborhood knew that Phil and Leonard's was where the wiseguys hung out. Most of the men who came in and out of there, or stood around in front when the weather was better, were friendly to the local kids, but not Jib Bufera. Roy heard that Jib's muscle shoved aside anyone who was in their path and that Jib never spoke to strangers.

"My dad says Uncle Paul told him Jib has trouble with the American language," said Chick.

"You mean he can't speak English?"

"He only talks Sicilian, keeps someone around to translate for him."

"How'd he get to be a U.S. citizen?"

"He ain't. A lot of them guys come over on a lost boat, like Lucky Luciano."

"I'm gettin' cold," said Roy.

A beat cop came around the corner by Phil and Leonard's and saw the black Cadillac parked there. Roy and Chick watched him give the car a once over, then glance at the entrance to the restaurant before walking on down Bavaria Avenue.

"Okay," said Chick, "let's go."

Roy only saw Jib Bufera once more. It was on a warm day about six months later. Jib was in the back seat of the black Cadillac, which was stopped for a red light at the corner of Sycamore and Racine. The window on Jib's side was down and he was blowing his nose into a white handkerchief. Roy stood on the corner waiting for the light to change so that he could cross. Just as it did, Jib Bufera threw the white handkerchief out the window and his car sped away. Roy stepped around it. When he got to the other side of the street, he looked back and watched a powder blue Impala run over the handkerchief.

When he was fifty-two, Jib Bufera was killed. An eighteen-wheeler rear-ended the car he was riding in and sent it over an embankment on Interstate 55 halfway between Chicago and St. Louis. At the time of his death, Bufera was fighting a deportation order. At his funeral, Jib's lawyer gave this statement to reporters: "Djibouti Bufera loved his adopted land and performed services on behalf of this country for which he should have been honored and decorated, instead of being deported. Despite the fact that he never did learn to speak our language, Jib was a great, if unofficial, citizen."

At the request of his mother, Jib Bufera's body was later disinterred from the Chicago cemetery in which he had been buried, and shipped to the little town in Sicily where he had been born and reburied there. Engraved on his tombstone, in English, were the words: He loved America more than she loved him.

Chick Ceccarelli died a month after Jib Bufera. He fell to his death from a balcony on the tenth floor of an apartment building on Marine Drive. According to his girlfriend, Loretta Vampa, who witnessed the accident, Chick was attempting to walk on top of the railing when he lost his balance. The apartment belonged to Loretta Vampa's mother's third husband, Dominic Nequizia, who had been Jib Bufera's lawyer.

Lonely Are the Brave

Many men in Roy's neighborhood had tattoos. Most of these tattoos were of military reference, such as USMC, Semper Fidelis, U.S. Navy, 101st Airborne, Dive Bomber or Tailgunner. Some of them were illustrated with an anchor, crossed sabers or rifles. The men who bore these tattoos had fought in World War II, the ink had faded and the men were middle-aged and generally overweight. Every once in a while Roy saw someone who had a woman's name, by itself or under a heart, or, less often, the word Mother or Mom, burned into his skin. A guy from West Virginia named Weevil, who worked the cash register at Rain Bo's Car Wash, had a drawing on his right forearm of a brunette with big eyes and bare breasts and the name Ava in cursive where her stomach might have been.

Most tattoo parlors in Chicago were located on South State Street, close to pawnshops and burlesque houses. Roy had never seen anyone actually getting a tattoo other than a drunken sailor or soldier until Flip Ferguson's older brother, Lefty, got one just before he went away to boot camp at Parris Island, South Carolina.

Roy and Flip, who were both fourteen, accompanied Lefty, who was seventeen, to Detroit Art's Tattoo Emporium on the corner of State and Menominee. Lefty had recently been expelled from high school for beating up the vice-principal, who had ordered him to put out his cigarette. Lefty put it out on the vice-principal's forehead, then popped him in the face a few times. Shortly thereafter, Lefty and Flip's father signed a release giving his oldest son permission as a minor to join the Marines. When apprised of this, the Board of Education and the vice-principal agreed to drop the assault charges they had filed against Lefty. By enlisting in the

Marines, Lefty saved his father a lot of money in legal fees, and himself a year in the reformatory at St. Charles.

Detroit Art was about sixty, tall and skinny with a pockmarked face Lefty later described to an uncomprehending prostitute in Saigon as resembling a Chicago street after a bad winter. The tattooist wore a green eyeshade and Coke bottle-thick glasses with heavy black frames, and smoked an unfiltered Old Gold in an ebony cigarette holder.

"What'll it be?" he asked Lefty. "You know what you want?"

"Yeah, I want it to say 'Lefty from Chi.'"

"You want a picture with it?"

"What kind of picture?"

"That's up to you," said Art. "How about a fist?"

Lefty thought about this for a few seconds, then nodded.

"Okay, a left-handed fist," he said, and held his up for Art's inspection.

Art peered at it for a moment or two, then asked, "You want upper and lower case or all capital letters?"

"All capitals," said Lefty.

"Over, under or around the fist?"

"Over."

"Biceps or forearm?"

"Biceps."

"Left, right?"

"Right, left," Lefty said.

He rolled up his left sleeve and presented the designated arm to Detroit Art.

"You're really gonna do it?" said Flip.

Lefty grinned. He wasn't all that big, or even especially tough. He just liked to fight, Flip told Roy, like their father.

"Sure, he is," said Art, who did not remove the cigarette holder from between his clenched teeth while he worked. "Won't take twenty-five minutes."

Flip and Lefty's mother had died a couple of years before under mysterious circumstances. According to the newspapers, their mother was found lying in the alley behind their house very early one morning. Her head had been bashed in from behind with a hammer or similar object and she was found dead when a neighbor, taking out his garbage, discovered the body and called the cops. Flip and Lefty and their father were asleep in their house when the police came. No murder weapon was ever found and the case remained unsolved. Nobody knew why Mrs. Ferguson had been in the alley at five thirty that morning, unless she had taken out some garbage, but no fresh garbage was found in the Ferguson family's trash can. Neither Flip nor Lefty had heard any unusual noises, they said, nor did their father. The only strange thing was that Mrs. Ferguson's body was entirely nude when the neighbor found her. It was late March, snow flurries were in the air and she didn't even have slippers on her feet. If the police ever had a suspect or suspects in this case, no mention of it was made public.

A little more than a half hour later, the three boys were back out on State Street. It was windy and cloudy but not cold. An old woman passed them on the sidewalk, pushing a baby carriage filled with empty beer cans.

"Set 'em up in the other alley!" she shouted.

"How does your arm feel?" Flip asked his brother.

"Probably how a calf feels after it just got branded," said Lefty. "It stings."

"You were really brave," Roy said. "You didn't say anything while he was writing and drawing on you."

Lefty took out a pack of Chesterfields and a book of matches from the right pocket of his navy blue windbreaker. He lit a cigarette, inhaled deeply, then let the smoke out slowly.

"Know why soldiers wear uniforms?" Lefty asked.

"So they'll know who's on the same side," said Flip.

"That's one reason," said Lefty. "But it's also so everyone feels equal. Nobody's better than anybody else and each man knows he's not alone, that they're a part of somethin' bigger than just themselves."

The boys began walking toward the el.

"You gonna show the old man?" asked Flip.

"I ain't that brave," said Lefty.

Force of Evil

Roy was sitting at the kitchen table with his grandfather on a rainy Saturday afternoon in November listening to the radio. Johnny Hodges was blowing the first chorus on "Gone with the Wind." His grandfather was eating smoked fish and drinking beer while Roy, who was nine years old, watched him wield fork and knife to pick apart the flesh from the bones with surgical precision. Roy hated the smell of the smoked fish but was fascinated by his grandfather's dexterity. Not once, it seemed to Roy, did even a very small bone elude his grandfather's diligence. When the record ended, a man with a deep voice began talking. The news on the radio included a report of an eight-year-old girl having been found behind a row of bushes in a park. Roy's grandfather reached over to the counter where the radio was and turned it off. Roy looked out the window. For some reason, the sky looked more red than gray.

"Terrible," said his grandfather. "Many years ago, the young son of a friend of mine was kidnapped and murdered by two older boys. The three boys knew each other, they lived in the same neighborhood. All of them came from well-to-do, respectable families."

"Why did they kill your friend's son?"

"The pair who committed the murder had planned everything carefully. Both of them were twenty years old, brilliant students at the university, and they devised what they thought would be a perfect crime. They considered what they were doing an experiment to prove to themselves that they could get away with it, that they were more clever than the police. Nobody else would ever know that they had done this; they pledged to one another that it would be their secret for the rest of their lives. Just the fact of knowing they had carried out the plan and succeeded in not being found out would be sufficient. It turned out not to be, of course."

"How did they get caught, Pops?"

Roy's grandfather put down his knife and fork, then took a swallow of beer.

"They couldn't stand the anonymity, Roy, not being given recognition for their ingenuity. After the boy was reported missing, they volunteered, as concerned friends of the family, to help the police find him. Convinced as they were of their own genius, they decided to amplify the experience by witnessing first hand how inept the investigators were, to share a private joke at the expense not only of law enforcement, but the parents of the dead boy and, of course, the public, who were certain to be horrified, frightened and mystified. Eventually, after they slipped up and one of them confessed, they led the police to a culvert by a drainage canal where they had hidden the body."

"What happened to them?"

"After a spectacular trial that was in the headlines for weeks, thanks to an outstanding defense lawyer who was a crusader against the death penalty, the murderers were given life sentences. One died in prison, knifed by a fellow inmate in a shower stall, and the other served more than thirty years before being paroled under special conditions. He volunteered to participate as a guinea pig in medical experiments, testing antiviral and anticancer drugs. He actually married and lived for many years following his release.

"The persons who suffered the most, of course, were the parents of the murdered child. As I said, I knew the father and considered him a friend. He was a good fellow, we belonged to the same club. He died of a broken heart not very long after the trial. His wife lived a few more years before she, too, had a heart attack. She survived but remained an invalid until her death. The boy was their only child."

Rain was pounding the roof and the windows harder now. Roy

shivered, even though the radiators were turned on all the way.

"That's really a terrible story," he said.

"Yes, it is. Books and plays have been written about the case. I read recently that a movie about it is in the works now. People just could not understand why these outstanding young men, both of whom were otherwise destined for great careers, would have risked everything by committing such a despicable act."

"Maybe that's why they did it," said Roy. "I mean, if school was so easy for them, if they were so smart and came from rich families so they had everything they wanted, maybe taking that chance gave them a kind of excitement they couldn't get any other way."

"You're right, Roy. The papers called it a 'thrill' killing."

"Did they ever say they were sorry?"

"One of them did, the one who eventually got out of prison. He said he wanted to try to make up for his crime by allowing himself to be used by medical researchers to discover drugs that could save lives."

That night, before Roy fell asleep, he thought about why people did terrible things. It wasn't enough to just say that people who do something awful are sick in the head, there had to be something more, a kind of evil force that exists inside them. Maybe it exists in everyone, Roy thought, but some people have more evil in them than others. Roy wondered when he would find out how much of this force he had in himself, and what he would do about it if he had too much. Perhaps there wouldn't be anything he could do, that the evil power would just take over his brain and use him as an agent or instrument of destruction. He was only nine years old, but Roy knew that this thought would be in his head for the rest of his life.

The Choice

Buckshot was scattered throughout the clouds, but no snow had fallen. In less than an hour the sky would be black and moonless, so Roy walked quickly. It was election day and he was headed to the ward office on Western Avenue to help count votes. Roy's friend Elmo's mother worked there for every election, and this year she had arranged for the boys, both of whom had recently turned fourteen, to assist her.

The presidential race had been hotly contested and everyone agreed that it was impossible to guarantee the outcome. The differences between the two candidates were substantial; the result of this election, both sides promised, would dramatically affect the direction of the country. For the first time in his young life, Roy felt engaged politically, and he was excited to be a part of the process.

However, as Roy walked toward the office, his thoughts were about the movie he'd just been watching on television, *White Cargo*, with Hedy Lamarr as a native temptress who drives all of the white men who oversee a British rubber plantation in Nigeria crazy. When a new man shows up, the artificially darkened Hedy slithers up to him half-naked in the shadows, flaps her false eyelashes, plants one knee gently into his crotch, and whispers, "I am Tondelayo."

Tondelayo is notorious in this region for leading men not only on but to their doom, and the head man, played edgily by Walter Pidgeon, having at one time himself succumbed to her wiles but survived, does all he can to prevent the newcomer from becoming infatuated and inevitably victimized by the dusky vixen. Nonetheless, she succeeds in seducing and then, to the collective dismay and even horror of the other white men, marrying him. Tondelayo is easily bored and within a very short time, despite her callow husband having bought her all the silks and jewels she desires, the devil girl pursues other men and tortures the poor wretch with vividly described revelations of her sordid history. Tondelayo slowly poisons the besotted fellow until he is on the brink of death, at which point the perpetually inebriated plantation doctor, who is at a loss as to what could be causing Tondelayo's husband's precipitous decline, and Boss Pidgeon arrange for him to be shipped back to England, listing him on the freighter's manifest as "white cargo."

Roy had to leave his house before finding out what happens to Tondelayo after the planters discover she's been poisoning her spouse. She would try to get to Lagos, Roy guessed, carrying with her as many of her jewels and precious silks as she could, and lose herself in the big city. Roy imagined Lagos was an African version of Chicago, a place where a devastating beauty such as Tondelayo would have no difficulty enticing, destroying and dispensing of countless men.

At the ward office, Roy and Elmo and several other boys stacked and unstacked boxes of ballots until two thirty in the morning, then loaded them onto a truck for delivery to election headquarters downtown. On the way home, Roy told Elmo about Tondelayo. As the boys walked through the quiet streets, snow began to fall.

"So she was good-lookin', huh?" said Elmo.

"Really good-lookin'," said Roy. "But she didn't look black, just kind of dusty, like she'd been down in a coal mine. It's hard to tell when the picture's not in color."

"Was she as pretty as your mother?"

"Yeah, I guess," said Roy. "Maybe even prettier."

"How many times has your mother been married?"

"Four."

"How many times was Tondelayo married?" Elmo asked.

"I don't know," said Roy. "Probably more than four."

Just as Elmo turned off Ojibway and cut down the alley between Mohican and Darrow to get to his house, he said, "When we wake up we'll find out who won the election."

Roy felt a little guilty that he didn't care so much any more about the election. His mind was on Tondelayo. He was surprised when he got home that his grandfather was still up, sitting in the living room reading a book.

"Hey, Pops," said Roy, "how come you're awake?"

"When you get old," Pops said, "you don't need so much sleep. How did it go?"

"Okay. Mostly we moved around a lot of boxes. They don't know who won yet."

"Neither of these fellows is a genius or a madman, I don't think," said Pops, "so things won't change much, no matter who wins."

"I thought this election was going to change the direction of the country."

Pops put down his book and looked at his grandson.

"I hate to sound cynical, Roy," he said, "but unless the Russians drop an atomic bomb on New York, or we drop one on Moscow, nothing is going to change. Not even the reprobate Quaker being elected president, God forbid, will derail the economy. The United States won the war, so we own both the groceries and the grocery. You understand?"

Roy nodded, then asked, "What do you know about Hedy Lamarr?"

"Her first husband was an Austrian Jew," said Pops, "who was Hitler's armaments manufacturer, an honorary Nazi. He married Hedy when she was fifteen or sixteen and kept her locked up in a castle, but she escaped and went to Czechoslovakia where she appeared naked in a movie. Her husband attempted to suppress it by buying up all of the prints, but the film got released anyway and created a scandal. After that she got on an ocean liner and sailed to New York. On the boat she met Otto Preminger, another Viennese Jew, the movie producer and director, who set her up in Hollywood. Hedy Lamarr was choice. For a while she was considered to be the most beautiful woman in the world. Why do you ask?"

"I just watched her in a movie called *White Cargo*."

"Isn't that the one where she's a native girl who says, 'I am Tondelayo'?"

"Yeah, she says it to a white guy who comes to Africa to run a rubber plantation. He marries her and then she poisons him."

"He was a fool to marry her," Pops said, "but some men are fools when it comes to women."

"Aren't women sometimes fools when it comes to men?"

"If you're thinking of your mother, Roy, you've got to remember that, depending on the circumstances, anybody can make a bad decision."

"Who did you vote for?" Roy asked.

"The Catholic fellow," said Pops.

"I thought so," said Roy.

Bad Girls

Jimmy Boyle asked Roy to go with him to Uptown to see a girl Jimmy had met the Saturday before at the Riviera theater.

"Why don't you just go by yourself?" asked Roy.

"She said she was gonna be with a girlfriend," said Jimmy. "I need you to help me out and talk to her friend."

"Are they hillbilly chicks?"

"I guess so. Babylonia told me her family moved here from West Virginia."

"Babylonia? Her name's Babylonia?"

"Yeah, but she says everyone calls her Babs."

"Most of the people who move here from the Appalachian Mountains live in Uptown," said Roy.

"Babs said she lived in some little town that didn't even have a stoplight until she was ten, then they moved to Wheeling and stayed there until a year ago. They came to Chicago the day after her thirteenth birthday."

"What does she look like?"

Jimmy shrugged. "I don't know. Light brown hair, blue eyes, kind of skinny. But her skin is white like on a statue. Whiter than milk."

"Where are you supposed to meet her?"

"On Kenmore, behind Graceland Cemetery, at one o'clock. She's tellin' her folks she and her girlfriend are goin' to the movies."

"Why the cemetery?"

"I guess she lives near there."

It was mid-November but not too cold. The sky was entirely gray without birds of any kind, a condition that made Roy feel as if he were among the last survivors on a dying planet. He and Jimmy Boyle walked down Ravenswood to Montrose, turned left and headed toward Kenmore Avenue. The streets were as empty as the sky.

"What if they don't come?" Jimmy said.

"Then we'll go hang around the Loop, maybe meet some girls there."

Nobody was on the corner of Kenmore and Montrose, so the boys turned south and walked along the east side of the cemetery.

"Know anybody who's buried in there?" asked Jimmy.

"No. My dad's buried in Rosedale."

"There they are," Jimmy said. "I told you she'd be here."

Standing halfway down the block were two girls, both wearing black scarves around their heads, navy blue pea coats, short black skirts with black tights and black fruit boots. One of them was smoking a cigarette.

"Bad girls," said Roy.

"I hope so," said Jimmy Boyle.

When the boys got closer, Roy could see that the girl who was smoking was also chewing gum. She had dark hair and dark eyes. The other one was Jimmy's.

"Hi, Babs," Jimmy Boyle said. "This is Roy."

"Hi, Jimmy," Babs said. "Hi, Roy. This is Sunny."

"Is that Sunny with a u or an o?" said Roy.

Sunny cradled her right elbow in her left hand. She held her cigarette in her right hand and did not smile. She cracked her gum.

"She spells it with a u," said Babs.

"Roy like in Roy Rogers," said Sunny.

"Roy Rogers is cute," Babs said. "My mother says he's part Indian."

Sunny was wearing makeup to conceal some pimples on her chin and cheeks, but Roy thought she was good-looking, maybe even beautiful like Gene Tierney. He'd heard his friend Frankie's mother, who read a lot of Hollywood fan magazines, say that

Gene Tierney was crazy and had to be put in a nuthouse on a regular basis. In any case, Sunny was a lot cuter than Babs, though what Jimmy had said about Babs's skin was true.

"We gonna go somewhere?" asked Babs.

"Where do you want to go?" said Jimmy.

"I'm hungry," she said. "Let's go to Billy the Greek's on Irving Park. We can cut through the cemetery."

Jimmy and Babs walked off first and Roy and Sunny followed. After a minute, Sunny said to Roy, "I'm Greek. My folks come from Piraeus. They had me here, though, so I'm Greek-American."

"I'm first-generation American, too," said Roy. "My father was from Vienna, Austria."

"I don't think I've ever met anyone from Austria."

Sunny tossed away her cigarette. She was about the same height as Roy.

"How old are you?" he asked.

"Fourteen, same as Babs. What about you?"

"I'm fourteen and a half."

They walked for another minute without talking, then Sunny said, "Do you like cemeteries?"

"Not since my dad died," said Roy.

Sunny stopped and put her right hand on Roy's left forearm. He stopped, too.

"Oh, Roy, I'm sorry I asked you that."

Roy looked into her eyes. They were dark brown with a tinge of red in them.

"It's okay," he said. "He died a couple of years ago."

Sunny curled her right arm through Roy's left and they began walking again. She took the chewing gum out of her mouth with her left hand and threw it on the ground.

"My mother died a year ago," Sunny said, "when I was in Chicago Parental."

"You were in the reformatory?"

Sunny nodded.

"What for?"

"Chronic truancy."

"What's chronic?"

"It means I cut school too much," said Sunny. "I was upset about my mom bein' sick and not bein' able to do anything to help her. Her husband? He's not my father. My real dad went to Korea in the army and never came back. He probably went back to Greece."

"What about your stepfather?"

"Oh, yeah. He's a drunk. Worked loadin' trucks in South Water Market. He tried to rape my sister on her sixteenth birthday, so now he's in jail. It was a bad atmosphere at our house, so I mostly just stayed out all the time. I was in Chicago Parental for three months. They let me out after my mother died and her sister, our Aunt Edita, came to live with me and my sister. She's really nice."

"Are you going to school again?"

"Oh, sure. I got a B average."

They walked slowly, letting Jimmy Boyle and Babs get way ahead.

"We've got some things in common, Roy. It's real important, don't you think? I mean, if we're going to be friends."

"Did your stepfather ever try to do anything with you?"

"Uh-uh. Valeria's prettier than I am, and she's got big boobs already. So he didn't pay so much attention to me. He's Hungarian."

"Well, I'm glad your aunt is there to take care of you."

"Her husband, my Uncle Ganos, went bughouse one day and wouldn't come out from a closet. When the cops tried to pull him out he bit one of 'em on his nose, almost tore it off the cop's face. My aunt said the poor man had to have it sewn back on. I was eight when that happened."

"Jesus," said Roy. "What happened to your uncle?"

"He's in Dunning, the state mental hospital out on Foster. He'll probably be in there for the rest of his life."

When Roy and Sunny got to Irving Park, Babs and Jimmy were not in sight.

"They must already be at Billy the Greek's," said Roy.

Sunny and Roy were facing each other.

"Roy," she said, "would you like to kiss me?"

Sunny leaned forward and pushed her tongue deep into Roy's mouth, then rolled it around a few times.

"Where did you learn to do that?" Roy asked.

"Valeria taught me," said Sunny. "She's a bad girl."

The Sudden Demise of Sharkface Bensky

The guy who cut Sharkface Bensky's throat in front of Santa Maria Addolorata that Saturday night got away clean. He ran down the alley next to the church so fast nobody going in or coming out of Carnival Night got a good look at him. Only a deaf kid standing on the steps came forward to say he'd seen it happen, and the description he gave to a hand sign reader the next morning at the police station wasn't much, just that the cutter used a straight razor with what looked like an ivory bone handle and wore a dark brown overcoat. Sharkface crumpled to the sidewalk like a squeeze box out of air and bled to death before anyone thought to call an ambulance. Two teenage girls stepped right around him, the deaf kid told the reader, kept right on talking and went up the steps into the church. A cop said they probably thought Sharkface Bensky was a drunk who'd passed out and was sleeping it off.

Roy and his friends went by on Sunday to see the bloodstains. It was the first week of December and there hadn't been any snow yet, though the temperature was below freezing.

"It don't look like blood, does it?" said the Viper. "It's so black."

"Maybe they already washed it with somethin'," said Jimmy Boyle, "to get the red out."

"Skull Dorfman says the church makes its living off the blood of others," Roy said.

"What's that supposed to mean?" said Jimmy.

"Means the fathers wouldn't be cryin' over a little spilt blood," said the Viper. "Not after what it says in the Bible. It's good advertisin', you ask me."

"The priest is probably talkin' about it right now," Roy said. "Comparing Bensky's blood to the blood of Christ."

"You coulda fooled me," said Jimmy Boyle. "I didn't think Sharkface had any blood in his body. He never let anyone slide."

"Skull said he was a kneebreaker who needed his knees broke," said the Viper.

"Think he done it?" asked Roy.

The Viper shrugged. "Who's to say?"

"The bulls ain't gonna knock theirselves out to solve this case, that's for sure," said Jimmy. "I wouldn't be surprised they was behind it even."

Sharkface Bensky's real first name was Moses. The moniker Sharkface came from his having had his nose slit open from bridge to tip with a stiletto by Bobby Battipalo, a soldier for Joe Batters, because he welshed on a bet, and Battipalo's having inserted in the wound a five dollar bill. He did it in such a way that the fin stood up like a shark's. Bobby Battipalo paraded Bensky around afterwards so that people could see his handiwork. It took thirty-two stitches to close up the cut and left a scar impossible not to notice. When Battipalo left Bensky, still stunned and bleeding, in front of Meschina's restaurant on Blackhawk Boulevard, he said to the bunch hanging out on the sidewalk, "Looks like a shark out of water now, don't he?"

Mass let out and the parishioners began leaving Santa Maria Addolorata and coming down the steps. Roy, the Viper and Jimmy Boyle had all stopped going to church a couple of years before, when they were twelve or thirteen, although Jimmy occasionally still accompanied his crippled grandmother to confession when his mother was unable to, to make sure she didn't fall.

Jerry Murphy walked over to the boys. Everybody called him Goat because he had been trying to grow a goatee ever since the first few hairs appeared on his face when he was fourteen. Goat was now almost eighteen, and he had hardly any more hair on his chin than he'd had four years before. His idol was the trumpet player and famous hipster Dizzy Gillespie, who wore a goatee, and Murphy often wore a beret and glasses, like Gillespie, even though there was nothing wrong with his eyes.

"Hey, cats," he said, "you come to scope out the murder scene, huh?"

"Hi, Goat," said the Viper. "Yeah, you know, we Shakespeare scholars are checkin' out the damn spot."

"For extra credit in English," said Roy.

"I bet I know who's the perp," Goat said.

The three boys looked up at him. Goat was six two; of the boys, Jimmy Boyle was the tallest at five eight.

"Remember Bird Man?" said Goat.

"Yeah," said Roy, "the ex-welterweight from Streator went to see *Birdman of Alcatraz* twenty times. Used to hang out with the Pugliese brothers at their garage."

"Right."

"Bird Man cut Sharkface's throat?" said Jimmy. "Why?"

Goat fingered the several thin hairs on his chin, then said, "Sharkface was collectin' for the Puglieses and keepin' part of the payoffs for himself, tellin' 'em some cats didn't pay up when they did. The Puglieses hired Bird Man to take Sharkface out of the count."

"Who told you?" asked the Viper.

Goat shrugged his shoulders. "Just a guess," he said. "Gotta split. Stay cool, cats."

Goat pulled his Dizzy beret out of one of his coat pockets, stretched it over his crewcut scalp and walked away.

As churchgoers continued to file past and around the boys, a squad car drove up and parked in front of Santa Maria Addolorata. Two of Chicago's Finest got out and hurried up the steps into the church.

"Somethin's up," said Jimmy Boyle.

"Yeah," said the Viper, "let's wait here."

Four more squad cars pulled up and blocked off the street in both directions. Eight cops ran up the steps into Santa Maria Addolorata and four more stayed outside and made sure no citizens lingered on the steps or on the sidewalk. One of the cops motioned for the boys to step away from where they were standing. The trio walked ten feet up the street and stopped.

A couple of minutes later, two officers exited the front door of the church clutching a man between them, each holding one of the man's arms. There was a black hood over their prisoner's head and his hands were handcuffed in front of him. He was wearing a long brown overcoat. The cops on the steps, the sidewalk and in the street all had their guns drawn and kept looking around. The prisoner was shoved into the back seat of one of the squad cars and wedged between two cops. The rest of them got into the cars and drove off with sirens blaring. Roy saw the head priest from Santa Maria Addolorata, Father Vincenzu, who was from Romania, standing on the top step watching the police cars speed away.

"Bird Man," said Jimmy Boyle.

"Maybe so," said the Viper.

"You think Father Vincenzu was hiding him?" Roy asked.

"More likely he talked Bird Man into turning himself in," said Jimmy.

"But why would Bird Man have been in the church in the first place?" said Roy.

The Viper put up the collar of the army field jacket his brother had given him after he'd come back from Korea. It was several sizes too large for him.

"What beats me," he said, "is how Goat knew it was Bird Man."

Suddenly the street was dead quiet. Roy looked up again at the entrance to the church. Father Vincenzu was still standing there. As he turned to go inside, he saw the three boys and waved at them. Roy waved back, and then the Viper and Jimmy Boyle waved, too.

Portrait of the Artist with Four Other Guys

As soon as Jimmy Boyle got back from Ireland, he went to see his friends. Roy, the Viper, Magic Frank, and Crazy Lester were hanging out under the viaduct on the corner of Warsaw and Bohemia, near Heart-of-Jesus Park. It was a late Friday afternoon in August, and Jimmy knew he'd find them there because the league games were over by four or four thirty and the boys liked to stay around for a while afterwards to talk about what happened. Jimmy had gone to Ireland for a holiday with his mother, his grandmother and his sister. They were there for two weeks and he was happy to be back in the neighborhood.

The Viper was the first to spot Boyle.

"Hey, Jimmy! Did you kiss the Blarney Stone?"

"Yeah, all of us did, even my grandmother. We had to hold her by her legs. You gotta bend over backwards to do it. My ma got pictures of me and my sister there. What'd I miss?"

"Roy hit two homers today," said Lester.

"He's always hittin' homers," said Magic Frank. "That ain't news."

"Red Dietz got killed," said Roy.

"No shit," Jimmy said. "How?"

"You know Red Dietz," said Roy, "the one-armed pitcher on Margaret Mary's?"

"Yeah. Lost his right up to the elbow when he stuck it out a window on the Illinois Central."

"A line drive hit him right between the eyes in a game last week," said the Viper. "Dietz died on the mound."

"Who hit it?"

"Vidinski," said Roy, "the third baseman for Mohegan Mortuary."

"They picked up the tab for the funeral," said Frank.

"Did you guys go?" asked Jimmy.

"Nobody liked Red Dietz," said the Viper. "I don't know anybody that went."

"My mother did," said Lester. "She dyes Dietz's mother's hair."

"He was all pissed off all the time," said Frank.

"You lost an arm, you'd probably be pissed off all the time, too," said Roy.

"So what was the best thing about Ireland?" the Viper asked Jimmy.

"It don't get so hot and humid in the summer like here. There's a river goes through Dublin that's pretty nice. Lots of old buildings and churches, stuff like that."

"Do the people speak English or Irish?" asked Roy.

"Both, I guess. Sometimes I couldn't understand what they were sayin' in English. You know, like Cunningham's mother. My grandmother speaks Gaelic pretty good and my ma, too, so we didn't have no problems."

"What about girls?" asked Lester.

"Didn't hardly see any except for my cousin, Kathleen. She's a couple years older, fifteen. We stayed with her family. One night after she took a bath, she came out in a towel and asked me if I wanted to use her bath water while it was still warm."

"She'd already bathed in it?" asked Roy.

"Yeah," said Jimmy. "They share it 'cause there ain't so much hot water."

"Too bad you couldn'ta shared it with her," said Lester.

"She showed me her tits," said Jimmy.

"Bullshit!" said Frank.

Jimmy nodded. "She did. Nobody else was around. Opened the towel and rewrapped it standin' in front of me. They were the two best things I seen in Ireland."

"Were they big?" asked the Viper.

"Average," said Jimmy. "There were freckles all over 'em and the nipples pointed up."

Clouds blocked the sun and suddenly the air felt cooler.

"Anybody hungry?" asked Roy.

"Let's go to the Cottage," said Frank, "get fries with gravy."

The boys began walking west on Warsaw, toward Pulaski. Roy and Jimmy Boyle trailed the others.

"Do you think your cousin wanted to do somethin' with you?" Roy asked.

"I don't know," said Jimmy. "You think girls in Dublin are any different than the ones in Chicago?"

Before Roy could offer an opinion, a police car drove up and stopped in the street next to them. There were two cops in it, one driving and one riding shotgun.

The cop in the front passenger seat leaned out his window and said, "Any of you seen two colored boys drive by in a lime green Cadillac?"

"I ain't," said Frank.

"Me, neither," said Lester.

Roy and the Viper shook their heads.

"What about you?" the cop asked Jimmy Boyle.

"I just got back from Ireland," he said.

"You go blind from drinkin' the water over there?" said the cop.

"No," said Jimmy.

"They got coloreds in Ireland?" the cop asked.

"I don't know," Jimmy said. "I didn't see any there."

"He seen his cousin Kathleen's tits, though," said Lester.

The cop stared at Lester for a moment. Crazy Lester was grinning.

"Are you Irish?" the cop said.

"No," said Lester. "I'm Lithuanian on my mother's side and Moldavian on my dad's."

"You better watch yourself," said the cop.

Then the police car drove away.

The Starving Dogs of Little Croatia

"Every man lives like hunted animal," said Drca Kovic.

"You make this just up?" asked Boro Catolica.

"What is difference," Drca said, "if it is truth?"

The two men, both in their midthirties, were seated next to one another on stools at the bar in Dukes Up Tavern on Anna Ruttar Street drinking shots of Four Sisters backed with Old Style chasers. Brenda Lee was on the jukebox belting out "Rockin' Around the Christmas Tree," just as she did every December. Boro Catolica lit up a Lucky.

"Ten years now Chicago," he said, "and no truth more than Zagreb."

"At least here we drink in peace," said Drca Kovic. "There we drink in war."

"Yes, but probably we end up lying still in alley with cats they are looking at us. Our eyes they are open but not being able see theirs."

It was seven o'clock on a Friday evening two days before Christmas. There were four inches of snow on the ground with more expected. Boro and Drca had been in Dukes Up since ten to five, thirty minutes after dark and twenty minutes following the end of their shift at Widerwille Meatpacking on Pulaski Avenue. The men worked full days Monday through Friday and half days on Saturday.

"You notice old man Widerwille not so often check line now?" said Boro.

"Probably too cold in freezer for him," Drca said. "Blood is thinner."

The front door opened and two boys, both about eleven or twelve years old, entered the tavern, bringing with them a blast of icy air accompanied by a spray of new snow.

Emile Wunsch, the bartender and part owner of Dukes Up, shouted, "No minors allowed! And shut that door!"

"There's a dead guy lyin' out on the sidewalk," said the larger of the two boys.

The smaller boy closed the door.

"How do you know he's dead?" said Emile Wunsch.

"He looks like Arne Pedersen did," said the smaller boy, "after he died from Sterno poisoning last February."

"His body froze overnight," the other boy said, "on the steps of Santa Maria Addolorata."

Boro and Drca went out, followed by the boys. Half a minute later the four of them came back inside.

"It's Bad Lands Bill," said Boro, brushing snow from his head, "the Swede was from North of Dakota."

"The flat-nosed guy used to work at the chicken cannery?" asked Emile.

Drca nodded. "His skin is blue and there is no breathing."

"We saw his eyes were open," said the smaller boy, "so we stopped to look at him."

"He wasn't blinkin'," said the larger boy, "his tongue's stickin' out and it's blue, too."

The two Croatian men went back outside, picked up the body and carried it into Dukes Up, where they set it down on the floor. Boro closed the door.

"I'll call the precinct," said Emile Wunsch, "tell 'em to send a wagon. You boys can stick around to tell the cops how you found him."

Drca and Boro went back to their stools at the bar.

"Boys, you want Coca-Cola?" asked Boro.

"Sure," said the smaller one.

"I am Drca, he is Boro."

"I'm Flip," said the larger boy.

"I'm Roy," said the other.

"Okay they sit at bar?" Boro asked Emile.

Emile was still on the phone to the precinct. He hung up and motioned to Flip and Roy to go ahead. The boys climbed up on stools next to the men.

"You think corpse we should cover?" said Drca.

"Why to bother?" Boro said. "Wagon coming."

"Did Bad Lands Bill drink here?" Roy asked.

Emile came over with Cokes for the boys.

"Not for a while," he said. "He got laid off a few months back. Last time I saw him was in July."

Flip sipped his Coke as he spun around on his stool and looked down at the body. The eyes and mouth were closed.

"Hey," Flip said, "weren't his eyes and mouth open when you carried him in?"

"Yeah," said Roy, "his tongue was hangin' out."

Everyone stared at Bad Lands Bill. His skin was not quite so blue.

"I guess gettin' warmed up changes the body," said Flip. "It's good for him to be inside."

"That's what Midget Fernekes said about himself," said Emile.

"Who's that?" asked Roy.

"A bank robber grew up in Canaryville," the bartender said. "He was the first person to blow safes usin' nitroglycerin. Midget said he learned more about safecrackin' in the pen than he ever could've on the street."

Drca and Boro drank in silence. Emile poured them each another shot of Four Sisters, then busied himself at the end of the bar. No other customers came in. Roy and Flip finished their Coca-Colas and sat quietly, too. For some reason it did not seem right to talk a lot with a dead man lying there.

"The wagon oughta be here by now," said Emile, who came around from behind the bar, walked over to the front door and looked outside through the small window.

"It's a full-on blizzard out there," he said. "Maybe you kids should go on home now, before it gets any worse. Drca and Boro and I can tell the ambulance boys what happened, if they can even get here."

"Go," said Boro. "Drinks on house. Yes, Emile?"

The bartender nodded.

"Be careful of starving dogs," said Drca. "They are hunting in group when weather is bad."

"This Chicago," said Boro, "not Zagreb. Here dogs eat better than people of half of world."

Roy and Flip got down from their stools and took one more look at Bad Lands Bill. His skin seemed almost normal now and there was a peaceful expression on his face. Emile opened the door a crack.

"Quick, boys," he said, "so the wind don't blow the snow in."

After Flip turned off Anna Ruttar Street to go to his house, Roy bent his head as he trudged forward and thought about packs of hungry wild dogs roaming the streets of Croatian cities and villages attacking kids and old people unable to defend themselves, feasting on stumblebums like Bad Lands Bill, especially if they were already dead. Roy brushed snow from his face. He wondered if Midget Fernekes was really a midget or if he was called that just because he was short. Roy worried that he could end up like Bad Lands Bill or Arne Pedersen, a rummy frozen to death on a sidewalk or in an alley. This was a possibility, he knew, it could happen to any man if enough breaks went against him. Roy tried to keep the snow out of his eyes but it was coming down too fast. He felt as if he were wandering in the clouds only this wasn't heaven. He was where the dogs could get him.

In the Land of the Dead

Roy dreamed that he was on the el on a hot, humid summer's day. He was not wearing a shirt, only a pair of khaki pants and shoes. It was in the afternoon and he stood looking through the windows on the train doors. His friends and other passengers were behind him, he heard but did not see them. The train stopped at a station, and at the last instant Roy stepped out of the car onto the elevated platform. The doors closed behind him and the train sped away. Roy realized that he had gotten off too soon. He and his friends had been headed downtown to the Loop.

Roy decided to walk to his house. When he got there, the three-story yellow brick building looked dirty and run-down, the lawn and bushes unkempt. He walked up to the front door and saw that it was not the door he remembered, it was badly abused and made of cheap material, the top layer peeling up from the bottom. Roy did not have a key. He stood still, sweating, wondering why he was there. Through the window in the front door he saw a woman in the hallway. She opened the door and came out of the building. She was middle-aged and, despite the heat, was wearing a blue cloth coat, a scarf around her head and glasses with black frames. The woman did not look at Roy and was unfamiliar to him. He caught the door before it closed and entered the building.

Inside the front hallway it was dark and cool but musty. He walked up the stairs, past the first-floor landing. Sunlight streamed in through a hallway window, but it was muted and he could see dust floating in the air. When he reached the second-floor landing he saw two nuns, one very young, one an older woman. Their habits were gray or light blue, not black and white. The young nun came over to Roy and looked closely at him, studying his face. She was short and her eyes were strange, one blue, one hazel, and they were cast in different directions. She said, "*Buona sera.*" Roy was surprised that she greeted him in Italian, but he replied, "*Buona sera,*" to her. The older nun took the younger sister by an arm and steered her back toward the apartment door on the second landing. Roy did not see the older nun's face and she did not speak to him, only to the other nun, whom she hurriedly guided into the apartment.

Roy continued upstairs. He stood in front of the door to the third-floor apartment. The hallway was dusty and shabby, the door much like the front door to the street. He reached into his pocket and found that he had a key to this door. He inserted it in the lock and entered the apartment. There were oriental rugs on the floor, as there always had been, but the apartment was stuffy, close, as if it had not been aired out in a long time, and over-crowded with furniture. His mother wasn't home, nobody was there. Roy decided to go to his room at the rear of the apartment to get a shirt. He walked through the rooms, particles of dust and dirt swirling in the shafts of sunlight that pierced through brown shadows. Even though he knew he was on the top floor of the building, Roy felt almost as if he were navigating his way through the entrails of a large animal.

In the back room, Roy realized his clothes were gone. He knew now that he had not lived there for a very long time. He looked out the windows of his old room at tar-covered garage roofs and back porches with wash hung out to dry on clotheslines. Roy understood that he had gotten off at the wrong stop, that this was the land of the dead, and he was not supposed to be there.

Roy would remember this dream for the rest of his life.

The Secret of the Universe

When he was eleven years old, Roy began writing stories. Using a lined yellow legal pad and pencil, the first story he wrote was about two brothers who fight on opposing sides during the War Between the States. One brother lived with their father in the South, the other with their mother in the North. They meet on a battlefield and recognize one another but are forced to fire their rifles and both brothers are killed. Roy titled this story *All in Vain.*

The next story Roy wrote he called *The Secret of the Universe.* It was about a boy who every day sees an old man, a neighbor, going into a little cottage next to his house. One afternoon, as the boy is passing by, he sees that the door to the cottage has been left open. The boy walks over to it and peers inside. Test tubes and vials of chemicals are on a work table, dozens of books are piled around and there is a large blackboard on which are chalked what appear to be mathematical equations or formulas. The old man comes up quietly behind the boy and asks him what he is looking for. The boy is surprised, a little frightened, but curious about what he has seen. He looks at the old man, who has a kind face, and asks him what he does every day in the cottage. The old man smiles and tells the boy that he is a scientist and that he is trying to discover the secret of the origin of the universe before he dies.

Before continuing his story, Roy wanted to know what the secret was. A few years later, when he read about Saul's conversation with Lazarus after Jesus had raised Lazarus from the dead, Roy thought he might have the answer.

"Tell me, Lazarus," said Saul, "what was it like? What is the difference between life and death?"

"Other than the light," replied Lazarus, "there really isn't much difference."

In an attempt to erase the evidence of Jesus's greatest miracle, Saul then stabbed Lazarus to his second and unrescued demise.

The more Roy thought about Lazarus's report from the other side, the more unlikely it seemed to him that the old man, no matter how dedicated a scientist he was, would succeed in solving the mystery of existence.

Roy never finished the story.

Far from Anywhere

Roy read in the newspaper that Doctor Death had escaped and was believed to be hiding out in South America. Doctor Death, whose real name was Aribert Heim, had supposedly murdered hundreds, if not thousands, of Jews, Gypsies, Communists, and other prisoners in unspeakable medical experiments at the Mathausen concentration camp during World War II. He had been captured by the Allies and held in custody with other Nazis for a short time following the end of the war, then, for some unexplained reason, released. Heim lived in Germany for fifteen years, until he was tipped off that he was about to be indicted and fled the country.

Walking to work after school, Roy stopped in front of Vignola's appliance store and watched the televisions in the window. There were three, each tuned to a different station with the sound off. At first, Roy watched the one showing a Porky Pig cartoon, then a picture of a man came on another set, the one in the middle. The man's face was darkly handsome but hard, the almost oriental eyes staring to the left of the camera, the grim mouth tight and turned down at the corners, his severely widow-peaked hair slicked back. The name "Doctor Death" appeared under the photograph. Wet snow began falling, melting before it could accumulate on the ground. The wind blew flakes into Roy's face, but he wiped them off and watched the TV with Doctor Death's face on it until it switched to another story. Then he remembered that old man Vignola was from somewhere in South America.

Roy went into the appliance store and saw the owner standing on a small stepladder, replacing a lightbulb. There were no customers in the store. Roy went over and stood next to the stepladder.

"Hi, Mr. Vignola," he said, "need any help?"

"Here," said the old man, handing down the dead bulb to Roy. "Hold this."

Roy took it and Vignola finished screwing in the new bulb, then climbed down.

"Thank you, Roy," he said. "What can I do for you?"

Roy handed back the old bulb.

"If you were going to hide out in South America," said Roy, "where would you go?"

Vignola stood half a head shorter than Roy, mostly because he was bent over and had a hump on his back. He had a head of thick, curly white hair, though, that made Roy imagine him wearing a tuxedo and conducting an orchestra with his hair flying.

"That's a strange question," said Vignola. "Why do you ask me?"

"You're from there," Roy said.

"From Argentina, yes," said the old man, "Buenos Aires. But not for forty years. I came to this country in 1922, and I have never gone back."

"This Nazi called Doctor Death that I saw on the news is probably hiding out down there."

Vignola nodded. "I heard. Heim. He and Mengele experimented on people in the camps. Beasts. Brazil, maybe. Many of them went there. Some to Argentina, sure, and Bolivia. Paraguay, too. Chile, perhaps, a little fishing village far from anywhere."

"Why are they allowed to live there?" asked Roy. "If they're fugitives, and it's obvious they're Germans, not Brazilians or Bolivians, why aren't they arrested?"

"Because in many cases the governments sided during the war with the Axis. Also, the Nazis escaped with enough money to pay for protection for years, or their children now support them."

"Were you born in Buenos Aires?"

The old man looked up and directly at Roy, who noticed for the first time that Vignola's eyes were blue.

"No," said Vignola, "in Napoli. My father was a cobbler, but in those days Italy was not united, not truly a country. There was a great schism between the North and the South, there still is. In Napoli, there were many factions vying for power, political battles in which men were killed just for an insult. Tribe against tribe. My parents took a boat with me and my sister to Montevideo, Uruguay, and settled eventually in Argentina, where there was already a large Italian population."

"Why did your father leave?"

"They wanted him to go into the army to fight in Abyssinia, and he didn't want to go there. The Abyssinians defeated the Italians in 1896, and after that Italy wanted revenge. They got it when Mussolini invaded again in the 1930s. This began the war for Italy."

"They sided with Germany," said Roy.

The old man shook his head, and said, "Italy has never ended a war on the same side on which it began."

"I've got to go to work," Roy said.

Vignola looked out the front window.

"It's snowing harder now."

"I've got a hat," said Roy.

"This Doctor Death," said the old man, "they'll get him. Maybe not right away, but they won't stop."

"Who won't stop?"

"The Jews," said Vignola. "The Americans won the war but they didn't finish the job. The Israelis will. They'll hunt down Doctor Death and the other Nazis, you'll see."

"Even if they're far from anywhere?"

"The world is shrinking fast, Roy. Anywhere is not so far any more."

"You're not Jewish, are you?" asked Roy.

"I wish I were," said Vignola.

"I never heard anybody say that before," said Roy, "that they wished they were a Jew."

"How old are you, Roy?"

"I just turned fifteen."

The old man smiled. "Put on your hat," he said.

Rain in the Distance

Roy was with Magic Frank and the Viper in Meschina's Delicatessen when he saw a girl sitting in a booth across from theirs who looked familiar. It was just before midnight on a Friday in April. The boys had been to a basketball game at Chicago Stadium and then gone to a party in their neighborhood, which turned out to be pretty dull, so they left and went to get something to eat. Roy couldn't remember right away where he'd seen this girl before. She wore her honey blonde hair up in a ponytail and had a slender, curvy shape. Roy couldn't take his eyes off of her. He did not recognize any of the other three girls who were sitting in the booth.

"You guys know who that girl is?" Roy asked his friends. "The one with the ponytail over there."

"She's good-lookin'," said Frank, "but no."

The Viper shook his head. "Wish I did. She looks older."

"What do you mean older?" Roy said.

"Older than us."

Roy and Magic Frank were sixteen, the Viper was fifteen and a half. The girl got up and one of her friends said, "Wait, Daisy, I'll go with you."

"Daisy Green," said Roy. "I saw her at a party a few years ago. Ernie Nederland knew her."

"Nederland?" said Magic Frank. "He piped a kid at Algren and got thrown out. I had a couple fights with him over at the park when we were in eighth grade. He was small but tough. Smart, too. Knew when to quit."

Roy said, "Let me out," and squeezed past the Viper.

He caught up with Daisy Green and her friend outside in front of Meschina's.

A cold wind came up suddenly and Roy shivered. He'd left his jacket in the booth.

"Hello," he said to Daisy Green. "We met once back in about sixth or seventh grade, at a party. My name's Roy."

"Gee, I don't remember," said Daisy.

"Well, we didn't actually meet. Ernie Nederland told me who you were."

Daisy Green laughed. She had a slight overbite, but other than that her teeth looked perfect.

"Ernie's probably in jail," she said.

"Or should be," said her friend. "I'm Donna."

"Hi, Donna," said Roy.

He looked at her, then immediately forgot what she looked like.

"That was a long time ago," Daisy said. "How did you recognize me?"

"I never forgot you since that night."

"How romantic," said Donna.

"Did we make out or anything?" Daisy asked.

Roy smiled. "No. Like I said, we weren't even introduced. I thought you were the prettiest girl I'd ever seen. You still are."

"He's dangerous," Donna said.

"Why didn't you talk to me at that party?" said Daisy.

"I think you were there with somebody," Roy said. "Do you want to come back in and sit with me and my friends? It's cold out here."

"There's rain in the distance," said Donna. "That's what my grandmother always says when there's a wind like this."

"I can't," said Daisy. "I've got to go home."

"Can I call you? What's your number?"

"Do you have a good memory?"

"I remembered you all this time, didn't I?"

"Rogers Park 4-32-32."

"I'll remember," Roy said.

"Nice meeting you," said Donna.

"Nice meeting you, too," said Roy.

The girls turned away and Roy went back inside.

"We ordered," said Frank.

Roy fished in a pocket of his jacket for a pen and wrote down Daisy's telephone number on a paper napkin.

"You get anywhere?" asked the Viper.

"I got her phone number."

"How old is she?" Magic Frank asked.

"I'm not sure," said Roy. "She's supposed to be dead by now."

"Dead?" said Frank. "Why?"

"Ernie Nederland told me she had a heart problem and had already had a big operation and that she wasn't supposed to live very much longer. She went with older guys he knew. Men. Nederland said she'd do anything."

A waitress brought Frank and the Viper's food to the table.

"You want something?" she asked Roy.

"He wants Daisy Green," said the Viper.

"She ain't on the menu," the waitress said.

"Corned beef on rye and a ginger ale."

The waitress left.

"Maybe she had another operation," said Magic Frank, "and she's okay now."

The two girls with whom Daisy and Donna had been sitting got up from their booth and put on their coats. One whispered to the other and then the one who did the whispering came over and stood and looked at Roy. She was short and heavy with stringy brown hair.

"I heard what you said about Daisy," she said. "About doing anything. I'm gonna tell her."

Both girls walked away.

Roy stared at Daisy Green's phone number on the napkin, then he folded it and put it into the right front pocket of his trousers.

"You should call her anyway," said the Viper.

Bad Night at the Del Prado

Roy's mother's third husband, Czeslaw Wanchovsky, was a jazz drummer whose professional name was Sid Wade. His fellow musicians called him Spanky, a reference to his style of appearing to slap or "spank" his drums as he played. Roy was ten years old when Sid Wade married his mother, and from the beginning Roy and his new stepfather did not get along. Wade was in his early forties and had not been married before, nor did he have any previous experience dealing with children. Wade had lived with his mother and was used to being taken care of: cooked for, having his laundry done, sleeping as late as he wished. During a meal, if he saw a piece of meat or other morsel on someone else's plate that he thought looked better than what he had on his own, Wade would spear it with his fork and then scrape his portion, or what was left of it, onto theirs.

About a year into the marriage, Roy and Sid Wade had a terrible fight that very nearly came to blows. Wade had taken to using Roy's room to nap in during the day, which meant that Roy could not go in there, for fear of waking him. One afternoon, however, Roy needed to get his baseball gear out of his closet, so he snuck into his room and, as quietly as possible, gathered up his glove, bat and spikes. Sid Wade woke up, saw Roy and yelled at him, cursing Roy for disturbing his rest. Roy talked back, one angry word led to another, and Wade, a big, bearlike guy who had wrestled in college, came at the boy as if he were going to mangle him. Roy dropped his baseball glove and spikes and held up the bat, ready to defend himself.

At this point, having heard the shouting, Roy's mother entered the room. Her husband stood glaring at Roy, breathing heavily, his large hands frozen inches from the boy's neck.

"What did you do?" Roy's mother yelled at him.

"I needed my stuff for the game," he said. "I had to get it out of the closet."

"You know Sid works nights," she said. "You should have taken your things out earlier."

"Next time, son," said Sid Wade, his barrel chest heaving like a gorilla's, "it'll be your ass."

Roy stared hard at this sweating, red-faced beast more than twice his size and said, "I'm not your son. And the next time, as you say, I find you sleeping in my room, I'll stick an ice pick in your ear."

"You hear that, Kitty?" said Wade. "He's just like his father."

Roy's mother spat on him.

Sid Wade said to her, "I told you he was going bad."

Roy did not wipe his mother's saliva off his face. He picked up his glove and spikes and, still holding the bat, walked out of the room without saying another word.

For the following few days, Roy made himself scarce. When he was home, he avoided both his mother and Sid Wade as much as possible, refusing to speak to her unless it was absolutely necessary, and not at all to him. Wade no longer took naps in Roy's room.

Ten days after the incident, on a Sunday, Roy's mother came into his room and said, "You and Sid should make up. He left his bass drum and some other things behind at the gig last night at the Del Prado Hotel and he has to drive down there this afternoon to get them. I thought perhaps you could ride with him and talk things over."

Roy looked at her. She was in her early thirties and still beautiful, but her eyes were not right, they were more red than brown and her gaze was unfocused. She seemed to be staring at an object other than him, something not in front of her or even in the room.

"There's nothing to talk about," said Roy. "If he lays a hand on me, I'll kill him in his sleep."

"Don't say that, Roy. Sid's a good man, really. He just doesn't know how to handle you. Give him a chance, for my sake."

There were tears in Roy's mother's eyes now.

"All right," he said.

An hour later, Sid Wade opened the door to Roy's room and said, "You ready to go?"

Roy followed him to his car, a green 1955 Pontiac Chieftain sedan, and got into the front passenger seat. The hotel was on the South Side, so Roy knew it would take at least forty-five minutes to get there.

Neither of them spoke for ten minutes, then Sid Wade said, "Your mother's a nervous woman. She's not always easy to live with."

Wade lit a cigarette and rolled down the driver's side window. It was early April but the real spring had not come yet. There was still a nasty chill in the air.

"Do you want to listen to the ball game?" Wade asked. "I think the Sox are on."

"Okay," said Roy.

Wade turned on the radio.

"What number is the station?"

"Ten something," Roy told him.

Sid Wade found the game and left the radio on with the volume low. Roy knew that he was not a baseball fan.

A few minutes later, Wade said, "It was a bad night at the Del Prado. First a drunken couple in the ballroom slapped the shit out of each other, then a guy got shot outside just as the band was packing up to leave. There was a lot of confusion and I left part of my kit behind."

"Who got shot?"

"A guest who was coming back to the hotel at around two a.m. He'd just gotten out of a taxi."

"Was he killed?"

"I think so, yeah."

"Do you know why?"

"I didn't hang around to find out."

They rode the rest of the way without talking. Roy listened to the game. By the time Sid Wade pulled the Pontiac up in front of the Del Prado, Chicago was up six to two over the Senators in the eighth.

"Wait here," said Wade. "If anyone asks, tell them your father is inside the hotel and he'll be right back."

Sid Wade got out of the car and took the keys with him. Roy could not listen to the radio, so he opened his door, got out and stood on the sidewalk. A doorman came out of the hotel.

"You c-c-can't park here," he said.

"I didn't park it here," said Roy. "I can't drive."

"Who th-th-this c-c-car belong to?"

"A musician who forgot something in the hotel last night."

The doorman was a tall but slightly stooped slender man wearing a red and yellow braided cap and a red and black coat that resembled the jackets the flying monkeys who worked for the Wicked Witch wore in the movie *The Wizard of Oz*. He looked around and up and down the block, as if he were desperate to speak to someone other than an eleven-year-old kid.

"I heard that a man got shot and killed here last night," said Roy.

"Um-hum," said the doorman.

"Do you know why or who did it?"

"All's I kn-kn-know is the p-p-police f-f-found a Re-Re-Remington ought-six Bu-Bu-Bushmaster d-d-deer rifle under a t-t-tree 'cross the street. Um-hum."

Sid Wade came out of the hotel carrying a large, round, black leather bag and a sock cymbal stand. He set them down on the sidewalk by the rear of the Pontiac, took out his keys and opened the trunk.

"Y-y-you c-c-can't park here, mister," said the doorman.

Sid Wade loaded the bag and stand into the trunk and closed the lid.

"Keep your shirt on, Pop," he said.

Wade walked around the back of the car to the driver's door.

"Get in," he said to Roy.

As the Pontiac pulled away, Wade said, "Old fool."

He lit a cigarette, then turned on the radio and tuned it to another station. A band was playing.

"That's 'Jive at Six,'" said Wade. "Ben Webster on tenor, Sweets Edison on trumpet."

He turned up the volume.

The Theory of the Leisure Class

Roy did not so much mind the two feet of new snow that had fallen overnight, but ice had hardened during the early morning hours and created a carapace upon the sidewalks that made them dangerous to negotiate. The elderly and enfeebled were advised to stay home. Stepping cautiously on his way to school, Roy stopped in front of Walsh's drugstore on Blackhawk to take a copy of that day's *Sun-Times* from the bundle on the ground in front of the entrance. Walsh's would not open for another hour, so Roy left a dime on the bundle, rolled up the paper, stuck it under his arm and continued toward the school.

He wished he could be with his father right now in Havana, Cuba, where the temperature was in the mid-80s and the trade winds were blowing. His dad had gone to Cuba on business and was staying at the Hotel Nacional, his regular place of residence when he was on the island. Roy enjoyed sitting out on the terrace there early in the morning, when it was coolest, drinking lemonade and munching lightly toasted and sweet-buttered Cuban bread. After breakfast at the Nacional, Roy would usually go swimming in the hotel pool, then he would get dressed and walk by himself over to the Sevilla Biltmore to have lunch with his father. Most of the time, Roy's father would be there already, seated in a booth at the rooftop restaurant with two or three other men. There were framed black and white photographs on the walls of the restaurant, in two of which his dad could be seen smiling and holding a cigar. Roy's mother was in one of the photos, taken at Oriental Park Racetrack in Marianao, her long, auburn hair pulled back tightly, wearing the calico jacket Roy liked so much. Often when he thought about his mother, he pictured her wearing that jacket.

Roy's parents had been divorced for five years. He was ten now, and he lived with his mother most of the time, but his parents remained close friends. Roy had never seen or heard them argue or say a harsh word to or about one another. It seemed to him that they got along better than many of his friends' parents who were still married and lived together.

Roy took a seat in the last row of his classroom and opened the newspaper on his desk. The first thing he looked at was the sports section, which was full of news about the Dodgers and Giants abandoning Brooklyn and New York City and moving to the West Coast. Both owners of those teams, Walter O'Malley and Horace Stoneham, had received dozens of death threats from furious and forlorn fans. Roy did not blame them for being angry; he would be, too, he knew, if the Cubs and White Sox left. On the front page of the paper was a story about a shooting on a river bridge in rural Wisconsin. Two teenagers, a boy and a girl, had been parked in a car with the motor running on the bridge at night when a man wearing an orange cap with earflaps came out of the nearby woods carrying a shotgun, walked up to the car and ordered the girl, who was sitting in the front passenger seat, to roll down her window. He then pushed the barrel of the gun into the car and fired it at the boy, blowing away most of his face. The girl fainted. When she woke up and saw the boy, she screamed, then got out of the car, its motor still running, and hiked three miles back to their hometown and told the sheriff what happened. She didn't know where the man who had shot the boy had gone, but he was not there when she regained consciousness.

The next morning, at first light, the sheriff organized a manhunt. His posse gathered on the river bridge, and as the sheriff was giving them their instructions, a man wearing an orange hat walked out of the woods holding a shotgun above his head with both hands and surrendered. The man gave his name, age and place of residence as Gunnar Hamsun, thirty-eight, from Duluth, Minnesota. The girl later identified Hamsun as the killer. No motive for the murder had been determined. One member of the posse was quoted as saying that the man taken into custody had a tattoo of a cross with a snake wrapped around it in the center of his forehead.

Roy's teacher told him to put away the newspaper and pay attention to what she was saying.

"School is for learning," she said, "not for leisure."

Roy pictured his father and his cronies sitting in a booth at the Sevilla Biltmore, smoking Montecristos and drinking mojitos or sipping the strong Cuban coffee that smelled so good. Roy did not like the taste of coffee so much as he loved the odor. The next time his father was going to Havana, Roy would ask him to take him along, even if it was during the school year. He could learn what he needed to in Cuba, Roy figured, as well or probably better than he could in Chicago. His father and his friends did business, but they conducted it, it seemed to Roy, at their leisure. They had the right idea, he decided, and the weather undoubtedly had something to do with it.

Innamorata

Roy's mother liked to go to foreign films.

"They're more realistic than American movies," she said to him. "Maybe realistic isn't the right word. Honest is probably better. Also, the actors and actresses seem more like real people, people you could meet on the street. Most of all, though, I like their faces because they're not perfect."

When Roy was nine years old, he went with his mother to see an Italian film at the Esquire theater called *Innamorata*. Sometimes he had difficulty reading fast enough to keep up with the subtitles, but he managed to get most of it. The story was about a girl of fifteen who loses everyone in her family during bombing raids on her town in Italy at the beginning of World War II. She wanders through the countryside trying to stay alive, to find food and shelter. Some of the people she meets are kind and generous, but others, especially men, treat her badly. She loses her virginity to a one-armed Italian soldier who deserted the army and is then maimed by a hand grenade thrown by a six-year-old boy. The girl helps nurse the wounded soldier until he regains his strength, at which point he rips off the girl's clothes, rapes her and runs away.

The girl is saved from drowning in a river during a torrential storm by a farmer, who then takes her home to stay with him and his wife. The wife hates the girl because she is young and beautiful, and the wife is middle-aged and worn down from years of laboring on the land. The wife compares her gnarled, scarred hands to the girl's lovely ones and is so upset that she attempts to chop off the girl's fingers with a hatchet. The girl escapes and hides in a cave where she cries and asks God why He created people if all He wants them to do is to suffer and then die.

The war ends two years later, when the girl is seventeen. She is very thin and dressed in rags when an American soldier with a patch over one eye driving a Jeep sees her sleeping near the side of a dirt road. He stops and carries her to the Jeep. She is only half-conscious and weak and unable to resist. He takes her to a hospital and visits her every day for several weeks. She slowly recovers her health and he is beguiled by her beauty. One morning he brings her flowers and a nurse tells him that his innamorata is now strong enough to leave the hospital. He asks the girl what innamorata means. "It's my name," she tells him, and the movie ends.

Outside the theater, Roy's mother said, "That one wasn't so good."

"I wish somebody had shot and killed the one-armed soldier," said Roy.

"Oh, I'm sure something bad happened to him later," said his mother. "But that's what I like about these European movies, Roy, they don't always tie the story up so neatly and explain everything. They leave you with something to think about."

Roy was thinking about the girl's naked breasts, which he'd gotten to see a lot. He also thought about the American soldier's eye patch, which was over his left eye when he was driving the Jeep but over his right eye when he brought flowers to the girl in the hospital. Roy was in the car with his mother when he told her about the eye patch.

"Good, Roy," she said. "I didn't notice that."

"And was her name really what they said at the end?" Roy asked.

"Innamorata," said his mother. "It means beloved."

"At the beginning," said Roy, "everybody calls her Lucia."

His mother drove for a few minutes without talking, then she said, "War changes everybody, Roy. Nobody is the same after a war as they were before the war started. Maybe that's the point. I just hope you never have to be in one."

"Have you ever asked God a question," he said, "like the girl did when she was in the cave?"

"No, Roy, I haven't."

"How come?"

Roy's mother laughed, and said, "Because I know I wouldn't get an answer, either."

The Exception

Tampa, Florida, was a quiet, sleepy fishing and cigar manufacturing city in the 1950s, when Roy's Uncle Buck, his mother's brother, moved there and went into the construction business. Roy enjoyed visiting Tampa, which was easy to do from either Key West or Havana, the two places Roy's mother preferred spending time when Roy was a boy, before they went to live in Chicago. Roy's mother would often leave him with her brother while she traveled elsewhere. Roy was happiest when he got to hang out with his Uncle Buck, taking fishing trips in the Gulf of Mexico or just accompanying him while he did business in Tampa.

One of Buck's closest associates was his poker buddy, Chino Valdes, who owned the Oriente Bank in Ybor City. Chino's real first name was Nestor, but everyone, including Roy, called him Chino because his narrow, slanted eyes gave him an Asian appearance.

"Know why I'm called Chino?" he asked Roy.

"No, why?"

"'Cause my grandmother had a little yen."

Chino was a partner in a nightclub on the outskirts of Tampa named El Paraíso Bajo las Estrellas, where he and Roy's uncle often met. Buck took Roy along with him to El Paraíso several times in the afternoons, letting his nephew sit at the bar and order Coca-Colas and watch the showgirls rehearse while he and Chino discussed matters of mutual importance.

It was on one of these afternoons at El Paraíso that Roy was present during a murder, an event about which he was sworn to secrecy by his uncle and Chino Valdes.

This incident occurred the day before Roy's twelfth birthday. He and his uncle arrived at El Paraíso shortly after two in the afternoon. Chino was already there, sitting at a table by himself, sipping Methusalem rum on the rocks. Roy and Buck walked over to Chino, who stood up and shook hands with both of them, then sat down, as did Buck.

"Go watch the girls, Roy," said Chino, and handed the boy a five dollar bill. "It's educational. The drinks are on me."

Roy smiled at Chino, thanked him, and went over to the bar and climbed up on a stool. He placed the fin down in front of him and when Alfredito, the bartender, came over, said hello and ordered a Coke. Roy liked Alfredito, a short, thin, baldheaded man with a mustache that looked like two caterpillars crawling towards one another. Alfredito never charged Roy for his drinks. The five dollar bill that Chino gave Roy, as he did every time Roy came in, was to be left on the bar as a tip for Alfredito.

The dancers were on the stage, practicing their routines. Most of them were coffee-colored Cuban girls. They wore short shorts and little tops that left their midriffs bare. Roy thought they were all beautiful.

"How come you never look at the dancers?" Roy asked Alfredito. "You always keep your back to them."

"I'm an old man, chico," said Alfredito. "I have grandchildren older than some of these girls. It is for their sake that I don't turn around. When they look at me, I see pity in their eyes. I want to spare them the pain."

Roy remembered a story his uncle had told him after the first time they'd gone together to El Paraíso. It was about one of the dancers, a brunette originally from Matanzas named Soslaya Zancera, who was billed as the Ava Gardner of Cuba. Soslaya was the star of the show, and the girlfriend of one of the owners, Morris Perlstein. One night Perlstein caught her in an unnatural embrace with the club bouncer, Roberto Bulto, in her dressing room, and shot Bulto dead. Perlstein then fired two bullets into the girl's buttocks when she attempted to flee. The owner was subsequently convicted of manslaughter and sentenced to twenty years in prison. His mistress survived, but her injuries put an end to her career as a dancer. Roy's uncle told him that Soslaya now walked with the aid of two canes and worked as a manicurist at the Hotel Khartoum in Miami Beach.

"It was a tragedy," said Buck. "Soslaya Zancera was exceptional."

Roy looked over at the table where his Uncle and Chino Valdes were sitting. A third man had joined them, a large, pale-faced person wearing a mauve guayabera, a Panama hat and dark glasses. Roy noticed that the man's fingernails were painted blood red. He had never before seen a man wearing nail polish.

"Who's that guy?" Roy asked Alfredito.

"Cherry Dos Rios," said Alfredito, "from Fort Lauderdale."

"What does he do?"

"He's in the construction business."

"Like my uncle."

Alfredito nodded, and said, "It's a good business to be in."

Roy returned his attention to the girls. Music came from a tape recorder because the band was there only at night. Alfredito told Roy the musicians slept during the day.

Suddenly, there was a loud popping sound, and the dancers stopped. Roy looked around and saw Chino Valdes hand a revolver to a man in a green seersucker suit, who walked quickly out of the club. Cherry Dos Rios sat slumped in his chair, a large, dark stain spreading under his mauve guayabera. His Panama was on the table. He still had on the dark glasses. Someone turned off the music.

Roy's uncle came over to him and said, "Vamonos, sobrino."

Chino stood up and came over, too.

"Chico," he said to Roy, placing a hand on the boy's left shoulder, "your uncle and I know that we can depend on your not having witnessed this unfortunate little accident."

Roy looked at Chino and nodded.

"Buck tells me that tomorrow is your birthday. Here's something from me."

Chino handed Roy a hundred dollar bill. Roy had never held one before.

"If you're anything like your uncle," Chino said, "I know you'll use it well."

"Thank you," said Roy. "I will."

The dancers had disappeared. Two men were dragging Cherry Dos Rios's limp corpse into a back room. As Roy and his uncle walked together out of El Paraíso, Roy saw Alfredito pick up Cherry Dos Rios's hat off the table at which he'd been sitting. Alfredito waved it at Roy and smiled.

As Buck pulled his white 1958 Eldorado convertible onto Gasparilla Road, he asked, "Would you like me to put the top down?"

"Sure," said Roy.

His uncle unhooked the latch on his side and Roy undid the one on his, then Buck flipped a switch on the dashboard and the top peeled back. The warm Gulf air felt good on Roy's face and in his hair.

"It's time you started to think about what profession you want to go into when you get older," said his uncle. "Do you have any ideas?"

"Not yet," said Roy.

"You can't go wrong in the construction business."

"Alfredito told me the guy who accidentally got shot was in the construction business."

Roy's uncle picked a cigar out of a box he kept on the front seat next to him, bit off one end, spit the leaves out his window and pushed in the dash lighter.

"Forget about him, Roy," said Buck. "He was the exception."

Close Encounters of the Right Kind

Oleg Bodanski owned and operated the Odessa Grill, a four-stool, two-booth diner on Kedzie Avenue next to the canal that separated the city of Chicago from its northwestern suburbs. He was a widower whose fifteen-year-old daughter, Fátima, had a reputation at her high school for being a fast girl. Roy, who was two years younger, shared the opinion of most of the boys he knew that she was, if not conventionally beautiful, certainly exotic looking, almost oriental, and undeniably sexy with her large black eyes, high-arched eyebrows and ample figure. Fátima was often seen with older guys, men who picked her up in their cars after school. She did not seem to be a part of any particular group of girls, though she was polite to everyone; Roy had never heard anyone say a bad word about her. Fátima was an average student, she participated in class but not in any extracurricular activities. Roy never saw her at any of the school athletic events, but he always kept an eye out for her in the hallways between classes.

Roy's friend Jimmy Boyle's father worked at a plumbing supply house near the Odessa Grill and he went in there from time to time. Jimmy, who had a long-distance crush on Fátima Bodanski the same as Roy, asked his father if he ever saw Fátima in there and he said only once. She had come in around three thirty in the afternoon, when Mr. Boyle was on a coffee break, spoken briefly to her father, stashed her school books on a shelf behind the counter and then went out again. Mr. Boyle said he saw her get into the front passenger side of a late-model Chevy and be driven away. He hadn't seen the driver.

Mr. Boyle told Jimmy that the girl's mother had supposedly run off with a knife thrower from a travelling carnival when Fátima was eight or nine years old. According to a pal of Mr. Boyle's who had been in a bowling league with Oleg Bodanski, the diner owner's wife was killed in an accident a few months later when the knife thrower's car went off an icy road and plunged into Lake Superior near Grand Marais, Minnesota. Both she and her paramour drowned before rescuers could pry open the doors of his automobile and extricate the bodies.

Roy knew that his chances of getting to know Fátima Bodanski better were slim, but he held out hope for the future, when their age difference would not matter so much. One rainy Saturday afternoon in August, Roy found himself near the Odessa Grill and decided to go in and get something to drink. He had been playing in a baseball game that ended prematurely due to the weather; he was dirty and wet and glad to get inside for a little while before walking the rest of the way to his house.

Oleg Bodanski was sitting on a high stool behind the counter reading a newspaper; there were no customers in the diner. Roy sat down on the stool nearest the front door. Oleg Bodanski was forty-two years old, slightly built, a couple of inches under six feet tall. He wore wire-rim glasses, was clean-shaven, and his bushy brown hair was graying at the temples. Fátima, Roy decided, must favor her mother as far as her looks were concerned. He noticed that the paper Bodanski was reading was the *Christian Science Monitor*.

"Hi," said Roy.

Oleg Bodanski looked up and said, "Do you know what you want?"

Before Roy could answer, Bodanski added, "Does anyone?"

The diner owner put down the *Monitor* and slid off his stool.

"I'll have a chocolate phosphate," Roy said.

Bodanski made the drink and set it down on the counter in front of Roy.

"Tell me if there's enough syrup in it," said Bodanski. "I'll put in more if you want."

Roy took a sip through the straw in the glass.

"It's okay," he said.

Bodanski nodded. "Sometimes people want it sweeter. Me, I don't like so much chocolate that it overpowers the seltzer."

Oleg Bodanski stood behind the counter and watched Roy sip the phosphate.

"You look like an intelligent boy," he said.

"How can you tell?" asked Roy.

"What would you think if I told you that I've had encounters with visitors from other planets?" said Bodanski. "And that you might have, too, even if you don't realize it."

"What happened to you?" said Roy.

Oleg Bodanski hovered over Roy from the other side of the counter, leaning more than a little in the boy's direction.

"They nabbed me once while I was driving my old Ford, the '51, and twice while I was asleep. Each time they kept me for exactly two hours."

"How do you know?"

"Lost the time. I was drivin' home from Racine one night, my cousin Boris lives there, and arrived two hours later than I should have. Lost two hours of sleep twice. Checked the Westclox next to my bed. Know what they wanted?"

Roy shook his head.

"My sperm. They milked me, then put me back where I'd been."

"How did the car keep driving without you at the wheel?"

"Don't really know," said Bodanski. "Didn't feel a thing other than a weakness in my groin. They got methods our scientists haven't thought up yet."

"Where were they from? I mean, what planet?"

Bodanski did not answer. He had a faraway look on his face, so Roy didn't ask him again. He did not want to know how Oleg Bodanski knew the aliens had deprived him of his sperm. Just then the door to the diner opened and in walked Fátima Bodanski.

"Hi, Daddy," she said. "Can I borrow five bucks?"

Her father emerged from his reverie and said, "What for?"

"Francine and Donna are waitin' outside in Donna's mother's car. They want me to go to the movies with 'em. I told 'em sure since it's so hot and rainin' and I don't have anything to do until eight when Ronnie's comin' to get me."

Oleg Bodanski turned around and punched open the cash register.

"Hi," Fátima said to Roy, and gave him a big smile.

She had perfectly straight, small teeth, and she was chewing Juicy Fruit gum. Roy could smell it.

Her father handed her a fin and said, "Have a good time, baby."

"Oh, Daddy, you're the tops!" said Fátima, as she took the money, then blew him a kiss and left the diner.

Roy looked out the window and saw Fátima climb into the back seat of a tan 1955 Dodge Lancer and close the door as the car pulled away from the curb.

"Ronnie," Bodanski said. "You know who Ronnie is?"

"No," said Roy.

"Neither do I."

Oleg Bodanski stood still. For a moment Roy thought the man might have gone back into his reverie.

"My daughter," said Bodanski. "I named her Fátima Portugal Bodanski because of the flying saucer sightings near Fátima, Portugal, in 1917. Called the 'miracle of Fátima.' Thousands of people saw 'em. One of the aliens, a tiny, woman-like creature, appeared, walked right out of a spaceship while it was still in the air and said she'd descended from Heaven, and declared that the only way further suffering on Earth could be averted was if people stopped offending God. Catholic Church verified the events. You can look it up."

Roy put a quarter on the counter.

"I enjoyed the chocolate phosphate," he said, and got down off the stool.

"Come again," said Oleg Bodanski. "You're a bright boy."

Walking home in the rain, Roy thought about Fátima Bodanski standing next to him, cracking her Juicy Fruit. He could still smell it. It was as close an encounter with her as he was likely to have, but if he did run into her, Roy decided, he would say hello and remind her that they'd sort of met in the Odessa Grill. He could tell her that her father had told him what he'd named her after and ask her what she thought about it. And he wouldn't say anything to Fátima about how spacemen had drained her father's sperm. Roy figured she didn't know anything about that.

Blue People

Roy's fascination with maps began before he was eight years old. His curiosity about what people in distant lands looked like, what languages they spoke, and their customs, accelerated the more he read about countries whose names and geography he discovered in the *Great World Atlas*.

In school one day, a substitute teacher named Arvid Scranton mentioned that just after the war he had been stationed in North Africa, and had traveled extensively in that region. In Morocco, he told Roy's class, he had been in a place called Goulimime, at the edge of the Sahara desert, where he had encountered the Blue People, a nomadic tribe called the Tuareg, who wore blue robes dyed with natural indigo that was absorbed by their skin and turned it blue. Many people believed, said Arvid Scranton, that the dye had become so pervasive over time that it entered the Tuaregs' bloodstream to the degree that their babies were born with a decidedly blue tinge to their otherwise black skin.

Roy was eleven when he learned of the existence of the Tuareg. A year later, he was playing in a basketball tournament at Our Fathers Out of Egypt when he saw a blue person. The center on the team from Kings of Assyria had skin that was exactly as Arvid Scranton had described: deep, dark blue that glowed under and despite the dull yellow gymnasium lights. The kid on Kings of Assyria was taller than anyone else on either team and extremely thin, so thin that he was easily pushed around and brutalized by shorter but stockier opponents. Occasionally, he lofted a shot high over a defender's head that was impossible to block, but more often than not it clanged harmlessly off the rim of the basket, or banged too hard against the backboard. The kid had no touch, as well as not enough strength, and his team was easily defeated.

After the game, Roy was tempted to ask him if he was related to the Tuareg of the Sahara, but he was afraid the kid would be offended, so he did not.

Later, at Meschina's Restaurant, Roy and Jimmy Boyle were sitting at the counter eating club sandwiches and drinking Dad's root beers, when Roy told Jimmy about the Blue People, and how he figured the kid on Kings of Assyria must be related to them.

"You ever seen anyone else with skin dark blue like that?" Roy said.

Jimmy's mouth was too full to speak, so he just shook his head.

Lorraine, a waitress who had worked at Meschina's for forever, stopped in front of the boys and said, "My skin is black upon me, and my bones are burned with heat."

"What's that?" asked Jimmy. "You ain't black, and it's freezin' outside."

"Job, 30:30," said Lorraine. "I heard you talkin'. Kid must be descended from those desert people, the ones move around all the time."

"Nomads," said Roy.

"Roy says they turn blue because of the dye on their robes," said Jimmy.

"Very clever," Lorraine said. "I wish I could just wear a red babushka over my hair to make it stay red, then I wouldn't have to pay the beauty parlor no more."

As Roy and Jimmy walked home from Meschina's, the sky got dark fast and snow began to fall. A hard wind made them duck their heads.

"The weather in Chicago'll turn you blue, too," said Jimmy, "you get stuck out in it too long."

"Good thing that blue kid couldn't shoot," Roy said.

"He could," said Jimmy, "nobody'd stop him."

"He's too skinny," said Roy, "but if he keeps playin', he'll learn how to score and beef up as he gets older. Probably be a pro, he grows more."

"Good thing for him his family moved here," said Jimmy. "I bet they don't play basketball much in the Sahara desert."

Call of the Wild

When Roy was eighteen years old, he learned that an old friend of his from the neighborhood, Eddie Derwood, had attempted suicide by placing a plastic bag over his head in an effort to asphyxiate himself. Eddie, Roy was told, had been committed to the Illiniwek Psychiatric Institute in Chicago, where he was undergoing treatment for severe depression. Roy was away at school when he received this news in a letter from a mutual friend, and when he returned to Chicago for the Christmas holidays, he went to see Eddie.

Roy did not know why Eddie Derwood, with whom he had been friends all through high school and had played with on many baseball, football, and basketball teams, had tried to kill himself. This was a mystery to Roy and Eddie's other friends, too, since Eddie had always seemed like a happy guy. Derwood was smart, handsome and well-liked by almost everyone in the neighborhood. He had gone off to college in Wisconsin, and two months into his freshman year his roommate found him unconscious on the floor of their dormitory room with the plastic bag over his head secured by rubber bands around his neck.

The Illiniwek Psychiatric Institute was a large, ugly brown brick building. Snow was falling lightly but insistently as Roy entered, registered at the reception desk as a visitor and was told to wait until an attendant arrived to escort him to the fourth floor, where Eddie Derwood was housed. Two other people were in the waiting room: an old man with a week's growth of white whiskers on his face, wearing a green hat with earflaps and a dark blue overcoat with a gray, fake fur collar; and a woman who looked to be in her late thirties or early forties, perhaps the old man's daughter, or even granddaughter, whose bleached blonde hair with black roots showing was partially covered by a bright red scarf, and whose thin, red cloth coat, Roy thought, could hardly succeed in keeping her warm. She was very skinny and had a long, sharply pointed nose that she kept wiping with a black handkerchief.

"Are you all right?" the woman asked the old man.

"Louise," he said, "you always ask the most terrible questions."

A large, powerful-looking man with carrot-colored hair brushed to a point on the crown of his head, wearing a dirty white smock, entered the waiting room and called Roy's name. Roy walked over to the man and stood in front of him.

"You here to see Derwood?" the man asked.

"I am," said Roy.

The man turned around and walked away. Roy followed him. They took an elevator to the fourth floor and got off. The attendant walked swiftly ahead without looking back and stopped in front of a door with the number 404 on it. He turned and faced Roy.

"You don't give him nothin'," said the attendant. "You don't take nothin' he try to give you. Don't touch him, even if he touch you. Don't say nothin' could disturb him. You do, I put you out real fast. You understand?"

Roy nodded.

The man opened the door and entered the room, followed by Roy. Eddie Derwood was standing in front of the only window. There were bars on it.

"Person to see you," said the attendant.

"Hi, Eddie," said Roy.

Eddie did not say anything. His eyes were foggy and the corners of his mouth had white crust on them.

"It's me, Roy. Don't you recognize me?"

Eddie stared at Roy for thirty seconds before saying, "You're just a bird, a big, dark bird without wings."

"I'm your friend, Eddie. I'm Roy."

Eddie stood still. His eyes did not move and did not blink.

"Is he on drugs?" Roy asked the attendant. "His eyes are messed up."

"You don't know that," he said.

"That's why I asked you," said Roy. "He's like a zombie."

The attendant went over to Eddie, bent down and put his face close to Eddie's. The attendant's body completely blocked Roy's view of his friend.

"You need somethin', Mr. Derwood?" the attendant said.

Eddie squawked like a crow.

"Caw! Caw!" he said.

The attendant straightened up and turned back to Roy.

"Visit's over," he said.

The attendant took Roy firmly by his right arm and led him out of the room, closing the door behind him. In the elevator going down were two men besides Roy and the attendant. Both of them wore thick-lensed eyeglasses and had wild, curly hair like Larry Fine of the Three Stooges.

"Don't ever say that again," one of them said to the other.

"Say what?" said his companion.

"That you run this place."

"But I do."

"No, you don't. I do."

The elevator stopped at the ground floor, the door opened and Roy got off. The attendant and the two curly-haired passengers stayed on. The door closed and the elevator started going back up.

The old man and the younger woman were no longer in the waiting room. Roy walked out of the building. It was snowing harder and the air seemed colder, but Roy decided to walk for a while before taking a bus back to his neighborhood.

The only time Roy could remember Eddie Derwood losing his temper was once when they were fifteen at Eddie's house and his mother told Eddie that he was not as smart as his older brother,

Burton. Eddie sprang from his chair like a leopard catapulting out of a tree onto an unsuspecting passing animal and grabbed his mother with both hands around her throat, pinning her against a wall. Eddie held her there for several seconds before letting go. He did not say a word and neither did his mother. Eddie sat down and his mother left the room. Roy did not go back to Eddie's house again for a long time after that.

Arabian Nights

Roy, the Viper, and Jimmy Boyle were sitting on top of the back of a bench at Heart-of-Jesus Park drinking grape Nehis after playing a football game. Their team had lost that afternoon to Our Father of Fearful Consequences, a school from Kankakee, and they were not happy about it.

"We shouldn'ta run the ball so much," said Jimmy. "We needed to throw it more."

"Three yards and a cloud of dust," said Roy. "Except we could only get two."

"It's what worked in ancient times," said the Viper, "when Coach was playin', but not no more."

It was a little windy and cold, but the boys didn't want to go home yet. Stan Yemen, the park janitor, came out of the fieldhouse carrying a long-handled rake and walked over to them. Yemen was in his midthirties and had been a janitor at Heart-of-Jesus ever since he had dropped out of high school at sixteen. He always wore a dark brown windbreaker zipped up to his neck, dark brown trousers, white socks and dark brown clodhopper shoes. He never wore a hat, even in winter and even though he had a crewcut. Yemen's most outstanding feature was his missing left ear. His family was from Arabia and Yemen said they were desert people. He had lived over there until he was nine.

The Viper had once gotten up the nerve to ask him how come he didn't have a left ear, and Yemen said, "When I was seven, an elder of our tribe tried to circumcise me, but I dodged his dagger and he sliced off my ear instead."

The boys didn't know whether or not to believe him, but all Yemen had where his ear should have been was a small lump of congealed flesh that looked like somebody had thrown a mudball at his head and part of it had stuck there.

"Hey, fellas," Stan Yemen said.

"Hi, Stan," said Jimmy Boyle. "You see our game?"

"No, I had to work. Lots of leaves to clean out of the gutters and rake up this time of year. I heard you tried to run on 'em and got beat."

"It was ugly," said Roy.

"Tell the truth, Stan," said the Viper. "You really lost your ear when they tried to circumcise you?"

Yemen smiled at him. The janitor had big brown eyes that matched his clothing; they jiggled in their sockets as he spoke.

"All Arab boys are expected to submit to circumcision in order to pass into manhood," he said, "but I had witnessed this ceremony performed on my two older brothers and seen and heard their suffering, and I vowed then not to allow it to happen to me."

"Didn't your father or mother try to make you?" asked Jimmy.

"Not really. They had already decided to try to leave the country, and my mother, especially, was not a true believer in many traditional Muslim customs. It is thanks to her, not Allah, that I still have my foreskin."

"What about your ear?" Roy said.

Again, Stan Yemen smiled.

"I confess," he said, "about that I lied. The truth is, it was bitten off by a lion one night when I was sleeping in the desert. In fact, on the same night I ran away from the circumcision ceremony to hide."

The janitor walked away, holding his rake over his right shoulder like a rifle.

"No way," said Jimmy Boyle. "A lion would have bitten off his whole head, not just an ear."

"You think he can hear out of the left side of his head," said the Viper, "even though he don't got an ear there?"

The wind picked up and suddenly the sky darkened. Roy jumped off the bench.

"Ask him next time," he said.

Last Plane out of Chungking

The little plane was barely visible through dense night fog as it sat on the ground. Then the engine turned over and the single propeller started to rotate, scattering mist as the plane nudged forward, feeling its way toward the runway. Chinese soldiers suddenly burst out of the airport terminal and began firing their rifles furiously in an attempt to prevent the plane from taking off. Tiny lights from the aircraft's cabin winked weakly from within its whitish shroud while the plane taxied, desperately attempting to gather speed sufficient for takeoff. The soldiers stood confused, firing blindly and futilely until the aircraft lifted into blackness and escape.

Roy fell asleep with the television on after watching this opening scene of the film *Lost Horizon*. He liked to watch old movies late at night and in the early morning hours, even though he had to be up by seven a.m. in order to be at school by eight. On this particular night, Roy dreamed about four boys his age, fourteen, in Africa, who discover a large crocodile bound by rope to a board hidden in bushes, abandoned by the side of a dusty dirt road. A stout stick was placed vertically in the crocodile's mouth between its upper and lower jaws in order to keep the mouth open as widely as possible and prevent its jaws from snapping shut.

The crocodile could not move or bite, so the boys decided to drag it by the tail end of the board to a nearby river and release it. As they approached the river's edge, it began raining hard and the ground suddenly became mushy and very slippery. To free the crocodile, they placed the board so that the croc's head faced the river. One of the boys tore a long, sinewy vine from a plant and cautiously wound it around the stick. Another boy had a knife and prepared to cut the rope. The other two boys kept a safe distance. The boy with the knife sliced the rope in two at the same time the other boy tugged forcefully on one end of the vine, pulling out the stick. The crocodile did not immediately move or close its enormous mouth. The boys stood well away from it, watching. After a few moments, the crocodile hissed loudly and slowly slithered off the board and wobbled to the water's edge, slid into the dark river and disappeared from view. The boys ran off as the downpour continued.

When Roy woke up, it was a few minutes before seven. He turned off the alarm before it could ring and thought about both the plane fleeing Chungking and the African boys rescuing the crocodile. What was the difference, he wondered, between waking life and dream life? Which, if any, was more valid or real? Roy could not make a clear distinction between the two. He decided then that both were of equal value, two-thirds of human consciousness, the third part being imagination. The last plane out of Chungking took off with Roy aboard, bound for the land of dreams. What happened there only he could imagine.

The Vanished Gardens of Córdoba

Roy was a Chicago White Sox fan until 1956, when the Sox traded their shortstop, Chico Carrasquel, who was Roy's favorite player, to the Cleveland Indians, to make room for a rookie, Luis Aparicio. Roy switched his allegiance to the Chicago Cubs, who had the home run–hitting newcomer Ernie Banks at shortstop, and he never forgave the White Sox for getting rid of Carrasquel. Aparicio, like Chico, was from Venezuela, and the Sox proved correct in exchanging one Venezuelan for another, since Little Looie, as he came to be called, went on to a Hall of Fame career, while Carrasquel quickly faded into obscurity. But Chico had been the first flashy Latin infielder in the major leagues and Roy, who was then a nine-year-old shortstop on his Little League team, never forgot him. Chico and Looie were the vanguard of Venezuelan star shortstops, to be followed by Davey Concepcion and Omar Vizquel, the latter being perhaps the best of them all. Roy became enamored of Ernie Banks, too, but more for his power stroke than his fielding. Banks had good hands—he set the major league record for fewest errors in a season (since broken)—but limited range. Carrasquel made more errors but he got to more balls, as did Aparicio, whom Roy eventually came to respect and admire. Alfonso "Chico" Carrasquel, whose father, Alex, had been a legendary pitcher in his native Venezuela, would remain Roy's baseball hero. When he grew up, Roy decided, he would write a biography of Chico Carrasquel even if nobody else remembered him. Many years later, when Roy read in a book about Prince Faisal saying to Lawrence of Arabia, "And I . . . I long for the vanished gardens of Córdoba," he pictured Chico Carrasquel on the vanished infield of old, since demolished Comiskey Park in Chicago, snagging a hard ground ball on the short hop and firing it to first base just in time to nail the runner. Roy knew exactly how Faisal felt.

Benediction

Years later, during the several days preceding her death, in her delirium caused by a stroke, Roy's mother imagined that her father, whom Roy had called Pops, was with her. Pops, of course, had died fifty years before, but Kitty believed that he was now looking after her and that they were dining together in a great restaurant. In reality, it was Roy's sister who sat by their mother's bedside in a hospital, listening to Kitty talk about her father, whom Roy's sister had never known.

When his sister told Roy about this on the phone, before Roy got on an airplane to see his mother for the last time, he told his sister it was a good thing because Kitty had long felt guilty about having acted coldly, even cruelly, to Pops in the years prior to his own death, believing that he had been entirely to blame for the divorce from her mother when Kitty was ten. Nanny, Roy's grandmother, had died when Roy was eight, so his sister, who was not born until four years later, had not known Nanny, either. This visitation from Kitty's father on her deathbed was a miracle of reconciliation, a touching resolution to Kitty's conflict. How wonderful, Roy told his sister, for their mother to release herself from what clearly had been her most profound regret.

"Well, after all," said Roy's sister, "she was raised a Catholic."

"Pops forgave her," Roy said, "not a priest."

As Roy stood in line waiting to board the plane, he remembered Pops standing on the sidewalk in front of the hotel he lived in in Chicago, waiting for his daughter to pick him up to go to lunch with her and Roy, who was then nine years old. It was a cold, blustery, overcast Sunday afternoon, and Roy felt sorry for his grandfather, who was almost eighty, waiting there alone in the bad weather, a black woollen scarf wrapped around his neck underneath a long, gray overcoat. Pops always dressed well and Roy had wondered that day why he was not wearing his signature Homburg hat.

After his mother had pulled her car to the curb and stopped, leaving the motor running, Roy, who was sitting in the back seat, opened the right rear passenger door of the midnight blue 4-door Oldsmobile Holiday and got out to greet his grandfather.

"Pops," Roy said, "it's really windy. Why aren't your wearing your hat?"

Pops smiled at Roy and gave him a kiss on the top of his head. Roy loved his grandfather more than any other person in his family. It always disturbed him when his mother spoke harshly to Pops.

"You know what the banker said to the poor farmer who'd come to see him about a loan?" Pops asked.

"No, what?"

"Here's your hat, what's your hurry?"

After they'd gotten into the back seat of the Oldsmobile and Roy closed the door, Kitty looked at her father in the rear view mirror and said to him, "Where's your hat?"

Pops put an arm around his grandson and said, "I must have left it in the bank."

Then he and Roy laughed.

Roy's sister told him not to expect that their mother would recognize him.

"She's lost at least thirty years of her memory," his sister said.

When Roy saw his mother on her deathbed, he asked her if she knew who he was.

Kitty opened her eyes, looked into his and said, "You're Roy. You run faster than anybody."

For God's sake let us sit on the ground
And tell sad stories of the death of kings.

—William Shakespeare,
The Tragedy of King Richard the Second

The Red Studebaker

ROY'S UNCLE BUCK

Alligator Story

A kid wearing a Tampa Tarpons t-shirt came running up the street shouting, "Some cracker just shot a gator!"

Roy and his uncle Buck were in the driveway of the house on Oakview Terrace, rinsing down the boat. They had just come in from fishing out of Oldsmar and had been gone since five o'clock that morning; it was now six thirty in the evening. They hadn't had much luck, having boated several kingfish and a few mackerel, but they'd run on sharks everywhere and had to cut lines to get rid of them. The weather had been spotty, the water in the Gulf was cloudy, and there were periodic brief showers. It was just the two of them, so they'd had a lot of time to talk. Roy was twelve and a half years old and he loved to listen to Buck, who was forty-five. Buck was full of information on almost any subject. He was well-traveled and well-read and today he had been teaching Roy about navigation, explaining a rhumb line, which is a course that makes the same angle with each meridian which it crosses; it is constant in direction throughout and always appears as a straight line on charts.

"But the curve of shortest distance between any two points on the earth is always an arc of a great circle," Roy's uncle told him, "the sort of circle which would be marked out if we were to slice the earth into two halves, passing the cut through the ends of the course and the center of the earth. The shortest path will always be a great circle course."

Buck had been a Lieutenant Commander in the navy during the war and he was a civil and mechanical engineer; sometimes his explanations were too esoteric or complicated for Roy to absorb, but his uncle was always careful to show Roy what he was talking about.

"It's the wind you have to pay the closest attention to," said Uncle Buck. "The winds will control the course more than mathematical considerations."

As the kid in the Tarpons t-shirt ran by, Buck asked him, "Where's he got it?"

"On the little pier at the end of Palmetto," the kid shouted.

Buck cut off the hose and went into the utility shed and came back out with a sheathed knife and a hatchet. He handed the hatchet to Roy and said, "Come on, nephew, let's go down there."

Roy and his uncle walked along River Grove under massive hanging moss and cut across the narrow skiff launch to Palmetto Street, which they followed down to the little pier. When they got there they saw a skinny man about forty years old wearing only a pair of gray trousers with the butt of a pistol sticking out of the waistband and a dark brown Remington Ammo cap slicing up the belly side of a six-and-a-half-foot-long alligator. The man's pants, chest, and arms were spattered with blood.

Buck and Roy watched him work for a minute, then Buck said, "What are you going to do with the hide?"

The man was working fast and he did not look up.

"Throw it away. There's a five hundred dollar fine you get caught with it. All I need's the meat."

Roy and his uncle and two boys who were about eight or nine years old and had been swimming in the Hillsborough River watched the man hack and tear feverishly at the carcass. It was still very hot although the sun had begun to go down. Roy knew that it was against the law to shoot a gator without a permit; he guessed that the man didn't have permission to kill alligators, so he wanted to take what was edible and get going.

When the man had finished carving up the belly, he crammed the meat into a canvas sack, stood up and wiped his knife on his right trouser leg and said to Buck, "I'll leave the rest to you, then."

The man walked off with the sack over his left shoulder. Roy noticed that he was barefoot and his right leg was considerably shorter than his left. The bag full of gator meat seemed to help keep him balanced as he made his way up the pebbly incline from the dock and disappeared behind the hanging moss.

Buck unsheathed his knife, flipped what remained of the alligator onto its stomach and told Roy to chop off the head.

Roy hesitated and his uncle said, "Come on, nephew, we don't want Fish and Game to find us. Run your fingers along the top of the spine and find the soft spot."

The ridges along the gator's back were hard as stones and sharp-edged but not abrasive like a shark's skin. Roy's fingers found what felt like a seam two inches behind the head and with both hands wrapped tightly around the handle of the hatchet raised it just above his right shoulder and brought it down into where he judged the seam to be. The blade cut a half-inch into the hide before meeting resistance from muscle and tendon. Roy dropped down from his squatting position and straddled the snout with a knee on either side of the gator's head resting on the planks. The two boys watched intently as Roy hacked away until the head began to separate from the rest of the body. It took about fifteen or twenty minutes to sever the head entirely. When Roy stood up his legs and arms were trembling and his hands hurt.

"Pull the head away," said his uncle, "and stand back."

Buck knelt on the gator's back from the opposite end and began cutting at the hide. Roy stood with the two boys and observed as Buck swiftly but carefully skinned the ancient-looking reptile. Sweat streamed down Roy's uncle's face as he worked, cutting evenly as he progressed from neck to tail, taking particular care not to mutilate the feet. The sun had been down for three hours before Buck completed the job. Roy and the two boys, who were cousins named Rupe and Rhett, were seated cross-legged on the pier.

"That was tough, huh?" Rupe said.

"Alligators have survived for tens of thousands of years," said Buck. "They don't live in houses, like people do, so they have to be protected from the elements."

"God made 'em tough," said Rhett.

"What you gonna do with the head?" asked Rupe.

"You can take it, if you like," Buck said.

Rupe and Rhett stood up and together they lifted the head.

"Whoa, it's heavy," said Rupe, and they dropped it. "We can't carry it all the way to my house."

"Your mama wouldn't let you keep it anyhow," said Rhett.

"Shove it into the river," said Buck.

The cousins slid the head to the end of the pier and pushed it over. There was a small splash when the head hit the water. It floated on the surface for a few seconds, then tilted backwards so that the mouth half opened and grinned at them before the head sank out of sight.

"Them were some terrible lookin' teeth," said Rhett.

Buck kicked what was left of the gator's guts, bones and intestines into the river, then lifted the hide under the front legs.

"Grab the tail with two hands," he told Roy. "Put your arms underneath. Adiós, muchachos."

Rupe and Rhett watched Roy and his uncle carry off the hide.

Back at the house, Buck brought out from the garage a board about six feet long and three feet wide. He and Roy centered the hide on top of it, then Buck tacked it down so that it was stable. He went into the house and came back out with a box of salt and sprinkled the salt liberally all over the hide.

"Pick up the other end," Buck said, and he and Roy carried the board with the gator skin tacked to it around to the backyard and set it down on the ground. Buck took two cinder blocks and placed them down five and a half feet apart, then he and Roy picked up the board and set it down end to end on the blocks.

"It'll be all right here for now," said Buck. "The sun will hit it first thing in the morning, then we'll hoist it up onto the garage roof in the afternoon to dry out."

Buck looped his right arm around Roy's shoulders.

"You did a great job, nephew. I know that head didn't come off easily."

"You did the real work, Unk. You skinned the gator like a Seminole would."

Both Roy and his uncle were covered with blood and gristle.

"How is it you were able to keep your concentration the way you did while you were skinning him?" asked Roy. "I mean, you hardly said a word for two hours."

Buck pulled his blood-stained shirt off over his head and threw it down.

"I started thinking about your grandmother's second husband, the one who raised your mother. He hated me and I hated him and so I imagined that I was skinning him instead of the alligator."

"Why did he hate you?"

"For no good reason, really. I'm almost fourteen years older than your mother. He disliked the fact that my mother had been married before, so he resented my existence. Some men are like that; some women, too."

"Did he hate my mother?"

"No, she was a young girl, and he sent her away to school when she was old enough. I was almost a man, it was easier for him to hate me."

"My mother never talks about him; all I know is that he died."

"He had a heart attack after he and your grandmother were married for ten years; then she remarried my father."

"You must have really hated the guy to imagine that you were skinning him."

"I pretended that he was still alive but barely conscious and that he knew what I was doing but was too weak to do anything about it. I imagined that he didn't die until after I skinned him entirely."

"Did he do anything terrible to you?"

"He banished me from his house, even though my mother and sister lived there. To see me, your grandmother had to meet me somewhere else, in a park or at a restaurant. Whenever she gave me money she made me promise that he would never know that she had."

"That's crazy, Unk. How could she allow that to happen?"

"I don't know, Roy. People do all sorts of crazy things."

Buck unfastened his belt and let his pants drop to the ground. His skinning knife was in its sheath which was still strung on the belt.

"I'm glad I never had to meet him," said Roy.

"He wouldn't have hated you, nephew. What's terrible is that I still harbor such awful feelings for a man who's been dead for twenty-five years. It's no good to keep that kind of poison in you because after awhile the poison starts to work on you. I hope you never have to hate anyone like that."

"I hope I won't, either."

"All right, let's wash up and get some dinner."

"Why didn't we save the head?"

"The only way to preserve it would be to soak it in formaldehyde. Too much trouble. The catfish are feasting on it."

"I bet those cousins are telling their folks about the alligator now."

"Come on, Roy, get your clothes off."

The head was scary, Roy thought, but it was beautiful, too. It was too bad that Rupe or Rhett hadn't kept it.

The Vast Difference

"My Uncle Laszlo told me sex controls a man," Harvey Orszag said, "a man can't control it."

Roy was walking to school with Orszag and another kid, Demetrious Atlas, who had recently moved to Chicago from New York City. Atlas talked a lot and was not shy about expressing his opinions even though he was new in the neighborhood. Roy had heard that was how people behaved in New York, that they weren't afraid to chime in whenever they felt like it. Atlas was thirteen, a year older than Roy and Harvey; he was supposed to be in the eighth grade but was being made to repeat seventh grade because the Chicago school system was different than the one in New York.

"Yeah," said Demetrious Atlas, "a man's sex comes from the vast difference. We learned about it in Personal Hygiene at Brother Ray, the junior high I went to in the Bronx. The school's name used to be Daniel Boone but because of civil rights or somethin' it got renamed after Ray Charles the year before I got there."

Atlas was shorter than both Harvey and Roy but he was wider and heavier. He said his father had once been a professional wrestler who was called Tiny Atlas, the Little Man Who Can Lift the World.

"What's the vast difference?" Roy asked.

"Vast means big, don't it?" said Harvey.

"It's the tube goes from a man's balls carries the juice. A guy gets a boner and shoots a girl the goods. Didn't you learn about it already?"

"They don't teach Personal Hygiene in Chicago," said Orszag.

"I get a boner every morning at ten o'clock," Atlas told them. "I can set my watch by it."

It was the kind of day Roy almost did not mind going to school. The sky was dark gray so he figured there was rain in it but there were no drops falling yet. Sometimes he could see faces in the clouds but today, even though it was the beginning of May, there weren't even wrinkles in them.

Roy and the other students took their seats in the classroom just as the bell rang but Mrs. Barbarossa was not there. Mrs. Barbarossa was a heavyset, middleaged woman who wore thick glasses with frames like television sets and an orange wig. The students knew it was a wig because often when Mrs. Barbarossa returned to the room after a bathroom break her hair was on crooked. Once, the wig was even on backwards and Mrs. Barbarossa had to keep pushing the orange hair out of her eyes. Finally she excused herself and presumably went back to the teachers' bathroom and readjusted the wig because when she returned it was on straight. Mrs. Barbarossa claimed that her husband, Barney Barbarossa, the Kitchen King, who appeared in commercials for his kitchen appliance store during the Midnight Movie on local television, was a descendant of an Algerian pirate from the fifteenth or sixteenth century, only she didn't call him a pirate, she called him a corsair, which is how Roy learned that word.

After a couple of minutes the door opened and a young woman walked in, closed the door behind her and set down the books and papers she was carrying on Mrs. Barbarossa's desk. She stood still for a few moments, looking over the students before she spoke. Roy stared hard at her. She was probably the most beautiful woman he had ever seen, with wavy black hair that fell to her shoulders, unblemished tan skin, large brown eyes and full red lips with sparkling white teeth under them that gleamed like a beam from a ray gun when she opened her mouth.

"Good morning, students," she said. "Or, as they say in my native country of Mexico, *buenos dias*. Mrs. Barbarossa is ill today so I will be substituting for her. My name is Señorita Rita Gomez, or Miss Gomez, if you prefer."

She turned around and wrote the name Miss Gomez with chalk on the blackboard behind the desk. Miss Gomez was slim and not very tall but Roy thought she was perfect. When she turned back around and began to speak, Roy could not hear what she was saying, especially once he noticed that she was wearing a sleeveless white blouse that permitted tufts of puffy black hair to protrude from her armpits. Roy had never seen hair exploding from underneath a woman's arms like this before. He looked over at Demetrious Atlas, whose eyes were glued to the coffee-colored substitute teacher. It was not yet ten o'clock but Roy guessed that like himself and most of the other boys in the room Atlas had a boner already.

By the time school ended that day, Roy was exhausted. He was tired even though he had done nothing other than study Miss Gomez. Her every movement mesmerized him and walking to his house he felt as if he were in a kind of trance. Even her voice captivated him; instead of speaking it sounded to Roy as if she were singing like Julie London only with a Spanish accent.

When Roy got home his grandfather, whom he called Pops, was sitting in an armchair in the livingroom reading the afternoon newspaper.

"Hello, boy," Pops said, "did you have a good day at school?"

"Mrs. Barbarossa was out sick. We had a substitute so we didn't have to do much. Her name was Rita Gomez and she's from Mexico."

Roy sat down on the sofa. He could see that Pops had the newspaper folded open to the sports section.

"If you want something to eat, Roy, there's ham and Swiss in the refrigerator."

"Pops, have you ever heard of the vast difference? A kid who moved here from New York says every guy's got one. It has something to do with sex."

"He must mean the vas deferens. It's a duct that carries sperm from a man's testicles into his penis in order to impregnate a woman."

"Can a man control it? Harvey Orszag's Uncle Laszlo says you can't."

"Well, Roy, that's a good question. I don't know how much Harvey Orszag's Uncle Laszlo knows about biology but I suppose the answer is that some men are better at controlling it than others."

"Señorita Gomez is from Mexico," Roy said. "She's very pretty and she doesn't shave the hair under her arms."

"There are a lot of pretty girls in Mexico," said Pops.

Roy imagined Rita Gomez standing in front of him in the livingroom.

"I think I'd like to go there," he said.

The Birdbath

In 1964, when Roy was a student at the University of Missouri, in Columbia, two friends of a recent acquaintance, Tom Booth, who occupied the room next to Roy's in their dormitory, stopped by to see Tom while he and Roy were in his room playing records. Bill and Bob were from Cape Girardeau, Missouri, where they had gone to high school with Tom, and where they still lived. Bill worked in a filling station and Bob in a lumber yard. They told Tom and Roy that they were on their way to Memphis, Tennessee, to visit Elvis Presley.

"He know you're comin'?" Tom asked.

Bill and Bob both snickered, and Bob said, "Naw, we thought we'd keep it a surprise."

Bill was a tall, lanky kid with sandy hair and a wispy mustache. Bob was shorter and even skinnier and already losing his hair. Both of them were eighteen, the same age as Tom and Roy.

"How do you know Elvis is at Graceland?" Roy said. "He might be off in Hollywood making a movie."

Bob removed a pack of Lucky Strikes from the rolled-up left sleeve of his white tee shirt, shook out a cigarette, put it between his lips and lit it. He offered the pack around. Tom took one and stuck it in his mouth. Bob lit it off the same match, then blew out the match.

"We just want to see the place," said Bill. "Be cool to check out the King's crib, maybe eyeball his pink Cadillacs. Heard he bought one for each of his Memphis Mafia, and his mama, too."

"I think she died," Bob said.

In Bill and Bob's honor, Tom put on a 45 of Elvis singing "You're So Square (Baby I Don't Care)". After it finished playing, Roy said, "I really like Buddy Holly's version of that one. You ever hear it?"

"Elvis does everything better than anyone else," said Bob.

"Know who Elvis says is his favorite singer?" Bill asked.

Tom and Roy shook their heads.

"Mario Lanza."

"I saw him in a movie," said Tom, "wearin' a pirate costume or somethin'. He's pretty fat."

"He's fat, yeah," Bill said, "but he's got a real deep voice that Elvis likes."

Bob nodded. "Elvis is startin' to sound more like Mario Lanza now," he said. "Like on 'Devil in Disguise'."

" 'Little Sister', too," said Bill.

Bill stubbed out his cigarette on the sole of his shoe, stood up and flicked the butt out the window. It was a late afternoon in October and the sky was getting dark.

Bob stood up and so did Tom and Roy.

"We'd best be movin'," Bob said.

Tom and Roy shook hands with both of them.

"Let me know how it goes with Elvis," said Tom. "Good to see you guys."

"Nice to meet you," Roy said. "Good luck."

"Say hi to the King for me," said Tom.

"You bet," said Bob.

About four thirty the next morning, someone knocked on Roy's door and woke him up. It was Tom. Roy let him in.

"What's the matter?" Roy said.

"Bill and Bob were just here again."

"They're here?"

Tom shook his head. "No, they're gone now, but they wanted to show me somethin' before they headed back to Cape Girardeau."

"What was it?"

"They got a cement birdbath in the back of Bill's Apache pick-up. Said they stole it out of Elvis's garden at Graceland."

"Why?"

"Elvis wasn't there. A guard at the gate told 'em the King was away in California or Hawaii makin' a movie, just like you said."

Roy got back into bed and Tom Booth stood by the window. The sky was turning pink.

"So they copped his birdbath?"

"Yeah. They snuck in somehow and took it, then drove back here for a pit stop. I went out and saw the birdbath in the bed of Bill's truck."

"Anything special about it?"

"Just looked like a regular old birdbath to me," said Tom. "Thought you'd like to know. I'm goin' to bed."

A week later, Tom told Roy he'd heard from Bill and Bob. Apparently, after they'd gotten home to Cape Girardeau, they called Graceland and told someone there that they were big fans of Elvis's, that they'd taken the birdbath and would return it if they could meet Elvis in person after he returned from Hollywood. They told whoever it was they spoke to that they would call back the next day, which they did. One of Elvis's buddies, a guy named Red, told them that he'd called Elvis and Elvis said his movie was finished and that he'd be back in Memphis in a couple of days. Elvis told Red to tell Bill and Bob that if they returned the birdbath he wouldn't press charges, and he agreed to meet them in person.

"Did they go back?" asked Roy.

Tom nodded. "Yeah, delivered the birdbath and the guard let 'em carry it to where it had stood in the garden and set it down. Elvis and Red came out and Elvis gave both Bill and Bob autographed pictures of himself and had Red take a photograph of the three of them with one arm around Bill's shoulder and one arm around Bob's. Bob told me that Elvis said they'd done a good service by showing him how his security at Graceland wasn't what it should be, that everyone wasn't as honorable as Bill and Bob. They told Elvis how they'd gotten onto the grounds and smuggled out the birdbath and Elvis said he reckoned as how one of these days they'd be doing bigger things and that he'd be reading about them in the newspapers."

"They're lucky he kept his word and didn't press charges."

"He made Bill and Bob promise to not tell anyone what happened because he didn't want other people to think that by stealing something like they'd done would be a good way to meet him."

"They told you," Roy said.

"Yeah, but I was kind of there about from the beginning. I told Bill I wouldn't tell anyone."

"You told me."

Tom looked down at his feet for a moment, then back up at Roy and said, "Well, I just thought you'd appreciate knowin' what a good person Elvis is."

Storybook Time

From the age of eleven, Cleveland Love never went anywhere without his hammer. In cold weather he kept it in a coat pocket, and when the weather was too warm to wear a coat he kept it tucked in his belt. Cleve was tall and thin, spindly, with curly red hair cut short and posture that gave him the appearance of angling his body backwards, leaning away from whomever approached him. He did not talk much. As Roy's friend Magic Frank said, "Cleve lets his hammer do his talking."

Cleve was put back in school twice, so he was a year or more older than Roy and Frank and their friends. Cleve did not hesitate to use the hammer in a fight, gaining a reputation for being both dangerous and a little looney. Roy never got to know him well but Cleve acted friendly enough and they played together on their eighth grade football team. All Roy knew about Cleve Love's family was what Magic Frank, who had been to Cleve's house a couple of times, told him.

"His old man was a brakeman on the Illinois Central," Frank said, "until he disappeared when Cleve was six. His mother's a hairdresser; so's his sister, Trudy. She's eighteen."

"What's Trudy like?" asked Roy. "Does she carry a hammer, too?"

"Carrot top, like Cleve. Also tall and skinny with a long nose. Freckles. I only seen her once. Cleve told me she knifed a guy when she was in high school, then dropped out and went to work with their mother."

"Maybe the old lady packs a rod," said Roy.

"Could be. She smokes Camels and half her left ear's missing. The top part."

Cleve Love played safety on defense for the Clinton School

Eagles. To Roy's knowledge, nobody on the team—for which Roy was a running back and Magic Frank a middle linebacker—had ever seen an eagle.

"Maybe they got eagles up in Wisconsin," said Jimmy Boyle, their quarterback. "If anybody here in Chicago saw one, he'd probably think it was just a giant pigeon."

During a game against the Black Hawk School Young Bucks at Green Briar Park, Cleve Love was beaten twice early for touchdowns by a kid named Jesse Ash, Black Hawk's best receiver. Midway through the third quarter, Ash caught a long pass and was headed for the end zone when Cleve, who was in full pursuit, pulled a hammer from the back of his pants and clubbed Ash on the head with it, splitting the receiver's helmet in two. Ash fumbled the ball, fell down on the ground and stayed there.

Nobody playing in or watching the game from the sidelines could believe what they'd just seen. Cleve Love stood over Jesse Ash's body for a few seconds, holding the hammer in his right hand, before running off the field and down Washtenaw Street without taking off his helmet. The referee and a couple of adults rushed onto the field and helped Ash stand up, then walked him slowly over to a bench. One of his teammates picked up the pieces of Ash's helmet. The Black Hawk School coach was shouting at Fat Porter, the Clinton School coach, and the referee declared the game over, giving the victory to the Young Bucks even though the Eagles were ahead twenty-one to fourteen.

Jimmy Boyle, Magic Frank and Roy took off their cleats, put on their street shoes and, since they lived near one another, began walking home together. A whisper of rain pelted their dusty faces.

"I asked Cleve once why he carried a hammer," Magic Frank told Roy and Jimmy. "He said that when he was little and went to Storybook Time at the library, he learned that Thor, the Norse god of thunder, used one to defend himself, and that when Thor threw his hammer at someone it returned to him like a boomerang."

"They got boomerangs in Australia," said Jimmy Boyle. "The Vikings must have invaded down there and given 'em some hammers."

"Thor wasn't a Viking," Roy said. "He was a mythical figure, part of a legend."

"That's what Cleve'll be now," said Jimmy, "a legend."

Fifteen years later, when Roy came to Chicago on a visit from San Francisco, where he was then living, he saw Magic Frank and they talked about the old days.

"Whatever happened to Cleve Love?" Roy asked. "I never saw him after he got out of reform school."

"He's around," said Frank. "He owns a vintage clothing store on Armitage."

Roy laughed and asked, "Is it named Thor's?"

"No. Dragstrip, or Stripjoint, something like that. I haven't been there."

"Does he still carry a hammer?"

"Bitsy DiPena, who used to work for him, told me Cleve keeps one on a shelf under the cash register," said Frank. "She says he's famous for going after shoplifters with it."

The Red Studebaker

Roy was twelve years old when his mother and her third husband, a jazz drummer named Sid "Spanky" Wade, told him that they were going to move out of Chicago to a suburb north of the city. They had already paid for the beginning of the construction of a new house and the foundation had been laid. The next day, a Sunday, the four of them—Roy's mother, her husband, Roy's one-year-old sister, and Roy—drove out to see it.

Roy had no desire to leave the neighborhood, and when he saw the property in Winnebago Gardens, a new development in the middle of nowhere, only sidewalks and streets and other houses under construction, no people, not even a kid on a bike, he knew immediately this place was not for him. The thought of being stranded like a lost Legionnaire in the Sahara made Roy shiver. He disliked Sid Wade and Sid disliked him; and Roy's mother, as always during her marriages, was either on the verge of a nervous breakdown or in the throes of collapse. His mother's marriages—of which there would eventually be five—inevitably and rapidly deteriorated into disappointment and fear which found expression in the form of hysteria and vicious vitriol, behavior that terrorized not only her husband of the moment but Roy and anyone else who had to deal with her. This proposed move to the suburbs, to "somewhere quiet and less stressful," as Sid Wade said, would surely salve her condition. City life made her nervous, agreed Dr. Martell, a heart specialist and old friend of Roy's grandmother's, who provided pills for his mother even in the middle of the night.

Several days after their excursion to Winnebago Gardens, Roy was having dinner with the family when Sid Wade began telling Roy what he could and could not take with him when they moved.

"I'm not moving," Roy said. "Don't worry about me, I'll take care of my own things."

Sid Wade dropped his fork onto his plate, his heavy-jowled face turned crimson, and he said, "Of course you're moving. We all are."

"No, I'm not. I've already made arrangements to live next door with the McLaughlins. Mr. and Mrs. McLaughlin said it's all right with them. Jimmy's going into the army next month, so I'll have his bunk in the room with Johnny and Billy. I told Mrs. McLaughlin I'd contribute money to the household out of my pay delivering for Kow Kow. I'll be fine there."

Roy's mother stood up from the table and put her dishes into the sink. Her face was green and her lips were trembling. Her body shook and she was crying.

"Look what you've done to your mother!" Sid Wade shouted.

Roy's little sister, upset by his loud voice, began crying, too.

"If your father were here," Wade snarled, "he wouldn't put up with your insolence."

"I'm not being insolent," said Roy. "And don't talk about my father. You didn't know him and he's dead. You don't know what he'd say or do. If he were alive, I'd go live with him. Johnny and Billy are my best friends and Mr. and Mrs. McLaughlin are good people."

Frank McLaughlin worked as a doorman at the Drake Hotel and his wife took in laundry. They were from Ireland and spoke Gaelic in their house. They let their sons drink coffee in the morning and Margaret McLaughlin made great peach and strawberry pies in the summer. Roy couldn't wait to go live with them.

Sid Wade and Roy's mother began arguing. She closed her eyes and fell down on the floor. The baby was screeching and Sid Wade wouldn't stop yelling, carrying on about how Roy should be sent to reform school, that he'd never be any good just like his gangster father.

"He did time and you'll do time!" Wade said. He snorted like a buffalo and his little eyes disappeared.

Roy could hear his mother moaning.

"You're killing your mother!" screamed Wade, though he made no attempt to pick her up off the floor, where she was now writhing like a Moroccan fakir's cobra being replaced in its basket.

Roy rose from the table and walked out the back door, down the steps, through the yard and into the alley behind the garage. It was windy and cold and he was wearing only a T-shirt. Mr. Anderson's old red Studebaker was parked in the alley between his house and the McLaughlins'. Roy knew that Mr. Anderson never locked it, so he walked over, opened the passenger side door and got in. He sat there looking through the windshield. The sky was almost dark, there was a thin, pale yellow ribbon running through the gray. At the far end of the alley two men came out of the rear door of The Green Harp tavern. They were smoking and laughing. One of them was wearing a blue zipper jacket and the other was wearing a brown one. Both men were hatless. Roy watched them standing and talking and smoking, their hair waving in the wind. Mr. Anderson had left an opened pack of Lucky Strikes on top of the dashboard. Roy took one, put it between his lips and punched in the lighter.

Three months later, Roy's mother told him that Sid had defaulted on their installments for the house in Winnebago Gardens and forfeited the down payment, so they weren't going to move there. A week after that, Roy came home from school one day and found Sid Wade picking up his clothes and other belongings from in front of the house where Roy's mother had thrown them. Later the same day Sid moved out and Roy's mother said she was divorcing him and going to work as a receptionist in Dr. Martell's office.

Jimmy McLaughlin came home from the army on leave for a few days after completing basic training. Roy and Johnny and

Billy were sitting on Johnny's bunk listening to him. Jimmy was lying on his bed in his uniform smoking a Chesterfield, telling them about life at Fort Leonard Wood in Missouri. Johnny had taken over Jimmy's job washing dishes at the Chinese restaurant, Roy had taken over Johnny's delivery days, and Billy, the youngest McLaughlin brother, a year younger than Johnny and Roy, who were five years younger than Jimmy, now worked at Kow Kow, too, sweeping up and taking out the garbage.

"It's good to be back home," Jimmy said, "even if it's only for a week. You don't know how much you miss it until you can't be there."

"What did you miss the most?" asked Johnny.

"Strange things, little things, mostly."

"Yeah? Like what?" said Roy.

"Oh, I don't know," said Jimmy. "Just seein' Mr. Anderson's red '52 Studebaker parked in the alley is one, I guess. It gives me a good feelin' knowin' it's still there."

The Trumpet

Marty the T worked at the Sinclair service station on the corner of Rosemont and Western when Roy lived in St. Tim's parish. Marty's last name was Sullivan but everybody in the neighborhood called him Marty the T or just T because he played a trumpet while he sat around when he wasn't pumping gas. Old man Poznanski, who was about fifty but was bald and always had a grizzled, gray, six-day beard, owned the station and did the mechanical work and tire patching. All Marty the T had to do was wait on the Two Dollar Bills and Bettys, as Poznanski called those motorists who stopped only for gas. T was sixteen when he began working there, right after he dropped out of high school. The first time Roy met him, Marty the T told Roy he had decided that he was going to be a jazz trumpet player. Poznanski didn't mind that T practiced the trumpet all day because he was half deaf and spent most of his time under cars on the garage side of the station. As long as Marty the T's playing didn't interfere with his taking care of the customers, the old man left him alone. T was a medium-tall, skinny guy with green eyes, crewcut red hair, a nose that would have been a comma but for a scar below the bridge that made it resemble a semi-colon, and a prominent chin with a few wispy, straw colored hairs sticking out from it. "All the jazz cats got chin hair," he said.

It was a drizzly, chilly March afternoon in 1962 when the station was robbed by two men wearing bandanna masks, one red, one black. Marty the T was working on Dizzy Gillespie's tune "Con Alma" when a gray and blue 1959 Chevrolet Impala pulled up to one of the pumps. T noticed the car out of the corner of his left eye, played a few more notes and put down his trumpet. By the time he'd stood up and begun to head out the office door, the two men were walking quickly toward him. Both of the men were of average height and weight and carried guns in their right hands, which they held at their sides, not pointed at T. They wore dark brown Fedoras and black car coats and were inside the office before Marty the T could do anything. As soon as T saw the guns, he put up his hands.

"Open the register," ordered one of the men.

Marty the T hit the No Sale key on the 1920 National and the cash drawer slid out. The man who had not yet spoken elbowed T out of the way, removed all of the bills and stuffed them into a pocket of his coat, then took out the drawer and dropped it. Coins scattered all over the room even before the drawer hit the floor. The man scooped out the larger bills, tens and twenties, that had been hidden underneath and crammed them into the same pocket.

The other man said, "Show us the safe."

"There isn't one," said T.

"Where's the old man?" asked the bandit who had cleaned out the register.

"In the garage."

That man left the office; the other one stood still and kept his eyes on Marty the T. T noticed that they were blue; the other man's eyes were brown but T didn't really look at them until the man returned to the office marching old man Poznanski in front of him.

"The boy's tellin' the truth," Poznanski said, "there's no safe."

"Get on the floor, both of you," said the man who'd herded Poznanski. "Face down."

"Close your eyes and stay put," said the other man.

Poznanski and Marty the T did what they were told. The robbers took a fast look around the office, one of them kicked over a waste basket that was next to the desk, then they left. Marty the T and old man Poznanski stayed down until they'd heard the men open and close the doors of their car, the engine start and the car pull away.

Poznanski stood up first, looked out the door and said, "It's okay, Marty, they're gone."

T got up and looked out.

"We're pretty lucky, I guess," said the old man. "They didn't shoot us, they only took the cash."

"No," said T, "they took my trumpet, too."

Poznanski looked at the top of the desk, which was where Marty the T always put the trumpet down when he left the office to pump gas.

"They'll pawn it for two bucks," he said.

When Roy and his friends found out that thieves had stolen Marty the T's instrument they chipped in and gave T nineteen dollars and seventy-five cents.

"That's great of you guys," he said. "Old man Poznanski gave me ten. Now I can buy a better horn than the one I had."

The next day, Marty the T bought a used trumpet at Frank's Drum Shop on Wabash Avenue for thirty bucks. He was playing it in the office at the Sinclair station three weeks later when the police called and told old man Poznanski they had found the '59 Impala that had been used in the hold-up abandoned in an empty lot on Stony Island Avenue. It had been stolen, then dumped. Marty the T's trumpet was on the back seat.

T went down to the precinct house across the street from City Hall to claim it. Roy and Tommy Cunningham went with him. When the claims officer handed the trumpet over to T, he laughed and said, "Look what they done to it."

The bell had been bent up at a forty-five degree angle.

"This is how Dizzy's horn looks," said Marty the T. "Whichever one of the stick-up men did it must know that."

"Can you still play it?" asked Cunningham.

Marty the T put the trumpet to his lips and squeaked out a few notes.

"No trumpet playin' in here," barked the claims officer.

"That's the intro to 'Night in Tunisia'," T told him.

"Yeah, well, it's late afternoon in Chicago," said the cop. "Take it outside."

Years later, when Roy saw Dizzy Gillespie perform in a night-club in New York, he told this story to the people he was with.

"Did Marty the T become a professional musician?" asked one of them.

"I don't know," said Roy. "I never saw him again after I graduated from high school and left the neighborhood. But Tommy Cunningham told me he heard that T had married a girl from Africa named Happiness Onsunde. I said that would be a good title for a song, 'Happiness On Sunday', and Cunningham reminded me that Marty the T told us when we were outside the police station that he was going to write a tune called 'Late Afternoon in Chicago' and send it to Dizzy."

Unspoken

Walking home together on Ojibway Boulevard, Roy and his grandfather passed Litvak's Delicatessen, and Roy, who was twelve years old, said, "I like the young guy, Daniel, who works behind the counter in Litvak's. He's always telling jokes and makes the best sandwiches."

"Do you know where the name Litvak comes from?" asked his grandfather.

"No, Pops. Where?"

"It was a name given to certain Jews from Lithuania, in Eastern Europe. These Jews were inclined to doubt the so-called magic powers of the Hasidic leaders, so Litvak came to connote shrewdness and skepticism."

"Who were the Hasidic leaders?"

"The Orthodox Jews."

"Tommy Cunningham told me that Daniel's father hanged himself."

"Nathan Litvak, yes. Two years ago."

"Why'd he do that?"

"It's a long story, Roy. An unhappy one, although there is a good ending, too."

"Can you tell it to me?"

"I didn't know Nathan Litvak but my friend Herman did."

"Herman who wears the hearing aid and always has a runny nose?"

"Yes, the jeweler on Minnetonka Street. He told me that Litvak came to Chicago after the war ended, almost seventeen years ago, in 1945. He was a Jew, of course, a survivor of the Holocaust, when the Nazis attempted to exterminate the Jewish population of Europe. He and his wife, Sarah, were arrested in Lithuania. She died in a concentration camp."

"What about Nathan and Daniel?"

"Daniel was five years old when his parents were able to get him out of the country, just before the Nazis invaded. He was sent to live with relatives here in Chicago. Nathan managed to stay alive and was eventually liberated by the Allies. He emigrated to America and was reunited with his son."

"Daniel is a real friendly guy," Roy said. "I like his wife, Ruth, too, although she doesn't talk much, just smiles a lot."

"It's an amazing thing, what happened to Ruth. She and her parents also were taken by the Nazis to a death camp, the same one as Nathan and Sarah. Ruth was younger than Daniel, three or four years old at the time. Her father, Mendel, died in the camp, but her mother, Esther, survived. How anyone survived in those circumstances I don't know, but she did, and saved her daughter, too."

"And they also came to Chicago after the war."

"Yes. For years, Ruth did not speak at all. She had been severely traumatized by her experience in the concentration camp. When she grew up she went to work as a seamstress with her mother. Then, as fortune—or misfortune—would have it, Esther and Ruth came to live in the same apartment building as Nathan and Daniel."

"Daniel and Ruth live in an apartment above the delicatessen," said Roy.

"They all lived there, right across the hall from each other. It happened that Esther's sister, Golda, had known Nathan in their home city of Vilnius, and she told Esther that Nathan had survived by cooperating with the Nazis; first in Vilnius, by identifying Jews in hiding, and then by supervising a brothel comprised of Jewish women for the exclusive use of German soldiers."

"What's a brothel?"

"A whorehouse, where men pay women to have sex with them; only in these places run by the Nazis, the soldiers didn't have to pay."

"What happened to Golda?"

"She was murdered by a Nazi officer. Naturally, Nathan was

hated by the other Jews. Esther confronted him after she and Ruth moved into the apartment here and she realized who he was. I suppose that's how Daniel found out about his father's betrayal of his own people. Esther later had a stroke and she was paralyzed for quite a while before she died, but not before Nathan, who could no longer live with his shame and guilt, hanged himself. It was Daniel who discovered his father hanging by a rope from a meat hook in the back room of the delicatessen."

"What's the good ending, Pops?"

"Well, Daniel had always had a crush on Ruth. As you know, she's quite pretty and he'd fallen in love with her even though she'd never spoken to him. After her mother had a stroke and couldn't work any more, Daniel paid their rent and gave them food. Ruth realized that Daniel was a good person, not like his father, and eventually she agreed to marry him."

"She talks to him now," said Roy. "I've heard her."

"Yes, of course she does. But it took a very long time to overcome the terrible memories she had. It's a miracle that Ruth is finally able to have a decent life."

"It's sad that Daniel's mother died in the concentration camp."

"He told Herman that he doesn't even have a photograph of her. Daniel said that whenever he used to ask his father about Sarah, Nathan would tell him, 'The best way to speak about the dead is to remain silent.'"

"That's an unhappy story, all right. I heard Jimmy Boyle's mother say once that what the Nazis did to the Jews was the world's worst crime."

His grandfather nodded and said, "An Argentine writer, Jorge Luis Borges, in a story called 'Death and the Compass,' has a character named Lönnrot say to the editor of the *Yiddishe Zeitung* newspaper, 'Perhaps this crime belongs to the history of Jewish superstitions.' To which the editor replies, 'Like Christianity.'"

"A superstition is something that isn't really true, right?"

"Correct. It's a belief that has no basis in fact."

"So is Christianity a superstition?"

"All religions are, Roy. Sometimes it makes people feel better to believe in one, and that's all right. It's when religion makes people mean and provokes or emboldens them to use their religion as an excuse or reason to harm those who don't believe as they do that it turns bad."

"Is that why the Nazis tried to kill all the Jews, because they had a different religion?"

"They did, but the Nazis thought the Jews were a tribe of troublemakers and wanted to get rid of them."

"Earl Borg, the one-armed guy who rents shoes at the bowling alley, says the Jews think they're better than everybody else."

It began to rain and Roy's grandfather said, "Come on, boy, let's walk a little faster."

"They're not better than everybody else, are they?" asked Roy.

"No, the Jews are pretty much the same as everyone. They made a lot of enemies, though, by calling themselves the Chosen People."

"Who chose them?"

"God, they said."

"You mean God spoke to them?"

"Anything is possible, Roy. Ruth spoke to Daniel, didn't she?"

Haircut

Roy overheard his mother telling her friend Kay that Rocco the barber, who lived next door, had molested her on the front steps of her house. Kay and his mother were sitting in the livingroom and Roy, who was nine years old, was standing in the front hallway where the women could not see him.

"He was very nice at first," said Roy's mother, "just making conversation, then all of a sudden he tried to kiss me on the mouth. I turned my head away but he kept trying, pushing himself at me and putting his hands on my breasts. I pushed him away and yelled, 'Rape!' I called him a whoremaster because his wife, Maria, told me he'd been a pimp in Naples during the war. She was probably one of his girls."

Kay was an on-and-off girlfriend of Roy's Uncle Buck, his mother's brother. She was a glamorous woman, a redhead who looked like Rita Hayworth and wore wonderful perfume. Roy was always glad to see her because Kay would kiss and hug him and he could smell her. She was married to a rich lawyer but she always went out with Buck when he visited Chicago. Once Roy had asked his uncle why he hadn't married Kay and Buck said, "Well, Roy, there are some girls you marry and some you're happy to see marry someone else, which doesn't mean you can't still see them sometimes."

"Are you going to tell Rudy?" Kay asked Roy's mother.

"I'm thinking about it. Rudy would have his legs broken."

Rudy was Roy's father. He and Roy's mother had divorced when Roy was five but they were very friendly and always spoke well of one another around Roy. Often when his mother needed a favor or money in a hurry she called Rudy.

"He deserves it, the pig," said Kay. "Rudy's had worse things done to guys."

Roy left the house quietly, closing the front door without letting the women hear him go. On his way to the park to play baseball, Roy could not help but picture in his mind Rocco the barber attacking his mother. He did not say anything about it to anyone at the park but later that afternoon, after his game had ended, Roy walked up to Ojibway Boulevard to where Rocco's barber shop was and stood across the street.

It was late August and the air was heavy. As the sky darkened, a few raindrops fell and a weak wind began to blow. Rocco's dog, a three-legged Doberman pinscher named Smoky, was chained, as usual, to a pole in front of the barber shop. One story was that Smoky had lost his left rear leg in a fight to the death with a wolverine when Rocco had taken the dog with him on a hunting trip to Michigan or Wisconsin. Tommy Cunningham told Roy that Rocco's son, Amelio, who was six years older than Roy and Tommy, said Smoky had killed the wolverine by biting it in the throat but that the wolverine had attacked Smoky first and torn off the dog's leg. Another story was that Smoky had been hit by a bus and run over on Ojibway Boulevard while he was chasing a kid and trying to bite him, which is the one Roy believed because Smoky tried to bite any kid who came close to him.

Roy took out his Davy Crockett pocket knife and opened it. He crossed the street and waited until there were no passersby watching. Just at a moment when Smoky had his big dark brown head turned to lick the stub of his missing leg, Roy darted at the dog and plunged the blade into Smoky's right eye. The animal howled and whipped his head around, dislodging the knife, which clattered to the sidewalk. Roy quickly picked it up and ran. He did not wait to see Rocco and other men come out of the barber shop to see what Smoky was howling and whimpering about.

When Roy got home, his mother and Kay were not there. He rinsed the blood off his knife at the kitchen sink, wiped it clean with a dish towel, then went into his room and buried it at the bottom of his toy chest. He went back into the kitchen and poured himself a glass of chocolate milk, carried it onto the back porch and sat down on the top step. The rain started coming down harder.

The next time Roy passed Rocco's barber shop, Smoky was not chained in front. Roy would go to Arturo's Barber College to get his hair cut, even though it was farther from his house. The guys learning to cut hair there were butchers but they only charged a quarter. Roy hated to go to the barber's anyway. He wished he never had to get a haircut again.

The Invention of Rock 'n' Roll

The first record Roy ever bought was a 45 rpm single of Little Richard singing "Good Golly, Miss Molly," when he was nine years old. Later the same year, 1956, he bought his first LP, the soundtrack album of the movie *The Man with the Golden Arm*, which featured Shorty Rogers, Shelly Manne, Conte and Pete Candoli, and other jazz musicians. Neither of these recordings were examples of the kind of music his mother and grandmother played on the piano and often sang; those tunes were standards and popular songs like "La vie en rose," "Satan Takes a Holiday" and "It Had to Be You." Roy liked those songs but as soon as he heard Little Richard banging out on the piano the first few chords of "Lucille" and screeching the lyrics, followed by "Good Golly, Miss Molly," "Tutti Frutti" and "Slippin' and Slidin'," he knew there was another world beyond "Autumn Leaves" or "If I Didn't Care" and he was crazy to find out about it.

There was a guy named Gin Bottle Sam who showed up now and again on Blackhawk Avenue sitting on a metal milk bottle crate playing his harmonica for change, which appreciative pass-ersby tossed into an upside down short-brimmed hat Sam kept by his feet on the sidewalk in front of him. Roy had stopped to listen to Sam a couple of times and the next time he saw him Roy asked Sam what kind of music it was that he was playing.

"Blues, mostly," he said. "Might put a little pep into a pop'lar tune peoples knowin', somethin' more famil'ar make 'em give up a few extry pennies."

It was an afternoon in mid-November when Roy asked Gin Bottle Sam about his music. The sky was gray-brown and full of black specks, so Roy knew it was about to snow. Sam warmed himself with a swig from a half-pint bottle he kept in a side pocket of his long blue overcoat. Roy's friend the Viper, who was two years older, had told him Sam's name, but Roy noticed that the liquid in the bottle Sam was sipping from on this particular day was dark brown, not clear like gin.

"Fo' zample, tune I just been playin's 'Sportin' Life,' wrote by Brownie McGhee. Fixin' now to do 'Long Distance' by Muddy Waters, real name McKinley Morganfield. Like me, he come up to Chicago from Miss'ippi make his bones. He the man invented rock an' roll, you best believe."

Sam slipped the bottle back into his overcoat pocket and began to sing.

"You say you love me, darlin', please call me on the phone sometime. You say you love me, darlin', please call me on the phone sometime. Give me a call, ease my worried mind."

Roy listened closely as Sam breathed in and out on his harmonica. A couple of pedestrians pitched a dime or a quarter into the short brim.

When Sam finished the song, Roy asked him, "Is it called the blues because you blew into the harmonica?"

"Well, no. It's all up in the feelin', though you do got to blow to make it happen. Don't need to be a reg'lar instrument you got to blow into, though. Can be hands beatin' on a log, or dogs howlin' with chains fix roun' they neck. Men, too, you best believe."

Roy only had a nickel on him but he put it into Sam's hat. Sam tooted twice on his harmonica, then chuckled and picked up the change he had earned. He was wearing red and green cotton gloves with the fingertips cut off. Sam rattled the coins in his left hand and grinned at Roy. Several of his teeth were missing and he had blood spots in the whites of his eyes.

"You got to listen, boy," he said. "You got to study on what it is you hearin' an' maybe one time you begin to understand."

Sam stood up and dropped the coins into the left side pocket of his overcoat. He put the harmonica into the other pocket, then shook Roy's right hand with his own.

"Thanks for talking to me," said Roy.

"I was a orphan," Sam said. "You know what's a orphan?"

Roy nodded.

"Was no good for me where I been put, so I was about your size I took out for my own self. And here now you askin' me questions. Ain't that good news."

The next morning Roy told the Viper about his conversation with Gin Bottle Sam. They were walking by the canal that cut through the neighborhood and the sky was already darker than it had been the previous afternoon. There had not yet been any precipitation but a heavy snow was predicted to arrive by evening.

"What do you think Sam meant by beating on logs and dogs howling with chains around their necks?" asked Roy.

"Slaves in the South would sing while they picked cotton and chopped wood," said the Viper. "Makin' music while they worked made 'em feel better."

"Do you know who Muddy Waters is?"

"Yeah, he worked on a plantation where he was discovered, then he came to Chicago to make records."

"Sam says he's the one who invented rock 'n' roll."

The Viper laughed.

"What's so funny?"

"Whenever I play a record by Little Richard or Elvis Presley," said the Viper, "my mother shouts, 'What's all that poundin' and howlin' about?'"

Infantry

It was in his eighth grade history class that Roy learned the word infantry had originated in ancient Rome to describe the youngest soldiers in the Roman legions. These were *infanteria*, children no older than Roy and his friends, who were put at the front of the invading army, almost certainly to be sacrificed so that the following troops, comprised of older, veteran soldiers, would be preserved for the most serious, decisive parts of the battles.

After school the day they'd learned about the infantry of ancient Rome, Roy said to the Viper, "I bet it was only the poorest families whose children were forced to fight. The rich people paid to keep their sons out of the army."

"Probably," the Viper said, "but at least the kid soldiers didn't have to go to school."

Roy thought a lot about the Romans' use of young boys in their army, and after he read about Hadrian's Wall he imagined a situation in which the boy infantry revolted and deserted and ran away to an isolated part of the empire and established their own encampment.

"What if the kids built a big wall like Emperor Hadrian did?" Roy said to the Viper and Jimmy Boyle.

The boys were standing together under the awning of Vincenzo's Shoe Repair near the corner of Dupre and Winnebago early on a Saturday morning. They were waiting for a few other guys to meet up with them before walking over to the fieldhouse at St. Rose of Lima where they were going to play basketball. It was a cold, gray, drizzly day and there weren't many people on the streets yet.

"Emperor who?" asked Jimmy.

"In 122 A.D., the Roman emperor Hadrian began building these enormous walls, like one-sided forts, to establish boundaries," Roy explained. "The longest one was about eighty miles and it was so tall and impenetrable that no enemy could get over or through it."

"They could go around," said the Viper.

"Yeah, but that would take a very long time and the far ends of the walls were built up against big, rugged rock formations or hills. The kid soldiers could protect themselves by constructing a smaller version of Hadrian's Wall. They could stockpile weapons, mostly crossbows that they could fire from the parapet at anyone who came to get them."

"What's a parapet?" Jimmy asked.

"A narrow platform or walkway at the top that ran the length of the wall."

"What about food?"

"They'd hunt," said Roy, "and they could bring along goats and chickens for milk and eggs."

"This didn't happen, though," the Viper said. "You're just makin' it up."

"I'm sure some kids thought of doin' it," said Roy. "The infantry knew they were doomed. Why would they stick around once they saw how the legions used them?"

Magic Frank, Billy Kristelis and an older kid Roy knew only by sight and reputation named Bobby Dorp jaywalked across Winnebago and joined Roy, Jimmy and the Viper.

"Hey, fellas," Frank said, "this is Bobby Dorp. He's gonna play with us today."

Dorp nodded at the other boys and they nodded back. Roy knew that Dorp had dropped out of high school after a girl named Mitzi Mink had accused him of molesting her in a hallway and that he now worked delivering groceries for the A & P on Minnetonka. The Viper had played basketball with him before, so he knew Dorp was good.

"Great," said the Viper. "Bobby can shoot with either hand, guys."

"He's ambidestric," said Billy Kristelis.

"Which hand are you better with?" asked Roy.

Dorp was at least two or three inches taller than the other boys but he was skinny. His coat was too small for him so his wrists stuck out. Roy noticed how long they were.

"I shoot about the same with either one," said Dorp. "When I'm off, I miss with both."

"Bobby's gonna join the army," said Magic Frank.

"When I'm seventeen," Dorp said, "in three months. My brother Dominic's in already."

"What happened to him?" asked Jimmy Boyle. "Is he okay?"

"Oh, yeah," said Dorp. "He's in Germany now, but he's gonna re-up so he can go to Indochina. Bein' in the army's the best way to see the world, Dom says. I'm goin' in the infantry, like he did. They're the ones who get to do the real fightin'."

Drifting Down the Old Whangpoo

There was a mysterious old guy Roy saw now and again walking in the neighborhood who would disappear for weeks or months until Roy thought he must have died or gone away and then suddenly there he was, wearing the same baggy brown suit and black slouch hat with a crumpled brim. Roy wondered who the man was and asked around about him but nobody had any information. Most everyone Roy asked had not noticed the guy, not even Don Diego Rosagante, who stood all day and night outside Phil and Leonard's Restaurant on Bavaria Avenue opening the door for tips. Don Diego Rosagante, whose real name was Emmanuel Snitzer, prided himself on being at the very least on nodding acquaintance with everybody in the neighborhood. He called himself Don Diego because, as he explained, "that was Zorro's real handle." He'd adopted Rosagante, which means "splendid" in Spanish, "because it's a lot classier-sounding than Snitzer." Don Diego was forty-six years old and lived with his mother over Rube and Ruby's Laundromat where his mother worked beating dust and dirt out of rugs in a lot out back.

After Roy described the man to him, Don Diego said, "Oh, yeah, I think maybe I seen him goin' by a few times, always from across the street, though. He looks like that actor got knifed or poisoned by a child prostitute named Little Kiss in a floating cat house driftin' down the old Whangpoo River in the movie *Shanghai After Midnight.* That Little Kiss was a real doll."

Roy figured the guy was in his late sixties or seventies because he was slightly stooped and shuffled his feet. A few months passed between sightings and then, just before Roy's twelfth birthday, on the first really cold day in October, the man was heading in Roy's direction on Washtenaw.

"Pardon me, mister," Roy said to him before the man could pass, "could I ask you a question?"

He stopped and looked at Roy. They were almost the same height. Roy had not noticed before how short the man was. His nose was very long and mottled like an old dill pickle, and his eyes were almost closed so that Roy could not tell what color they were.

"You already have," the man said.

Roy hesitated for a moment, then smiled and said, "You're right, I did."

"What's your next question?"

"Do you live around here?"

"There's no price on my head, if that's what you're looking for. No reward for turning me in."

The man spoke with an accent that Roy did not recognize.

"Where are you from?"

The man raised his head slightly and from under his heavy lids studied the boy's face. He kept smiling.

"Before Chicago, you mean?"

Roy nodded.

"Why do you stop to ask me this?"

"I don't know. I've seen you around and I'm just curious, I guess."

"Hongkew."

"I never heard of that place. Where is it?"

"If you're really curious, you'll find out," the man said, and walked away.

The next time Roy was in the library he looked up Hongkew in the encyclopedia. Hongkew, it said, was a ghetto in Shanghai, China, where Jewish refugees from Europe lived after Germany invaded their countries before and during World War II.

Roy told Don Diego Rosagante that he might be right about the old man after all.

"What do you mean?" asked Don Diego.

"I ran into him walkin' on Washtenaw and he told me before he came to Chicago he lived in Hongkew, which is part of Shanghai. So maybe he was in that movie you saw where the guy gets murdered on a boat in the river."

"The Old Whangpoo. He said that, huh?"

"He didn't say the name of the river, or even Shanghai. He just told me Hongkew, so I looked it up in the encyclopedia and it said that's where Jews went to in China to escape the Nazis during the war."

"How about that?" said Don Diego. "Hey, next time you see him, ask how well did he know Little Kiss."

The Wicked of the Earth

Roy and Jimmy Boyle were shooting pool on a rainy Saturday afternoon in Lucky's El Paso when Mooney Yost, a Lucky's regular, came in and sat down on a bench near the boys' table. Yost was about fifty years old, a fin and a sawbuck hustler who was always kind to Roy and his friends. He liked to tell slightly off-color jokes. "What's the lightest thing in the world?" he'd ask, then answer himself: "A man's penis—it only takes a thought to lift it." He didn't look happy sitting on the bench, though, and after Roy and Jimmy finished their game they sat down on either side of him.

"What's wrong, Mooney?" Jimmy asked. "Your dog get run over?"

"Dogs don't dig me," Mooney said. "They take one sniff and head for the hills. Must be something in my blood reminds 'em of bein' beaten in Egypt back in the days of the pharaohs. No, I was just talkin' to my sister, Rita, in Peoria, and she told me that our mother's last husband died a bad death. He was her fourth or fifth, not even my mother remembers any more. His name was Reno Mott. He was Rita's stepfather, she's twelve years younger than I am, and I was gone by the time our mother married him. Rita's father was my mother's third or fourth husband, a cat burglar named Slippery Elmo Daniels.

"Anyways, this last husband had been divorced from our mother for more than twenty years. He wasn't smart or rich or even very goodlookin', but my sister says he was always nice to her. I met Reno Mott a few times but I had no use for his ass. Despite his religious dishonesty, constant lies and penny ante swindling, he never made even a modest living and lost every cent my mother had, including whatever I give her or Rita did.

"He remarried, my sister said, and he and his new wife lived in a trailer on the outskirts of Phoenix, Arizona. He worked odd jobs, Rita told me, the final one for a messenger service deliverin' small packages in his old Buick that didn't have headlights. His wife worked as a bank teller. Reno kept at it until he was eighty, then his vital organs began to go one by one. Rita went to see him in the hospital a few days before he died. Drove all the way from Peoria, Illinois, to Phoenix. She's a good girl, Rita. He was hooked up to a few machines and he was scared. He told my sister that he'd lived a bad life, cheatin' people all the time, pretending to be a big shot and failing at everything he tried. Mott lost his messenger job after he drove into a kid on a bicycle and killed him. The police let him off because the kid had darted out from an alley or a side street without lookin' to see if any cars were comin'. It was typical of his bum luck, Mott told Rita. He'd done everything the wrong way, he said, and now he was about to die without money, love or peace of mind.

"My sister talked to his wife after he died and the woman told her it had been a real ugly deal. She was in the hospital room when the nurses pulled the plugs. He stood up next to the bed and howled, 'I don't want to die! I've led a mean life, I've hurt everyone I've ever known. I've stolen money from children, I've killed people! Now I'm goin' to hell, I have to go to hell and I'm afraid! Oh, Lord,' he cried, 'you know me only as one of the wicked of the earth and my flesh trembleth for fear of thee!'

"Reno carried on like this, his wife said, for more than a minute before he collapsed to the floor and was pronounced dead. His eyes were rolled back in his head and his mouth was open. Almost all of his teeth were gone. His tongue was green and hung out of one side of his mouth. Rita told his wife that Mott had been nice to her when she'd been a young girl. The woman thanked her for saying so, and said once Reno had read about a boy who'd been hit in the head and lost his ability to remember anything after that. The child's mind was frozen in time. Not only could he not remember anything new but also did not even recognize himself in the mirror as he grew older. Reno thought that would be the perfect way to live, with nothing terrible in your mind to haunt you forever.

"When my sister told our mother that Reno Mott had died, she said, 'I thought he died years ago.' Rita said he believed he was going to hell and was afraid to burn. 'I'm not surprised,' my mother said. 'He never did any good in his life.' 'He was always nice to me,' said Rita. Out mother looked at her and said, 'I don't believe you.' "

Mooney stood up, stretched his lanky frame, and said, "Be thankful, boys, you don't have a Reno Mott messin' with you. Guess I'll see if I can scare up a game of one-pocket."

"I don't really feel like playin' any more," said Jimmy.

"Neither do I," said Roy.

They racked their cues, walked to the door and pulled their jackets up over their heads before going out into the rain.

Christmas Is Not For Everyone

When Roy was seventeen years old, his mother got married without telling him. He found out when he came back home to Chicago from college for Christmas. Roy was sitting at the kitchen table having breakfast the morning after he arrived and his mother was standing at the sink washing dishes when she told him that she and his little sister were going to move from Chicago to Ojibway, Illinois, on the Wisconsin border.

"Why?" he asked. "And when?"

"Right after the new year," she said. "In about ten days. I've already sold my half of the apartment building to Uncle Herman."

"What's in Ojibway?"

"That's where Eddie Lund lives. He has a nice house there on Sweden Road. Your sister will have her own room, at least during the months Eddie's daughter is away at nursing school in Ohio."

"Who's Eddie Lund?"

"His family owns a steel company in Rock City, close to Ojibway. Eddie works for Rock City Steel."

"Ma, who is this guy?"

Roy's mother did not answer right away, then Roy realized that she was crying.

"What's wrong, Ma?"

"I'm going to marry him, Roy. Actually, we're already married."

"When did this happen?"

She turned off the water at the sink and wiped her eyes with her apron, but did not turn around to look at Roy.

"On my birthday, the day after Thanksgiving."

"Why didn't you tell me?"

"I didn't want to bother you while you were at the university. I thought it would be better to tell you when you were home."

Eddie Lund was his mother's fifth husband. Roy knew she was embarrassed by this and had been afraid to tell him she'd gotten married again, especially after promising Roy, following her divorce two years before from her fourth husband, a drug addict jazz drummer named Spanky Wankovsky, that she was finished with matrimony.

"Eddie's a good guy, Roy, you'll see. He's coming here today, so you'll meet him."

Roy's father had been his mother's first husband; he died when Roy was five. Each of the husbands who came after him had considered Roy a nuisance, if not a burden. None of them had any interest in assuming responsibility for him. Roy was his mother's son, and he learned to keep his distance from her husbands. Since these men never lasted very long with his mother, Roy just waited them out, hoping, of course, that there would not be another. He soon realized, however, that the only control he had was over himself, and since the age of nine knew that he was on his own.

The intervals between his mother's marriages were when Roy and she got along best. Christmas, though, was always difficult because his mother was so often either getting married or divorced around that time. When she threw her third husband, Dion Braz, a sailboat salesman, out of the house for the last time on Christmas Eve, he said to Roy, "Christmas is a trick on kids."

Finally she turned and faced Roy and said, "Remember when you were little and I would play the piano and you'd sing? You had such a sweet voice. Why don't we do it now, Roy, while your sister is sleeping and before Eddie gets here? I always loved it when you sang 'Count Your Blessings.' Do you remember that song?"

Roy looked at his mother's face. She was not yet forty years old and she was still very beautiful. Before he could answer her, the doorbell rang.

"That must be Eddie," she said, taking off her apron. "He's early."

The Cuban Club

ROY'S GRANDMOTHER ROSE

"To die is nothing, it's only going from one room to another."
—Major-General James Hope Grant, *Incidents in the China War*

"You may be witched by his sunlight . . . but there is the blackness of darkness beyond."
—Herman Melville, "Hawthorne and His Mosses"

"Shortly before his death, [a man] discovers that the patient labyrinth of lines traces the image of his own face."
—Jorge Luis Borges

Roy and the River Pirates

Roy had no idea that this would be the last summer of his father's life. Roy was eleven years old and his father was forty-seven. His dad had always appeared strong and healthy. He smoked cigarettes and cigars and drank Irish whiskey but did not exhibit any obvious respiratory problems, nor did he ever give the slightest indication, in Roy's presence, of a lack of sobriety. The cancer that took Roy's father's life appeared in the fall and by the end of that winter he was dead.

His father and his father's second wife, Ellie, along with Roy's younger brother, Matthew, and older female cousin, Sally, were staying in a house his father was considering purchasing on Key Biscayne, Florida. Matthew was six and Sally, the younger daughter of Roy's father's sister, Talia, was almost fifteen. All of them lived in Chicago, although Roy, who lived mostly with his mother, frequently resided wherever she decided to spend time, alternating among Chicago, New Orleans and Havana. This summer of 1957, Roy's mother was with her current boyfriend, Johnny Salvavidas, in Santo Domingo, or travelling with him somewhere in the Caribbean. Roy did not expect to see her again until sometime in September.

Roy had a crush on Sally; he thought she was very pretty, with honey-blonde hair cut short, hazel eyes, unblemished skin and a slim figure. The best thing about her, though, was how naturally kind she was, even-tempered with a good sense of humor, and not at all stuck up. Sally was a straight talker, too, and she could be silly in a good way; she kidded around easily with both Roy and Matthew. Roy's father said that Sally did not get along very well with her parents, and she had asked him if he would take her to Key Biscayne for the summer if it was all right with her mother and father. Talia told Roy's father that Sally was "different," that she had her own way of thinking and doing things, which too often conflicted with Talia and her husband Dominic's ideas of how Sally should behave. Roy's dad didn't know exactly what Talia meant but he and Ellie liked Sally so they agreed to take her with them to Florida.

"What do you think Talia and Dominic don't understand about Sally?" Roy's father asked his wife.

"She's too airy fairy for them," said Ellie. "Her parents are all about business. If it's not about money, it's not worth their time. Sally's not like that."

Roy liked looking at his cousin. Sally was the first girl he knew who made him feel a little goofy just by looking at her. Whenever Sally noticed Roy staring, she smiled at him and sometimes brushed the hair off of his forehead with her hand.

The river pirates struck on the third night. Roy, Matthew and Sally had draped their bathing suits to dry over the back fence after they were finished swimming late that afternoon and left them there overnight. When they came out to get them the next morning, the bathing suits were gone. The intracoastal canal flowed right behind the house, making it easy for anyone on a boat to steal items of clothing hung over the back fence.

"We have to find out who took our bathing suits," Roy told Sally and Matthew. "It had to be river pirates."

"This is a canal," said Sally, "not a river."

"You mean real pirates?" asked Matthew. "With swords and patches over one eye and a black flag with a skull and crossbones on it?"

"Probably just kids in a rowboat who live around here," said Sally.

"We'll find out," Roy said. "Come on."

"Come on where?" Sally asked.

"Talk to the neighbors. Somebody might have an idea about who the thieves are."

None of the residents on the block had any suggestions about who could be responsible for the thefts, so Roy, Sally and Matthew decided to camp out at night in the yard and surprise the pirates if and when they came by again. As before, they hung their new bathing suits over the back fence after they had ended swimming for the day, and as soon as it was dark outside prepared their bedding on the grass. Ellie and Roy and Matthew's father both agreed that it was a good plan but asked what the kids intended to do if the thieves returned.

"Shoot 'em!" said Matthew. "I've got my bow and arrow set."

"The arrows have rubber tips," said Sally.

"We can describe 'em and get the name of their boat and track them down," Roy added.

"We'll give the information to the cops," Matthew said.

"No cops," said his father. "Handle it yourselves."

Roy and Sally and Mathew camped out in the yard several nights in a row but the river pirates did not appear. Of the three, Matthew was the most obviously disappointed. Roy was disappointed, too, but he enjoyed sleeping on the ground next to Sally. Early in the morning after what they decided would be their last night camping out, Mathew shot a few of his arrows over the fence into the canal.

"What did you do that for?" Roy asked him.

"I was pretending the pirates were there. They were probably afraid to come back."

Matthew walked over to the fence and shouted, "Chickens!"

For the remaining few weeks, Roy stole looks at Sally whenever he thought she wouldn't notice. She was always nice to him but this was not enough for Roy; he made up his mind that before they returned to Chicago he would try to kiss her.

Roy waited until the night before they had to leave, when Sally was alone in the yard standing by the back fence. He went out and stood next to her. His father and Ellie and Matthew were inside the house, packing.

"What are you doing out here?" Roy asked her.

"Oh, just looking at the water," she said. "I like seeing the reflection of the moon in it."

"It's too bad we never caught the pirates," said Roy,

Sally didn't seem so tall to him now; Roy figured he must have grown two or three inches since they'd been in Florida. He leaned over and kissed Sally on the corner of the right side of her mouth.

"What did you do that for?" she asked.

Sally was calm and smiled at Roy, as if she were not surprised.

"I like you a lot," he said.

"I like you a lot, too. I'm going to miss being down here with you and Matthew and your dad and Ellie."

"We'll see each other in Chicago."

"Sure, but it's not the same as Florida. The air is sweet and warm here, and the sky is always beautiful, especially at night."

"You're beautiful, too," said Roy.

Sally looked directly into his eyes. She was not smiling.

"Thank you, Roy," she said.

"I wish I were older," Roy said, "so I could be your boyfriend."

Sally looked back at the water, then up at the moon.

"There aren't any river pirates," she said. "Your father took the bathing suits and made me promise not to tell you and Matthew."

Roy didn't say anything. A large white bird flapped past them.

"You're not angry at me, are you?"

Roy walked back into the house.

"Come on, son," his father said, "give us a hand."

Dingoes

Roy liked to ride his bike up to Indian Boundary Park to look at the dingoes. There was a little outdoor zoo with a variety of smaller animals at the northern edge of the park, among them llamas, monkeys, ostriches and a patchy-furred, old brown bear. But it was the wild dogs of Australia that interested Roy the most. The dingoes were feisty, beige- or dun-colored knee-high canines that constantly fought among themselves and bared their fangs at the zoogoers who stared at them for more than a few seconds. Roy wondered why dogs were in a zoo, even supposedly wild ones. He guessed that in Australia dingoes ran in packs across a vast desert in the western part of the continent. He'd read about Australia in his fourth grade geography book which only mentioned dingoes in passing; most of the information about fauna in Australia was about kangaroos.

"Nasty little critters, aren't they?" a man said to Roy. "Now they're cooped up in this hoosegow."

Both Roy and the man were standing in front of the dingo enclosure on a cloudy day in August. Roy was nine years old and the man looked to Roy to be in his thirties or forties. Roy straddled his bicycle and watched and listened to the dingoes nip and yip at one another.

"The cage is too small for them," Roy said. "They need to be out running around in a desert."

The man was only slightly taller than Roy and thin with a grayish-brown mustache. He lit a cigarette then flicked the match through the bars at the dingoes.

"Wild dogs," the man said. "In China they'd be beaten to death. They've got police squads over there that do nothin' but run down stray dogs and club 'em over the head, then throw the bodies in a pile and burn 'em."

"These dogs are from Australia," said Roy. "They're not domesticated."

The man gave a little laugh with a hiccup in the middle of it. Roy had never heard anyone with a strange laugh like that before.

"Pretty fancy word you got there, kid. Domesticated. You learn that one in school?"

"Dingoes aren't meant to be pets," Roy said.

"Neither is that fat, scabby bear," said the man. "He shouldn't be in durance vile, either. These cages here are like cells in the Chateau d'If."

"What's that?" Roy asked.

"Prison island off the coast of Marseilles, in France. Like Alcatraz in San Francisco Bay. Nobody escapes from there."

"These animals can't escape from here, either. You seen the Chateau Deaf? Is it for deaf criminals?"

"Nope. It's d'If, not deaf. Name of the island is If. I read about it in *The Count of Monte Cristo*, a novel by Alexandre Dumas. Man named Edmond Dantes gets put away for life but after sixteen years digs a tunnel to the sea and swims away."

"I thought you said nobody escapes from there."

"Not in real life they don't. *The Count of Monte Cristo* is a story takes place in the nineteenth century. Edmond Dantes is an innocent man and after he gets out he finds a treasure a dying inmate at the Chateau d'If told him about and changes his name to Monte Cristo before taking revenge on the three wrong customers who were responsible for having him take the fall for a crime he didn't commit."

The man dropped his butt then lit up another cig and again flicked his match at the dingoes.

"How come you're not in school, kid?"

"Summer vacation."

"I'm kind of on vacation, too."

Roy looked at the man again: his pale blue shirt had dark brown stains on it, as did his khaki trousers. When the man turned his head Roy saw that his left ear was missing; there was only a misshapen lump of skin where an ear should have been.

Roy climbed onto his bicycle seat and started to ride away but the man took hold of the handlebars with both of his hands.

"If you're clever," said the man, "you won't ever let anybody take advantage of you."

"What's that mean?"

"There are evil spirits haunt this earth who beguile good men and women and render them useless."

Not only was the man missing an ear but Roy noticed the mean-looking red and blue-black scar that ran almost the entire length of his hairline.

"I've got to go, mister. Let go of my bike."

The man released the handlebars, removed his cigarette from the right corner of his mouth and flicked it into the dingo cage.

As he was riding Roy remembered his grandfather telling him to listen carefully to what even crazy people said because the information might be useful later. When he got home Roy would ask him what in durance vile meant.

The King of Vajra Dornei

One of Roy's most interesting childhood friends was Ignaz Rigó, who, following high school, had vanished into the greater world. Ignaz Rigó was a Gypsy kid whose family owned a two-story building on Pulaski Road next to the tuberculosis sanitarium. Roy had been to Ignaz's house a few times between the ages of thirteen and sixteen, and there never seemed to be fewer than twenty people, apparently all related, living there. The Rigó clan also occupied a storefront on Diversey, where the women, including Ignaz's mother and sisters, gave "psychic readings" and sold herbal remedies for a variety of complaints.

Ignaz, Senior, Roy's friend's father, called Popa, was always at the house on Pulaski whenever Roy went there. Regardless of the weather, Popa and an old man, Ignaz's maternal grandfather, named Grapellino, sat out on a second floor balcony on lawn chairs overlooking the street, talking and smoking. Both men were always wearing gray or brown Fedora hats, long-sleeved white shirts with gold cuff links buttoned at the neck, black trousers and brown sandals. Roy asked Ignaz what Popa's work was and Ignaz said that his father kept the family in order; and that Grapellino was a king in Vajra Dornei, which was in the old country. Roy asked Ignaz why, if his grandfather was a king in Vajra Dornei, he was living in Chicago. Ignaz told Roy that Lupo Bobino, a bad king from Moldova, had poisoned Grapellino's first wife, Queen Nardis, and one of his daughters, and commanded a band of cutthroats that drove the Rigó clan out of Romania. Grapellino and Popa were planning to return soon to the old country to get their revenge and take back the kingdom stolen from them by Bobino's brigands.

"I'm goin' with them," Ignaz said. "We're gonna cut the throats of Lupo Bobino and everyone in his family, including the women and children. Last July, when I turned thirteen, Popa showed me the knife I'm gonna use. It once belonged to Suleiman the Magnificent, who ruled the Turks back when they kicked ass all over Asia. The handle's got precious jewels on it, rubies and emeralds, and the blade is made from the finest Spanish steel. Popa keeps it locked in a cabinet in his room. It's priceless."

Roy lost contact with Ignaz, who did not finish high school with him. Just before Christmas when Roy was twenty-one and back in Chicago on a visit from San Francisco, where he was then living, he went into the storefront on Diversey and asked one of Ignaz's older sisters, Arabella, who told fortunes and gave advice to women about how to please their husbands, where her brother was and what he was doing. Arabella, who was not married, had big brown eyes with dancing green flames in them, a hook nose, a mustache, and a thin, scraggly beard, as well as the largest hands Roy had ever seen on a woman. She told him that Ignaz was on a great journey, the destination of which she was forbidden to reveal. Arabella then offered Roy an herb called Night Tail she said would bring him good fortune with women, which he declined with thanks. Looking into Arabella's eyes, Roy remembered, made him feel weak, as did the thought of what she could do to him with her huge hands.

A year or so later, another former high school classmate of his, Enos Bidou, who worked for his father's house painting business in Calumet City, called Roy and told him that he'd run into Ignaz in East Chicacgo, Indiana, where Ignaz was repairing roofs and paving driveways with his uncle, Repozo Rigó.

"Remember him?" Enos Bidou asked. Roy did not, so Enos said, "He went to jail when we were still at St. Tim the Impostor. Got clipped for sellin' fake Congo crocodile heads and phony Chinese panda paws."

"When we were thirteen or fourteen, Ignaz told me he would

go one day to Romania or Moldova with his father and grandfather Grapellino to take back Grapellino's lost kingdom."

"Well, I seen him a month ago in Indiana," Enos said. "He's got a beard now."

"So does his sister," said Roy.

Real Bandits

Roy was fourteen when he read a story about the Brazilian bandit Lampião in a book entitled *Famous Desperados*. Baseball practice had been called off because of rain, and he did not want to go home and have to listen to his mother complain about the short-comings of her current husband, so Roy went to the neighborhood library and found the book lying by itself on a table. He sat down and looked at the contents page; there were chapters about Jesse James, the Dalton Gang, Baby Face Nelson, even Robin Hood, among others, all of whom he already knew something about, but Lampião—whose real name was Virgolino Ferreira da Silva—Roy had never heard of.

Lampião, it said in the book, means lantern, or lamp, in Portuguese. He lived and marauded with his gang in the 1920s and '30s in Northeastern Brazil, in the back country, or back-lands, called the *sertão*. After his father was killed by police, when Virgolino was nineteen years old, he vowed to become a bandit and was given the nickname Lampião because he was the light that led the way for his followers, who included both men and woman. His girlfriend's name was Maria Bonita; she left her rancher husband to go with Lampião and ride with his band of outlaws, leaving her daughter, Expedita, to be raised by Lampião's brother, João.

The Brazilian word for bandits was *cangaceiros*, which came from the word *canga* or *cangalho*, meaning a yoke for oxen, because a *cangaceiro* carried his rifle over both of his shoulders like a yoke on an ox. Roy was enraptured by the place names of towns and backlands provinces that Lampião and his outfit traversed: Pernambuco, Paraíba, Alagoas, Chorrocho, Barro Vermelho, Campo Formoso, Santana do Ipanema, and many others. Lampião achieved a reputation similar to that of Robin Hood, sharing the spoils with the poor while robbing the rich. There was no real consistency about this, of course, as Lampião's generosities were often arbitrary, but nonetheless the myth grew over the years that he and his band, which varied in number between ten and thirty, moved freely about the backlands. He was regularly written about in newspapers and magazines throughout Brazil and dubbed the King of the *Cangaceiros*. A Syrian named Benjamin Abrahão even made a film starring Lampião and Maria Bonita.

Lampião and ten of his bandit gang, including Maria Bonita, came to an ignominious end, however, when they were gunned down by police in their hideout on the São Francisco River. The soldiers cut off hands and feet of the outlaws, to preserve as souvenirs, and each of the dead desperados was decapitated. Their heads were put on display first in Piranhas, and then in the local capital of Maceió. Finally, the heads of Lampião and Maria Bonita were sent to Salvador, the capital of Bahia, where they were exhibited in a museum. A photograph in the book of several of the heads, surrounded by their guns, hats and other belongings, fascinated Roy, especially since one of the faces closely resembled his own.

It was just drizzling when Roy came out of the library and there was very little light left in the sky, which was deep purple. As he walked toward his house, he thought about Lampião and his bandit brother, Ezekiel, nicknamed Ponta Fina, "Sureshot", escaping on horseback across the São Francisco, pursued by government soldiers, described by a witness as rawboned, dirty and desperately tired-looking. The bandits were constantly on the run, and in addition to their practice of thievery and murder, Lampião and some of his men occasionally castrated, branded or sliced off ears of those who opposed or offended them, believing that these particularly brutal acts of violence would intimidate others who would dare refuse to assist them or get in their way.

The rain began again, harder than before, so Roy stopped

underneath the awning in front of Nelson's Meat Market on Ojibway Boulevard. The downpour reminded him of an episode described in the book of the time monsoon rains came suddenly one year near Raso da Catarina when Lampião and several of his cohorts were fleeing after raiding the property of a wealthy rancher. They were caught in open country and forced to take shelter under their standing horses and had to endure it when the horses urinated on him. Lampião was proud of the legend of himself as a rough, roguish, romantic character, glorified by journalists—some of whom he paid to propagate his myth—in the faraway big cities of Rio de Janeiro and São Paulo. Roy wondered if the dwarfish, skinny, half–blind bandit king had consoled himself with these thoughts as his bedraggled steed pissed on him.

A man and woman came and stood under the awning with Roy. The man was tall and thin and was wearing a brown suit with a red tie. The woman was wearing a green dress and her blonde hair was wet and matted from the rain. She fussed with it a little, then they both lit cigarettes. Roy noticed that the woman had a deep two–inch blue scar under her right eye she tried to conceal with make–up that had been mostly worn away by the rain.

"I heard they tied him to a tree," she said to the man, "then slit his throat and stole his wallet."

"No kiddin'," said the man.

"Yeah," she said, "took his shoes, too. They were real bandits."

Haitian Fight Song (Take Two)

Roy stood on the front steps of his school waiting for the car that was supposed to pick him up. An associate of his dad's, he'd been told, would be there at three o'clock to drive him to his father and his father's second wife Evie's house. Roy's mother, his father's first wife, from whom he'd been divorced since Roy was five, three years before, was out of town with her current boyfriend, Danielito Castro, so Roy was staying at his dad's until she came back to Chicago. His mother told Roy that Danielito Castro, whom Roy had briefly met once, wanted her to meet his family in Santo Domingo. She had been gone now for a week and had been uncertain about when she would return.

"I'll see how things go," his mother had said. "I don't think any of Danielito's family speaks English, other than Danielito, of course, so it probably won't be very long since I can't speak Spanish. You'll be fine with your dad and Evie, she's a nice girl. You won't even miss me."

Roy asked her where Santo Domingo was and she told him, "The Dominican Republic, it's on half of an island in the Caribbean Sea. The other half is a different country called Haiti. Danielito says the people there speak French. He told me the two countries are separated by a big forest and high mountains. He says the Haitians are very poor and are constantly trying to sneak into the DR, which is a richer country, so Dominican soldiers are permanently on guard along the border to keep them out."

"Probably a lot of the Haiti people hide in the forest until night when it's harder for the soldiers to see them and then sneak across," Roy said.

"Maybe, Roy. I'm sure I'll hear all about it when I'm there. Danielito says the Haitians are no good, that they don't like to work."

It was pouring when school let out. He did not have an umbrella or even a hood on his coat to pull up over his head so he hoped the person who was picking him up would not be late. Roy stood on the steps in the rain watching the other kids head for home or wherever they were going until he was the only one left. He waited for half an hour before he decided to walk to his father's house, which was more than two miles away. His own house, where he lived with his mother, was only a few blocks from the school, but nobody was there and he didn't have the key. He thought about going to one of his friends' houses but he knew that Evie was expecting him so he kept walking, hoping the rain would stop.

The rain did not stop. Other than for a few short intervals it continued in a steady downpour. On Ojibway Avenue, the main shopping street that led directly to his father and Evie's house, people hurried past him. Had he the fare, Roy would have taken a bus but he had not asked his dad for any money when he had dropped him off at school that morning. At the intersection of Ojibway and Western, in front of Wabansia's sporting goods store, where Roy had bought his first baseball glove, a Billy Cox model, a maroon Buick clipped a woman as she was stepping off the curb. She fell down in the street and the car's right rear tire ran over her black umbrella. The Buick turned the corner onto Western and kept going. The woman, who was wearing a red cloth coat, got up by herself. She bent down and picked up her umbrella, saw that it was broken and tossed it next to the curb. Roy was across the street from her when the accident happened. Nobody came to help her or ask her if she was all right and she walked across Ojibway and went into Hilda's Modern Dress Shop. Her right leg wobbled and Roy figured she'd been injured or the heel of her right shoe had broken off.

It took Roy a very long time to get to his dad and Evie's house and by the time he knocked on the front door the rain had weakened to a steady drizzle. When Evie opened the door and saw him looking like a drowned rat, she was horrified.

"Roy, what happened? Didn't Ernie Lento pick you up?"

"No, I walked. I didn't see anyone in a car at my school."

"You should have called me," said Evie. "I would have called a cab and come for you."

"I didn't have any money, or I would have taken a bus."

Evie took Roy in, helped him take off his wet clothes and wrapped two big towels around him.

"I'll make you some soup," she said, and headed for the kitchen.

Roy sat on the couch in the livingroom, covering his head with one of the towels. He looked around and for the first time noticed that there were no pictures on any of the walls, no paintings or photographs.

Evie came in and said, "The soup is heating up. I called your father and he said that Ernie Lento told him he was a few minutes late getting to the school but that you weren't where you were supposed to be."

"He must have been more than a little late," said Roy. "I waited on the front steps for around a half hour. Evie, how come you don't have any pictures on the walls in this room?"

"We have some framed photos on the dresser in our bedroom," she said. "Family photos. You've seen them. My parents and grandparents. Your grandparents, too, taken in the old country."

Evie left the room. Roy thought about Haitians creeping through a thick forest and waiting until night fell before hiking over a mountain range to get to the Dominican Republic. They probably didn't have umbrellas or any money on them, either. Danielito Castro had told Roy's mother that the Haitians didn't like to work but it had to be really hard work just to get from their side of the island to Santo Domingo or wherever they tried to get to in the Dominican Republic; and once they got there, if they survived beasts in the forest and bad weather in the mountains, the people spoke a different language.

Evie came into the livingroom carrying a bowl of tomato soup and a plate with Saltine crackers, a spoon and a napkin on it.

"Here's your soup, Roy. Blow on it because it's hot."

"Evie, what do you know about Haiti?"

"Why?" she asked. "Is that where your mother is?"

"No, she's in the Dominican Republic, another country that shares an island with Haiti. Are the people in Haiti really poor?"

"I think so, Roy. Most of them, anyway, certainly not all of them. There's always a ruling class who have more of everything. The only thing I know about Haiti is that it's the only country that was taken over by people who once were slaves. They had to fight for their freedom."

"My mother's friend Danielito Castro says the Haitians are no good and don't like to work."

"I'll tell you who's no good," Evie said. "I'll bet that crumb bum Ernie Lento stopped in a bar and was drinking with his race-track buddies. That's why he wasn't at your school on time, if he even got there. Your dad will find out. Eat your soup."

The Cuban Club

Roy met Tina at the Cuban Brotherhood Club and Dance Hall in Tampa, Florida, when he was fourteen. Roy was spending the summer with his uncle Buck working construction on weekdays, resting on Saturdays and fishing on Sundays. Tina was a local girl who went with her girlfriends to the dances at the Cuban Club on Saturday nights.

Roy and his friend Ralph were fascinated by the big-eyed, dusky Cuban girls who had come to Florida with their families in the first wave of emigrés who fled the island following the revolution. These girls wore make-up, bright red lipstick, large gold hoop earrings and short skirts. They danced only with one another and did not speak to white boys. Mostly they sat together in folding chairs in a corner of the dance hall and never stopped chattering and gesturing dramatically. Roy spoke some Spanish but when he got close enough to overhear their conversations they spoke so rapidly and without fully pronouncing most of their words that he could not understand anything they were saying.

Tina didn't like the Cuban girls. She was tall and blonde, as was her friend, LaDonna. When Roy asked Tina to dance she asked him what he thought of the Cuban girls. Before he could answer, Tina said, "They're cheap. They have big asses and dress like whores. LaDonna says her mother told her that their fathers have sex with them starting when they're five."

Roy found this hard to believe. He worked laying sewer pipe and shooting streets with Cuban men and liked them. They were good workers, glad to have a job, and they laughed a lot. Most of the time Roy didn't get their jokes—they spoke as rapidly as the girls at the dances—but they always offered to share their homemade lunches with Roy. He loved the Cuban food: lechon and pollo asado, platanos maduros, black beans and yellow rice.

Tina had blue eyes with yellow spots in them, an almost pretty face and a terrific figure. She and LaDonna wore as much or more make-up as the Cuban girls.

"Are you from around here?" Tina asked Roy. "You don't talk like you are."

"I'm from Chicago," he said. "I'm down here staying with my uncle for the summer."

"I'm almost seventeen," said Tina. "How old are you?"

"I'll be sixteen in October," Roy lied.

Tina was a little taller than Roy. She had slender, muscular arms and held him tightly, pulling him around during a slow dance. Her new breasts were as hard as her arms. She pushed herself against Roy and he got excited.

"I can tell you like me, Roy," Tina said, and smiled. Her teeth were crooked and up close Roy could see the pimples beneath cracks in her make-up.

Ralph was trying to get one of the Cuban girls to talk to him and LaDonna was dancing with a big, heavyset guy whose ears were perpendicular to his head. Tina told Roy that his name was Woody and that he was one of LaDonna's exes. "She's got a lot of 'em," Tina said.

After the slow dance Roy and Tina got cups of lemonade at the host table and stood off to the side.

"Do you want to walk me home?" Tina asked him. "I live four blocks from here. I don't much like the music they're playing tonight and my parents make me come home early."

When they got to her house, a white, wooden bungalow set on concrete blocks with a wide front porch with a swing on it, Tina said, "Come in with me. My parents go to bed right after *Perry Mason* and then we can sneak out and go down to the river."

Tina introduced Roy to Ed and Irma, both of whom Tina

addressed by their given names, not Mom and Dad, which Roy had never heard a kid do before. Ed and Irma sat in separate armchairs in the small livingroom watching Raymond Burr be a lawyer on their black and white Motorola. Roy and Tina sat slightly apart from each other on a lumpy couch. Ed and Irma did not say anything until the program was over. Ed stood up and turned off the television set after the theme music finished playing over the end credits.

"Man never loses a case," he said.

Ed had a huge belly and big arms. So did Irma. They both said goodnight and left the room. Tina put her right hand on Roy's left leg and squeezed his thigh. As soon as Tina heard the door to her parents' bedroom close and lock click, she turned to Roy and kissed him hard on the mouth.

Tina stood, took Roy's left hand and said, "Let's go down to the river and sit on the pier."

The river was at the end of Tina's street. She led him past a dwarf palm tree that was bent halfway over to a short pier and pulled him down onto the planks.

"Lie back," she said.

There were no boats moving on the water and except for insect noises it was quiet. Tina lay on top of Roy and rubbed her body against his. They kissed a few times with their mouths closed, then Tina rolled onto her side and with one hand unzipped his fly. Roy's cock popped up like a jack-in-the-box and Tina wrapped her right hand around it. He stared at the crescent moon as she stroked him slowly for a minute or so and then Roy tried to get up and lie on top of her. Tina pushed him back down, held him prostrate with her ropey arms, straddled his legs and put his cock into her mouth. Roy came immediately.

Tina rolled off of him and spat into the water, turned back to Roy and said, "You have a good dick, I think."

She stood up, so Roy did, too. He zipped up his pants. Tina had already begun walking back off the pier. They walked to her house without saying anything. Tina stopped in front of her porch steps. No lights were on. She stretched out her arms and rested them on Roy's shoulders.

"I won't be at the Cuban Club next Saturday," she said. "I'm going with Ed and Irma to Milwaukee on Monday. That's where Mamie, Irma's mother, lives. I have a cousin there, Ronnie. He's the only boy I let fuck me. He's twenty-one."

"How long have you been letting him do it?" Roy asked.

"Since a couple of months before my thirteenth birthday. This will be the fifth year. I only see Ronnie in the summer when we visit Mamie. Ronnie's getting married in September."

Tina kissed Roy on the mouth and this time she stuck her tongue in. Roy watched her go up the steps and into the house. He saw Irma sitting on the swing in the dark, smoking a cigarette.

"Go on now, boy," she said.

Appreciation

It was Roy's mother's third husband, Sid Wade, who told Roy that his father had died. Roy and Sid did not get along. Roy's mother had married Sid two years before, when Roy was ten, and it had since been obvious to Roy that if this husband had a choice, he would prefer Roy were not part of the deal.

Roy had gone home from school to have lunch and Sid took him into what had been Roy's grandfather's room before he moved to Florida to live with Roy's Uncle Buck. Ice coated the windows.

"Listen, Roy, your father died this morning," Sid said.

Roy knew his father was in the hospital being treated for colon cancer. He'd had an operation a few months before and needed to sit on a rubber pillow at the kitchen table. Also, since then Roy had seen his father's second wife, Evie, giving his dad shots with a large hypodermic needle. Despite the illness, Roy's father did not appear to have lost his strength or his sense of humor. The only difference Roy noticed was that his dad was at home more. Usually he was at his liquor store from early afternoon until three or four in the morning, and sometimes he didn't go home for twenty-four hours.

"In my business, there's always something going on," he told Roy. "If I don't pay attention, I'll end up paying in other ways, and if that happens too many times pretty soon I won't be in business."

There were always people coming in and going out of his dad's store, and men hanging around talking or whispering to each other or just standing and waiting. His dad seemed to know all of them and did not mind that none of them ever bought any liquor. The only times Roy saw a bottle of whiskey or gin change hands with one of them was when his dad gave it to him and did not ask for money. Sometimes a showgirl from the Club Alabam next door came in and without saying anything went down the rickety inside staircase into the basement with Roy's father. They would come back up a few minutes later and the girl would kiss his dad on his cheek and say, "Thanks a million, Rudy," or "You're a swell guy," before leaving. The showgirls came in on a break from rehearsals wearing only high heels and a skimpy costume under a coat. Roy thought they were all knockouts and he asked his father what they wanted to see him about.

"They need a little help from time to time, Roy," his dad said, "and I give them something to make 'em feel better."

"What do you give them?"

"It's not important, son. They're poor girls and I like to help people if I can."

"They always kiss you goodbye."

Roy's father smiled and said, "That's how they show their appreciation."

Roy wanted to go back to school in the afternoon after Sid Wade told him about his father, but Sid said he couldn't, that he would drive Roy to his father's house so he could be with Evie and his father's relatives. Roy asked his mother if he had to go to Evie's and she said yes, to show his respect. "She'll appreciate it," his mother said.

Years later, long after Sid Wade, his mother and Evie were dead, Roy, in recounting the events of that day for his own son, explained his asking to be allowed to go back to school as his desire to act normally, a way of denying to himself for the moment that his father was dead.

"I didn't really understand what it meant," Roy told his son, "that I'd never again see my father hanging out with his cronies or being kissed on the cheek by a showgirl from the Club Alabam. I wanted to help him and I couldn't."

"You help a lot of people now, though, Pop," Roy's son said. "Have you ever been kissed by a showgirl?"

The Awful Country

When Roy's mother returned from her birthday trip with her companion Nicky Roznido, Roy asked her how it was and she said, "Everybody in Mexico carries a gun."

Roy was eight years old and his mother was twenty-nine for the second time. She didn't look thirty, she said to her friend Kay, and she saw no reason to admit to her real age until she absolutely had to.

"I was twenty-nine until two years ago," said Kay, "when I turned thirty-eight. I admitted it to Mario and he told me he didn't care so long as I looked good to him. I asked him what he would do when that day came and he said he'd have to buy a younger wife."

Kay and Roy's mother snickered and Roy, who was in the room with them, asked Kay, "Did Mario buy you?"

"He knew what he was getting when he married me," she said. "Be smart, Roy, don't ever get yourself into a situation where you're paying for more than you can afford."

"Cut it out, Kay," said Roy's mother. "He doesn't know what you're talking about."

Kay had flaming red hair and green eyes with black dust smudged around them. She was wearing a double strand of tiny pearls and diamond rings on the third fingers of both hands.

"Your mother's right, Roy," she said, and smiled, displaying more teeth than he could quickly count accurately. "Don't listen to me, it won't matter, anyway. Everyone makes their own mistakes."

Kay returned her attention to Roy's mother and said, "Come on, honey, I'm going to buy you a fancy lunch to celebrate your return from that awful country. Did Nicky have to shoot anybody this time?"

After Kay and his mother left the house, Roy went into his room and lay down on the bed. He could hear thunder but it was far away. He thought about what Kay had said about everyone making their own mistakes. He knew she meant something other than giving a wrong answer on a test. Roy remembered the morning his mother threw her second husband, Des Riley, out of the house. He was six then and his mother had said, "We won't have to listen to his bullcrap any more, Roy. That one was a mistake."

"Was my dad a mistake?" Roy asked her.

"No, Roy," she said, "I was just too young to know what I was doing."

His mother was really thirty now, not twenty-nine. How old did a person have to be to not be too young? If his father were still alive, Roy would ask him. It was not a question, he decided, that his mother could answer.

Deep in the Heart

After she graduated from high school in Chicago, Roy's mother had gone to the University of Texas in Austin. When he was ten, Roy asked her why she had gone to college so far away.

"Your Uncle Buck was training to be a pilot at the Naval air station down there and he thought it would be a good idea for me to get away from the nuns and our mother. I was very shy. I'd spent ten years in boarding school being bossed around by the sisters and the priests, I'd never been on a date alone with a boy."

"Did you like Texas?"

"The girls were nice but sometimes they played tricks on me."

"What kinds of tricks?"

"Oh, one time at breakfast instead of two sunnyside up eggs they put two cow's eyes on my plate. But I liked how blue and enormous the sky was and singing 'Deep in the Heart of Texas' and 'The Eyes of Texas Are Upon You' at the football games."

"How long did you stay there?"

"Almost two years. My brother washed out of pilot school and got stationed in Philadelphia. He and Diana were married by then. My girlfriends talked me into entering a beauty contest at the university and I won. I was offered a modelling job in New York, so I went there and stayed with my Aunt Lorna and Uncle Dick."

"Aunt Lorna's the one I punched in the eye when I was two."

"That's right, when she came to Chicago to visit. She and Uncle Dick had a beautiful house on 65th Street off Fifth Avenue. I was making my own money for the first time so I didn't see the point in going back to college."

"I got sick, though, so after a few months I came back to Chicago and spent a few weeks in the hospital being treated for a severe case of eczema. The doctors said I had a nervous condition and should avoid stress. Eventually I went back to work modelling furs for wholesale buyers in the showroom at the Merchandise Mart. I was only nineteen then. That's when I met your father. He was twenty years older and knew how to take care of me. Boys my own age didn't. So I married your dad and we honeymooned in Hollywood and Las Vegas. He arranged a screen test for me and his friends out there introduced me to some movie stars."

"Like who?"

"Oh, Errol Flynn and William Holden were the most famous ones. And that terrible Lawrence Tierney."

"What was terrible about him?"

"He was forward with me at the studio but then your dad's friends let him know the score and he apologized."

"I didn't know you could have been in the movies."

"I couldn't act, Roy, I didn't have any experience, so nothing came of it. Hollywood is full of pretty girls. I had fun, though. Your dad had business to do in Las Vegas so we spent quite a bit of time there. In those days everyone stayed at the El Rancho, it was the place to be before Ben opened his hotel."

"Who was Ben? Was he a friend of Dad's?"

"Yes. He was murdered in Los Angeles while we were with his girlfriend's brother in Vegas."

"Who killed him?"

"They never found out. When you're in business, it's easy to make enemies. People never know who their real friends are, anyway."

"I've got real friends."

Roy's mother smiled at him. She had beautiful teeth. They were sitting at the kitchen table and she patted him on his hand.

"Of course, Roy," she said. "I wasn't talking about you."

Unopened Letters

"Roy, would you please take out the placemats that are in the bottom drawer of the dining room dresser? The red ones underneath the candlesticks."

"Sure, Mom."

Roy's mother was preparing the house for a dinner party that evening in honor of her Aunt Lorna, who was visiting from New York. Roy was fifteen and had not encountered his great-aunt since he was about two years old, an occasion of which he had no recollection. Lorna had helped Roy's mother establish herself as a model in New York twenty-five years before and she had always been grateful to Lorna for her kindness and generosity; having a dinner party for Lorna during one of her rare visits to Chicago was the very least his mother could do.

"Ma, who's Frank Jameson?"

"What, Roy? Did you find the placemats?"

"Yes, but there was a marriage certificate and a bundle of unopened letters with a string tied around it underneath the placemats. The marriage certificate is between Nanny and a man named Frank Jameson. Who is he?"

Roy's mother came into the dining room and Roy handed her the certificate.

"And these letters all have a return address in Kansas City. They were sent to Nanny here in Chicago."

"The letters are from your grandfather to Nanny. She never opened them because she was married at the time to Frank Jameson."

"You mean that she and Pops got divorced? You never told me."

"No, Roy, I didn't think it was necessary for you to know. Maybe I was wrong not to tell you, but you and Pops were so close I didn't want anything to interfere with that."

"How long was Nanny married to Frank Jameson? You must have been a little girl then."

"Ten years, from when I was six to sixteen. He had a heart attack and died on Christmas day, just after my sixteenth birthday. Pops wanted to re-marry my mother but she didn't want to. He used to stand in a doorway across the street from our house and when she came out he'd try to talk to her. He'd gone to live in Kansas City after they divorced, then he moved back to Chicago after Frank died. Pops still loved Nanny and wrote her letters but she wouldn't open them. Half of those letters he sent while Frank was still alive."

"But she lived for twelve years after Frank Jameson died, until you were twenty-eight. Why didn't she open them for all those years?"

"I don't know. I only discovered them after Nanny died. I didn't want to just throw them away."

"Did you tell Pops you had them?"

"No. I meant to but I never did. I don't know why exactly except that because of things my mother said I blamed Pops for breaking up their marriage. And after he died, I hid them away."

"Along with Nanny's marriage certificate to Frank Jameson. You grew up with him, Ma. Did you like him? What was his profession? And why did Pops and Nanny get divorced?"

"Frank was all right to me but not to my brother. I was sent away to boarding school, so I didn't spend much time with him. He didn't want anything to do with your Uncle Buck, and since Buck was fourteen years older than me he was already pretty much on his own. The Jameson family were fairly well-to-do. They were Irish, the father and mother were born in County Kerry, and there were four brothers, including Frank. They owned warehouses in and around Chicago. Frank was a devout Catholic, so Nanny began going to church regularly. She became close friends with the Mother Superior at St. Theresa's, near where we lived."

"She was in our house a lot when Nanny was dying. I remember her. I'd never seen a woman with a mustache before. What about Pops and Nanny? Why did they split up?"

"Pops had a girlfriend, Sally Carmel, who lived in Kansas City. I guess he met her on one of his business trips. He still loved Nanny, though, and wanted her to go back with him. I think that's what's in those letters."

"Love letters."

"I suppose."

"Are you ever going to open them?"

"I don't know. Perhaps it's better to leave them unopened. They're addressed to my mother, not to me. I've often wondered why she kept them. I should probably burn them."

Roy's mother replaced the letters and the marriage certificate in the bottom drawer of the dresser and closed it.

"Let's not talk about this any more now, Roy. I've got to have everything ready for the dinner. Aunt Lorna will be here at five."

She went into the kitchen. Roy sat down on a chair in the dining room and looked out the window. The sky was gray with black specks in it, a snow sky. He wondered what else his mother thought was unnecessary for him to know.

Walking to St. Tim's the next morning, Roy asked his friend Johnny McLaughlin if he thought either or both of his parents kept secrets about their family from him and his brothers.

"The Catholic church is all about secrets," said Johnny. "It's the mysteries keep people comin' back for more, hopin' they'll some day get filled in on the real goods. My Uncle Sean is always goin' on about the Rosetta stone, you know, that hunk of rock found in Egypt over a hundred years ago has pictures of birds and half-moons on it symbolize something important. My parents ain't no different. They just tell me and Billy and Jimmy what's necessary to keep us in line. Only the dead know the meaning of existence, and they don't answer letters."

"They don't even open them," said Roy.

Chicago, Illinois, 1953

Roy and his mother had come back to Chicago from Cuba by way of Key West and Miami so that she could attend the funeral of her Uncle Ike, her father's brother. Roy was six years old and though he would not be going to the funeral—he'd stay at home with his grandmother, who was too ill to attend—he looked forward to seeing Pops, his grandfather, during his and his mother's time in the city.

It was mid-February and the weather was at its most miserable. The temperature was close to zero, ice and day-old snow covered the streets and sidewalks, and sharp winds cut into pedestrians from several directions at once. Had it not been out of fondness and respect for her father's brother, Roy's mother would never have ventured north from the tropics at this time of year. Uncle Ike had always been especially kind and attentive to his niece and Roy's mother was sincerely saddened by his passing.

She and Roy had first stopped on the way in from the airport to see Roy's father, from whom his mother had recently been divorced, at his liquor store, and were now in a taxi on their way to Roy's grandmother's house when she told the driver to stop so that she could buy something at a pharmacy.

"Wait here in the cab, Roy," she said, "it's warmer. I'll only be a couple of minutes."

Roy watched his mother tiptoe gingerly across the frozen sidewalk and enter the drugstore. The taxi was parked on Ojibway Avenue, which Roy recognized was not very far from his grandmother's neighborhood.

"That your mother?" the driver asked.

"Yes."

"She's a real attractive lady. You live in Chicago?"

"Sometimes," said Roy. "My grandmother lives here. Right now we live in Havana, Cuba, and Key West, Florida."

"You live in both places?"

"We go back and forth on the ferry. They're pretty close."

"Your parents got two houses, huh?"

"They're divorced. My mom and I live in hotels."

"You like that, livin' in hotels?"

"We've always lived in hotels, even when my mom and dad were married. I was born in one in Chicago."

"Where's your dad live?"

"Here, mostly. Sometimes he's in Havana or Las Vegas."

"What business is he in?"

Roy was getting anxious about his mother. The rear window on his side of the cab kept steaming up and Roy kept wiping it off.

"My mother's been in there a long time," he said. "I'm going in to find her."

"Hold on, kid, she'll be right back. The drugstore's probably crowded."

Roy opened the curbside door and said, "Don't drive away. My mom'll pay you."

He got out and went into the drugstore. His mother was standing in front of the cash counter. Three or four customers in line were behind her.

"You dumb son of a bitch!" his mother shouted at the man standing behind the counter. "How dare you talk to me like that!"

The clerk was tall and slim and he was wearing wire-rim glasses and a brown sweater.

"I told you," he said, "we don't serve Negroes. Please leave the store or I'll call the police."

"Go on, lady," said a man standing in line. "Go someplace else."

"Mom, what's wrong?" Roy said.

The customers and the clerk looked at him.

"This horrible man refuses to wait on me because he thinks I'm a Negro."

"But you're not a Negro," Roy said.

"It doesn't matter if I am or not. He's stupid and rude."

"Is that your son?" the clerk asked.

"He's white," said a woman in the line. "He's got a suntan but he's a white boy."

"I'm sorry, lady," said the clerk, "it's just that your skin is so dark."

"Her hair's red," said the woman. "She and the boy have been in the sun too much down south somewhere."

Roy's mother threw the two bottles of lotion she'd been holding at the clerk. He caught one and the other bounced off his chest and fell on the floor behind the counter.

"Come on, Roy, let's get out of here," said his mother.

The taxi was still waiting with the motor running and they got in. The driver put it into gear and pulled away from the curb.

"You get what you needed, lady?" he asked.

"Mom, why didn't you tell the man that you aren't a Negro?"

Roy's mother's shoulders were shaking and tears were running down her cheeks. He could see her hands trembling as she wiped her face.

"Because it shouldn't matter, Roy. This is Chicago, Illinois, not Birmingham, Alabama. It's against the law not to serve Negroes."

"No it ain't, lady," said the driver.

"It should be," said Roy's mother.

"How could they think you're black?" the driver said. "If I'd thought you were a Negro, I wouldn't have picked you up."

The Colony of the Sun

Gina Crow played Hoagy Carmichael records every Saturday morning. Certain records she played more than once. One day Roy heard "Hong Kong Blues" and "Old Man Harlem" twice, and "Memphis in June" three times. Usually, the last song Mrs. Crow played was "Stardust". All of these versions featured Hoagy Carmichael with solo piano, except for "New Orleans", on which he sang a duet with a woman. Roy liked to sit on his back porch from about eight to nine o'clock listening to the records during the year Gina Crow and her daughter, Polly, lived next door. Polly was twelve, a year older than Roy. She had cat's eyes, billiard ball black with yellow flames in the center. Polly looked and acted older than she was, and she had a sharp-edged manner of speaking that made her sound mean or angry. She made Roy feel uncomfortable but excited at the same time.

"Martha Poole told me that Gina Crow's husband is getting out of prison."

"I didn't know she had a husband."

"Martha said he was busted in Toledo, where they used to live."

"What for?"

"Embezzlement. She thinks he worked in a bank."

Roy's mother and her husband were washing and drying dishes while Roy was sitting at the kitchen table eating a bowl of cereal.

"What's embezzlement?" he asked.

"It means he stole money," said his mother.

"Is he coming to live with them?" her husband asked.

"Martha doesn't know."

"If he's on probation, he'll have to stay in Ohio. For a while, anyway."

"I'm just glad he didn't rape or murder anyone. I wouldn't feel comfortable having a murderer living next door to us."

Walking home from school the next day, Roy was following behind Polly Crow and her friend Vida when he heard Polly say that her father was coming home soon, and that she had not seen him for a long time.

"Where's he been?" asked Vida.

"Far away, in the Colony of the Sun."

"I've never heard of that place. Is it in the United States?"

"I think it might be in Canada, or Antarctica."

"What was he doing there?"

"Working on a big project. My mother told me he was exploring for something that could save the planet."

"You mean Earth?"

"Yeah. My mother says pretty soon there won't be enough coal to heat all of our houses."

"Maybe he was digging oil wells. They use oil to heat houses, too."

"Could be. She says the men there have to shoot polar bears and seals to have meat."

After Vida turned off at her street and Polly was by herself, Roy caught up to her and said hello.

"Oh, hi, Roy. Were you walking behind me and Vida?"

"Yes. I heard what you said about your father being in Antarctica."

"It gets even colder there than here in Chicago. We might move to New Orleans, where it's a lot warmer. My mother lived there when she was a little girl."

Polly was taller than Roy. She had long brown hair and very white skin. The wind blew her hair across her face and she kept pushing it back into place.

"How long has it been since you've seen him?"

"I was eight. We were in Toledo then."

"I like the records your mother plays. Sometimes I sit on our porch and listen to them."

Polly stopped walking and turned and faced Roy. Her lips were purple and she brushed her hair out of her eyes.

"Two nights ago my mother got drunk on vodka and told me my father isn't my real father, and that my real father was a boy named Bobby Boles and that he was killed in a bar fight in Houston, Texas. At least that's what she heard because he abandoned her when she told him she was pregnant. She married my father when I was a year old. She told me she still loved Bobby Boles, even though he was dead, and that every time she looks at me she sees him in my face and it makes her want to cry."

Roy stared at the jumpy yellow flames in Polly Crow's eyes. They got bigger, then smaller, then big again.

"She never told you this before?"

Polly shook her head. The wind whipped her hair around.

"Why do you think she wanted you to know now?"

"She made me promise not to tell my father that she told me. She said Bobby Boles had been her sister's boyfriend, my Aunt Earlene, who's older and lives in Little Rock, Arkansas. I've never met her. My mother says when Earlene found out Bobby Boles fucked my mother she called her a whore and swore she'd never speak to her again, and she hasn't."

Roy had never heard a girl say fuck before. Polly started to walk, so he did, too. She didn't say anything else and when they got to her house Polly went in without saying goodbye.

As far as Roy knew, Gina Crow's husband never showed up, and a few months after Polly had told Roy about her real father she and her mother moved away without telling Roy or his mother and her husband or Martha Poole to where.

"Gina's an odd woman," Roy's mother said one night at the dinner table. "Her daughter, too. She'll be trouble when she grows up, if she's not already. Where do you suppose they went?"

"The Colony of the Sun," said Roy.

"There's no such place," said his mother's husband.

Creeps

Roy noticed the creepy little guy following him right after he got off the bus. Roy was on his way to the Riviera theater to see a double feature of *The Alligator People* and *First Man Into Space*. His friends Buzzy Riordan and Jimmy Boyle were meeting him there. Buzzy had once been thrown out of the Riviera for shouting "Fire!" and ordered never to return, but that had been more than a year before so he figured the manager and the ushers wouldn't recognize him, especially since he now had a crewcut and was taller. Buzzy told Roy he'd done it so that he could get a better seat; he'd gotten to the theater late and all the seats except for ones in the first row were taken and he hated sitting so close to the screen because he had to look up all the time and the actors' heads were too small. Lots of kids ran out into the lobby and Buzzy moved back and sat down in the center seat of a middle row. When the kid who had been sitting there came back after learning it was a false alarm told Buzzy to move Buzzy told him to get lost. The kid called an usher and a girl who'd been sitting in the front row near Buzzy and was now walking back to her seat pointed at him and said, "That's the creep who yelled fire!"

Buzzy and Jimmy Boyle were in the same fifth grade class at Delvis Erland grammar school, which most of the kids called Devil's Island. The grades went from kindergarten through eighth so if a student spent the entire time there he or she could say that they'd done nine years of hard labor at Devil's Island. The school had been built in 1902 and resembled an asylum or prison out of Victorian England. When Roy saw the movie of *Jane Eyre* on TV he thought the similarity between Lowood Institute and Devil's Island was unmistakable.

The creep who was following Roy was very short, no more than five feet tall, with splotchy bleached blonde hair, a frog-faced kisser and a pudgy build. Roy guessed his age at about forty. The man trailed Roy from the bus stop toward the theater, keeping a few feet behind him. Roy hurried but did not run, hoping that Buzzy and Jimmy would be in front of the Riv waiting for him.

Roy had to wait across the street from the theater for the light to change. He saw his friends standing under the marquee sharing a smoke. Before Roy stepped off the curb the creep was standing next to him.

"Hello, sonny," he said, "are you hungry? I'd like to buy you a hamburger."

Just then the light changed to green and Roy ran over to Buzzy and Jimmy.

"Hey Roy," said Buzzy, "we thought maybe you weren't comin'. *The Alligator People*'s gonna start."

"Yeah," Jimmy said, "Buzzy was just sayin' how if we couldn't get good seats right away he'd have to yell 'Fire!' again."

"Uh uh, I was gonna shout 'Rat!'"

When the blonde babe in *The Alligator People* who's wandering lost in a spooky southern swamp sees that her husband has turned partly into a gator, she screams, reminding Roy of the creep with bleached hair who had followed him on the street. The skin on the creep's face was scaly looking, like an alligator's, and his hair was almost as long as the actress's. Roy hoped the guy wouldn't be waiting for him outside the theater when he got out. Buzzy and Jimmy would be with him, though, so he figured the creep wouldn't try anything. The boys would stay for both movies unless Buzzy pulled some stunt that would get the three of them tossed before *First Man Into Space* was over. The show wouldn't let out until dark. Roy was sure the creep would have found another boy to follow around by then.

Achilles and the Beautiful Land

Roy enjoyed listening to the old guy who fixed zippers tell stories. The man would come through the back door into the kitchen of Roy's house and sit down on the rickety little wooden chair with the left rear leg that was a quarter of an inch shorter than its other three. Roy's mother kept the crooked chair because it had belonged to her grandmother and when his mother was a little girl she would sit on it. A daffodil had been painted in yellow on the inside back of the chair but it had faded badly over the years and Roy knew the vague shape was once a daffodil only because his mother told him so. Roy asked her why one leg was shorter than the others and she said she didn't really know but that her grandmother had owned a brown and white mutt named Blackie who liked to chew on the chair's legs; teeth marks, presumably Blackie's, decorated all four of them.

The man who fixed zippers called himself Achilles. He was eighty-eight years old, he said, when he first appeared at the back door and asked Roy's mother if she had any zippers that needed repairing. He spoke English but with a strange accent punctuated by a cloudy cough that sometimes made it difficult for Roy to understand him. Roy was five when he met Achilles, who remained a regular visitor for more than a year. Even when there were no zippers on Roy's mother's dresses or jackets to fix Achilles would come in and sit on the crooked chair by the door and talk to her and Roy, often telling stories about his childhood in a place he called the beautiful land. The beautiful land, said Achilles, was in another country, much smaller than America, a half-step from the Orient, where he had been born. Roy asked him what the name of the country was but Achilles said he didn't know any more; the country had been invaded by soldiers from many other countries over the years and each time the name had been changed. The old man preferred to recall it only as the beautiful land, describing the forests and rivers and hills and villages where a boy such as he had been was welcomed into any hut or house to eat or sleep.

"Why did you leave there?" Roy asked him.

"When an army wearing helmets sporting blue feathers arrived from the East everyone in every village was forced to abandon their homes and belongings and march together for many days and nights to a train station. I was thirteen years old then and I had never seen a train, so I was curious, and even though I did not want to leave the beautiful land, I did not really mind going. I had heard people describe trains and when I finally saw one I was thrilled that I was going to ride on it. The train was puffing white smoke and hissing like a big long dragon."

"Where did it take you?"

"Far away from the beautiful land to a place I have forgotten."

"Did your parents bring you to Chicago?"

"My parents were made to travel on a different train. One day I did not see them and ever since there has been another day."

"What kinds of animals were there in the beautiful land?"

"Deer, tigers and birds, and fish, of course, in the rivers and lakes."

"Didn't the tigers eat the deer?"

"Yes, Roy, and hunters killed and ate both of them, as well as the fish."

"Did the tigers ever eat the people who lived in the villages?"

"A tiger once spoke to me. I was walking in the woods, looking for mushrooms, when a magnificent orange and black and white beast appeared in my path."

"How old were you?"

"No more than ten. I was a small boy, only a bit bigger than you are now."

"You're still small, Achilles. For a grown man, I mean."

"Being small has its advantages. I assumed the tiger was going to eat me but he just stared with his yellow eyes and said, 'Come back when you are larger and will make a better meal.' Then he disappeared into the trees."

Roy told his mother that a tiger had spoken to Achilles and she said, "That was in a time when people and animals were still polite to one another."

"Achilles said the tiger wouldn't eat him because he was too small."

"That's what I mean," she said.

Roy did not see Achilles for a while so he asked his mother if she had.

"No, Achilles has gone back to the beautiful land. He told me to tell you that he looks forward to seeing you there in about a hundred years."

"Can you show me on a map where the beautiful land is?"

"Achilles said, 'Tell Roy that when the time comes he'll know how to get there. I'll be waiting for him.'"

"A hundred years is a long time to wait," said Roy.

"Maybe not," said his mother, "not if you're in the beautiful land. Achilles won't ever leave there again."

Men in the Kitchen

"So you were already in the basement when this man attacked you."

"Yes, I was doing the laundry."

"You didn't hear him approaching?"

"No, the washing machine was filling with water. I'd just put in a second load, and I was putting the wet things from the first load into the dryer, so I couldn't hear over the noise."

"Do you always leave the basement door open when you're doing laundry?"

"Yes, to have some fresh air, unless it's cold and raining or snowing. The ventilation down there isn't very good, and it was a warm, sunny day."

"You were loading up the dryer. Then what happened?"

"A hand came over my mouth and he wrapped his other arm around my chest. The knife was in his left hand."

"Left-handed. Go on."

"The man said, 'Don't try to scream or I'll cut your throat.' Then he dragged me away from the washing machine and dryer into the passageway by the storage area. He forced me to the ground and took his hands away. That's when he saw that I'm pregnant and cursed."

"What did he say exactly?"

"God damn it. He said it three or four times. I kept saying, 'Don't hurt my baby, don't hurt my baby.' He took out a piece of rope and cut it with his knife, then turned me onto my left side, facing away from him, and tied my hands behind my back. He told me to shut up and I heard him making sounds."

"What kinds of sounds?"

"I think he was masturbating."

"How long did this go on?"

"You mean his masturbating?"

"Yes."

"It couldn't have been for very long, maybe a minute or two."

"You didn't scream or call for help?"

"He would have stabbed me or cut my throat if I had, I'm sure of it. When he was finished he walked out of the basement, out the back door. He didn't run. I didn't try to look at him, I didn't want to see his face. I stayed on the ground for several minutes before I got to my feet. It was difficult because my balance isn't good. I'm in my eighth month."

"It sounds like the same guy who attacked the other women. None of them were pregnant."

"Did he rape them?"

"Yes, ma'am. He cut one."

"Did she die?"

"No, she's recovering."

"Nobody could recover from that."

Roy's mother and two men were seated at the kitchen table when he came home from school. Roy stood and looked at the men, both of whom were wearing coats and ties and hats and were clean shaven. One of them wore glasses and the other had a bluish scar on the right side of his chin.

"Hi, Mom," he said, "are these guys friends of Dad's?"

She hugged him and said to the men, "This is my son, Roy. He's seven."

"Hello, son," said the man wearing glasses.

"No, Roy," said his mother, "they're detectives. They're investigating a case, something that happened nearby. They're asking me if I know anything about it."

"Do you?" Roy asked.

"The boy wasn't home when it happened?" said the man with the scar.

"No, he was at school."

The detectives stood up.

"We'll get back to you about this. Are you sure you don't want to go to the hospital?"

"No, I'm all right. I'll call my doctor myself."

"Thank you for your cooperation, ma'am," said the man wearing glasses.

"We'll find our way out," said the other detective.

The men left and Roy sat down in the chair in which the man with the blue scar had been sitting.

"Mom, are you okay? Why did they ask if you wanted to go to the hospital?"

"They were being kind because I'm pregnant."

"Can I help you with anything?"

"Not now, sweetheart. I'm going to take a sponge bath and then I've got to finish the laundry. You can help me carry the baskets upstairs when it's dry."

"What kind of case are they investigating?"

Roy's mother placed her hands flat on the table and pushed herself up.

"I'll tell you later," she said, "How was school today?"

Anna Louise

Roy's cousin Skip's mother, Anna Louise, was an alcoholic. The first thing she did every morning after she got out of bed was go into the kitchen and put a teaspoon of sugar into a chimney size glass, fill it with gin, stir it up and drink half of it. Then she lit a gold-papered, unfiltered cigarette and took a long drag before finishing off her glass of gin. She was a natural platinum blonde with unblemished ghost-white skin. Anna Louise was Roy's Uncle Buck's first wife; after him, she married Karl von Sydow, a Swedish construction magnate. Von Sydow died of a heart attack six years after marrying Anna Louise and left his fortune to her. She and Skip, who was fifteen when von Sydow died, lived north of Chicago on an estate fronted by a high brick wall. A stream ran through thick woods that bordered the other three sides of the property. Anna Louise owned the land the woods and stream were on. She was forty-two and still beautiful when her second husband died. After she'd drunk the glassful of gin, she puffed on her cigarette for a minute or two before returning to the bathroom that adjoined the master bedroom and began running water into the sunken tub. She remained entirely nude during this routine no matter who else was in the house. Roy was thirteen when he first witnessed his aunt's diurnal performance. Anna Louise had perfect posture, having as a girl and young woman been a dancer and an actress before working briefly as a teacher of calculus and poetry at a private girls' school. She was twenty-two when she married Roy's uncle, who, Anna Louise unembarrassedly informed Roy, had not been her first lover, though she had let him believe so.

"Your uncle was good to me and an ardent paramour," she said, "until he impregnated me. After that, I seldom saw him. It wasn't much of a marriage. Von Sydow was consistently hands on, shall I say. I don't know which was worse. I should have married a Jew."

Roy's aunt delivered this information to him while he and his cousin Skip were seated at the breakfast table eating cereal, the only food Anna Louise kept in the house. She had yet to run her bath.

Roy saw her infrequently during his teenage years, the last time being when he was seventeen and she was living in a motel in an unfashionable suburb of the city. This was after she had unintentionally set fire to her house, which burned to the ground. Anna Louise had passed out drunk in her bedroom, where firemen found her collapsed on the floor and carried her out just before the roof caved in.

According to Skip, most of his mother's money was gone, swindled by von Sydow's attorney whom she had trusted to manage her financial affairs, and she spent the majority of her waking hours drinking gin out of the bottle from a case on the floor next to her bed positioned so that to extract a new bottle all she had to do was reach down and lift it up to her lips.

The last Roy heard of Anna Louise was that she had been admitted to an assisted living facility in Indiana, where she had relatives. By that time, however, her mind was gone, as well as what little money she had left, and she died sober and fully dressed sitting in a wheelchair. Skip was overseas in the army at the time and did not come back for the funeral, which was paid for by his father.

Roy always remembered Anna Louise naked in the morning in her big house standing in the kitchen holding her tall glass of sugared gin and a golden cigarette; but he never understood what she meant when she said she should have married a Jew.

Mules in the Wilderness

Bruno and Lily had moved to a new house since Roy had last seen them, which had been at the funeral of Grandpa Joseph, his dad and Bruno's father, five years before, when Roy was fourteen. Roy's uncle and aunt had not made an effort to keep in touch with him since his dad died, two years before the death of Grandpa Joseph. Roy had been living in Europe for the last two years and was visiting his mother in Chicago before continuing on to the West Coast. He decided to stop by Bruno and Lily's just to say hello and see their house. He had always liked his aunt Lily, a lively, attractive woman who at one time had been quite friendly with his mother, even after his parents divorced. "Give my best to Lily," Roy's mother said to him.

Bruno was another story, as were Roy's cousins Daria and Delilah. Daria was a year younger than Roy and Delilah five years younger. Ever since Roy could remember both Daria and her father seemed always to be in a bad mood, and Delilah uncommunicative, keeping very much to herself. Roy's mother told him that his Uncle Bruno had wanted sons, not daughters, and made his feelings obvious in his behavior toward Daria and Delilah; he remained cold and distant, leaving Lily with the responsibility of raising them. Besides this and catering to her husband, Lily devoted much of her time to work on behalf of Mother Wolfram's Mission for the Misshapen and other charitable organizations.

When his uncle answered the front door, he did so by peering through a narrow slit. Not recognizing Roy, he asked who he was. Roy identified himself, which caused Bruno to pause for several seconds before informing him that there were too many locks to undo on the door and instructing him to come around the side of the house where he would be admitted through the servants' entrance.

It was Lily who admitted him. She smiled and seemed pleased to see Roy. His aunt had worn heavy pancake makeup ever since he'd known her and dark red, precisely applied lipstick so Roy was not surprised when she air-kissed him on both sides of his face. Lily guided Roy up a winding staircase and through an enormous kitchen into a den that he could see connected to a livingroom. Daria and Delilah, she informed him, were away at boarding school in the East. Bruno was sitting in a high-backed chair and motioned with his right index finger for Roy to sit in an armchair across from him.

"Is your mother still alive?" Lily asked.

"She is," said Roy.

"Say hello to her for me," his aunt said, then left the room.

Roy looked around. There were paintings on the walls of older men in suits, none of whom Roy recognized.

"What do you want?" asked Bruno.

Roy's father's only brother was a large man, a couple of inches over six feet tall and he weighed in excess of 220 pounds. Bruno wore his pants fastened just below his chest, a blue dress shirt and dark brown tie; he had a bushy mustache and a full head of gray-brown hair that stood up like a stiff brush.

"I came to say hello to you and Aunt Lily," said Roy. "I've been living abroad for two years."

"Do you plan to stay in Chicago now?"

"No, I'm on my way to California."

Bruno was an auctioneer; he handled sales of restaurants, auto-mobile dealerships, private estates and business properties. Roy recalled his mother once commenting that Bruno could for the right price acquire anything anyone wanted. He was Roy's father's older brother by four years but he seemed to Roy to belong to an earlier time, a Biblical epoch when kings ruled unchallenged. Bruno scrutinized his nephew as if Roy were a freak in a carnival.

"I can have the maid make you a sandwich if you're hungry," he said.

Roy shook his head. "Who are the men in these paintings?"

"Mules in the wilderness, ones who survived."

Roy and his uncle sat in silence until Roy stood up.

"Use the servants' door," said Bruno.

When Roy returned to his mother's house she asked him if he'd seen Bruno and Lily.

"Lily says hello. She wasn't sure you were still alive."

"Does she still look the same?"

"Like a Kabuki actress," said Roy. "She still wears more makeup than Lon Chaney."

"What did Bruno have to say?"

"He asked me what I wanted."

"And what did you tell him?"

"Nothing. We didn't talk much. He asked me if I was hungry. He said the maid could make me a sandwich."

Roy's mother was sitting on a couch in the livingroom. Roy sat down in a chair on the opposite side of the coffee table.

"You know that was my father's favorite chair," she said.

"I remember Pops sitting in it in the afternoons reading the *Daily News* when I came home from school. I sat on the floor next to him and he read to me from the sports section."

Rain streaked the windows behind Roy's mother.

"Looks like I got home just in time," he said.

"When your father died he didn't leave a will. Intestate, it's called. He left Bruno in charge of all of his affairs, but he told me you would be taken care of. Bruno said your dad didn't have anything to leave, that he had to pay off his brother's debts and there was nothing left for you. My brother knew Bruno was lying and so did I. Your dad kept money in safe deposit boxes in hotels and God knows where else. He didn't want the government to know what he had and he never trusted the banks. Your Uncle Buck talked to Bruno about it but there was nothing he could do. If your dad left a will my guess is that Bruno burned it."

"Why didn't you tell me this before?"

"You were twelve years old, there wasn't any point. What was done was done."

"He acted like I'd come there to kill him."

Roy's mother gave a little laugh. "Bruno was afraid of you, that you knew he'd stolen whatever your father had."

"Did Aunt Lily know?"

"Bruno never told her anything about his business."

A year after Roy saw his uncle, Bruno died. In a letter Roy's mother told him an article in the *Chicago Tribune* said the police suspected foul play, that Bruno had been poisoned and that Daria and Delilah were being held in protective custody on suspicion of murdering their father. In her next letter Roy's mother enclosed a newspaper clipping featuring a photograph of Lily that said she had committed suicide by ingesting an overdose of sleeping pills and that she had left a note confessing that she, not her daughters, had poisoned her husband. Her estate, she instructed, should be divided equally between her children and Mother Wolfram's Mission for the Misshapen.

In her second letter Roy's mother wrote, "Your dad told me that when he was four years old and Bruno was eight, Bruno hammered a nail through one of his fingers into a piece of wood on purpose to test himself to see if he could do it and not cry. I asked your dad if Bruno cried and he said yes but that his brother promised him if he told anyone he would nail your father's fingers to a tree."

The Boy Whose Mother May Have Married a Leopard

When he was eight years old Roy had a dream in which his mother, who in real life had already been married three times, came home one day with a leopard and told Roy that the leopard was her new husband. The leopard was very big and he was not tawny but black with even darker spots that could be seen only if a person looked closely at his skin.

"How could you marry a leopard, Mom?" Roy asked. "I didn't know that human beings and animals could marry each other."

In the dream Roy's mother did not answer his question. The following morning when he told her his dream she laughed and said, "I may have married a leopard when I was younger, before you were born. I can't remember, my memory's not so good about those things."

"You'd remember if you married a leopard."

"Did I have him on a leash?"

"I don't think so."

"Figures." she said.

Walking to school Roy told his friend Jimmy Boyle about his dream and Jimmy said, "Nobody would ever pick on a kid if they knew his old man was a leopard."

Roy did not like the men his mother married. His real father had died when Roy was three years old, so he had not really known him, but Roy convinced himself that these other husbands were different. Maybe, he thought, the leopard in the dream was how he wanted his real father to have been, powerful and beautiful, someone who would always be there to protect him.

A few days later Roy's mother's friend Kay, who wore a lot of make-up and whose bright red lipstick was always slightly smeared, said to him, "Kitty told me you had a dream that she'd married a wild beast."

"A leopard," said Roy.

"It was a symbol," Kay said.

"What's that?"

"Something that represents something else, like a desire or a feeling you didn't know you had. I've got lots of repressed desires. My doctor says it's why my skin breaks out."

"Don't confuse him, Kay," said Roy's mother.

Kay was holding a lit cigarette in her right hand; she ran the fingers of her left hand through Roy's hair.

"Your father had thick dark hair like yours," she said.

Roy saw an old black and white movie on TV in which a black leopard escapes from a zoo and turns into a woman who gets hit by a car and dies but before she does she turns back into a leopard. He told Jimmy Boyle about it and Jimmy asked him if he ever had the dream again about his mother marrying a leopard.

Roy shook his head. "No, it probably got run over, too."

A few months later Roy overheard his mother telling someone on the telephone that Kay had divorced her husband and married one of his mother's ex-husbands, but that had not worked out so Kay was going to divorce him, too. Not long after this Roy came home and found Kay and his mother sitting in the livingroom drinking highballs, smoking cigarettes and talking.

"Hello, Roy," said Kay, "how nice to see you. What are you doing with yourself these days? "

"Playing baseball and going to school. What are you doing?"

Kay puffed on her cigarette. Her lipstick was smeared more than usual.

"Waiting for you to grow up," she said.

Stung

When Roy's mother swam into a bevy of jellyfish and got stung by them he was walking along the beach smashing men-of-war with a board. He liked hearing them pop and seeing their blue ink spurt onto the white sand. Roy took care to stand a couple of feet away from the cephalopods, not wanting to step on their invisible poisonous tentacles. He heard his mother's screams and saw her walking unsteadily out of the ocean. She was crying and two teenage girls who were sunbathing on the beach got up and ran over to her. Roy dropped the board and ran over, too.

"It was terrible," his mother said, sobbing between words. "I was swimming close to shore and all of a sudden I was surrounded by jellyfish. They stuck to my back and I couldn't get away from them. They kept stinging me."

"Jesus, lady, your back is full of wounds, your shoulders, too," said one of the girls. "You should see a doctor right away."

"They're hairs," said the other girl. "The stingers are actually hairs that grow out of their tentacles. I learned it in biology."

Roy and his mother were in Miami Beach, staying at the Delmonico Hotel, waiting for his father to come over on the ferry from Havana. Roy knew that his parents were getting a divorce but he didn't know exactly what it meant. He understood that his father would not be living with him and his mother any more, but his dad had seldom been with them in the past few months anyway, so Roy didn't think that would make much of a difference.

At the doctor's office, Roy was made to sit in the waiting room while his mother was being attended to. A receptionist asked him how old he was and when he told her five but almost six she gave him six Tootsie Rolls. Roy didn't like Tootsie Rolls but he took them from her anyway, said thank you, and stuffed them in the right hand pocket of his silver-blue Havana Kings jacket.

Later, Roy decided, he would distribute them to the bus boys at the Delmonico. Roy had gotten to know them well during the five weeks he and his mother had been there. They had all been nice to him—especially Leo, Chi Chi, Chico and Alberto—giving him dishes of ice cream and Coca-Colas while he hung out in the hotel kitchen and talked to them about baseball. They were all Cubans and Roy often went to the Sugar Kings games with his father when he was in Havana. In December, Roy's father had introduced him to El Vaquero, "The Cowboy," the Cuban League home run champion who had for many years played third base for the Cienfuegos team. El Vaquero, whose real name was Raimundo Pardo, had recently had "una taza de café" with the Washington Senators, but he'd struck out much more often than he'd hit home runs for them so the Senators had cut him loose. El Vaquero was going to play now for the Sugar Kings. Roy was looking forward to seeing him hit home runs out of Gran Stadium, but when he told this to Chico and Leo they laughed and said El Vaquero was too old, that his nickname should be changed to El Viejo, "The Old Guy."

"What did the doctor do, Mom?" Roy asked when they were in a taxi going back to the hotel.

"He washed and disinfected the places where I was stung and then applied ointment to them. He said they'll take a few days to heal. You'll rub the ointment on my back for me at night, won't you, Roy?"

"Sure, if you want me to. But I go to sleep before you do. When Dad gets here, he can do it if I'm already in bed."

Roy's mother looked out the cab's window on her side. The sidewalks were very crowded and the taxi couldn't go fast because a wagon filled with plantains being pulled by a horse was in front of it.

"Don't talk about your dad," she said. "Not right now."

"Why, Mom? He's coming to Miami, isn't he?"

"It hurts, Roy. I didn't think it would, but it does."

"Don't worry, Mom, they're just jellyfish stings. You'll be okay in a few days."

El almuerzo por poco

The girl was sitting at a corner table next to a window, gently knocking ash from her cigarette into an empty cup. The café was crowded due to the rain; nobody wanted to leave until it stopped or at least let up a bit. Customers were standing, holding cups and saucers and plates in their hands, ready to pounce if a table became free. She didn't want to give up hers, even though she had finished her coffee.

Roy was with his mother having a quick lunch before her appointment at the dermatologist's. After both of them had ordered grilled cheese sandwiches and coconut milkshakes, Roy's mother told him that she had to make a phone call. He had noticed the girl in the corner as soon as they'd sat down and now could hardly take his eyes off of her. She was about seventeen or eighteen, Roy guessed. Her thick black hair fell over one eye but he thought she looked a lot like Elizabeth Taylor in the movie *Suddenly, Last Summer*, which he'd seen the day before with his mother. Roy was twelve years old and a sign at the theater had said No Minors Allowed but his mother had bought two tickets anyway and nobody tried to stop him from going in with her. After they'd taken their seats, Roy whispered to his mother that children weren't supposed to see the movie.

"It's a matinee, Roy," she whispered back to him. The theater's not even half full. They're just glad to sell tickets."

When the girl at the corner table leaned back in her chair and brushed the hair off of her face, Roy felt a little flutter in his stomach. She had almost the identical expression as Elizabeth Taylor had when she was telling the story of how the desperately poor and starving kids on the beach had devoured Montgomery Clift.

The grilled cheese sandwiches and coconut milkshakes arrived before Roy's mother returned but Roy ignored the food and continued to stare at the girl. The café was in Little Havana, on Southwest 8th Street, close to the dermatologist's office. Roy had been there twice before and he and his mother always ordered the same thing. Everyone in the café, which was named La Cafetería Fabuloso, was speaking Spanish, so Roy assumed the beautiful girl was Cuban, like most of the people in this part of Miami. He wondered why she was alone and imagined she worked in a shop somewhere in the barrio.

His mother came back and said, "Oh, good, I'm starved. Aren't you, Roy? I couldn't get Margie to stop complaining about Ronaldo. I told her to just tell him to go back to his wife."

Roy took a sip of his milkshake through the straw in the glass and thought about those wild boys biting into Monty Clift's flesh. Elizabeth Taylor told the psychiatrist, or Katherine Hepburn, who played Montgomery Clift's mother, Roy couldn't remember who, how there had been nothing she could do to stop them.

"Come on, Roy, we don't have much time."

The girl stood up. She was taller than Roy expected her to be, and slender, not short and buxom like Elizabeth Taylor. She still had a terrified expression on her face, as if she expected something bad to happen to her as soon as she left the café.

"I'm glad it's raining today," said Roy's mother. "Too much sun makes me want to wriggle out of my skin like a snake."

Roy watched the girl walk out. She was wearing a pink cotton dress and did not carry an umbrella. Roy wanted to get up and follow her.

"We're late, Roy. If you're not hungry now, wrap up your sandwich in a napkin and we'll take it with us. You can eat it at the dermatologist's."

Vultures

"In Africa, some tribes believe that wearing a freshly decapitated vulture head can give a person the ability to see into the future."

Roy was sitting on a bench against a wall in Henry Armstrong's second floor boxing gym in Miami listening to Derondo Simmons, a former middleweight once ranked number five in the world by *Ring* magazine. Derondo was forty-two years old and worked as a sparring partner for up-and-comers. Mostly he hung around Henry's and talked to whoever would listen. He was a great storyteller and a voracious reader, especially in the areas of ancient history and anthropology. Roy, who was nine, was a willing audience for Derondo's lectures, and Derondo appreciated it.

"You're a great listener, Roy," he said. "It will pay off for you in the future."

"Pay off how?"

"If you listen carefully, you can figure out how a person's mind works, how they think, then you know what you've got to do to get them to pay you."

Roy's father often dropped him off at the gym when he had business to do downtown. He'd make a contribution to Armstrong's Retired Fighters Fund and press something into Derondo's hand and know they would keep a close eye on his son until he returned.

"Did you ever have a vulture head?" Roy asked Derondo.

"Only seen 'em in pictures and the movies."

"There's vultures in the Everglades."

"Don't take to snakes and gators, Roy, and I don't want snakes or gators takin' to me. I don't go into the 'glades because I can't figure how those creatures think, or even if they do think. Did you know that in ancient Rome soldiers rode two horses at a time, standing up?"

Henry signaled to Derondo and he got up and went over to the larger of the two rings where Henry was talking to a small, well-dressed man wearing a Panama hat. Standing above them leaning down over the top rope was a lean young guy with boxing gloves on. Roy pegged him as a welterweight in the making, a few pounds shy, sixteen or seventeen years old. Derondo nodded his head while Henry spoke to him, and when Henry stopped talking Derondo walked around to the other side of the ring, slipped a sleeveless sweatshirt over his T-shirt, let one of the ring boys grease his face then wrap his hands before fitting on the gloves and fastening his headgear. The kid in the ring began bouncing around, shadowboxing, getting warm. Derondo climbed through the ropes, did a few deep knee bends, practiced a couple of combinations and uppercuts then motioned to the kid.

Roy went over to ringside and stood near Henry and the man wearing the Panama. Derondo outweighed the boy by twenty-five pounds, so Roy knew he would not throw any hard leather. For the kid's part, it was not unexpected that he would be faster both with his hands and feet. Neither Henry nor the man in the hat, who Roy figured was the boy's manager, said a word for the first minute, then Panama shouted, "No baile! Pégale!"

Roy understood that Panama wanted his boy to prance less and punch more. The kid could not get inside on Derondo, who took whatever the boy offered on his arms and shoulders and did not himself do more than feint and tap. Printed in cursive in gold letters on both sides of the boy's black trunks were the words El Zopo. Suddenly, Derondo threw a left hook off a jab that landed flush on the kid's right temple. The little welter tilted onto his left leg and froze for a moment like a crane or heron in the shallows before toppling over and landing on his left ear. Henry jumped into the ring and he and Derondo bent over him. Panama stayed put while Henry and Derondo helped the boy to his feet.

Roy looked over at Panama and examined his face. He had a

thin, dyed black mustache, almond eyes with pale flecks in them and no chin. Roy thought the man resembled a small monkey, a marmoset. When Panama walked around to where Henry and the ring boy were talking to the kid, Roy went back to the bench and leaned against the wall.

A few minutes later, Derondo came and sat down next to him. He had removed the headgear, gloves and sweatshirt and sat still, staring straight ahead for several seconds before saying, "I tell you, Roy, if I'd had a decapitated vulture head I could have told you that kid has no future as a fighter."

Roy's father picked him up an hour later. When they reached the bottom of the forty-seven steps Roy asked him what el zopo means in English.

"Deformed. A deformed person, like in a sideshow. Why?"

"A boxer had it written on his trunks."

"Did he look weird?"

"No, he looked okay. He was just a kid. He was sparring with Derondo Simmons and Derondo knocked him down. I don't think he meant to."

Roy felt safe walking on the street with his father. There were always a few stumblebums on 7th Street outside Henry's; people who had lost their way, his dad called them.

"All fighters get deformed sooner or later, son. You don't need a crystal ball to tell you that."

"Or a vulture head," said Roy.

I Also Deal in Fury

"Then that greaseball actor shows up, and guess who's with him?"

"What actor?"

"Guy with black, curly hair was in the picture where the giggling creep pushes the old lady in a wheelchair down the stairs."

"The actor pushed the woman in the wheelchair?"

"No, the other one, the cop. He's got the rich kid's wife with him, the brunette the queer actor falls for so he drowns his pregnant girlfriend."

"The same movie?"

"No, another one."

"I don't go to the pictures much. I get antsy. Half of the show I'm in the lobby smokin', waitin' on Yvette."

"*I Also Deal in Fury*, you didn't see it?"

"No."

"Anyway, they don't want nobody to know they're in Vegas together, but after ten minutes it's all over town."

"What did they expect?"

"In for the weekend."

"They want privacy they go to the springs, get a mud bath."

Roy was sitting next to the men on a pile of unsold newspapers waiting for his father. It was three-thirty in the morning and his father had said he'd be back at the liquor store by three. Phil Priest and Eddie O'Day were keeping an eye on the boy.

"You okay, kid?" Eddie asked. "Your dad'll be here soon."

"Here," said Phil. "Take it by the grip."

Phil Priest pulled a snubnose .38 out from inside his coat and handed it to Roy.

"You ever handled a piece?"

"Phil, you nuts?" said Eddie. "His old man won't like it, he finds out."

"Be careful, kid," Phil said, "Don't touch the trigger."

"Is it loaded?" Roy asked.

"You got always to assume a piece is loaded. And never point it at anyone other than you mean business."

"It's heavy," said Roy. "Heavier than I thought."

"How old are you now, Roy?"

"Ten. How old are you?"

"Thirty-two."

Roy's father came in and saw Roy holding the gun. Phil took it from him and replaced it inside his coat.

"Roy," said his father, "go stand outside for a minute. By the door, where I can see you."

Roy slid off the stack of newspapers, walked out and stood by the entrance. He liked being up late and looking at people on the street. They were different than the people he saw during the day and in the evening who hung around his father's place. Their faces were hidden even under the lights from the signs on the clubs and restaurants. Phil and Eddie came out of the store and walked away without saying anything.

"Dad, can I come back in now?"

Roy's father came out and stood next to him and draped his right arm around Roy's shoulders. He was wearing a white shirt with the long sleeves rolled up to his elbows and a blue tie with a gold clasp with his initials engraved on it.

"It's cooler out here," he said. "Chicago gets so hot in the summer."

"Are you angry at Phil for showing me his gun?"

A girl came by and stopped and whispered into Roy's father's ear. Her high heels made her taller than his father. She walked around the corner onto Rush Street.

"What did she say, Dad?"

"Thank you."

"For what?"

"I helped her out with something the other day."

"What's her name?"

"Anita."

"She's tall."

"She's a dancer at The Casbah."

"Dad?"

"Yes, son?"

"Are you still angry at Mom?"

"No, Roy. I'm not angry at your mother."

"What about Phil?"

Hour of the Wolf

When he was eleven years old, Roy began waking up between four and four-thirty in the morning, four hours before he had to leave for school. His mother, her husband and Roy's sister were asleep and so long as he kept to the back of the house he did not disturb them. No matter what the weather was, even if it was freezing or raining, Roy liked to go out onto the back porch to feel the fresh air and watch the sky. He could imagine that he lived alone, or at the least that this third stepfather did not exist. Roy had come to understand that his mother gave very little thought to how her bringing these men into his life might affect him. He knew now that it was up to him to control his own existence, to no longer be subject to her poor judgment and desperation.

It was on a morning in mid-December when Roy was standing on the porch wearing a parka over his pajamas looking up at a crescent moon with snow beginning to flurry that he heard a scream. It came from the alley behind his house. Roy could not identify the sound as having come from a woman or a man. He waited on the porch for a second cry but none came. Roy went inside to his room and exchanged his slippers for shoes and went back out. He pulled the hood of his parka over his head and walked carefully down the porch steps, not wanting to slip on the new snow, and continued through the yard along the passageway that led to the alley. Flakes were falling faster, translucent parachutists infiltrating the darkness.

Roy looked both ways in the alley but did not see a person. He stood there waiting to hear or see someone or something move. He was about to go back to the house when he saw a shadow creep across the garage door directly opposite his own. Instinctively, he retreated a few steps toward the passageway. The shadow was low and long, as if cast by a four-footed animal, a large dog or a wolf, although he knew there were no wolves in Chicago. What if one, or even a panther, had escaped from a zoo? But could an animal have emitted such a human-like scream? Roy knew that he should go back inside the house but his curiosity outweighed his fear, so he waited, ready to run should a dangerous creature, man or beast, reveal itself.

A car appeared at the entrance to the alley, its headlights burning into the swirling snow. Roy watched the car advance slowly, listening to its tires crunch over the quickly thickening ground cover. As the vehicle came closer, he stepped back further into the passageway, wanting not to be seen by the driver. The car crept past his hiding place and slid to a stop twenty feet away. Roy could not see the car clearly enough to identify the make. Nobody got out. The car sat idling, its windshield wipers whining and thunking.

Roy imagined the driver or perhaps a passenger was looking for the person or animal responsible for the scream. If so, why didn't someone get out of the car and call out or look around? What if the object of their search were injured or frightened, unable to make its distress and location known? After a full minute, the car moved forward, heading toward the far end of the alley. When Roy could no longer see its tail lights, he walked back through the passageway to his house.

His mother's husband was standing on the porch holding a flashlight.

"The back door was open," he said. "What are you doing out there?"

Roy remained at the foot of the porch steps, looking at this man he never wanted to see again. He could feel the snow leaking around the edges of his parka hood, water dripping onto his neck.

"I heard a scream," Roy said.

"You probably had a nightmare. Lock the door after you come in."

The flashlight clicked off and Roy's mother's husband went inside. The snow let up a little but there still was no light in the sky. Roy sat down on the bottom step. It was almost Christmas and he knew that what he wanted was what he didn't want.

Lost Monkey

Secret Jones cleaned windows in rich people's houses during the day and returned to the houses when he knew the occupants would be away and burglarized them. Secret worked alone and made a steady living. He lived modestly in a small apartment on North Avenue but took a two or three week holiday once a year, usually a luxury cruise to either Caribbean or Mediterranean ports-of-call during the fierce Chicago winters.

Nights he wasn't working, Secret Jones often stopped into Roy's father's liquor store to mingle with other characters who used the store as an unofficial meeting place. Secret was one of the few Negroes among mostly Italian, Irish, Jewish and Eastern European men who hung out at the sandwich counter, seated on stools nursing lukewarm cups of coffee, nibbling stale doughnuts and smoking cigarettes and cigars, or just stood around talking or pretending to be waiting for someone. The liquor store was in the center of the nightclub district and stayed open 24 hours. Roy's father was usually there or in the vicinity from noon until four or five in the morning. Nights when he didn't have school the next day, his father let Roy hang around "to figure out for yourself what bad habits not to pick up."

Secret Jones was one of the men Roy enjoyed listening to.

"You know how I got my name?" Secret said. "My daddy was sixteen and my mama was fifteen when I was born and they wanted to keep me a secret, so that's what my grandmama called me, Mamie June Jones, my mama's mama. She was the one raised me. This was in Mississippi. My daddy bugged out before I could know him and my mama got on the stem and died of alcohol poisoning when I was four years old. How old are you now, Roy?"

"Nine."

"I been on my own since I turned thirteen, after Mamie June passed. I come up to Chi on the midnight special with nothin' but what I was wearin', no laces in my shoes, no belt for my trousers. Thirteen years old stood in Union Station with nothin' in my pockets, that's for real. You're lucky you got a daddy looks out for you. That's what life is about, Roy, or should be, people lookin' out for each other, whether they be blood related or not. Here it is 1956, ninety-one years since President Abraham Lincoln freed my people and there's still places in this country I get shot or strung up I go there. Ain't that a bitch! Same all over, some folks bein' left out or rubbed out and nobody do anything about it."

"Quit cryin', Secret," said Hersch Fishbein. "It ain't only your people catch the short end. How about my six million Hitler done in?"

Hersch, Secret and Roy were sitting at the counter. Hersch worked days at Arlington Park racetrack as a pari-mutuel clerk and sometimes at night at Maywood when the trotters were running.

"You hear about Angelo's monkey?" Hersch asked.

"The organ grinder?" said Secret.

"Angelo's my friend," said Roy. "Dopo sits here at the counter with me and dunks doughnuts in Angelo's coffee."

"Somebody stole him."

"Why would anyone steal Dopo?" Roy asked.

"Sell him," said Secret Jones. "Smart monkey like him. People pay to see him do tricks."

Hersch nodded and said, "A carnival, maybe."

"How'd you hear?" Secret asked.

"Saw Angelo on Diversey, grindin' his box. Had a tin cup on the sidewalk. 'Where's Dopo?' I asked. 'Disappear,' said Angelo. 'I can no passa da cup anna play at same time.'"

"We should look for him," said Roy.

"Hard findin' a little monkey in a city as big as Chicago," Secret said.

Roy went outside where his father was standing on the sidewalk in front of the store talking to Phil Priest, an ex-cop.

"Dad, Hersch says someone stole Dopo, Angelo's monkey."

Phil Priest laughed and said, "A wino probably ate it."

Roy punched Phil on his right arm.

"Take it easy, son," said his father.

"You've got to do something, Dad. Angelo can't make a living without Dopo collecting coins and tipping his hat."

"I'll see what I can do, Roy."

Roy remembered the time he was sitting at the counter doing homework and Angelo and Dopo came in and Dopo picked up a pencil and began imitating Roy, making marks on a piece of paper.

"Dopo helping you," Angelo said.

Roy looked up and down the street. It was ten o'clock at night, not a good time to start hunting for Dopo. Roy would begin the next day asking around the neighborhood if anybody had seen Angelo's monkey, although Angelo had probably already done that.

Phil Priest took off and Roy's father said, "If Dopo doesn't turn up, the organ grinder'll get another monkey."

"I don't like Phil Priest, Dad. Mom says he was a crooked cop, that's why he was kicked off the force. I didn't like what he said about Dopo. It'll take a long time for Angelo to train a new monkey."

Roy walked back inside. Hersch and Secret were arguing about the best way to fix a horse race. Hersch said you had to have the jockeys in your pocket and Secret said it was better to juice the nags.

"None of the bums who hang around your dad's store are on the level," Roy's mother had told him. "Some are worse than others."

"Why does Dad let them stay there?"

"Those men are just part of the system, Roy. Being on the game is all they know, they grew up with it."

"I'm growing up with it, too."

"You won't be like them," said his mother.

Roy's father was still out on the sidewalk, talking to a man Roy had never seen before. The man walked away and Roy went out again.

"Dad?"

"What is it, son?"

"Mom says when I grow up I won't be like the men around here."

Roy's father looked at him and said, "How does she know?"

When Benny Lost His Meaning

Roy was sitting at the counter in the Lake Shore Liquor Store on a Saturday morning in November sipping a vanilla Coke listening to Lucio Stella and Baby Doll Hirsch talk.

"Remember Mean Well Benny?" asked Lucio.

"Worked for Jewish Joe. Spidery little guy. Got rung up for killin' a crooked cop."

"McGuire, in Bridgeport. The Paddy guarded the mayor's house."

"What about him?"

"He's out. Mastro seen him at Murphy's day before yesterday, eatin' a steak without his teeth in."

"What happened to his teeth?"

"Guess he had 'em yanked in prison. Mastro said Benny put his choppers in a glass of water while he gummed the steak."

"He got plans?"

"Probably."

"We should find out."

"How'd he get that tag, anyway?"

"It was Jocko named him Mean Well because too often he did things he wasn't told to do that didn't turn out well."

"Such as?"

"Time he offered Lou Napoli's girl, Ornella, a lift to Lou's crib, only Lou wasn't expectin' her and happened he was entertaining a waitress from Rickett's at the moment. Napoli worked for Jocko and when Lou told him how it had come about Ornella stabbed him and he almost lost a kidney, Jocko said, 'You know, Benny, he means well.' After that, he was Mean Well Benny to everyone in Chicago, even the cops.

"Shootin' McGuire was a mistake, too. He thought it was

McGuire had leaned on Jewish Joe, so he threatened him one evening in Noches de San Juan, a PR bar on North Damen. McGuire took offense, busted Benny in the mouth, so Benny parked a pair in the cop's chest. This was after McGuire got thrown off the force."

"Maybe why he got false teeth in the joint."

Roy liked going with his father to his liquor store on Saturday mornings. All kinds of people came in and Roy liked looking at and listening to them, even and especially if they were a little or a lot crazy. A week later, a day before his ninth birthday, Roy heard Lucio Stella tell Baby Doll Hirsch that Mean Well Benny's corpse was found with his throat cut stuffed into a garbage can in an alley in Woodlawn.

"What could he been doin' in that neighborhood?"

"Probably lookin' to do some woolhead a favor he didn't need."

After Lucio Stella and Baby Doll Hirsch left, Roy asked his father if he had known Mean Well Benny.

"He used to come around. Why do you ask?"

"I just heard Mr. Stella tell Mr. Hirsch that Mean Well Benny's body was found in a trash can."

"Some men's lives don't amount to much, son. They get on the wrong road and don't ever get back on the straight and narrow."

The following Saturday morning Roy's father took Lucio Stella and Baby Doll Hirsch aside and said something to them Roy couldn't hear, then they left without finishing their cups of coffee.

"Dad, did you tell Mr. Stella and Mr. Hirsch to leave because of me?"

"I did."

"Are they on the straight and narrow?"

"They don't know what it means."

Sick

A girl's dead body was found on Oak Street beach by a man walking a dog at five o'clock in the morning of March 5th. The body was clothed in only a black raincoat; there was no identification in the pockets. The girl was judged to be in her late teens or very early twenties, the most notable identifying mark being a six-inch scar on the inside of her left calf. She had light brown hair and brown eyes, height five feet four inches, weight one hundred and five. When discovered, the body was coated with a thin layer of ice. Forensics determined that the girl had been dead since approximately seven o'clock the previous evening. Her stomach and abdominal tract contained only particles of food; she had not eaten for at least two days.

Twelve days later, at four p.m. on March 17th, St. Patrick's Day, perhaps the most festive day of the year in Chicago's substantial Irish community in 1958, a forty-eight year old woman named Mary Sullivan, a native of Belfast, Northern Ireland, who had been a resident of Chicago for twenty-two years, filed a missing persons report at the Division Street precinct, claiming that her daughter, Margaret, had not been in contact with her since March 2nd. Margaret, who fit the description of the corpse found on Oak Street beach on the 5th, including the scar on her leg, worked as a waitress at Don the Beachcomber's restaurant—a strange, or perhaps not so strange, coincidence—and had been living with another girl, Lucille Susto, twenty years old, a recent arrival in the city from West Virginia, who also worked as a waitress in a coffee shop in The Loop. When questioned by police, Lucille Susto told them that she had not seen her roommate since the morning of the 4th, before going to work. Her recollection was that Margaret was not scheduled to work at Don the Beachcomber's that night, a fact corroborated by the manager of the restaurant. Mary Sullivan's husband, Desmond, Margaret's father, had been living in Ireland for the past three years and was not presently in contact with either his wife or daughter; Mary did not have a current address for him. At six-thirty on the evening of the 17th, Mary Sullivan identified the body lying in the morgue as that of her daughter, Margaret.

The man who discovered the body was Paddy McLaughlin, a doorman at the nearby Drake Hotel, who had been walking a standard poodle belonging to a resident of the hotel. McLaughlin, whose brother, James, was a sergeant in the Chicago police department, reported his find to the police immediately upon returning to the Drake Hotel with the dog.

"Look, Roy," his mother said to him while they were having breakfast on the morning of March 6th, "Paddy McLaughlin's picture's in the *Trib*."

The McLaughlins were Roy and his mother's next door neighbors; their sons, Johnny, Billy and Jimmy, were Roy's best friends. Roy, who was eleven years old, looked at the photograph of Mr. McLaughlin dressed in his epauleted doorman's uniform, the brim of his military-style hat fixed precisely in the center of his forehead, the tip of his aquiline nose almost touching his long, thin upper lip.

"He found a dead body,"

"I read the article, Roy. He must have had quite a shock."

When Roy saw Johnny that afternoon he asked him what his father had told the family.

"He said there was nothing to tell other than seeing the girl lying on the sand wrapped in a black raincoat and then calling the cops. My Uncle James says if the body's identified my dad'll be called to appear at an inquest, if there is one. I'm thinkin' about goin' down to the beach to search for clues. Want to come with me?"

Johnny was six months older than Roy. He was interested in science and read all about fingerprinting, blood types and various procedures involving detection.

"The police are doing that," said Roy. "What makes you think we can find something they won't?"

"Happens all the time. In the Hardy Boys books they're always solving crimes the cops can't. The other night on *Ned Nye, Private Eye* a kid discovered a foreign coin in a murderer's apartment that could have belonged only to the victim, brought it to Ned, and that cracked the case."

A light snow was falling at eight-thirty the next morning when Jimmy and Roy arrived at Oak Street beach.

"It's freezing out here," Roy said. "The snow's covering up whatever evidence might still be around."

Waves collapsing on the sand sounded like cats knocking over garbage cans in an alley. Lake Michigan was wrinkled gray and black.

"You can't see anything," said Roy. "Not more than a few hundred yards, anyway. No ships in the distance, no planes in the sky. We should go to the Drake and get hot chocolate in the coffee shop."

"My dad doesn't come on duty today until ten," said Johnny. "We'll go over then. The manager's a pal of his so we won't have to pay. Come on, let's see if we can find something."

After forty-five minutes of searching all Roy had found was a broken pencil and a used rubber. After he unearthed the rubber he asked Johnny if he knew if the girl had been raped.

"If she was, it probably didn't happen on the beach in bad weather. She didn't have any clothes on under the coat, so if the killer molested her he did it somewhere else before he dumped the body here."

Johnny found a toothbrush, cigarette butts, one child's size pink mitten and a broken neck chain. He held up the chain for Roy to see and said, "This might be something."

A cop came along and said to them, "What are you boys up to? This is a crime scene."

"It isn't marked off, officer," said Johnny.

"The snow's coverin' up the markers. You lads had best be moving along."

"Do you know Sergeant James McLaughlin?" Johnny asked. "He's my uncle. I'm Johnny McLaughlin."

"Well, when I get home tonight I'll be sure to tell my wife, Kathleen, guess who I encountered on Oak Street beach this mornin' in the sleet and snow but Sergeant James McLaughlin's nephew, Johnny. Go on now, both of you."

"And my father's Paddy McLaughlin, the head doorman at the Drake Hotel. He found the body."

"Next you'll be tellin' me your mother's Rose of Sharon."

In the Drake coffee shop the boys sat at the counter and ordered hot chocolates.

"I think the killer's a rich guy who lives in a fancy apartment around here, on Lake Shore or Marine Drive," said Johnny. "Probably somebody she knew who worked or she met at Don the Beachcomber's. He raped the girl, strangled her—or maybe, if he was a real pervert, strangled her before raping her—then carried the body down in the dead of night."

Johnny and Roy were finishing their hot chocolates when Paddy McLaughlin came into the coffee shop and sat down on the stool next to his son's.

"Top o' the mornin', fellas," he said. "Bobby, the night man, told me you were visiting. May I inquire as to your purpose?"

"We were searching for clues to the murder," said Johnny.

"A cop ran us off the beach," said Roy.

Mr. McLaughlin put two quarters on the counter and stood up.

"I'll be goin' on the job now," he said. "See that you get home safely, detectives. Don't hitchhike, take the bus."

The girl's killer turned out to be a regular customer at Don the Beachcomber's, who, as Johnny figured, lived a few blocks from the beach.

"Johnny got it right," Roy told Jimmy Boyle. "He pegged where the creep met her and where he lived. "Johnny knew it the morning we went to Oak Street to see if we could find a lead."

"Did you find something?"

"No, Johnny just put it together. Maybe he got a feeling from the spot his dad discovered the body."

"I heard on the radio about people who have a special talent to tune in to the sick mind of a killer," said Jimmy, "to identify with him. It's called havin' a sick sense."

Margaret Sullivan's rapist-murderer was a 42 year old bachelor named Leonard Danzig, an architect, who told the judge at a pre-trial hearing that he had been searching for several years for a direct descendant of the sister of Jesus Christ, whom he believed, like her brother, claimed to have been fathered by the Holy Ghost. Danzig said he felt it was his duty to abort what he described as an immoral lineage in order to cease the false prophesies that had wrought chaos since the blasphemy of immaculate conception. Danzig's rationale for the rape was to anneal "the unspeakable insult."

Leonard Danzig did not stand trial but was instead committed for the remainder of his natural life to the Hermione Curzon Institution for the Hopelessly Irreparable in Moab, Illinois.

"Jimmy Boyle's father says Danzig should have gotten the electric chair," Roy told his mother. "What do you think?"

"You can't execute all of the sick people in the world, Roy. There are too many. Once you start doing that it would never stop."

"Don't you think the world would be better off if Leonard Danzig wasn't in it?"

Roy's mother, who had already been divorced twice and had a third marriage annulled, said, "Him and a few other men I can name."

The Best Part of the Story

Roy and four other boys, all of them twelve or thirteen years old, were standing in front of Papa Enzo's Pizza Parlor talking and smoking cigarettes, just hanging out even though the temperature outside was well below freezing. A foot of snow had fallen the day before, most of it had hardened and iced over, but the boys, wearing parkas or peacoats, did not mind the cold, they were used to the Chicago winters; only when a fearsome wind was tearing in from the lake did they not gather on the street, especially on weekend nights such as this one. They could hear Buddy Holly's new record, "Maybe Baby," coming from the jukebox inside Enzo's.

It was almost ten o'clock when Jimmy Boyle noticed Logo Leberko lurking next to the doorway of Papa Enzo's restaurant.

"Hey, guys, look—there's that creep Leberko standin' by the entrance. I thought he was still locked up at St. Charles."

"Nah," said Tommy Cunningham, "Bobby Dorp told me yesterday they couldn't keep him in the reformatory after he turned eighteen. They either had to release him or transfer him to Joliet."

"He and another guy robbed Koszinski's Bakery, didn't they?" Roy asked.

"Tried to," said Boyle. "It was so stupid. Leberko's mother works there and when he and Dion Bandino stuck up the joint Logo's old lady was behind the counter. Accordin' to the article about it in the *Trib*, Leberko said, 'Ma, I thought you weren't workin' today,' and she said she was fillin' in for someone who was out sick, so she identified him for the cops."

"That's crazy," said Roy. "They really went through with the robbery even though his mother was there?"

"That's the best part of the story," said Richie Gates. "They had guns, my brother told me. He used to deliver cakes for Koszinski's, so he heard all about it. Both Leberko and Bandino had 'em in their hands when they went in."

"Did Bandino get sent to St. Charles, too?" asked Roy.

"Yeah," said Cunningham, "but he got out sooner 'cause he was only fifteen."

"Leberko's a moron," Jimmy said. "Remember how he was always shakin' down younger kids for their milk money at Clinton? He'd take their change then stomp on the kids' lunchboxes and slap 'em around even though they'd already come across."

"He got me once," said Richie. "After that I took off if I saw him in the schoolyard. He didn't get past fourth grade, then they had to let him out when he turned sixteen."

"His old man was murdered in prison," said Tommy Cunningham. "Other inmates set him on fire in his cell."

"No shit," Jimmy Boyle said.

"Yeah. My father thinks he was snitchin' for the guards."

The door of Papa Enzo's opened and two people came out, one of whom was Dion Bandino. Leberko came up quickly behind him and with an eight inch switchblade cut Bandino's throat clear across. Blood exploded out of Bandino's neck like flames being tossed out of a bucket, turning the snow at his feet into a sea of vermilion. For what seemed to Roy a long time, though it was only a few seconds, nobody moved except Leberko, who disappeared. Dion Bandino was dead and didn't know it as his body accordioned down and knelt with his chin resting on his chest.

Roy and Jimmy Boyle took off in one direction and Richie Gates and Tommy Cunningham in another without looking back.

After they'd run as fast as they could for a few blocks, Jimmy and Roy stopped to catch their breath, and Jimmy said, "I thought Bandino would fall forward. He just dropped and didn't topple over."

"I never saw anybody get their throat slit before."

"We can't say nothin' about it, Roy. Don't tell nobody we were there. We don't want the cops to make us be witnesses against

Leberko. If somehow he beat the rap he'd come after us like he done Bandino."

"Why do you think he did it?"

"Bandino must've caved, maybe said the stick-up was Logo's idea, that he'd been forced into it by an older guy."

Roy was still gasping for air; even in the darkness he could see his breath.

"I'm goin' home," he said.

"Me, too," said Jimmy. "Remember, don't tell anyone we were there."

When he got home, Roy's mother was sitting alone at the kitchen table. Her eyes were red and her face was swollen.

"Hi, Ma, why're you cryin'? Are you all right?"

"Not really, no, Roy, but it's nothing you have to worry about. Did you have a good time with the boys?"

"It's too cold to be outside."

"I'm going to make a pot of tea. Do you want some?"

"No, thanks. I'm pretty tired. I'm going to lie down in my room. Are you sure you're okay?"

"Yes, Roy. It's just that Dan and I have decided to not see each other any more. It's for the best, I know, we're really not a good match, but I feel like my dog just died."

"We've never had a dog."

"Oh, you must know what I mean. It's not the end of the world, but it's a kind of death, nevertheless. There are all kinds of deaths. Some stay with you more than others, you'll see."

Four days later the police found Logo Leberko hiding in the boiler room of an apartment building a few blocks away from Papa Enzo's Pizza Parlor; scraps of food he'd scavenged from garbage cans were scattered on the floor and he was covered with rat bites. Roy and his friends were not questioned about the incident; other witnesses, including Dion Bandino's companion that night, Arvid Gustafsson, whose mother also worked at Koszinski's

Bakery and was the person Leberko's mother was substituting for the day of the robbery, fingered Logo as the killer.

On their way to school one day the next week Richie Gates told Roy that his brother was delivering cakes again for Koszinski's.

"Is Leberko's mother still working there?"

"Yeah. Floyd heard her tellin' a customer that Logo'll get the chair unless he gets whacked in stir first, like his father. She says her son is already dead to her and it's like he never even existed. Think she means it or she's just sayin' that to make herself not feel bad?"

"Both, maybe," said Roy.

"I'm sure if somethin' happened to me," Richie said, "my mother wouldn't try to convince herself I'd never been alive. What about yours?"

Tell Him I'm Dangerous

Roy came home from work at the Red Hot Ranch around ten-thirty and found his mother sitting alone on the couch in the livingroom watching TV. He was fifteen years old and his mother was thirty-eight. She had recently been divorced from her third husband, by whom she had a child, Roy's sister, Sally, who was almost four.

"Hi, Ma, Sally asleep?"

"Yes, Roy, just now. I let her stay up late. I was teaching her how to play gin rummy. She caught on fast."

"That doesn't surprise me, Sally's smart."

"I was smart once, too," said his mother. "How was work?"

"All right. Busy, like every Saturday. I thought you were going out tonight with Kay and Harvey."

"They wanted me to meet a friend of theirs, a guy who's in town from Minneapolis, to show him Chicago. A business associate of Harvey's. Made a lot of money in jukeboxes, Kay told me. But I'm not up to it. Besides, Madeleine couldn't babysit tonight, she's got a date."

"She's a cute girl," said Roy, "lots of boys like her. She's sixteen. I think her babysitting days are over."

"Madeleine's a nice kid, I hope she makes good choices. I'm off men for now."

"I'm a man."

"You're my son, my beautiful boy. Come sit and watch a movie with me. It's just about to come on. I saw it when it came out, in 1948, just before you were born. Roxanne Hudnut and Diane Root as sisters."

"One good, one bad?"

"Both kind of bad, if I remember right. One more than the other."

"Okay, Ma, I'll wash up a little first."

The movie's title was *Tell Him I'm Dangerous*. Roxanne Hudnut and Dianne Root were still in their twenties when it was made, as had been Roy's mother when she'd seen it in a theater. She always identified with Roxanne Hudnut, whom she resembled. Both of them were brunettes with slightly slanted chestnut eyes that gave their faces an almost oriental look. When they looked up at you slowly or sideways it was easy to believe they were keeping dark secrets. *Tell Him I'm Dangerous* was in black and white, as were most of Roxanne Hudnut and Diane Root's movies, many of which were mysteries of some kind involving crimes of passion. Roy sat down on the couch half way through the opening credits. His mother had a blanket over her legs.

"Tell me if you get chilly, Roy," she said. You can share the blanket."

The time of the movie was present day late 1940s. A young woman named Ann Rivers, played by Roxanne Hudnut, arrives in a small midwestern town, asks for and gets a job in a flower shop run by an older woman, Mrs. Morgan. Ann tells her that she's recently dropped out of business college, secretarial school, in the capital city. She needs a break from that hectic life. Ann says she has no immediate family, that both of her parents are dead and she has no siblings. Mrs. Morgan is a kind lady and helps her find a room to rent in a local boarding house with a good reputation run by Mr. and Mrs. Drummond, a middleaged couple.

At the Drummond house Ann meets another resident, Lee Lockwood, a contractor and structural engineer, who is in town working on the repair of a bridge. He's a few years older than Ann, calm with a pleasant manner.

"He looks a little like Dick Brothers, only shorter. Remember him, Roy? That car dealer I had a few dates with?"

A few days after their first meeting, Lee Lockwood invites Ann out to dinner. They begin spending time together but she avoids giving him any detailed information about her background other than what she's told Mrs. Morgan. Three weeks later another young woman arrives in the town, also a stranger, and tells people that she's searching for her younger sister, Ann Rivers. Her name is Sarah Rivers. Sarah is directed to Mrs. Morgan's flower shop, where she introduces herself to Mrs. Morgan. Ann enters and does not seem surprised to find her sister there. Mrs. Morgan is surprised because Ann has told her she had no family. Sarah explains that she and Ann had a falling out and Ann left home, that's all, but Mrs. Morgan remains suspicious, as if there is something left unexplained.

Sarah also rents a room at the Drummond house, where she encounters Lee Lockwood, to whom she introduces herself as Ann's slightly older sister. The sisters argue in Sarah's room. Ann had accused Sarah's fiancé, Bob Dean, of attempting to rape her. He was found guilty of sexual assault and sentenced to six months in prison. Sarah has never believed this accusation. Bob Dean denied it, but Ann has stuck to her story.

Ann abruptly stops seeing Lee Lockwood without giving him a reason. He's puzzled but doesn't demand an explanation; after all, he doesn't really know her very well. He becomes friendly with Sarah, who finds a job as a ticket taker in the box office of the local movie theater, the only one in town. Sarah tells Ann that Lee has asked her about Ann's refusal to go out with him any more, to which Ann replies, "Tell him I'm dangerous," that he's better off not seeing her.

Lee is a straight shooter, well-liked in the community, doing a good job on the bridge. He and Sarah begin going around together, then become intimate. One night he comes back to his room and finds Ann there, she's been waiting for him. Ann tells Lee that the only reason Sarah is pretending to be interested in him is out of jealousy, that Sarah wants to cause her trouble because of what happened with Bob Dean. She tells Lee about Bob Dean trying to rape her, that Sarah claimed Ann was lying. This is why Ann left home, to escape the controversy and the gossip. "I stopped going out with you because I knew Sarah would try to poison our relationship," Ann says. She then seduces Lee.

"Do you think I look like her, Roy?" asked his mother. "People used to compare me to Roxanne Hudnut all the time."

"Your hair is the same color," Roy said. "Her eyes always seem a little out of focus. When she's supposed to be looking at someone her eyes are staring in a different direction."

Lee Lockwood is mixed up, vulnerable to both sisters. A few days after Ann seduces Lee, Sarah is found dead, hanging in the early morning from the bridge Lee is repairing. People initially assume it was suicide, but then Ann accuses Lee of murdering Sarah because she was pregnant with Lee's child. Lee admits he has been sleeping with Sarah but swears he didn't kill her. Lee is arrested. At his trial Ann tearfully testifies that Sarah told her she was afraid of Lee, of what he might do since Sarah has told him of the pregnancy. She tells the court that she went to see Lee and that he raped her. He denies both charges of murder and rape, and says that Ann formerly accused Sarah's fiancé of attempting to rape her. The prosecuting attorney declares that information to be irrelevant to this case and forces Lee to admit that he made love to Ann when she came to see him about Sarah. Lee is sentenced to life in prison for the murder of Sarah Rivers.

"I told you one sister was worse than the other," said Roy's mother.

"Sarah wasn't good, either. Maybe she was trying to set Lee up," said Roy, "that she was really pregnant by Bob Dean."

"That's good, Roy. I didn't think of that."

Soon after the trial, Ann is found dead hanging from the bridge. A crowd has gathered to watch the removal of her body by the police, which is shown through the point of view of a man among the spectators. After Ann's body is loaded into an ambulance and driven away, the man walks to a car and begins driving. As he drives, the movie flashes back through his mind, reliving the sequence of events that have led up to Ann's death: Ann seducing this man, whom we now realize is Bob Dean, then accusing him of attempted rape; his being confronted by Sarah after Ann tells her that Bob attacked her; Bob's contention that Ann acted out of jealousy over Sarah's relationship with him; and finally Bob is shown appearing in Ann's room at the boarding house and forcing her to write a letter confessing that she killed Sarah and hung her from the bridge, which is also shown in flashback as Ann writes.

The movie switches back to present time as Mrs. Morgan is opening a letter in her flower shop. It's the confession Bob Dean forced Ann to write. Also enclosed in the envelope is a second letter, written by Bob. Both letters are heard in voice over by Ann and Bob as Mrs. Morgan reads them. In Bob's letter he admits that Sarah was in fact carrying his child and that he killed Ann and hung her body from the bridge. The final two shots in present time are of Bob Dean driving away into the distance and Lee Lockwood being released from prison.

Then comes a surprise, a coda in which two little girls, each about four years old, are sitting next to each other on chairs playing with dolls. One girl says to the other, "I couldn't sleep last night." Girl number two says, "What did you do?" Girl number one answers, "I woke up my sister." "Why?" asks girl number two. "If I can't sleep, she shouldn't either," says girl number one. Girl number two asks, "Do you like your sister?" "I hate her!" answers girl number one, who then tears her doll apart.

Roy got up from the couch and turned off the sound on the television as the end credits rolled, then sat back down.

"Do you think that was a good idea to have a scene with those two little girls?" asked his mother.

"Sure, it's so you know that Ann was jealous of Sarah from the beginning. Ann was more evil than her sister."

"Do you really think Sarah was evil?"

"Yes, like I said, she stole Lee Lockwood away from Ann and wanted him to believe that he was the father of her unborn child."

"But Ann had stopped seeing him."

"I think she was still keeping him on the hook, to make him uncertain of how she felt, to control him."

"Roxanne Hudnut played bad good," said Roy's mother. "When they put her in more sympathetic roles she was never completely believable, especially musicals. She couldn't dance."

"Why did she stop making movies?" Roy asked.

"She got involved with the actor who played Bob Dean, Mark Brown. She married him. They had a couple of kids, then she had a nervous breakdown, maybe even tried to commit suicide, and was in and out of mental hospitals for years."

"Is she still alive?"

"I think so. Brown divorced her. It's a rotten business, the movies. A girl gets old, you're no use to them. The producers need fresh faces. Beauty sells. Once it fades a girl gets desperate."

"There are parts for older women."

His mother threw off the blanket and stood up.

"It's not the same, Roy. A pretty girl gets used to the way the world looks at her. Not just men, women, too. Roxanne Hudnut wasn't prepared for life after she changed, and she probably didn't have any help, the right kind of help. I guess the same thing happens to everyone. Good night, sweetheart, I'm going to bed. Thanks for staying up with me."

Roy stared at the TV with the sound off for a few minutes before he got up and turned it off. He knew his mother thought of herself as being a little like Roxanne Hudnut, even though she hadn't been a movie star, as if she didn't have much to look forward to, even the lives of her children. Roy was old enough now to know there was nothing he would ever be able to do about it.

The Shadow Going Forward

Roy's father never spoke to him about his illness. Roy was ten when he first noticed that anything was wrong. Since his parents were divorced and he lived with his mother Roy did not even know that his father had been in the hospital let alone had surgery. It was not until he was at his father's house a month or more after the surgery that Roy saw his father sitting on a round rubber pillow at his kitchen table.

"How come you're sitting on that pillow, Dad?" Roy asked.

"Well, son, when somebody gives me a pain in the ass this makes me feel better."

"Was it Moe Jaffe? You always say he's a pain in the ass. Like the time he went to the track before depositing the receipts in the bank and dropped everything on a longshot named Remy's Desire?"

"Not this time."

"Does it hurt?"

"Only when I think about my trusting Moe or some other vecchio rimbambito to do something."

"Jimmy Boyle couldn't sit at his desk in school for two days after Angelo's monkey Dopo bit him on the ass."

"Why did Dopo bite him?"

"He saw Jimmy snatch a doughnut from Angelo's stand and start eating it without paying for it first."

His father gave a little laugh but Roy could see him grimace whenever he moved, so he didn't ask him about it again.

A few months later Roy's father began spending more and more of his time at home in bed and didn't want to have any visitors, even Roy.

"He needs to rest, Roy," his father's second wife, Ellie, told him. "You can see him when he feels better. I'll let you know when it's a good time."

Roy liked Ellie and trusted her, so he waited, but before he was allowed to go over to his father's house again Roy's mother told him he was dead.

"Your dad fought hard," his mother said, "you know how tough he was, and the doctors did everything they could for him."

Roy's father was only forty-eight when he died. Too young to die, Roy heard a dozen or more people say at the wake. Moe Jaffe was there, and he draped his long right arm around Roy's shoulders. Roy looked up at Moe's nose, which also was very long and dotted with pockmarks; the tip of it hung over his upper lip. Everything about Moe was long, even the lobes of his ears reached to his shirt collar.

"God must've needed him," Moe said to Roy. "He must need your father to help straighten somethin' out, somethin' he can't fix all by Himself. Trust me, Roy, Rudy'll be the man for the job. You can be sure of that."

"Do you know what a vecchio rimbambito is?" Roy asked him.

The deep wrinkles in Moe Jaffe's forehead tangled together like vines in the Amazon jungle and his eyes crossed and uncrossed before he said, "No, Roy, I don't. What is it?"

"My dad's not one, so maybe you're right."

Moe removed his arm from Roy's shoulders and Roy walked away, past his mother and Ellie, who were talking to one another, past a bunch of people he didn't know who were eating pastries and drinking wine and whiskey, and out of what had been his father's house. It was hot outside, so Roy took off his sportcoat, dropped it on the ground next to the front door and walked down the street.

Some older boys were playing baseball in the park at the end of the block. Roy sat down on the grass next to the field and watched them. God didn't need his father, he thought. The kid playing shortstop kept booting ground balls. He didn't have soft hands. One thing Roy knew for sure was that if you want to play shortstop you have to have soft hands.

Years later, when Roy was in Rome, he asked an older Italian man, a writer, what "vecchio rimbambito" meant. The man raised an eyebrow, laughed briefly, and said, "That's a very old world expression, Roy. It means old fool or dotard, someone who behaves in a childish manner, perhaps due to senility. Where did you hear it?"

"When I was a boy my father used those words to describe someone who worked for him, a person who sometimes acted foolishly."

"You grew up in Chicago, didn't you?"

"Yes, I was born there, but my father didn't go to live in America until he was ten years old."

"It's the kind of description you could still hear in Napoli or Reggio Calabria, more-likely in Sicily. Yes, it's Siciliano, a term an elderly mafioso might use. What was your father's family's business in Chicago?"

Feeling the Heat

Standing outside in the oppressive heat and humidity of Miami at eleven o'clock in the morning was not what Roy's mother expected. She and Roy, who was five years old, were waiting in a long line to enter a theater in order to attend a free advance screening of the new Hopalong Cassidy movie and have an opportunity to obtain the autograph of William Boyd, the actor who had portrayed "Hoppy", as the cowboy hero was familiarly known, in movies and in a television series for more than twenty years. William Boyd had been a leading man in silent films and early talkies before taking on the black-clad character of an Old West crime fighter. Boyd had been a matinee idol in his youth, was renowned as a ladies man, and now, in his fifties, he sported a full head of wavy, snow-white hair that crowned a still-handsome face.

"I don't know how much longer I can take this," Roy's mother said to him. "There's no shade and no place to sit down. I know how much you like Hoppy, Roy, but maybe we just ought to wait and see the movie when it opens."

This was in 1952, when westerns were very popular. Most of the kids waiting in the hot sun were dressed like Hopalong Cassidy, wearing stovepipe-high black cowboy hats, black shirts and pants, with a white bandanna tied around their neck and double holster gunbelts housing a pair of white-handled cap pistols.

"But Mom, Hoppy's here!" Roy said. "I want him to sign his name on my hatband."

Before Roy's mother could complain again, many of the kids began shouting and pointing.

"Look!" cried Roy. "There he is! It's Hoppy!"

William Boyd, dressed in full Hopalong Cassidy regalia, was walking slowly along the line, shaking hands with the kids, nodding politely and tipping his hat to their parents. When he got to Roy and his mother, the actor stopped and looked her over carefully. Kitty was in her mid-twenties and still as attractive as she was only a few years before when she had been chosen the University of Texas beauty queen.

"Is this your son?" William Boyd asked her.

"Yes, his name is Roy. He's a great admirer of yours."

"Of Hopalong Cassidy's, you mean," said Boyd. "Howdy, Roy. And, if I may ask, what is your name Roy's mother?"

"Kitty."

William Boyd smiled and took off his hat. Even though there was no breeze, it seemed as if his long white hair were blowing in one. His teeth were sparkling white and even.

"It's extremely hot standing out here, Mr. Boyd. I don't think Roy can take the sun much longer. I know I can't."

"Come with me, Kitty, and Roy. I should be getting back inside anyway."

Roy and his mother stepped out of line and accompanied Hopalong Cassidy to the theater entrance.

Once they were inside, Roy's mother said, "Oh, thank God, it's air-conditioned."

The night before, Kitty had told her friend Kay on the phone that she had decided to leave her husband, Roy's father, who was in Havana, Cuba, doing business with the Morabito brothers, both of whose wives Kitty disliked. She would send her husband a telegram this afternoon, then take the phone off the hook. It would be nice to live someplace that was cooler, Kitty thought, like San Francisco. She and Roy's father had gone there on their honeymoon. Nights were windy, she could wear her fur coat and not have to pin up her hair every day to keep the back of her neck from sweating.

"I'd like to send Roy a few souvenirs, Kitty," said William Boyd. "Where can I reach you?"

A young woman wearing a red-satin cowgirl blouse with a yellow bandanna tied around her neck came over and stood next to him. She was smiling brightly and holding a clipboard and a pen.

"Penny here will take down your contact information," Boyd said. "I have to go backstage now to get ready for the show. It's been swell meeting you, Roy."

The actor reached down and shook Roy's right hand.

"And a pleasure to have met you, Kitty."

"Thank you for rescuing us, Mr. Boyd," she said.

"Bill, you can call me Bill. I'll be in touch."

"Hoppy, could you sign my hat?" Roy asked.

"Please," said Kitty.

"Please," said Roy.

William Boyd replaced his tall black hat on his head. Penny handed him her pen, he signed Roy's hatband, gave the pen back to Penny, tipped his hat to Kitty and walked away.

Roy's mother gave Penny the telephone number of the Delmonico Hotel, where they were temporarily living, she explained, and Penny thanked her, then hurried after the actor.

"Do you think he'll really send me something, Mom?"

"He said he would, Roy. Yes, I believe we'll be hearing from Mr. Boyd."

"He said to call him Bill, remember?"

The other kids and their parents began filing into the theater.

"Come on, Mom, we've got to get seats."

"Oh, Roy, I don't think I'm up to it. The sun really took a lot out of me. We'll see the movie another time. Soon, I promise."

Kitty took Roy's hand and they fought their way through the crowd until they were back outside on the sidewalk.

"Don't be sad, darling," Kitty said, "you got to meet Hoppy personally and he signed your hat. He even knows your name."

"He knows yours, too."

"Uh huh. I could go for a cold milkshake, couldn't you?"

The Sharks

Roy was eight years old when he flew with his mother and her boyfriend Johnny Salvavidas from Miami to the Bahamas for a long weekend. There was a casino in the hotel on the island where they stayed and Johnny liked to gamble. During the day, Roy and his mother went to the beach or hung out at the hotel swimming pool while he played blackjack. At night, after dinner, Roy watched TV in their room and Johnny played roulette while Roy's mother watched him lose.

"The wheel is best challenged in the night time," he told Roy. "It's a game that requires witnesses."

"Why?" Roy asked.

"To play boldly, with daring, a man must be brave, and bravery demands an audience. Alone every man is a coward. The ability to conquer one's fears is enhanced by the arousal of blood in others."

"It takes skill, too," said Roy. "My Uncle Buck says to win consistently you have to do the math, that you can't succeed unless you know the odds. He says at roulette the odds are always against you, especially when the wheel has a double zero."

"Johnny knows what he's doing, Roy," said his mother.

The third day they were there the three of them had lunch together on a terrace of the hotel. Both Roy's mother and Johnny Salvavidas were sipping from big glasses with tropical fruits impaled on the rims. Roy was nibbling giant prawns that he dipped into a spicy red sauce. The pieces of chipped ice in the bowl under the prawns melted faster than he could eat them.

"Bob Donovan invited us to go with him and some other guests this afternoon to a beach on the other side of the island," Roy's mother said. "It's supposed to be very beautiful and uncrowded."

"I'm sure it will be," said Johnny.

Johnny Salvavidas was from the Dominican Republic, which was on an island Roy had never been to. His mother had been there once with Johnny. When she came back from that trip to get Roy, whom she had left with his grandmother Rose in Chicago, he overheard his mother telling Rose that in the capital city of Santo Domingo everyone is a thief.

"Johnny told me to never carry any money except for a few coins and not to wear my rings if I went out by myself. He always carried a pistol while we were there."

"Surely not everyone in Santo Domingo is a thief," Rose said. "People work in the sugar mills and the cane fields. Besides, Johnny carries a gun when he's in Chicago, too."

"How do you know that?"

"He told me. He probably thinks everyone in Chicago is a thief."

Roy and his mother accompanied Bob Donovan, who was from Cleveland but had been living in the Bahamas for a few years, and six other hotel guests to Emerald Beach. Bob Donovan drove them in a rusty, blue Chevy van and told them on the way that there was a good restaurant at the beach with a bar in case anyone got hungry or thirsty. The trip took forty minutes over a rough road. Roy's mother asked Bob Donovan what business he'd been in in Cleveland and he said, "Cement. You can't go wrong in cement."

Emerald Beach looked like both of the other beaches Roy and his mother had already been to but it was uncrowded. In fact, no other swimmers or even sun bathers were there. Roy and his mother went into the water right away. It was crystal clear, like all of the water around the island, and shallow for a long way out. A couple of other people went swimming, too; the rest of the group went to the bar with Bob Donovan and did not go into the water at all during the two or three hours they were there.

When they got back to the hotel, Roy and his mother took

showers and then lay down on their beds. Roy fell asleep but woke up when he heard Johnny and his mother talking in loud voices.

"How was I supposed to know it was dangerous?" she said. "You could have warned me."

"Donovan takes tourists there because he gets a kickback from the bar. Nick Turco told me Emerald Beach is shark-infested. That's why no locals go there."

"Who's Nick Turco?"

"A guy I know from Fort Lauderdale. I ran into him in the casino. He's in the construction business. He's down here on a gambling junket."

"You're supposed to take care of us, Johnny. You could have come and taken us back."

She sat down on Roy's bed and held him close to her. Her skin was soft and hot. She was slim with large breasts, long legs and flaming chestnut-colored hair. Roy was beginning to understand why men were attracted to her.

Johnny Salvavidas stood and patted his thick, black mustache with the fingers of his right hand as if it were the top of a dog's head, then he left the room. He said something in Spanish when he was outside in the hallway.

"We're lucky no sharks were at Emerald Beach today, aren't we, Roy?"

"I read in a book about sea creatures that a moray eel has an even stronger bite than a shark's," Roy said. "After it's sunk its teeth in, a moray never lets go. To kill it you have to cut off the head with a machete."

The early evening sun was streaming into the room. Roy's mother got up and drew the curtains.

"Johnny shouldn't be upset," said Roy. "He wasn't the one who could have been bitten by sharks."

Smart Guys

"The girl used to dance at La Paloma. Jasmine Ford. I don't know if that was her real name."

"It wasn't. Not her first name, anyway. Marlene, Marla, something like that. You thinkin' what?"

"Where's she's got to, that's all."

"You ready to do something dumb again, huh?"

"I'm not a smart guy like you, Freddie."

Harry Castor walked toward LaSalle. He had a room there, a basement. A real comedown, he thought, every time he woke up there or came back to it. No place to bring Jasmine Ford. Castor came from Kansas City, Kansas. He was a musician, a drummer. In Chicago he jammed with guys he met hanging around the clubs, sat in here and there when the opportunity arose. Harry was getting in until he got shot one night in a currency exchange where he'd gone to cash a check from one of his rare gigs. A teenager was killed trading gunfire with a security guard and Castor got caught in the crossfire, taking a slug from the punk in his left hand. The bullet passed through the palm and put a permanent crimp in his career as a percussionist.

After he recovered from the gunshot wound, Harry partnered with Freddie DiMartini selling phony home burglary insurance policies. Roy's friend Jimmy Boyle's uncle, Donal Liffey, had done time at Joliet with DiMartini; according to Jimmy, Liffey was the mastermind behind the insurance scam.

"Uncle Donal says this hustle is foolproof," Jimmy told Roy. "He has his own guys rob an insured house once in a while and he pays off. Those homeowners tell their friends about the Midnight Insurance Company and they sign up, too. It's just him and DiMartini and a new guy, Harry Castor, used to be a jazz drummer. I like Harry. He has a hole in the palm of his left hand he keeps a hundred dollar bill in."

Roy and Jimmy were in the same fifth grade class. They were walking to school together when Jimmy told Roy about his uncle's operation.

"What do you mean he keeps a C-note in a hole in his hand? How'd he get the hole there?"

"Some yom was tryna stick up a currency exchange and Harry walked in on it. The guard draws on the yom, they go high noon, and Harry takes one in the hand."

"Who shot him, the stick-up man or the security guard?"

"I don't know, and neither does Harry. I asked him and he said the slug went out the other side. Could've been from either gun."

A couple of months after Jimmy Boyle told Roy about the scam, the two boys were sitting in the kitchen in Jimmy's house after school eating liver sausage sandwiches when his Uncle Donal came in with Freddie DiMartini and Harry Castor. Donal Liffey, Jimmy's mother's brother, lived with them. He had supported his sister and her son since Jimmy's father was run down and killed walking home at one A.M. from Milt's Tap Room on Elston Avenue two years before. The driver kept going and there were no eyewitnesses. Donal, a bachelor, moved in a few days later and had become the most significant male figure in his nephew's life. Jimmy thought his Uncle Donal was the smartest man in Chicago.

"Hey there, me bucko," Donal said to Jimmy. "Who's your pal?"

Donal was a small but well-built man with thick black hair and squinty blue eyes. He'd been a pretty good amateur lightweight in his youth, and at forty-two he maintained his fighting weight. Donal idolized James Cagney, the way he'd been in *City for Conquest*, where he played a boxer who gets blinded by an opponent's unscrupulous corner men. "All the pros thought Cagney had been a boxer," Donal liked to tell people, "but he hadn't. He was a good dancer and knew how to move, he had the footwork. He spoke Irish and Yiddish, too. Did you know that?"

Freddie DiMartini was only slightly bigger than Donal but he leaned to his right both when he walked or stood still. He said it was because when he was a kid a horse pulling an ice wagon had kicked him in his back, but Donal knew Freddie had taken a beating in reform school that partially crippled him. A guy who'd been in reform school with Freddie told Donal that DiMartini had been stealing the other boys' comic books and they had ganged up on him.

Harry Castor was a large man with big shoulders and big hands, one of which had a hole in it.

"Harry," said Jimmy, "Roy wants to see the Benjamin."

"Harry walked over to where Roy was sitting and held out his left hand, palm open. There was a corner of a bill that had been folded over a few times with the number 100 showing.

"Your dad owns Lake Shore Liquors, doesn't he?" Donal asked Roy.

"Yes," Roy said.

"He's a stand up guy. His name's Rudy, right?"

Roy nodded.

"He did me a good turn once. You got good taste in friends, Jimmy."

Donal shook Roy's hand and then the three men went into a back room and closed the door.

"Does your mom work?" Roy asked Jimmy.

"At Woolworth's on Minnetonka. She's the head of the sewing counter. Uncle Donal tells her she should quit but she likes doin' it. She has friends there she says she'd miss if she didn't see 'em every day. Uncle Donal pays the bills but my mother says what if somethin' happens to him like happened to my father?"

Six weeks later something did happen to Jimmy's Uncle Donal and to Freddie DiMartini, too. They were shotgunned by a man whose house they were breaking into at three o'clock in the morning. Donal was killed and DiMartini was blinded.

"What about Harry?" Roy asked Jimmy Boyle.

"He split," Jimmy said. "He was probably there, maybe drivin' the car, but nobody saw him. My mother got a letter yesterday and the only thing in the envelope was a folded-up hundred dollar bill."

Apacheria

Roy and his friend Jimmy Boyle were walking to school on a rainy morning when a car passed them going too fast and went out of control, skidding on its two right side wheels before crashing into a telephone pole. The woman who had been driving was thrown from the car and was lying in the street. Roy and Jimmy ran over to see if she was all right. She was on her back with her eyes closed and her mouth open but she was not bleeding. The driver was young, in her late teens or early twenties, and her dress was up around her waist exposing her bare legs and underwear. A few cars passed by without stopping.

"We should call an ambulance," said Jimmy.

A man wearing denim overalls came out of an apartment building and looked at the girl.

"I heard noise," he said. "I'm janitor here."

"Call an ambulance," said Roy.

"I call cops, too."

The man went back into the building. The girl was not moving. She had fluffy, medium-length brown hair, high cheekbones, a short, straight nose and full red lips.

"She's really pretty," Roy said.

"You think we should pull down her dress?" asked Jimmy. "Cover her up?"

"Probably better not to touch her before the ambulance comes."

"Think she's dead?"

"She's breathing. See? Her chest is going up and down."

Rain was still falling lightly when two police cars arrived, followed a few seconds later by an ambulance. By this time a few passersby and residents of nearby houses were gathered on the sidewalk.

"Anybody see how this happened?" asked one of the cops.

"We did," said Jimmy Boyle. "Roy and I were walkin' to school and we seen the car skid and smash into the pole. It's a '56 Chevy."

"Were there other cars on the road? Maybe coming toward her?"

"No," said Roy, "just this one."

He and Jimmy watched as the ambulance attendants tucked a blanket around the unconscious girl from the neck down and lifted her onto a gurney then loaded it into the wagon.

"She have any passengers?" the cop asked. "Anybody walk away from the vehicle after the collision?"

Both Roy and Jimmy shook their heads.

The janitor, who had come back out and was standing next to the boys, said, "I call ambulance. Nobody run."

A tow truck arrived and one of the cops told the spectators to move away from the wrecked car. The ambulance drove off, its siren blaring.

"Okay, boys," said the cop who'd been asking questions, "you'd better go on to school."

Another cop came over and said, "Let's go, Lou. Eisenhower'll be at the Palmer House quarter to ten."

"We're late," Jimmy said to the first cop. "Can you give us a note?"

He removed from one of his pockets a pad of traffic tickets, scribbled on it, ripped out the page and handed it to Jimmy.

"When you boys are old enough to drive remember not to speed on a wet street."

Roy and Jimmy watched the tow truck guys attach cables to the car and signal to the winch operator to pull the car right side up. After that was done they hooked up the front bumper and hauled it away. The cops got back into their cars and headed for The Loop.

"I didn't know the president was comin' to Chicago today," said Jimmy.

"What did the cop write?" Roy asked him.

Jimmy showed the yellow ticket page to Roy, who read it out loud.

"These two boys witnessed a traffic accident this A.M. Car hit pole corner Granville and Washtenaw approx. 8:45. Please excuse them being late. Ofc. P. Madigan, Badge 882."

"Look at this," said Jimmy.

Lying next to the curb where the car had been on its side was a pink make-up compact with a cracked cover. Jimmy picked it up.

"Maybe she was puttin' on make-up while she drove," he said, and put the compact into his right jacket pocket.

"You gonna keep it?"

"Yeah. If the cops come back to inspect the scene I don't want her to get in trouble."

The janitor and the other observers had all gone back into their houses and the boys began walking toward the school.

"You're right," Jimmy said.

"About what?"

"She was pretty. Her legs and everything."

"I felt bad," said Roy, "lookin' at her that way. Part naked, I mean. I hope her neck's not broken."

"Me, too. I couldn't stop lookin' either."

That afternoon in American History Roy was reading about the war with the Apache Indians on the U.S.-Mexico border in the 1870s when he thought about the girl. He wondered if Apaches came across a white woman lying alone and unconscious on a desert trail, maybe thrown from a horse, would they have stopped to help her or leave her to burn in the sun and be nibbled by insects and torn apart by coyotes. He knew that the Apaches did not take scalps but they did bury living enemies up to their necks in the ground and lather their faces with *tiswin*—corn liquor—in order to attract killer ants that ate out their eyeballs and invaded their noses and ears.

After school Roy asked Jimmy Boyle what he thought the Apaches would have done and Jimmy said, "Are you kiddin'? Those young bucks wouldn't leave a pretty girl to rot. Not once they seen her legs."

Dark and Black and Strange

As a boy, Roy often stayed up much of the night watching movies on TV. Most of them were old, black and white films from the 1930s and '40s. When he and his mother were living in hotels in Miami, Havana or New Orleans, she was usually out during the late night and early morning hours, leaving Roy by himself, which he did not mind; when they were in Chicago, staying at his grandmother's house, he had a little television in his room to watch the all-night movies on channel nine, a local station that owned an extensive archive of classic as well as obscure films.

The movies Roy preferred were mystery, crime and horror pictures such as *The End of Everything*, *Stairway to Doom*, *Three-and-a-Half Jealous Husbands*, *Fanged Sphinx of Fez*, and *Demented Darlings*. By far his favorite was *Snake Girl*, starring Arleena Mink, a purportedly Eurasian actress of uncertain provenance, who never made another movie. Unlike *Cult of the Cobra*, also one of Roy's favorites, which featured a woman who turned into a viper in order to commit murders, *Snake Girl* was about a child abandoned, supposedly by her parents, in a swamp for unexplained reasons.

When first we see Arleena Mink, an exotic-looking, stunningly beautiful teenage girl, unclothed but covered in strategic places by what appears to be a sheer coating of dark moss, her amazingly long, dark hair entwined around her neck, upper arms, waist and legs, she is not really walking but *gliding* in a dreary landscape both jungle and swamp. She deftly navigates her way through and beneath hanging moss and reptilian vines, sinuously evading gigantic Venus flytrap types of plants and overgrown vegetation. The only noises come from invisible birds that constantly squawk and screech. Her passage is interrupted briefly by an apparent flashback showing a car stopping on a road next to a swamp, the right front passenger door opening, and a person's hands and arms holding and then rolling a bundle—presumably containing the body of an infant—down an incline into the murk. The door closes and the car is driven on. We do not see the driver or passenger's faces.

Arleena Mink does not utter a sound other than an occasional hiss. Four men carrying rifles, machetes and nets appear, attired in khaki bush jackets and safari hats. They don't talk much as they plod past waving leaves and wade through brackish shallows. We assume they are hunting for the snake girl, whose existence, we learn from their minimal dialogue, may be only a rumor. Having seen Arleena Mink, however, we know her presence in the swampland is not a myth and she is apparently endeavoring to avoid capture.

Arleena slithers, slinks and crawls as her pursuers become increasingly frustrated due to biting insects, unidentified moving things rippling the waters, and debilitating heat. The action concludes when one after another of the men are eliminated: the first two sucked under and swallowed by quicksand, the third strangled by a serpent-vine, and the fourth dragged into dense foliage by the hairy arm of an otherwise unseen beast, the victim's cry muffled by one huge, sharp-clawed paw.

The snake girl may or may not have even been aware that she was being stalked by men; behaving cautiously is her natural condition. In the last shot of the movie she rises to her full height, stares directly into the camera, her slanted eyes burning and sparkling like black diamonds, and from between her puffy lips darts a shockingly long, whiplike tongue. The forked tip of Arleena Mink's quivering organ flaps and twists as she emits a sudden, deliciously hideous, spine-shriveling hiss.

Whenever Roy saw *Snake Girl* listed in a TV movie guide—without exception in the middle of the night—he watched it.

Arleena Mink disappeared from public display after 1944, the year her one film was made. It wasn't until almost fifty years later that by chance Roy noticed an obituary in *Variety* that read: "Arleena Mink, actress, born Consuelina Norma Lagarto in Veracruz, Mexico, on January 1, 1930, died June 20 in Asunción, Paraguay. Her husband, Generalissimo Emilio Buenaventura-Schmid, whom she married when she was fifteen years old, preceded her in death, date unknown. Miss Mink's only film appearance was in *Snake Girl*, rumored to have been secretly directed in Brazil by Orson Welles, using the name Mauricio de Argentina. Writing in *Le Monde* (Paris), the eminent critic Edmund Wilson described *Snake Girl* as 'an erotic masterpiece, uniquely dark and black and strange. One can easily imagine being bitten by the vixenish, barely pubescent Arleena Mink and expiring without regret.'"

The Vagaries of Incompleteness

After they moved from Florida to Chicago, Roy's mother hired a maid named Wilda Cherokee. Wilda, a sweet-tempered woman in her mid-twenties, had a son, Henry, who, like Roy, was seven years old. When Wilda could find nobody to take care of Henry, which was often, she brought him with her to Roy and his mother's house. After Roy came home from school he and Henry played together. Roy asked him if he ever got in trouble with his school for being absent so much and Henry said, "Not so much trouble as when I'm there."

"How come your last name is the name of an Indian tribe?" Roy asked.

"My mother's people are from North Carolina," Henry said. "They're part Indians."

Roy wished he had a great name like Cherokee and whenever he introduced Henry to someone he always said, "This is Henry Cherokee," not just Henry.

"He ain't an Indian," said Roy's friend Tommy Cunningham, "he's a Negro."

"He's both," Roy said. "His great-great grandmother was married to a Cherokee chief."

"What was the chief's name?" asked Tommy.

"Wind-Runs-Behind-Him," said Henry.

"You're makin' that up."

"No, I'm not. My grandmama Florence told me."

Roy, Tommy and Henry were standing in the alley behind Roy's house. Roy and Henry had been playing catch with a taped up hardball when Tommy came out of Jimmy Boyle's backyard, which he'd been cutting through.

"How come you're here?" Tommy asked.

"His mother works for us," said Roy.

"What's her name, Princess Summer-Fall-Winter-Spring?"

"Wilda," said Henry.

"Can you do a war dance? Say somethin' in Cherokee,"

A red Studebaker crept slowly up the alley and parked a couple of houses away behind a garage.

"That's Mr. Anderson," said Roy.

He waved at the tall, fair-haired man who got out of the car and the man waved back. Mr. Anderson walked over to the boys.

"Hello, Roy. And you're Paulie Cunningham's son, aren't you? How's your dad? He hasn't been around Beeb's Tavern lately."

"He's in jail," said Tommy. "But my ma says he's gettin' out soon."

"Tell him Sven Anderson says hello and that the first one's on me."

"Yes, sir."

"And who's this?" Mr. Anderson said, looking at Henry.

"This is my friend Henry Cherokee," said Roy.

"Do you live around here, Henry?"

"No."

"His mother works for my mother," Roy said.

Mr. Anderson fingered a cigarette from an open pack of Lucky Strikes in his shirt pocket, put it between his lips, then took out a green book of matches with the name Beeb's written on it in white letters, and lit the Lucky.

"I hired a colored fella to work at the bottling plant," he said. "Two years ago, I guess it was. He was a good worker. After about six months he didn't show up one Monday, didn't call in either. Turned out he'd been shot and killed in a bar Saturday night before."

"Henry's part Indian," said Roy.

"His grandfather was a chief," said Tommy Cunningham.

"My great-great grandfather," said Henry. "His name was

Wind-Runs-Behind-Him."

"That's poetry, that is," Mr. Anderson said. "Our names aren't nearly as colorful, or descriptive. He must have been a fast runner."

"I don't know," said Henry.

"Nice meeting you, Henry. It's not every day I get to meet the great grandson of an Indian chief."

Mr. Anderson walked back toward his garage.

"What's poetry?" asked Tommy.

"Words that rhyme," said Roy.

"Wind-Runs-Behind-Him don't rhyme."

"What's your father in jail for?" Henry asked.

Tommy, who was almost nine and a head taller than Henry, bent over and put his nose on top of Henry's and said, "He's a horse thief."

Roy thought Tommy might try to beat Henry up so he got ready to hit Tommy in his head with the hardball, but Tommy backed off and began running down the alley.

"Does his father really steal horses?" asked Henry.

The sky had clouded over in a hurry.

"Come on," said Roy, "let's play catch before it rains."

King and Country

In January of that year a monumental blizzard hit Chicago, forcing the city to shut down for four days. Virtually all businesses closed except for a few neighborhood bars and liquor stores. Only police, firefighters and emergency services remained available. Residents were advised not to try to drive; the only way around was on foot.

Roy was thirteen and by the night of the second day cabin fever compelled him to venture out to visit his friend Jimmy Boyle, who lived a couple of blocks away. Wading down the middle of Ojibway Boulevard through the hip-and even chest-high drifts, Roy encountered a man coming out of Beebs and Glen's Tavern carrying two fifths of Murphy's Irish whiskey, one under each arm.

"I'm goin' to Peggy Dean's house and I'm not comin' out for a week!" he shouted.

Just before Roy reached Jimmy's block another man came toward him, also struggling to make a path for himself. He was wearing a purple turban and wrapped around his body were layers of different colored robes, rags and rugs. The man's barely visible face was brown and bearded. He was pulling a two-wheeled cart laden with what Roy assumed were his belongings, piled high and covered with more rugs and pieces of material. As Roy and the man approached one another, Roy could see that beneath his robes, which reached to his ankles, the man was barefoot.

"Ah, I saw you from afar!" the man said to Roy, and stopped in front of him.

The man's eyes blazed like blue moons in the darkness.

"You look like a king," Roy said.

"I was a king in my own country," replied the man.

"Aren't you afraid your feet will get frostbite?"

"I come from a strong and powerful people who walk in the

footsteps of Arphax, he who lived more than four-hundred years and paved a fiery path. My feet are like unto fine brass, as if they burn in a furnace. My servant Isaiah walked naked and barefoot for three years through a hostile and terrible land. Though I hath cometh out of prison to reign again am I also he who becometh poor."

The man began to move forward, dragging his cart.

"What's your name?" Roy called after him.

"To know me," said the man, "you must first solve the mystery of the seven stars."

When Roy got to Jimmy Boyle's house he told him about the biblical character who said he'd been a king in his own country.

"His name is Morris Jones," said Jimmy. "He used to be a fry cook at the Busy Bee on Milwaukee Avenue. He went batshit about a year ago and started tellin' everyone he was the son of God. He lives under the el over there. My father gives him a buck or two when he sees him."

"Is he dangerous?"

"He carries a carving knife under his robes. He took it from the diner. Elmer Schuh, who owns the Busy Bee, let him keep it to protect himself."

Roy did not see Morris Jones again until the following August. It was a boiling hot day and Morris was sitting in the back seat of a police car parked in front of the el station with his hands cuffed, wearing his purple turban. Roy asked a cop standing next to the car why Morris had been arrested.

"He carved up a dog and was tryin' to sell the parts to passengers gettin' on and off the trains."

"Is that against the law?"

"It is when you're not wearin' nothing but a turban."

"He was a king in his own country," Roy said.

"He should have stayed there," said the cop.

The next day Roy told Jimmy Boyle about his having seen

Morris being arrested, and what for.

"He was naked?"

"Except for his turban."

"I don't think Morris would ever hurt anyone on purpose," said Jimmy. "He always gave me extra bacon whenever I went into the Busy Bee with my dad."

House of Bamboo

Roy was sitting at the kitchen table eating a ham and cheese sandwich when his mother appeared from the front of the house pushing Marty Bell toward the back door.

"I hope you don't mind going out this way, Marty," she said. "I thought it would be easier since you're parked in the alley."

Marty Bell was one of Roy's mother's boyfriends. He wanted to marry her but despite the fact that he made "a good living," as she said, Roy's mother would not marry him.

"Too bad he's so short," she had told Roy. "He only comes up to my shoulders. How could I be seen with him?"

Roy's mother allowed Marty Bell to kiss her on the cheek before he went out the back door. Just as she closed it behind him, the front doorbell rang. She hurried through the house to answer it and returned less than a minute later to the kitchen accompanied by Bill Crown, another boyfriend of hers. Bill Crown was considerably taller than Marty Bell. His right arm was wrapped around Roy's mother's shoulders, and she was smiling.

"Look, Roy, Bill brought you a present."

"Here," said Bill Crown, "you can practice with this."

With his left hand Bill handed Roy a small polo mallet. He knew that Crown played polo on the weekends, but Roy knew practically nothing about the sport, other than it was played on horseback and the participants rode around trying to hit a small, hard wooden ball into a goal. None of his friends knew anything about polo, either.

"I'd like you and your mother to come out to Oak Brook on Saturday to watch me play. It'll be a good match."

Bill took a scuffed white ball out of a pocket of his brown leather coat and set it on the table.

"This is from last week's match," he said. "You can knock it around the yard."

Roy put down his sandwich and held the mallet in both of his hands.

"Put your hand through the strap when you grip the handle. That way you won't drop the mallet. It's made of bamboo. It'll bend but won't break."

"Thanks," Roy said. "I have a baseball game on Saturday."

"We play on Sundays, too, sometimes. I'll let you know. You'll come this Saturday, Kitty, won't you?"

"I'll be happy to," said Roy's mother.

She and Bill Crown left the kitchen. Roy placed the mallet on the floor and finished eating his sandwich.

The next day, Roy was batting the wooden ball around in front of his house when his friend Johnny Murphy came by.

"What kind of a club is that?" asked Johnny.

"A polo mallet. Bill Crown, a friend of my mother's, gave it to me. You ride horses and sock this ball with it."

Roy handed Johnny the mallet.

"The shaft is made from bamboo and the head is hard wood, like the ball."

"Sounds like hockey."

"Yeah, only on horseback."

"I think just rich guys play polo," Johnny said. "Maybe he'll give you a horse."

"Uh huh. We can keep it in our apartment."

"Is your mother gonna marry him?"

"I don't know."

"How many times has she been married?"

"Twice."

"My mother says it's rough on kids who come from broken homes. Do you want this guy to be your father?"

"I have a father. I've only seen Bill Crown a couple of times.

He's okay."

Johnny hit the ball and it rolled into the street.

"What does your mother like about him?"

"He's tall," Roy said, and went to get the ball.

The Unexpected

"You think Miss Peaches is terrific, you shoulda seen Little Egypt that time Gus Argo and I were in East Saint Louis at Miss Vivian's Evening in Havana."

"The original Little Egypt was a Syrian dame made her bones at the Columbian Exposition in 1890-somethin'. Married a Greek guy owned a restaurant. Other girls stole the name and her act, only they done it dirtier."

Roy was in Meschina's Delicatessen sitting in a booth with Jewish Joe, who wasn't Jewish, and Al Martin, who was. Roy ran errands for the men when he needed extra money. He was fourteen years old, Joe and Al were both in their forties. They'd done time for making book and extortion, but they never involved Roy or any of the other kids who worked for them in anything the kids knew was illegal. Mostly the men used the boys to deliver messages to people when they didn't want to use a telephone. The messages were in code. Joe or Al would tell a kid to go over to the Time Out, a bar on South Mohawk, and tell Big Lloyd, the bartender, "Ali Baba had twenty-five thieves, not forty." The kid would keep a few newspapers under one arm to make out like he was a newsboy in case any no good law was around, and Big Lloyd would say, "No minors or peddlers allowed, kid. Take the air."

For this or similar endeavors, Roy would get five bucks. He got a kick out of the gangster talk but he didn't consider Jewish Joe or Al Martin real mobsters. They were small-timers hustling a living. Chicago was full of guys like them. Roy figured it was the same in any big city and so long as he didn't have knowledge of any of the particulars he wouldn't get in trouble.

One Friday night Al Martin handed Roy a menu from Meschina's and told him to take it to 1432 Water Street. A woman would answer the door, a blonde in her late twenties, and Roy should give her the menu. On the way over to Water Street, which was a good sixteen blocks from Meschina's, Roy examined the menu and saw at the bottom of the second page a telephone number written in pencil. Al said if anybody other than the blonde opened the door Roy should say he'd made a mistake and bring the menu back to Meschina's.

"What if somebody chases me?" Roy asked.

"Run," said Al. "Don't drop the menu."

Roy lived with his mother and younger sister. His father was dead. Roy's mother worked as a receptionist at a hospital and Roy worked three nights a week delivering Chinese food on a bicycle. He gave half of the money he made from the Chinese restaurant to his mother. She didn't know he ran errands for Joe and Al.

He knocked on the door at 1432 Water but nobody answered right away. It was a cool, windy night, and Roy had not minded the long walk. Jewish Joe and Al Martin and every other denizen of Meschina's smoked cigarettes and cigars even while they ate, so Roy was glad to be out in the fresh air. He did not smoke because when he began boxing at the YMCA two years before his trainer, Pat Touhy, told him, as he told all the boys, not to smoke, drink alcohol or lift weights.

"When you roll out of the sack in the morning," Pat Touhy instructed, "get down on the floor and do a hundred sit-ups and as many fingertip push-ups as you can, then go take a piss and brush your teeth. Don't touch a weight or your muscles will tighten up. I want you long and loose and fast. Weight work cuts quickness. And you run—run to school, to the gym, to work. Walkin's a waste of motion."

Roy knocked again and this time a woman opened the door but she was a brunette and she looked a lot older than twenty-something. Roy heard a man's voice from inside ask, "Who's there, Phyllis?"

"I made a mistake, lady," said Roy. "I got the wrong house."

He walked away but before he'd gone fifteen steps someone came up behind him and said, "Did Al send you?"

Roy turned around and saw a blonde woman with a bad complexion who looked even older than the brunette who had opened the door. The blonde's face was vaguely familiar.

"What are you holding?" she asked.

Roy wasn't sure what to do. He looked back at the house; the front door was open and the dark-haired woman was standing on the sidewalk watching him and the other woman.

"Is that for me?" said the blonde, pointing at the menu in Roy's left hand.

"Al Martin sent you, didn't he?"

"How old are you?" asked Roy.

The woman hesitated a moment before saying, "What do you care?"

A man came out of the house, brushed past the brunette and walked toward Roy and the blonde. Roy did not recognize him. The man was mostly bald and was wearing an unbuttoned white shirt with the sleeves rolled up to his elbows. He was holding a gun in his right hand against his right leg. Roy turned and ran. After he'd gone four blocks he stopped and looked back. Nobody was chasing him.

Jewish Joe and Al Martin were still at their table in Meschina's when Roy came in. He put the menu down in front of Al.

"Nobody home?" Al said.

"A brunette answered the door, then a bleached blonde about forty years old came out and wanted what I had that you'd given me."

"Yeah, then what?"

"A bald guy came out of the house carrying a gun, so I took off."

"A bald guy," said Joe. "Kind of heavy?"

"I guess so. Maybe. I saw the piece, I ran."

"Sorry about that," said Al.

He reached a hand inside his suit jacket, took out a billfold, opened it, removed two fives and handed them to Roy.

"Why the extra fin?" Roy asked.

"The unexpected."

"I got scared when I saw the guy had a gun."

"Sure you did," said Jewish Joe.

"Okay, kid, go home," said Al Martin. "See you next Friday."

Roy looked in both directions on the street in front of Meschina's. The temperature had dropped and sweat dried cold under his shirt. The blonde used to do the weather report on channel two. She looked better on TV.

The Way of All Flesh

"You boys know about Oriental girls? Their slits go sideways, so you have to prop 'em up perpendicular to yourself goin' in or you'll have a bent pecker comin' out."

Roy and Eddie Hay were standing under the awning outside Myron and Jerry's Steakhouse on South Mohawk getting the goods from Sonny Lightfoot. Sonny worked for Jib Bufera, who ate lunch every afternoon except Sunday at three o'clock at Myron and Jerry's. Sonny's real last name was Veronesi, but he earned his nickname when he weighed forty pounds less and burglarized houses while the residents were sleeping. He became famous for his ability to tread so softly that nobody woke up while he pilfered jewelry and other valuables. These days he drove for Jib Bufera.

"Jib's got me on call twenty out of twenty-four, so I snooze in the Lincoln while he's havin' meetings."

"You like workin' for Jib?" asked Eddie Hay, who the other boys called Hey Eddie, which he hated.

"Can't complain. Less stressful than breakin' and enterin'. Jib's generous. He and his goombahs speak Sicilian most of the time, which is okay by me because then I don't know nothin' when the wrong guys ask me what I know."

A steady, warm rain had put an early end to the boys' ballgame but Roy did not mind since he was fighting a summer cold.

"Hey Eddie," he said, "I'm goin' home. Take it easy, Sonny. And thanks for the anatomy lesson."

"Any time, kid. Shake that cold."

Roy was twelve years old and didn't know much about girls. He had his doubts, though, about Sonny Lightfoot being a source of reliable information.

When he got home, Roy's grandfather was asleep in an armchair with a book on his lap. Roy looked at the title: *Germany Will Try It Again*. He went into his room and turned on the little red and white portable TV he kept on a table next to his bed, then took off his shoes and lay down. There was an old movie on about a terminally ill man, a philosophy professor, who decides to do the world a favor and murder a truly evil person before he himself dies. The professor shoots and kills a spider woman who is having an affair with the husband of a colleague of his. The spider woman is a crook who has seduced the husband, an artist, and blackmailed him into creating paintings in the styles of old masters and selling them as lost or stolen masterpieces to private collectors. The professor confesses his crime to the police, goes to trial and is sentenced to die in the electric chair. Before he is executed, however, the professor is horrified to learn that another man, having read in a newspaper about the professor's reason for committing the murder, has subscribed to the professor's philosophy and mistakenly killed an innocent person.

The spider woman, when confronted by the professor, was unmoved by his plea that she relinquish her hold on the husband. Her smug, nonchalant attitude infuriated him but intrigued Roy. If a diabolical but goodlooking dame like this got her hooks into a man, he realized, she could compel him to do almost anything.

Roy's grandfather appeared in the doorway.

"Hello, Roy. I didn't hear you come in."

"Hi, Pops. You were sleeping. I didn't want to disturb you."

"Are you hungry?"

"No, I'm okay. Pops, do you think there are people who are really evil? Or are they just mentally ill?"

"I'm sorry to say, Roy, I believe in the existence of evil. Hitler, for example, was an evil man who had the ability to inspire and manipulate people into committing the most gruesome acts of villainy."

"I saw the book you're reading about Germany. Hitler was a

German, wasn't he?"

"No, he was Austrian, but he became chancellor of Germany."

"There had to be a lot of evil people in Germany to do what they did."

"That's what the book is about. The author theorizes that their society is genetically predisposed to waging war, that they possess an imperative biological desire to control others and force them to submit to their will."

"A woman can do that to a man."

"Yes, and a man can do it to a woman."

"How much does sex have to do with it?"

"Sometimes everything, sometimes nothing. Do you have any more questions before I make myself a sandwich?"

"Just one, but it can wait."

"What's it about?"

"Oriental girls."

Some Products of the Imagination

Roy did not realize he was lost until a woman hanging wash on a line in her backyard asked him what he was doing there. Roy was walking home alone from kindergarten. It had been his second day at school and he had decided to take a shortcut through the alley between Washtenaw and Minnetonka streets and then cut through a yard to get to Minnetonka.

"Where are you going, little boy?" the woman asked him.

Sheets and towels on the line were fluttering in the wind and the sun was half-blinding him.

"Home."

"What street do you live on?"

"I'm not trying to steal anything, lady. I was just cutting through."

"You don't look like a thief. What's your name?"

"Roy. I live on Rockwell, with my mother."

One of the sheets kept flapping up in Roy's face so he ducked under it and stood directly in front of the woman, who seemed very big. She was wearing a gray and white checked housecoat, and her long black hair was being blown back and forth across her face.

"Well, Roy, Rockwell is one block over. Is your house closer to Ojibway or to Minnetonka?"

"Ojibway."

"Then you'll turn left on Rockwell."

"Can I walk through your yard or should I go back to the alley?"

"Of course you can walk through the yard. How old are you?"

"Five."

"You're very young to be walking to or from school by yourself. It's more than half a mile from your house."

"I can do it. I just got confused trying to take a shortcut."

"My name is Mrs. Miller, Roy. You can cut through my yard whenever you want to."

"Thanks. Do you have a dog?"

"No, no dog."

When Roy got home nobody was there. Both his mother and grandmother, who was visiting from Miami, were out. His mother had left a note for him on the kitchen table.

> *Roy, I hope you had a good day at school. Nanny and I have gone downtown to buy her a coat. She is not used to the cold weather in Chicago. There is roast beef left over from last night's dinner in the refrigerator. Make yourself a sandwich if you are hungry. The bread is in the bread box. Drink a glass of milk. Nanny and I will be home soon.*
>
> *Mom*

Roy wasn't hungry, so he went into his room and lay down on the bed. The next thing he knew his mother was sitting on the bed talking to him.

"Hi, sweetheart. Did you eat something?"

"No, I guess I was too tired. I dreamed I was lost in a desert and the wind was blowing sand around so I couldn't see very well and then a beautiful lady appeared out of the sand and held my hand and led me out of the desert."

"Did you recognize this beautiful lady, Roy? Was it me?"

"No, she had black hair."

"Did she tell you her name?"

"Yes, it was Mrs. Miller."

Both Roy's mother and grandmother, who had come into the room, laughed.

"Maybe Mrs. Miller was a mirage," said his mother.

"What's a mirage?"

"Something you think you see but it's not really there. It's a product of the imagination."

"How do you like my new coat, Roy?" his grandmother asked. She was wearing a bright pink coat.

"Anyone can see me in this," she said, "especially drivers when I'm crossing a busy street."

"Tell me if you want to eat something," said his mother.

She smoothed his hair back off his forehead, then she stood up and both women left Roy's room.

On his way home from school the next afternoon, Roy opened the back gate to Mrs. Miller's yard, closed it behind him, and was about to walk through when a man came out of the back door of the house and said, "Where do you think you're going?"

The man was very big, bigger than Mrs. Miller, and he had a mean look on his face. He walked toward Roy.

"Mrs. Miller said I could cut through her yard on my way home from school."

"If I see you in this yard again, I'll let my dog out."

The man's head was completely bald and red. His face and eyes were red, too. Roy backed away, opened the gate and stepped into the alley.

"What happened to Mrs. Miller?" he asked.

"Something will happen to you and any of your friends if I catch you in here."

"She said she didn't have a dog."

The man pulled on the gate and closed it with a loud clang, then he turned around and stomped back to the house.

Each day for the rest of that week Roy stopped in the alley and looked into the yard but Mrs. Miller was never there. After that, he walked home a different way.

About a month later, Roy was with his mother on Ojibway Boulevard when he saw Mrs. Miller walking toward them. He was about to say hello but Mrs. Miller passed by without looking at him. Roy stopped and looked back at her. She was holding a big brown dog on a leash.

Roy remained curious about Mrs. Miller and the man who had kicked him out of the yard. Why did she tell him she didn't have a dog? Roy decided to go back one more time to ask her. He stood in the alley behind the Miller house and waited for twenty minutes before the back door opened and the brown dog bounded down the steps followed by Mrs. Miller.

Roy went up to the fence and said, "Mrs. Miller? Can I talk to you?"

She came over to the fence, as did the dog.

"Hello, Roy. I haven't seen you for a long time."

"I tried to cut through your yard one day and a man came out and told me I couldn't. He said if I tried to again he would let his dog out to attack me. I told him you said I could and that you said you didn't have a dog. After that, I saw you on Ojibway Boulevard walking with this dog."

Mrs. Miller smiled and said, "I'm sorry for the confusion, Roy. The man is my brother, Eugene. He was staying here for a few days. He lives in St. Louis. This is his dog, Grisby. Eugene went back to St. Louis and left Grisby with me until he finds a new place to live. I'm afraid Grisby isn't properly socialized, so it's probably a good idea while I have him here that you don't cut through the yard. He might bite you."

"Okay, I won't."

"I'm sorry, Roy. I don't think he'll be here too much longer, though I don't mind having his company."

Grisby propped his large front paws on top of the fence and barked at Roy. He had a long, green tongue and sharp teeth.

"Your brother is scary," Roy said.

"He's had a difficult life, Roy. I'm trying to help him out."

"Was he ever in prison?"

Mrs. Miller stared at Roy for a few moments before answering.

"Yes, as a matter of fact, he was. How could you know? Did Eugene tell you?"

"Was it for murder?"

"I think you'd better go home now, Roy."

Grisby got down from the fence and followed her. Roy noticed that part of the dog's tail was missing; it looked as if half of it had been chopped off.

Just as he arrived at his house, Roy's mother ran out and shouted something Roy could not hear clearly at his grandmother, who was standing in the doorway. He watched his mother get into her car without saying anything to him and drive away.

"What happened, Nanny?" he asked. "Where's my mother going?"

"I couldn't stop her, Roy. Like most really beautiful women, she's often overwhelmed by her insecurities."

"I don't know what that means."

"It doesn't matter. Come into the house."

"Is she in trouble?"

"I hope not."

"Mrs. Miller is really beautiful and I think she's in trouble."

"Who's Mrs. Miller?"

"I told you and Mom about her. Her brother Eugene is a murderer. He escaped from prison and killed Mrs. Miller's husband."

The Comedian

On the hottest day of the summer Roy and his friend Elmo Rubinsky played Fast Ball at the schoolyard. It was a two man game, one pitching, one batting, exchanging places after three outs in an inning. The pitcher threw to a box marked in chalk on a brick wall; this was the strike zone. Lines were drawn in the gravel on the ground behind the pitcher; a ball hit past him on the fly was a single, past the first line was a double, against the fence was a triple, over the fence a home run. Foul lines were drawn on both sides of the field. The pitcher called balls and strikes; often, if the batter protested a call, it didn't count and the pitcher had to throw it again.

After their game was over, the boys were exhausted and dehydrated, so they staggered over to the Standard gas station two blocks away to buy bottles of cold Nehi soda pop for a nickel apiece from a machine inside the station waiting room. Elmo had won the game that day largely due to his use of what he called his "back up" pitch, which looked to the batter like a fast ball but appeared to slow down—or back up—after the batter had already begun his swing, causing him to pop up the ball or miss it entirely.

Elmo drank half a dozen grape sodas and Roy half a dozen orange. The sports section of that morning's *Tribune* was on a table in the waiting room where Roy and Elmo sat on wooden folding chairs draining Nehis from the bottles. Roy examined the box scores from the previous day's major league baseball games and saw that a rookie on the San Francisco Giants named Willie McCovey had made his debut by going four for four, hitting two triples and two singles. This was the first game of what turned out to be McCovey's hall of fame career.

Across the street from the gas station was a synagogue and

when the boys looked out the window of the waiting room they saw that a crowd was gathering on the sidewalk in front of the steps leading to the entrance. After they had finished the last of their bottles of pop, Roy and Elmo left the station and went across the street to find out what was going on.

"We're waitin' for George Burns to arrive," said a kid. "The rabbi here died and his funeral is today. George Burns was his brother and he's supposed to be comin' in from New York or Hollywood for the burial."

George Burns was a famous comedian. He and his wife, Gracie Allen, had acted in many movies and currently had a popular television show. The crowd had gathered not necessarily out of respect for the deceased rabbi but to see if it was true that George Burns was his brother and that he would show up for the funeral. Most of the people waiting around were not Jewish and had never been inside the synagogue nor did they even know the name of George Burns's brother. Elmo asked a man what the rabbi's name was and he said, "Birnbaum. George's real name is Nathan Birnbaum. He changed it to George Burns because he was in show business, because of anti-Semitism. He didn't want people to know he was a Jew."

The crowd surged to the curb as a long, black limousine pulled over and stopped. The driver got out, came around the car and opened the curbside rear passenger door. George Burns got out, holding a big cigar in his right hand. He was a very small man; he smiled and waved. He wore glasses and a bad toupée. People shouted his name over and over and shouted, "Where's Gracie?" Everyone was genuinely excited to see that it really was the famous comedian.

George Burns and his brother had grown up in New York City. They were from a poor family that lived on the Lower East Side. Nathan had become an entertainer when he was very young, beginning his career in vaudeville, eventually changing his name and moving to Hollywood. Some people in the crowd tried to get his autograph but his chauffeur pushed through the throng clearing a path ahead of the comedian and the two of them went up the steps of the synagogue and disappeared inside. Two police cars drove up and parked behind the limousine. Two uniformed cops got out of each car and waded into the crowd, telling people to move away from the synagogue entrance.

Nobody left; they were determined to wait until George Burns came out so they could see him smile and wave his cigar at them again. A black hearse pulled up and stopped in the middle of the street. Roy and Elmo crossed the street to get away from the people pushing and shoving one another in order to be in better positions to watch the mourners leave for the cemetery. More cars came and parked in a line behind the hearse.

Two mechanics from the gas station came out from the garage and stood on the sidewalk with Roy and Elmo. The name patches on their coveralls were Rip and Don.

"I didn't know George Burns was a Jew," said Rip.

"I like his wife on the show," said Don. "She's always getting' things mixed up and he stands around holdin' a big cigar and explains what she said."

"I know a guy named Bill Burns," Rip said. "He's a Lutheran."

Roy and Elmo did not wait to see George Burns come back out. They were walking to Elmo's house when he said, "What if George Burns changed his name back to Birnbaum now? He's sixty years old or older and famous, not just starting out, so he shouldn't be worried about anti-Semites preventing him from getting work. Everyone knows who George Burns is, right? Everyone in the entertainment business knows he's a Jew. So do his fans."

"Rip, the grease monkey at the Standard station, didn't know."

"It would be an important statement against anti-Semitism, I think," said Elmo.

"You should write him a letter," Roy said, "and tell him that."

When the boys got to the house Elmo's father was in the gangway digging up dirt around his tomato plants. Elmo told him his idea and that Roy had suggested he write to George Burns. Big Sol Rubinsky owned a salvage business on the south side of Chicago and had fought in the Pacific with the Marines during World War II.

"Them guys don't think like that," he said. "You'd just be wastin' a stamp."

The next day Roy read in the *Sun-Times* that George Burns had been in town for his brother's funeral. The article said that due to personal differences the brothers had not talked to or seen each other in many years. When asked the reasons for their estrangement, George Burns was quoted as saying the only difference between them was that his brother did not smoke cigars.

Lament for a Daughter of Egypt

When he was a small boy, Roy's mother liked to throw parties. She was a good dancer, especially of the Latin variety such as the samba, mambo and cha-cha-cha. After her divorce from Roy's father, when Roy was five years old, his mother invited several couples to their apartment on Saturday nights every other week or so. Her own companions during the three years between the divorce and her second marriage were a succession of over-smiling, iron-handshaking, smooth-dancing guys who were always surprised that she had a child. It was obvious to Roy that she had not mentioned his existence to any of them prior to the evenings of her parties.

On one of these occasions, while her guests were shuffling tipsily to Art Blakey's "Jodie's Cha-cha," Roy's mother and her date, a broad-shouldered, slick-haired man with a dark brown paint-smear mustache named Bob Arno, got into a tiff over his having danced once too often with someone's wife. Roy usually hung out on the periphery observing the action. His mother's wrangling with Arno began in the kitchen, where he was in the process of mixing himself a drink, then continued into the diningroom before ending abruptly in the front hall, where he hammered the remainder of his cocktail, handed the empty glass to her and left the apartment.

Three women immediately surrounded Roy's mother, each of them chattering like monkeys about the incident, indicting the wife as the instigator. A tall, blonde woman appeared in the hallway, a mink stole draped around her otherwise bare shoulders, said good night to the other women and made a swift exit. A few seconds later, a husky man in a baggy gray suit approached them.

"Have you seen Helen?" he asked.

His face was green and his eyes were bloodshot.

"I believe she just went out to get a pack of cigarettes," said Kay O'Connor, a skinny redhead about whom Roy had once heard his mother say never left her house without make-up on and a gun in her purse.

"Helen doesn't smoke," said the man.

"Come on, Marty," Roy's mother said to him, "let's dance."

She handed Bob Arno's empty glass to Roy, took one of the man's hands and led him into the livingroom.

"Didn't you used to date Bob Arno?" one of the women asked Kay O'Connor.

"He's afraid of me," Kay said.

"You mean he's afraid of Harvey," said the third woman.

"What's the diff?" said Kay.

The three women walked into the livingroom.

Roy watched his mother doing the cha-cha with the husky man. His face had turned from green to bright red and Roy's mother was laughing, showing all of her teeth.

After the cha-cha number ended, someone put on another record. A woman's voice, high-pitched with a tremble in it, delivered the song's lyrics slowly and directly, but somehow a half-step behind the band without dragging the beat. Everyone stopped talking and laughing and listened.

"I still remember/the first time you said/If I can't be free/I'd rather be dead/Now that you're gone/and nothing has changed/the answer to my question/can be arranged."

Somebody took off the record and put on a mambo and people started talking and laughing again. Roy went to the kitchen, put the glass in the sink, then went to his room and closed the door.

The next morning, he asked his mother if she thought it had been a good party.

"Not all bad," she said, "but not all good, either."

"Are you going to see Mr. Arno again?"

His mother reached far back into a cabinet, found a clean cup, and poured coffee for herself. The kitchen was a mess.

"He's not in our plans any more, I don't think," she said. "You don't like him, anyway, do you, Roy?"

The Old West

Like most young boys in the 1950s, Roy often wondered what it would have been like to have lived in the Old West. Movies and television shows mostly glorified those days, despite frontier lawlessness and having to fight hostile Indians. The reality that not many people lived into let alone past their thirties did not enter into Roy's thinking; to a seven or eight year old, thirty or more years might as well be two hundred. Neither did the idea of men killing one another without remorse deter Roy and his playmates in the least. Growing up in Chicago, they were used to hearing and reading about gangsters strangling and shooting their adversaries; also, most of the boys were sons of men who had fought in World War II, some of whom had been wounded or had brothers who died in battle. Violent death was a not unfamiliar circumstance, nor was it devoid of meaning; but this did not preclude their pantomiming violence in their fantasy scenarios.

Rube Danko, a ten year old cousin of Roy's friend Billy Katz, had, thanks to Billy, the reputation of being an exceptionally fast draw. Danko lived in a rough neighborhood, and Billy bragged about how tough his cousin was. When Billy brought him around one day, Roy was surprised that even though Rube was a couple of years older, he was short and pudgy. Danko didn't look tough and had a seemingly permanent grin on his puffy-cheeked face. He did not say much, and agreed to participate in whatever games his cousin and the other boys were playing. Danko wore a shiny silver and black gunbelt and badly scuffed brown and white cowboy boots, a black cowboy hat, blue jeans and a green T-shirt with the words Logan Square Boys Club written on it in white lettering.

Jimmy Boyle, Tommy Cunningham and Roy were the good guys; Katz, Danko and Murphy were the bad guys. Following a big shootout, only two boys were left standing: Roy and Rube Danko. The final showdown was between them, a quick-draw gunfight. Whoever pulled their gun and fired first won; the losers would then have to buy cokes for everyone.

Roy and Danko faced off ten feet apart. Katz's cousin was grinning, fingering the butt of his gun. Roy drew, pointed his revolver at Rube and shouted, "Bang!" Danko did not draw, just stood there smiling. Finally, he pulled his pistol and fired it twice into the air.

"Don't worry," he said, "they're blanks, and I'll buy the Cokes."

Later that day, after Rube had left, Jimmy Boyle said to Billy Katz, "Your cousin is weird. What if those bullets weren't really blanks?"

"His father works for the government," said Billy. "The FBI, maybe. I'm not sure. The gun must belong to him."

"Did you know it was real?" Roy asked.

Katz shook his head.

"The kid's crazy," said Tommy. "Why's he always smiling?"

Johnny Murphy pushed Billy in his chest and said, "Don't bring him around to play with us any more."

A couple of years later, Billy told Roy that his cousin Rube had gotten killed playing Russian Roulette.

"He was probably smiling when he pulled the trigger," Roy said.

Incurable

"Your father was a very generous man. He'd give you the shirt off his back, if he liked you. But in business he was tough, even ruthless; nobody got the better of him. Your mother shouldn't have divorced him; but then she shouldn't have married him, either."

Roy and his Uncle Buck, his mother's brother, were riding in Buck's Cadillac convertible on Dale Mabry Boulevard in Tampa, Florida, having just inspected a prospective site for a housing project Buck's company, Gulf Construction, was considering for development. Roy was thirteen years old; his father had been dead for almost two years. Since his parents had divorced when Roy was five, he had not known his father as well as he would have liked. During most of his childhood, Buck had been the primary paternal figure and influence in Roy's life.

"Were you and my dad friends?"

"We were friendly. He was only one year older but he had been in business since he was very young, so he was more experienced. I was just getting started as a civil engineer when your mother married him; and then for the first two years they were together I was up in the Yukon building the railroad. He knew most of the important people in Chicago, he made a good living. Your father made sure your mother had whatever she wanted and she enjoyed the nightlife. He was a twenty-four hour kind of guy."

"He was much older than my mother."

"Fifteen years older. He was good to her, and he really loved you."

"Why didn't Nanny like him?"

"Your grandmother didn't dislike him, Roy. She was just protective of your mother. She was afraid of some of the people your dad did business with."

"I met a lot of those guys. They were nice to me."

"Why shouldn't they have been? You were a little boy and nobody wanted to get on the wrong side of your father."

"Nanny said they were dangerous."

"Even after your parents were divorced, if my mother had a problem she called your dad."

"Did he always fix it?"

"He loved your mother, so I'm sure he did what he could."

"I remember once when a guy my mother didn't want to see any more kept calling her and coming around, and Nanny said to her, 'If you don't call Rudy to take care of him, I will.'"

"There's a good Cuban place up here, La Teresita. Feel like eating?"

"Sure."

Buck pulled the Caddy into the parking lot of the restaurant. The sun was going down and when they got out of the car a strong breeze was blowing in off the Gulf.

"Just a minute, Roy. I'm going to put up the top in case it rains."

"I'll do it, Unk."

Roy slid into the driver's seat, turned the key in the ignition and pushed the button that controlled the top. Once it was up, he fastened both the driver's and passenger's sides, turned the key off, removed it, got out and handed the key to his uncle. The wind felt good and Roy stood still for a moment watching the sky turn different shades of red. This was one of the best things about Florida, he thought, the sunsets.

His mother had had three husbands since she divorced his father. Roy felt better when he was with his uncle. They went fishing together and Roy worked on construction jobs for him. Buck taught him about navigation, mineralogy, the correct way to build a staircase and the architecture of bridges. He treated Roy differently than other men, not exactly as an equal, but Roy felt that he could trust him, that he could talk to his uncle about almost anything.

"I don't think I'll ever get married," Roy said.

Buck's first wife had divorced him and Roy knew that his uncle's second marriage was on the rocks.

" 'Weak you will find it in one only part, now pierced by love's incurable dart.'"

"What's that?"

"Lines from a sonnet by John Milton. I had to memorize it when I was in high school. Do you remember Rameses Thompson, who used to work for me?"

"The black guy who had a holster for his handgun on the inside of the driver's side door of his pickup truck. Is he still around?"

"No. He killed his common-law wife, Rosita, and her girl-friend."

"His wife had a girlfriend?"

"They were stepsisters, from Panama City. Thompson got caught in Mobile, Alabama, and a cop shot him in his spine. I hear he's alive but can't use his arms or legs."

"He was very strong. He could lift two chairs at the same time holding each one by only one leg."

"Rosita was ugly and lazy, but Thompson was crazy about her."

Another thing Roy liked about the west coast of Florida was that rain was never far away. It started a few minutes after he and his uncle were inside La Teresita.

Shrimpers

Roy and his friend Willy Duda were looking for a summer job. They were both fourteen years old and temporary work that paid decently in Tampa, Florida, in 1961, was hard to find. Tampa was a small southern city then, a fishing and cigar town with a large ethnic Cuban population. Roy's uncle Buck, with whom Roy lived during the summer months, was in the construction business; he would have employed both his nephew and Willy Duda, as he had in better times, but the building trade was slow at the moment so the boys had to look elsewhere to make money. Buck, who had been a lieutenant commander in the navy during the second world war, suggested they sign up to work on a shrimp boat.

"These little boats have small crews," Buck told them, "usually only the captain and two or three helpers. The boats go out for ten days, two weeks, maybe three at most, then bring in their catch, sell it, take a few days off, and go back out again. Come on, I'll take you down to the docks and we'll see if someone needs hands."

Roy and Willy didn't know anything about shrimping but Roy's uncle said the work was pretty simple. It was a cloudless, sunny day, as usual, and Buck talked while he drove.

"You toss out the nets into the shrimp beds, haul 'em in and load 'em in a cooler. It's repetitious, hard work, and there's nothing to do but work on a shrimp boat in the middle of the Gulf of Mexico. You sleep on deck."

"It's hot as Hades out there," said Willy. "We'll fry like catfish being on the water twenty-four hours a day."

"You boys can hold up for a fortnight," Buck said. "It'll be a good experience."

The shrimp boats docked under the Simon Bolívar Bridge.

Roy's uncle drove his 1957 Cadillac Eldorado convertible right onto the wharf, parked, and he and the two boys got out. Most of the boats were empty or their captains were asleep under a canopy. Buck, Willy and Roy walked along the wooden planks until they came upon a man in a boat mending nets. The boat's name, painted on the stern in faded black letters, was *Lazarus*.

"Ahoy there, captain," Roy's uncle called out to him. "I've got a couple of strong young men here looking for work. Are you hiring?"

The man had a lobster-red face with a six day beard and a dead cigar sticking out of the right side of his mouth. Roy thought he looked to be about forty years old, maybe older. The man's left eye was closed and did not open during the time he spoke to them. He was wearing a sleeveless green sweatshirt inside out that had brown and black stains on it.

"These boys are young but they're able bodied," Buck shouted.

The man took a quick look up at Roy and Willy then returned his attention to the nets.

"Too young," he said. "A shrimp boat ain't no place for clean cut kids. Only lowlifes work shrimpers. Alkys, criminals, cutthroats, perverts. Nothin' to do but haul, mend, swill bad hooch like the devil's slaves and bugger each other."

"Maybe this isn't such a good idea, Unk," said Roy.

Two weeks later he and Willy were watching the TV news when a picture of the shrimp boat captain Buck had talked to came on the screen followed by a female reporter standing on the dock under the Bolívar Bridge.

"Albert Matanzas," said the reporter, "captain and owner of a shrimp boat out of Tampa, was discovered by the Coast Guard drifting in Tampa Bay close to death tied with a rope to the wheel of his boat with stab wounds in his left arm and shoulder and a bullet wound in his right leg. Two men were lying dead from gunshots on the deck. According to a statement Captain Matanzas gave to the Coast Guard, a third man was lost overboard in the Gulf after being shot by one of the dead men. It has not yet been determined what caused the dispute among the men. Matanzas remains in critical condition in Tampa General Hospital."

"Let's not ask your uncle if he has any more ideas," said Willy.

Learning the Game

"Hey, kid, what you think? We take this car, sell it, make big money."

Roy was waiting for his mother in her Buick Roadmaster convertible while she was inside her boyfriend Irwin's building on Clinton Street. Roy was six years old. It was mid-July but the late morning air was still cool and the car's top was up. His mother had said she'd be back in a couple of minutes, just long enough for her to pick up a few things from Irwin. His company manufactured women's undergarments: slips, panties, girdles, brassieres and hosiery. He owned a factory in Jackson, Mississippi, where the goods were made, and the building on Clinton Street in Chicago, where the design and shipping departments were located.

The small, brown man peered into the car. He had thick eyebrows and a thin mustache and was wearing a Panama hat.

"We get the money, go to Puerto Rico. I am from there, have many friends. We get the money, we are rico there, muy rico."

Roy's mother had left her keys dangling from the ignition. Roy, who was in the back seat, saw them and crawled into the front seat and took out the keys. Irwin's building was on the south side, neighbored by factories and meatpacking plants, all brown and gray brick buildings.

"What you say, chico? We go, huh?"

"No," Roy said. "This is my mother's car, she needs it."

"She rich. She get a new one."

"My father will shoot you."

Roy's mother came out of Irwin's building carrying two bags. The small, brown man walked away.

"It took a little longer than I thought it would, Roy. Were you worried?"

"No, Mom."

She put the bags on the back seat.

"You stay up front with me," she said.

"Did you see that little guy in the straw hat?"

His mother slid in behind the steering wheel.

'Where are my keys?"

Roy handed them to her.

"They were in the ignition. I took them out."

She adjusted the rear view mirror, then started the engine.

"What little guy, Roy?"

"A Puerto Rican man. He wanted me to steal the car with him."

"Don't be silly. He would have to be crazy to steal a car with a child in it."

"I told him Dad would shoot him if he did."

"You have such an imagination."

Roy's mother started driving.

"What if I told you that I'm thinking of marrying Irwin? After my divorce from your father is final, of course."

"He's too short for you, Mom."

"He is short, but he's very nice to me, and to you, too."

"Where are we going now?"

"I have to make one more quick stop, and then we can have lunch. Would you like to go to the Edgewater?"

"Have you ever been to Puerto Rico?"

"Yes, twice. Once with your father, and once with Johnny Salvavidas. Remember him, Roy? You were on his boat."

"Did Irwin ask you to marry him?"

"Not yet."

"Maybe he won't."

Roy's mother was a good driver. He always felt safe in the car with her. She drove for several blocks before Roy saw that she was crying.

"What's wrong, Mom? Are you upset?"

"Not really, Roy. Maybe you're right. Maybe Irwin doesn't want to get married."

"You could get anyone to marry you. You're beautiful and smart."

"And I have a good sense of humor. Don't I, Roy? We laugh a lot, don't we?"

"Yes, Mom. You're really funny."

"Hand me my dark glasses. They're in the glove compartment."

She put the glasses on.

"Did you stop crying?"

"Don't worry, Roy. I'm fine now."

They were driving next to the lake. The water was calm and many sailboats were out.

"What if I had been a girl?" Roy asked. "I mean, if you had a daughter instead of a son."

"What are you talking about?"

"Would you act different with her than you do with me?"

"What a strange question. I don't know, probably. Why did you ask me that?"

Roy watched the sailboats struggle to catch some wind. He didn't feel like talking to his mother any more.

The Fifth Angel

Roy fell asleep while he was watching a movie on TV about a twelve year old boy who's living in an isolated mountain cabin with his parents. His father is a failed writer, a novelist, and he's sickly; he should be living in a better climate, not in a snowbound redoubt with a wife who doesn't love him and a child who is not really his own. The boy's real father is the sick man's brother who the boy thinks is his uncle, a bank robber who shows up at the mountain retreat during a blizzard with a bullet wound in one leg, accompanied by two cohorts, a third having been captured during the getaway wherein two cops were killed. The bank robber is the boy's mother's old boyfriend; his brother married her to give the boy a home and a family. She's still in love with the bad brother, who intends to escape the manhunt by hiking over a supposedly impassable mountain trail. There's also a bleach blonde floozy, a warbler who can't carry a tune, who's hung up on the bank robber, as well as a handyman who lusts after the boy's mother and begs her to let him take her away from the invalid novelist. The boy is the hero, the only one who can lead the criminals over the dangerous pass.

Roy woke up just as the movie was ending. He was ten, two years younger than the intrepid boy, and he wondered if, given a similar circumstance, he would behave as bravely. His own mother had married her third husband a few months before, but Roy knew it wouldn't last. They were fighting all the time and Roy did not want to continue living with them. He loved his mother but she was constantly on the verge of a nervous breakdown; Roy had overheard her talking on the telephone to his grandmother telling her she needed to be hospitalized or sent to a sanitarium, somewhere she could rest. Otherwise, his mother said, something terrible might happen. Roy figured this meant one of three things: that she would kill herself or her husband, or that her husband would kill her.

Roy didn't care about his stepfather. The best solution, Roy thought, would be for him to go away, to admit the marriage had been a mistake and leave Roy and his mother alone. It was a week before Christmas and snow was falling. Roy put on his parka and galoshes and went out the back door. He decided that if his mother and her husband did not separate, he would be the one to go. It was five o'clock in the afternoon and there was no light left in the sky. Roy walked into the alley behind his house. He was standing still, letting the snow cover him, when he heard shots, four of them in rapid succession.

Teddy Anderson, a nephew of Roy's neighbors Sven and Inga Anderson, came into the alley from behind the Andersons' garage holding a gun, an automatic. Teddy saw Roy and waved to him with his hand holding the gun. Teddy was twenty years old, he had always been nice to Roy, but Roy knew that Teddy was often in trouble with the law and that his uncle and aunt were trying to straighten him out. Teddy fired a shot into a garbage can behind Johnny Murphy's house, then he fell down and stayed there. Roy went over to him and saw that in his other hand Teddy was holding a bottle of brandy. He had passed out. Roy took both the gun and the bottle out of Teddy's hands and put them on the ground just inside the passageway next to the Andersons' garage, then he went back and dragged Teddy by his left leg out of the middle of the alley and propped him up against the garage door, just in case a car came through and the driver couldn't see Teddy lying in the snow.

When he'd heard the shots, Roy thought they could possibly have come from inside his house. If his mother was dead, since his father had died two years before, a court would probably order him to live with his grandmother, which he did not want to do.

In this circumstance he would just run away, get out of Chicago, hop a freight train or hitchhike west, to California or Arizona, somewhere warm, like the writer in the movie should have done.

He looked at Teddy Anderson leaned against the garage door, sound asleep. Roy was surprised nobody had come into the alley after hearing the shots. He did not feel guilty about being disappointed that neither his mother nor his stepfather had been murdered. Roy walked back into the passageway, picked up the automatic and put it into his coat pocket. He would hide the gun somewhere in his room until he really needed to use it.

A Long Day's Night in the Naked City (Take Two)

Roy's father had a friend in Cicero, Illinois, named Momo Giocoforza whom Roy visited once in a while when he was in high school. He died a few years later but in those days Momo hung out at the Villa Schioppo, a restaurant on Cermak Road next to the Western Electric Company plant. Momo was part owner of Hawthorne Racetrack, which was on the boundary between Cicero and Stickney. Roy could usually find him in a back booth of the Villa talking to men who always looked like they were in a hurry. Momo, on the other hand, not only never seemed to be in a hurry, but he hardly moved except to put a fork or glass to his mouth. Momo was a fat man, close to three hundred pounds, with very small hands, fingers no bigger than a ten year old child's. He rarely shook hands. Momo always seemed glad to see Roy and have plenty of time to talk with him. He insisted that Roy eat something and would order food for both of them. Roy guessed that Momo never stopped eating.

From what little Momo shared with him about his relationship with Roy's father, Roy gathered that they had done business together during and after Prohibition, and he never asked Momo for details. Once afternoon when Roy and Momo were having linguini with clam sauce and discussing the vicissitudes of the Chicago Blackhawks, of whom Momo was an avid follower, a short, wiry guy entered the Villa Schioppo and came over to their table and held out to Momo a white envelope.

"It's all there," the man said. "I'm t'rough wid it."

Momo did not reach for the envelope so the man put it down on the table.

"Siddown," said Momo. "Have some linguini."

"Thanks, Mr. Giocoforza, but I can't. I got my cab outside. I'm workin'."

The man shifted his weight from foot to foot and looked nervously around the restaurant. He was about thirty-five years old, five-nine or ten, ordinary features. His eyes were so small Roy could not tell what color they were.

"So we're up to date now, right?" he said.

Momo barely nodded and said, "If you say so, Brian. I'm always here for you."

'No offense, Mr. Giocoforza, but I hope to Mother Mary I won't."

The man was jumpy, like he badly needed to take a piss.

"I'm goin'. Thanks a million, Mr. Giocoforza."

The man left and Momo picked up the envelope and slid it inside his coat pocket.

"Funny guy," Momo said to Roy. "He was a cop. He's moonlightin' one night, guardin' some buildin's onna Near North Side, and almost gets his eye shot out. Some fancy broad, a white girl, she's stoppin' cars—Mercedes, Jags, Cadillacs, expensive models—and tellin' the drivers she's got a flat tire or somethin'. As a driver's about to give her a lift, opens a door, a black guy dressed like a bum comes up behind her and drags her into an alley. Most drivers take off, but one hero gets out, chases the mugger.

"Now the broad's a real doll, dressed to the nines, and the hero's gonna save her, right? Thinkin' what she'll give in return. The black guy drops the woman when he sees the hero comin' to help her. The driver comforts the broad, takes her into his car, asks her where she wants to go. She pulls a pistol out of her purse, puts it to the hero's head, and the black guy jumps into the back seat, also wid a gun, tells the hero to drive. They go to his house or apartment, which they clean out the jewels and cash. Primo scam. Worked thirty-two times inna row until my pal here, the cop who's moonlightin' in order to save money for his weddin', spots the pair in the act.

"The cop attempts to pull the black guy out of this Mercedes, doesn't figure he an' the broad are workin' together, an' she plugs Brian point blank in the skull. Brian's lyin' onna sidewalk next to the car and the bum tumbles out right on toppa him. Brian's bleedin' all over but takes out his own piece and shoots the black guy, then passes out. When he wakes up, Brian's inna hospital wid his eye bandaged. He's barely alive an' doctors tell him maybe he won't lose the eye. The black bum's dead, the broad got away clean.

"While Brian's inna hospital, his girl never comes to see him. She thinks he's gonna die. He's already given her ten, fourteen thousand for the weddin'. She's why he was workin' a second job inna first place, right? So while he's inna hospital fightin' to recover, she runs off wid another joker. By the time Brian's on the street again he's in deep shit. The police department insurance policy won't cover him 'cause he was off duty workin' for a private security firm, and they don't cover part-timers. So he comes to me, knows a guy knows me. Brian's suin' the insurance company, the owner of the buildin' he was guardin' that night, the police department, everybody he can think of, payin' some ambulance chaser to do it. On toppa that he's afraid to go see the girl threw him over 'cause he'd put six inna her. Now he's pushin' a hack tryna get back on his feet. I give him a good deal, plenya time to pay me back, right? Why not? Your dad, he helped out plenya guys."

The Religious Experience

"I was in Brazil, with Antonio. When we flew into Rio the plane passed over the big statue of Christ on top of Corcovado and for the entire time I was there I couldn't get that out of my head. The statue, I mean, the way it commanded everything below, in every direction. When I had an orgasm the image of Jesus on the mountaintop was in my mind, like I was coming with Him, not Antonio."

"How old were you?"

"Twenty-five. Rudy and I were separated and when Antonio invited me to go with him to Brazil, I just said yes, without thinking. I left Roy with my mother in Miami and we flew from there."

"And that was the first time?"

"Uh huh, and it didn't happen again—not with Antonio, anyway. I only saw him two or three times after we got back to Chicago."

Roy's mother and her friend Kay were standing in the lobby of the Oriental Theater. Kay was smoking a cigarette. Her husband, Harvey, and Kitty's son, Roy, who was eight years old, were inside the theater watching the last few minutes of *The Proud Ones*, a western starring Robert Ryan as a sheriff in a Kansas town who's going blind.

"Do you think if I went to Brazil I could have an orgasm with Harvey?"

The two women laughed and Kitty said, "Maybe you should go with Antonio."

"Is he my type?"

"He looks like Chico, the Mexican gunfighter in the movie, only taller. But Antonio was only an instrument of the Son of

God."

"You should do a commercial for the Catholic Church, Kitty, standing in a mink coat, saying, 'Jesus made me come.' Or, 'I came for Christ.'"

"I'm sure the nuns believe it when they masturbate."

"I thought they weren't allowed to."

People began coming out of the theater.

"Mom, you missed the best part. The sheriff can't see but he uses his hearing to figure out where the bad guy is and shoots him down, anyway."

Kay's husband lit a cigarette and watched the crowd leaving.

"See anything you like?" Kay asked.

"The movie was okay. The kid liked it."

"I mean the women in the lobby."

"Lay off, Kay."

"Kitty was just telling me about the time she went to Brazil."

"I remember when you went there, Mom. You brought me back a little statue of Jesus Christ standing on the top of a mountain."

"Did you have fun there, Kitty?" Harvey asked.

"She certainly did," said Kay. "She even had a religious experience."

"What kind of religious experience?"

"Kay's just being silly."

"No, really. She had an epiphany."

"What's that?" asked Roy.

"It's when you see God," said Kay, "or you feel Him inside you."

"Do you have to be a Catholic to have one?"

"No, Roy," Kay said, "but it probably helps."

The Familiar Face of Darkness

"You're a godsend, Rudy. Thanks for helping me out. I won't forget it."

"I'm the one doesn't forget."

"I know, I know. You didn't have to do this."

Rudy turned around and entered Lake Shore Liquors. His partners in the store, Earl LaDuke, who was Rudy's uncle, and Dick Mooney, were waiting for him. Moe Herman, to whom Rudy had just handed a double sawbuck, went on his way. Rudy never loaned money to anyone; either he gave someone what he or she needed or refused without providing an explanation. All anyone in dire straits wants to hear is yes or no. If he was paid back, so much the better, but there never was a reason to count on it.

Earl and Dick were seated at a card table in the basement. Rudy's uncle was smoking a cigar with his eyes closed, and Dick was scrutinizing the previous day's results at Sportsman's Park. Rudy sat down and poured himself a finger of Jameson's from a bottle on the table.

"Good afternoon, Rudy. How's Kitty?"

"Fine, Earl."

"You'll tell her I asked."

Dick put down the paper and took off his glasses.

"Nothing yet," he said.

"If it's not here by tonight, I'll call. Not before then."

Earl LaDuke opened his eyes and stood up. He was a big, ungainly man. Rudy wondered how he could have outrun the hussars in the old country when his name was Sackgasse.

"I'll be home. Your Aunt Sofia would like it if you and Kitty came for dinner."

"We will, Uncle Earl. Not tonight, but soon. Kiss her for me."

"I can still kiss her for myself, I want to. I can still do that."

Earl walked slowly up the stairs.

"You're not worried?" Dick asked.

"The roads are icy."

"Emily wants to leave Chicago. Her sister's in Atlanta."

"Earl and I can cover your share."

Dick was thirty-two, ten years younger than Rudy and twenty-seven years younger than Earl LaDuke. He had bought into Lake Shore five years before and his third was worth twice as much now.

"I could be your man down there."

"Atlanta belongs to Lozano."

There were footsteps on the stairs. The two men looked up and saw Lola Wilson, a dancer from the Club Alabam next door, coming down. She was wearing a fur coat over her rehearsal costume. When the front of the coat swung to either side, they could see her legs. Lola descended cautiously, placing her high heels delicately on each of the rickety wooden steps. She came over and stood behind the chair on which Rudy's uncle had been sitting.

Dick got up, said, "Hello, Lola. See you later, Rudy," and started up the stairs.

Lola sat down, took out a crumpled pack of Camels and a book of matches from a pocket of her coat, then changed her mind and replaced them in the pocket.

"You don't like it that I smoke. Sometimes I forget. Kitty doesn't smoke, does she?"

"No, she doesn't."

"I saw Roy down here with her the other day. He's getting big. He must be about ten now."

"Eight. What can I do for you, Lola?"

Lola had a sharply upturned nose, rose-colored full lips, dark brown swampy eyes and blonde hair translucent at the ends. Her face fascinated most men and women, especially women, very

few of whom were gifted with such dramatically contrasting features that so exquisitely combined. Lola's teeth were crooked and
tobacco-stained; they embarrassed her so when she smiled she
determinedly pressed her lips together. Before he married Kitty,
when Lola was eighteen, fresh off the bus from West Virginia,
Rudy had offered to pay to have her teeth straightened but she
had demurred, and then it was too late.

"You'll hate me," she said.

"What is it?"

"I picked up a dose. Can you give me a shot?"

Rudy got up, walked to the rear of the room, opened the door
of a small refrigerator and took out a little round bottle. He
opened a drawer in a cabinet next to the refrigerator and removed
a hypodermic syringe and a thin packet containing needles, one
of which he shook out and fitted to the syringe, then drew fluid
from the bottle before replacing it in the refrigerator. Rudy picked
up a brown bottle, took a cotton ball from a box and walked back
to the table.

Lola stood, turned her back to Rudy and held one side of the
fur coat away from her body. Rudy sat down, daubed the exposed
part of her left buttock with the piece of cotton he'd soaked in
alcohol from the brown bottle, then inserted the needle into the
sanitized spot and injected the penicillin, after which he again
brushed the spot with the cotton ball before standing up and
walking back to a sink next to the cabinet and placing the items
he had employed into it.

"How long were you in medical school, Rudy?"

"A year and a half. I've told you this. When they rolled the
cadaver in, they rolled me out. After that I transferred to pharmacy school."

"Do I need a band-aid?"

"You'll be all right."

Lola sat down again, as did Rudy. She balanced herself carefully on her right buttock.

"Really, I don't know what I'd do if you weren't in my life."

"I thought you were going to marry Manny Shore."

"I can't go on dancing forever. I figured at least it would get me off my feet, but no. I realized it wasn't going to work. I haven't seen him in months. Weeks, anyway. Rudy, do you think I'm a trollop?"

"Where did you learn that word?"

"Monique said somebody called her one and I asked her what it meant. She didn't know exactly, so I looked it up. Did you think I was a trollop when we met?"

"You're not Monique. You have to take better care of yourself." Lola stood up.

"I have to get back to rehearsal."

She leaned down and kissed Rudy behind his right ear.

"Am I still pretty? Not as pretty as your wife, I know, but tell me."

Rudy stood and looked into her murky eyes.

"Yes," he said, "you are."

Lola turned and walked up the stairs. When she reached the top step she paused and said, loud enough for him to hear, "I'm twenty-nine."

Las Vegas, 1949

"Mr. Randolph is very nice, Rudy. He offered to let us use his house in the Bahamas any time we want."

"It's all right for you to be polite to Mr. Ruggiano, Kitty. Or anyone else, for that matter. Just keep your distance."

"Who's Mr. Ruggiano?"

"Ralph Randolph is the name he uses when it suits his purpose."

"What about Marshall Gottlieb?"

"What about him?"

"Is that his real name?"

"It was something else when his family came from Poland or Russia."

"Like yours."

Kitty stood up and put on her candy-striped terrycloth robe.

"I'm going to the room to call my mother and talk to Roy," she said, and walked around the pool into the hotel.

Kitty and Rudy were staying at El Rancho Vegas. Their son, Roy, who was almost three years old, was being looked after by his grandmother in Chicago. Luchino Benedetti came over and sat down in the chair Kitty had been using.

"Your wife is a real doll, Rudy," he said. "Everybody likes her, even the other wives."

"Thanks, Lucky. She's having a swell time. We both appreciate your hospitality. You keep a good house."

"Kitty got a lot to show, but she don't show it. She has class."

"She was raised right."

"Leave it to the sisters. How is your boy?"

"Growing up fast. He's back home with Kitty's mother."

"My Rocco joined the Air Force. He wants to be a pilot."

"I heard. I'm sure he'll do well."

"So, our thing with the Diamond brothers."

"All I know is, the goods are always on time, and they're always what Sam and Moses say they are."

"They move."

"If they didn't, Rugs would know."

"Did you hear about Sam's wife?"

"Dolores. A nice woman."

"She run off with Solly Banks's son, Victor."

"Run off? Where to?"

"New York. Sam's there now, it's why he ain't here. Rugs is afraid this will interfere with our business, and that can't happen."

"I'll talk to Moses."

"Do it now."

Kitty came back and Lucky jumped up.

"Hello, Kitty. I was just telling Rudy what a hit you are with everyone."

"Thank you, Lucky," she said, and sat down in the chair.

"See you at dinner," said Lucky, and walked away.

"Did you speak to Roy?"

"Yes, he's fine. The janitor found a dead rat in his fire truck and showed it to him. The tail was as long as Roy's arm."

"Did they bury the rat in the yard?"

"No, the janitor burned it in the furnace. Roy was about to take his nap. He told me to kiss his daddy for him."

Kitty kissed her husband on the cheek.

"And Rose?"

"I'm worried about her heart condition. She doesn't have the energy she used to."

"Has she seen Dr. Martell?"

"Unless he's operating, he comes to the house every evening to have a glass of wine."

"Your mother will be all right. Martell would leave his wife for her in a minute if Rose gave him some encouragement."

"My mother says he has a tax problem. He could lose his hospital."

Marshall Gottlieb and his wife, Sarah, came over.

"Come with me, Kitty," Sarah said. "We're going to have our fingernails and toenails done."

Kitty got up and went with her. Marshall sat down.

"Lucky told you?"

"About Sam Diamond? I told him I'll talk to Moses."

"Moses just called Mr. Randolph two minutes ago. His brother shot and killed Dolores and Victor Banks in their room at the Waldorf, then he phoned Moses to tell him what he'd done and that he was going to kill himself. Next thing, Moses hears a shot."

Arlene Silverman, Art and Edith Silverman's seventeen year old daughter, dove into the pool. Rudy and Marshall Gottlieb watched her swim.

"Arlene's a lovely girl, isn't she?" said Marshall. "How is it she has gorgeous blonde hair when neither of her parents do?"

"She's adopted," said Rudy.

"Oh yeah? I didn't know."

Arlene Silverman swam the length of the pool twice before Ralph Randolph helped her climb out.

"Lotsa times," Marshall said, "after you get what you want, you don't want it. That ever happen to you?"

In Dreams

Roy's grandfather was watching a baseball game on television when his grandson came home from school.

"What's on, Pops?" Roy asked.

"The White Sox are playing the Senators. Two outs in the ninth. Billy Pierce is pitching a perfect game."

Roy sat down on the floor next to his grandfather's chair. Ed Fitzgerald, Washington's catcher, was the last chance for them to break up the no-hitter.

"Fitzgerald bats left-handed," Roy said. "Since Pierce is a southpaw, shouldn't he just throw breaking balls?"

"He might hang one, Roy, but Pierce is crafty. He'd probably do better to start him off with a fastball high and outside, then go to the curve."

Fitzgerald lined one off the right field fence for a double.

"Pierce went with the fast ball, Pops."

"It caught too much of the plate. He should have gone away with it."

The game ended when the next batter made an out. Roy's grandfather turned off the set.

"Too bad," said Roy. "A pitcher doesn't get many chances to throw a perfect game."

"There have only been about twenty perfect games in the history of major league baseball. How was school, boy? What grade are you in now?"

"Fourth. I don't know, Pops. I think I learn more important things talking to you and some other people. I like it when you tell me stories about your life."

"Don't ignore dreams, Roy. You can learn a lot from them."

"I don't always remember what I dream."

"Write them down as soon as you wake up, even if you're groggy and only half awake. For me, the most interesting dreams are the ones in which people who have died appear."

"Like who?"

"I recently had a dream about a very old, close friend of mine who died about twelve or thirteen years ago, before you were born. His name was Warren Winslow. In my dream someone told me he heard that Warren was living in Chicago in the house of a person I didn't know. He gave me the address so I went there and found Warren, looking much as he had when both of us were younger. He was calm, sitting on a couch with a blanket across his legs. I asked him how this could have happened, how he had recovered, why he hadn't told me and let me know he was here in Chicago."

"What did he say?"

"He said that he had died but come back to life and was rather embarrassed to have done so. He asked the doctors in the hospital where he had been treated not to tell anyone, and he left everything he owned and came to stay with a fellow he did not know very well who was willing to keep his existence and whereabouts a secret."

"Why?"

"Warren himself was not entirely certain other than he felt satisfied that at the time of his death he was not displeased by the state of his affairs and his relations with those closest to him. I told him I had missed him and Warren said he had always valued our friendship highly. Now that I knew where he was, Warren told me, I could visit him if I chose to, but warned me that he didn't know how much longer he would be there. It wasn't so much that his attitude was one of indifference—at least I didn't take it that way—so much as his having moved on from the past."

"What did you do?"

"I left the house, then I woke up. This is the way the dead visit us, Roy, in dreams. It's the only way we can be with them again."

"That's pretty spooky, Pops. See, this is the kind of stuff they don't teach us in school."

Lucky

"You sure the coal man's comin' this mornin'?"

"He usually comes around nine or ten every other Saturday during the winter. Depends on how many deliveries he has."

Roy and his friend Johnny Murphy were standing in the alley behind Roy's house waiting for the coal truck to arrive. Two feet of snow had fallen during the night, then the temperature had dropped, so the ground was covered by a frozen crust. The boys, who were both eight years old, liked to slide down the coal chute into the pile in front of the furnace in the basement. The best time to do it was on delivery day, when the pile was highest.

"I'm freezin'," said Johnny. "I shoulda worn two pairs of socks."

It was almost ten o'clock when they heard and then saw the big red Peterson Coal truck turn into the alley. The truck crunched ahead and skidded to a stop in front of Roy's garage. Alfonso Rivero, the driver, climbed down from the cab and tromped over to where Roy and Johnny were standing. Alfonso was a short, stocky man in his mid-forties. He was wearing a black knit hat pulled down over his ears, a navy blue tanker jacket and steel-toed work boots. An unfiltered Camel hung from his lips.

"You waiting go slide?" he said.

"Hi, Alfonso," said Roy. "Yeah, I thought you might be late because of the snow and ice."

"We been out here since nine," said Johnny Murphy.

"I hate the nieve," Alfonso said. "In Mexico, no hay snow and ices, except in los montañas."

"Why do you live in Chicago?" asked Johnny.

"We don't have no work in Mexico, also."

Roy and Johnny watched Alfonso take down a wheelbarrow mounted on the back of the truck and set it on the ground, then open the two rear doors and hoist himself inside. He pulled a thick glove from each of his side pockets, put them on, picked a shovel out of the coal pile and began shoveling it down into the wheelbarrow. When the barrow was full, he leaned down holding the shovel.

"Take la pala, chico," he said to Roy.

Roy took it and the deliveryman jumped down. Roy handed Alfonso the shovel. He stuck it into the pile of coal in the wheelbarrow and wheeled it through the passageway leading to Roy's backyard. The boys followed Alfonso, who stopped in front of a pale blue door at the rear of the building, undid the latch on the door and swung it open. He shoveled most of the contents of the wheelbarrow down the chute and dumped in the rest, then headed back to the truck for another load.

After six trips back and forth, Alfonso said to the boys, "Es todo, muchachos. Okay now for deslizamiento."

"Muchas gracias, Alfonso," said Roy.

"Yeah, mucho," said Johnny.

Roy went first, sliding all the way down and landing in front of the furnace. As soon as he got up, Johnny did the same. They went out the basement door and ran up the steps into the yard.

"Once more, Alfonso!" Roy shouted.

"Si, uno mas," said the deliveryman, and lit up a fresh cigarette.

After the boys emerged from the basement, Alfonso closed the door to the chute, latched it, and pushed the wheelbarrow back into the alley. Roy and Johnny trailed him and watched as he tossed in his shovel, closed the doors and re-attached the wheelbarrow.

"See you dos semanas, amigos," Alfonso said, then climbed into the cab, started the engine and drove slowly away down the alley.

Roy and Johnny's faces were covered with coal dust, as were their hands and clothes. They picked up clean snow, washed their faces and hands with it and rubbed it on their coats and pants.

"I wouldn't mind havin' Alfonso's job," said Johnny. "You get to drive a big truck and stand around smokin' cigarettes in people's yards."

"Alfonso's a good guy," said Roy. "He probably lets any kid who wants to slide down the piles."

"It don't seem so cold now," Johnny said. "You hear about Cunningham's mother?"

"No. What about her?"

"She died yesterday."

"Tommy didn't say anything about her being sick."

"My father says she committed suicide. It's a mortal sin, so now she can't get into heaven."

"Maybe it was an accident."

"My father says she ate a bullet."

"What's that mean?"

"Shot herself in the mouth. She's probably already in hell."

"Don't say that to Cunningham."

"My mother said she thinks Tommy's father pulled the trigger."

"Why would he murder her?"

"When husbands and wives are arguin' they're always sayin' how they're gonna kill each other. I hate hearin' it when my parents fight. You're lucky you only got a mother."

Danger in the Air

Roy liked to fly with his mother. Most of the time they drove between Key West or Miami, Florida, and Chicago, the places in which they lived; but if they needed to be somewhere in a hurry, they took an airplane. Roy's mother always dressed well when they flew, and she made sure Roy did, too.

"You never know who you might meet in an airport or on a plane," she told him, "so it's important to look your best."

"Even a little boy?"

"Of course, Roy. You're with me. I'm so proud of you. You're a great traveler."

"Thanks, Mom. I'm proud of you, too."

One afternoon when they were flying from Miami to New Orleans to see Roy's mother's boyfriend Johnny Salvavidas, their plane ran into a big storm and lightning hit both wings. The plane tilted to the right, then to the left, like Walcott taking a combination from Marciano, only the airplane didn't go down.

"We're really getting knocked around, Roy. Better keep your head down in case things start flying out of the overhead compartments."

"I want to look out the window, Mom. I have a book about lightning, remember? The worst thing that can happen is if the fuel tank gets hit, then the plane could explode. Also, lightning can make holes in the wings and pieces of them can fall off. If it strikes the nose, the pilot could lose control and even be blinded. And during thunderstorms ball lightning can enter an airplane and roll down the aisle. That's pretty rare, though, and the fireball burns out fast and leaves a kind of smoky mist in the air. Some scientists even believe ball lightning might come from flying saucers."

"Don't be silly, Roy. There's no such things as flying saucers. That's just in movies and comic books."

When the plane landed at the airport in New Orleans, Johnny Salvavidas was there to meet it. He asked Roy's mother if it had been a good flight.

"It was horrendous," she told him. "We ran into a terrible thunderstorm and there was a lot of turbulence. My stomach is still upset."

"What about it, Roy? Was the storm as bad as your mother says?"

"Lightning hit the wings," Roy said. "We could have gotten knocked out of the sky, but we weren't."

Johnny smiled and said, "That can't happen."

He smoothed back both sides of his hair with his hands. His hair was black and shiny and fit tightly to his scalp like a bathing cap. He took Roy's mother's right arm and they walked together toward the terminal to pick up her suitcases.

The sun was going down and the sky was turning redder. What did Johnny Salvavidas know? There was a kind of lightning that moved across rather than up and down called spider or creepy-crawly lightning that can reverse itself and probably bring down a spaceship. Roy watched his mother and Johnny enter the terminal. He wanted to get back on an airplane.

Child's Play

The two Greek brothers, Nick and Peter, had settled in Jackson, Mississippi, in 1935, three years after they emigrated with their parents from Patnos. Their father, Constantin, had worked in a grocery store for a Jewish family in New York City, where the immigrants had landed; but when the Great Depression cost Constantin his job, rather than join a bread line he used the few dollars he had saved to move his family south, where, he'd been told, it was cheaper to live. The Jewish grocers had a cousin who traveled in a wagon throughout Mississippi peddling household goods who apparently made a decent living, so Constantin informed his wife and sons, ages six and nine, to take only what they could comfortably carry, and they entrained to another, quite different, country.

In Jackson, the state capital, Constantin and his wife, Josefa, found part-time employment as night cleaners in government buildings, then Constantin got a job scrubbing down a diner frequented by local businessmen and politicians. After six months, he was hired on as a waiter, and within a year the owner died. With the assistance of several of the patrons, Constantin bought the diner, which he renamed The Athens Café. Josefa and their sons worked with him and soon The Athens was the most popular restaurant in town. After their parents died, Nick and Peter took over.

During the year or so that Roy's mother had a boyfriend named Boris Klueber, who owned a girdle factory on the outskirts of Jackson, they often accompanied him when he traveled there from his headquarters in Chicago. Roy and his mother always stayed in the Heidelberg Hotel, as did Boris. The Heidelberg was the best hotel in Jackson, located only a few blocks from The Athens Café.

This was in 1955, when Roy was eight years old.

Negroes were not allowed to eat in the diner, but all of the kitchen workers, including the cooks, were black. To get to the toilets, which were accessible only by a steep flight of stairs, customers were required to go through the kitchen. It was in this way that Roy became friendly with the employees. He was friendly, too, of course, with the owners, who enjoyed showing him photographs they took in Greece on their annual vacations. Neither of the brothers ever married, but Roy's mother told him that according to Boris both of the brothers kept Negro mistresses.

"What's a mistress?" Roy asked her.

"Women who aren't married to the men who support them."

"Why don't they marry them?"

"Well, in Mississippi, it's against the law for white and black men and women to marry each other. Don't repeat what I'm telling you, Roy, especially to Nick and Peter. Promise?"

"I promise."

"It's a sensitive issue in the South."

"Can Negroes and whites get married to each other in Chicago?"

"Yes, Roy. Laws are often different in different states. In Mississippi, and some other southern states, a white man can get arrested for dating a black woman; and a black man can be put in prison or even murdered for being in the company of a white woman. I know this doesn't make sense, but that's the way it is. As long as we're here we have to respect their laws."

"What if you went on a date with a Negro man? Would you be arrested and the man murdered or thrown in jail?"

"Let's not talk about this any more, Roy. I shouldn't have told you about Nick and Peter. And don't mention it to Boris. Promise?"

"I already did."

couple of days later, while Roy was cutting through the kitchen of The Athens Café to use the toilet, one of the cooks, Emmanuel, who was taking a cigarette break by the back door, said to him, "How you doin' today, little man? You enjoyin' yourself?"

"Sort of. There's not much for me to do. I don't have anyone to play with."

"I got a boy about your age. His name's John Daniel."

"Can I meet him?"

Emmanuel removed his wallet from one of his back pockets, took out a photograph and handed it to Roy.

"That's John Daniel, that's my son."

"He's white," said Roy, "like me."

"That's on account of his mama is white. He's got her colorin'."

"My mother says white and black people can't get married to each other in Mississippi."

"That's right. John Daniel's mama and I ain't married, not to each other. I don't get to see him except his mama sneak me a walk by."

"There's a Negro boy in Chicago I play with. His name's Henry Cherokee, and he's part Indian."

"Me, too. My grandmama on my daddy's side is half Choctaw."

Roy returned the photo of John Daniel to Emmanuel, which he replaced in his wallet.

"Gotta get back to work," he said, and tossed his cigarette butt into the street.

That evening Roy and his mother were having dinner with Boris in the dining room of the Heidelberg Hotel when Boris whispered to her, "See that waiter there? The one who looks like Duke Ellington."

Roy's mother looked at the waiter, who, like the other waiters, was wearing a tuxedo.

"He's quite handsome," she said.

"He's Mrs. Van Nostrand's back door man."

"Sshh. Don't talk that way around Roy. Why do you have your factory here, Boris? I don't like Jackson."

"Manufacturing's cheap. No unions, no taxes. It would cost me four times as much to have a plant in Chicago like I have here."

Roy watched the waiter Boris had said resembled Duke Ellington as he served an old white man and an old white woman at another table.

"Mom," he said, "the next time we come here, could we bring Henry Cherokee with us?"

The Message

Roy was alone in the hotel room he shared with his mother when the telephone rang. It was ten to four in the morning and Roy was less than half awake, watching *Journey into Fear* on TV. He'd fallen asleep on and off during the movie, and when the telephone rang Roy looked first at the television and saw Orson Welles, wearing a gigantic military overcoat with what looked like dead, furry animals for lapels and a big fur hat littered with snow. The picture was tilted and for a moment Roy thought that he had fallen off the bed, then he realized it was the camera angled for effect.

"Kitty, that you?"

"No. She's not here, I don't think."

"Who's this?"

"Her son."

"She's got a kid? How old are you?"

"Seven. Six and a half, really."

"Your mother didn't tell me she had a kid. How many more kids she have?"

"None."

"What's your name?"

"Roy."

"You sure she's not there?"

"No. Yeah, I'm sure."

"Know where she is?"

"She went out with some friends, around ten o'clock."

"It's almost four now. She was supposed to meet me at one. Said she maybe would, anyway."

"Do you want to leave a message?"

"Yeah, okay. Dimitri, tell her. If she comes in, I'll be in the bar at the Roosevelt Hotel until five."

"All right."

"She leaves you alone this time of night, in the room?"

Orson Welles was growling at someone, a smaller man who kept his head down. The picture was lopsided, as if the camera had been kicked over and it was lying on the floor but still rolling.

"Kid, she leaves you by yourself?"

"I'm okay."

"She's kind of a kook, your mother. You know that?"

Orson Welles did not take off his coat even though he was in an office.

"Go back to sleep, kid. Sorry I woke you up."

Roy hung up the phone. He and his mother had been in this city for a week and Roy was anxious to return to Key West, where they lived in a hotel located at the confluence of the Gulf of Mexico and the Atlantic Ocean. A beautiful, dark-haired woman was on the screen now but she kept turning her head away from the camera so Roy could not see all of her face. She looked Cuban, or Indian.

When Roy woke up again, the television was off and his mother was asleep in the other bed. He looked at the clock: it was just past ten. The heavy drapes were drawn so even though the sun was up the light in the room was very dim. Roy's mother always hung the Do Not Disturb sign on the outside doorknob. She was wearing a blindfold. Roy lay listening to her breathe, whistling a little through her nose as she exhaled.

What was the name of the man who had called? When she woke up, Roy would tell his mother that a general or a colonel with a strange accent had called from a foreign country. Roy could not remember his name, only that the man had said it was snowing where he was calling from.

River Woods

Roy's father drove as if his powder blue Cadillac were the only car on the road. In the fall of 1953 there wasn't much traffic between Chicago and the western suburb of River Woods, where they were headed. It was mid-October, Roy's favorite time of the year. Sunlight slithered through the trees and the air was comfortably cool; in a month they would have to keep the car windows closed and the heater on.

"Who are we going to see, Dad?"

"A business associate of mine, Jocko Mosca. He has a classy layout in River Woods."

"Does he have kids?"

"Two sons, much older than you. They don't live here."

"Did you tell him tomorrow's my birthday?"

"You can tell him."

"Jocko is a funny name."

"It's short for Giacomo. He was born in Sicily, which is an island off the heel of Italy."

The houses they passed were set far back from the road. Most of them had long, winding driveways leading to buildings you couldn't see from a car, and some were behind iron fences with spikes on the top. Jocko Mosca's house had an iron fence in front of it but the gates were open. Roy's father drove in and stopped next to the house. Just as he and Roy got out of the car, a man came out and shook hands with Roy's father.

"Rudy, good to see you," he said. "This is your boy?"

"Hello, Lou. Roy, this is Lou Napoli. He works with Mr. Mosca."

Lou Napoli was not a large man but he had very big hands. He shook hands with Roy and smiled at him.

"You're fortunate to have a son, Rudy. And one handsome enough to be Italian. Quanti anni ha?" he asked Roy.

"He wants to know how old you are," said Roy's father.

"I'll be seven tomorrow."

"A lucky number," said Lou. "Let's go in."

They descended three steps into an enormous living room. The ceiling was very high with little sparkling lights in it. The walls were made of stone. There were five or six couches, several armchairs, lots of tables and lamps and a stone fireplace that ran nearly the entire length of one wall. A swimming pool snaked under a glass door into the rear of the room.

"I've never seen a swimming pool in a living room before," Roy said.

"This is only part of the pool," said Lou. "The rest of it is outside, on the other side of that glass door. It's heated. You want to take a dip?"

"I didn't bring a bathing suit."

"If you want to go in, let me know and we'll find you one. I'll tell Jocko you're here."

"Pretty swank, isn't it, son?"

"Jocko must be really rich."

"Call him Mr. Mosca. Yes, he's done well for himself. When his family came to America, from Sicily, they had nothing."

"Your parents didn't have anything when they came to America, either, Dad, and you were ten years old. How old was Mr. Mosca when his family came?"

"Probably about the same age I was. None of that matters now. We're Americans."

"Jocko is here," announced Lou Napoli.

Jocko Mosca was wearing a dark gray suit, a light blue shirt and a black tie. He was tall, had a big nose and full head of silver hair. He entered the room from a door behind a bend in the pool. Roy noticed that there was no knob on the door. Roy's father waited for Jocko to walk over to him. They embraced, then shook hands, each man using both of their hands.

"It's good of you to come all the way out here, Rudy," Jocko said.

"We enjoyed the drive. This is my son, Roy."

Jocko Mosca leaned down as he shook hands with Roy. His nose was covered with small holes and tiny red bumps.

"Benvenuto, Roy. That means welcome in Italian."

"I know. Angelo taught me some Italian words."

"Who is Angelo?"

"He's an organ grinder. He has a monkey named Dopo. They come into my dad's store and have coffee and Dopo dunks dough-nuts in the cup with me. Dopo means after."

Jocko stood up straight and said, "Rudy, you didn't tell me your boy's a paesan'."

They laughed, then Jocko said to Roy, "I hope you'll be com-fortable in here while your father and I go into another room to talk."

"I'll be okay, Mr. Mosca."

"Call me Jocko. We're paesanos, after all."

The two men left the room and Roy sat down on a couch. A pretty young woman with long black hair, wearing a maid's uni-form, came in carrying a tray, which she set down on a low table.

"This is a ham sandwich, sweet pickles and a Coca-Cola for you," she said. "If you need something, press that button on the wall behind you."

Roy felt sleepy, so he lay down and closed his eyes. When he reopened them, Lou Napoli was standing in front of him, holding a cake with eight candles on it.

"Did you have a nice nap, Roy?" he asked.

Jocko Mosca and Roy's father were there, as was the maid.

"He must have been tired from the drive," said Roy's father. "We got up very early today."

Lou passed the cake to the maid, who put it on a table and lit the candles. Lou, the maid, Jocko and Roy's father sang "Happy Birthday", then Lou said, "Make a wish and blow out the candles. The eighth one is for good luck."

Roy silently wished that his father would come back to live with him and his mother. He blew out all of the candles with one try.

Later, while his father was putting what was left of the cake, which the maid had put into a blue box, in the trunk of the Cadillac, Jocko Mosca handed Roy a little white card.

"This is my telephone number, Roy," he said. "If you ever have a problem, or anything you want to talk about, call me. Keep the card in a safe place, keep it for yourself. Don't show it to anyone."

"Can I show it to my dad?"

"He knows the number."

Roy's father started the car. Roy and Jocko shook hands, then Jocko opened the front passenger side door for him.

"Remember, Roy, I'm here for you, even just to talk. I like to talk."

Jocko closed the door and waved. He and Lou Napoli watched as Roy's father navigated the driveway.

"You all right, son? Wasn't it a nice surprise that they had a cake for you?"

"Do you want to know my wish?"

"No. You should keep what you wish for to yourself. Remember that you can't depend only on wishing for something to come true. It will always be up to you to make it happen."

"Always?"

"Always."

The gate in front of one of the houses had a metal sculpture of a fire-breathing dragon's head on it.

"River Woods is a beautiful place, isn't it, Roy? Would you rather live out here or in the city?"

"I don't know, Dad. I like when we're driving and we're not anywhere yet."

"So do I, son. Maybe, now that you're older, we're beginning to think alike."

The History and Proof of the Spots on the Sun

Roy accompanied his friend Frank to see a foreign movie Frank wanted to see at a little theater near The Loop.

"What language is it in?" Roy asked him.

"French. It'll have the translation in English on the bottom of the screen, but the words are only on for a few seconds so most of the time I can't finish reading it."

"I know. My mother likes to see foreign movies. I used to go with her when I was younger."

Both of the boys were thirteen years old. They had been close friends since the age of nine. Frank lived with his mother and two older brothers in a tenement on the same block as Roy and his mother. Frank's mother worked selling vacuum cleaners door to door. She slept in a bed that folded down from a wall in their livingroom, and the three boys shared a room with two beds in it. Roy and his mother lived in a larger apartment that she had inherited from one of her grandfathers. She worked as a receptionist in a hospital. Both Roy and Frank's fathers were dead, Frank's from a heart attack when Frank was seven, and Roy's from cancer when Roy was ten. Roy was an only child, his mother had been married and divorced twice; Frank's mother remained a widow.

Once Roy had heard her say to Frank and his brothers, "Men are like spots on the sun. Who knows what they are or how they got there? A woman can't even be sure they'll still be there the next day."

"But Ma," Frank's oldest brother, Ronnie, who was sixteen, said, "we'll all be men soon."

"I suppose you'll take care of me when I'm old, won't you?" she asked.

"Of course we will," answered Arnie, the middle brother.

"Proof! I don't have any proof!" their mother shouted, then put on a coat, picked up her purse and left the apartment.

The theater was only half full. Roy and Frank were the youngest people there. The movie's title was *Cela ne fait rien* (*It Makes No Difference*). The actors did not do anything much except talk and smoke cigarettes, and at the very end a woman took off her clothes, walked into the ocean and disappeared.

When they were back outside, Roy asked Frank, "Why did you want to see that movie?"

"My brother Ronnie's girlfriend, Rhonda, said her cousin, Lisa, who's studying to be an actress, told her it was smart and sexy."

"The woman who drowned herself kept her back to the camera," Roy said, "so we didn't even get to see her tits. In most of the foreign movies my mother took me to the women always showed their tits."

"Yeah, that was disappointing," said Frank, "and the translation went by so fast I couldn't get it all."

"There was too much talking," Roy said, "but the part where the boy found a gun under his mother's pillow was interesting."

"I wouldn't have put it back," Frank said. "I thought he should have shot her boyfriend when the guy hit her."

"After the guy walked out and she was lying on the floor, did you catch what she said to her son?"

"Yes," said Frank, "the boy asked why he'd hit her and she said, 'Because he loves me.' I would've gone into her bedroom, gotten the gun and run after the guy and plugged him. All she did was put a cigarette in her mouth and tell the boy to get a match and light it."

It was already dark and beginning to snow when Roy and Frank came out of the movie theater, but they walked slowly anyway. The top of the head of the statue in front of Our Lady of Insufferable Insolence was white. As Roy and Frank passed the church Roy remembered his grandmother Rose telling him that Saint Pantera had been born in Africa but the archdiocese would not allow her face and hands to be painted black.

"Do you think the kid was better off after his mother committed suicide?" Roy asked.

"I don't know. We never got to see his father, who lived in a different country. Switzerland, someone said. Maybe the kid went to live there with him."

"One thing about European movies," said Roy, "there's always more to think about afterwards than with American movies."

"Probably because they've got more history there," Frank said. "That's why more stuff happens in our movies. Americans don't like to think so much."

War is Merely Another Kind of Writing and Language

Walking into the A&P to buy a quart of milk, Roy spotted a tall, thin guy wearing an oversized hooded sweatshirt with the hood up and floppy pants watching a bunch of little kids playing in an empty lot. The guy had his back toward him but even though Roy could not see his face, Roy thought there was something peculiar about the way he was standing there, slightly slumped over, bent, not moving. The kids were very young, four, five and six years old, running and jumping around in the dirt and weeds. Roy was nine. He knew a few of the kids, one of whom was his friend Jimmy Boyle's younger brother, Paulie, who was six and a half.

Roy stopped and watched the guy frozen at the edge of the lot. It was a boiling hot day in July. The guy shouldn't be wearing a big sweatshirt with the hood up over his head, Roy thought. If he made a move toward the kids, Roy figured he could brain him with a rock. The empty lot was full of rocks and leftover half-bricks from when an addition to the Rogers house next door was built. Roy picked up a broken broom handle from the gutter in front of where he was standing. It had a sharp point on it.

The guy watched the kids for about two minutes more before he began shuffling away in the opposite direction from where Roy was headed. The kids probably had not even noticed him. When the guy turned the corner and was out of sight, Roy tossed the broom stick back into the gutter, then walked to the store.

When Roy came back carrying the milk, the kids were no longer in the empty lot. He walked to the corner the hooded guy had turned and Roy saw him about a quarter of the way down the block sitting at the edge of the sidewalk with his feet in the gutter. Roy still could not see his face. Nobody else was around. It was dinner time so the kids had gone to their houses. Roy stood looking at the curved figure on the sidewalk. He thought about going back for the broken broom handle, taking it and poking the guy and telling him to get up and keep moving. Just after he had this thought, the guy toppled forward and his entire body collapsed into the gutter.

A woman came out of a house next to where the guy was lying. She had a small dog on a leash, a black, brown and white mutt. The dog strained at the leash, trying to sniff the body, but the woman jerked him away. She walked the dog toward Roy.

"I saw that guy a little while ago watching some little kids playing in a vacant lot around the corner," Roy told her. "I thought he might be a child molester."

"It's Arthur Ray, Grace Lonergan's boy," said the woman. "He's not right in his head. I'll knock on her door and tell her to come and get him. He was hurt in Korea."

Roy knew there had been a war in Korea, which was a country near Japan and China, but he was not really sure where those countries were, only that they were very far from Chicago. Arthur Ray Lonergan probably had not known where or just how far away Korea was either until he went there.

The End of the Story

The dead man lying in the alley behind the Anderson house was identified by the police as James "Tornado" Thompson, a lone wolf stick-up man from Gary, Indiana. After robbing the currency exchange on Ojibway Boulevard in Chicago, he had gone out the front door holding a gun in one hand and was confronted on the sidewalk by two beat cops who were shooting the breeze before one of them went off duty. A clerk from the currency exchange appeared in the doorway and shouted, "Stop that man! He just robbed us!" Thompson pivoted and shot him. The cops pulled their guns but the thief dashed next door into the Green Harp Tavern and ran through the bar out the back door. One of the cops followed him; the other called for back up and for an ambulance to attend the wounded clerk, who was lying on the sidewalk.

Tornado Thompson ran down the alley. Roy and Jimmy Boyle and two of the McLaughlin brothers were playing ball when they saw Thompson speeding toward them holding a gun, followed by a cop.

"Holy shit!" yelled Jimmy Boyle. "Get down!"

The cop shouted, "Stop or I'll shoot!"

Thompson did not stop but stumbled over a crack in the uneven pavement and fell down, still gripping the gun. He twisted around and fired once at the cop, who stopped, dropped to one knee, aimed, and shot Tornado Thompson in the head.

"Stay down, boys!" said the cop.

He crept forward in a crouch, keeping his revolver trained on the robber. When he got to the body he determined the man was dead, then took the gun out of Thompson's hand and replaced his revolver in its holster.

Jimmy Boyle got up and rushed over to the body.

"Wow," he said, "you plugged him right in the forehead."

Roy and Johnny and Billy McLaughlin stood up and walked over. The cop stood up, too. A patrol car entered the alley from the Hammond Street end.

"Move away, boys," the cop said.

The car stopped and two cops got out. Another police car entered from the same direction and pulled up behind the first car. Two cops got out of it, too. They surrounded the body and the cop who'd shot Thompson told them what happened. A few neighbors, including Mr. Anderson, came out of the gangways of their houses. Three more police cars approached from the Ojibway Boulevard end of the alley. They stopped and six more cops joined the others.

"There ain't been so many people in the alley since Otto Polsky's garage burned down," said Johnny.

"He was refinishing a rowboat he'd built," Roy said, "and the shellac caught fire."

A few minutes later, an ambulance, its siren off, drove in off Hammond Street, stopped, and two men in white coats got out. One of them removed a stretcher from the rear of the ambulance, then they both walked over. After exchanging a few words with one of the cops, they lifted Thompson's body onto the stretcher, carried it to the ambulance, slid it in, and backed the ambulance out of the alley.

"What happened?" Mr. Anderson asked the boys.

"A guy come runnin' down the alley," said Jimmy, "with a cop chasin' him. The guy fired at the cop, the cop fired back and killed him."

"Hit him in the forehead," said Billy.

"Who was the guy?"

"I heard one of the cops say his name was Tornado Thompson, from Gary," Roy said. "He held up the currency exchange next to The Green Harp."

"He was a black guy," said Billy. "Why would he come all the way from Gary, Indiana, to Chicago to pull a hold up?"

The neighbors went back to their houses and all of the police cars left. Two cops remained in the alley, the cop who'd shot Tornado Thompson and the beat cop who'd stayed on Ojibway Boulevard.

"The detectives are at the currency exchange," said the beat cop.

"How's the clerk?"

"Dead."

"You fellas all right?" asked the cop who'd done the shooting. The boys all nodded.

"Come on, Dom," said the other cop. "We got time to stop in the tavern, have a shot and a beer."

"Why was he called Tornado?" asked Roy.

"He was a halfback at the University of Indiana, eight, nine years ago," said Dom. "I saw him run back a kick-off ninety-four yards against Northwestern. It's how he got his nickname. I wish I hadn't had to shoot him."

The two cops walked up the alley. They boys watched them go through the back door of The Green Harp.

"I think I'd like to be a cop," said Billy.

The next afternoon, Roy's grandfather read to him from an article in the Chicago *Daily News* about the incident. The basic facts were there along with the additional information that a four year old Negro boy was found alone in a 1952 Plymouth parked a block away from the currency exchange. The boy was Tornado Thompson's son, Amos, who had been told by his father to wait in the car until he came back. A woman walking by had seen Amos Thompson sitting in the back seat of the Plymouth, crying. When she asked him what was wrong, the boy told her his father had been gone for a long time, that he didn't know where he was. The woman told a cop about the child in the car and he took Amos to the precinct station, where he informed the sergeant in charge that his mother and both of his grandmothers were dead and that he and his father had been living in their car because they didn't have any money. Amos was given over to The Simon the Cyrenian Refuge for Colored Children.

That's awful, Pops," said Roy.

"Yes, Roy, it is. And for Amos, it's not the end of the story."

Innocent of the Blood

From the first time he met him, Roy disliked Buddy Dobler. Dobler had an identical twin named Marty, so kids called them Buddy and Marty Double. It was easy to tell them apart because Buddy was taller and heavier and was more assertive than his brother. Marty was quiet and good-natured, whereas Buddy was abrasive and mean-spirited. The twins attended a different grammar school than Roy, but they lived not too far away from Roy's neighborhood, and hung out with his friends Johnny Murphy and Tommy Cunningham, whose families were members of the same church as the Doblers.

Buddy and Marty were in the eighth grade and Roy was in the seventh, as were Johnny and Tommy.

"Buddy beat up a grown man by himself," Johnny Murphy told Roy. "Tommy saw him do it."

Johnny and Roy were walking on Ojibway Avenue going to meet Tommy and the Doblers at Blood of Our Savior Park. It was the first day of December but no snow had fallen yet in Chicago. The temperature was just above freezing and wind was gusting hard off the lake. Both boys were wearing leather jackets, earmuffs and gloves.

"Who'd he beat up?"

"A wino on Clark Street was bummin' for change. Tommy said Double clobbered the guy with a garbage can lid."

"Was the guy big?"

"Tommy didn't say. He was just a regular-sized wino."

"I don't like him."

"Who? Buddy Dobler?"

"Yeah. I think he's a jerk. He likes to push people around."

"He do somethin' to you?"

"I don't hardly know him. His brother's okay, though."

"Their mother was in a mental hospital."

"How do you know?"

"I heard my parents talkin' about it. My dad said Mrs. Dobler cut her wrists and her throat and almost died."

"When was this?"

"She got out of the bin two or three months ago. Maybe Buddy's angry about his mother so he takes it out on other people."

At Blood of Our Savior the Dobler twins were kneeling on the ground next to the basketball court shooting craps with Tommy Cunningham and another kid Roy didn't recognize.

"Who's that?" Roy asked Johnny. "The guy with the right side of his head shaved."

"Harley Fox. He's fourteen or fifteen. Remember him? He got sent to St. Charles after he set his five year old cousin on fire. They kept him in a year. He goes to a special school now."

Buddy Dobler was holding the dice. Coins and a few dollar bills were on the ground. Buddy kissed the dice, said, "Come on, eight," and threw them.

One die rolled off the concrete into the dirt. It turned up three. The other die showed four.

"You lose," said Harley Fox.

"It don't count," said Buddy, and scooped up both dice. "One of 'em fell off."

"The hell it don't," said Harley. He picked up the money. "Pass the dice."

Buddy Dobler chucked the dice hard at Fox's face and jumped on him. Both Tommy and Marty Dobler stood up quickly, got out of the way, and watched Buddy and Harley wrestle, as did Roy and Johnny Murphy.

Buddy got to his feet, grabbed hold of Harley's left leg and dragged him around in the dirt. Fox was on his back and Roy could see that on the shaved side of his head were several stitches.

Fox was trying to twist away but he couldn't until Buddy tripped backwards over the low curb bordering a footpath. Harley Fox sprang to his feet and kicked Buddy in the head. He was wearing motorcycle boots and Dobler stayed down. Fox kicked him a few more times and then stomped down as hard as he could with the heel of his left boot on Buddy's face.

Harley was shorter than Buddy but he outweighed him by twenty pounds. Dobler wasn't moving or saying anything. Blood ran out of his nose and the sides of his mouth and his eyes were closed. Fox took a book of matches out of the right pocket of his bomber jacket, struck one, lit the matchbook, bent down and set fire to Buddy's hair. Marty took off his coat and tried to smother the flames but Harley stopped him, wrenched the coat out of Marty's hands and tossed it aside.

"The old lady nurses at St. Charles are tougher than your brother," Harley Fox said to him.

Fox turned and walked away. The back of his head and jacket were covered with mud. Marty picked up his coat and went to cover his brother's hair, but the fire was already out. Buddy's forehead was singed and the front of his hair had been burned off. He still was not moving.

"We gotta call an ambulance," said Tommy.

Johnny Murphy picked a dime out of the dirt and said, "There's a pay phone in the drugstore next to the park. I'll go call."

Marty Dobler was sitting on the ground, staring at Buddy. Tommy came over and stood by Roy.

"I guess Fox learned how to fight like that in the reformatory," he said.

"Setting someone on fire is his own idea," said Roy.

Johnny Murphy came back and said, "I told the drugstore owner what happened, so he called."

When the emergency medical crew lifted Buddy onto a stretcher, he groaned a little, but he did not move or open his eyes. Marty went along with him in the ambulance.

"I should go tell Buddy's parents so they can meet him at the hospital," said Tommy.

"Here's the dime I was gonna use," Johnny said, digging it out of his right front pants pocket and handing it to him. "Talk to Mr. Dobler. You know his wife's not right in the head."

"What do you think'll happen to Harley?" asked Tommy.

"Buddy started the fight," said Roy.

"True," said Tommy, "but Harley torched him. Walk over to the drugstore with me. After I make the call we can get somethin' to eat."

As they passed the sign Blood of Our Savior Park, Roy thought about why he did not feel bad or upset about Buddy Dobler being hurt; he wondered if he should, even though he didn't like him. When Tommy went into the drugstore, Johnny and Roy waited outside.

"I guess Buddy deserved a beatin'," Johnny said. "None of us jumped in to help him until Marty tried to put out the fire on his head. Maybe Buddy is a jerk, like you said."

"When Jesus was carrying the cross," said Roy, "nobody jumped in to help him, either."

The Italian Hat

Roy's mother's friend June DeLisa was the kind of woman who would fly from Chicago to Venice, Italy, just to buy a hat. She did this in September of 1956, and when she returned Roy's mother asked her what was so special about the hat.

"It's handmade, of course, and designed by a man named Tito Verdi, who claims to be related to the famous composer. He's very old, in his late eighties or early nineties. The materials he uses are woven by crones in the hills of Puglia. Anyway, how do you like it?"

The hat perched perilously on the right side of June DeLisa's head. Other than an extraordinarily brilliant yellow-green feather attached to the radically raked left side of the tri-corner, Kitty thought the hat unremarkable; even the crumpled blue material that formed the construction looked like it could have been purchased for a dollar ninety-eight at Woolworth's.

"I like the feather. I've never seen such a radiant yellow before."

"Plucked from a rare species in the Belgian Congo."

"Dare I ask what you paid for it?"

"You daren't."

June DeLisa's husband had made a fortune on the commodities market. Kitty and June had met before either of them had gotten married, when they both modelled fur coats at the Merchandise Mart.

"How was Venice?"

"It's always lovely at this time of year, unless there's a hot spell. You've never been, have you? Crowded, but still like being in a dream, especially just after dawn."

"Did Lloyd go with you?"

"Oh, no. He has his polo to occupy him. And Mrs. Gringold."

"I thought he'd ended it with her."

Roy came into the livingroom, where his mother and June DeLisa were seated on the sofa.

"Goodness, Roy," June said, "you're growing up so fast. How old are you now?"

"I'll be eight next month."

"Mrs. DeLisa has just returned from Italy. She's telling me about her trip."

"Do you like my new hat, Roy? I had it made for me over there."

"It looks like the one Robin Hood wears, only his is brown, not blue."

"What is it, sweetheart? I thought you were going to play outside with the Murphy boys."

"It's raining, so I'm going to build a model in my room."

"Let me know if you need anything. If June and I decide to go out, I'll tell you."

Roy left the room. He did not dislike June DeLisa, but seeing her made him think that she was going to go home and jump out a window from her apartment on the 30th floor of the building she lived in on Lake Shore Drive.

"So he's seeing Anastasia again."

"He never really stopped. I'll probably have to kill her, or get a divorce. If I decide to have her killed, would you mind if I asked Rudy about getting someone to do it? You and he are still on good terms, aren't you?"

"Stop it, June. Don't even talk like that. Of course Rudy and I are on good terms. We're very close, and he sees Roy once or twice a week. Rudy loves his son more than anything."

"What about your mother?"

"She's too sick now to do anything about it."

"As if she hasn't already done enough."

"Since I divorced Rudy, she's actually begun to be more

respectful of him."

"Rose respects what he can do, or have done, you mean."

"He provides very well for Roy."

"And for you, too, I hope."

"I can't complain."

"He still loves you, Kitty. He always will. You're luckier for that. Lloyd never cared for me the way Rudy does you."

"He doesn't love Anastasia, I don't think. Does she love Lloyd?"

"If Maurice Gringold didn't own two banks and half the state of Ohio, I doubt she would stay married to him."

"Take off that hat, June. Just looking at it makes me nervous."

June removed her hat and put it down on the coffee table.

"I feel useless, Kitty. If Lloyd and I had children I don't suppose I would."

Rain was coming down hard. The two women sat without talking and listened to it bang against the windows and the roof.

"I asked old Signore Verdi how he had come to be a hat maker and he told me it was because he was a lousy violinist. Isn't that funny?"

Kitty looked at June's hat.

"Did Verdi tell you that feather came from the Belgian Congo?"

The Senegalese Twist

Roy had walked for several blocks before he realized he was lost. His friend Danny Luna had moved with his family to a new neighborhood and Roy was looking for their house. Danny had told him it was on the edge of Chinatown on Rhinelander Avenue, an apartment above the Far East Laundromat, a few blocks south of Superior. Danny's father worked as a drover in the Stockyards pens and his mother, a seamstress, was from Tell City, Indiana, a Swiss community. Danny said she had run away from Tell City when she was sixteen and come to Chicago, where she met his father, an illegal immigrant from Juarez, Mexico.

Since Danny was born, the Luna family had moved twelve times, one for each year of his life. He and Roy had played together on baseball teams for the past two years and Roy wanted to get him to play second base on the Tecumseh Cubs, for whom Roy was going to be the shortstop. The Lunas did not have a telephone, otherwise Roy would have called him.

Roy found himself on the corner of Menominee and Van Buren streets. He had no idea where Rhinelander Avenue was, so he decided to ask someone. He went into a beauty shop called Miss Racy's Powder Room, figuring there had to be a woman in there who could give him directions. Roy was surprised to see that all of the women in Miss Racy's Powder Room, both the customers and hair stylists, were black.

A slender girl with skin the color of maple syrup came up to Roy and said, loud enough for everyone to hear, "Don't tell me you're lookin' for your mama, baby, 'cause she ain't been here."

All of the women laughed, and the girl, who looked to Roy to be about eighteen, poked Roy on his chest with the long, purple painted nails on the two middle fingers of her right hand. She had red hair that stood up at least eight inches from her head, brown eyes with blue shadow on the lids, and freckles all over her face.

"What's your problem, sweetness?" she asked.

"I'm looking for Rhinelander Avenue. A friend of mine lives there over the Far East Laundromat."

"What your friend can do for you I can't?"

Most of the women were no longer paying attention to Roy and the girl, but the few who were giggled and shouted, "Rock that cradle, Red!", "His mama do find her way here, she gonna close us down!" and "Quit scarin' that boy, Charleen. He ain't big enough to do you right no how!"

"How old are you, sugar?" the girl asked Roy.

"Twelve and a half."

"That's what my milkman delivers every Tuesday and Friday," said a woman with a scalpful of green paste, which made one woman howl and say, "Uh huh."

Roy looked around the walls, which were decorated with posters from the Regal Theater and Aragon Ballroom featuring photographs of Ruth Brown, Chuck Jackson, Sarah Vaughan and Nat "King" Cole. Also tacked up were signs advertising hair straightening, skin lightening, manicures and pedicures. But the one that intrigued Roy read, "We Do Senegalese Twist".

"You got good, wavy hair," the girl said. "Be longer than most boys."

"I don't like getting haircuts," said Roy.

She ran her painted fingers through his hair from back to front, then front to back.

"I could do somethin' nice with it."

"What's the Senegalese Twist? It sounds like a kind of dance."

"Show it to him, Charleen," crowed Green Paste, "out back!"

"It's okay," said Roy, "I'll find Rhinelander. Thanks, anyway."

He opened the door to the street and went out. Before he could walk away, one of Charleen's hands was on his left shoulder. Roy turned around and looked at her.

"We call it Chopsticks Street," she said. "Go up a block on Van Buren, then right until you run into it. What's your name?"

"Roy."

"Mine is Charleen. C-h-a-r-l-e-e-n. You tall for your age, Roy. Almost tall as me, and I'm seventeen. I be in Miss Racy's every day but Sunday and Monday you want to take me up on my offer."

"I live pretty far away from here."

Charleen's freckles glittered in the sunlight. A butterfly landed on top of her high-piled hair.

"There's a butterfly on your head."

"Those ladies, they get raunchy, don't they? Miss Racy say the reason I'm attracted to very young boys is because my stepdaddy messed with me. He's gone now. Marleen, my sister, she cut off his privates while he was sleepin' and he bled to death. He was messin' with her, too. The butterfly still there?"

"Yes."

"He like me. You like me you know me better."

She tilted her head and the butterfly flitted off.

"Thanks, Charleen. I've got to go."

Later, Roy asked Danny Luna how he liked living in the neighborhood, and Danny said, "I don't know anybody yet except for the Chinese kids downstairs."

"I know where your mother can get her hair done," said Roy.

Kidnapped

Foster Wildroot disappeared on a Tuesday morning in early November of 1956. He was last seen on his way to school, walking on Minnetonka Street at a quarter to nine as he did every weekday morning. Foster's mother told police on Wednesday that before he left the house her son, who was ten years old and in the fourth grade, had eaten a piece of rye toast with strawberry jam on it, drunk half a cup of black coffee and taken with him an apple to eat at recess. The weather was unusually warm for November, so Foster wore only a blue peacoat, which he did not button up, and did not take either a hat or gloves. He was small for his age, said Frieda Wildroot, and very shy. Foster did not have many friends, almost none, really, she told them; he kept mostly to himself. He had brown hair, cut short, and wore black-framed glasses to correct his severe near-sightedness. Foster stuttered badly, she said, an impediment that hampered his ability to orally answer questions put to him in the classroom. As a result, Foster disliked school. She did not, however, believe he would run away from home, as that was his sanctuary, where he spent his time alone in his room building model airplanes.

Foster's father, Fred Wildroot, did not live in Chicago with his wife and son. At present, Frieda told the authorities, her husband was working in a coal mine in West Virginia, from where he mailed her a support check every month. The police asked if she thought it was possible that Foster would try to go to West Virginia to see his father, and she said that Fred Wildroot had neither seen nor communicated with his son since the boy was six years old.

"Fred moves around a lot," said Frieda. "Foster wouldn't even know where to go to find him."

Foster Wildroot was in Roy's class but since he did not talk much or participate in sports on the playground, which was Roy's main interest, they did not really know each other. None of Roy's friends knew much about Wildroot; like Roy, they saw him only in school, where he sat by choice in the last seat of the back row in the classroom. Foster had been absent from school for a week or more before Roy noticed he was not there. Even after he did, Roy figured the kid was sick or that his family had moved away. Many people left Chicago during the 1950s, most of them relocating to the West Coast, primarily to Los Angeles.

"Wildroot lives on your block, doesn't he?" Roy asked Billy Katz. "What do you think happened to him?"

"My mother thinks he was kidnapped by a pervert," said Katz. "She says Chicago's full of perverts. Wildroot's probably locked in a basement where the perv feeds him steaks and ice cream to keep him happy after he does shit to him."

"I just hope they don't find his body dumped in the forest preserves with his head cut off, like those sisters," Roy said. "They were our age, too."

"He stayed inside his house all the time," said Billy. "I hardly seen him. He didn't play with any of the other kids on the block, neither. My mother says his mother works part-time ironing sheets and stuff at the Disciples of Festus House for the Pitiful on Washtenaw, but I don't know how she knows."

"What about his father?"

"Never around. Maybe he don't have one."

Foster Wildroot was never seen again, at least not in Roy's neighborhood. Billy Katz said Mrs. Wildroot still lived in the same house, though, and one day, about six months after Foster went missing, Mr. Wildroot showed up.

"My mother seen him," said Billy. "Tall, skinny guy, walked with a cane."

"How'd your mother know it was Foster's father?"

"He went to every house on the block and handed a card to whoever answered the door, or else he put one in the mailbox if nobody was home, then he went away. My mother said he didn't talk to anyone."

"What does it say on the cards?"

"If anyone knows what happened to my son, Foster Wildroot, please write to Mr. Fred Wildroot at a post office box in Montana or Utah, someplace like that."

A year later, Roy and Billy Katz were playing catch with a football in the alley behind Billy's house when Billy pointed to a woman dumping the contents of a large, cardboard box into a garbage can behind a garage a few houses away.

"That's Mrs. Wildroot," he told Roy.

After the woman went back into her house, Billy said, "Let's go see what she put in there."

The garbage can was full of model airplanes, most of them missing wings or with broken propellers.

"See any you want to take?" asked Billy.

The Dolphins

Roy's Uncle Buck built a house on Utila, one of the Bay Islands of Honduras. It was an octagonal structure with eight doors on a spit of land accessible only by boat when the tide was in. Buck had transported a generator, refrigerator and other appliances on the ship *Islander Trader* from St. Petersburg, Florida, to Utila, and when he returned on the same boat two and a half months later, Roy met him at the dock.

"I had to go to Teguci for a few days to renew my residency visa and take care of some other business," Buck told him, "and I was walking down a street with my friend Goodnight Morgan, who used to live on Utila but now lives on Roatan, when a car came by, slowed down, and someone fired three shots at us, then sped away. Neither of us were hit. Drive-bys are common in Tegucigalpa, it's the murder capital of Latin America, if not the world, but I didn't know why anyone would want to kill us. Goodnight Morgan used to be High Sheriff of Utila, so I asked him if he thought he could have been targeted by a political rival or a criminal who held a grudge against him. Goodnight said either was possible, but he didn't think so. 'Gangsters in Teguci kill for no reason other than to intimidate the population,' he said. 'That's why almost nobody is on the streets. To shop they go to malls where there are security guards with automatic weapons to protect them.'"

Roy and his uncle were driving on the bridge over the bay on their way to Tampa when Buck said, "The *Islander Trader* started leaking fuel when we were a day from port, and the radio was on the fritz. We barely made it to Roatan. The leak had to be patched up before going on to Utila. Then came the shooting in Teguci. Keep in mind, nephew, when a person walks out the door you might never see him or her again."

It was a hot and humid day, which was not unusual, but the exceptionally heavy cloud cover, without wind, portended rain, at the very least.

"This weather reminds me of the time I was in Callao, waiting for a ship to take me to Panama City, where I could get a plane to Miami," said Buck. "Hundreds of dolphins invaded the harbor, making it impossible for boats to get in or out. They sensed that a giant storm was coming and they were trying to get out of its way. I'll never forget the sight of those blue-green dolphins crowded together like cattle in the stockyards in Chicago. Dolphins are big, the adults average seven feet long, and they were jabbering to each other, loud, squealing and honking that drowned out everything else."

"Did a big storm hit?"

"About four hours later, the rain started, then huge waves inundated the Peruvian coast, followed by a hailstorm, the kind you get in Kansas or Oklahoma. Nobody there had even seen hail before. All of the ships tied up or at anchor in and near the harbor were damaged, and a number of boats out at sea capsized."

"What about the dolphins?"

"They dove deeper to avoid the hail. But when the bad weather passed, the dolphins were all gone, no sight or sound of them. They were already miles away in the Pacific."

"How long were you stuck in Callao?"

"About a week. I went to Lima for a couple of days, then went back to get my ship."

Rain hit the windshield, so Roy slowed the car down. They were almost across the bridge.

"Dolphins are smart, Roy, they know when and how to escape from the weather and other cetaceans. Human beings are the biggest threat to their existence. I told Goodnight Morgan about the dolphins in Callao, and you know what he said?"

Roy shook his head.

"That's why you never see any dolphins walking down the street in Tegucigalpa."

Dragonland

Roy's mother was having trouble sleeping. When she mentioned this to her friend Kay, she recommended that Kitty make an appointment to see Dr. Flynn.

"Is he a sleep expert?" Kitty asked.

"He has a medical degree in orthopedics," said Kay, "but he specializes in hypnotherapy now."

"I don't want to be hypnotized. I just need a scrip for sleeping pills until I'm myself again."

"Better to see Flynn than take pills. You'll get strung out on them and have a bigger problem. Dr. Flynn is kind of a genius. He uses hypnotism to correct bodily deformities based on his theory that malformations of the body are caused by psychological conditions."

"You mean he cures cripples by hypnosis?"

"I know it sounds daffy, but apparently he's had great success."

"Where did he go to medical school, in Tibet?"

"Go see him, Kitty. Try it once, then tell me if you think he's a quack. And even if he is, if what he does cures your insomnia what difference will it make?"

The day after Roy's mother saw Dr. Flynn she called Kay to give her the report.

"He's a nice man with good manners. Dyes his hair. We talked for a while, and he asked me if anything in particular had been bothering me lately. I told him I've had trouble sleeping periodically since I was a child. Now, since my divorce, I've been having difficulty again, and that when I do fall asleep I often have bad dreams."

"Did he hypnotize you?"

"I suppose so."

"What do you mean 'suppose'? Did he or didn't he?"

"He said he did. He didn't swing a watch or anything in front of my eyes. He just spoke to me and then I felt a little dizzy. I guess I passed out for a few minutes. Afterwards I felt relaxed. That's all."

"Did you sleep better last night?"

"Roy had to wake me up this morning to get his breakfast. I'm always up before he is."

"How did you feel?"

"Like I didn't get enough sleep. Not exhausted but vague. I think yesterday tired me out."

"What did Flynn say? Are you going to see him again?"

"I don't know, Kay. He left it up to me. I had a strange dream last night."

"Do you remember it?"

"I was walking alone on a city street in the middle of the night. I had no destination, I was just walking. There were other women like me, walking, because they were crazy and couldn't stop. I was afraid and some of them laughed at me. One of the women said, 'Welcome to Dragonland.' I wanted to go home but I was lost and only these crazy women were there."

"Did you ever have this dream before?"

"It wasn't only a dream, Kay. I did this for real lots of times. I never told anyone."

"Rudy didn't know?"

"It happened once when he and I were first together. I told him I was restless and needed to get some fresh air. We were in a hotel room, three o'clock in the morning. I told him not to worry, to go back to sleep, and I went out."

"What about Dr. Flynn? Did you tell him?"

"Maybe, when I was hypnotized."

"What about Roy?"

"What about him?"

"Do you want him to stay with me and Marvin for a couple of days? Until you're feeling better."

"I feel all right. Thanks for offering. Roy's no trouble."

That night Kitty couldn't sleep. She had an urge to leave the house, to walk, but she was afraid to leave Roy alone. She looked at herself in the bedroom mirror and thought about what Dr. Flynn had told her before she left his office.

"There's nothing terribly wrong with you," he said, "Go back to work."

"I used to be a model," she told him.

Kitty went into the livingroom and turned on the TV. Ava Gardner was dancing barefoot in the rain. She didn't look happy, either.

Role Model

On Roy's fourteenth birthday he came home from school and found his mother sitting alone at the kitchen table drinking a cup of coffee and reading *Holiday* magazine.

"Hi, Ma," he said. "What are you reading?"

"An article about Brazil. You know I was there once."

"You told me. Who were you there with?"

"Oh, a boyfriend. It was before I met your father. We spent a week in Rio. The beaches were lovely, the sand was so white, but very crowded, as crowded as Times Square on New Year's Eve. The Carioca girls were almost naked, brown and slithery and beautiful. I had a wonderful time."

"Why haven't you ever gone back?"

"Rio's not the kind of place your father would have liked, and since he died I've not had the opportunity."

It was a dreary day, drizzly and gray and colder than usual for the time of year. Roy knew his mother preferred warm weather.

"It's my birthday today."

"I know, Roy. Are you going out with your friends?"

"Later, maybe. Right now I'm going to work. I just came home to change my clothes."

"Your father always dressed well. People used to dress better in the old days."

"You mean in the 1940s?"

"Yes. Before then, too."

"Well, I'm going to be boiling hot dogs and frying hamburgers. It wouldn't be a good idea for me to wear a suit."

"No, Roy, of course not. That's not what I mean. It's just that people cared more for their appearance when I was young."

"This is 1961, Ma, and you're only thirty-four. You're still young."

Roy was standing next to the table. His mother looked up at him and smiled. She really is still beautiful, he thought. She had long auburn hair, dark brown eyes, perfect teeth and very red lips.

"I know you miss your father, Roy. It's a shame he died so young."

"He was a strong person," Roy said. "People liked and respected him, didn't they?"

"Yes. He handled things his own way. People trusted him. You know your father never gave me more than twenty-five dollars a week spending money, but I could go into any department store or good restaurant and charge whatever I wanted. I'll tell you something that happened not long after he and I were married. We were living in the Seneca Hotel, where you were born, and there was another couple in the hotel we were friends with, Ricky and Rosita Danillo. Rosita was a little older than I—she was from Puerto Rico—and Ricky was a few years younger than your dad, who was nineteen years older than me."

"What business was Ricky in?"

"Oh, the rackets, like everybody in Chicago, but he wasn't in your father's league. He looked up to Rudy. Anyway, late one afternoon your father came home and I was wearing a new hat, blood red with a veil, and he said it looked good on me. I told him I was just trying it on. He asked me where I'd gotten it and I said it was a gift from Ricky Danillo, that I'd come back to the hotel after having lunch with Peggy Spain and the concierge handed me a hatbox with a note from Ricky."

"What did the note say?"

"I don't remember exactly, something about how he hoped I'd like it, that when he saw it in a shop window he thought it suited my style. Your dad didn't say anything but the next day when I went down to the lobby I saw that one of the plate glass windows in the front was boarded up. I asked the concierge what happened and he told me that Rudy had punched Ricky Danillo

and knocked him through the window, then told the hotel manager to put the cost of replacing it on his bill. That night I said to
your dad, 'You knocked Ricky through a plate glass window just
because he bought me a hat?'"

"What did he say?"

"'No, Kitty, I did it because he didn't ask me first.' That's the
kind of guy your father was. I didn't say another word about it."

"What happened to the hat?"

"I never wore it. I gave it away to someone."

Roy did not tell anyone at work that it was his birthday and
afterwards he was too tired to go anywhere. When he got home
there was a chocolate cake on the kitchen table with fifteen yellow
candles stuck in it. His mother wasn't home. He picked up a book
of matches that was on the stove and lit the candles, then took off
his wet jacket and draped it over the back of a chair. Roy thought
about making a wish but he couldn't think of one. He blew out
the candles anyway.

Mona

"What's goin' on?"

"Two guys held up the Black Hawk Savings and Loan. A teller set off the alarm and the cops showed up just as the robbers were comin' out. They shot the first one out the door, he's dead, but the other one ran across the street into the Uptown. He's holed up in there."

"What's playin'?"

"*Tell Him I'm Dangerous*. You seen it?"

"No. How long's he been in the theater?"

"Twenty minutes, half hour. The cops got the exits covered. They don't want a shootout inside, innocent people get hurt."

Roy had been on his way home from Minnetonka Park when he saw a crowd on the sidewalk on Broadway. He spotted Bobby Dorp right away because Dorp was six foot six and towered over everybody. Bobby was a junior in high school, two years ahead of Roy, who knew him from pick-up basketball games.

"I was goin' into Lingenberg's to get a cake for my mother when I heard the shots," said Dorp. "I come over here and saw a body lyin' in front of the bank with blood pourin' out of it. He musta been drilled twenty times. The other robber was already in the theater. He might be wounded."

"It's a matinee, so there probably aren't too many people in there," said Roy. "It'll be dark in less than an hour. I think the cops'll wait him out."

By now the street was clogged with police cars and patrolmen had the theater surrounded.

Dorp said, "I gotta get my mother's cake before Lingenberg's closes. Don't let the shootin' start until I get back."

Marksmen with high-powered rifles were positioning themselves on the roofs of buildings around the Uptown. The only way the robber could escape, Roy figured, was to pretend he was a patron. To do that, the guy would have to ditch his weapon and the bank money, if he had any. Hiding a bullet wound might be tough, though, depending on where he'd been hit.

As darkness fell, spotlights were set up on nearby rooftops. No traffic was moving in the immediate vicinity. Bobby Dorp came back carrying a cake box.

"I got there just in time," he said, "or they woulda sold this cake, too. Lingenberg's is sellin' out the place. Seein' men die makes people hungry, I guess. I never seen it so crowded."

"I wonder if they're sellin' popcorn and candy in the Uptown," said Roy.

A middleaged woman in front of the boys fainted and fell off the curb. Two men helped her to her feet and led her away. The sun was gone.

"I can't stay no longer," said Dorp. "Gotta get the cake home. Anyway, it's gettin' cold. Maybe I'll come back after dinner."

After Bobby Dorp left, Roy moved closer to the front, so that he had an unobstructed view of the theater entrance. Sawhorses had been lined up along the curb. Every cop in sight had his gun drawn.

Men and women began walking out of the theater with their hands held above their heads. Some of them were crying. Police took each person into custody as soon as they reached the sidewalk. Thirty or forty people came out and were loaded into paddy wagons. The cops kept their guns trained on the entrance.

"He's still inside," a man said.

"Go in and get him!" yelled another man.

"There he is!" screamed a woman, pointing at the roof of the theater.

Everyone looked up. A man was standing near the edge of the roof, directly over the marquee. He was bareheaded and was wearing a brown hunter's vest over a red and black checkered shirt and dark green trousers. He looked to be about twenty-five or thirty years old.

"Put your hands on your head!" a policeman ordered through a bullhorn.

The man did not comply. He just stood there with his hands by his sides.

"Place your hands over your head or you will be shot!" warned the cop with the horn.

The man said something but Roy could not make out the words.

"What did he say?" asked the woman who'd spotted him on the roof.

The man spoke again and this time Roy heard him say "Mona."

"Mona?" the woman said. "Did he say Mona?"

The riflemen fired, hitting him from sixteen directions. The man fell forward into the well of the marquee. A dozen pigeons fluttered out. All Roy could see now was the theater sign, black letters on a white background: tell him i'm dangerous plus cartoons.

Roy elbowed his way out of the crowd and started walking. All that was missing, he thought, was snow falling on the thief's lifeless body. Lingenberg's Bakery was still open. Roy went inside.

"Do you have any doughnuts left?" he asked a pink-faced, blonde woman behind the counter.

"Yust one," she said. "Chocolate."

"I'll take it."

"I hear many noises together. Something happen?"

"The police shot and killed a man."

Roy gave the woman a dime. She took it and handed him the doughnut wrapped in wax paper.

"What reason for?" she asked.

Roy took a bite, chewed and swallowed it.

"Mona," he said.

Mud

When Leni Haakonen was eight and nine years old she liked playing war or cowboys and Indians with Roy, who was the same age. She was a Swedish girl who lived with her mother in a tenement apartment on the corner of the block, two buildings down from where Roy lived with his mother. Her father had been killed in the war and Roy's parents were divorced. There was a vacant lot next to the building Leni lived in where she and Roy often played. Leni was as tough as any boy Roy knew, including himself, and she was very pretty. Most of the time she wore her honey-brown hair in two long braids; she had gray-blue eyes and a small red birthmark on her left cheek, and for as long as Roy knew her Leni never wore a dress.

One afternoon in late August they were pretending to be soldiers, rolling in the dirt and weeds of the vacant lot, when Leni asked Roy to kiss her. She was lying on her back and her face was dusty and smudged.

"I'm going to be nine tomorrow," Leni said to Roy, "and I've never kissed a boy. I want you to be the first."

Roy had kissed girls before but he had not thought even once about kissing Leni. He hesitated and looked at her. She had a fierce expression on her face, the same as when the two of them wrestled.

"Kiss me, Roy. On the lips."

There was mud on her mouth. Roy wiped it off with his right thumb and kissed her. Both of them kept their eyes open.

"My mother wanted me to only invite girls to my birthday party," she said. "That's why you didn't get an invitation."

The kiss had lasted two seconds. Leni rolled away from Roy and stood up. He stood up, too.

"Which girls did you invite?"

"None. It's just going to be me and my mother and her sister, my Aunt Terry, and her daughter, my cousin Lucy. Lucy's twelve. I don't like her but my mother says she has to come because of Aunt Terry. I don't like her, either. I'm getting a new winter coat, a white one with a red collar. I can save a piece of cake and give it to you the day after tomorrow. It'll be a yellow cake with chocolate frosting."

Leni and her mother moved away before she and Roy were ten. Seventeen years later, a few months after Roy's first novel was published, he received the following letter in care of his publisher in New York. The name on the return address on the envelope was Mrs. Robert Mitchell.

Dear Roy, I hope you remember me. We used to play together when we were children and I lived in Chicago. My mother and I moved to Grand Rapids, Michigan, when I was ten, or almost. Now I live in Detroit with my husband who is a dentist. I work as a receptionist in his office.

I bought your book and wanted to tell you. I have not read all of it because there are too many parts I do not really understand but I like the photograph of you on the back cover. You look like I thought you would.

Robert and I do not have children. I don't want any but he does. My mother lives in Grand Rapids with her sister.

I probably should not tell you this in writing but I want to. Sometimes I can still feel your thumb on my lips when you wiped off the mud that time. It was on the day before my ninth birthday. I don't expect you to remember.

If you ever come to Detroit look me up. On the book it

says that you live in Paris, France, so I don't really think I'll see you here or ever. You probably get other letters like this.

Sincerely,
Leni (Haakonen) Mitchell

The Phantom Father

Roy's father was born on August 13, 1910, in the village of Siret, in what following World War II became Romania, close to the border of Ukraine. Soon thereafter, he moved with his family to Vienna, the capital city of the Austro-Hungarian empire. They were Austrian citizens. In 1917, the family resided at number five Zirkusgasse in the neighborhood of Leopoldstadt, near the ferris wheel in Luna Park Roy would first glimpse in director Carol Reed's film *The Third Man*. Roy's grandfather's profession as listed in the Vienna city directory of that year was printer. The Great War ended in December of 1918, at which point the family—father, two sons, one daughter, mother—made their way to Czernowitz, where they remained until April 1921, when they left for Antwerp, Belgium, from which port they took ship on the 14th of that month aboard the S.S. *Finland* bound for New York. From New York City they continued to Chicago, Illinois, where the family established residence for the remainder of their lives. They were Jews, fortunate to escape Europe before the Nazis perpetrated their murderous campaign to expunge the race from the continent.

Roy's father, who died at the age of forty-eight on December 5, 1958, not quite two months after Roy's twelfth birthday, never spoke to him of his Austrian childhood, nor did Roy ever hear him speak either German or Yiddish, as his father did. (Roy's grandmother died before he was born.) He became an American, a Chicagoan, and a criminal who was arrested several times for receiving stolen property and violations of the Volstead Act, known as Prohibition, during the years when the sale of liquor was illegal in the United States. His longest jail term was one year. Roy was, therefore, by birth a first-generation American, the son of a gangster who died young. Like his father, Roy eventually made his own way without much help. He wanted to know where his father came from, so he travelled first to Vienna, later to Romania, and found out. What Roy discovered did not surprise him; what did surprise him was that among those who had been closest to him, Roy was alone in his interest: neither his brother nor his mother particularly cared. Roy was not sure why he thought they would.

For Roy, the question that remained was why, during the twelve years he knew him, his father chose never to share with him any information, let alone details, of his or his immediate family's pre-American existence. As William Faulkner famously stated, "The past is not dead, it's not even past." This was a sentiment with which Roy agreed, and so he hated knowing that he would never know.

For his seventh birthday, in 1953, on an unseasonably cold and snowy October afternoon in Chicago, Roy's mother took him and a few of his friends to see the movie *Phantom from Space*. It was in black and white and the title figure could appear and disappear at will; one moment visible to earthlings, invisible the next. This is how Roy's father remained in his memory, a kind of phantom, there but not there, and no longer here; not enough for Roy.

Roy's Letter

Dear Dad,

It's almost Christmas of 1962. You died four years ago, when I was twelve. We didn't talk after you went into the hospital for the last time. Mom told me to call you there and I tried the night before you died but the nurse said you couldn't talk. The next day Mom asked me why I hadn't called you and I told her I did but she didn't believe me. I don't know why. She was acting crazy maybe because you were dead saying she was going to faint. She went out on a date that night and didn't tell me you might die. She's talking about getting married again which would make this her fourth marriage since you and she were divorced. I was five then and didn't really understand what that meant. By the time I was eleven I understood that it was up to me to take care of myself. You had a new wife and the man my mother was married to and I did not like each other. Anyway, he didn't last much longer with her. You remember I got a job delivering Chinese food on a bicycle for 25 cents an hour and a dime a delivery plus tips. I've been working ever since, mostly in hot dog and hamburger places. I give Mom money every month for her and my sister, who was born a few months after you died. Mom is working part time as a receptionist in a private hospital. I hope she doesn't get married again until after I graduate from high school. I'll be gone then and not have to deal with another guy who doesn't want me around. I'm not sure what I want to be yet but I write stories and articles about sports. I'm a pretty good athlete, especially in baseball. I remember all of the times we spent together in Chicago and Key West and Miami and Havana. I wish we could still go to Cuba. I miss the people and the food there. I remember one morning when we were having breakfast on the terrace at the Nacional and there were some very beautiful girls sitting near us and you told me Cuban women didn't usually have big breasts but their rear ends were exceptional. I liked the weather there even though it got so hot. I won't live in Chicago after I finish high school. I don't know if I'll go to college even though Uncle Buck says I should. He wants me to be a civil engineer like him, or an architect, but I don't think I will. I just want to go places, to travel everywhere that interests me and see what happens and write about it. You were only a few years younger than I am now when you came to America from the old country. Other than wishing you were still alive I wish I could have known you when you were a boy, that both of us could have been boys at the same time and that we could have been friends.

Love, your son,

Roy

The
World in the
Afternoon

ROY'S GREAT-GRANDFATHER BORIS, CONSTANTINOPLE, 1889

The World in the Afternoon

"Come on, Roy, I don't want to be late."

"Why do you want me to go with you?"

"For protection. Just in case Billy's acting strange."

"Do you think he's dangerous?"

"I don't really know what to think, baby. Get your coat, the blue parka."

"Where are we meeting him?"

"In the lobby of the hotel he's staying at. Then we'll go somewhere, a public place where other people are around."

Roy's mother was going to meet her soon to be ex-husband, her second, to have him sign papers declaring their marriage null and void, as if it never existed. Roy was eight years old and did not quite understand what was happening, only that Billy Cork, whom he liked, had for the past six months been his stepfather and now he wasn't going to be and according to the law never was.

"Are you getting a divorce, Ma?"

"No, an annulment. It means we were never married."

"But you were married. I was at your wedding."

"The Catholic church doesn't allow people to get divorced, Roy. Billy didn't tell me before we were married that he wasn't right in his head, so the church granted permission for me to have the agreement annulled. This means that in the eyes of God and the church Billy and I were never legally wed, and that's all that matters. Take your gloves."

It was mid-November and already cold in Chicago. Roy's mother drove toward downtown and parked a block away from Billy's hotel.

"Put up your hood, Roy, we're near the lake so it's very windy."

They walked to The Cass, a rundown, semi-residential hotel

on the Near Northside. Before he and his mother entered, Roy saw Billy through the glass doors standing in the lobby. He was wearing a dirty beige trenchcoat.

"He's there, Ma."

"I see him. This won't take long, I hope."

"Hello, Kitty," Billy said when she and Roy were inside. "Hello, son," he said to Roy.

It appeared to Roy as if Billy were trying to smile but couldn't make the corners of his mouth turn up. He was unshaven and needed a haircut. His right eye was bloodshot.

"Hi, Billy," Roy said, and smiled.

Billy stuck out his right hand to shake and Roy put his own into it.

"Too cold for you, hey, me bucko? I'll bet you wish you were down in Havana with your father, or with Uncle Jack in Florida, fishing in the Gulf."

Billy liked to call Roy bucko. His family were Irish, from Donegal. Billy had come with his mother and father and sister to Chicago when he was about the age Roy was now. Roy had never met any members of Billy's family. He knew only that Billy's sister, Marjorie Anne, was married and living in West Virginia, where her husband, Billy said, was a foreman in a coal mine.

"My dad is in Las Vegas right now," Roy said. "He'll be back in Chicago next week for Thanksgiving."

"You're looking fine, Kitty. Where would you like to go?"

"I don't want to go anywhere, Billy. I just want to get this over with."

"We'll take a walk, then. I'd like to get out in the air."

The three of them left the hotel lobby and headed in the direction of Lake Michigan, which was a few blocks away.

"There's a cozy park on the next street," said Billy. "We can sit on a bench there and talk."

As they walked, Billy put an arm around Roy's shoulders. Kitty kept her distance from Billy and looked straight ahead, not saying anything. The last time Roy had seen Billy was when he refused to get out of bed and just sat up staring at nothing without speaking or moving. Roy's mother had shouted at him for a while, then run screaming out of the house. She called a doctor from the McLaughlins' house next door and did not come back until the doctor was with her.

Roy had gone into his mother's bedroom and stood at the foot of the bed. Billy sat still. He didn't blink. Roy had only known him for a few months but he and Billy had gotten along well. Billy was tall and handsome and a good athlete. They had played catch with baseballs and footballs and gone swimming with his mother in lakes in Northern Illinois and Wisconsin. Billy smiled a lot and seemed happy to have a family of his own, which he told Kitty and Roy he'd not had before. This turned out to be a lie. Kitty found out later from Billy's sister that he had been married to a woman in Minneapolis with whom he had two children, a boy and a girl. Billy had abandoned them without warning, just walked out of their house one morning two years before and not contacted them since.

Roy heard the doctor say that Billy was catatonic, a word Roy had never heard before. The doctor called for an ambulance to come and take Billy to a hospital. Roy's mother told him to go to the McLaughlins and stay with them until she came to get him.

Roy sat on a bench separate from the one his mother and Billy sat on in a small park from which they had a view of the lake. Roy watched the gray-black waves gnash at the sand and die there. He thought about bait fishing with nets in Tampa Bay with his Uncle Jack. To do this you had to hold one end of the net with small weights attached in you mouth and throw the other weighted end into the water and make sure to open your mouth when you threw the net so that your front teeth didn't go with it. Roy did not like the extreme heat there any more than he disliked the freezing cold winters in Chicago but when he was on the water in Jack's boat or in a skiff off Varadero with his dad and a guide he felt good. Snow flurries began falling and blowing around.

"Let's go, Roy," his mother said.

She was standing in front of him, shivering in her thin calico coat. Neither she nor Billy wore a hat.

"Kitty, wait," said Billy, who remained seated on his bench. "Can't we just talk?"

Roy's mother brushed snowflakes from her face with a few folded up pieces of paper, then put them into her purse. She didn't reply to Billy, just took Roy by one hand and led him out of the park without looking back. Roy did, though, and saw Billy still sitting, letting the snow pelt his head and the shoulders of his trenchcoat.

Once Roy and his mother were back in her car, he asked her if Billy had signed the papers.

"Yes, Roy. Now we'll never have anything to do with him again."

"He didn't act crazy," Roy said. "If he had attacked you I couldn't have stopped him, he's too big and strong."

"You would have run and gotten help, maybe found a policeman."

"I was a little afraid he would hit you."

Kitty drove home without saying anything more to Roy. She walked into the house and into her bedroom and closed the door behind her. Roy stood in the hallway until he heard her talking to someone on the phone. He went back outside and sat down on the front steps. There were a couple of inches of snow on the ground and the sky was darker than it should have been at two o'clock in the afternoon, even in November.

Wing Shooting

When she was in her twenties, Roy's mother enjoyed shooting skeet at a club on the shore of Lake Michigan in Chicago. This is a form of trapshooting in which clay targets are sprung upwards in such a way as to duplicate the angles of flight found in wing shooting. Skeet was a very popular pastime in the 1940s and '50s, and Kitty often went shooting with one or another of her boyfriends when Roy was a young boy, occasionally taking him along.

When she shot skeet Roy's mother wore a club jacket with a padded right shoulder that afforded protection from the kick of her shotgun. "Pull!" she'd shout, and the clay bird would be launched into the sky. Kitty was a pretty fair shot, regularly outscoring her mostly male partners. Roy would watch her for a little while, then wander off by himself and walk on the nearby beach.

He was seven years old on a Saturday afternoon while his mother was plugging pigeons with projectiles when Roy came upon a woman standing knee deep in the water staring into the distance. Roy guessed the woman was younger than his mother but not too much younger. She let the waves roll gently over her legs, she hardly moved. It was a sunny day in late September, Indian summer, still warm with as yet no hint of the violent winter certain to come. Before the first snow, Roy knew, he and his mother would head south to spend the cold months in Key West, Florida, the southernmost point in the United States.

Roy stood on the sand and watched the woman. She was wearing a thin black dress, the lower half of which was already wet, but she did not seem to mind. Two coastwise freighters and a barge were visible in the distance; the freighters, Roy figured, were headed north toward the St. Lawrence seaway. He had gone sailing on Lake Michigan several times with his Uncle Buck, his mother's brother, on Buck's sailboat, the *Friendship*, before it split almost in half during a severe storm. The wreck occurred while Buck and his wife, Marguerite, were competing in the annual race to Michigan. A large wave crashed into the *Friendship*'s bow as the boat approached the apex of a preceding swell at an angle that caused its hull to crack. Buck and Marguerite were rescued by a passing freighter after taking down the sails and spending twelve hours below deck wrapped in blankets, but the *Friendship* was lost. It had been a beautiful yawl, built in Sweden, and Roy missed going sailing with his uncle.

"Your dress is getting wet," Roy shouted to the woman.

She turned and said, "It feels good. Take off your shoes and socks and roll up your pantlegs and come in. You'll like it."

She motioned with her left arm for Roy to join her, so he did as she suggested and stood near her in the water allowing the waves to soak him from the waist down.

"Do you live around here?" he asked.

The woman shook her head. "No, honey, I don't live anywhere at the moment. I'm free as a bird. What about you?"

"I live with my mother. She's shooting skeet over there."

Roy pointed toward the club.

"You're very pretty," he said. "So is my mother. Your hair is dark red, like hers."

The woman looked more closely at him and smiled.

"I'm sure she is. What's your name?"

"Roy."

"My name is Florence, like the city in Italy."

"Where do you sleep at night?" he asked.

"Oh, I have many choices, Roy. I suppose it depends on my mood."

"Do you have a boyfriend? My mother has a lot of boyfriends. They buy her lots of things and sometimes take her on trips to other countries. She can speak French and some Spanish. I can speak some Spanish, too."

"Your mother sounds like an interesting woman. What's her name?"

"Kitty. Everybody calls her Kitty but her real name is Katherine."

"Roy! Roy! Time to go, boy! Get out of the water!"

Roy and Florence both looked behind them and saw a man with thick, shiny black hair and a big black mustache standing on the beach. When he saw Florence's face he came closer.

"I hope he wasn't bothering you, miss," he said.

"This is Rome," Roy told Florence. "He drove us here."

Roy walked onto the dry sand and picked up his shoes and socks.

"Her name is Florence," he said, "that's a city in Italy."

Rome smiled at her and said, "We have something in common, then, both of us being named after Italian cities. Do you live around here?"

"She doesn't live anywhere."

"You're quite beautiful, Florence," Rome said, still smiling.

"Her hair is the same as my mother's, isn't it?"

"Can I help you with anything?" Rome asked her.

"No, thank you," she said. "I'm fine just as I am. It was nice meeting and standing in the water with you, Roy."

"I liked meeting you, too. Maybe you'll be here the next time I come back."

Florence smiled at Roy and waved at him.

Rome kept smiling and said, "I hope to see you again sometime, too."

Florence turned away and looked out at the lake. The freighters had disappeared but the barge was still in sight.

Roy walked barefooted toward the shooting club with Rome, who no longer was smiling.

"Florence didn't tell you her last name, did she? Or where she lives?"

"I told you, she doesn't live anywhere. She said where she sleeps depends on her mood."

"I'm sure it does," said Rome. "These beautiful dolls are all a little mixed up in their heads, some more than a little."

"Is my mother mixed up in her head?"

"Here's a bench. Sit down and put your socks and shoes back on."

Acapulco

Roy was eight years old when he and his Uncle Buck, his mother's brother, flew from Chicago to Mexico City. They were going to visit Buck's former father-in-law, Doc Wurtzel, at his house in Cuernavaca. Roy's cousin Kip, Buck's son by his first wife, Doc's daughter Juliet, had been living with his grandfather and his housekeeper, Pilar, for the past ten months, ever since his parents divorced. Kip was twelve now, and neither Roy nor Buck had seen him for a year. Juliet had had a nervous breakdown before the divorce, and Buck travelled often for his work as a structural engineer, mainly as a consultant on designing or reinforcing bridges, so Doc suggested that until a more suitable situation could be arranged, Kip come to live with him at his villa. Doc Wurtzel was a widower, a retired mineralogist; he and Buck had much in common and were fond of one another. It would be beneficial, both men agreed, for Kip to learn Spanish and to be away from his mother, whose instability prevented her from paying proper attention to her son. Buck told Doc he thought the best solution would be for Kip to be sent when he turned thirteen to a military academy; until then, Doc could provide the boy with valuable life experience.

It was January of 1954 when Roy and his uncle left freezing cold Chicago for sunny Mexico. Roy had been to Cuba, where his father had business, he spoke a little Spanish, and he looked forward to being in another Latin American country. Despite the four year difference in their ages, Kip and Roy had always gotten along well, as had Roy's mother, Kitty, and Juliet. Both women were beautiful and smart, said Buck, but troubled.

"Your mother and Kip's mother aren't really suited to raising children," Buck told Roy on the plane. "They're too self-absorbed to be responsible for others. Kip is better off for now with his grandfather and you with your father."

"What are we going to do at Doc's?"

"We'll stay at his place in Cuernavaca for a couple of days, it's not far from Mexico City; he's got a beautiful swimming pool lined with big white rocks, surrounded by flamboyana trees. I designed his patio and helped him build the pool. Then the four of us will drive cross-country to Puerto Vallarta and go fishing. Doc has a special place he likes to hunt for marlin. After that maybe we'll stop over in Acapulco for a day or two."

"My mom and dad went to Acapulco on their honeymoon, I've seen pictures of them there."

"We'll rough it most of the way. Your dad tells me you're a good traveler."

"We once drove to Oriente from Havana, a lot of the way over mountains. It was kind of spooky sometimes. My dad kept a gun on the front seat between us, a .38. He showed me how to hold it with both hands and aim just below the target before I pulled the trigger."

"Did you have to shoot anybody?"

"No. Dad said there were bandits in the hills but all of the people we met were very nice. They were mostly black on that side of the island, different from in Havana. There are lots of pretty girls there."

Buck laughed and said, "There are pretty girls everywhere, Roy."

Doc's house was simply furnished and comfortable, with rattan chairs big enough for two people to sit in at the same time, and lots of doors to the outside that were always left open. Roy and Kip were happy to see each other again and Doc was a friendly, large man with a white beard and big hands. Kip told Roy that his grandfather could fix or build anything and that he was a championship fisherman. Pilar, Doc's live-in housekeeper, was a short, stout young woman with very long, shiny black hair.

"Pilar grew up in a small village near here," said Kip. "She's never even been to Mexico City and doesn't speak English. She doesn't speak good Spanish, either, mostly a local lingo Doc has trouble understanding. She's twenty-four. Doc sleeps with her sometimes, he says he does it to keep her happy because she's never been married and doesn't have any boyfriends."

"What if she gets pregnant?"

"I don't know. I guess the kid would live here with us. Pilar's parents never leave the village. Her sister, Tentación, comes to see her sometimes. She's only eighteen and has two kids already, a boy and a girl. Her husband, Pablo, breaks horses for ranchers around here. I've only met him once. He's shorter than I am but Doc says he knows how to sit a horse better than any man he's ever seen. Tentación told me Pablo's busted every bone in his body at least once."

"What does Tentación mean?"

"Temptation."

Doc and Buck sat and talked for two days, then the four of them loaded fishing and camping gear into the back of Doc's station wagon and headed for the west coast. The trip was uneventful but Roy enjoyed seeing what Mexico looked like. The country they drove through was not as verdant as Cuba; Doc said you had to go further south, to the state of Chiapas, to get into the forest.

"There's some serious jungle down that way," Doc said. "The Lacandon Indians live there and keep pretty much to themselves. They don't welcome outsiders. I hear they're tough folks to tangle with."

The men traded off driving and Roy got a little nervous when Doc drove because he sipped tequila all the time, but Kip told Roy Doc's secret to staying sober was to suck on venenoso limes while he drank. After a while Roy believed him because Doc was always steady on his feet and handled his customized, reinforced steel-bellied Willys expertly over bad roads.

"What's in the limes that keep him from getting drunk?" Roy asked Kip.

"Poison. That's what venenoso means."

The fishing at Puerto Vallarta wasn't so good. The marlin weren't running because of what Doc said was an unexpected cold spell, but he and Buck didn't seem to mind. All of the roads around the town were unpaved and the good weather didn't hold. Rather than camp out they stayed at a guest house that wasn't much more than a glorified lean-to. Kip taught Roy how to carve a resortera, a slingshot, out of a tree branch and they used stones to kill lizards. After three days of windy, wet weather and bad luck hunting marlin, Doc declared they should pack it in and make for Acapulco. There was a casino there, he said, and good restaurants.

In Acapulco, Doc decided they should check into a good hotel and clean up, then find the best place in town for martinis and steaks. After dinner, Kip and Roy walked with the men to a building next to the ocean with lots of steps leading up to the entrance.

"You boys wait here," Buck ordered when they were halfway up the steps. "Doc and I will be back in a little while."

The men continued up to the front door and Kip and Roy sat down on the steps and looked out at the Pacific. The sun was down but there was still a stripe of green light in the sky. The waves were gray-black and kicking up.

"Is this a casino?" Roy asked Kip.

"No, it's a prostibulo, a whorehouse. They're going to get laid."

A few men went up and came down the steps while the boys sat there.

"Do you miss your mother?" Roy asked.

"Sometimes, but only when she's not drinking, and she was always drinking before I got shipped down here to Doc's. Does your mother drink?"

"No, not really. She says if she has more than one drink she falls asleep. She has other problems, though."

"Like what?"

"She faints a lot. Sometimes she screams for no good reason and her body shakes. My grandmother gives her pills and puts her to bed."

"Remember that time she showed us how to play craps on the sidewalk in front of my house and my mother came out and yelled at her and made me go inside? Your mother just laughed and picked up the dice then got into her car and drove away."

"Her maroon Roadmaster convertible."

"Yeah. Doc says she's as beautiful as Gene Tierney, maybe even more beautiful."

"Who's Gene Tierney?"

Doc's favorite movie star ever since he saw her in *The Return of Frank James*. He said she went crazy and got put into an insane asylum."

After about an hour Doc and Buck came out of the house and walked down to where the boys were sitting. Roy and Kip stood up.

"How'd it go, Doc?" Kip asked.

"We got out alive, that's good enough. Let's go to the casino, I'll teach you to play craps."

"We know how to play, Roy's mother taught us."

"Kitty's my kind of woman," Doc said. "Don't you think so, Buck?"

When he got back to Chicago, Roy's friend Jimmy Boyle asked him if he'd had a good time in Mexico. They were on their way home from school, walking against a strong wind that made their faces feel like apples being sliced into by paring knives.

"I don't know," said Roy. "I liked being with my Uncle Buck and being in better weather than this."

"Did anything bad happen?"

Roy didn't answer. He lowered his head, bent his body half over and thought about the gentle breezes that ruffled the leaves of the flamboyana trees around Doc Wurtzel's swimming pool.

When he and Jimmy got inside the front hall of Roy's house, Roy rubbed his face with his hands and said, "Nothing bad happened, it was only that I didn't feel like I belonged there."

"Do you feel like you belong here?" Jimmy asked.

His Truth

In 1950, when H.T. was born, his mother, Thelma Louise Booth, named him Henry Thomas Booth, after her father. The man who impregnated her, a G.I. on leave whom she very briefly knew only as Monty, had disappeared from her life a few days after their liaison. It was Thelma Booth's misfortune that she had gotten knocked up at eighteen years old and was forced to fend for herself. Both of her parents had died in a car crash outside Terre Haute one year before she became pregnant. Adrift and alone, Thelma relocated from Indianapolis, where she gave birth in the Hilda Brausen Paupers Hospital, to Chicago. It was there with infant in arms that she joined The Church of Blood on Their Houses and was born again. Shortly thereafter, she renamed her son His Truth. For brevity's sake most of the time she called him H.T., which is what he came to be familiarly known as he was growing up.

Thelma Booth worked weekdays as a typist in the offices of Widerwille Sausage Company and played organ for the choir at The Church of Blood on Their Houses three evenings a week and on Sundays. She told her fellow parishioners that her husband had been killed in combat in Korea. H.T. did not like going to church and hated school but he liked to read. He went often to the Halsted Street public library and read history books and biographies, mostly about military leaders such as Hannibal of Carthage, Alexander of Greece, Alaric of the Visigoths, and Geiseric of the Vandals. His favorite, though, was Attila, commander of the Huns. H.T.'s mother had told him that her father's family, originally named Boethenius, had emigrated to the United States from a part of the Austro-Hungarian empire that had included eastern Ukraine and the northern Caucuses, the largest mountain range in eastern Europe. Thelma's great-great grandfather, Georgescu, she said, had led a rebel band opposed to the oppressive rulers of his province; according to what her mother had told her, Georgescu was known as The Almighty Destroyer of Pests. Armed with the false belief that his own father had been a warrior slain in battle, the tales of his mother's ancestors militant history, along with his own studies of great fighters and conquerors, at the age of eleven and a half H.T. organized a neighborhood gang of boys that called themselves the Halsted Street Huns. In their private meetings, members were instructed to address H.T. as His Truth.

On a late afternoon in February of 1961, H.T. and two other members of the Halsted Street Huns robbed Paddy Flannery's liquor store on Belmont Avenue. In the process, one of the boys shot the proprietor in the heart with a .22 caliber pistol purchased from a black Jew on Maxwell Street for five dollars, killing Flannery instantly. The three boys absconded with the proceeds from this misguided exercise in villainy and disappeared into the fast-closing winter darkness. Several passersby, however, had observed the miscreant trio as they fled the scene of the crime. One of them told the police that he believed it was a redhaired kid who was holding a gun in his left hand as he ran. The only one of the marauders who was lefthanded and had red hair was H.T.

Thirty-six hours following the robbery and murder Regis Furtwanger was apprehended outside of The Red Hot Ranch carrying a bag containing a dozen hot dogs with the trimmings and three bottles of Coca Cola. Against the advice of his co-worker, Roy, Spooky Spiegelman, a teenage employee of the Ranch, called the cops and identified Furtwanger as one of the Halsted Street Huns who were suspected of having knocked over the liquor store.

"My father told me to never call the cops," Roy told Spooky. "Something bad may have happened, but it will get worse once the police are involved." When confronted by six of Chicago's Finest with their guns drawn, Regis Furtwanger, whose father,

Adolph, played poker on Wednesday nights with the group of men who until that week had included Paddy Flannery, immediately blurted: "They're hidin' out in the belfry of The Church of Blood on Their Houses on Southport next to the Nazi beer joint."

Within minutes of Furtwanger's capture, a police squadron surrounded the church. It was just past five o'clock in the morning. When H.T. and his cohort Cornelius Slivka heard a voice over a bullhorn order them to come out with their hands high, Cornelius began moving toward the stairway. H.T. did not follow suit. He held tightly to the gun with which he had plugged the Irishman and thought of his heroes: Attila had died of alcoholism; Alaric, Hannibal and Alexander from malaria. He heard someone coming up the stairs, then a woman's voice, his mother's.

"H.T., it's me. Please give yourself up. The cops'll kill you if you don't."

Thelma Booth stepped into the belfry and saw her only child standing in a corner holding the .22 pistol. Suddenly, he sprang forward and used it to break the glass in a window overlooking Southport Street, leaned out, and rapidly fired four shots before receiving a rifle bullet between his eyes.

Thelma did not approach her boy's body. She stood still for a few moments, then slowly began descending the stairs. Police officers rushed past her on their way up to the belfry. Once back on Southport Street in front of The Church of Blood on Their Houses, a cop said to Thelma, "We didn't want to shoot him, lady. That's God's truth."

"His, too," she replied.

Disappointment

Bernie Zegma could hardly complain about business. His Mohawk gas station on the northeast corner of Ojibway and Thebes on the northwest side of Chicago had kept up a steady trade ever since he'd purchased it seventeen years before with his wife Helen's money. Their marriage of twenty-one years was uneventful, a generally calm alliance based not on passion but respectful understanding. Having married relatively late in their lives—Bernie's age kept him out of the war—by mutual agreement they had no children. Now in their fifties, Bernie and Helen enjoyed their individual privacy, he with his reading and she with her music. Bernie harbored a desire to someday write a novel, and Helen was a competent, devoted classical pianist.

Bernie retained only two employees at the station, high school kids named Roy and Ralph, who came to work after school to pump gas and change tires. Bernie took care of the gasoline trade in the morning hours and read books in his office in the afternoons. He no longer provided mechanical services as he had during the first fifteen years, doing only oil changes, replacing windshield wipers, headlamp and taillight bulbs.

One afternoon Bernie read about a remote part of French Polynesia called The Islands of Disappointment. Comprised of two small islands with a combined population of approximately three hundred, they had been named in 1752 by the grandfather of the poet Lord Byron, also named Byron, captain of an English trading ship that had been refused landing by the islanders. Byron applied the word "disappointment" to these bodies of land because of his displeasure at having been unable to explore the possibility of farming coconuts for the copra trade, coconut oil being a valuable commodity in Europe. Drawings of the islands made them seem a veritable paradise, unbothered by strife in the greater world, protected by their isolation. Bernie decided to go there.

That he murdered his wife could not be positively determined. The official reason given for Helen's death was a heart attack, but Ralph told Roy that his parents suspected Bernie had done away with her in order to inherit her family money.

"She was lying on the kitchen floor," Bernie told investigators. "I thought she was sleeping so I went out to buy cigarettes. When I came back she was still lying there. That's when I called the police."

"Did your wife often fall asleep on the kitchen floor?" an investigator asked.

"I don't know," Bernie answered. "I'm at work every day from five o'clock in the morning until eight p.m., when I close up the station. During the winter our kitchen is the warmest room in the house."

Once Helen's estate was settled, Bernie sold both their house and the Mohawk station. He gave each of the boys a twenty dollar bill and disappeared from the neighborhood.

"Remember when Bernie told us about those disappearing islands in the South Pacific?" Ralph asked Roy.

"Islands of Disappointment," said Roy. "Yeah, why?"

"Maybe that's where he went, to get away from the lousy Chicago weather. It don't snow out there. I seen what they look like in that dumb movie *South Pacific* my mother made me go with her to see."

"Hurricanes," Roy said. "There's floods and winds hundreds of miles an hour. Even worse than Chicago."

"Probably that's when the natives harvest the coconuts. They wait until the big winds blow 'em off the trees, then they pick 'em off the ground. Easier than climbin' up to get 'em.

"Could be. Do you think your parents are right, that Bernie killed his wife?"

"Who knows? I never heard him say nothin' about her. He was always the same, with that Gloomy Gus expression on his face. You know. I bet nobody around here ever hears from him again."

"He was a good enough guy to us," said Roy.

"I think he should have given us more than a double sawbuck," Ralph said. "He must have got plenty for sellin' the gas station."

A little more than a year after Bernie Zegma left Chicago, Roy got on a bus at the corner of Minnetonka and Western and saw him sitting in the last row. Roy walked back and sat down next to him.

"Hi, Bernie. I thought you were camped out with a bunch of beautiful brown island girls like in those paintings in the Art Institute."

"Hello, Roy. I was, but then I got sick, very sick, so I came back. I just got out of the hospital. I'm still not completely well."

"Are you going to buy another gas station?"

"No, I'm not going to stay in Chicago."

"Where are you going to?"

"I'm not sure yet."

Roy looked closely at Bernie's face. He wore the same gloomy expression as always but his face was pale, not bronzed by the Polynesian sun.

"I guess it's not paradise out there," Roy said.

"I'm getting off here. It's nice to see you. Say hello to Ralph."

Before the bus stopped, Bernie stood by the rear door. He looked back at Roy and said, barely loud enough for Roy to hear him, "Paradise is a dark forest."

Then he got off.

The Navajo Kid

"How old was The Navajo Kid when the Apaches killed his father?"

"Two or three, I think."

"Then the Navajos found him and he was raised by them?"

"Right. His father was the Indian agent for the Arizona territory. The Apaches moved back and forth across the border with Mexico. Mescaleros, I think."

Roy and Jimmy Boyle were walking to school together discussing the movie they'd seen on TV the night before. They were in the same fourth grade class.

"The guy who played the Kid after he was grown up also played a killer in a Bogart movie. He punched Bogey in the face holdin' a bunch of nickels in his fist."

"That must hurt."

"Knocked Bogey out."

"Didn't The Navajo Kid have a mother?"

"She was never mentioned. Maybe she was already dead."

"I read a book about a white boy who lived with an Indian tribe but his mother was an Indian. He had blue eyes and blonde hair so he always felt like he didn't belong."

"I bet. The full blood kids musta picked on him."

"Yeah. When he got old enough he went away to find out the truth about what happened to his father."

When Roy got home late that afternoon he found his mother in bed with bandages wrapped around her neck. He'd seen her this way numerous times applying ointments prescribed to treat her frequent outbreaks of eczema.

"Hi, Ma, your skin's bothering you again, huh?"

"It's pretty bad, Roy. I've been upset ever since I heard about cousin Norma having to go back into the sanitarium. I'm sure that's what triggered this attack. Norma's always been good to me, especially in the time after your father died."

"Do you need me to bring you anything?"

"Not right now. My back is getting itchy. I might ask you to apply the salve to my back and shoulders if it gets any worse."

"Sure, Mom. I'll leave the door to my room open. Just call me, I'll hear you."

"I didn't have a chance to go to the grocery store, Roy. If you want to get something take money out of my purse, it's on the dresser."

Kitty often talked about moving back to Florida to get away from the freezing cold Chicago winters. Her eczema bothered her in Florida, as well, but the sun made her feel better, she said, as if it were caressing her skin. Roy and his mother had lived in Key West from soon after his birth in Chicago until he was six. They had moved north so that Kitty could take care of her mother, Rose. Rose died the following year from heart trouble and Kitty decided to stay to be closer to Norma and a few other members of their family. Roy missed his friends in Key West, mostly Cuban kids, and being able to play outside year round, but he had good friends in Chicago now and didn't want to leave.

About an hour after he'd returned, Roy got hungry. He went into his mother's bedroom and saw that she was sleeping, so he quietly removed two dollars from her purse and left the house.

Roy's father died when Roy was five but Roy had never been given a satisfactory explanation as to how or why. Rudy had been twenty years older than Kitty, Roy knew that, but his mother told him only that his father had just collapsed one day and not recovered. Roy identified with The Navajo Kid. He had not been adopted by an Idian tribe but he needed to know more about his father's life, in particular what he did for a living. His mother said that Rudy was a businessman who helped out other people in their businesses, and that as a child he had come to America from a faraway corner of Eastern Europe when he was ten years old.

"Your dad didn't go to school, Roy," Kitty told him, "he always worked, doing all kinds of jobs because his family was very poor. I think it was because he had to work so hard that he died young."

Roy had light brown hair and blue eyes, unlike his father, who had black hair and brown eyes. Roy looked more like his mother. The Navajo Kid did not resemble the Navajo boys and girls, he knew he was different, and he wanted to know what his real parents looked like and where they had come from before they—or at least his father—were in Arizona.

On his way to Pooky's hot dog and hamburger stand it began to rain, lightly at first, then harder, so Roy stopped under the awning in front of a Chinese laundry. A heavyset, middleaged woman came out of the laundry carrying a green duffel bag. She took a look at the rain and stood next to Roy.

"Wattaya think, kid, this a real storm or only a passin' cloud?"

"Probably if I were an Indian, I'd know," said Roy, "but I'm not."

The woman looked at him. Her hair was tied up on the top of her head with a pink bandana and she had bright red lipstick smeared unevenly around her mouth.

"I just get through arguin' with them overchargin' charmers and then I get a smartass punk answer from you. Am I in hell yet or only dreamin'?"

The woman slung the duffel bag over her right shoulder and walked off in the downpour. Roy had not meant to be rude to her, he didn't know why he had spoken to the woman that way. The rain continued coming down hard. Did it rain like this in Arizona? Or in the part of Europe his father had come from? He wondered why he had wound up here in Chicago standing in front of a Chinese laundry watching raindrops the size of bullets beat into the sidewalk. What if he just kept going and never saw his mother again? What would happen to him? Suddenly the rain slacked off, then stopped entirely. Roy put up the collar of his jacket and continued on his way to Pooky's.

Roy remembered when he was little and used to stand next to the piano in the livingroom and sing while his mother played. One of her favorites was *Autumn Leaves.* "The autumn leaves/drift by my window/the autumn leaves/of red and gold." Roy sang the words softly out loud as he walked. His mother didn't play the piano often any more; sores on her fingers made it too painful, she said. Roy's grandmother used to play the piano and sing, too. Rose and Kitty sometimes played duets and Rose taught Roy how to read notes on the sheet music. He missed singing along with them. From now on, Roy decided, whenever anyone asked him about his parents he'd tell them his father had been murdered by Apaches in Mexico and that his mother was part Navajo.

In My Own Country

Robinson Geronimo was an old man who lived in a two-room apartment above a Mom and Pop grocery store on the West Side of Chicago during the 1940s and '50s. The entrance to his walk-up was accessible only from the alley behind Nelson Avenue up two flights of rickety porch stairs that had not been painted or repaired for more than forty years. When Joe and Ida Divino bought the building and opened Divino's Grocery in 1946, Robinson Geronimo was already in residence. Nobody in the neighborhood knew how old he was, and perhaps he did not himself know. Robinson Geronimo claimed that he was a son of the Apache chief Geronimo. He told Ida and Joe that he had been born "in Apacheria before the coming of the White sickness." Despite his advanced age, Robinson still did odd jobs around the neighborhood, mostly plumbing. The Divinos never raised his rent, which was ten dollars a month. Robinson Geronimo did not talk much. When Ida Divino asked him how it was he had come to live in Chicago, all he said was, "In my own country I was a chief's son."

Roy and his friends, who in 1955 ranged in age from seven to ten years old—Roy was eight—were naturally curious about the Apache Indian who lived above Divino's Grocery. They especially wanted to know if he really was Geronimo's son, and if so what life had been like for his tribe back in the old days.

"We should go ask him," suggested Jimmy Boyle.

"You mean go to his apartment over Joe and Ida's?" asked Chuck Danko.

"Sure, why not? We walk upstairs and knock on his door. Worse can happen is he don't open it."

Chuck, Jimmy and Roy cut down the alley between Nelson

and Poland streets and stopped behind the grocery building. It was two days before Christmas, cold and cloudy.

"Who's goin' up first?" asked Jimmy.

"We should all go up together," said Roy, who began walking toward the stairs.

The other two boys followed him. Several of the steps were missing, so they had to climb slowly.

"Robinson should replace these broken steps," said Chuck. "He's a handyman, isn't he? What if he's comin' home late at night after he's had a couple pops too many at Beeb's and Glen's and puts a foot into a hole? He'd break a leg."

"He probably already done it," Jimmy Boyle said. "I know my old man would. He trips all the time on our back porch comin' in the gangway from Beeb's and it's only got six steps which none of 'em are broken."

When they reached the apartment door, Chuck said, "Let me knock."

Roy and Jimmy stood behind him as Chuck knocked twice. Nobody came to the door.

"Knock three times," said Roy.

"Why three?" asked Jimmy.

"You know that song, 'Hernando's Hideaway'? It's about some guys goin' to a secret club or bar and they're supposed to knock three times and whisper low so they'll be let in. My mother plays that record a lot."

Chuck knocked three more times. After a few seconds the door opened. Robinson Geronimo stood, tall and still, looking down at the boys. When he spoke his lips did not move.

"Somebody sent you?" he asked.

"No," said Roy. "We'd like to talk to you."

Robinson Geronimo's face was gray, the color of smoke, his narrow eyes were dark and brown without light in them, and his nose was broad, almost round, and had no tip to it. For an old man, his face had very few wrinkles, only pockets like crevices in the smoky skin.

"Talk about what?"

"Was Geronimo really your father?" asked Chuck.

"Did he kill a lot of soldiers?" asked Jimmy.

"How old are you?" asked Roy.

Robinson Geronimo did not say anything for almost a full minute. He stood looking at them, then turned and went back inside his apartment, leaving the door open. The boys waited on the porch without talking. When Robinson Geronimo returned, he was holding a small, black and white photograph which he placed against his chest so they could see it. After each of the boys had examined the picture closely, Robinson spoke.

"My father, forty-eight years ago, 1907, two years before he died. On his horse, Takes Far Away. On horse next to him, my uncle, Wolf Once Was A Man. On other horse behind them, my little brother, nine years old, Nobody Sees Him In Moonlight. He died next year from White man's sickness. Our mother, too, same year."

The three boys stared at the photograph. There were cracks in it and some discoloration but the faces of the two men and a boy on horseback were discernible.

"How come your name is Robinson?" Roy asked.

"I keep Apache name. You can't have it. Go home now. The sky is in trouble."

Robinson Geronimo went back inside and closed the door. The boys walked down the stairs, stepping carefully.

When they were back in the alley, Roy said, "In a movie I saw one of the Indians was named No Enemy of Horses, but I don't remember what tribe he belonged to."

"Indians back then had better names than us," said Chuck.

"Yeah, Jimmy Boyle said, "even their horses did."

Rinky Dink

The wind came hard off the lake. Lights were on in the big houses as Rinky Dink roared by, his Harley nudging the white line between the inner lanes. The party he'd been to in Milwaukee had lasted four days past New Year's and he was looking forward to telling the gang about it. He knew they'd be at The Torch on Paulina and wanted to get there before midnight, while Bo Crawford and Johnny Kay and the others were still there. Rinky Dink cut in and out of the slowgoing traffic, skidding slightly every so often on an icy patch, but he was too crack a rider to let that bother him, and he was only twenty minutes away.

The woman who hit him with her brand new 1962 Packard Caribbean never looked in her side view mirror, only the rear, and knocked him sideways off the bike into the path of oncoming traffic. His head hit the ground an instant before a Buick ran over his back. Rink wasn't big, about five-eight or nine and slender, and he had a three inch long scar on his forehead that turned red whenever he laughed or was angry. The accident did not leave a mark on his face, only a bruise on his right temple that would never heal. When she saw him in his coffin Bonnie Hodiak said, "Why he looks cuter now than ever."

Fifty-five years after Rinky Dink was killed he appeared in Roy's dreams. Why now? Roy wondered. He had been in his last year of high school then. Rinky Dink, Bonnie Hodiak, Bo Crawford and the rest of that crowd were Roy's cousin Kip's friends, all of them several years older than Roy. None of them had ever gone to college, the boys worked as automobile mechanics or at other blue collar jobs, the girls as waitresses or counter clerks in department or dime stores. A few of the girls did a little hooking on the side— "soft" hookers Kip called them, meaning they were independents who worked the local bars whenever they needed extra cash for a new dress or coat or pair of shoes.

Roy was fourteen or fifteen when he began hanging out with Kip's pals. They interested him because they didn't live straight lives, kept irregular hours and occasionally committed crimes, usually holdups, thefts of some kind, sometimes got caught and did time. The girls were sexy, they smoked and drank hard liquor even if they were underage, and talked tough. In the places they hung out the bartenders never checked to see how old they were. The beat cops who came in never bothered anybody, just took their payoff, knocked back a shot or two and left quietly.

One of Bo Crawford's girlfriends, Cindy Purdy, twice gave Roy a blow job in Bo's car while he was in a bar. Cindy was nineteen then, four years older than Roy. She was a pretty little blonde who'd come up to Chicago from Oklahoma, sipped grain alcohol cut with orange juice from a flask she kept in her purse, and carried a switchblade knife. Cindy disappeared about a year later. Roy asked his cousin what happened to her and Kip said she'd taken off with "a gray hair" who worked in the oil business and was living with him somewhere in Texas, so Roy never saw her again.

Kip told Roy that Rinky Dink used to "run errands," as Rink called them, for Johnny Kay and a cohort of Johnny's named Teddy Fitts. Kay would scope out a target, figure the best time of day or night to hit a retail store, usually the day before a bank armored car picked up the week's receipts, and send in Teddy Fitts to knock it off. After Fitts came out of the place, Rinky Dink, who'd been waiting nearby on his Harley, would swoop in, grab the swag and speed away. Johnny Kay then pulled up in a stolen car he'd changed the plates on, Teddy jumped in, and Johnny drove off in the direction opposite to the one Rinky Dink headed in. This gambit worked well until the bandit trio chose to rob a grocery store in Kenosha, Wisconsin, where a sixteen year old bag boy got the drop on Teddy Fitts and drilled him three times with a .22 caliber handgun he carried in a back pocket. When Teddy didn't come out of the store right away both Rink and Johnny split. Teddy didn't die until the next day and never said a word to the authorities before he did. After that, Rinky Dink quit the holdup business, telling Johnny Kay, "I had a bad feelin' in the morning. There was a cold, noisy wind blowin', what the Apaches call the devil's breath. We shoulda called it off."

Rinky Dink worked part time in a salvage yard pulling parts out of wrecked cars and trucks. All he really cared about was his motorcycle, which he had painted bright red and kept in perfect running condition. Cindy Purdy told Roy she had a "ditch deep" crush on Rinky Dink but that he just pushed her away when she went for his fly. Rink hung out with the group but kept quiet most of the time, just grinned and drank beer from the bottle. In Roy's dream, Rinky Dink was leaning against a parked car at nightfall in front of a bar with an orange neon sign in the window that blinked the name "Armando's" on and off. He was wearing an unzipped navy blue windbreaker and his caramel-colored pompadour rippled in the breeze. As usual, he was grinning. There was a blonde-haired girl sitting in the front seat of the car on the passenger side. Roy could not see her face but he thought it might have been Cindy Purdy.

Where the Dead Hide

"Look in the bottom drawer of the dresser in the dining room, Roy. The placemats are underneath a burgundy tablecloth."

Roy's mother was having a dinner party that night and Roy, who was fourteen, was helping her prepare the table. He knelt down and felt around under the tablecloth and found the placemats, which he took out, as well as a thick piece of paper that was partially stuck to the underside of the placemat on the bottom. He carefully separated the paper from the placemat without tearing it and read what was printed on it.

"Hey, Ma, who is James O'Connor?"

His mother walked from the kitchen into the dining room and said, "Who?"

"I found this document in the bottom of the drawer. It's a marriage certificate with Nanny's name on it and a James O'Connor. I didn't know she'd been married to anyone other than Pops."

"Let me see it."

Roy handed her the certificate and stood up. His mother scanned it, then said, "Yes, Roy, she was, for about ten years, from the time I was six until I was sixteen."

"So she and Pops got divorced."

"Yes."

"Why didn't you ever tell me?"

"I didn't think it was important, I guess. O'Connor died when I was in my last year of high school, and Nanny died when you were eight, so I didn't really see the point. Also, since you and Pops are so close, I didn't want to say anything that might affect your relationship with him."

"So you really grew up with this guy O'Connor. He was your stepfather."

"Oh, I was away most of the time at boarding school, and then in the summer I went to Kansas City to visit my father, who was living there for much of the time Nanny and O'Connor were married."

"Did you live here then, in this house?"

"No, O'Connor had a house in Norwood Park, about thirty miles west of Chicago. After O'Connor died, my mother sold that house and we moved back into the city."

"Did Pops own this house?"

"Yes, he still does. Half of it, anyway. I own the other half."

Roy's mother rolled up the certificate and said, "I'll tie a ribbon around this."

"Why did you keep it?" Roy asked.

His mother looked at him but didn't say anything.

"What about Uncle Buck?"

"What about him?"

"Did he live in Norwood Park, too?"

"No, Roy, my brother is twelve years older than I am, he was already pretty much gone by the time Nanny married O'Connor. He was at the University of Alabama for a couple of years before he went into the navy."

"What about when he came back?"

"He and O'Connor didn't get along. I'm not sure why, but O'Connor didn't want Buck around, so he stayed with friends in Chicago. It was easier for him to find jobs in the city."

"I wonder why Uncle Buck never told me about Nanny being married to O'Connor."

"It was a difficult time for my brother. O'Connor wouldn't even let Buck see Nanny at their house. She used to meet him at restaurants and other places in Chicago. I guess it's painful for him to talk about that time."

"Did O'Connor like you?"

"He was always polite and nice enough, I suppose. I was just a little girl. As I said, I was off at a Catholic boarding school, so he didn't have to deal with me very much. My mother took care of me. Besides, O'Connor spent a lot of time with his brothers, they were in the warehouse business in the Chicago area and other cities in the Midwest. He was always busy or going out of town somewhere."

"Did you call him Dad?"

"No, Mr. O'Connor."

Roy's mother walked back into the kitchen. Rain began beating at the windows. Roy went into the livingroom and looked outside. The sky was darkening quickly and rain was hitting the windows harder in the front of the house. He thought about Pops living alone in a hotel in Chicago. Roy's Uncle Buck had recently moved to Florida and wanted Pops to live down there with him and his wife and daughter. Pops was almost eighty years old, the winters in Chicago were hard on him, so Roy figured it would be better for his grandfather to live somewhere warm. Roy loved Pops more than anyone else in his family. Pops was his best friend and Roy knew he would miss him a lot. James O'Connor didn't sound like he was such a good guy, especially his not having been kind to Buck, whom Roy loved almost as much as he loved Pops. Roy's father had been dead for two and a half years now. Maybe, Roy thought, he would go to Florida, too.

Bar Room Butterfly

Roy's grandfather subscribed to several magazines, among them *Time, Field & Stream, Sport,* and *Reader's Digest,* but the one that interested Roy most was *Chicago Crime Monthly.* One afternoon Roy came home from school and found his grandfather reading a new issue.

"Hi, Pops. Anything good in there?"

"Hello, boy. Yes, I've just started an intriguing story."

Roy sat down on the floor next to his grandfather's chair.

"Can you read it to me?"

"How old are you now, Roy?"

"Ten."

"I don't know everything that's in this one yet. I wouldn't want your mother to get mad at me if there's something she doesn't want you to hear."

"She's not home. Anyway, I've heard everything."

"You have, huh? All right, but I might have to leave out some gruesome details, if there are any."

"Those are the best parts, Pops. I won't tell Mom. Start at the beginning."

BAR ROOM BUTTERFLY
by Willy V. Reese

Elmer Mooney, a plumber walking to work at seven a.m. last Wednesday morning, noticed a body wedged into a crevice between two apartment buildings on the 1800 block of West Augusta Boulevard in Chicago's Little Poland neighborhood. He telephoned police as soon as he arrived at Kosztolanski Plumbing and Pipeworks, his place of employment, and told them of his discovery.

The dead body was identified as that of Roland Diamond, thirty-four years old, a well-known Gold Coast art dealer who resided on Goethe Street. He was unmarried and according to acquaintances had a reputation as a playboy who had once been engaged to the society heiress Olivia Demaris Swan.

Detectives learned that Diamond had been seen on the evening prior to the discovery of his corpse in the company of Miss Jewel Cortez, 21, at the bar of the Hotel Madagascar, where Miss Cortez was staying. When questioned, Miss Cortez, who gave her profession as "chanteuse," a French word for singer, told authorities she had "a couple of cocktails" with Diamond, with whom she said she had only a passing acquaintance, after which, at approximately nine p.m., he accompanied her to her room where he attempted by force to have sex with her.

"He was drunk," Cortez told police, "I didn't invite him in, he insisted on walking me to my door. I pushed him out of my room into the hallway but he wouldn't let go of me. We struggled and he fell down the stairs leading to the landing below. He hit his head on the wall and lay still. I returned to my room, packed my suitcase and left the hotel without speaking to anyone."

Jewel Cortez confessed that before leaving the hotel she removed Roland Diamond's car keys from his coat pocket and drove to Detroit in his car, a 1954 Packard Caribbean, where, two days later, she was apprehended while driving the vehicle in that city. Miss Cortez was taken into custody on suspicion of car theft. Upon interrogation by the Detroit police she claimed not to know that Diamond was dead, that he had loaned her his car so that she could visit friends in Detroit, where she had resided before moving to Chicago. Miss Cortez also said she had no idea how his body had wound up in Little Poland. When informed that examination of Diamond's corpse revealed a bullet wound in his heart, Cortez professed ignorance of the shooting and declared that she had never even handled a gun let alone fired one in her life.

Betty Corley, a resident of the Hotel Madagascar, described Jewel Cortez as "a bar room butterfly." When asked by Detective Sergeant Gus Argo what she meant by that, Miss Corley said, "You know, she got around," then added, "Men never know what a spooked woman will do, do they?"

Chicago, May 4, 1955

•   •   •

"What does she mean by 'spooked'?" Roy asked. "Frightened?"

"Yes, but her point is that women can be unpredictable."

"Is my mother unpredictable?"

Pops laughed. "Your mother is only thirty-two years old and she's already been married three times. What do you think?"

Absolution

After Kitty suffered her second stroke within a week, she could not talk, walk or recognize anyone. What she could do was smile, and when she did her face appeared virtually unlined, as it had been when she was in her twenties and her son, Roy, was a little boy. The last coherent sentence she had spoken, following her first stroke, came when Roy visited her in the hospital, and was directed at him: "You were always different," she said.

Kitty died a few months later at the age of ninety-one. There was no funeral; Roy's sister, who lived in the same city as their mother, had her cremated the next day. The afternoon Roy had seen her in the hospital, he had brought with him his cousin Peter, whom Kitty had not seen for fifty years. Peter wore a dark blue shirt under a black sportcoat and stood at the foot of her bed while Roy sat on a chair close to her.

"Who is that?" Roy's mother asked him.

"Our cousin, Peter, Dora's son. You haven't seen him in a very long time."

"Padre Pietro," she said. "Please tell the sisters I'm sick tonight, that I won't be coming down to dinner."

Later, Peter told Roy, "I didn't expect your mother to recognize me."

"She thought she was back at boarding school, with the nuns," said Roy. "You were a priest."

"Padre Pietro."

"Better him than one of her ex-husbands."

"How many were there?"

"Five."

"How many of them are still alive?"

"Two that I know of. My father died when I was five."

"She knew who you were."

"I could have been anybody."

"No, she knew."

That evening at dinner Roy's sister asked Peter if Kitty had spoken to him.

"Not really, she thought I was a priest."

"There'll be a real one there to give her the last rites."

"She thought she was still a girl at Our Father of Frivolous Forgiveness," said Roy.

His sister laughed and said, "She never could."

"Never could what?"

"Forgive herself for not having been a better wife or mother."

"Padre Pietro forgives her," said Peter.

Roy and his sister looked at him.

"Absolution is my business," he said.

After his mother died, Roy reminded Peter of his joke about forgiving Kitty and told him about the time he was seven years old when she went with their neighbor, Mrs. McLaughlin, to St. Tim's church to commit a novena. Upon her return, Roy had asked her what a novena is.

"A novena is an act of devotion," his mother explained. "It's a pledge to honor a specific religious object or figure for nine days by saying prayers, usually to request a favor."

"Did you go to confession, too?"

"Not today."

"That's when you tell a priest about any sins you committed, right?"

"Yes, Roy."

"Does committing a novena rub out those sins?"

"No, the priest listens to your confession and decides which prayers you should recite and how many times you say them in order to expiate your sins."

"What does expiate mean?"

"To atone, to make up for having done something you shouldn't have or regret."

"What bad things did you tell the priest about the last time you went to confession?"

"Nothing really bad, only impure thoughts."

"Did you tell him about the time you said you wished your boyfriend Phil Rogers would rot in hell because he went back to his wife? Was that an impure thought?"

"No, that doesn't count."

"Do I have impure thoughts?"

"Of course not."

"And the priest forgave you for thinking them?"

"He did."

"How do you know if something you're thinking of is wrong?"

"If you feel in your heart and soul it's not good, then it's not. What the priest does is grant absolution, so you don't have to feel bad about it anymore."

"I thought only God can make things right."

"A priest is an agent of God, His emissary. God speaks through him."

"Why doesn't God do it Himself?"

"Oh, Roy, you know He can't be everywhere. He needs help."

"I thought God *is* everywhere."

"I can't explain it any better, sweetheart. You'll understand more about how God works when you're older."

"I heard Mrs. McLaughlin say that her Great-Uncle Declan in Ireland is older than God."

Roy's mother laughed. "That's just an expression. It means she thinks he's very old."

"There's a lot I don't understand about how religion works, Mom."

"I know, Roy. There's a lot I don't understand about it, either."

"Did your mother continue going to confession for the rest of her life?" Peter asked.

"No," said Roy, "at least not that I know of. Only when I was a kid, and then not consistently."

"I don't ever remember her going," said his sister.

"She remembered the last words of the Lamentations from the Old Testament, though," Roy said. "'But thou hast utterly rejected us.' Kitty quoted that line every once in a while when something bad happened or she'd been disappointed by one of her husbands or boyfriends."

"She figured God had given up on His people," Roy's sister said, "so why should she bother talking to Him? After all, He was just another man."

The Goose

Roy's mother's fourth and final husband, Barney Roper, was a member of the Brotherhood of Ganders Lodge, a secret and fraternal organization. Wives of those members were referred to as The Gathering of the Geese. Privately, however, many of the Ganders jokingly called them "The Waggle Gaggle Gals." Four times a year, to celebrate the seasons, the Ganders had balls, which were really more on the order of drunken parties. Formal wear was required to attend, and Barney insisted that Kitty accompany him on these occasions.

It happened that Roy, who was eighteen years old, was visiting his mother and sister, Sally, who was six, in Rock City, Illinois, a town of 150,000 in the central part of the state, when one of the seasonal balls was held. Barney Roper worked for his two older brothers, Ben and Bradley, as a plant foreman at Roper & Roper Dry Ice. Kitty's husband, the third Roper, was an employee, not a partner, a position, he assured Kitty, that he would at some point achieve. This never happened due to Barney's eventual mishandling of certain accounts receivable for which his brothers decided to terminate his employment but declined to prosecute him.

During Roy's brief visit, his mother and her husband attended the Ganders event honoring the winter solstice. Kitty wore her best dress and jewelry given to her by Roy's father, her first husband. Barney Roper, as was customary, wore a tuxedo.

Roy and Sally were seated on a couch in the livingroom where Roy was reading to her a Nancy Drew mystery story when Barney and Kitty arrived home. Barney Roper was at the wheel of his 1962 Pontiac Bonneville when it smashed into the garage door, shaking the house and shocking both Roy and Sally. Kitty came rushing through the front door, shouting and crying, her hair and clothing awry.

"That's it!" she yelled. "It's over! I'm through! I'm getting a divorce!"

She passed through the livingroom without looking at her children and went directly into her bedroom, slamming the door shut behind her. Kitty continued ranting and raving, scaring Sally. Roy embraced his little sister, expecting Barney to appear momentarily, but he did not. Roy heard the car back down the driveway and be driven away.

"I'll be back in a minute," he told Sally, and went outside to inspect the damage.

The garage door had a large hole in it and was dangling from one of its hinges. Pieces of splintered wood were strewn on the ground, along with the outdoor lamp that had been mounted above the door.

Roy reentered the house but Sally was not in the livingroom. The bedroom door was open so he walked over and looked in. Sally was sitting on the bed watching her mother throw the contents of a closet and then belongings from a dresser onto the floor. As she was madly flinging shirts and socks and underwear out of the drawers, she suddenly stumbled and collapsed on the piles of clothing. Sally screamed and Roy bent down and attended to Kitty. She had fainted so Roy tapped her cheeks and spoke to her.

After several seconds Kitty regained consciousness and looked up at Roy. Her brown eyes were bloodshot and there was no light in them. The top half of her dress had fallen off, exposing most of her breasts. A strand of pearls had broken, leaving only a few still attached to the string.

"I'm not beautiful anymore, Roy," she said. "I used to be, you remember, when you were a little boy, how I looked then, how everyone stared at me, how the other girls envied me, my complexion, my hair, my figure."

"Yes, Mom, I remember."

"It's gone now, I'm gone."

"You're not gone, Ma, and you'll look fine again. You've got to get out of this marriage, that's all. Move back to Chicago with Sally. You've got to be well and take care of her."

Kitty closed her eyes and fell asleep.

"Is mom all right, Roy?"

"Yes, Sally. She just needs to rest for a little while."

Kitty laughed, softly at first, then louder but gently, without opening her eyes.

"My goose is cooked," she said. "Isn't that funny, Roy? It's me, I'm the goose."

She fell back to sleep but her breathing was labored and a whistling noise came from her nose.

"Are we going to move back to Chicago?" asked Sally. "I want to."

Spooky Spiegelman and
The Night Time Killer

Roy remembered an old guy named Rooftop Perkins who ran a radio repair shop in the neighborhood and sold dirty books under the counter. Spooky Spiegelman, a kid Roy had played ball with a few times in the schoolyard, brought customers to Rooftop who kicked back to Spooky a quarter or fifty cents for the hustle. Spooky approached Roy one day and asked him if he was interested in being a puller. Roy said he didn't think so but agreed to accompany him to Rooftop's place of business where Spooky wanted to collect what the old guy owed him.

"He owes me five bucks," said Spooky. "This way you can meet Rooftop, I'll get the gelt, then we can go to The Pantry and get a couple burgers and fries, my treat."

Spooky's real first name was Spencer. It was his mother who hung his nickname on him because of what she described as his strange behavior, his habit of lurking silently in empty hallways, doorways and otherwise deserted rooms of their house, "doin' nothin' but waitin'," Mrs. Spiegelman said, "standin' around, like waitin' on a bus. He's a spooky kid, he disappears but don't really go nowhere, you don't see him but you know he's there, like a ghost."

Spooky was a year older than Roy but they were both in fifth grade, which Spooky had flunked the year before.

"Mrs. Clancy told me she was puttin' me back on account of my spellin' and penmanship ain't good enough. Penmanship! Only ship I'll be on is when I join the navy."

Rooftop Perkins was sitting on a high stool behind the counter in his shop on Washtenaw Avenue when the boys entered. The old man was reading a paperback book the title of which, Roy noticed, was *Night Time Killer*. The illustration on the cover depicted a snarling, drooling, wildhaired man dragging a blonde woman wearing a torn green dress into an alley.

"Still bonin' up on the classics, I see," Spooky said.

"This was a best seller," said Rooftop, without lifting his eyes from the page. "Whadda you know about literature?"

"I know you owe me five pins."

"Four and a half. Al Prince didn't buy nothin'."

Using only his left hand Rooftop opened a cigar box that was on the counter, reached in and fingered four dollar bills, laid them down, then fished out two quarters and placed them on top of the singles.

"I'm gonna ask Al Prince if he didn't."

Spooky scraped up the money and stuffed it into his right front pants pocket.

"Your friend wanna have a look at the merch?"

"He can't read."

"I got some don't need readin'."

As the boys walked toward The Pantry, Roy asked Spooky why the old guy was called Rooftop.

"He fell off a garage roof after burglarizin' an apartment what I hear. Broke both legs, got caught and did a nickel for B and E. It was a light sentence cause he'd dropped the goods, so technically they weren't in his possession. Chicago's Finest found him crawlin' in the alley."

"What's his real name?"

"Baumholz. Don't know his first."

"Could be he's related to Famous Frankie Baumholz played outfield for the Cubs."

"You ever met someone famous?"

"I don't think so," said Roy, "but my Uncle Buck told me and my mother he and his new wife, Odile, who's French, were on an ocean liner comin' back from France and they met Ernest

Hemingway, the writer, who was also a passenger. My uncle said when Hemingway found out Odile was a singer he asked her to sing a song for him in French and she did, so they got friendly and had dinner with Hemingway and his wife a couple times during the voyage."

"This guy ever wrote a best seller?"

"Lots of 'em, I think. My mother said his picture was on the cover of *Life* magazine."

"Maybe he's the author of *Night Time Killer*."

Just as the boys entered the diner rain started coming down hard.

"My older brother Ben's friend Skinny Fazzoletto says the best time to rob houses is when it's rainin' because rain makes it easier to get away without bein' seen or identified. People are too busy tryin' to get where they're goin' without gettin' wet to notice you."

"Is Skinny Fazzoletto a burglar?"

"Not at the moment. At present he's sittin' out a jolt in Indiana. Got nabbed bein' in a truck full of stolen furniture after the driver lost control and went off the road durin' a rainstorm."

Roy lost track of Spooky Spiegelman after fifth grade when the Spiegelman family moved away from Chicago. Roy always remembered when Spooky moved because it was the year the White Sox traded Chico Carrasquel to Cleveland and Luis Aparicio took over at shortstop. Thirty years later Roy watched a movie on late night television called *Night Time Killer*. It was crudely made and the plot was simple: a deranged man, played by the hunky but sullen-faced actor Steve Cochran, stood half-hidden in doorways at night waiting for an unaccompanied female to pass by, then following and attacking her from behind before dragging her into an alley where he strangled her to death. No attempt at an explanation for the strangler's aberrant behavior was made except for a cop's comment to another cop that "The world is full of maniacs whose only excuse is that when they were a kid their mother didn't pay 'em enough attention. Well, I couldn't wait to get away from my old lady, she was always gettin' on me for somethin' I done wrong." The other cop grunted and said, "Yeah, me, too. Maybe that's why we're cops." In the end the killer assaults a female cop wearing a sexy dress who struggles out of his grasp, pulls her revolver and shoots him dead. Roy scrutinized the credits and saw that the movie was based on a novel by a woman named Juanita Mimoso, and the screenplay had been written by S. Spiegel.

Roy was surprised that the author of the novel was supposedly a woman but he was convinced that S. Spiegel was really Spencer "Spooky" Spiegelman. Roy never saw the movie again, nor did he ever notice another screenwriting credit attributed to S. Spiegel, about whom Roy did some research but failed to unearth any information other than that one credit for *Night Time Killer*. A few years later, however, Roy saw an episode of a cops and criminals tv show about a man who burglarized houses on rainy days whom the newspapers dubbed The Rainy Day Robber. The writing of the episode was credited to Rooftop Perkins.

Constantinople

Roy was eight years old when he learned from his mother that her grandfather, Roy's great grandfather Boris, had been a violinist in an orchestra in Constantinople, Turkey, during the penultimate decade of the 19th century. Originally from Russia, Boris had gone from there to Constantinople with his wife, Hattie, Roy's great grandmother, in the 1880s, then emigrated to Chicago, Illinois, in 1890. Roy's great aunt, Sophia, was born in Constantinople, and his grandmother, Rose, the family's first American, was born in Chicago in 1892.

Many years later research into family genealogy revealed a photograph of Roy's great grandfather with his violin seated among other members of a little orchestra in Constantinople. He was thrilled. This small orchestra consisted of men on tuba, flute, clarinet, bass fiddle and three violins (of which Boris played one), and two children, boys, one on drum, the other on trumpet.

When Roy was in the fifth grade, in 1955, during the course of a class discussion about family histories, he mentioned that his great aunt Sophia had been born in Constantinople. Several boys in the classroom laughed at him, certain that he was lying in order to make his family sound more exotic and colorful. After these students stopped laughing, Roy added that his great grandfather had been a violinist in an orchestra in Constantinople, which provoked more derisive laughter. After class, in the schoolyard, a boy named Eddie Koslov, one of the kids who had doubted Roy's claims, repeated his accusation that he had invented this story, so Roy punched him in the face. Koslov cried and ran away. When decades later Roy saw the photograph of his great grandfather Boris with the orchestra in Constantinople holding his violin, he wished that he could show it to Eddie Koslov and punch him in the face again.

The Same Place in Space

"There's a bunch of guys followin' us," said Chuck Danko, "black guys."

Three other boys, including Roy, all of whom were thirteen or fourteen years old, turned and looked behind them as they walked.

"They're pretty big," Jimmy Boyle said. "Older than us."

Roy and his friends were walking on Lake Street in The Loop on a freezing cold and windy late Saturday afternoon in February. They had just come from seeing the movie Giant at the State & Lake theater.

"If they start somethin'," said Richie Gates, "we should split in four different directions."

"No," Jimmy said, "if they get one of us then the rest of us can help him. There's six of them."

One of the black kids ran up and shoved Richie.

"Where you goin', punk?" he said.

Richie turned around and shoved him back. The kid was three or four inches taller than Richie. The other black guys walked up and stared hard at Roy's back. Everybody stood still.

"Y'all in a hurry?" said the kid who'd shoved Richie.

"How much money you got?" another kid said. "Prob'ly all you boys got your allowances, huh? How much allowances you get?"

"Chester!" said Roy. "How are you, man?"

The tallest and most muscular-looking one of the black kids looked at Roy, then smiled and said, "Hey, Roy, what you up to?"

Roy and Chester both came forward and shook hands.

"Just saw *Giant*, the new James Dean movie."

"Any good?"

"Yeah, long, though. James Dean looks kind of funny made up as an old guy."

"He was killed in a car wreck, wasn't he?" asked Chester.

"Yes, drivin' a racing Porsche on a highway in California. Farmer in a pick-up truck named Donald Gene Turnupseed ran into him from a side road."

"You know this kid, Chester?" said the boy who'd asked about allowances.

"We played ball together last summer," Chester said.

"Chicago Park District All-Stars," said Roy. "Chester was the catcher, I played third."

"How old are you now, Roy?"

"Fourteen."

"Roy was the youngest player on the team. He can hit."

"You gonna play again this year?" Roy asked.

Chester shook his head. "Too old, I'm seventeen now. Playin' football, basketball and baseball for Lost Sons of Egypt."

"You're a great catcher, Chester, and a real power hitter."

"A coach from Notre Dame come to see me play football, says I can be a good linebacker, maybe make All-American."

Roy's friends huddled behind him and Chester's boys backed off.

"You guys just hangin' out?" said Roy.

"Omar here only messin' with your friend. Nobody be botherin' you."

"Great to see you, Chester."

They shook hands again.

"Let's get goin' fellas," Chester said. He and his bunch turned and walked away. Omar lingered for a few seconds and sneered at Richie before joining Chester and the others.

"Wow, good thing you recognized that guy, Roy," said Jimmy Boyle.

The wind began blowing harder, twisting its way around corners of the downtown buildings.

"Yeah," Chuck Danko said, "but even more amazing is that you know the name of the driver who killed James Dean."

The Good Listener

Roy's Uncle Buck and his friend Tony Grimaldi, who owned the Abeja Bank in Ybor City, played poker with two or three other men on Thursday nights. This was in the 1960s when Tampa, Florida, was still a relatively small city, a shrimp and cigar town, as Grimaldi called it. Ybor City was the center of the Cuban-American community, which it had been since the mid-19th century. Tony Grimaldi wasn't Cuban but, having grown up there, spoke Spanish like one.

"C'mon, Gus, you want cards or not?"

"Tony, you know how much time it takes you to okay or refuse a loan?"

"No time. You need a loan or cards?"

"One."

"Buck?"

"I'm good."

"Art?"

"Dos."

"Ralph?"

"I'm out."

"Speakin' of loans?"

"Art?"

"What about Don Kay? You know he's goin' away for torchin' the Riviera Terrace."

"Don Kay don't worry me. You worry me, always takin' two cards."

Buck, Art, Tony and Gus showed their hands. Buck scraped up the pot. After the game ended and only Tony and Buck were still seated at the table, Buck asked Tony about Sam Lowiski.

"He's in Dallas with that puta, the counterfeit rubia makes stag films."

"You like her, Tony, don't you?"

Tony lit a Chesterfield, puffed on it a few times, then said, "Mary Duckworth is her real name."

"Lowiski calls her Deronda LeMay. Anyhow, he come through?" Grimaldi stubbed out his cigarette.

"I could use another beer."

"Gus killed the last one."

"If he don't show by tomorrow, we'll go get him. I can send Izzy."

"You mean Lefty, whose left arm got shot off by that runt Martinelli?"

"Israel Izquierda, yeah."

"Funny he's called Lefty when it's his left arm's the one missing."

"To remind him be more cuidado how he goes about his business. Unless you want to go. We could drive up together Saturday."

"Can't. Taking my nephew fishing."

"Roy's a smart boy. How old's he now?"

"Twelve."

"Good you're there for him. His mother's still got her looks but she's a wreck."

"My sister's never recovered from the break-up of her second marriage. She had a nervous breakdown, plus she has a skin condition puts her in the hospital."

"You teachin' Roy the construction business?"

"He wants to be a writer."

Tony laughed. "He's just a kid, he needs to learn how to make a livin'. Writin' what?"

"Stories."

"I'll talk to him."

"He's got his own mind, like his father."

"When my old man died, I was fifteen," Tony said. "He was from Trapani, in Sicily. He had old country rules. They still apply."

Two days later, when Buck and Roy were on Buck's boat in the

Gulf of Mexico, Buck said, "You ought to go see Tony Grimaldi, he likes you. You could get some good stories from him."

"I like Tony, too. He lets me sit in the chair behind his desk when I go in the bank. One thing I know already is that to be a writer it's important to be a good listener."

"Your dad had plenty of stories."

"He told me some things that happened in Romania when he was a boy, about people who lived in his village that believed in magic. There was an older boy who talked to pigs and the pigs talked to him. One of the pigs predicted everybody's future, how some of them would have accidents like falling off a roof or drowning when they were drunk, or being stabbed by their wife. But somehow the way my dad told the stories, even though the fortune-telling pig predicted someone being torn apart by wild dogs or run over by a train, they were funny. Those are the kinds of stories I want to write, funny tragedies. If death is the worst thing that can happen to a person but there's something funny about it then it might not be so bad. What do you think, Unk?"

"Well, I've seen men die with smiles on their faces. Not many, a few. When I was with the Seabees, stationed on an island in the South Pacific, Vanua Levu, we built Quonset huts to house the men. It was my idea, modelled on Narragansett tribal construction, that I studied in engineering school. One of the men fell off a ladder and broke his neck. He died, but not right away. His name was Bentley, from Alabama. Bentley asked me why we were building Quonset huts and I told him the Indians built them for protection from freezing cold winters. 'There's no winter here, Commander,' he said. I explained that the long, high ceilings not only kept heat in during the cold months but kept the temperature down in the hot months. 'The Indians figured that out, did they?' he asked. I said yes, in Rhode Island. 'My granny Calwallader was right,' Bentley said. I asked him what she was right about, and he said, 'If you got some curiosity in you, you can learn something new near every day.' Then Bentley died, smiling. Calwallader must have been his mother's family name."

"What do you think happens to a person after he dies?"

"Nothing. There's just no person anymore."

"Dead people live in other people's memories, Unk, like my dad. He'll always be there in my mind."

Years later, after Tony Grimaldi, Roy's Uncle Buck and Roy's mother were dead, Roy refused to forget them. Instead, he wrote about them as they were, as he imagined they were, and as they never were or even could have been. He figured if he had known them as well as he thought he'd known them then what he wrote would be as close as he would ever come to the truth.

The Garden Apartment

Roy was eight years old when he and his mother moved from Key West, Florida, where they lived in a hotel, to an apartment in Chicago, Illinois, where his grandmother had lived until she died a few months before. It was a large, high-ceilinged, six room apartment on the first floor of a three-flat building. There was also what was called a "garden" apartment on the basement level, even though there was no garden attached to the building. Roy was unhappy about having to move from the hotel, which was located at the confluence of the Gulf of Mexico and the Atlantic ocean. In Key West he spent his time swimming and fishing, playing with the Cuban kids who lived in the houses around the hotel, and attending school irregularly. His mother, who suffered from a nervous condition that doctors determined caused her chronic eczema and other, mostly unspecified ailments, explained that the move was for financial reasons, given that her mother had been half owner of the apartment building, which his mother inherited. They could now live rent free and share income derived from the third floor and garden apartments. Cousins of theirs, who were co-owners of the building, occupied the second floor apartment.

The garden apartment comprised a livingroom, bedroom, kitchen and bathroom, with ground floor windows in the livingroom that looked out at the front lawn and sidewalk. The tenants were a childless married couple, a man and a woman, both in their late twenties or early thirties, who always wore black clothes, most often turtleneck sweaters, black trousers and jackets or coats. The man had a neatly trimmed beard, a short haircut—his thinning hair was dark brown—and wore wire-rimmed eyeglasses. His wife had shoulder-length black hair with bangs that covered her forehead, and wore heavy blue-black eyeshadow. According to Roy's mother, the man worked as a librarian at Loyola University, and the woman as a typist in a law office. They were quiet and clean, said his mother, had lived in the building for two years, paid their rent on time and had never caused his grandmother any trouble.

Roy often heard music coming from the garden apartment, mostly jazz, sometimes classical. He learned that the tenants' names were Joyce and Michael, and that they were originally from Canton, Ohio. One day after school Roy came home at the same time Joyce was arriving. He said hello and told her he liked hearing the music she and Michael played, especially the jazz.

"That's cool, Roy," said Joyce. "Would you like to come in and listen to some records?"

"Sure," he said, and followed her down the stairs.

Roy had been in the garden apartment only once before, during a visit to his grandmother when he was five years old. An elderly lady had lived there at that time. The first thing Roy noticed were long strands of beads that hung in the doorways between rooms. The beads were red and black, Joyce put on a record.

"Have a seat," she said. "Would you like something to drink?"

"No, thanks, not right now. Who's that playing piano?"

"Thelonious Monk. John Coltrane's on tenor saxophone, Shadow Wilson on drums. Keen, huh?"

"I guess," said Roy. "It's pretty different from what my mother plays."

"I've heard her, she's good. This tune's called 'Nutty'. Michael digs Monk the most, so do I."

Joyce went into the kitchen, brushing aside the beads, which clacked together loudly before settling back into place, then came back out with a glass in her right hand containing something red.

"What're you drinking?" Roy asked.

"Wine. It's sweet. I'd offer you some but you're a little young. Maybe if we were in France it would be all right, but we're not. You might not like it anyway, and neither would your mother. My giving you some, I mean."

"That's a strange picture," said Roy, pointing to a large, framed painting on one wall.

"Not strange, Roy, it's an abstract. Michael's grandfather did it before the war, twenty years ago, in 1938. His name was Mikhail Nev. He's quite famous."

"Was?"

"He and his wife were murdered during the war, in a concentration camp in Poland. Michael's parents took this painting with them when they came to America in 1939. Michael was fifteen then."

"It reminds me of an octopus I saw caught in a wire fence below the surface of the water in the Gulf, only the painting's got different colors in it. Why was he killed?"

"He was Jewish. The Germans tried to kill all the Jews in Europe. The title of this painting is 'Schreck'."

"I don't know that word."

"Schreck is German for fear or horror. Michael says his grandfather meant it to represent what the Jewish people were feeling at that time."

Roy looked around the room. There were other paintings and drawings and photographs on the walls but none of them were anything like Michael's grandfather's painting.

"What's the name of this tune? I like it."

"'Functional'. I like it, too. Monk can be way out there sometimes, but this one makes me feel there's a reason for living."

"Not like that painting," said Roy.

"No, not like that painting."

"Why do you have it on the wall?"

Joyce did not answer right away. She took a long sip of wine before she did.

"It's important to not forget, Roy. To not forget there are other people who don't think the same way you do. Mikhail Nev knew what could happen, what was already happening, that it was unspeakable, so he painted it."

Roy sat and listened to 'Functional' until it was over and the record ended. He stood up and told Joyce he had to go.

"Come visit any time," she said.

Later, when Roy and his mother were having dinner, he told her he'd been with Joyce that afternoon in the garden apartment.

"She's very nice, I think," said his mother, "and smart, too. Of course I don't know her well. What did you talk about?"

"Music and painting."

"They're very arty people, Roy. You can probably learn a lot from them."

"Michael's grandfather is a famous painter."

"Really? Perhaps you'll meet him sometime."

"No, he's dead. He was killed in the war."

The telephone rang. Roy's mother got up from the table and went to answer it. Roy tried to remember the title of the painting, the German word, but he could not. He wondered what the painting would sound like if it could be turned into music.

Kitty's World

Several years after their mother died, Roy's sister, Sally, told him that she had recently had dinner with Kitty's former sister-in-law, their aunt Isabelle, whose first husband had been Kitty's brother, Buck. During their conversation, Sally said, Isabelle remarked that Buck had warned her when they were newly wed that his sister was only out for herself, that Isabelle should be cautious in her dealings with Kitty, who was twelve years younger than he.

Hearing this made Roy angry, given that Isabelle, now in her mid-eighties, was, in his experience, one of the most cold-hearted, ungenerous, selfish persons he had ever known. He'd not seen Isabelle in more than thirty years, but her behavior when he was a child had made an indelible impression on his memory. Not that Kitty hadn't been vain, self-absorbed, even neurotic, but she had not been a snob, an *arriviste*, as was Isabelle.

"Isabelle has no right to disparage Kitty," Roy told his sister. "Our mother had a very different history than Isabelle. Being raised in a convent insufficiently prepared her for the world, married off at nineteen to a man two decades older, having to suffer from a chronic, misdiagnosed illness since adolescence. Kitty had her faults, we know that, serious psychological as well as physical problems. She was a very beautiful woman who learned early on how to use her looks to get what she thought she needed or wanted. Isabelle must always have been envious of Kitty's natural beauty, how most men were instantly attracted to her even well into her middle age."

"Isabelle was pretty when she was young," said Sally.

"Yes, but she couldn't compare to Kitty. And despite her failings our mother had a good sense of humor, which Isabelle never did. It bugs me that Isabelle still can't let it go, that she said this to you now."

The night after Sally related to Roy her conversation with Isabelle, he had a dream in which he was a very young boy accompanying his mother, she was driving and Roy was seated next to her on the front seat of her midnight blue 1953 Oldsmobile Holiday convertible. The top was down and the car was zooming down the old seven mile bridge on Highway A1A in the Florida Keys. For a moment Roy was again in Kitty's world, she was in her late twenties, telling a joke and then laughing, flashing her perfect white teeth and tossing her long auburn hair as the wind caught it. There were no other cars on the road.